Where The Guitars Play

LM Foster

This is a work of fiction. Names, characters, places and incidents are products of the author's imagination. Any resemblance to actual events, locales, organizations, or persons, either living or dead, is entirely coincidental.

ISBN-10: 0692589090
ISBN-13: 978-0692589090

Cover
Two Satyrs
Peter Paul Rubens, 1619

9th Street Press
www.9thstreetpress.com

This then is our proposition: devils by their act do bring about evil effects through witchcraft, yet it is true that without the assistance of some agent they cannot make any form, either substantial or accidental, and we do not maintain that they can inflict damage without the assistance of some agent, but with such an agent, diseases, and any other human passions or ailments, can be brought about, and these are real and true. How these agents or how the employment of such means can be rendered effective in co-operation with devils will be made clear in the following chapters.

– *Malleus Maleficarum,* 1487

ONE

My phone signaled a text and I looked at it curiously.

How the hell r ya, Cal?

Well, I'll be goddamned, I thought. The message was from Ernie LaBelle, my old high school buddy, my bandmate. Once upon a time, I was the drummer for Sonic Daydream, and he'd been second-guitar. We were one of the planet's premier acts; we'd toured the world, played before the crowned heads of Europe and a million screaming fans in hundreds of cities. We'd still be touring if our singer hadn't decided to call it quits. Now it was all long ago and far away, almost twenty years past.

Ernie and I had started Sonic Daydream in high school, along with Leonard Whitly, who played bass. The band never would've been any bigger than the Riverside bar scene if Lenny's little brother Dennis hadn't joined us. Even I had to admit that. Denny was the most bankable talent in Sonic Daydream. It was his pretty face and his catchy tunes that made us famous, made us rich. Even I couldn't deny that Dennis Whitly had *made us.* He ended us, too.

Ernie's text was a surprise. I hadn't heard from him in a long time. When Denny decided that our band was over, Ernie hadn't even changed his guitar strings before joining another band. Azomite was never as big as Sonic Daydream, and *Rolling Stone* pronounced them as having the same sound, but Ernie had done all right. He'd gotten to stay on the road, on tour. It was the place he best liked to be, because that's where the groupies were.

How's the band? I asked him.

Just out of the studio, he replied. *On hiatus. No tour this summer.*

What will u do for a date?

☺ *I've got a surprise 4 ya, Cal. I'm a daddy.*

If it was anyone else but Ernie, I would've thought, *Well, it's about time you settled down.* I would've pictured some blushing local girl, someone to whom the ol' man had taken a shine. He would've paid court to her, asked her to marry him. Their child would be the pride and joy of his old age, a late in life, surprise blessing, something to give his existence new meaning.

But since it was Ernie, groupie-slayer par excellence, I knew that it hadn't happened that way. This baby was no doubt the product of a quick, sweaty tumble in the back of the tour bus, the living, breathing, squalling result of Azomite's charismatic lead-guitar servicing one of his adoring fans, as was his wont, his avocation. Even if he was old.

Grab it, live it up, long as you can get it up, The Knack had advised in 1979. Sonic Daydream consisted of only the three of us then, just sixteen-year-old boys who called themselves a band. Lenny and I did all right with the girls, but it would be Ernie LaBelle that took Doug Fieger's advice, every single time he got the chance. Fieger had been in the ground since 2010, but apparently neither that fact nor a few decades had slowed down Ernie's appetites. *It's better to burn out, then to fade away. Hey, hey, my, my.*

I frowned. I wasn't bitter – the groupie scene had never been my thing – it was just that . . . Oh, I dunno. It was just that everyone seemed to have found someone now, even Ernie. Everyone but me.

Ernie was still getting action eighteen years after the defunction of Sonic Daydream. Denny and the bride of his youth were living happily-ever-after in connubial bliss; at the tender age of twenty-seven, their daughter Valerie, creator of the world famous Talk To a Movie Star service, was a millionaire.

Lenny, too, had a companion – Barbie, ten years his junior. She used to be our rep from Sony. She still made sure we got our royalty checks, and she'd been keeping Lenny warm at night on his ranch in the wilds of Anza for about fifteen years now.

Congrats, Ernie, I texted.

I want you to meet her, Cal.

The universe was not without a sense of irony, it would seem, if it had given Ernie LaBelle a daughter. I pictured him, positively geriatric by the time the boys started sniffing around, impotently trying – now there was a turn of phrase – impotently trying to keep them away from her. Then I figured, he probably wouldn't live long enough to see it. He was fifty-five, the same age as me. A grandfather's age, not a father's. By the time Ernie's baby was old enough to date, he'd probably be in his grave, as was The Knack's frontman. As I would be. Not too many of us former rock stars live into our seventies.

Sure, Ernie. I'll bring her a teddy bear.

There was a pause, then Ernie texted, *Ur not picking up what I'm putting down, Cal. Lisa's not a baby. Can I call u?*

By all means.

The phone rang immediately, and I was greeted by Ernie's familiar, always-laughing voice. "Dude," he said. Ernie called everybody *dude*. I'd known him since high school; our band had hit the big time in 1988, and we'd toured together for twelve years. I thought vaguely that if I had a dime for every time I'd heard Ernie say *dude* in all those years, it would rival the royalties I still received when one of our long-memoried fans bought a CD, or when they requested one of our tunes on the oldies station. It was pleasantly nostalgic to hear him say it now.

"Lisa's not a baby. She's eighteen. I got a letter from her."

The picture in my mind changed. Baby-mama was not some diehard fan, down to make it with a past-his-expiration-date, once-famous guitar player. She wasn't a fan of Azomite, where he played lead. She wasn't a fan of his new stuff. Baby-mama was from the old days, a Sonic Daydream groupie. She was from when we were still big, still touring; she was one of the literally hundreds that had waited around after our shows to see what they could get. I did the math: if the kid was eighteen, she was born in 2000. Her mom must've been one of Ernie's last Sonic Daydream groupies. We'd quit touring in May of 1999.

"Well, I'll be damned, Ernie. You have to tell me all about it. You wanna have lunch?"

"You read my mind, Cal."

"Are you still in Riverside?"

"Yep. Same place."

"I'll meet you in an hour."

I'd moved to Temecula when the band ended, close enough to home to visit my parents, but far enough away to not have to relive bad memories. I lived in a succession of overpriced apartments until I'd finally knuckled down and bought a house, after my parents passed. I hadn't been to Riverside in years.

"We can grab a beer at The House of Ale," Ernie suggested. "For old times' sake."

We had once been the house band at The House of Ale, had gone from there to conquer the known rock and roll universe.

"Do you think anybody'll recognize us?"

"They've still got our picture above the bar."

I laughed. "From thirty years ago. Things have changed since then."

"Wait to you hear about this, dude. It's something else."

"I'm glad you're happy about it, Ernie. I'll see you in an hour."

TWO

The House of Ale was unrecognizable, compared to how it had been when we used to play there. They had gutted the inside, knocked down a wall and taken over the space from an adjoining building. The bar was where the tiny stage used to be; the new stage was higher, larger.

But it was true what Ernie had told me: our picture was still over the bar. There we stood, smiling, arms linked, beneath the sign out front. That hadn't changed with the interior renovations. God, how young we all were! Denny was just twenty-one, and Ernie and Lenny and I were twenty-five. Denny had scrawled across the bottom of the eight-by-ten, *To all our friends from The House of Ale, management, staff, and fans – we'll never forget you!* And we had all signed our names, legible then, before a decade of signing autographs made our signatures into meaningless squiggles.

But we *had* forgotten them, I thought, management, staff, and fans. At least Denny had, abruptly, way back in 1999. And more importantly, they had forgotten us.

The bartender, a girl of about twenty-five herself, saw me looking at the picture and smiled. "My mom was tickled to death when I started working here. She told me all the stories, how they used to play every Friday and Saturday night. She was a big fan."

"They all were, honey." Ernie LaBelle appeared at my shoulder. He took a pen out of his pocket with a flourish, slid a napkin from a stack on the bar so it was in front of him. He paused, smiled at the bartender. "What's your mom's name?"

The girl blinked blankly at him, and Ernie nodded at the picture. "See that devilishly handsome longhair on the right? That's me. The one on the other end? That's him." The girl looked at the picture then back at us, twice. I smiled at her expression of astonished recognition. "What's your mom's name?" Ernie asked again.

The bartender was speechless for another heartbeat. Sonic Daydream had been *big.* Then she stammered out her mother's name.

Ernie wrote, *To my good friend Bianca – Long live rock and roll!* He signed his name and then handed the pen to me. I also signed, and Ernie slid the napkin across the bar. "Could you send us over a couple of Buds, honey?" He glanced around at the now unfamiliar layout of The House of Ale. "We'll be in that booth over there."

The girl nodded, still speechless, and Ernie winked at her.

On the way over to the booth, I said, "You should've asked her when she was born. Maybe you have two daughters."

Ernie grinned wryly, shook his head. "Denny got all the action in the old days. Remember?"

How could I forget? The interior of The House of Ale had changed, but I was sure that the little alley-alcove behind it was still there. It was where we'd park my truck to load-in and load-out when we played here. There was a chain-link gate across one end, and I remembered the girls, red-lacquered fingernails gripping the metal, calling to Denny while we packed up our instruments. In the good old days, he never failed to answer them. He and Lenny had lived just around the corner then, and Denny took a different girl home to see his etchings after every set.

That had all ended when he met Sophia.

The bartender brought our beers personally, and when Ernie tried to pay, she insisted that they were on the house. "My mom's your biggest fan."

"Keep 'em coming, then," Ernie said and winked at her again. Flustered – she was talking to a real rock star; wait 'til Mom hears about this! – she walked away quickly.

"Remember how Elise used to sneak in here to see us?" Ernie asked.

I corrected him. "Elise snuck in here to see Denny. She didn't know the rest of us even existed."

Ernie shrugged. "I almost hit that once. Did you ever –?"

I shook my head. "We were friends. She only had eyes for Denny. You know that."

"I can't say as I paid all that much attention at the time, dude. I had my hands full."

"Comforting Denny's spurned groupies."

Ernie grinned. "But I learned the whole story when I read your book."

"You and three or four other people."

Ernie looked steadily at me. "Denny read it."

And that was why this was just Ernie and me having a beer together for old times' sake, why it wasn't a Sonic Daydream hometown reunion. I hadn't talked to Denny or his brother since our greatest hits compilation had been released, years ago; I doubted if I would ever speak to them again in this life.

My book was called *Sonic Nightmare.* In it, I told the band's story, the way I saw it, the way I'd lived it. Elise Carlin had been sixteen when she met and fell in love with Dennis Whitly. But he wasn't having any; she was underage, and unlike my good friend Ernie here, that was a line Denny wouldn't cross. Elise introduced Denny to her older sister Sophia, and they fell in love.

Sonic Daydream hit the big time. Sophia came with us on tour, and so did her little sister. Over the years, Elise became our de facto road manager, relieving Lenny of a job he didn't like in the first place. Though she was just a slip of a teenaged girl, no one was more of a pit bull than Elise when it came to dealing with promoters and hoteliers when we were on the road. Sony eventually put her on the payroll; our rep, Barbie, frequently said that Elise was the best road dog in the business.

When I first met Elise, I was a soon-to-be-famous drummer, who, at twenty-five, had been around the block, seen more than my share, whatever cliché you wanted to choose to indicate a not-innocent musician. At sixteen, Elise was at a time in her life when she should've been worried about prom and getting her eyeliner just right and the opinions of other high school chickies like herself.

Elise ignored me at first, and Lenny and Ernie; like I'd just reminded him, she'd only had eyes for Denny. But at first, she kept it to herself. We didn't get to be friends, she didn't start telling me about how she and her sister's boyfriend were going to live happily-ever-after someday, until a year or so after we'd met. Not until after Sony had signed us, after we'd started to tour.

But before you start thinking that I befriended an innocent young thing because I was bored and wanted to laugh at her impossible desire, let me disabuse you of all that. Elise was no innocent. At sixteen, she had already *run wild*; it was Sophia's expression. *In the bars, with the men who play guitars.*

And in addition to telling me what she wanted to do to Denny, Elise bragged about what she had already done with the high school football captain, and Sammy the bouncer, and Carl (who actually played guitar, though not well, according to her), and various and sundry fortunate young men in between. Elise told me about them because she liked to talk, and she liked to talk about herself most of all. I didn't judge, and she didn't care if I did. Elise and I shared a love of music, that old time rock and roll, and that was the initial thing that made us friends. But she also wanted to let me know that she was an adult; that her groupie-love for Denny wasn't only some passing adolescent infatuation.

Ernie hit on Elise once, and she'd politely turned him down. She loathed Lenny, worshipped his brother. She couldn't or wouldn't talk to the three of them too much, so by the process of elimination, it was me she befriended. As the years have slipped inexorably by, I've come to the realization that I was in love with Elise back then, at least a little bit. These things happen when you spend your days and nights with someone for twelve years, on tour, in a different town every other night.

I didn't think that I loved her at the time, however, because she was in love with Denny. That was the only reason she was there with us, day in and day out, year after year. She was immersed in an unshakeable delusion, an impossible dream from which she refused to awaken: someday, Denny would be hers. Even after Denny and Sophia got married, had a baby; someday, he'd divorce her sister, abandon their child. Someday, Denny would see Elise. He would return her love. They'd be together forever.

Denny saw this adoration; we all did. But Elise only confided her passion to me. I thought all along that the most honorable thing for Denny to have done would've been to send Elise home, so she could forget her obsession with him, get on with her life. But that never happened. At first, Sophia wanted her along with us to keep an eye on her, but after their daughter was born and Sophia stayed home, Elise was still there. Denny took advantage of her managerial skills, as did Sony and the rest of us – Elise had made herself indispensable to Sonic Daydream. So she toured with us. And she told me about how she would be with Denny someday.

When we weren't on tour, Elise lived with Denny and Sophia and their daughter in a big cave of a house in Malibu. Still, for twelve years, Denny managed to never be alone with her.

Then the inevitable happened. Denny had arrived home a day earlier than he was expected, in order to surprise his daughter for her eighth birthday. But Sophia had made plans; a birthday party was scheduled for Valerie at the country club, and Sophia took her to it, leaving Denny at home. With Elise. Alone.

The universe was finally smiling on Elise. She had given twelve years of indefatigable service to Dennis Whitly and his band, and at last she was gonna get her reward. The only thing she'd ever wanted, since she was sixteen years old: to consummate her love for her sister's husband.

From what followed, I figured that Elise seduced Denny. I figured that he had an attack of conscience about it afterward. I said as much in my book.

Elise left me a voice mail, but I didn't get it until the next day, until it was all over. We frequently spoke to each other via song lyrics. It was our thing. The words written by the great legends of music were our shorthand, almost like our own secret way of communicating. A lot of meaning and emotion could be packed into a few short verses.

She sighed heavily into the phone. *"This is the end, my only friend, the end. Of our elaborate plans, the end. Of everything that stands, the end. No safety or surprise, the end. I'll never look into your eyes again.*

"I really wanted to talk to you, Cal. It's chickenshit to do it like this, but you would've just tried to talk me out of it, anyway. You would've said, *there's still time to change the road you're on.*

"I guess I've been kind of a one trick pony for as long as you've known me, huh? All I ever talked about was Denny, wasn't it? I want to thank you for listening.

"I finally got to touch him again, after all these years. *All you touch and all you see, is all your life will ever be.* We were finally alone . . . Then he told me that things couldn't go on like they had been. He told me that it would never be just the two of us." She sighed again.

"I have seen the writing on the wall, Cal. Denny showed it to me, so now, I *don't think I need anything at all. No. Don't think I need anything at all.*

"I know you'll miss me – you'll be the only one – and for that, I'm truly sorry. *But I don't need to fight to prove I'm right. I don't need to be forgiven.*

"I saw him first. He would've, *should've* been mine, all along. She doesn't deserve him. She never has." Elise sighed a third time.

"Just what you want to be, you'll be in the end. Goodbye, Cal."

The message was over, but the next line of the song played in my head, Justin Hayward's plaintive, lamenting, haunting voice: *And I love you, yes, I love you, oh, how, I love you. Oh, how I love you.* I felt Elise's unendurable pain.

I don't know for sure what happened between her and Denny that night. But whatever it was, it was too much for Elise. She picked up Sophia at the country club; Valerie remained at the party for a while longer, then stayed overnight with one of her school chums.

Elise drove Denny's black Mercedes through the guardrail on Mullholland Highway. Investigators found no skid marks. She hadn't tried to brake at all, yet they put it all down as simply a tragic accident. A young woman had lost control of a big, powerful car on a dark, twisty, California highway. Many such heartbreaking events happened yearly in the area.

But I knew better. The heartbreak had come earlier in the evening for Elise. Whatever had occurred between Denny and his sister-in-law, it ended with rejection, and it undid her. If Elise couldn't at last have the object of her desire, then her sister wasn't going to have him anymore either.

I'll never look into your eyes again.

Sophia was severely injured in the wreck. Denny sold the beach house, moved his family back to Riverside to get away from the bad memories. He nursed his wife back to health. He converted the garage in the back into a recording studio, and we released two more albums. But we never toured again. Sonic Daydream was finished.

Ernie joined another band; Lenny moved to Anza with the record company rep and more or less retired from the world. I did a little studio work.

It took eight years of nightmares and recriminations and self-loathing and alcoholism to realize that I'd been in love with Elise, that if anyone could've saved her, it would've been me. *For of all sad words of tongue or pen, the saddest are these: "It might have been!"*

Love or no love, there was nothing I could do for Elise. She was gone. To exorcise the demon of my own guilt, I wrote *Sonic Nightmare.* I told the world how Denny had taken advantage of a young girl's love for him, how she'd killed herself because of that love, how she'd tried to take her sister with her. I told the world that Dennis Whitly had killed Sonic Daydream because he didn't want to risk the adoration of another psychotic fan, as his sister-in-law had been.

Writing it had made me feel better. I stopped blaming myself and shifted the blame to where it belonged, directly onto the talented, cowardly shoulders of Dennis Whitly, guitar god. The nightmares stopped. I quit drinking. Elise's ghost was appeased.

The book enjoyed a brief, moderate success. It could've been bigger, but I declined a book tour. I wasn't out to make money off of the one great tragedy of my life. I just wanted to tell the story. *Sonic Nightmare* had been successful enough; it had reached its target audience. Ernie had read it. And Denny.

"Was any of it true?" Ernie asked me now.

"It says *Non-fiction* on the spine."

"But –"

"You lived it as much as I did, Ernie."

"I'm telling you, Cal, I never paid that much attention to her. You were the one that was friends with her."

"And I told it as I saw it. You can believe it or not. I've already got your $9.95." I knew that referring to the price of the book would appeal to Ernie. I was right: he grinned.

Then I sighed. "I really don't want to talk about it. It was a long time ago – Christ, it's been almost twenty years. It's all over. The past is gone forever. You wanted to tell me about your daughter."

The word felt strange in my mouth, in this context. *Ernie LaBelle's daughter.*

"Okay. I got this letter about six weeks ago. All melodramatic and shit. *Hi, my name is Lisa Corson. My mother says you're my father.* It was like six pages long, in this rounded, little-girl-looking handwriting.

"The killing part of it is – the story she tells about me and her mom? I *remembered it,* Cal. I remembered her."

I reckoned that it was an exclusive enough club: perhaps a thousand singers, including Mick Jagger, Robert Plant, David Lee Roth; no doubt even Justin Bieber, and of course, Ernie LaBelle. Musicians that'd had so many women that it was an anomaly to be able to remember any particular one. And Ernie wasn't even a singer. He had simply comforted all those girls that had come out with hopes of getting at Dennis Whitly. It hadn't bothered him in the least.

"I remembered her, particularly, for two reasons. The first one was that she said she was there to see me, that she thought I was a better guitarist than Denny." He grinned. "Of course, I'm not, but it was nice of her to say so."

Ah, Ernie, still sticking up for that son of a bitch, even after all these years. I'm a drummer, and guitar players are all pretty much the same to me. The fans and their wallets thought Denny was good; he'd never seemed any better than Ernie to me, nor Lenny the bass player, for that matter.

Despite his avid love-‘em-and-leave-‘em antics over the years, Ernie was a better person to me, however. He was what he was. Dennis Whitly, singer, songwriter, multi-platinum recording artist; fine, upstanding, solid husband and father – he’d driven a young woman to suicide. From Day One, I’d never been overly impressed with Lenny’s little brother as a musician. It had been the fans that had recognized Denny’s talent, not yours truly. But after what happened to Elise, as a human being, he’d always be nothing but a cowardly son of a bitch to me.

“I met her in Frisco,” Ernie was saying. “After what would turn out to be our last show.”

The day before Elise died . . .

“She was waiting backstage. I don’t know how she got through – you know how Denny frowned on that –”

“Yet you never had any trouble.”

Ernie shrugged. “I just waited until he left. You know how he always went and got on the bus or went back to the hotel right away.” Ernie grinned slyly. “There were always girls lingering around the barricades between the doors and the bus. I’d just look out there, check them out, and have one of the roadies –”

“I remember how it worked, Ernie.”

“But this girl got backstage somehow. Denny walked right by her, and she didn’t even look at him. She was waiting for me.”

“Lucky you.”

“Yeah, she was all *Hi, Ernie, I’m you’re biggest fan.”*

I rolled my eyes. I’d had my own share of biggest fans, and just like Ernie said, they would stand outside the barricades and wait, and scream my name when I tried to get on the bus. On more than one occasion, I’d put my arm around Elise, pretending that she was my girlfriend, in an attempt to shut them up. But it never worked. They didn’t care if I had a girlfriend or a wife. Such is the life of a touring musician in a famous band: all the women you could ever want. Denny hid out, Lenny and I ignored it, and Ernie took full advantage of it.

“I thought I might’ve seen her on the rail before, so I asked, and she said yeah, she always came to all our West Coast dates.”

Elise had termed such fans *camp-followers.* One performance wasn’t enough for them; they would attend as many shows as they could afford, sometimes ranging hundreds of miles from home. If he hadn’t been married to her sister, thereby allowing her to be on tour with us, to *be with the band,* Elise would’ve camp-followed Sonic

Daydream, just for a glimpse of Denny. She'd told me so all the time.

Ernie continued. "She said she got backstage there, in Frisco, instead of somewhere else, because it was her hometown. She had a little place right around the corner from our hotel."

A memory struck me. "Was that the one –? You almost missed the bus the next day. You had a bunch of weird spots on you. You said it was some kind of ritual –"

"Oh, my Christ, Cal! You remember it, too!"

"The devil-worshipping chick!"

"The very one. I don't know if she was a devil-worshipper per se, but she wasn't a Jehovah's Witness. Some kind of witchy thing, definitely. Her apartment was tiny, painted all in blacks and dark greens. She had a stuffed goat's head on the wall. She lit candles and incense; she mumbled a few words. In the middle of it, she's on top of me, and she reaches over and picks up a brush and a little paint pot from the night stand and starts painting symbols on my chest, on my forehead; on herself. She says it's to help us commune with the spirits in ultimate tantric pleasure or some such bullshit, and I said, *Whatever's clever, honey, I'm down. Whatever gets you there."* Ernie grinned crookedly. "It only got freakier and kinkier after that."

"What was it that she painted you with?"

Ernie shrugged. "She said it was the blood of the firstborn of Egypt or some such. Anything for a good time, dude. But it wasn't blood. Blood washes off. This stuff stayed on me for days."

I remembered Ernie showing up at Cedars-Sinai, where they'd taken Sophia after the accident. He'd still had faded splotches of red on his forehead. *Anything for a good time.*

"So, fast forward eighteen years, and I get this letter in the mail. This girl is telling me this story, about the ritual and the painted symbols, and I remember it. Her mother had said it was to make everything better, and I have to admit that it was pretty good in an out-of-the-ordinary, witchy kind of way, but apparently, the ritual wasn't just to make the sex better. It was also some kind of fertility thing. Seems Mom had closely followed my career –" again Ernie grinned, "– and was rather obsessed with me. Thought I was the best guitarist ever and all that. Apparently her daddy was some blues piano player who OD'd when she was a kid or something, so she *knew* music. She'd drifted into this witchy shit, but she never forgot about Dad and his piano . . . She heard our band, thought I was great, and decided that, with the help of the spirits, my son would be the greatest musician ever. So she looked me up –"

"She got pregnant on purpose?"

Ernie nodded, sipped his beer. "With the help of the spirits."

"And her daughter told you all this? And none of it strikes you as weird at all? Creepy?"

Again Ernie shrugged. "What do I care? Remember the guys that opened for us in Portland? On the first tour?"

I nodded. "Black Winter."

"Yeah. The front's name was Mike. He had a pentagram tattooed on his palm, like in *The Wolfman.*"

"What?"

Ernie shook his head. "It's not important. They were all sitting in their little van before the show and I walk over there, and they're passing around a horn-cup looking thing, like they're Vikings or something, and Mike says it's blood wine or blood rain or something like that, for luck, would I like some, and I said I'd pass."

"Yeah. Their drummer told me that he had irrefutable proof that Lars Ulrich had sold his soul to the devil. *Watch him when he drums, man,* he told me. *Watch his feet. You can see Satan's mark. There have got to be cloven hooves inside his shoes.*"

"That's my point, Cal. Who cares what these people believe? They're allowed. As long as you don't start believing it and I don't start believing it. This chick wanted to have my son. She wanted to make another great musician, just like his daddy." Ernie winked.

"You said you have a daughter."

Again Ernie grinned. "Apparently the spirits screwed up. Lisa told me that her mom was pissed about it, that she was a girl."

"Jesus, Ernie."

He held up a hand. "Mom changed her mind. She realized a girl could be a musician just as easily as a boy. So Lisa took lessons. All her life."

"What does she play?"

"The guitar. Like her daddy."

I raised my eyebrows at Ernie's paternal pride, but asked the question anyway. "Is she any good?"

Ernie laughed. "Would I waste your time with a shitty musician, Cal? Even if it is my kid? You should know me better than that."

"So you're saying she's –"

"She's *phenomenal. Amazing.* She plays guitar like falling down the steps, and her voice is flawless. The rest of them are okay –"

"All girls?" I thought, *The Runaways Redux,* and the next thought was *novelty act.*

"No. Three dudes, all in their thirties."

"How did she end up in a band with –"

"The second-guitar is Mom's current boyfriend. Like I say, as a band, they're all right. Nothing spectacular. They don't have much original material; all they do are covers of the Jurassic classics. But Lisa is amazing, a standout."

"What's the name of this girl-fronted band?" I asked him with a grin. I had no trouble humoring Ernie. We had been friends for a lifetime.

Ernie rolled his eyes. "They call themselves Phenex."

It was an easy fallback, recognizable, the name of a town. Before Sonic Daydream had hit the big time, I'd suffered through a cramped, sleep-in-the-van-with-your-instruments tour with a band called Scranton. I'd referred to it as the *1987 Fire-Trap Tour.* It was a nightmare, the road trip from hell, and when it was over, I'd never been so glad to see home.

Sonic Daydream was signed the next year, and even our first tour was luxurious compared to Scranton's. We had a bus, and a roadie named Perry; we slept in hotels. The guy from Sony knew talent went he saw it. From there, we went on to tour the globe, to become wealthy, rock and roll legends.

In contrast, Scranton would never play a venue that served more than a hundred people. Their tour had been a case-study in the hard life of an unsigned band, the depressing travelogue of a bunch of mildly talented nobodies playing for beer and a pittance in a collection of West Coast dives. But for Pete and Allie and the rest of them, it still beat a day job. *It's the work that we avoid, and we're all self-employed.* I figured it would probably be the same for Ernie's daughter's band.

"Who's from Arizona?" I inquired.

Ernie shook his head. "Not like the town, Cal."

"So somebody's a poet?" I said with a grin. "Rising from cover band ashes to assume the mantel of derivative mediocrity?"

It was a mean thing to say, but Ernie could take it. My bank account allowed me to indulge in quite a bit of mockery of ambitious bands with tired, trite mythological monikers, as did Ernie's. If all the band names of the electrically amplified-era were listed in some kind of rock and roll roll call, I imagined that there would be quite a few Scrantons and Black Winters and Phoenixes, all as forgotten as high-button shoes. But there'd been only one Rolling Stones, one Beatles, one Pink Floyd. There had been only one Sonic Daydream.

Again Ernie shook his head. "It's P-H-E-N-E-X. It's not the town, and it's not the bird, exactly. I don't fucking know."

It was another of his familiar expressions, right up there with *dude,* and I smiled at the memories. *What time do the doors open, Ernie? What town are we in? What was her name?*

Dude. I don't fucking know. Always accompanied by his *nor do I care* grin.

I asked Ok Google to enlighten me, to give me a definition of P-H-E-N-E-X. I read the Wikipedia entry; now it was my turn to roll my eyes.

"What?"

"It says, *In demonology, Phenex is a Great Marquis of Hell and has twenty legions of demons under his command. He is depicted as a phoenix, which sings sweet notes with the voice of a child, but the conjurer must warn his companions (for he has not to be alone) not to hear them."*

I clicked on a Tumblr page, swathed in purple. There was a diagram in a circle. *The Sigil of Phenex*, the caption read. *"Another demonic muse for the creative. Invoke Phenex during fire baptisms and rebirth rituals including creative path working."*

I grinned as I read a warning from a site called Deities Daily, another colorful Tumblr dedicated to the netherworld. *"Sources say that although Phenex follows commands, he is very deceptive, and after tricking one into trusting him, will destroy them spiritually and psychologically.*"

Ernie shook his head, shrugged. "Yeah, all that bullshit has to go. They're not a metal band."

"Thank Christ."

Ernie nodded in agreement. "They need to come up with another name. If nothing else, people'll misspell it."

"You thinking of promoting the demon Phenex's band, are ya, Ernie?"

Again my old friend shrugged. "I love the road, Cal, you know that."

Just like Elise did, I thought fleetingly.

"But just between you and me, Azomite is getting stale. This last album . . . It's like our *In Through the Out Door."*

Ah, Ernie, my egomaniacal friend. Azomite was no Led Zeppelin, but I understood his point. *In Through the Out Door* had been the juggernaut's last release before the death of John Bonham. It demonstrated a band in flux, trying something different. In was mellower – there was nothing like *Black Dog* on it. It still sold a bazillion copies, because it was by Zeppelin, but *Rolling Stone* roundly panned it way back in 1979, and rock and roll history never got any kinder to it. I'd always thought *Fool in the Rain* was brilliant, but it really wasn't representative of the same band that had given us *Dazed and Confused.*

Ernie was telling me that like *In Through the Out Door,* Azomite's latest studio effort might just be their swan song. I grinned inwardly at my own pun.

"I'm not ready to give up the road," he was saying. "What would I do with my time then? A whole lotta nothing, like . . ." He let the *you* go unsaid.

But he was right. Time was all I had: it wasn't like I had to work. Sonic Daydream's long ago success kept me funded. The money had been obscene in the old days, and the interest remained more than sufficient, plus I still got royalties from our tunes, and a few bucks when someone bought my book. I knocked around the big McMansion I owned in Temecula; I read a lot. I wrote a few fanciful short stories about bands and the road, stuff that would never see publication.

A guy my age had recognized me at Starbucks a few years before. We chatted, and before I knew it, he'd talked me into giving drum lessons at the YMCA. I volunteered my time – I paid enough taxes.

When the kids heard my name, there was no recognition. I was just old Mr. Bascomb, twirling my sticks and telling them to hold theirs loosely. But if they typed my name into the Google search box, then they'd be a little more impressed, because Sonic Daydream had been big. They'd heard of the band, had heard our music, even if they were too young to remember when we toured. After they found out who I was, there were a few requests for autographs, mostly for parents and even grandparents who had come out to see us in the old days.

But there always had to be that internet search first – no one remembers the drummer's name, not even from world-renowned, famous bands. If you think that sounds bitter – everyone remembers Keith Moon and Jon Bonham, you say – but that's only because they're dead, victims of the excesses of the rock and roll lifestyle. You know Anthony Kiedis and Flea, and you know their drummer looks like Will Ferrell, but what's his name? Or, quickly – name the drummer from Pink Floyd. Or Black Sabbath. Or Pearl Jam. Sure, you know the singers' names, and maybe even the guitarists', but the drummers' . . . I'm not bitter about it. It's just how things are.

"So, I was figuring, maybe I could try it from a different angle for once," Ernie continued. "Backstage, behind the scenes this time." He studied my expression for a second to see how I was taking the novel idea of *Ernie LaBelle, Ridiculously-Named-Band Promoter*.

"You gonna bankroll it?"

Again Ernie shrugged. "Why not? Like I say, it would be something different."

"Maybe you should call Lenny. Get Barbie to give 'em a listen. Get 'em signed. Have Sony bankroll it."

"They're not anywhere near ready to be signed. They need work; they need a new name. Lisa's great though, I'm telling you. She could go far with a better band, or even this one, if they clean it up a little bit, and get some new songs. Forget about Lenny and Barbie and Sony for right now. I want *you* to come and hear them." When I still looked dubious – an eighteen-year-old, undiscovered female singing sensation sounded like some kind of Hollywood Cinderella-story – Ernie repeated, "I wouldn't waste your time if they weren't any good, Cal. I'm telling you, I see a lot of potential."

It wasn't like my life had a whole lot going on in it at the moment. "All right. I'll give 'em a listen. I haven't been to Frisco in decades."

"We don't have to go to Frisco, Cal. Lisa lives here. I guess her mom is originally from here. She was only fourteen or fifteen when we were signed, so she never got the chance to see us play this dive, but she's been a fan since our first CD. That's when she first noticed me."

Again I did the math in my head. If Lisa's mom was only fourteen when we were signed, then she was a good eleven years younger than Ernie and myself, had been far too young to come out and express her appreciation for the guitarist when our eponymous CD was released in 1988.

Unlike Denny, age differences had never meant anything to Ernie. Once we made it big, he tried to make sure the groupies he chose were at least twenty-one, but if the pretty thing screaming his name at the barrier was exceptionally pretty, it was a risk Ernie was willing to take every now and then.

Denny had never dabbled in jailbait, no matter how eager or attractive, although he was no saint. It was the only rule he had regarding his fans in the early days. Elise would've gotten him – he had already taken her home – if it wasn't for his brother pounding on his bedroom door at the last possible minute, telling him that the cute little thing that he'd just picked up had only managed to slip into The House of Ale because she was dating the bouncer. She was only sixteen.

Denny had immediately shown Elise the door, and that should've been the end of it. The girls already lined up around the block to hear him sing; he had more than his share to choose from, none of them underage.

Denny wouldn't have given Elise a second look after her first attempt to get at him – not only was she too young, she was a devious schemer who had wormed her way into the bar just to see him. The worst kind of fan. He would've forgotten all about her, if she hadn't introduced him to her sister.

Sophia was twenty-one, the same age as Denny. He liked to tell people that it was love at first sight. And since she was her little sister's legal guardian – their parents were dead – Elise Carlin remained at Denny's side, on the road with us after we made it big, always hoping, always dreaming that he'd forget about Sophia and take up with her. She remained Dennis Whitly's Number One Fan until she killed herself over him.

Denny gave up groupies the day he met Sophia, and Lenny had never been much for them either. He sampled a few when we toured Europe – the foreign chicks were more apt to intrigue him, at least until the next day, *when the morning sun comes streaming down* and they woke up in their town. But when we were in the States, he occupied himself with the managerial tasks of looking after a touring act, and left the groupies to Ernie.

And me? There had been one of two girls before Denny joined Sonic Daydream, before his face and voice and guitar put us on the map. But after that . . . I told Elise that I'd never been one for the sex-crazed groupie thing. I told her that I'd been drumming since childhood, that I didn't join a band to pick up women. And that was true to an extent – I'd never been what you'd call a womanizer, and being in a famous act hadn't changed that.

And I figured that the girls were all there to see Denny, anyway. The ones that called my name from behind the barriers – maybe that was because the lead-guitar, the singer, the face of the band – he was already gone, already on the bus or back at the hotel with his beloved Sophia. Ernie was second-guitar, and he didn't mind playing second-fiddle – age differences, the fact that he was probably the groupies' second choice – none of that mattered to Ernie. It was all the same in the dark to him.

But it wasn't my scene, and Elise was my constant companion on the road, anyway. She was beautiful and vivacious and funny. She loved the road, she loved rock and roll. We were never lovers, only friends. It was enough for me.

Don't get me wrong – I enjoyed *looking* at the fans. All that intensity: the eager, shining faces, the screams; all that unleashed, hormonal enthusiasm. There is nothing more beautiful than a young girl in the crowd, singing along to one of your songs. It was the best part of touring. But I was content just to look, to smile, to sign autographs, to toss my sticks to them at the end of the show. Anything more than that, well . . . it wasn't me.

Ernie had never found a steady girlfriend either, not in our touring days, and apparently not since. He was still single, a loner like me. But his wilder days had caught up with him. The mother of his kid had been just a kid herself when we'd released our first album, but time marches on, and she was no child when the spirits bade her to conceive Ernie's baby. She had to have been about twenty-six by then, to Ernie's pushing-forty. She was a little younger than Elise, who, like many of the musical legends she had admired, had joined the 27 Club on a dark, twisty, California highway, apparently the day after Ernie and the spirits and some groupie had conceived his now grown daughter.

Ernie was saying, "Lisa's mom – her name's Candy –"

Of course it is. Candy Corson, alliteratively named, the Sonic Daydream groupie, the camp-follower. Ernie LaBelle's biggest fan, his daughter's mother.

"She moved back here to Riverside when Lisa was a kid."

"It's a small world after all," I opined.

"When do you want to see the band?"

"Whenever you want," I told him and finished my beer. "My calendar is clear." For the rest of my life, if the future was to be anything like the last ten or fifteen years.

"Never been a better time than right now."

THREE

Ernie continued Candy and Lisa's backstory as we walked out to the parking lot. *Candy and Lisa. His family.* It was so odd to think of Ernie with such a thing. Like me, he was now an orphan: his parents were dead. I'd met his little brother a few times when we were still in high school; he was almost-retired from the military nowadays, stationed overseas somewhere. They talked online, sent a few texts. They'd never been close.

Ernie pulled out of the parking lot into the light Saturday afternoon traffic and nodded at the occult bookstore as we passed it. "That's where Candy works," he told me.

The sign said, *Mohini's House of Dreams.* It had been there for as long as I could remember, although I seemed to recall that the name had been a little different when I was younger – *Mohini's House of Something Else.* I'd never been inside.

"Again with the witchy thing." The occult and bands named after demons. It was all nothing but ridiculous to me.

Ernie nodded, grinned. "It's Candy's shtick. And I guess it's as real as any other religion to Lisa, because she was raised in it." Ernie forked the Evil Eye at me, as he had done during a thousand shows – it was also the universal symbol for rock and roll.

It was refreshing and a little amazing to hear Ernie talk about these people as if he'd taken the time to get to know them. In-depth interest in the lives of others had never been a part of his personality in the past.

I thought it'd always been a combination of absent-mindedness and self-absorption on his part. On the bus the day after a show, he'd regale us with tales of his adventures with the groupie from the night before, but her name and sometimes an actual physical description were often lacking. Like Candy and her kinky paint-by-numbers fertility ritual, if there was something unusual about her, he'd remember that, but mostly it was just a standard story of another anonymous quickie or two.

Life on the road had always been like living, breathing pornography to our second-guitar. If one liked to look at dirty pictures, one didn't pause to wonder what the girl's name was, or how she came to be in such a position – so it was with Ernie and his accommodating fans. He didn't waste space in his mind with the details of their lives – he wasn't ever going to see this one again, and there would be another one soon enough.

Even Elise, who'd lived with us, who'd traveled with us for twelve years – Ernie hadn't paid attention to her tragic longing for Denny, the sole motivation of her existence. He'd been intrigued enough to proposition her once, but after she'd turned him down, he'd ceased to notice her.

But Ernie had taken the time to learn about the *religion* of his daughter and her mother. Perhaps encroaching old age had worn away a patch of my old friend's narcissism.

"Do they really worship Satan?" I asked with amusement. I'd heard that such things existed, but the idea was just silly to me. Black robes and candles, prayers to the arch-fiend. How did any of them keep from laughing?

Ernie shrugged. "Who knows? Who cares?"

That was more like the Ernie of the old days.

"They put a lot of store in good luck charms, I know that. Like Black Winter and their horn full of fake blood."

And he took the cup, and gave thanks, and gave it to them, saying, "Drink ye all of it; for this is my blood of the new testament, which is shed for many for the remission of sins." It was all about what you decided to believe, what your parents passed down to you, I reckoned. My mother had been a staunch Catholic, and I still remembered the Bible verses, but they held no more meaning to me now than they ever had.

Ernie reached into his shirt and removed a medallion on a chain and handed it to me. "They've got their own little machine. You put a blank in it, then choose a stamp. You squeeze it together, and voila! Good luck abounds."

I ran my finger over the strange squiggly lettering, not unlike the Sigil of Phenex I'd seen on the internet.

"Is this a real language? What does it say?"

"I have absolutely no idea, Cal. It's all gobbledygook to me. Lisa and Candy said a few words, made some gestures."

He made a vague approximation of the Sign of the Cross. *Spectacles, testicles, wallet and watch.* I grinned.

"Then they gave me the thing, said it would protect me from evil influences or some such. I don't fucking know. I put it on for them. What possible difference could it make?"

"The power of suggestion . . ." I suggested.

"Yeah, that only works if you believe in it in the first place, right? Like voodoo dolls? I make my own luck, Cal." Ernie grinned, batted his eyes at me. "But they gave it to me – they believe all this mumbo-jumbo. I thought the least I could do was wear it for them."

Anything for a good time, I thought and handed the medallion back to him.

"Wait 'til you see their place. It's as odd as they are."

FOUR

The *Casa de Ernie's Familia* was out in Arlanza: a couple of turns off of Arlington Avenue and we had indeed stepped off the beaten path.

There was a tall, ivy-choked fence; chain link, I guessed, but I really couldn't tell. Ernie pulled up before an automatic gate, like the kind they have at apartment complexes. He retrieved a clicker from the dashboard and pointed it at the sensor. The gate began to clank open, disappearing into the ivy, and again I thought that he'd gotten to know these people quite well, if they'd already bestowed upon him the keys to the castle. He'd said he'd only received Lisa's letter six weeks ago.

The lawn wasn't a lawn at all; just more ivy, a dense tangle that covered the fence behind us and the fence to our right, and all of the gentle slope up to the house. The fence to the left of the dirt driveway was of planked wood, once white, but now faded to colorless gray. I noted that it was impossible to see into the neighbors' yards on either side: the plank fence and the ivy obscured the views completely. *Apparently, Candy and Lisa like their privacy,* I thought, and since there was nothing else to draw my attention, I looked up the hill at the house.

I could see that it was ramshackle, even from this distance, contrived of dark-brown clinker bricks of all things, with a shake shingle roof, decaying, the wood faded to the same color as the unmaintained fence.

Ernie pulled the car around to the grassless backyard. The lot stretched for another thirty feet or so, and was again contained in the back by the wooden fence. A few feet ahead of it, the ivy began again and climbed the slats. There was an old Chevy van parked with its grill almost touching the fence. Like everything else, it was decrepit, painted a non-descript primer gray, coated with dust. A few tendrils of ivy tentatively considered embracing the tires; it had evidently not moved in quite some time. Beside it was a turn-of-the-most-recent-century Honda Accord, the shit most definitely beat out of it. And last but not least was an old Triumph motorcycle. It was the best of the bunch, but still it wasn't much.

Like the neighbors' houses on either side, the property behind was obscured. I got the lonely impression that Candy's place was like an island, solitary in a sea of ivy and sandy dirt and lack of upkeep. It was a silly feeling; if I listened, I was sure I'd be able to hear the endless swoosh of the traffic on busy Arlington Avenue, just a few blocks away. But the place felt isolated, nonetheless.

We got out of the car and I could hear music from within, loud, live. Ernie nodded in the direction of the side door: above it were affixed two Gibson Flying V's, a black one and a white one. Runes similar to the ones on Ernie's good luck charm had been painted in red across them. All pickups and strings were intact; their necks were crossed like swords.

I looked at him in astonishment. He grinned. "What did I tell ya?"

"Let me guess. It says, *Long live rock and roll.*"

"Probably."

He knocked on the door, then after a moment, he opened it and we entered. No one could've heard his knock over the band anyway. We walked down a short hall, passing the entrance to the kitchen on the right and a bathroom on the left, and then we were in the huge front room.

There was a massive fireplace, constructed of clinker bricks, just like the house's exterior. Mounted above the mantel was Ernie's old friend, Candy's stuffed black goat's head. His weird yellow eyes regarded me impassively.

The drummer and a large, mismatched kit were in front of the blackened mouth of the fireplace, flanked by a couple of nice big amps, and a couple smaller ones on stands. Predictably, I recognized the demon Phenex's sigil, hand-drawn in black on the white bass drum. There was a grand piano, battered now, which must've been something to see in its heyday. The bass player smiled at me; the second-guitar was looking down at his pedals and hadn't noticed us come in.

The lead-guitar, the singer, Ernie's daughter – like a shy Jim Morrison, she had her back to her newly arrived audience. She was wearing a white tank top and a pair of khaki cargo pants. A mass of curly dark hair was done up in a high pony tail. When she glanced down at the floor, I could see the nubs of her spine; the bones of her shoulder blades showed through the thin material of her shirt. She had the zodiac symbol for Aquarius tattooed at the base of her neck.

From the back, she wasn't much to write home about, with her frizzy hair and her commonplace tattoo and her baggy, unflattering pants; just another skinny teenage girl with a guitar. So far, I was unimpressed.

They were halfway through a familiar AC/DC standard, released twenty years before she was born. Ernie was right: they needed some new material.

Still not noticing that anyone was in the room, she turned and approached the mike. *"Rock and roll ain't noise pollution,"* Lisa sang. She didn't attempt to imitate Brian Johnson's rough screech. *"Rock and roll, it will survive."* Instead, she imbued the lyrics with a low-pitched, sly quality. *"Yes it will."*

The bass player nodded to indicate that they had an audience, and Lisa looked out at me. An incredible expression of astonished pleasure crossed her face. It was a look of old friend, almost old lover recognition, and it surprised the hell out of me. I'd never seen this girl before in my life.

Then she looked me in the eye and sang the next lines with the curled lip and challenging leer of a woman twice her age.

'I took a look inside your bedroom door
You looked so good lyin' on your bed
Well, I asked you if you wanted any rhythm and love
You said you wanna rock and roll instead."

She was much better-looking from the front, and the lyrics were sexy, and she was sexy. But I was unmoved. That smoky stare would undoubtedly work on the boys in the crowd someday, but . . . *I've seen every blue-eyed floozy on the way,* honey, I thought unkindly.

Maybe I was uncomfortable with Ernie's daughter looking at me like that, even if it was just a rock and roll pose. It put me in mind for a moment of Denny's onstage persona: a columnist from *Rolling Stone* had once gushed, *Sensuality clings to him like sweat. He grins, he pouts, he winks; he makes you believe he'd be amenable to damn near anything you could think up, for the price of a return smile or pout or wink. Dennis Whitly broadcasts an easy availability, an irresistible, Hey, baby, ya wanna? attitude . . .*

Elise had put it more bluntly, had called a spade a shovel, as my father used to say. "Watching Denny onstage – there's just something in his voice, in the expressions he makes when he sings, when he plays his axe . . . It's like the act simulated." Elise wanted to see Denny make those same faces, but just for her, in private. As did a million girls, worldwide; as did the columnist from *Rolling Stone,* who should've known better.

It was all just an act. Once offstage, Denny was certainly not *available;* he was married, a one-woman man. All the guitar god sexuality was a put-on, a pose; it was what had made him famous, what sold records, what packed venues around the world. But he had only lived it for the first six months after he'd started fronting for Sonic Daydream. After he met Sophia, it was all just part of the set.

And I suspected it was the same with Lisa. Surely, she sang the sexy, raucous lyrics just to me, but then, I was the only one there. She wasn't going to *broadcast availability* to her daddy. Making eyes at the only other audience in the room, a man her father's age – she was just practicing for better days.

Phenex finished the AC/DC anthem; Lisa looked over her shoulder and said something to the drummer. And then she was singing *Break It To Me Gently,* and I felt my haughty, worldly-wise, once-famous-musician's contempt slip a notch. Perhaps several notches.

Like Lisa, Brenda Lee had been just a teenager when she'd recorded the song, and like Brenda, Lisa loaded it with the same mournful, soul-rending pain. The grown-up sadness in her voice had put Brenda on the map, and while Lisa's voice was devoid of the legendary singer's country twang, she nailed all the agony just as well.

Again, she sang directly to me, gazing sadly into my eyes. It was as if she'd read my mind, as if I'd dismissed her as just another skinny girl with a guitar out loud, to her face; as if I'd dismissed her, period. It was as if we were indeed lovers, and my scorn had hurt her. It was as if my contempt had positively *wounded her.*

"Break it to me gently, let me down the e-e-e-asy way." The words rolled out of her like poisoned honey, sweet, unbearably painful. *"Make me feel that you still love me, if it's just, if it's just for one more day."*

I wanted to look away. I didn't want to feel the way that she was making me feel, that I had wronged her, that I was leaving her. *"If you must go, then go slowly. Let me love you 'till the last."*

But I couldn't look away. She made me feel every syllable of her pain, and worse, that I was the source of it. No one had ever made me feel like that from just a song, as if I was the cause of some irretrievable loss. It was just a corny, whiny old ballad, but oh, my God, *her voice . . .*

Ernie was right. His daughter was a phenomenal singer. She would go far.

Lisa finished the sad old tune: *"'Cause I'll never lo-o-o-ove a-a-again,"* and then she smiled at me. I thought there was a tiny, almost imperceptible glint of triumph in her eyes; probably from the astonished expression on my face.

"Calvin Bascomb," she whispered into the mike, and her speaking voice, amplified, was just as low and melodic as her singing voice. "As I live and breathe."

Lisa's first words to me were odd, unexpected. A subtle mockery in her lyrical voice pinged in my brain, and the superiority of an old, once-famous musician returned to me instantly. Sure, she was good, but who was she? She was nobody, the offspring of some kinky witch and my old friend Ernie. So what?

Lisa had seen that I'd been impressed with her performance, and I would be goddamned before I would let her see it anymore. *It's a long way to the top if ya wanna rock and roll, baby. Maybe you should include that AC/DC standard in your Cenozoic set list.*

Ernie opened his mouth to introduce us, but Lisa spoke again, cutting him off. "I've seen your picture."

She set her axe on its stand and approached with her hand outstretched, and I shook it, feeling all of a guitarist's inevitable callouses on her fingers. Her grip was firm, very strong, her manner straightforward as she told me her name. There was no nervous reverence in the presence of legendary rock and roll greatness about her, not like the rest of the band, who hung back, bashfully waiting to be introduced. Again, it was if she already knew me.

No, in no way was Lisa a shy teenager, and in this she reminded me of Elise at the same age. They had similar blue eyes, though Lisa had dark hair, whereas Elise had been a blonde. Lisa's coloring was similar to Ernie's in his youth, but to my immense relief, she resembled him in no other way. She was definitely his, however: he'd informed me with a crooked grin that a DNA test had confirmed it. *She must take after her mother,* I thought.

Lisa said, "I read your book." She glanced around the room, and to my utter surprise, she snatched a dog-eared copy of it off of one of the amps. "Maybe you can autograph it for me."

But she made no move to find a pen, or to hand it to me. She was kidding. I was her daddy's drummer; no more nor less famous than he'd once been. She didn't need my autograph.

"We've all read it." The second-guitar stepped up and introduced himself. He told me that his name was Sonny and that he was a big fan of my music. It was evidently true: he pumped my hand enthusiastically, and bestowed upon me that familiar, slightly dazed fan-smile.

"Are you a drummer?"

"I have been," he replied, the shy smile remaining. "I also play the piano. And the guitar. Mostly, we play whatever Candy says we should, so James is our drummer."

James shook my hand. He was a large man, bull-like, unsmiling. He had shoulder-length, blazing red hair, which would've made him seem comical if it weren't for his size and his glowering, unamused biker's expression, not to mention the tattoo of a goat on his beefy shoulder, similar to the stuffed head above the fireplace. "Nice to meet you," he said gruffly, unconvincingly. Unlike Sonny, James was not a fan. I was just another old guy to him.

The bass player's name was Roy, and he was James's opposite: small and wiry, with close-cropped, dyed blonde hair. He also enthusiastically shook my hand, told me he was a fan. But it struck me that his smile, while wide and seemingly welcoming, didn't quite reach his eyes. Roy was just kissing my ass, which was entirely unnecessary. I was left with the impression that he was not someone to turn my back on.

Lisa had thumbed through the beat-up copy of *Sonic Nightmare,* had found the *About the Author* page at the back, complete with a flattering likeness, if I say so myself, of the smiling drummer from a famous band. My expression in it was chock-full of a successful musician's bravado. *Ah, those were the days.*

I remembered the publicity chick from the publisher, pawing thru stacks of Sonic Daydream concert stills. "Why are there so many of everybody else and so few of you?"

"I'm the drummer, honey. You know, back there, behind the kit? I only come out to the front of the stage to take a bow at the end."

She had not found that funny, but had been delighted when she'd discovered this one good picture of me.

"You haven't changed a bit, Cal," Lisa stated.

Inexplicably, I was again mildly offended at the *familiarity* of her words. Who was this *kid,* to be calling me by my first name, once more, like she knew me? It was a bizarre reaction – what was she supposed to call me, *Mr. Bascomb,* like the kids at the Y?

I didn't know where my annoyance was coming from. Maybe I suspected that she was making fun of me, giving me back some of the derision that she'd read on me earlier, because I certainly had changed from the cocky, long-haired, twenty-six-year-old in the picture. But Lisa wasn't making fun of me, and even if she was, so what? I surely wasn't sensitive about being old.

It occurred to me that maybe I just didn't like her. Or maybe I liked her too much: *Christ, but she could sing,* and she knew it. Maybe it was that ever-present twinkle of triumph in her eye. It was arrogant, off-putting in someone so young. Maybe I thought she should be a little awestruck, like Sonny, who was a good ten or twelve years older than her. Maybe it was because her confidence imbued her with a subtle yet stunning beauty, and I just didn't know how to handle the unexpected surprise of that.

"Rock and roll. The fountain of youth," Ernie said, and slapped me on the back.

Lisa's momentary spell on me was broken, and I was left to ponder the idea that I was attracted to Ernie's eighteen-year-old daughter, like I'd never been attracted to another woman. I didn't like the idea, not in the least. I was a staggering *thirty-seven* years older than her, and from that undeniable fact of chronology, of seasons passed and long years lived, came the basis for my offense, for my dislike: how dare she affect me so? It wasn't right for her to look at me like she did, to speak my name with such familiarity, as if I was some *boy* who might be interested in a little slap and tickle behind one of the big amps once the rest of the band went home. It was . . . *disrespectful,* that's what it was, and I should've and would've been amused by it, were it not for the fact that I had discovered that I was rather helplessly responding to it.

That would have to stop immediately.

It wasn't because she was Ernie's daughter. I'd known Ernie for forty years, and he wouldn't care if I made a play for her. He'd only been a daddy for six weeks, and a lifetime of *Anything for a good time* didn't evaporate because of a positive DNA test. Ernie was a true feminist: whatever the women wanted from him, he was more than happy to give it to them, and I had no doubt that this philosophy extended to his old bandmate as well. If his daughter wanted me, well . . . hell. Age was just a number.

I wanted to dislike Lisa because I wasn't like Ernie. I'd never had *that give 'em what they want, because, hot damn, ain't it fun?* attitude. At this late date, I should've been immune to the charming come-hither-old-guy smile of an eighteen-year-old girl; for my entire life, I'd been mostly immune to the charm of such looks in general. Like Freddie had said, *Their beauty and their style wear kinda smooth after a while.* They wanted what they wanted; it didn't mean that I wanted it, too. There had been girls, especially in my youth, but there had been no monumental love in my life, except for maybe Elise, and the realization of that hadn't come until years after it was too late.

But I recognized immediately that here was a girl who could make a fool out of me, could lead me to make a fool out of myself. And I'd lived too long to allow such a thing to occur. I was too old to even entertain the thought of such impossible ridiculousness.

"What would you like to hear next?" she asked. "I've always been a big fan of Pink Floyd. David Gilmour's one of my idols."

David Gilmour's got guitar strings older than you, I thought immediately. My sense of self-preservation returned, again manifesting itself as scorn for her youth. I was again in control, no longer allowing myself to be dumbstruck by her confident beauty, by the way she looked at me, by her voice.

She glanced at Sonny and he pulled the guitar strap over his head, set his instrument on its stand and seated himself at the piano. The rest of the band resumed their places, and Sonny began the intro to *The Great Gig in the Sky.* Lisa again smiled at me, and I suddenly felt trapped, like the oft-mentioned rat, lost in a maze of memories.

There had been a girl once, whose name escaped me at the moment. It had to have been about 1983, I had to have been about twenty, and the unmistakable slow piano reminded me of the exquisite manner in which we had enjoyed each other, while Clare Torry wailed and screamed through just this song in the background. I hadn't gone through as many women as Ernie, or even Denny, but I'd had my share, and this particular nameless chick and the night we'd spent together had been a standout in the sexual history of Calvin Bascomb.

Sonny's intro had put me in mind of a spectacularly steamy adventure from my long-ago youth, and I didn't want it playing through my mind and my nerve endings while Lisa recreated the tune in her remarkable voice, whilst she stared at me with her triumphant, knowing blue eyes. I was not *frightened of dying,* but Ernie's daughter singing *The Great Gig in the Sky* to me would be entirely too much. Hence the feeling of being trapped.

The piano picked up tempo; Roy and Lisa slid their fingers up the necks of guitar and bass; James drummed the first few beats. But before Lisa could open her mouth and utter a single *Oh,* Phenex stopped abruptly, and I was saved the psychological ravages of listening to this incredible young woman's rendition of surely one of the most erotic songs in all of rock and roll. And least it had always been so to me.

I realized that I'd been holding my breath, anticipating. I let it out and reflected that it had been quite a day. I'd seen my old friend for the first time in years; had discovered that he was now a family man, proud papa to the girl-front of a band named after a demon. I'd met his child – though she was no child. From the way she looked at me, I realized that she'd probably already had the kind of adventures Floyd's old tune had brought to mind. Yeah, Lisa had been around the block – she was no innocent. She was just exceptionally young, a beautiful, dark-haired, blue-eyed woman with a phenomenal voice. I'd had her stare at me from behind her guitar, and at her stare, I'd felt stirrings I hadn't felt in decades.

Lisa now smiled at someone behind me, and I turned. It was the arrival of the lady of the house that had stopped Phenex. Lisa's mother, Ernie's long ago groupie, Candy.

She gave Ernie a lengthy, luxuriant hug, which I noticed he did not return. He only smiled at her; then he glanced almost guiltily at Sonny, who frowned. I remembered Ernie's words: *The second-guitar is Mom's current boyfriend.*

Candy had long ago communed with the spirits and Ernie LaBelle; it had been a concerted effort on her part to conceive the unbelievable young woman before me now. Candy had called herself Ernie's biggest fan, had certainly proved herself to be such. How was his reappearance in her life affecting the young musician with whom she was communing these days?

I didn't have time to reflect on that sticky situation at the moment. Ernie was introducing us; Candy was extending her hand.

I clasped it, said it was nice to meet her. She had incredibly long fingernails, painted black, and various bulky rings. She regarded me with a little curious smile, her hand lingering in mine, which gave me the opportunity to get a good look at her, to fully appreciate the image she attempted to project.

She could've been an attractive woman for her age, if she would've only accepted that she was indeed her age. Joe Gillis, William Holden's doomed character from *Sunset Boulevard,* spoke in my head: *There's nothing tragic about being fifty. Not unless you're trying to be twenty-five.*

Candy wasn't fifty; my earlier calculations had placed her at about forty-three or four. But she was surely trying to be twenty-five, or more accurately, she was trying to be eighteen. Her daughter's age.

A ghost of the girl she must've been remained: her figure was ample but trim. I could see that she had rivaled or even surpassed Lisa in big-eyed, black-haired beauty once upon a time. But now the raven color obviously came out of a bottle; it was too monochromatic in its blackness to be anything but artificial. The great volume of it, wild, unkempt, only added to the failure of the illusion of youth. The heavy eye make-up she wore was flawlessly applied, and on a younger woman it would've lent a sultry, smoky-eyed allure. Against the mild crow's feet around her eyes, it made Candy look like a somewhat startled raccoon.

Her full mouth, slightly slack, would've benefitted from a lighter shade of lipstick. But of course, she'd opted for a young, tough girl's scarlet. She wore a pair of impossibly tight jeans and an ancient, black Sonic Daydream t-shirt – are concert t-shirts ever any other color? It was not one of those vintage reissues you can pick up for your grandkids at Target, however, but the original article. The groupie image was completed by a studded belt and black leather, high-heeled boots.

If I'd seen her from behind, Candy could've stepped right out of 1989, chosen from the hopeful throng by a grinning roadie's summons, ready and eager and willing to satisfy her favorite guitarist's every whim. But once she turned around and I got a look at her face, the intervening years would've been painfully apparent. Candy still dressed like a groupie; she had chosen to ignore the indignities of age. In revenge, age made her look ridiculous.

Surely, there are men that fight Father Time, too, men that dye their hair and get their tummies tucked – and they look just as ridiculous as Candy did. Madison Avenue had given us a truism with the old Parkay commercial: *You can't fool Mother Nature.*

But men are allowed to age gracefully, or monstrously, depending on how they decide to let themselves go. I considered that Ernie and I had done pretty well: we were both gray, but were still as trim as we'd been in our prime. I wondered how the Whitly brothers were faring these days. Had they allowed themselves to get fat, to go to seed, in the secure love of their good women?

But for the ladies – aging itself was deemed letting themselves go, especially if they were involved in a profession where looks are paramount, such as show business or real estate or politics – or even groupiehood.

I reflected that though Candy seemed a little garish to me – she reminded me somehow of a big black spider in a Sonic Daydream tee – she had done all right for herself. She'd ensnared Sonny in her web, and he couldn't be a day over thirty-two.

Candy said it was nice to meet me, ceased staring curiously at me, dropped my hand. She told the band, unnecessarily, to take five, then suggested that we all go out to the kitchen and have lunch. Ernie mentioned that he and I had just drunk ours, so a little food would be nice, and I thought, is it still lunch time?

Like in Vegas, there was no clock in the giant room where Phenex rehearsed. It couldn't be termed a studio by any means, but in its lack of a timepiece, it could've been Abbey Road. I'm sure Richie Blackmore would back me up – I'd wager there'd been no clocks at the casino in Montreux or in the mobile or at the Grand Hotel. Musicians tend not to like to mark the passage of time while they're recording or rehearsing. *Beth I hear you calling, but I can't come home right now . . .*

When I thought about it though, I realized that Ernie and I couldn't have been there more than maybe ten or twelve minutes. Phenex had been halfway through *Rock and Roll Ain't Noise Pollution* when we'd walked in. Lisa had then belted out *Break It To Me Gently,* and in doing so, had captured my full attention. She'd said a few words, Ernie introduced me to the band. Then Lisa aimed to torment me further by subjecting me to *The Great Gig in the Sky.* But I'd been spared by her mother's appearance.

All told, not more that fifteen minutes, tops. Yet I felt as though I'd stood in this big, ugly room for hours, with its shabby instruments and its cold, blackened fireplace. Surely, the stuffed goat's head had been silently regarding me for longer than a mere quarter or an hour? But it wasn't so – this feeling of a longer passage of time, this almost-drugged feeling of transformation – it was all in my head. It was all just my reaction to Lisa's confidence, her incredible voice, the things that her enticing smile hinted at, promised, if I hadn't been so painfully cognizant of the insurmountable gulf of the decades that separated us.

I shook my head and watched her leave with the band and Ernie and her mother. I was entirely too old for this shit, for the illusions of a possibility of something that had long ago passed me by.

Sonny lingered at the piano, idly played a few notes. Then he looked up and met my gaze. Without preamble, quite unexpectedly, he said, "I get the feeling that I'm not long for this band."

I tried to keep my face expressionless, but of course I knew what he was talking about. He nodded down the hall. "The greatest guitar player ever, and all that."

A short guffaw escaped me. "He's not hardly the greatest –"

"He's not even in the top twenty, if you ask me. He's surely no Dennis Whitly."

"I wouldn't put him in the top twenty, either."

"*Rolling Stone* said –"

"Christ, Sonny! How do you know what *Rolling Stone* said? That was almost thirty years ago."

He grinned. "The internet." Then he shrugged, looked down at the piano, played a few more notes. "Regardless, I still get the impression that I'm about to be replaced. On all levels."

I walked around the amps and the mikes, the guitars; I stepped over the pedals and myriad cables duct-taped to the floor, and sat on the end of the piano bench next to him. "I really don't think you have anything to worry about."

"Candy thinks he's the greatest guitar player ever. And he's Lisa's father."

I felt for Sonny a little bit. That groupie-love had been known to overshadow real relationships, even if it was just for one night. Diehard fans that would never think of cheating on their boyfriends forgot about fidelity in a heartbeat if the opportunity arose to nail their favorite guitar player. It was usually a once-in-a-lifetime chance, not to be passed up.

Candy had taken her chance, and it had produced dividends – enough to attract the attention of her favorite guitar player again, eighteen years later. I thought that Ernie wouldn't have given Candy a second look, otherwise: she was quite a bit long in the tooth for his tastes.

And Sonny was no love-struck kid, even if he was ten years younger than Candy, but still I felt for him. It was obvious that his woman still had a bit of a warm for the old rock star, and Sonny didn't feel like he could compete with that.

"But you're her man, right? How long have you been together?"

He considered. "It's been about ten years. She picked me up after a gig in Frisco one night. I was in a band called Emerald Beach." When I raised an eyebrow at the moniker, Sonny shrugged. "Yeah, I know. The singer got laid there once. Maybe it was the first time he got laid. I don't really remember. It was a long time ago. I was only twenty-one.

"Emerald Beach wasn't going anywhere, any more than Phenex has, just a few not-much-pay gigs around town. I was bagging groceries for a day job. I'd seen Candy at a couple of our shows, once with James and once with Roy. I figured one of them was her boyfriend, and when she came up to me after our set and told me how much she like the way I drummed, I asked her about it. She said no, they were just her *familiars . . .*"

"She said it like that?"

Sonny nodded, played the intro to *Bad Company;* I could almost hear Paul Rodgers humming along. "They were just her companions, she said, along on this path to help her look after her daughter."

Sonny stopped playing and glanced over at me, to see how I was taking all this oddness. I remained expressionless, and he continued. "But she said she liked me, wanted something more from me than companionship." He grinned crookedly, and I grinned back. "I was pretty sure what that was, so I went home with her."

I remembered Ernie's description of Candy's witchy little apartment in Frisco, all blacks and dark greens, with the goat as silent sentinel and a pot of blood and a paintbrush by the side of the bed. I waited for a similar description from Sonny, but he talked of other things.

"Yeah, she wanted that from me, but there was something else. It didn't become readily apparent until we'd been together for about six months. And by then I was hooked."

Candy was surely not much of a fisherman these days – and it was as if Sonny read my mind. "She was something back then, wild, like a force of nature. *So hot.* And the things she told me, how much she loved me, how we would be together forever, what a great musician I was, almost as great as . . ." Sonny gestured down the hall, then frowned a little sheepishly, embarrassed at how he'd gone on about Candy, someone whom he thought might just be getting ready to dump him. He tinkled out a few bars of *Thunder Road* to cover his sentimentality, only to inadvertently express it further. *You ain't a beauty but hey, you're all right.*

"There were other incentives, besides just Candy herself," he went on with another crooked smile, and rolled into *Werewolves of London.* I smiled at his talent, at his fanciful accompaniment to the story, and he smiled back at my appreciation of it. "I quit Emerald Beach and James and Roy and I started Phenex. I was the singer, if you can feature that. I'm no singer. It was all Candy's idea. The whole witchy thing . . . She picked out the name and she claimed that she used the influence of the demon himself to get us gigs.

"There've never been too many, but she's always told us that the forces are aligning – we're gonna hit the big time someday." Sonny grinned and played a few unmistakable bars of *Don't Stop Believin'*.

Maybe with Lisa fronting for you, I thought. *Maybe with Ernie's money helping you along. But you're gonna have to change that ridiculous name, and you're gonna have to get some new material.*

"The other good thing about being with Candy . . . It also happened about six months after we met. Her grandmother died. Left her this house, and a small fortune. We moved here to your little town, me and Candy and James and Roy and Lisa. I miss Frisco sometimes, but except for playing a couple gigs around town . . . I'm just like you. Not famous, of course, but I haven't worked a day in the last ten years. No more bagging groceries. Candy supports all four of us, from the interest on Grandma's money. She's not what you'd call wealthy –"

"I thought she worked at that occult bookstore downtown? Mohini's?"

"That's just so she can keep in touch with the local coven."

"Really?" I was amazed. "There's a local coven?"

"Yeah. They hold their rituals out there in the dark on Box Springs Mountain. They go a couple times a month. Candy and James and Roy, and since she was about thirteen, Lisa's gone with them."

"But not you?"

Sonny shrugged, ran his fingers across the keys tunelessly.

"I'm surprised they allow an unbeliever in their midst," I said with mock gravity.

"Not so much an unbeliever as a non-practitioner, anymore. My level of involvement in her . . . *faith* . . . that's not the reason Candy keeps me around, anyway."

"It has to do with your level of involvement *with her,"* I opined with a crooked grin of my own.

"There's that, but it's never been entirely about that. Like I say, I didn't figure out the real reason Candy chose me until we'd been together for a while." Sonny sighed. "From talking to the other guys in Emerald Beach, she'd found out that I could read music, that I could play damn near any instrument . . ."

Sonny paused and I waited. At last he sighed again and spit it out. "Lisa was eight when I met Candy. She'd been through a succession of music teachers, all uptight straights who didn't particularly care for her mother's looks, regardless of how green her money was. I'd learned a lot of what I know from similar types, when I was a kid, but Candy didn't like any of them, didn't think any of them were good enough to teach Ernie LaBelle's daughter. But once she met me . . . May God have mercy on my soul. I was good enough. I taught Lisa how to play the guitar, Cal. I taught her how to read music. I taught her how to sing."

"And a fabulous job you've done," I told him genuinely.

He shrugged. "She has the genes for it, right?" Again he nodded down the hall. "So it was never that important to Candy that I wasn't as abject a believer as her *minions.* I believe enough. I know all the scripture, the rituals. I used to go with them, but . . . standing around in the woods, chanting, all the other shit they do out there . . . Once Lisa started going with them, I lost interest.

"I still do the Invoking and Banishing Rituals with them . . ." He pointed at four colored circles painted on the walls, one in each of the cardinal directions. I hadn't noticed them before. "To rid us of evil influences. But overall, I'm become disillusioned with the whole thing. Phenex still isn't famous." He grinned to indicate that he didn't think that was ever going to happen. "And now, Candy's reunited with the world's greatest guitar player. There's nothing more I can teach Lisa, so like I say, I get the feeling that my tenure here is about to be revoked."

"I really don't think you have anything to worry about, Sonny," I repeated. "Let me tell you a little something about the world's greatest guitar player." I couldn't say that without cracking a smile, and Sonny smiled back at me. "I've known him for forty years, so you can believe it. Ernie doesn't want Candy."

His smiled faltered. I couldn't tell him that Ernie didn't want Candy because he wasn't into aging groupies, although that was certainly one of the reasons. So I told him another truth. "He knows she's your girl. There've always been plenty of fish in the sea to Ernie – literally, overflowing nets full. So he's never been one to be snatching any off of someone else's boat. You get what I'm telling you? Ernie would never make a play for someone else's girlfriend, Sonny. No matter how . . . *hot* she is. It's just not how he operates. Trust me on this. I've known him for a long time."

"I appreciate your advice, Cal, and I appreciate your friend's integrity. But the decision isn't up to him. It's up to her. So don't be surprised if you come back here someday in the not too distant future, and find out that I'm gone."

"Seriously, man, I don't think you have to worry about –"

"Hey. Sonny."

We looked up. Lisa was standing at the end of the hallway.

"Mom says, *Let's eat.* The food's getting cold."

"Tell her we'll be right there."

Lisa looked at us inquisitively for another second, then she shrugged and went back down the hall. When he was sure she was gone, Sonny leaned closer to me. He pulled a medallion on a chain out from under his shirt. It was the same type that Candy and Lisa had gifted to Ernie, only older, worn a little smooth around the edges. Sonny whispered, "If they try to give you one of these, don't take it."

"What? Ernie already has –"

"Yeah, Ernie's already in way over his head. He just doesn't know it yet. James and Roy and I, we all wear one, but . . . I like you, Cal. You're an awesome drummer. One of the greats. You've sat here and sympathetically listened to me bitch about the unfair cards I've suddenly been dealt. They will fall where they will, and there's nothing I can do about it now. Again, may God have mercy on my soul. But I'm telling you, if they try to give you one of these, refuse it."

"How –"

"I dunno. Make something up. Tell them you're allergic to silver or something. Just don't take it. Don't carry it, don't put it around your neck – "

"What the hell, Sonny?" Now it was Candy standing in the mouth of the hall, hands on hips, obviously annoyed. "I made cheddar-onion cheeseburgers, just for you, and now they're getting cold." The scarlet mouth formed into a pout, and I again thought that the expression had probably been cute twenty years ago. Now it just communicated exasperated impatience.

Sonny stood, dropped the medallion back into his shirt. "We're coming right now," he told her. When she didn't turn and leave as Lisa had done, he closed the cover on the piano and said to me, "Don't forget what I asked you about that score."

Score? We hadn't discussed any music . . . Then I realized he was referring again to my refusal of groupies bearing gifts.

Whatever. The whole scene was just too bizarre. “I won’t,” I assured him.

“Great.” He glanced at his woman, waiting for us, then back at me. “Do you like cheddar-onion cheeseburgers, Cal? Candy makes the best ones in town.”

As we walked down the hall to the kitchen with her, I wondered if she’d gotten the recipe from the demon Phenex. Amused at my own wit, somewhere in the back of my mind, I heard Tim Curry sing, *I’ll get you a satanic mechanic . . .*

FIVE

For the next six weeks or so, Ernie and I – for lack of a better word – *mentored* Phenex.

In the beginning, before they would act on any suggestion we offered, the four of them would first look to Candy for permission. She was road manager, promoter, music critic and house mother all in one. Phenex was *her* band. Except that they had never been on the road under her dubious management, and she'd only promoted them to a couple of gigs at dives around Riverside, scintillating nightspots that made the sixty-five soul capacity and ragged bonhomie of the old The House of Ale look like the vaster space and we're-on-our-way professionalism of The House of Blues.

Candy immediately deferred to our experience as musicians – she neither sang nor played any instrument. She'd only ever been a fan. To make a comparison to the medical profession, Ernie and I were heart surgeons, whereas Candy was just a country, herbal-remedy witch. She told her band gleefully to do whatever we said, then stopped coming to rehearsals altogether, so they wouldn't be nervous in her presence. As the saying goes, Candy knew on which side her bread was buttered. Sonic Daydream-caliber rock stars didn't just drop by to counsel nobodies like Phenex every day.

Before Denny came along, Ernie had once alternated with Lenny as songwriter and singer for Sonic Daydream, so he and Lisa came up with some new tunes. I found it strangely pleasant to hear father and daughter harmonize, while Sonny tinkled out melodies on the piano and wrote down the words and music.

The new material sounded like Sonic Daydream – the same had been said for the stuff that Ernie had written for Azomite. It was odd that it turned out that way: Denny had penned all of Sonic Daydream's hits; every single one of them. Ernie had never written any of the money-makers, plus, his style was different. I don't think Ernie intended for his Azomite and Phenex songs to sound like Denny's; perhaps he unconsciously mimicked the younger Whitly's formulas because he'd never stopped believing that Denny was a great guy. Or at least a great musician.

Roy was an adequate bass player, competent but not imaginative. So Ernie imagined for him, and Roy doggedly memorized and gave back the licks Ernie showed him. Similarly, James was a serious, heavy-handed drummer. He kept the beat well enough, but he attacked the high hat as if it owed him money. I tried to teach him a little flair, a little subtlety, a little whimsy. It was an uphill battle: like Roy, the big redhead lacked imagination. I did coax a smile out of him when I taught him a few extraneous stick twirls, however.

"The ladies love that," Ernie said.

"The drums are the backbone to the piece," I told James. "Point and counterpoint to the listener's heartbeat. They are the first instruments developed by mankind. The guitars might affect the listener's emotions . . ." As if on cue, Sonny wailed effortlessly through the opening solo to *All Along the Watchtower.* Sonny had talent; he needed no mentoring.

"But without the drums, it might as well be chamber music. The drums make it rock and roll."

I figured that millions of Jimmy Page and Eddie Van Halen and Dennis Whitly and Ernie LaBelle fans would disagree with me. They were entitled to their opinions, but no one could convince me otherwise: the drums made the song.

Ernie was holding Roy's bass at the moment, and I happened to be seated behind James's kit. Lisa smiled and turned on her mike, removed it from its stand. She said, "Show him, Cal."

"All right."

It was a guitarist's song – Dylan was no drummer – but there was still plenty of room to get down. Sonny was nothing if not skilled, and of course, Ernie had not made it to the top of the known rock and roll universe by being mediocre; he could play six-string or bass equally well. With good musicians playing with me, I was surprised at how not rusty I was.

Lisa again turned her back on our non-existent audience and sang directly to me. It was something she always did whenever I was present, wherever I was in the room. But this was a brooding song, not a sexy one, and I returned her smug smile. Who felt that *life was but a joke* more than me?

I hadn't played with anybody but myself for years – an apt turn of phrase on so many levels – and it felt good. I wasn't exhilarated, reborn with a new desire to mount the stage and perform before a screaming audience again, or any of that claptrap. Despite the handful of old rockers that still toured, including my pal Ernie himself, I considered the rigors of the road to be a young man's sport. But hammering out a timeless classic behind talented guitarists and a great singer did bring back a little bit of the thrill. I would certainly enjoy doing it every now and again, playing just for the joy of it, like Ernie and Lenny and I had done a million years ago in my parents' garage.

We finished the song and Lisa turned hopefully to Roy and James. I guess we'd had a kind of an audience, after all. Roy was open-mouthed in stunned amazement. I reckoned that a guitar player always recognizes a superior talent, even if he's not prepared to admit it to himself or them. Not surprisingly, after a second, Roy blinked and his awed appreciation vanished. The look on his face now said that he thought that the second-guitar for world-renowned Sonic Daydream was all right on the bass, and his own second-guitar was passing-fair, but it wasn't anything he himself couldn't equal. He was kidding himself. Phenex would never sound this good with its actual drummer and bassist.

If she looked for some spark of sudden understanding in James, Lisa was disappointed. He just shrugged at her expectant, *do-you-get-it-now?* gaze. He failed to grasp from my demonstration that there was nuance to rock drumming; it remained only time marked out on a scale to him, no different than the cadence of a marching band.

This was what Ernie and I had to work with.

Still, things went well. The mood at the dilapidated clinker-brick manse was always light and enthusiastic, hopeful. Ernie had promised them a couple of good gigs, when he thought they were ready. I had no idea how he planned to accomplish that, but figured that his face and his name would at least get them a sight unseen show at The House of Ale.

Candy paid more attention to Sonny and less attention to her baby-daddy. There were no more luxuriant, lingering hugs, and I could tell that Ernie didn't miss them. He liked Sonny, and just as I'd said, he had no desire to steal his woman, even though it would've been easy enough for him to do so. It just wasn't Ernie's style.

Sonny whispered no more warnings to me against accepting good luck charms, maybe because none had been offered. We spoke almost exclusively about music, as if our impromptu heart-to-heart had not occurred. I talked him into drumming for me once – Big Red certainly didn't care – and as was not unexpected, he showed himself to be a better drummer than James could ever dream of becoming, even if he practiced every day for the rest of his life. But the band played the instruments that Candy wanted them to play, and James didn't know a fret from a pick-up on a guitar.

Lisa eased up on the come-hither stares. Don't get me wrong – I still caught her looking at me sometimes, appraisingly, almost like she was studying me. But when I did so she would just give me a sly smile or a quick wink and look away. Her promise-filled, wordless invitations before had of course lasted only seconds, though they had seemed like minutes to me. I'd stared back at her, helpless to look away, like the transfixed mongoose of legend. I feared that at any moment she might verbalize it – *Hey, Cal, ya wanna?* – and then I'd be just as helpless not to refuse.

Or maybe it was all in my head. Maybe I thought Lisa was silently coming on to me because I wanted her to, because her incredible voice and her youthful beauty had affected me as had no other woman's. That was all most assuredly my problem alone.

But I wasn't entirely imagining it – maybe just giving it more weight and importance than she did. One time she questioned me as if I was some sort of a curiosity to her. It seemed that Lisa was far more interested in the motivations of an aging drummer than was to be expected in a normal world, one in which beautiful young girls could not possibly care less about aging drummers.

The rest of the band had gone to eat lunch; only James and I remained in the big room. He wanted to review a piece from one of Ernie's new songs. Ernie and I had of course collaborated as seamlessly as we had in the pre-Denny, Sonic Daydream days, but James was having a little trouble with his part. I was standing by dutifully, listening to him ham-handedly bang his way through it, when Lisa materialized next to me. It was just like that: one minute she was not there, and in the next, the air beside me seemed electrified, like before a storm, full of compelling potential. I felt the hair on my arm stand on end; I looked, and there she was, smiling at me. It seemed that my body reacted to her before my mind was even aware that she was near.

James finished up with the simple fill that ended the passage. As with everything he or Roy produced, it was adequate. More practice would make it more technically accurate, maybe – but more practice wouldn't imbue James with any more talent.

He didn't wait for my critique, but glanced at Lisa, then said, "I'm gonna go grab something to eat. I'll try it again later." He set his sticks on the snare and departed.

I couldn't follow him because Lisa was more or less blocking my path. I again became aware of a tingling sensation – *please don't stand so close to me* – or maybe it was all in my mind. I breathed and

I could smell the fresh scent of her hair, her skin, and maybe I just imagined that it made me light-headed. Like a coward, I retreated behind the drums to get away from her. I played the fill the way it should be played, then idly twirled one of the sticks and watched her. I waited.

"The ladies always like that." She smiled and her eyes twinkled. She paused until I smiled back, then she said, "What is it that you want out of life, Cal? Do you want hot and cold running women, like Ernie, until the day you can't get it up anymore?"

I suppressed a wince at her straightforwardness, and gave her a rim shot for her whimsy. Mark Knopfler sang in my head, *When my ugly big car won't-a climb this hill, I'll write a suicide note on a hundred dollar bill . . .* But I remained silent.

"Or maybe you want to be famous again, tour the world, like you did with Dennis Whitly's band?"

This reference stung a bit – it had been *my* band, with Ernie and Lenny, *our* band, long before Denny had ever decided to pick up a six-string. But Lisa's sting was minimal, because what she said was true: when we were famous, when we toured the world, Sonic Daydream *was* Dennis Whitly's band. And fame had never been what I'd sought anyway, had never meant anything to me. Calvin Bascomb had always just been along for the ride. In my mind, Roger Waters slowly intoned, *Shall we set out across this sea of faces, in search of more and more applause?* Still I said nothing.

"Or do you want happily-ever-after with a family, like Denny, or without a family, like his brother? Pretend I'm the genie in the bottle and can grant your three dearest desires, Cal. What would make you happy? What is it that you want?"

And she stared steadily at me, big blue eyes searching. But her smile said that she already knew what she was looking for, that she already knew the answer to her own question.

No famous lyrics came to my mind now; just the simplest of three letter replies. *You. I want you. Not for just a day or a night, but every day, for whatever time I have left. I want to forget about the loneliness I've inflicted upon myself for most of my life. I want to forget about Elise, the tragedy I allowed to happen. I want you.*

But of course I didn't say that. Wanting Lisa was like wanting to live in the glittering town I'd glimpsed one time, strewn out like jewels on the slope of a dark mountain. I could have her – she was just that curious about me – all I'd have to do was say the word.

But in the morning, the magical-looking town that I'd seen from the tour bus window had turned out to be nowhere more enchanted than Albuquerque, New Mexico of all godawful places. Yet my spectacular memory of the panorama of its lights through the smudgy glass remained, and I wished it had been real.

And so it would be in the morning, with Lisa. Her curiosity satisfied – probably her curiosity and nothing else – I'd just be another old guy to her, another experience to be filed under, *Well, I'll Never Do That Again.*

But I would still want her. I would always want her.

So I said, "When you get to be my age, it's happiness just to see another sunrise. At my age, the guiding philosophy is, *Any day above ground is a good day."*

"You're not that old, Cal."

"I'm not that young, Lisa." I felt a shot of daring and asked, "What is it that would make you happy? What is it that you want?"

She answered immediately. "I want revenge."

This reply took me completely by surprise. Of all the things I might've guessed she might say, this was not even on the list.

"Revenge? Against who? For what?"

"What've you got?" Lisa smiled brightly. "I'm just kidding, Cal." She stepped closer to the kit, closer to me, and her eyes practically glowed. She lowered her voice to a husky whisper. "You know what I think?" She ran her fingers lightly over the snare, making it hiss like a rattlesnake. "I think I could –"

But then Ernie and the rest of Phenex were coming back into the room, laughing and talking noisily. Lisa turned and scowled at them, and to my immense relief, she did not look back at me again.

Oh, you definitely could, I thought. Now Sarah McLachlan wailed in my head, *Into the sea of waking dreams, I follow without pride. Nothing stands between us here, and I won't be denied.*

But I had pride. I would not follow, and I would deny myself. Lisa could sing, she was beautiful, and she enjoyed toying with me, making eyes and now almost making suggestions to her newfound daddy's old bandmate, simply because she could, because it obviously amused her for some unfathomable reason. But I wasn't going to let her make a fool of me. I wasn't going to make a fool of myself.

After this exchange, the looks seemed to slow down, and I became more relaxed around her. They didn't stop entirely, however, no matter how much I alternately wished and feared that they would.

Phenex responded well to our coaching. After six weeks, they coalesced as a group, even if they didn't stand out as an overly talented one.

SIX

It was a long, tiresome drive from Temecula to the Arlanza area of Riverside. I'd been staying with Ernie at his place on Victoria Avenue while we tutored Phenex, however, even though there were plenty of empty rooms in Candy's big, clinker-brick house. The dim staircase that led upstairs was just off the band room, and she constantly invited us to stay there and take advantage of the accommodations. But in that way might trouble lie for Ernie as well as for me, so every night when rehearsal and dinner and conversation concluded, the two of us dutifully returned to his expensive, secluded manse, nestled there amongst the orange trees.

But I still had to go home every now and then, to make sure the McMansion hadn't burned down, that it hadn't been robbed in my absence. Nothing was ever amiss; my home remained secure, another huge, cookie-cutter house on a small lot in a subdivision full of them, indistinguishable from all the others.

When I returned from one of these sojourns, there was an unfamiliar car parked in Candy's grassless backyard. Beside Ernie's dusty, baby-blue, rock star's Porsche – Candy's dirt driveway was murder on a detail job – sat a slick black Jag, equally dusty.

It wasn't a limo, and the license plate didn't read *Ms Big,* but when I saw her standing there with Ernie and Candy and Lisa, I smiled at Ernie's business sense, nonetheless. He'd taken my half-kidding advice and summoned Barbie, our old rep from Sony, to give Phenex a listen.

Barbie hadn't discovered Sonic Daydream. That had been an astute A&R man from the entertainment mega-corporation, and after our first couple of tours, he'd moved on to scout other acts to feed to the ever-hungry, record-buying public. After that, Barbie was our rep, and with her in LA and Elise on the road, we toured for another ten years. Lenny would sometimes spend the weekend with her when we were in town – *just another lost angel in the City of Lights* – and when his brother ended the band, she and Lenny eventually took up full time together at his hacienda in Anza.

Barbie was retired now, but she undoubtedly still had more than a little clout with her former employer. She'd represented one of the biggest rock acts on the planet, after all, even if she hadn't been the one that had turned over the rock that was The House of Ale and found us wriggling in the beery slime underneath. I knew that somebody at Sony would listen if she filed a good report on Phenex.

I got out of the car and she gave me a welcoming hug, told me I looked great. I told her the same. She *did* look great: she had dressed the part of a make-or-break record company rep; Candy was speechless with wonder. Barbie wore a snug-fitting black jacket and skirt, daring enough to show a little leg and a little cleavage, but not too much. She was subtly made up, her hair confined in a no-nonsense, businesslike bun. The black was now streaked with gray, but it looked good on her. Fine and sexy in her youth, Barbie had aged gracefully into a handsome, middle-aged woman. Candy, standing beside her, looked like a macabre clown in her tight jeans and boots and groupie regalia.

I realized with not a little amazement that the two of them were about the same age, and it occurred to me that perhaps it was the difference between the fantasy and the reality that had made them turn out so dissimilarly. Candy had dreamed of a rock star, of surrendering to the satyr-like potency that she imagined for the world's greatest guitar player. *(Wait 'til Barbie hears that one,* I thought and grinned to myself.) Ernie had allowed her to surrender, in all her witchy, blood-painting kinkiness, and after Ernie moved on, Candy had in due course found herself another guitar player, younger, to continue the fantasy. For what was Sonny, other than just another version of Ernie? He certainly had the talent; had he been backed by a better band, had he scored the same breaks, I had no doubt that he could've been as famous as Candy's baby-daddy.

Contrast all this to Barbie. She'd actually kept the rock star she'd caught, had loved him not as some pornographic vision of guitar god sensuality, but as a regular guy who just happened to also be *God's bass player,* as *Rolling Stone* had once put it. They'd grown old together, mellowed, whereas mellow was something that I thought Candy would never be.

Ernie smiled apologetically. "I thought it was time a professional checked them out, Cal."

"We're not professionals?" I retorted archly and winked at Barbie.

Ernie gave Lisa's shoulders a fatherly squeeze. "Sure we are. But maybe we're biased."

"Let's light this candle then," I proposed.

The happy little rock and roll family led the way into the house, followed by Barbie and me. As we passed the door to the kitchen, I glanced in that direction and beheld Leonard Whitly talking to Sonny. I should've realized that Barbie wouldn't make the long trip down from Anza without him.

Our eyes met and Lenny stopped talking. Sonny looked at me, then back at Lenny. He mumbled some excuse and quickly fled the kitchen. He'd read my book, in which I'd portrayed Dennis Whitly as a cowardly, cheating son of a bitch. Sonny suspected that there was apt to be a showdown now with Denny's brother because of all that. He wanted neither to witness it nor participate in it.

Lenny ignored Sonny's departure; he gazed at me expressionlessly. I'd heard he kept horses and a couple of cows up there in Anza; he looked tan and a little weather-beaten. He'd lost a great deal of his hair, and I noted that he'd also grown a little paunchy in his role as gentleman rancher. No doubt from all of those hearty, cowboy, chuck-wagon style meals.

I waited. He was the leader on the path that this reunion would follow. My attitudes and opinions about his brother and the ending of our band were a matter of published record; he knew where I stood. I'd already acted, said my piece years ago. What remained, now that we were face to face, was for Lenny to react to it.

I figured it could go either way. I'd met him forty years before, in junior high. We'd been best friends, bandmates, for a quarter century after that, through the lean years as a trio, playing covers at frat parties and a few dive bars; through the obscenely successful years, touring the globe, raking in the cash, after his brother had joined the band.

Lenny could choose to remember the good old days, the friendship of our long association, or he could take his brother's side, his flesh and blood. I'd placed the blame for Elise's death squarely upon Denny, on the fact that he'd ignored her love for him for twelve years, but still kept her with the band because she looked after our interests so well on the road. I'd postulated that he'd stopped ignoring her on the last night of her life, when they were at last alone. I'd told the world that I believed that Denny had afterwards rejected her, and it had been this rejection that had precipitated her suicide, as well as the attempted murder of her sister.

I had not painted the world-renowned, multi-platinum guitar god in a good light. Not a good light at all. What was his brother going to say to me about it now?

I waited, and Lenny let me wait. For the span of a good half a minute, the guy with whom I'd started one of the world's premier rock bands just stood there and wordlessly, solemnly stared at me.

At last he said, "I didn't read it, you know."

So we were going to get right to the heart of the matter. "I didn't miss your $9.95."

Lenny ignored this flippant remark. "Denny told me about it, though. He said he never slept with her."

Two paths diverged in a yellow wood; the conversation could again go either way. I could restate the facts of *Sonic Nightmare,* I could remember history for him, make him recall Elise's obsession with his brother; Lenny had witnessed it as thoroughly as I had. I could tell him just what I thought about Denny's protestations of innocence.

But these responses would cause Lenny to naturally leap to his brother's defense. I had no desire to provoke him – he certainly hadn't tried to provoke me, hadn't called me a son of a bitch, hadn't taken a swing at me. He hadn't defended Denny's response to *Sonic Nightmare;* he'd only informed me of it.

And like I'd told Ernie, it was all water under the bridge anyway, all ancient history. The dead were buried; my words had been spoken, published, forgotten, no doubt by all except those they concerned most.

I said, "What do you think?"

Lenny replied immediately, "It was a tragedy, Cal. Whatever I think – it can't change anything, so mostly what I think is that it's none of my business."

And that was the end of it. Leonard Whitly had taken the high road. Denny's business was Denny's business; Lenny was neither his brother's keeper nor his defender. *Each man's soul's his own.*

This crisis in friendship having passed, Lenny smiled at me. "You look great, Cal."

I returned his smile. "It's all that clean living."

"I have to thank Ernie for calling Barbie about this. Sometimes I think she misses the record biz. Sometimes I thinks she gets bored on the ranch."

"Barbie. Now there's someone that looks great. Always has."

Lenny slapped me on the back. "It's all that clean living." He paused for another smile, then lowered his voice. "So tell me about . . . all this. The little girl . . . She's Ernie's kid?"

She's hardly a little girl. You should see the way she looks at me sometimes. But I didn't say that. The way that Lisa looked at me sometimes . . . Maybe that was all in my head. Maybe it wasn't, but either way, just like David Gilmour, Lenny had guitar strings older than Ernie's daughter. Of course she was a little girl to him.

"And the mother? She's . . . She was one of . . ."

"Ernie's groupies."

Call a spade a shovel, son, my dad had always told me. *The truth's not always pretty, but it's always the truth.* My religious mother had added, *And ye shall know the truth, and the truth shall make you free.*

The freedom in the truths of this situation remained to be seen.

"Wow," Lenny said. "Who'da thunk it? Ernie LaBelle's got a kid. And a looker, too."

"For a little girl," I replied. Lenny grinned at me. All his golden-years', settled happiness hadn't blinded him to the undeniable fact of Lisa's attractiveness. He just had a better handle on his reaction to it than I did. *Well, good for you, old man.*

"But is she any good?"

I blinked in surprise. My old friend was asking me to speculate upon something about which I had often caught myself speculating, but I surely wasn't going to speculate about it aloud, and surely not with him. Then I realized that he was asking me about her talent.

I shrugged, wishing to appear noncommittal. "She can definitely sing. How she plays the guitar . . ."

"I know. Guitar players are all the same to you." He slapped me on the back again.

"The rest of the band . . . They're all right. I don't think they're ready, but apparently Ernie –"

"Ernie says he's ready to put his money where his mouth is. The way the business is these days, he might have to."

I shrugged again. "Ernie's ready for a professional opinion. And he's got plenty of money."

SEVEN

Candy and James retrieved folding chairs from the mysterious abyss that was the upstairs of the ramshackle house. They lined them up near the mouth of the hallway, and Candy gestured wordlessly for us to sit. She continued to be so impressed that an actual record company rep was here to see her band that speech eluded her. Ernie beamed his proud papa smile at Lisa; he gave Sonny a thumbs-up. Lenny and Barbie and Candy sat down beside us and the performance began.

They ran through the four songs that Ernie and Lisa had written. Lenny watched them, and did not exchange any looks with his lady-love. They had both heard Azomite, and perhaps expected that Phenex's material might sound a little like Sonic Daydream, and of course, it did. In all fairness, it probably wouldn't seem so to a non-musician, but to professionals, the chord progressions and time signatures were pure Dennis Whitly.

After their own material, Phenex covered *(I Can't Get No) Satisfaction* to show that the band could carry a tune, and *Show Me How To Live* to prove that Lisa could sing, and ended the set with yet another cover, of Sonic Daydream's *Tomcats,* to kiss Lenny's ass, no doubt. It had been our first number one hit, way back in 1989, another classic from the vaults. There was something just the tiniest bit surreal about listening to lovely Lisa warble her way through a song that I had played countless times, on hundreds of stages worldwide, for years before she was a twinkle in her daddy's eye.

Her daddy sat beside me and smiled. He was satisfied with the set. As always, I thought they were adequate; I agreed with Ernie's initial assessment, that Lisa was great, and could go far with a better band. But she didn't have a better band. She had Phenex, an okay band.

I snuck a peek at God's bass player and the good-looking gal from Sony Records. Both of them wore neutral, unreadable expressions, so I guessed. Lenny, I imagined, was unimpressed. He wouldn't let it show on his face, out of respect for his old bandmate, but if Ernie asked him straight out what he thought, I had no doubt that Lenny would be truthful.

Barbie was a professional, and her neutral expression was just part of the game. She could've thought that Phenex was as talented as Zeppelin, that Lisa was Janis Joplin and Joan Jett and Gwen

Stefani all rolled into one, but she'd never let it show on her face, not until the signatures were dry on the contract. Then it would be *I've always had a deep respect and I mean that most sincere,* but at this juncture, too much enthusiasm wouldn't be good for Sony's interests. Even though Barbie didn't actually work for them anymore, old habits die hard.

Candy whooped and jumped to her feet, applauded wildly. The band ignored her, and after a moment, she again realized that she was in the presence of a real record company rep, and put a leash on her stage-mother's zeal.

"That was great, guys," Barbie said with a tight little smile. "If you'll just allow me a moment to have a word with my associates?" Phenex dutifully set down their instruments and filed out of the room. Candy hesitated, then deciding that she was not an associate, at least not quite yet, she quickly followed them.

The four of us remained seated in the folding chairs, and I was inexplicably reminded of a parole board. Ernie leaned forward expectantly.

"How many covers are on their demo?" Barbie began.

"Demo? They don't have a –"

"Jesus, Ernie!" Lenny exclaimed. "You got us all the way down here to listen to a band with no –"

"They're just a garage band, Lenny! Where would they record it? Here? Even if they had the equipment, the acoustics in this room –"

"We were a garage band," I pointed out. "We had a demo." Recorded, stereotypically, in my parents' garage, it was awful, acoustics-wise.

"Capshaw ignored our demo, remember?"

Capshaw was the astute A&R man who had come to hear us at The House of Ale. He was there because of word-of-mouth, he'd told us, and he'd signed Sonic Daydream on the spot, after just one set. Ernie was right – nothing from the demo had made it onto the first album, because nothing on the demo had included –

"He said he signed us because of Denny. Lisa's as good as Denny ever was . . ."

Barbie raised a manicured eyebrow at this statement. Dennis Whitly was rock and roll royalty, and Lisa was perhaps a minor princess, and that was only by blood, so far.

"Things are different these days, Ernie. If I had a demo, maybe I could get Sony to promote them at a couple of festivals, put them in a line-up as an opening act for a bigger band. But they wouldn't sign them right away. It's not like it used to be. There are just too many acts these days, there's too much exposure . . . Nobody gets signed on just some rep's opinion anymore. There are committees, how are they doing with this demographic . . . And without even a demo . . ."

Ernie grinned. "We'll get you a demo."

Barbie didn't speak to the band. She'd given them a listen as a favor to her old friend Ernie, and she'd delivered her opinion to him. It wasn't like it was necessary or even professional to pretend that she was friends with them. Lenny said a few words to them, though, because he was a nice guy, and I imagined that he figured he'd never be talking to them again.

We walked Lenny and Barbie out to their Jag and bid them farewell. Ernie said he'd send a demo before the month was out, and Barbie said she'd pass it along. She of course guaranteed nothing, but promised Ernie that the right ears would hear it. After that, it was out of her hands.

The band was assembled again behind their instruments, Candy hovering nearby. James held his sticks like a knife and fork, like he might eat his kit; Roy gave his full concentration to adjusting the strings on his bass; Lisa paced back and forth with a dead mike in her hand; Sonny tinkled tunelessly on the piano. It was the only sound in the room. When we entered, they skewered us with nervous, expectant, hopeful eyes.

"Barbie said she liked you," Ernie lied. Barbie had said no such thing. "But she needs a demo, to pass along to the . . ."

"Decision makers?" Candy suggested.

"Right. So we have to make a demo."

My old friend Ernie paused then, and I could read his mind as clearly as black upon white. Dennis Whitly had a recording studio, right behind his house, right here in Riverside. And Denny had been a fair mixer in his day. But of course we wouldn't be using Denny's studio, nor would we be seeking Denny's advice, because I had written a book once upon a time. Ernie wouldn't be able to impose on his friendship with Denny as he had with Barbie, and it was all my fault. Ernie told me all this with one glance.

"Fuck Denny," I said and Ernie blinked. He hadn't realized that his thoughts had shown so plainly. "There's a studio in Temecula. I did some work there a few years back. It's state of the art." Phenex was gonna need that. "Let me make some phone calls."

EIGHT

A few days later, I was back at the band house with good news for Phenex. I'd managed to set up a session at the studio for the following Wednesday.

"Don't forget your checkbook," I told Ernie. "Oscar had to move some big names around. That doesn't come cheap."

"You got Oscar?"

I nodded. "He runs the place."

"I always wondered what he's been up to all these years. Scott and Dave have their own guy for Azomite."

Oscar Woodbine had been the audio engineer on all of Sonic Daydream's releases. He was one of the best in the business, and he was my good friend. Ernie wasn't the only one that still had connections.

Phenex had of course never heard of Oscar, but once I described his pedigree, they were again nervously stoked. None of them, not even talented Sonny, had ever been anywhere near a recording studio.

"We need two more songs," Ernie told them. "A good demo should be six songs."

"How are we gonna come up with two more songs by next Wednesday?" Sonny asked.

"I didn't say it was gonna be easy," Ernie countered.

"Why not one new song and a cover? How about *Satisfaction Guaranteed?"* As always, Lisa sang to me, and her incredible voice was as intimate as a caress, as if it was just the two of us in the room. *"Now then, tell me baby, do you need my love? Tell me baby, are you thinkin' of me? Tell me baby, what it is you need? What kind of satisfaction guaranteed?"*

There was a heartbeat of silence. Alarmed, guilty, I thought everybody must now be witnessing her attempt at seduction, and they had to be shocked at it, hence the silence.

I stole a glance at Ernie. He looked amazed, but not because his daughter was singing love songs to me. To my relief, I discovered that this little gem had passed him by, him and everyone else. Something else amazed him. "How could you possibly know that ancient song?"

"It's Paul Rodgers, Dad." I'd noticed some time ago that Lisa called him *Dad* to his face, but referred to him as *Ernie* when he wasn't present.

Her explanation would've been sufficient, coming from anyone over, oh, maybe forty or forty-five. Paul Rodgers had fronted Free in the 60s, and the legendary Bad Company in the 70s. The tune Lisa had so exquisitely sung was from his days with The Firm, in the 80s.

The guitarist for that band had been none other than Jimmy Page, but they'd only put out two albums and had called it quits by 1986, fourteen years before Lisa was born. She'd surely heard Bad Company's tunes; they were as big in the 70s as Sonic Daydream was in the 90s. But The Firm had been just a short (though successful) note in rock and roll history, and this was why Ernie was amazed.

"But how do you know that particular song?" he insisted.

And so thoroughly, I thought.

Lisa waved her hand at her mother and smiled affectionately. "I know all the music she knows. I've heard it all my life."

"That's actually a psychological phenomenon," Sonny said. Everybody looked at him in a kind of mild surprise. He was one of those people that didn't say much, but when he did deign to speak, what he had to say usually caught people's attention.

"I read an article about it once. It's an interlayering of memories. A parent remembers good times associated with a song or an album or a band, so she plays it for her kids. The kids associate the music with good times with their happy parent, and voila! The kids later remember the old stuff fondly, as if they'd heard it when it was new."

Lisa hugged her mother. "Just like I said. Mom's played great music for me all my life, and for that I'm grateful." She kissed Candy's cheek. The normal friction that occurred between teenage daughter and aging mother was absent from their relationship. Beyond a doubt, Lisa was her mom's biggest fan.

She again smiled at me. "And a lot of it was your music, Cal. I heard Sonic Daydream in the womb."

Another reason why you shouldn't look at me the way you do, I thought. Maybe it was the reason that she did, some kind of girlish adolescent curiosity about one of the guys from the band that had so ensorcelled her mother as a girl. Ernie was her daddy, Lenny had a girlfriend, legendary (though ersatz) sex god Denny wasn't here, so she had imprinted on me. It was like my friendship with Elise, all those years ago, arrived at because all the other possibilities were unsuitable.

"Aw, I'm just the drummer, Lisa. All I do is keep the beat –"

"And bad com-pan-y," she sang, and winked at Ernie. It was other line from a song from twenty years before she was born. Lisa knew Dire Straits, too.

It struck me that she knew the lyrics to as many songs as Elise had, again, all those years ago. There was no mystery to the similarity; it was just as Sonny had said. All it took was a kid that appreciated the tunes that a music-loving parent played for them. Elise's dad had been the same as Candy, after a fashion: he'd been a big fan, had proudly maintained an entire room filled with records.

Candy returned her daughter's hug. "I guess we should count ourselves lucky that you don't sing just like Dennis Whitly, for as much as you've heard Sonic Daydream." Candy's smile disappeared when she mentioned the front for her all-time favorite band. She said his name with more than a modicum of disgust, in fact.

Unable to hide my surprise, I asked, "You didn't care for Denny?" How could she not like the singer for the band she worshipped? Loathe as I was to admit it, Dennis Whitly *was* Sonic Daydream.

"I liked the other guitar player." Candy beamed a smile at Ernie, and out of the corner of my eye, I saw Sonny roll his. Then Candy's smile again vanished. "Dennis Whitly killed the greatest band in the world. I'll never forgive him for that."

I had known Denny, been friends with him once, unlike Candy, who, callous as it may sound, was nothing more than one of Ernie LaBelle's numberless groupies. Yet I'd never taken his ending the band personally, at least not like Candy obviously had. I'd never forgive Denny for the way he'd treated Elise, but ending the band? I hadn't liked it, but in the final analysis, I had to admit that it was his prerogative. It was just one of those things. I'd missed being in a band over the years, but it was what it was.

The undisguised vitriol of Candy's words – she would not only never forgive Denny, she clearly hated his guts – it reminded me how much their favorite band was sometimes an integral part of the lives of some fans. Past the posters on the wall and the concert t-shirts, something about those three or four or five guys up there on the stage and the sounds they made became so much more than just mere entertainment.

It was not only the sex-crazed groupie thing, although surely the sobbing, hysterical young girls at Beatles' concerts had felt more than just a passing appreciation for the music of The Fab Four. Musicians affected guys, too: it was not just young girls that had packed venues around the world to see Zeppelin and Floyd, Metallica and Sonic Daydream.

There had been fan suicides when John Lennon was murdered, and copycat acts of desperation when Kurt Cobain had taken his own life. Bands meant a lot to their fans.

Not long ago, I was standing in line at Starbucks and overheard the guy ahead of me tell his companion how Tool had changed his life. His friend had said that it had been Korn for him, that *Freak on a Leash* and *Falling Away From Me* had summed up the entirety of his emotions at one point in his life. "Johnathan Davis is a god, man!" he'd enthused.

Sonny and I had recently gone out for a beer after rehearsal, and the bartender we'd encountered at the little hole in the wall tavern had had an impressive sleeve of religious tattoos: Mary and Jesus were rendered with astonishing skill in bright, stunning colors on his pale shoulder. Sonny had complimented the bartender on his ink, and the guy then told us that he originally hailed from Bremerton, Washington, and he'd been inspired to get this subject matter by the early Christian punk music of a band called MxPx.

I'd heard some of their later stuff, and I asked the bartender how he'd liked that. They were pop-punk by the time I'd heard them; there had been no mention of God. But this guy was still a fan.

"Mike Herrera's one of the greatest bassists ever."

Without looking at me, Sonny mentioned, "*Rolling Stone* once said that Leonard Whitly was God's bass player."

The bartender shrugged. "He's all right. Sonic Daydream was always a little too laid-back for me. It's all about what you like, I guess."

And that was really the crux of it, I figured. It's all about what you like, and how much you like it. For some fans, the band they liked became an obsession, and when the band broke up, well . . . like Candy, they took it really hard. It wasn't just one of those things to the fans. Blame had to be laid somewhere and someone had to be the bad guy. For every Yoko Ono, there was a selfish singer who wanted to go solo, a money-hungry guitarist who wanted to start another band. For Candy, the bad guy was Dennis Whitly, who'd just wanted to quit, who had simply *killed* her favorite band.

Musicians learn early to be a little leery of the obsessive fans. Ernie had never had any experiences that turned him off from dabbling in groupies entirely, but on the other hand, Candy and her painted-blood ritual hadn't been the weirdest he'd experienced. There'd been the one, he told us, who had suddenly produced an exceptionally large pair of scissors, claiming that she wanted a lock of his hair as a keepsake.

"Those scissors, dude. They scared me. They were just too damned big. And she just pulled them out of nowhere. She could've cut off anything with scissors that big." He'd made her come up with a smaller pair, and had left her with one of his famous curls, but the episode had shaken him a little bit. I remembered that he'd yelled at Perry the roadie about picking out psychos, and he'd laid off the groupies for at least the next three shows after that.

The vast majority of even the most obsessive fans aren't in any way dangerous, but still it pays to be cautious. After all, it just takes one. Ask Taylor Swift about the guy that grabbed her leg while she was on stage.

And it's not that we feel ourselves to be above the fans. They pay the bills, buy the records, and most musicians start out with a little bit of idolatry ourselves. There's always someone great whom we seek to emulate. For me, it was my dad. He wasn't famous, just a drummer for a local jazz band. Dad was the greatest drummer in the world to me, but of course, he gave that title to Buddy Rich. I thought Buddy was good, true, but I never thought he was all that – as far as I was concerned, he was no Teddy Bascomb. I always believed that if I could be half as good as my dad, I'd be good indeed.

After a few years of success, the politics of the record business and the rigors of touring can beat a lot of that fan-like idolatry out of you. It's a business after all, and once you find out how it works, a little of your respect and awe for the famous musicians of yesteryear fades. Sure, the great ones did all this, but here we are, doing it, too. And look, we have our own legions of screaming fans, telling *us* how great *we are.* Maybe we're just as good as the stars we once worshipped.

Don't get me wrong – being a rock star is the greatest job in the world. But it's still a job for all that – what we do, not entirely who we are. But of course, the fans don't see it that way. We're not just people to them. How could we be? Mere people don't have the ability to change lives through their words and music. Mere people don't have the power to make women swoon, to make dudes quit school and try to become musicians themselves. People don't spend thousands of dollars and travel around the country following other regular folk like themselves; regular people don't inspire tattoos. Famous musicians aren't people; they're gods.

And Dennis Whitly, from his place on high, had thrown a Jovian thunderbolt and brought ignominiously to earth this other god that Candy worshipped: Ernie LaBelle.

But Ernie had not stayed earthbound for long. He'd ascended again, to take a lesser place in the firmament, surely – Azomite was no Sonic Daydream. Though moderate, Ernie's second success should've ameliorated Candy's dislike for Denny somewhat. I couldn't understand why it hadn't.

"You don't care for Azomite?"

She shrugged. "They're all right. I really like the lead-guitar." Again she smiled at Ernie.

Lisa said, "Sonic Daydream will always be Mom's favorite band. There's just something about how you guys played together."

She was just parroting her mother's opinions now; Lisa had never seen Sonic Daydream play together, past the now-dated looking videos – which had all concentrated on Denny – and maybe some grainy concert footage.

"You guys were the greatest band in the world."

Lisa's voice had the ring of a true believer, and I was suddenly transported back in time. I was ten years old again, in church beside my mother. The priest held up the communion wafer and spoke: *Behold the Lamb of God, behold him who takes away the sins of the world. Blessed are those called to the supper of the Lamb,* and I watched my mother soundlessly speak the words with him. Deep philosophical discussions of the transubstantiation of the bread and wine into the body and blood were unnecessary for her. This was truth right here, from the mouth of God to her listening ear. Her eyes shone in wonder.

Lisa bore a similar expression when she said, "You guys were the greatest band in the world." She recited the words like a catechism, something that was believed without reflection, because it had come from her mother, a trusted source. Words memorized, practiced, recited; truth distilled, with a capital *T.* The earth is round, the sun rises in the east and sets in the west, God is good, Sonic Daydream was the greatest band in the world.

This belief and her statement of it were disconcerting to say the least, and if I had any doubt as to the depth of it, Lisa made it clear. "Mom's your biggest fan, so I was born into being a fan, too. I've read every interview, watched every video. I know every song, every chord. I read your book, Cal."

"That's very flattering, honey," Ernie said. He avoided my gaze, because, while it *was* very flattering, it wasn't that unique. All the great bands had obsessive fans who'd learned every available detail about their idols. It was part of being a fan.

"You guys were the greatest band ever," Lisa solemnly stated again.

Now Ernie looked at me, and his expression wondered how we had gotten into this, playing mentors and counsellors to a group of barely adequate musicians, led by two women that worshipped the magnificent fantasy of the greatest band ever, and worshipped us because we'd been part of it.

But what did these suppliants at the altar of rock and roll *want* from their gods?

Ernie gave me just the ghost of a grin, the remnant of incompletely suppressed mirth. He said, "Maybe Phenex will be the greatest band in the world someday."

Ernie knew better, as did I, as did Sonny, who again rolled his eyes. But this proclamation seemed perfectly possible to James, and of course, Roy, who was a legend in his own mind.

Candy said, "I have scryed –"

"Cried? There's no reason, to cry, Candy. We're gonna cut a demo –"

"Not *cried,* Dad. *Scryed.* It means to foretell the future. With a crystal ball."

Ernie glanced at me again and the mirth in his eyes grew. But he kept it in. He didn't care what these people believed, but they were his family, newfound, and he was trying really hard not to bust out laughing at them.

Candy began again. "I have scryed, and it's been revealed to me that Phenex will succeed. I have long sought the aid of those forces unseen, and they assure me that the season is at hand. Some prophecies have been fulfilled." She smiled at Ernie, patted his hand. "Others await fruition. Rituals must be performed, and sacrifices must of course be made."

"The forces unseen aren't generous," Lisa added. "But they can be persuaded, their favors bought with the proper sacrifices."

"What kind of sacrifices?" Ernie closed one eye and glanced over his shoulder at the stuffed goat head, then back at me. I could see that he wasn't going to be able to hold it in much longer, nor could I keep one corner of my mouth from quirking up in a half-smile. Ernie's ladies, God or Satan or whoever love 'em, were just as silly and ridiculous as clowns to us.

"Simply prayer and ritual," Candy replied crisply, perhaps sensing his amusement. "Cleansing and fasting. Meditation. Nothing to concern the uninitiated."

"So mote it be," Sonny said expressionlessly, and I sincerely could not tell if he was kidding or not.

Ernie considered him blankly for a split second, then clapped his hands. "Right. Well, you guys can work on all that. In the meantime, we need to come up with two new songs. No covers. Record companies don't like covers. The licensing cuts into their profits." He grinned hopefully at the members of Phenex. "I'm open to suggestions."

NINE

Wednesday, August 29, 2018 dawned foggy in Temecula, California, but the mist had burned off by the time hopeful newcomers Phenex, accompanied by Candy and all the members of Sonic Daydream (save legendary frontman Dennis Whitly) arrived at Oscar Woodbine's recording studio.

The moment Oscar beheld the three of us, the mood was immediately like Old Home Week. It had been a while since I'd seen him, but it seemed like a million years since he'd seen Ernie or Lenny, who'd driven down the hill to watch Phenex record and contribute to the walk down Memory Lane with our old engineer.

Oscar asked after Denny, and Lenny said that his brother was still in Riverside.

"Still happily married?" Lenny nodded and Oscar said, "I would've been surprised, otherwise. I never saw two people more in love than Denny and Sophia."

I stifled an urge to roll my eyes at this observation. Leave it to Oscar to talk about love; he'd been married three times. Never having been in love, especially not like Denny and Sophia's storybook romance, unlike Oscar, I had my doubts about the wonderfulness of it. Like I say, I guess I'd loved Elise. She had been so vibrantly alive, she'd lived for music; she'd been my best friend. But I had seen what love had done to her. Elise had killed herself for love.

I caught Lisa smiling at me. Yeah, love. Whatever joys it might encompass, it had passed me by. I could've loved Lisa, if only she hadn't been born too late.

Ernie introduced the nervous members of Phenex to Oscar; they each nodded numbly and shook his hand. Candy managed a *So nice to meet you,* then fell silent again. Oscar gave them a brief overview of what was going to occur, then sent them on into the live room and told them to feel free to warm up a little bit.

Sonny and Lisa and Roy had brought their own guitars, but Oscar and I had arranged for a nice Yamaha Recording Custom for James, since the lugs on his own beat-to-death set would've rattled far too much. Ernie went into the live room with them and helped them plug in and adjust mikes and headphones. Maybe he didn't realize that the pick-up to the control room was on, or maybe he didn't care, but I heard him clearly say, "I wish Denny was here. He was always so much better at this stuff than me. Goddamn Cal."

"It's not Cal's fault that Denny's not here . . . Dad," Lisa retorted immediately, and I glanced at her in surprise through the glass. She was considering her father scornfully, and didn't look in my direction. "Nobody would've wanted him here, especially not Mom. He killed –"

"Yeah, yeah, the greatest band in the world." I was surprised again, at Ernie's annoyed tone with her. "I know. I used to be their second-guitar."

Oscar looked at me curiously. "Why *isn't* Denny here? He always liked working with new talent."

"Talent being the operative word," Lenny said.

Sonic Daydream's bass player didn't care if he offended Candy, as she was just an unnecessary hanger-on to him. This was the business end of the music business to Lenny, no place for groupies, especially aging ones. He felt that the studio should be the realm of musicians only.

I remembered that he hadn't even particularly liked Sophia's presence in the control room, and he had positively scowled at Elise. He'd never liked Elise anyway, had never trusted her because of her obsessive yen for his brother. Except when she was handling managerial tasks on the road, all the tedious odds and ends that had started out as his responsibilities; then he was her biggest fan.

Oscar directed his inquisitive expression at Lenny now. He was getting paid an ungodly amount of money; it mattered not in the least to him if Phenex was any good. But he hadn't expected the former members of Sonic Daydream to bring him a lukewarm band, and he certainly hadn't expected Leonard Whitly to as much as state it, not with their . . . whatever she was sitting right there in the room.

"It's a long story, why Denny's not here," Lenny told Oscar, and left it at that. It occurred to me that the engineer hadn't read my book. Sensational rock and roll tell-alls about a bunch of guys he knew personally were probably not high on his reading list.

The band ran quickly through the first of the tracks that they wanted to record. Ernie stayed in the live room for this warm up, doing a few last minute instrument adjustments. I knew he didn't care for the task; it had flabbergasted the guy from *Guitar Player* that he'd allowed Perry the roadie to tune his axes when we were on tour.

"He can't play worth a shit, that's why he's a roadie," Ernie had said, and the guy had printed it. "But he can tune a guitar like no one I've ever seen. Perry's the Guitar Whisperer."

Oscar listened for not more than five or six bars, then he flipped a switch and the control room went silent. He turned away from the live room and asked Lenny how life was treating him on the ranch, and Lenny shot me a quick glance before saying everything was great. Lenny and I knew that Oscar's muting the new talent, turning his back on them and making small talk was not a good sign; even Candy knew it. It indicated that he was not even remotely impressed with Phenex. She frowned at the engineer, then smiled brightly at Ernie when he gave a tentative thumbs-up through the glass.

"I think they're ready now," she volunteered.

Oscar looked at her as if he'd just noticed her presence; as if she was the chair in which she sat and it had suddenly acquired the power of speech. He didn't care for non-musicians in his studio, either.

Ah, the politics of the biz, how the power was wielded! Who was made to feel important and who was made to feel like dirt. Candy had longed to learn about all this for her entire groupie-life. She wanted so badly to be in the music business, to be *with the band.*

You'll always be a nobody to this guy, Candy. He doesn't care if you're the singer's mommy, or one of Ernie's stray pieces of ass from the good old days. How's all that sitting with ya?

Yes, I'm afraid it's true. I've always been a bit of a snob myself.

Ernie returned to the control room. He sat in a chair beside Oscar, beside the mixing board. Oscar was a professional audio engineer, one of the best in the business; if Phenex needed any coaching or direction, it was up to Ernie to provide it. Oscar was used to seasoned acts that needed no instruction, that knew what they were doing. He would not speak to Phenex.

Ernie flipped on the mike. "All right, dudes. Just relax. This is just like we're at home. Pretend the goat's on the wall behind you."

Oscar looked over his shoulder at me and I smiled innocently at him.

"Okay, James. Count it off." Ernie turned off the mike and a small sigh escaped him.

The session started badly. Phenex was nervous and their tenuous cohesion as a band suffered because of it. Ernie was unsatisfied, and had them repeat the tracks over and over. He was kind in his directions, however. He didn't yell at them, although I thought that they might've benefitted from a firmer hand at this point. Ernie was patient; he didn't care about how much the session was costing him, as long as they played as well as they could. But they weren't. Even Sonny, the most experienced musician in the band, was late a couple of times, and the nerves were showing in Lisa's voice.

At last, Candy spoke up. "Can I go in there for a minute?"

Ernie looked at her as if it was the chair come to life this time, as Oscar had earlier, as if he suddenly wondered who had let this refugee from 1989 into a professional recording studio. Oscar waved his hand, giving her permission to achieve the inner sanctum. It all paid the same.

Candy hugged Lisa, told her she was doing great. Then she gestured for the five of them to join hands. They formed a circle and closed their eyes, and Candy chanted low, unintelligible words.

Oscar squinted in disbelief at Ernie. "Are they religious?"

Ernie looked at him in helpless embarrassment. This kind of shit might fly with a more famous group, but it was just ridiculous for a mediocre garage band to be taking up the time of an engineer of Oscar's caliber in this manner, no matter how much money he was being paid.

"Yeah, they're religious," I supplied, to save Ernie the further mortification of an explanation. "But not like you think."

Candy returned to the control room. "They'll do better now."

Oscar ignored her. "You know, we could wrap this up in short order if you guys would just go in there and back this chick up." When nobody spoke, he continued. "She's pretty good –" high praise indeed from Oscar Woodbine, "– but at this rate, we're gonna be here all day. There's only so much I can do, Ernie . . ."

"What is it that you're suggesting?" Candy asked.

"He's suggesting that Cal and Ernie and I lay down the music behind Lisa's vocals," Lenny explained.

He didn't know the songs, but they were simple, Sonic Daydream knock-offs, after all, and he was God's bass player. Lenny could pick up the bass lines and make them sound better in less time than it was apparently going to take Phenex to get their act together.

Ernie liked the idea. "It would still say *Phenex* on the demo, Cand. No one would know it was us."

"It's called using studio musicians," Oscar told her, and gave me a little wink.

I'd been a studio musician, on and off, since the end of Sonic Daydream. If you look at the small print on the liner notes, you'll discover that it's me drumming on the CDs of a few of the bands you've been paying good money to see, not the charismatic longhair twirling his sticks onstage.

Candy studied each of us for a moment, then shook her head. "No. In order for them to achieve success, the demon requires . . ."

At Ernie's supremely embarrassed look, she stopped, then abruptly began again. "It has to be them. They have to sink or swim on their own, and I have it on good authority that they're gonna succeed."

Oscar looked at me and Lenny to see if it had been one of us that had made that unlikely prediction. Lenny shook his head.

Candy raised her chin in defiance. Not even her gods were going to dis Phenex. "They're gonna be great. They don't need help from the dregs of Sonic Daydream."

Oscar's mouth fell open in amazed incredulity at this remark. Lenny smirked, somehow not surprised at all. Insulted groupies had been known to turn bitchy. He waited for Ernie's reaction.

"Look, Candy –"

She cut him off. "They have communed with their . . . muse. They'll do better now."

There was another heartbeat of silence. Lenny grinned at me; Oscar looked through the glass at the band to keep from laughing at this crazy old groupie chick who'd just said that she preferred a bunch of third-rate wanna-be musicians to the members of one of the most famous rock bands in history; Ernie blinked in dismay at her.

He opened his mouth, then closed it again. "Fine. Whatever you want." He nodded at Oscar and his next words were pure Ernie LaBelle, dripping with the sarcasm that his experience, his talent, his fame and his bank account allowed him. "Let's light this candle. *They'll do better now.*"

And they did do better; they were as good as they were gonna be. I wanted to remark that the chant had apparently pleased their namesake demon, that he must now be guiding their collective fingers upon the holy instruments of rock and roll, but there was no call to be disrupting the now smoothly running session with my infidel's derision. Like Ernie had said, who cared what these people believed? Phenex's nervousness had dissipated. They did better.

TEN

Finally, the long session ended; Phenex's six demo tracks were safely stored inside Oscar's expensive electronics. He wouldn't need the demon's assistance to create the illusion that the band was much better than they actually were: Oscar was an absolute sorcerer at this particular brand of magic. Sony might just be pleased with our offering.

As Candy and the band loaded their guitars into the van, Ernie tried to apologize to the engineer for the lumpy session, for the outré pause for invoking the demon. Oscar waved his hand in dismissal, smiled at his old friend.

"All in a day's work, my brutha. I've been dealing with you weirdo musicians all my life."

And it has made you a millionaire, I thought. "Just make sure that check doesn't bounce," I said to Ernie.

Oscar winked at me. "Give me a week or so and I'll have it to you."

This remark produced a sidelong glance from Lenny. A week wasn't very long to mix six songs; perhaps Oscar was in a hurry to rid himself of his old friend's daughter's so-so band and their dubious demo. I shrugged and murmured, "So mote it be."

A brand-new fifth wheel, pulling a shiny white trailer, arrived in front of the studio, followed shortly by a black limo. Oscar shook hands with us hastily, bid us a quick, *It was great seeing you guys again, I'll be in touch.* With what could only be described as relief, he went to greet the next set of musicians. They probably weren't paying him any more than Ernie had, but they were obviously more established.

Candy and the members of Phenex lounged insouciantly against the side of their own tired and dented transport, waiting for direction, elaborately communicating that they had not a care in the world. It amused me to see that they ignored the members of the clearly more successful band as they began carrying their instruments into the studio. Who were these guys? Who cared? The demon had come through: Lisa and Roy and James and Sonny were *recording artists* now. If these other guys wanted to speak to them, perhaps they could have their people contact Phenex's people. How quickly they had adopted the rock star attitude!

Ernie noticed it too, and chuckled. *"Welcome to the machine."*

"Instruct them, Road Dog. They're waiting for you."

We walked over to the van and were greeted by five ear-to-ear grins. Candy and the band were pleased with their performance. They knew that, in the end, they'd been the best that they could be, and now it was all recorded for posterity.

"Well?" Candy asked.

"It's all good," Ernie assured her. He smiled proudly at his protégés. "But I want you guys to forget about the demo for the time being. It's Oscar's baby for right now."

"Let him gestate it," I said, a little proud of them myself. I had caught the band's excited, keyed-up mood; Lenny raised an eyebrow at my enthusiasm.

The hell with you, old man, I thought, but not unkindly. The studio was where the rubber met the road, where musicians had to prove what we were made of. No adoring fans, no gushing columnists from *Rolling Stone;* just a cold (or hot) room full of unfamiliar microphones and headphones and an unawed, impatient engineer who didn't care what the fans or *Rolling Stone* thought. When the session was finally over, there was a need to blow off all that pressure.

Ernie echoed my thoughts. "Now it's time to celebrate. Where do you want to go?"

Sonic Daydream's celebrations after recording had taken the form of drinking and listening to other bands' music, turned up to eleven. They had then invariably devolved into plugging guitars into amps for drunken cover attempts as well as recreations of the tracks we'd just laid down. I figured that it would no doubt be the same for Phenex, and the other band that they'd want to cover would undoubtedly be Sonic Daydream. I wasn't really looking forward to hearing *The Fastest Draw* blasted through the clinker-brink house while James messed up my rolls and Roy tried desperately to keep up with a bass player that was out of his league.

That bass player was reliving the same memories of drunken celebrations past, but decided that he was too old for any repeat of the good old days. "I've gotta be getting back up the hill to Barbie. You kids have fun." Lenny put the emphasis on *kids* and slapped me on the back.

We told him goodbye and watched him hop into his sleek British car.

"I'm gonna have one of those someday," Roy declared, and the old admonition about not holding one's breath crossed my mind.

Ernie answered his own question about where the party should take place. “I guess we can just go back to the house.” He put his arm around his daughter’s shoulders. “It’s not like we can take you to a bar.”

Lisa allowed herself an underage pout. It was of course adorable. “It’s such a long drive back home, Dad.”

Indeed it was, and most of the excitement of their first-ever recording session would dissipate by the time they slogged through traffic all the way back to Riverside.

“Let’s go to my house,” I suggested. Why not? The McMansion was only a few subdivisions and meandering sidewalks away, and I hadn’t had guests in, oh, let me see – I hadn’t ever had guests. Just a couple of students from my drum classes at the Y.

“Give us the address,” Roy said. “James and I’ll go get the beer.”

Ernie took Lisa in his Porsche, and Sonny and Candy accompanied me. Another lack of rock star excess on my part was my modest Cadillac sedan, even if it was this year’s model. Denny had preferred expensive: he’d always owned a Mercedes. And Ernie liked fast: he bought Porsches. Lenny *loved to drive in his Jag-u-ar:* he went for expensive *and* fast. I liked comfortable and dependable, four doors to provide plenty of room for that family I’d never have. Whatever. Sonny liked it, even though I suspected that Candy would’ve preferred a ride with the world’s greatest guitar player in his baby-blue 911.

Candy was equally unimpressed with my digs. It was a big house, though not an unusual one – no Bengal tigers or stripper poles or other outlandish rock star accoutrements. I thought Roy might be similarly unimpressed. I did have a pool, however.

I think Candy was also surprised that there weren’t battalions of beer bottles and overflowing ashtrays laying around. “You have a girlfriend we don’t know about, Cal? Who keeps this place for you?”

“Ah, you caught me, Candy. Her name’s Amanda. Sometimes she brings her sister along, too.”

Candy blinked in shock: evidently I had not one secret girlfriend, but two. Again I felt the snobbery of wealth. I hadn’t been born into it, so Candy’s ignorance seemed all the more glaring to me.

“I have a maid service, honey. They come in a couple times a month to tidy up after my wild parties.”

She had a rock star fantasy, didn’t she? Why not tell her what she wanted to hear? I wondered fleetingly if this could be another source of her daughter's strange fascination with me. Born into Sonic Daydream fanhood, did Lisa believe that I still lived it up like Black Sabbath on a bender?

It was all bullshit. Sonic Daydream had never been hard partiers after *the seats were all empty and the roadies took the stage.* Sex/guitar god Dennis Whitly was married, had a kid; Lenny did a lot of paperwork, at least when we were in the States. I'd been known to have a drink, true; maybe more than one. But that was because I had Elise to look after me, and it was always back at the hotel, because for the first couple of years, she was like Lisa, too young to go to the bar. It was only Ernie that lived up to the rock star hype in any manner, and he was no drinker. He just liked the ladies.

"No wild parties lately, huh, Cal?" Sonny said with a grin. "You've been stuck in Riverside with us."

"It's been fun," I told him truthfully.

And it had been fun, but not because of his band. That had been somewhat tiresome, even a little depressing. Phenex was adequate, another garage band dreaming of the big time, like the neighbor kid down the block who shot hoops incessantly in his short driveway, dreaming of the NBA. He might have a moment in the spotlight in college, but I thought he'd better study his accounting textbooks, because the NBA was going to pass him by. It was the same for Phenex. Ernie's money and connections might get them a couple of gigs opening for better acts, but I still doubted that they'd ever be the headliner.

Spending time in Riverside with Phenex had been fun because it had allowed me to have my own dream of what had already passed me by. It had let me be near Lisa, alive and exciting, sassy and amusing, just like Elise had been. But unlike Elise, whose heart and soul had belonged to Dennis Whitly – even though he hadn't wanted them – Lisa made eyes at me.

It was fun, it was infinitely flattering, it was bittersweet. Lisa had no idea that what she thought she wanted, what she imagined – wild parties with a rock star – all that would be pretty damn boring in real life. There were no parties, and I hadn't been a rock star since before she was born.

A life with Lisa would be great for me, everything I'd never thought I'd ever have, someone to love and to love me, all that sentimental romantic bullshit that I'd be ashamed to admit to thinking about. I'd never really thought about it, actually, had never really wished for it – I'd always been a loner – until I'd met her.

If I gave in to Lisa's curiosity, it would all be great for me, until the day – and it wouldn't be long in coming – when she'd realize that an old rock star was no different than an old anybody else. Then she'd leave. Without a backward glance, she would leave.

Life was lonely for me, that was a fact, but it had always been that way. I'd just never recognized how profoundly empty it truly was until this incredible young woman had started coming on to me. She showed me that things could be infinitely better if I had someone, like Denny and his brother did.

But that someone couldn't be her. I was just a passing curiosity, a notch that she inexplicably wanted to carve onto her up-and-coming, bad-girl rock singer's bedpost. Lisa thought she'd get to tell *Rolling Stone* someday, *Oh Romeo, yeah. You know, I used to have a scene with him.*

Life was not overly exciting to me. I was healthy and wealthy, although I was beginning to doubt that the years had lent me very much wisdom. I was supremely comfortable; I surely didn't have 99 problems, like the song said, and a bitch certainly wasn't one. But if I allowed Lisa into my life the way she wanted in, when she inevitably left, I would have one big problem. I would be devastated.

I wasn't going to do that to myself. I wasn't going to let the prospect of a few glorious days or weeks with her allow me to forget the pain that would follow. Loneliness, which had always been my companion, would then become my master. I wouldn't do it. No matter how much I wanted to.

ELEVEN

Ernie and Lisa and the rest of the band arrived, James and Roy laden with cases of beer, chips and various other munchies. This was a party that was going to last, until all memories of the rocky start to their first recording session were forgotten and only the achievement of its successful completion remained.

After a few beers relaxed them, Phenex wanted to hear stories about Sonic Daydream's recording days, long past, and that in turn led to a discussion of bass guitars and six-strings, mikes and amps and drum kits. Musicians are basically one-trick ponies, and when they get together, they talk shop.

Candy tried to join the conversation, saying that the thing she remembered about me from the shows she'd attended was that it was always hard to see me behind all those drums.

Sonny giggled, downed the rest of his beer, crushed the can. "Still have *all those drums,* do ya, Cal?"

"As a matter of fact I do," I replied.

Detecting a tiny slur in my own voice, I set the beer I was drinking down. I'd been quite the alcoholic once upon a time, and I recognized oncoming drunkenness when it was oncoming. The uncharacteristic beer intake was going straight to my head – who did I think I was, a rock star, that I could keep up with a bunch of kids? Better to slow it down now, before it snowballed into something I would be ashamed of in the morning.

"In storage, no doubt," Candy opined imperiously.

Ah, Candy, I really don't care for you, I thought. *You know nothing whatsoever about music or musicians, past the fact that you nailed a famous guitar player once, and you wanted your kid to have a band just like he did. Yet you open your big, slack mouth and utter the most ludicrous statements.*

Sonny again laughed at her ignorance. That was twice now. The beer was going to his head, too.

"Show me, Big Daddy."

Sonny knew. He was a musician. I'd gotten a haircut, grown old; I didn't tour anymore, wasn't even in a band, but my drums would never be in storage. Sonny knew; he practiced, played music every day. It was not a chore, not something he *had* to do, not for Candy or for Phenex. It was something he wanted to do, as natural as breathing. Playing music was not a means to an end for Sonny, not a way to get women or to make money. It was what he did because it was a part of him, and he recognized that I was the same way.

My kit was upstairs, on the third floor of the McMansion. There was only one room up there at the top of the house, actually, plus a little bathroom.

James and Sonny and I left Candy and Roy and Lisa and Ernie behind – guitar players and an old groupie weren't interested in checking out *all those drums.* Did I really stagger a little bit as we left the room? It was a distinct possibility, and I decided that I was done drinking for the evening.

As we climbed the two flights of stairs, I mused that before this recent reappearance in my life, I had last actually seen Ernie on the very day I'd purchased this big, empty house. It had been about five years before, and it had been just like this time, a random phone call out of nowhere.

Azomite had been scheduled to appear in LA in a few days, and Ernie was at odds and ends until then, back in his hometown with nothing to do. I'm sure he'd visited Lenny and Denny, although he mentioned neither of them; nor did he mention my book, which was already five years old at the time. Maybe he hadn't yet read it back then.

But the Whitly brothers were settled family men and Ernie's surprise visits to them had no doubt been brief. What were they gonna do, cruise The House of Ale for hometown groupies with him? He had always been closer to me, the other lone wolf in the band, even though my motivations for always being single were completely different from his. Ernie LaBelle had missed his old drummer, and was more than happy to go house-hunting with me.

The place was barely finished when the development company realtor gave us the tour; there were still a few buckets of paint in the garage waiting for disposal, and the unit two lots down was only half built. There was no water in the pool.

Like I say, the place is big: there's a nice open kitchen and dining area on the first floor, with a sliding glass door that leads to the patio and pool, and a hall that leads to the huge two car garage. There's a small room off the vaulted entranceway – "It could be an office or a guest bedroom," the realtor said, although the bathroom was not connected but adjacent, a few steps down the hall.

The house-tour moved upstairs. The master bedroom on the second floor had its master bath, and the two smaller bedrooms shared a bath between them. What I needed with three bedrooms –

four, if you counted the one downstairs – I didn't know. But I had to live somewhere, and it surely wasn't going to be back in Riverside, now that my parents had passed on.

But it was the lone room at the top of the house that sold me on the place. There wasn't what you'd call a living room on the first floor – just the big dining area. It had a fireplace, true, but it wasn't a living room, and it wasn't a den, and it wasn't any place to set up a drum kit. But this room was perfect.

The development company rep told us that it was designated *the entertainment room* – to me it was as if the absent living room had been transported upstairs, and the rep confirmed that impression. "You gentlemen could perhaps set up a home theater system here," she had suggested. "The television could go there –" she gestured at a blank expanse of wall, "with the speakers beside, and maybe a nice couch set right here."

She was several years younger than us, and pretty in her wine colored suit and black pumps. Ernie smiled at her. "We're musicians, honey. We call our speakers *amps,* and we don't need a television for entertainment." His grin widened. "Or for theater."

"Musicians?" I could see her running my credit it her head. When she actually saw it in black and white, she was gonna be surprised. "Have I heard of you?"

It was a standard, flippant question. She expected the answer to be negative, expected Ernie to say that we weren't really musicians, not like we did it for a living. We actually had some other high-paying day jobs, belonged to some other profession that was really a profession. We were two clean-cut guys pushing fifty – surely the flirty one meant that we were musicians only as a hobby. A couple of old guys still plinking around in the garage couldn't afford a house like this.

Again I knew she was gonna be astonished, would feel stupid about her glibness. Ernie told her who we were, and before she had a chance to doubt him, he told her to Google it. He even handed her his phone.

Surprise, surprise, I thought. *Charming Ernie LaBelle wouldn't lie to ya, baby. Once you know who he is, he doesn't have to.*

The realtor was gob-smacked, just as the young bartender at The House of Ale had been. It was really us, and now she told us how much she'd loved the band when she was a teenager. I thought about how some of the lunch money she'd saved to buy tickets to see us back then had transmogrified over the years into part of my ability to purchase this McMansion from her now. I smiled to myself.

Ernie's own smile didn't even dim when she asked, "What's Dennis Whitly really like?"

"Ah, he's a great guy. He and his wife live right up there is Riverside. It's our hometown."

This was news to the woman from the development company; she wasn't a chapter and verse fan like Candy, but she was fan enough, especially of Sonic Daydream's singer. Enthralled that she was talking to his second-guitar, she forgot for several minutes that she was trying to sell his drummer a house.

Ernie didn't mind talking about Denny; Denny wasn't there. And I'm not one to be telling tales out of school, as the old saying goes, so I can't state for certain that the realtor went right on home with Ernie, and I can't say that it was because Denny wasn't there. But when the showing concluded and I told her that I'd take the house, she looked at me as if she'd forgotten *I* was there, and told me that she could meet me at the sales office first thing in the morning. And Ernie, who'd left his car at the IHOP on Highway 79 where we'd had breakfast that morning, suddenly didn't need a ride back to fetch it.

The rep locked up and the three of us walked down the short driveway. She and I shook hands, and she repeated that she'd see me at the office in the morning to sign the papers and start the escrow. Ernie smiled innocently at me and opened her car door for her, then got in on the other side. A few minutes later, he sent me a text: *It's only rock & roll but I like it.*

Ernie went back on tour with Azomite; he wasn't on hand to help me move in. I got a few texts from him in the ensuing years, but hadn't actually spoken to him again until he'd called to tell me about his newfound family.

In the room at the top of the house, Sonny smiled in pleased wonder at my drums. I handed him a set of sticks and he absently twirled one of them, considering where he would begin, I imagined. But then he stopped and offered them to James, the de facto drummer in his band.

James looked at the sticks, looked at the drums, looked at me, then shook his head.

I was reminded immediately of my students from the YMCA. I'd invited several of them to the house over the years, in groups of twos and threes, my aspiring young drummers, those who'd mentioned that they'd like to see what a real rock star's kit looked like. After the first couple of groups, it became an experiment to me. I was fascinated because they always reacted in exactly the same manner.

Some of the kids really wanted to drum; some of them even had talent. But the majority were just bored. They didn't have anything to do after school, and Mom had signed them up for drum lessons to keep them off the street and out of the house. Often it was not possible to tell which category the student before me fell into – kids affect disinterest in the presence of adults, even if they're secretly interested. Didn't you?

But like an oracle, the big drum set at the top of the stairs revealed the truth. Every single time. The kids that didn't really care about drumming, the ones that would sign up to try their hand at guitar or ceramics or synchronized swimming next time – they behaved just like James. They balked, shook their heads – *all those drums* intimidated them. They didn't really know, hadn't really practiced, didn't really care.

But the ones that were truly musicians – even if they weren't any good; even if they *knew* that they weren't any good – they always got the same ear-to-ear grin that Sonny had now. Obviously Mr. Bascomb didn't care that they were just learning, that they always flubbed the end of the bridge with the time change, that they would never make it out of the garage. Or maybe he thought they might, because he was handing them a pair of sticks and offering them a go at *all those drums.*

Regardless, an opportunity like this didn't come along every day. And they would smile and sit down and attack my big, expensive, professional kit like it had insulted their sisters.

So it was with Sonny. He had a great deal of talent, and it was a pleasure to listen to him play and to see his appreciation for a good set of instruments. James lingered for a moment, then went back downstairs. His beer was empty.

Again I thought that it was a shame that Sonny wasn't Phenex's drummer. He was unquestionably a good guitarist, but it was clear that percussion was his first love. It was just another strange aspect of the whole strange scene.

I would've thought that Candy, ambitious, would've long ago cut James in favor of her boyfriend's vastly superior talent. It would've been just business, this business that she so longed to be in, and I didn't think the big redhead would've minded all that much. If he had any passion at all, it certainly wasn't for drumming. They could've found another guitarist anywhere. How did that old joke go? *What do you call a guitar player without a girlfriend? Homeless.* They would've lined up around the block for the free room and board Candy provided to her band.

And then I thought of the demon Phenex, their *muse.* Perhaps he had spoken to Candy through her crystal ball, decreeing what the line-up should be. *Mostly, we play whatever Candy says we should,* Sonny had told me. Maybe it wasn't that easy to just dump one's *minions.*

TWELVE

I couldn't actually say that it raged, but the party wore on. Surprised that two or three beers had indeed seemed about to cause me to reenact a few of my more scarcely remembered drinking days, I stopped early. Roy and James took up my slack, and Sonny soon joined them, about the time that Candy once again started checking Ernie out with an inappropriate appreciation. When she asked if he wanted to dance, even though there was no music, Ernie exercised the better part of valor: he retreated all the way to the top room of the house and passed out on the couch in the drum room.

Candy's attentions returned to Sonny after Ernie's departure. *Once a groupie always a groupie,* I thought nastily. If one guitar player decamped, the remaining one would serve just as well. Ernie had utilized this phenomenon for his entire career with Sonic Daydream, comforting all the disappointed girls that had dreamt that they might have a shot at Dennis Whitly.

Sonny was drunk, so he didn't notice that he was second choice. I directed them to one of the two smaller bedrooms upstairs.

Unlike her mother, Lisa didn't drink very much. I thought this was a good sign, as she wasn't old enough to be drinking anyway. When the party was reduced to myself and her sloppy-drunk bass player and drummer – they were attempting to play beer pong on the wide expanse of granite countertop in the kitchen – she announced that she was tired, it had been a long, exciting day, and asked me where she could sleep. I was relieved that she said it with no innuendo. Roy and James wouldn't have noticed, absorbed as they were with their game. But Lisa seemed to have something else on her mind for a change; I thought maybe she was reliving her very first recording session.

I directed her to the room off the entranceway. I had set it up as a guestroom, for all those guests I never had. What did a drummer need with an office? I figured that she probably wouldn't want to be just a shared bathroom away from her mother and Sonny, and it was also the farthest room away from mine. She said thanks and goodnight, and walked away with nary a *Would you like to join me?* glance. My relief was immense: Roy and James wouldn't have noticed, had I followed her, and I realized that I was just drunk enough that I might've if she had offered.

I sighed and turned back to the gamesters at the kitchen counter.

"I'm sorry, guys, but there's only one room left. I'm afraid you'll have to share it."

"It won't be the first time," Roy said.

There was only one bed: I realized that one of them would have to sleep on the floor, unless the two of them were chummier than was immediately apparent. On the other hand, they were pretty chummy. There were blankets and pillows in the closet – whoever got the short straw would be comfortable enough on the floor, and I figured that they were both too drunk to notice anyway.

"It's upstairs, turn right, second door on the left." Like I say, it was a big house; I didn't want them accidentally taking a wrong turn and staggering into my room. "I'll see you in the morning."

They nodded and gave me a disinterested wave, concentrating again on their game.

I didn't even pause as I walked through the entranceway and started up the stairs, didn't even glance in the direction of Lisa's room. *Oh, that way madness lies. Let me shun that. No more of that.* I felt as old as Lear at that moment.

I thought that I'd have a hard time getting to sleep. I hadn't drunk enough to simply pass out, like Ernie, and the idea of Lisa's presence in my house, just downstairs . . . I thought that would surely cause me to toss and turn. But I was mistaken. I was asleep, as the saying goes, almost before my head hit the pillow. Evidently, it *had* been a long day.

THIRTEEN

I awoke with a start, and it took a split-second to orient my place in the universe. I was in my own bed, instead of the one I'd slept in at Ernie's house for the last two months. Oh, yeah: Phenex had recorded yesterday, there had been a party. Lisa was asleep downstairs . . .

I got up and took a shower, and the hot water washed away any remaining cobwebs in my head. I thought about the band: there was really no reason for me to go back to Riverside with them. The tracks for the demo were completed. Ernie and I didn't have to oversee rehearsals anymore. There wasn't much more we could show them, really. There was nothing left to do now but wait for Oscar to deliver the finished product.

I got out of the shower and discovered that there was only one towel left. When she did the laundry, Amanda liked to stack them all in the closet downstairs, next to the washer and dryer, and sometimes she forgot to bring some up to my bathroom.

Amanda had been leery of my kit upstairs, never having been around any musical instruments. They were brightly colored, shiny and foreign to her, obviously expensive. She imagined that they were delicate in some way. After I had assured her that she couldn't possibly hurt them, I think she actually enjoyed dusting *todos esos tambores.* Amanda took great care of my house. Forgetting to bring up towels sometimes was the only error she made.

I got dressed and padded barefoot down the stairs, coffee in mind. The house was silent. I paused in the entranceway at the bottom of the steps, and the thought of towels crossed my mind again. The bathroom down the hall from Lisa's room was nearly as far away from the washer and dryer as my room was, plus there was the fact that I never had any guests. Had Amanda *ever* bothered to put any towels in there? I should check.

That's my story and I'm sticking to it. It was the idea that I might be a poor host, that there might not be any towels in the bathroom for Lisa to use when she wanted to take a shower, that guided me down the hall. *Towels.*

The door to her room was ajar, standing more than halfway open, actually, and I looked in. It was already nine o'clock in the morning, and bright sunshine streamed into the room. She was sleeping on her back, naked, and I looked. God help me, I looked.

One hand was thrown behind her head, the other lay on the whisper of roundness that was her flawless belly. I looked past the tips of her fingers; only a glimpse of curly fur was visible above the curve of her thigh. She wore a chain and a medallion similar to her father's. For what seemed like a lifetime, or an impossibly split second, I watched the gentle rise and fall of her breasts as she breathed.

I glanced at the floor in shame, moved away from the door, came back, looked again.

Words cannot describe how beautiful she was. A picture, as they say, being worth a thousand words, if you Google *Pre-Raphaelite Paintings, sleeping*, you could get the general idea.

But paintings of naked young girls sleeping are different than naked young girls, actually sleeping, now aren't they? On so many different levels. My psyche was instantly at war, right and wrong, the angel and the devil, what could not possibly matter and what mattered impossibly.

I felt like a prisoner already caught and condemned, a filthy voyeur. Yet one part of my mind defended me, rationalized. *It's not like you opened the door and peeped in at her. Maybe the wind blew it open, or maybe . . . maybe she left it open! Maybe she wanted you to see her!*

Ah, yes, blaming the victim, always a winning tactic.

She's no victim. It's not like you're standing in the doorway beating off, looking at her. It's not like you're gonna go in there. You're not going to wake

her, touch the incredible pinkness of her nipples, kiss her perfect belly, bury your nose in . . .

Again I looked at the floor, and again I looked at her. My rationalizing self was of course right and of course wrong. It was not a premeditated act. I wouldn't ever have dreamed in a million years of opening the door and peeping in at her, all that was true, but still I shouldn't be looking at her. I shouldn't be thinking about what it would be like to go in there, shouldn't be imagining that she would be anything besides mortified and possibly horrified if she should awaken and find me in her room or even standing in the doorway, regardless of the way she'd flirted with me all this time.

It was bad enough that I should be savoring, reveling, in the pleasure of just looking at her. I shouldn't be allowing myself to experience the exquisite ache that came from the impossible desire to touch her. It was all unbidden, unhoped for, just an innocent glance through an open door, turned shameful, indecent.

She'll never know you saw her, my mind tried to assuage me. *But I'll know,* I returned. *I'll always know.* It was just an innocent accident; she was in no way harmed by my seeing her. I was feeling ashamed over nothing.

But, ah, Christ, she was so perfect and the shame gave me a sick feeling for a moment, because she was eighteen years old and I was fifty-five, and the things I knew about life, the things I wanted to do to her. . .

There's no sin in that, the voice in my head said. *There's no sin in desire, in wanting to possess a beautiful naked girl. She surely acts like she wants you.*

The sin was in the quality of the desire, the ache; I would love her if I touched her. I loved her already from just the way she looked at me, from just hearing her sing. And loving her was insane, it was impossible. She would never love me back, at least not for very long. I was old enough to be her father. Her father played guitar on stage beside me for decades, had done so the night she was conceived. The years were just so impossibly wrong, it was all just so impossibly wrong.

But I couldn't stop looking at her. The shame, the love, the lust . . . I just stood there.

A car door slammed outside, and I was jarred out of my reverie. Somebody was going to catch me staring through the half opened door at Lisa, or she was suddenly going to open her eyes, and then *she* would catch me.

I gently pulled the door closed. I walked into the bathroom, turned on the tap. I splashed water on my face and considered my reflection. The crow's feet, the gray; Jesus Christ, I felt so old, despite the fact that I had become aroused like a schoolboy, by glimpsing a naked sleeping girl. I had not experienced this kind of exquisite longing in decades – oh, Christ, it hurt *so good.* I looked at myself in the mirror, laughed shakily – the impossibility of acting on the desire was what made it so arousing. I waited for it to go away.

Then she said my name and I jumped. She was standing in the doorway to the bathroom, wrapped in the sheet from the bed. She took a step into the tiny room and I caught her scent; she smelled just like she looked: young and fresh and alive and infinitely desirable.

I blinked and tried to swallow, but my mouth was suddenly dry. I caught my reflection in the mirror out of the corner of my eye, and of course I was every inch the 8th grader called to the front of the class at exactly the wrong time. It showed on my face as if someone had written it with a Sharpie on my forehead.

Lisa pushed the bathroom door closed with her foot. There was only a small touch of triumph to her smile this time, something about the quality of the curve of her mouth. She read me like sheet music, and all my silent dismissals before, all the haughtiness and control of age and maturity and wisdom – she discarded them as easily as she dropped the sheet to the floor. She had me now. There was no escape, no other people around, no drum kit to hide behind. The desire was plain on my face, as plain as that schoolboy's. It showed in my eyes – I wanted her more than anything I'd ever wanted before, would ever again. Yet still, I had self-control. I would not act. So she acted for both of us.

Lisa was neither shy nor inexperienced. These were not illusions that I had about her. The way she'd looked at me, from the moment I'd walked into that big ugly room full of scruffy instruments – I didn't hesitate because I thought she was an innocent, because I thought I'd be taking advantage of her. She was a fully aware, fully functioning eighteen-year-old girl, but still she didn't know everything that I knew about the world, nor the fatigue and sorrow of knowing it for so many years. I knew I would fall for her, I'd worship her, not because she was a blushing virgin, but because she was young and perfect and everything I'd ever wanted, and it was entirely too late to even dream that I could ever have such a thing.

She glanced demurely at the floor – it was a pose – and slid her hand purposefully over the front of my jeans. When I gasped, her eyes flicked immediately back to mine. She put her other hand on my cheek. The triumph in her eyes intensified; she molded her perfect naked body against my clothed one. She pressed her mouth to mine and it was like some kind of electric current switched on, galvanization to dead flesh. I reacted immediately.

Gentlemen of the jury, I could not stop myself. When Lisa kissed me, I kissed her back. When she undid my pants and dropped them to the floor, I kicked them away. I leaned back on the sink; I picked her up by the hips and impaled her on me. I thrilled to her cry of utterly triumphant ecstasy.

I cannot tell a lie: it was quick. She stayed where she was for a moment, her feet on the back of the sink, her arms around my neck, her head on my shoulder. I heard a door slam upstairs, and the specter of getting caught *gouged* at me, the question of *What have I done?* running like a corrosive acid through my brain.

Still she clung to me, and suddenly I was afraid to look at her, fearing that when I did, the confident, knowing young woman would be gone. Like some kind of changeling, I would find myself holding a regretful, disgusted, ashamed teenager.

When nothing else came to mind, I whispered, "You . . . you wanted this?"

She raised her head and smiled into my eyes, and the triumph was still there, larger now. No shame. No disgust. No regret. "Someday, maybe I'll be able to explain it, but right now, the short answer is yes. I wanted this. From the moment I saw you."

Again I felt like a schoolboy: from some unguarded part of me came the desire to say, *Really?* Because even though I'd seen it there in her eyes all along, I'd fought against it, shamed myself for even considering such a ridiculous, impossible thing – it was all too good to be true, that this beautiful, talented young woman would want me.

Not a jury in the world would've believed it, that *she* had seduced *me,* yet that was exactly how it had occurred. I was having more than a little trouble believing it myself, yet here she was, her perfect nakedness perfectly perched upon me. To my amazement, the very thought of it threatened to create the conditions for a repeat performance. *Somebody call Guinness,* I said to myself. *Once a king always a king, but once you're past forty . . . once a night's enough.* This had to be some kind of record.

But Lisa wasn't amazed. She grinned in delight and started to kiss me, the only fuel necessary to rekindle this unbelievable fire. But then we heard voices at the top of the steps. The rest of the band was awake; they'd be downstairs in a minute.

"Let me get rid of them," she murmured into my neck. "Hold that thought."

The thought had dissipated as abruptly as it had manifested at the noises of life from upstairs, but Lisa had already dropped gracefully to the floor, so it didn't matter anyway. I admired the exquisite roundness of her faultless ass as she bent to recover the sheet. She caught me looking, and playfully flung my jeans to me.

Lisa wrapped the sheet around herself, then kissed me quickly. Some kind of guilty look must've showed on my face, because she told me in a serious whisper, "Like I said. From the moment I saw you. This is destiny, Cal."

She didn’t wait for my reply – I didn’t have one, anyway. She cracked the door and peeped around it. The coast was clear, and she slipped out into the hallway, pulling the door closed silently behind her.

FOURTEEN

An insane voice in my head told me to stay right there and wait for her to get rid of the houseful of people, wait for her to come back. And I listened to it for perhaps the span of two or three minutes, standing there motionless in the downstairs bathroom, naked except for a t-shirt, clutching my jeans in my hand.

Then the voice of reason, struck dumb by the impossibly fantastic activities of the past several minutes, harshly reasserted itself. *Put your pants on, Cal, you fucking idiot! How can she possibly get rid of everybody? She's not coming back now. She's probably never coming back. In fact, maybe you dreamed the whole thing.*

I did as reason bid, and peeped around the door in the same manner as Lisa had done, as if I expected them all to be standing there staring accusingly at me. But of course the hallway was empty, as was Lisa's room, and the entranceway to the house. Voices drifted out to me from the kitchen/dining area. I took a deep breath and followed them.

Ernie and Sonny, Roy and James alternately lounged or leaned against the granite counter. Phenex's singer and her mother sat on the sofa which was in front of the fireplace. I couldn't bear to make eye contact with Lisa, nor Candy either, so I assessed my fellow musicians.

Phenex's guitarists and drummer were bright-eyed and bushy-tailed. They were each barely thirty, after all, and a fairly tame night of drinking hadn't fazed them in the least. Ernie, on the other hand, looked bleary-eyed, a little worse for wear, as the saying goes.

"Where the hell have you been?" he asked irritably, not quite half kidding. "Why is there no coffee?"

"I'll get right on that, Boss," I replied, not getting right on it at all. Ernie wanted coffee? He could make it himself. The fixings were right beside him on the counter. I'd just experienced something incredible; every nerve-ending in my body still spoke to me of it, and I was not quite ready to relinquish the conversation to start stepping and fetching for a hung-over guitar player.

"I don't wanna wait for coffee," Roy said. "Where can we get something to eat around here? I'm starving."

Ernie managed half a grin. "IHOP. Breakfast of champions."

So we caravanned to IHOP, the same way we had from the studio: Roy and James took the van, Sonny and Candy rode with me. I was both glad and a shade disappointed that Lisa opted to again accompany her daddy in his Porsche. She had not yet looked at me, and again the crazy little voice in my head suggested that perhaps I'd dreamed the whole thing.

It was the same at breakfast. Lisa made eye contact with me now, when the conversation warranted it, but her smiles and words were so completely devoid of any hint of our shared secret that I began to give credence to the idea that perhaps it hadn't happened at all. But it *had* happened, damn it. I could still smell her on my shirt. The faint perfume lingered, from where she'd been pressed against me, whilst we . . .

And then I realized what was going on. Given a moment to reflect, now that she was back with her band and her mother and her newfound father – my contemporary – Lisa had reconsidered *destiny.* She was pretending it hadn't happened because she now wished it hadn't.

When the lumberjack's repast of bacon and eggs and whipped-cream-drowned pancakes was demolished, as the waitress cleared away the detritus, Candy said, "What shall we do with this day the Lord hath made?"

I wondered fleetingly to which Lord she referred, my mother's Christian God or one of his fallen angels, but before I had the opportunity to give it much thought, Sonny said, "We should rehearse."

Roy guffawed around his coffee cup and James grinned at him. "Rehearse? I'm done rehearsing for a while. I think we should take a vacation from rehearsing until this guy gives us the demo. I think we should go to the beach."

Personally, I hate the beach. I watched Sonny and James and even Roy look to Candy for a decision, on whether they should rehearse, go to the beach; whether they should take another breath. It was amazing and a little disconcerting how they deferred to her. They really were her minions.

"I don't think we're really dressed for the beach. And our instruments are still in the van. We should just take 'em home and then decide on something to do from there."

Why had she asked them what they wanted to do if she'd already made up her mind?

"What do you think, Ernie?"

Ah, there it was, the pecking order on display. Candy hadn't really been asking her underlings what they wanted to do. She had been asking her deity.

"Sounds good to me." There would be no profound proclamations from on high at the moment. Ernie still had a hangover. I would've bet the price of breakfast that what he most wanted to do was rid himself of Phenex and go home to his cool, shaded house and sleep the rest of the day.

Lisa said, "You guys do whatever you want; go home, go to the beach. Cal told me last night that he was thinking about writing another book." She held her fingers up like quotation marks. *"The history of Phenex on the cusp of fame.* I want to be the first one interviewed."

"That's a great idea, Cal!" Candy enthused. "Your first book . . . It's awesome. I can't tell you how many times I've read it."

I searched for something to say, and at last came up with a simple thanks. Beyond that, I was dumbstruck. Of course I hadn't mentioned anything about a new book to Lisa. We'd barely spoken to each other during the party. The whole idea was laughable; what was there to write about a ridiculously named, doubtfully talented, garage band out of Riverside, California? Who would read it?

Lisa smiled at me blankly, her expression unreadable. After ignoring me throughout breakfast, why had she suddenly come up with this completely off the wall excuse to be alone with me? Then I grasped her motivation. She wanted to make sure no one was around to overhear when she told me that she was sorry, she'd made a mistake; what had happened this morning could never happen again.

Ernie paid the tab and we went out to the parking lot. He said he'd call me later and approached his car, then frowned when Candy trotted up beside him. Her smile was gleeful; she was *so* looking forward to that Porsche ride, to being alone with her favorite guitar player.

I hesitated outside the restaurant. I was not looking forward to taking Lisa back to the McMansion so she could deliver the bad news, then silently driving her all the way back to Riverside. Conversely, Lisa wasn't depressed by the anticipation of the pathetic scene to come: she walked out to the van with her drummer and her bass player, chatting happily.

Sonny hung back with me. He wasn't anxious to go home either, to get in the hot van with Roy and James, whilst his woman roared off in air-conditioned comfort with a famous rock star. Sonny had always seemed a little above his bandmates, and I'd always put it down to his superior talent and his relationship with the boss. But now I wondered if James and Roy would kid him about it, if they'd make a joke out of the fact that his woman so obviously wanted to again make a play for her baby-daddy.

At Sonny's bleak expression, I again said, "You don't have anything to worry about, man."

"You don't understand, Cal. The cards were shuffled a long time ago. It's only now that they're being dealt."

I liked Sonny; he had talent. Unlike Roy and James, he was truly a musician, and I felt a connection to him because of that. It made us friends. But when he started talking in riddles like this, I didn't really know how to respond.

He peered at me, and I was dismayed at the sadness in his eyes. Then he looked away, nodded toward Lisa. "I guess she didn't have to give you the charmed token. She's the charm herself."

Denial leapt up immediately, but before I could voice it, Sonny shook his head. "She believes it's her destiny."

Shocked to hear Lisa's silly, girlish words come out of his mouth, I actually managed to say the tired, liar's cliché before he cut me off again. "I don't know what you're talking about, Sonny."

"It's all been foretold, Cal." He watched Ernie and Candy exit the parking lot. "The cards begin to fall. The day of reckoning draws nigh, the season of cosmic revenge."

Revenge for what? "Look, Sonny, I don't know anything about revenge or any of this witchy mumbo-jumbo, but I'm telling you, Ernie's not interested in –"

James honked the van's horn. Lisa looked across the parking lot at us impatiently, hands on hips.

Sonny clasped my hand in both of his; I felt the guitarist's callouses on his fingers. He smiled ruefully, and I was again struck with the sadness, the resignation in his eyes. "It's been great knowing you, Cal. Like I said, I've always been a big fan." Roy honked again, and Lisa started striding purposefully across the parking lot towards us. Sonny dropped my hand. "Thanks for letting me play your kit."

He walked away then, head down, with the finality of a man walking to the gallows. He didn't acknowledge Lisa, nor she him, as they passed. I felt for him – it was this love thing. Sonny really believed he was about to lose his woman, that he was powerless to prevent it.

Lisa stopped, again smiled expressionlessly at me, nodded toward the Caddy. *Come on, Cal,* I imagined her thinking. *Let's get this over with. I might still have time to make it to the beach.*

Sonny had had his woman a lot longer than I'd had mine, but I reckoned that what she had to tell me when we got back to the house wasn't going to hurt any less than what Sonny imagined was in store for him in Riverside. I knew he was mistaken: Ernie didn't want Candy. But I was just as sure that Lisa didn't want me, either.

FIFTEEN

On the short drive home, Lisa burbled happily about how cool the recording studio had been, how much fun she'd had making the demo, how excited she was that a real rep from Sony was going to listen to it. I offered only perfunctory replies, because I wanted to get it over with, too. I allowed myself to be annoyed, savored a kind of petulance. We were alone now; why did she have to wait until we got back to the house? If she told me now, I could just get on the freeway and take her home.

A small portion of my superiority surfaced: maybe she didn't know exactly how to end it. She was just a kid, after all; perhaps she was having difficulty coming up with the words. My petulance expanded. That was her problem. I wasn't going to say anything, wasn't going to demonstrate that I knew the unavoidable truth. She'd started this, she had made the mistake. Now she could stammer through the ending.

I parked the Caddy in the garage. Lisa got out and trotted ahead of me into the house. I followed slowly, with the same shuffling, dejected strides Sonny had used crossing the parking lot at IHOP. She flung her purse carelessly onto the granite countertop in the kitchen, then turned and smiled brightly.

Before I had a chance to speak, Lisa launched herself at me, leaping lithely from the floor into my arms. I instinctively caught her. She wrapped her legs around my waist, her arms around my neck. She kissed me eagerly.

When I failed to respond, she said, "What's up, Cal?" Then she sang, *"I think we're alone now. There doesn't seem to be anyone around. I think we're alone now, the beating of our hearts is the only sound."*

Jesus, that one was almost older than me. Even Tiffany's version was decades before she was born. But her voice! Long after she was gone, I knew I'd still hear Lisa's voice in my dreams.

She tried to kiss me again and I said, "Lisa, you don't have to do this. You don't have to pretend like you . . . I'll just take you home now. I understand."

Now the crafty, triumphant smile returned. "I don't think you do, Cal. I want to stay here with you. When we were at breakfast, that's when I pretended. I figured that you needed a little time to think, that you wouldn't want me hanging all over you in front of everybody, in case you decided that you didn't want . . ."

Her stunning blue eyes darkened; her bottom lip trembled. "Is that what you've decided, Cal? That you don't want me?"

I should've said something right then. I should've faced reality, spelled out the impossibility of the situation to her *right then.* I should've said, *Lisa, this is crazy, it can never work, I can't possibly be what you want . . .*

But I was unable to speak, and the expression on my face revealed everything that I didn't want to say. Not the truth of a thirty-seven year age difference, of *what will people think, what will they say,* of how soon I knew boredom and embarrassment were going to come to her. The look on my face communicated the hope, the wish, the dream: yes, I wanted her. I would always want her. She was everything I'd *ever wanted.*

"That's what I thought," she said, and the triumph was complete. "Now kiss me."

She leaned in and I met her halfway this time, because a demon had popped up on my shoulder. It wasn't Phenex, of course, just the shrewd little guy that lives inside damn near all of us. He's the one that says, *Go ahead, have that second piece of pie. Have another drink. This girl's young, but she's of age; go ahead and give her what she wants.*

In those of us that are weak – and I was certainly one of them at the moment – this little fella's voice drowns out all the truths that we know to be self-evident: that pie's gonna make me fat, that drink's gonna make me drunk. Lisa's gonna break my heart. To me, he didn't represent sin so much as pleasure, pleasure that should be denied because the pain that would follow would be absolute.

But Lisa's kiss burst the dam of my sense of self-preservation. The sun would rise tomorrow or the next day or the next week, *racing around to come up behind me again.* And Lisa would be gone, and I would be nothing more than *older, shorter of breath and one day closer to death.*

But you're gonna be that anyway, the demon cackled, *and here she is, right now, convinced that it's her destiny to love a has-been drummer, more than three times her age. The smart money says go for it, Cal, ol' buddy, and worry about tomorrow when it gets here.*

So I did. As Sonny would say, may God have mercy on my soul.

We spent the entire afternoon in bed. Lisa commanded a youth from me that I thought had passed, or more likely, she just commanded all the sex I hadn't been having for all these years. She made my self-imposed celibacy sit up and beg, roll over and play dead.

She seemed to want me as much as I wanted her, even more sometimes, and that was the strangest, most dangerous part of all. I was in thrall to her at the first touch – even before that. When I first saw her perfect nakedness, I was her slave. But she was also my slave at some moments; the equality of our desire was frightening. Better for me to be a mistreated peon who only gets the master's occasional kindness, than to realize that this perfect young woman was perfectly, infinitely satisfied with a man as old as her father. With me.

It was almost enough to make a guy believe in destiny.

SIXTEEN

When the sun began to slant in from the west, we took a swim. I asked Lisa if she was hungry; she grinned and splashed me. "Aren't you?"

I nodded. "And I'm gonna sleep like the dead tonight."

"Don't bet on it," she said and molded herself against me in the water. "I've waited a long time for this."

You haven't been alive for a long time. But I wouldn't talk down to her. She had disappeared our age gap, at least for the moment. When we were alone together, we were equals.

But the rest of life would intervene, and soon. "I have to take you home. You can't stay here with –"

"Why not?" She kissed my nose. "My mother knows where I am."

At the mention of her mother, a horrifying thought occurred to me. The demon that had urged me to *go for it* earlier in the day now cackled in glee. *Time to pay the piper, Cal, ol' son.*

As I've mentioned, I'd had my share of women in my youth, and some of the encounters had been quite wild. But there had always been a plan, a calculation, a certain aloofness on my part. Unlike my good friend Ernie, I had never, not once, made the mistake that I suddenly realized that I'd made today.

Candy, obsessed with Sonic Daydream's second-guitar, had propagated his legacy, simply because Ernie had been too lazy and too arrogant to make sure that no such propagation occurred. Anatomy is reality, biology is destiny, and all that. And I, in the throes of a passion unimagined, had done exactly the same thing. It had not crossed my mind, until now, when it was too late, that the reason why there are so many people in this big old world is that the act that produces them is sometimes so enjoyable and utterly surprising that one forgets to plan, to calculate . . .

What if Lisa, in her fascination with me, had decided to emulate her mother? What if I, in my helpless, thoughtless enthusiasm, had gone right on ahead and accommodated her?

The water in the heated pool suddenly seemed glacial; I shivered. It must've shown on my face, because Lisa looked at me with concern, asked me if I was all right.

"We . . . you . . . you're not . . . because we didn't . . . you couldn't be . . ." I was unable to form a complete sentence, so I took a deep breath and tried again. I felt like the worst possible kind of careless oaf. "I'm so sorry, Lisa. This was just all so . . ." *Incredible.* "I didn't think to use a . . ."

The demon cackled again. *It's not like you have a supply on hand, anyway, now is it, Lover Boy?*

She furrowed her brow, concentrated on my panicked face, trying to figure out just what the hell I was trying to say. My panic increased, iced over by a new shame – maybe I'd misjudged her worldliness. Maybe she didn't even know about . . . But that was just ridiculous. Lisa had shown herself to be an experienced adult today; I'd never doubted it before. Surely, there was no way that she couldn't know . . .

Her eyes widened in comprehension. Then she started to titter, putting a hand to her mouth in a girlish attempt to cover her mirth, because she was laughing *at* me, you see. But the giggle wouldn't be contained; it soon grew into snorting hilarity. She tried to stop once, but was unable. It was literally a fit of laughter.

Finally, her giggles subsided enough for her to speak. "Oh, Cal! I'm gonna be a rock star! I don't have time for a baby!"

If wishes were horses, then beggars would ride, the demon in my head opined, unconvinced.

My expression must've said that I agreed with him, because Lisa explained, "I'm one of the initiated, my darling." She kissed my nose again, squeezed me. "I'm of the blood, a member of a sisterhood stretching back to the dawn of time. *We know things.* We don't get pregnant unless we want to, and I certainly don't want to." She attempted a serious expression, but her amusement remained, dancing in her gorgeous blue eyes. "You gotta trust me on this one."

All righty, then! the demon exclaimed. *One more layer of all-good to an already all-great situation.*

"And I don't want to go home just yet." She curled the hair at the nape of my neck around her rough, guitarist's fingers, and I shivered again, but for an entirely different reason.

I gave in. Her mother had no reason to suspect that she was anything but safe here with me.

"Your wish is my command." I kissed her, knowing that I had never uttered a truer statement.

She offered me that triumphant smile, and I wondered again, *What can she possibly see in me?* Wanting to know the why of it made me bold, bold enough to ask. I began, "Hey, Lisa –"

"I said, 'Hey, what's your name? Maybe we can see things the same.'"

Another famous song, almost older than me. So I returned her another line from it. It was like going back a million years, trading lyrics with Elise.

"Look, what's your game? Are you tryin' to put me in shame?"

Lisa grinned in delight. "*Slow, don't go so fast, don't you think that love can last?"*

"Love? Lord above. Now you're tryin' to trick me in love."

She sang the chorus: *All right now, baby, it's-a all right now.* She knew the old tunes, just like Elise had known them. The difference was that Lisa could actually sing them.

"I do love you, Cal."

Now I asked the sixty-four thousand dollar question. "Why is that, Lisa?"

Her surprise at this inquiry left her at a loss for words. I thought it straightforward enough. I wasn't going to give her any hints or offer any explanations as to why I thought she did. I didn't really want to speculate on that.

"I've always loved you, Cal," she said at last. "I'm your biggest fan."

I might've been shocked, might've been appalled, but I couldn't say I was surprised. "Oh, Christ, honey, don't say that!"

As I'd suspected, it all went back to her from-the-womb Sonic Daydream fandom, and the fact that I was the only guy from the band that didn't have previous and ongoing entanglements.

"You sound just like . . ." *your mother and Ernie, Ernie and a staggering number of other girls.* Girls that didn't know him, didn't want to know him, didn't need to know anything more than that the way he played guitar got their collective motors running. That wasn't love.

A part of me didn't want to believe it, although I'd known it all along. Beautiful, talented eighteen-year-old girls didn't just imprint on old drummers because of our irresistible attractiveness. But the part of me that didn't want to believe it had hope, and that part looked out at her and waited for her to say that it wasn't some kind of unrealistic, cross-generational groupie-lust that she felt for me. That it wasn't some kind of weird obsession that I'd gone right on ahead and culminated for her.

"Listen," Lisa sang, and squeezed me to her. *"Do you want to know a secret? Do you promise not to tell? Closer. Let me whisper in your ear."* She bit my ear.

Then she sighed and looked at me seriously. "I've loved music all my life, Cal. My Mom's got a video of me. If you stick around long enough –"

Where could she possibly think I was gonna go?

"– I'm sure she'll get around to playing it for you. I'm about five years old. I've got this little plastic play guitar, and I'm singing *Tomcats."*

Dennis Whitly's chart-topping ode to a Saturday night. I'd played it a million times. I sincerely hoped that Lisa wouldn't sing it now.

"Mom sent me to music lessons for as long as I can remember. Before Sonny, there were some regular classes, after school, and I can remember that some of the other kids . . . It was a chore to them. Their parents were *making* them go, and they couldn't wait to be done, so they could go and play and ride their bikes, do what *they* wanted to do.

"But it was never like that for me. I liked learning music, and it always made me feel good, how *proud* Mom was of me. My grandpa played piano, and she'd always told me that my dad played guitar. But she didn't tell me who he was until after your book came out."

Lisa paused to let that sink in.

"I guess I was about eight or so. Mom used to read it to me – like a bedtime story. I would find out later, when I was older, when I read it for myself, that she had paraphrased, that she had glossed over things, that she had exaggerated things, to make them sound more . . . *magical* to a little kid." Lisa grinned. "She made it into a fairytale for me. There was a beautiful girl, who loved music, just as much as I did. She knew all the words to all the songs, just like I did. She fell in love with a mean man that didn't love her back –"

"And she killed herself over him." *Yes, indeedy, that was quite the fairytale.* It crossed my mind, not for the first time, that Candy might just be the littlest bit touched in the head, and her insanity had perhaps twisted her daughter in ways that I didn't really want to know about.

Lisa shook her head. "I didn't find out about that part until I was old enough to understand it."

You're still not old enough to understand it. I don't know if I'm old enough to understand it, if I'll ever be.

"The story that Mom told me was about a beautiful girl that loved music. She showed me the pictures in the middle. There she was – smiling. There was my dad – he knew her. There was the bad man, and his brother – but Mom didn't dwell on them, not when I was little.

"And here was the man that was the beautiful girl's best friend. The one that had brought us her story. The one that loved music as much as she did. As much as I did."

Lisa shrugged abruptly. "That's what I got out of *Sonic Nightmare* when I was a kid, that you and Elise were great friends, that you and she shared the same love of music that I did. The idea of that made me curious about you, not Ernie or the other guys.

"It wasn't until I was sixteen – I stayed out all night with this guy." Lisa giggled. "He wasn't even a musician. I've never been much for musicians, actually."

Except for old, fairytale-telling drummers.

"Your mom liked musicians . . ." *So you wanted to be different.*

Lisa grinned. "The whole groupie thing. I understand that, I guess. If you don't play yourself, a guy's talent can make him seem . . . *magical.*" That was the second time she'd used that word. "It can make him seem extra-sexy, I guess. Before Ernie came back . . . Mom would stare at Sonny when he played, and as I got older, I could tell . . . The fact that Sonny played guitar, and she couldn't, just made him extra special to her.

"People like Mom . . . I guess it's a difference between liking the guy versus liking the music. It's the difference between seeing someone who is attractive to you, and feeling like, *He's so cute, and he's singing to me,* as opposed to, *He's just some guy, but he's singing* about *me,* or, *He's singing about something that's going on in my life.* Or maybe he's just singing in the background when something important occurs."

"Part of the soundtrack of your life."

Lisa nodded. "It's always been about the music to me, not the musicians. I mean, I think David Gilmour is the greatest guitarist ever, and Waters is the greatest lyricist. Mom played Floyd for me almost as much as Sonic Daydream. But I don't find either of the attractive. They're both . . ."

Go ahead, honey. Say it. They're both old.

But she wouldn't say it. "It's always been about their music. Like you say, the soundtrack of my life. It's the subtle things – the little sax breakdown near the end of *The Dogs of War* . . . I've always liked to think that I was the only one who noticed how absolutely awesome that is." She grinned.

"And of course, I've always liked your band, *for your music.* Mom does too, of course, but she also liked Ernie. Considerably, as events have shown."

Now I grinned. "But she didn't like Denny."

Lisa shrugged. "I've never cared for him either."

It was so bizarre to me. How could you not like the singer, the songwriter, the *front* for your favorite band? I said playfully, "You've never met Dennis Whitly. His charm is legendary. How do you know you wouldn't be charmed, too?"

She paused and gave this off the cuff remark way more deliberation than it merited, even saying, "I've never thought about that before. Would I be charmed by Dennis Whitly?" She looked at me as if she expected me to answer the question for her. "I can't rightly say."

"Chances are you'll never meet him. Not with me around."

But she was still considering the question. "Somehow, I don't think I'd be charmed by him." She kissed me on the nose. "Maybe he'd be charmed by me."

I shook my head sadly, as if I had the worst news in the world for her. "I don't think so. You're a trifle young for him. And he's married."

"I dunno, Cal, baby." She slid her hand across my back and scratched me gently. "I have a way with . . ."

Again I waited for her to say it, to call a spade a shovel. *I have a way with older men.* But again she didn't say it. She rubbed noses with me. "I have a way with . . . *musicians."*

She kissed me then, and for a moment I forgot what we'd been talking about; the entire thread of the conversation was just blotted from my mind. But then I remembered, and Lisa did, too. She had been telling me about why she thought she loved me.

"So, yeah. I'd just turned sixteen, and I stayed out all night with this guy. Mom was pissed. It was the only argument we've ever really had. This guy – his name was Ryan – he was my friend Ellen's older brother. He was twenty-one –"

And you were sixteen. Just like Denny and Elise.

"He gave us a ride home from school, then I wound up more or less spending the weekend with him. I lied and told Mom I was with Ellen, but when I came home on Sunday afternoon, she knew. We got into a fight. I said I loved Ryan."

Just like Elise loved Denny after watching him sing half a set of covers at a frat party.

"That was when Mom told me that I was stupid, and didn't know what love meant. She said that I couldn't possibly love someone I'd just met. She said that it wasn't real, that I'd talked myself into it. She said that talking myself into such a thing was dangerous."

Mother, did it need to be so high?

"She was so pissed! She said, 'Here's a cautionary tale about love at first sight.' And she dug out her copy of *Sonic Nightmare.*

"So I read it, from my new perspective of thinking I was in love. Mom was right, of course. I hadn't known Ryan long enough to really be in love with him, and here it was Sunday night, and he wasn't calling me back, so he certainly wasn't in love with me. I was just an eager girl that thought he was cute and liked touching him, so he had gone right on ahead and let me."

Did she pause so I could liken that to our own situation? I wasn't sure.

"Even at sixteen, I realized that it was the idea of it, that Mom wasn't going to approve, and therefore our relationship would then be fraught with . . . with . . . I don't even know. Thinking I was in love with Ryan was the only spurt of rebellion against Mom I've ever had.

"Waiting for Ryan to call – he never did – I read your book, and then I knew the whole story, past the fairytale Mom had invented. The beautiful, music-loving girl had really been a sad, lost soul.

"I wondered what that kind of longing must be like. I searched my own soul and discovered that I surely didn't feel it for Ryan. What I felt for Ryan, what I thought was love – that was something else entirely." She grabbed me unexpectedly and I flinched.

"That was fun and all, but it wasn't love. It wasn't what poor Elise felt."

That wasn't love either. It was obsession, delusion . . .

"I thought a lot about her. She'd only had one friend in the world, the person that told her story. Before I knew how it had actually ended, I'd been curious about you, the storyteller. Now that I was grown . . ." Again she giggled. "I was curious in a different way. You wrote so eloquently of Elise's longing . . . I wondered what it would be like to long for somebody like that, and I guess, after a while . . . I started to long for you.

"I have a bunch of pictures of you, did you know that? Besides the one in the book, and a couple of posters. On my phone – do you want to see 'em?"

I shook my head. None of them could possibly be recent. The latest would've been from years ago, maybe a publicity shot from when *Sonic Daydream's Greatest Hits* was released.

Lisa had talked herself into being in love with me before we'd ever met, but it was a much younger me. I asked her, "Is all of this how you thought it would be? I don't look like those pictures anymore."

"Christ, Cal! You act like you've gone fat and bald like Leonard Whitly! You and Ernie – you both look great for your age."

"That's quite the compliment from someone your age," I said with mock humility.

"I know what I like. I know what I want. And it's you." She grinned mischievously now. "What is it you love about me?"

"Your consummate taste in men."

She splashed me. "Seriously."

"Mellow is the man who know what he's been missing."

Lisa smiled, and again I was reminded of Elise. Just as it had been with her, it was unnecessary for me to go into a long, complicated explanation for why I loved her. Like Elise, Lisa already knew all the words. Zeppelin had said it in a song, eons ago.

"So stop *guessing 'bout a thing you really ought to know,* Cal. I love you. I've always loved you. This is destiny."

Maybe it was. I allowed myself to hope that Lisa was more than a groupie; she *wasn't much for musicians.* She dug the sounds, the lyrics, just as I always had.

In addition to her unfortunate insanity about Denny, Elise had also loved the music. And she'd been my best friend.

SEVENTEEN

I awakened on Friday morning suddenly; it was starting to become a habit. The bed beside me was empty, cold, and again I had the impression that I'd dreamed the whole thing. Then the same idea I'd had the day before reasserted itself: despite it being destiny and all that bullshit, Lisa had changed her mind.

Because she certainly was gone; the big house was as silent as a big mausoleum. I sat up and sighed and did what comes naturally to anyone under thirty, a habit I'd also inexorably picked up, despite being way past thirty. To see what the day might have in store, our ancestors had looked at the sky; our grandfathers had turned on the radio or opened the newspaper. Our fathers had turned on the television. Just like everyone else in the first world today, I checked my phone.

I took the train home, Lisa's text said. *Mom reminded me that I promised 2 go 2 the Lammas festival w/her.* Lisa had included an emoji picture of a bunch of grapes. *Shall we handfast? J/k. It's somewhere in Glen Helen, all weekend. She wants 2 take the van and camp out.* ☹ *But we'll be back on Monday. Say you'll come see me then?*

I Googled *Lammas* and *handfast.* The former was a pagan festival, one of eight *sabbats,* part of their Wheel of The Year, according to Wikipedia. *Handfasting* was a kind of temporary or permanent marriage that often commenced at such festivals. I blanched; but Lisa had said *j/k.*

Text me when you get home, I replied, feeling modern. I also wished to appear nonchalant. I wasn't going to put anything into electronic black and white that might be read by anyone else. I wasn't going to give away our secret.

Our secret. That would have to be addressed, eventually, if she didn't change her mind after a weekend with her own witchy kind, and I tried to picture the look on her mother's face, and the one on the face of her newly found daddy, my old – the operative word being *old* – pal Ernie.

But I drew a blank. The cards would just have to fall where they would on all that, as Sonny was fond of saying. Regardless, it wouldn't be before Monday, so there was no sense in worrying about it now. I'd just have to burn that bridge when I got to it.

I took a shower and returned to bed. I could still smell the faint perfume of her on the sheets, and soon I drifted off into an uncharacteristically contented, dreamless sleep.

The phone was ringing. I opened one eye and looked at the clock on the nightstand: it was four pm. A perfectly good Friday had passed me right on by, was now relegated to the history books. I'd slept all goddamn day, like some kind of rock star. I grinned.

The number was unfamiliar.

"Hey, Cal. It's Lenny. Ernie gave me your number."

How nice of him.

"I realized that you haven't been up here in years."

Lenny lived barely forty-five minutes away up twisty California State Highways 79 and 371, but I'd been up there exactly twice, if memory served. And it hadn't been for years, since before my not-at-all-a-fairytale book had ended contact between us.

"Why don't you come up and see us, Cal? If you're not . . . busy? I'll show you how to ride a horse."

That prospect held no anticipation whatsoever, but I was touched by Lenny's reaching out to me. We'd once been best friends, and it looked like he wanted to be so again. That was awesome.

"When did you have in mind?"

"How 'bout right now? I'll hold the steaks until you get here."

EIGHTEEN

I pushed the button and the garage door slid open. I put the Caddy in reverse, checked the screen to the back-up camera; and there was Katie standing in my driveway, her teenager's I-could-not-possibly-give-a-shit smirk firmly in place.

Ah, young Katie. Being out of town for the past month and a half, I'd more or less forgotten about my littlest non-fan. She lived with her mom and dad across the street, in a McMansion practically identical to my own.

Being indulgent, as wealthy and loving parents often are of their only fledgling, they allowed Katie and three of her peers to whale ceaselessly on a set of somewhat overpriced instruments in the garage. Since there was thereby no room at the inn, Mom's Lexus and Dad's Audi were relegated to the driveway, where they offered but a minimal sound barrier.

Katie and her friends called themselves The Piglets. They were each fourteen years old. I'd never actually met the other members of the band, but had seen them earnestly rehearsing on a regular basis. Katie played lead-guitar, and a mop-headed boy – I think it was a boy – was the singer. The drummer, definitely a boy, was a rock and roll refugee from the trenches of childhood obesity, and the bass player was a tall, rail-thin, stork-like girl. When the two of them stood together at the cavernous mouth of Katie's garage, they looked like the number 10.

When the band played their own tunes, The Piglets' sound was not quite punk, yet neither was it metal. Like most garage bands – like a one-time unknown called Sonic Daydream – they mostly mangled covers of the classics of yesteryear. All across the decades, the genres: Zeppelin, Sabbath, The Sex Pistols, Green Day, The Arctic Monkeys, Soundgarden – the boy was no Chris Cornell, not in this lifetime – they all got The Piglets' interpretation. They were the hope, the future of rock and roll. Or maybe not.

I first met Katie when she was about twelve. She'd rung my doorbell; she was selling Girl Scout cookies. In her green uniform, she looked like an average little girl then, instead of a curveless escapee from a Joan Jett lookalike contest, like she did now. But the music germ was already alive and well, infecting her system, even at twelve.

I dutifully bought one of each kind, filled out the form. I figured it was the neighborly thing to do, even though I wasn't going to eat them. I hadn't kept my girlish figure by stuffing my face with Girl Scout cookies. I figured that I could always give them to Amanda or her sister, for their kids.

"Thanks so much, Mr. –" Katie consulted the slick, slightly grimy form. "– Bascomb. Calvin Bascomb." She peered up at me. "I don't know if you know this, but there used to be a drummer named Calvin Bascomb. He was in my mom's favorite band. I only know his name because she liked him the best."

So I had a fan, and right in the neighborhood. How quaint.

"I'm taking guitar lessons," Katie continued. "This band – Sonic Daydream – now the guitar players were awesome. Dennis Whitly and Ernie –"

"LaBelle. I know, –?"

"Katie." She politely extended her hand and I shook it. "So you've heard of Sonic Daydream, too?"

"I'm that Calvin Bascomb, Katie."

I expected a big smile, a little of that second-generation fan admiration, just like Sonny had talked about. It bloomed on Katie's face, but it wasn't for me. "So you know – you actually *know* Denny and Ernie?"

I nodded. "They live in Riverside."

"Really? Wait 'til I tell Mom. She'll be so amped!" Katie studied me suspiciously. "You're really – you really know them?"

"When you get back home, look at your mom's CDs," I advised.

She still wasn't sure, and she certainly wasn't impressed, at least not with me. "Okay. Thanks for buying cookies."

I didn't see Katie again until it was time for delivery. She arrived at the house with a red wagon, a mountain of cookie boxes strapped precariously into it with bungee cords. Apparently I wasn't the only one in the neighborhood that had been feeling neighborly.

Katie's mom stood beside the wagon. She was a pleasant-looking woman, made girlishly attractive by the fact that she blushed and stammered nervously when she said it was *so* nice to meet me.

Katie rolled her eyes in annoyance. "Go ahead, Mom. Ask him."

She looked at the ground in embarrassment, then produced a copy of *Sonic Daydream's Greatest Hits* and a Sharpie. "Could you sign it for me?"

I smiled humbly. "Sure. What's your name?"

"Allison."

"With two Ls?"

She nodded and I stole Ernie's standard line: *To my good friend Allison – Long live rock and roll!* and signed my name.

I handed the CD back to her and my good friend Allison just stared at me speechlessly, eyes aglow, amazed. I knew she was reliving the good old days of her prime, before marriage and motherhood, when going to a Sonic Daydream concert was surely the most exciting thing in the world. And if she was lucky, the long-haired drummer might just toss his sticks to her at the end of the show . . .

Katie sighed theatrically. "Mom. Go ahead and talk. He won't bite you."

Allison ignored her daughter, and at last found her voice. "I've heard you playing . . ."

"Is it too loud?" I'd had soundproofing installed, but the room at the top of the house was open, doorless. And there were all those drums.

"No. it's very faint. I always thought you were good, but I never knew you were . . ." She blinked. Now would come the same question that her daughter had asked: *You really know Dennis Whitly?* Or the realtor: *What's Dennis Whitly really like?*

But Allison just smiled blankly at me, and I remembered what Katie had said, that she only knew my name because Mom had liked me best. This was *my* fan.

When the silence lengthened, Katie at last said, "Well. We have more deliveries to make." She consulted the form, grimier now, and handed me my cookie selections. "On behalf of the Girl Scouts of America," she intoned, "thank you for your purchase, Mr. Bascomb." Again she rolled her eyes at her mother. "Come on, Mom."

Allison quickly shook my hand and reiterated that she was so glad to meet me. "You were always my favorite," she said unnecessarily.

"Come on, Mom!"

They turned and walked down the sidewalk. Allison looked at her autographed CD – now priceless to her, I thought with no humbleness at all – and over the squeak of the wagon wheels, I heard her say, "*To my good friend Allison* – your dad's gonna love that."

"Jeez, Mom, why you gotta embarrass me? He's just a drummer."

I smiled to myself and went back into the house.

NINETEEN

Now I backed the car out until I was even with Katie, and returned her bored, I've-seen-it-all-already stare. Katie hadn't seen anything yet, not even puberty.

"'S'up, Cal."

"'S'up, Katie."

"I brought you a copy of our demo." She handed me a CD in a paper envelope. A sticker of a smirking pink pig making an obscene gesture graced one corner of it. "Sound quality's a little rough. Casey recorded it on his computer. But it's good enough to get us out there."

I thought that if there was no such thing as snobbery in the music business, if time truly was only money, then like a rich and incredibly beneficent uncle, I could buy an hour or two of Oscar Woodbine's expensive time, and then gift it to Katie and The Piglets. But that would just be insulting to my friend. It was bad enough that he'd had to put up with Ernie's flesh and blood and her band, adults who actually aspired to being professional musicians, despite a glaring lack of talent. Oscar wasn't in the business of humoring children, no matter what I could offer to pay him. It just wasn't done.

"Thanks, Katie. I'll give it a listen."

"Tell me what you think. And be honest," she said sternly.

"Always," I replied. I placed it reverently on the passenger side seat.

Katie paused for a second, then quickly blurted, "I saw Ernie's LaBelle's Porsche here yesterday."

Katie was not in touch with the forces unseen; she wasn't a pint-sized seer, or a clairvoyant sensitive. She hadn't even guessed. She knew it was Ernie's car because like any guitarist worth her strings, Katie had a subscription to *Guitar Player.* Last month's issue had featured an article on Azomite's upcoming release, including a picture of Ernie, holding his axe and leaning against his baby-blue 911. *That's all right, we told you what to dream.*

Katie's face betrayed a glimmer of emotion, a flash of unrestrained excitement. But before you think that the fourteen-year-old had become a groupie-in-training, that she had developed little girls' dreams of whatever it was big girls longed to do with aging rock legends, or even with guitar players less famous but more age-appropriate – allow me to quickly disabuse you of that idea. That had not occurred.

Katie worshipped Ernie LaBelle, there was no question about that, although she hid it exceptionally well. If I saw her outside and she trotted over to speak to me, she always feigned just a polite, passing interest when she asked if I'd seen him lately. The answer had always been in the negative.

"He's on tour," I'd tell her, and she'd make a face.

"He needs a new band," she'd opine. "Azomite's second-guitar sucks."

The light in her eyes now was not groupie-love, not by any means. Young Katie didn't want to *do* my old friend, or anyone like him. She wanted to *be him.*

"Are you guys starting a new band?"

Katie couldn't know that my uncharacteristic guests were a band unless she'd snuck across the street and peeped into the van, saw their instruments. It wasn't like *Phenex* was emblazoned across the gray primer.

Katie was aloof, yet she was still nosy, always interested to know what I'd been up to. She was too proud to openly let me know that Sonic Daydream was one of her favorite bands, even though we had ceased to tour long before she was born. It was more than just her mother's influence. I knew she was a fan because she came over and knocked on the door and asked me musical questions sometimes, even though I was only a drummer. And I knew Katie was a Sonic Daydream fan because of the sincerest form of flattery of all: I frequently heard The Piglets' barely recognizable covers of *Tomcats* and *Worlds Have Passed* and a few others, thumping off-tempo from across the street.

But Katie was not worshipful of my old band to my face, because while she might have progressed enough in her studies to know her natural minor from her natural pentatonic, her six-string plunker's superiority had not changed. Guitar players were all the same to me, and Katie took great pains to demonstrate that drummers – even famous ones – were all the same to her.

"They call themselves Phenex."

"Like the town?"

And the confusion begins. I pictured road dog Ernie yelling into a phone somewhere. *No! It's P-H-E-N-E-X.* They really should come up with a different name, but I knew that was never going to happen.

"Something like that," I told Katie, not in the mood to give a dissertation on demonology to a fourteen-year-old. "They spell it differently than the town."

"And the girl? Is she the singer? She asked me how to get to the train station." I imagined Katie, without her Ibanez for a change, riding her bicycle through the neighborhood this morning, like a regular kid. "I told her it was pretty far, so she called a cab."

Katie wasn't old enough to wonder why a girl not too much older than herself would be leaving an old drummer's house early in the morning; but I was sure her mother's assumptions would be right on the mark. I was reminded that I lived in a nosy little neighborhood, and speculation as to who my new friend might be was probably already the subject of gossip along the street.

"She also plays guitar. Just like you."

"Really?" Katie allowed pleased surprise to show. "That's great." Then she frowned. "She's very pretty, though. Is she any good?"

"You're pretty, Katie." This was stretching it. Katie was a skinny, gangly tomboy, despite the raccoon-style eye make-up she wore. She didn't do it to attract boys – she did it because she thought it made her look girl-guitar-player tough. Whether the ugly duckling would morph into a graceful swan once the hormones kicked in, remained to be seen. "And you're –"

"I don't want to be pretty. I want to be good." She grinned. "You know, I didn't quite believe you really knew Ernie until I saw his car here yesterday."

It amused me that she referred to Ernie like she knew him; like Lisa, she'd heard him play her whole life, when Mom busted out the old CDs at the barbeque. Because she played guitar, because she wanted to be *good,* like he was, she *felt like* she knew him.

"I was in the band, Katie," I reminded her. "I know Dennis Whitly, too."

An idolater's grin, undisguisable. "When is *he* coming to your house?"

"Don't hold your breath."

She looked down, scuffed the driveway with her Chucks. "You will introduce me to Ernie, though, won't you? The next time he's here? I would've come over when I saw his car, but we were going out to dinner, and when we got back, Mom said it was too late for me to ring your bell."

It was past your bedtime. Allison didn't want her little girl venturing across the street to the old rock star's no-doubt debauched party after dark.

Oh, yeah. There was gonna be gossip. I'd never had guests before, Porsches and vans parked in the driveway. And I'd surely never had overnight guests, two days in a row.

"Yeah, I'll introduce you. Are ya gonna ask for his autograph, like your mom?"

Katie glared at me. She was not a fan, not a groupie. She was a fellow musician. "I'm gonna ask him to show me the breakdown in *Cerulean.*"

Ah, yes, *Cerulean.* Denny's paean to his wife's eyes. Elise's eyes had been the same color as her sister's, but he'd never written any songs about them.

"I'll send him over to your house, the next time he's here."

"Really? That would be so cool, Cal!" More unguarded enthusiasm from the snooty teenaged guitar player. It was my lucky day.

I certainly wasn't going over there. I'd already caught of few frowns from Katie's dad when he was out cutting the grass. When I'd first moved in, he'd always smiled and waved. That ceased when he'd found out that his wife's favorite drummer lived directly across the street.

"I'm actually going to see Lenny right now."

No recognition in the black-banded, Ranger Rick eyes. "Who?"

"Leonard Whitly. He played bass."

Katie snorted. "Not enough strings." She was unimpressed with God's bass player, or Sonic Daydream's drummer. But Ernie and Denny were golden.

TWENTY

Lenny and Barbie and I grilled steaks and reminisced. The memories were quite redacted however: it seemed that Elise and what she'd done for the band, for Sony, had been blacked out with a large marker. It was like she'd never existed, had never toured with us for twelve years, for as often as Lenny or Barbie mentioned her.

But it was all right. Elise was gone, and if we starting talking about her, it would inevitably lead to all the things I'd said about Lenny's brother in my book, and all that would've surely snuffed out the fire of friendship he was trying to rekindle. It was just a little blaze so far: we were not yet again as comfortable with each other as we'd once been. If the fire grew, I knew we'd get around to talking about Denny and Elise and what had or hadn't happened between them. But not tonight.

Tonight was for talking about the good parts of the good old days, and leaving the touchy parts alone.

And there had been many and varied good parts, even before Denny joined the band. There had been high school and its formative parties, and playing frat bashes full of drunken college girls. And there had been The House of Ale, also pre-Denny, for a while. Barbie pretended to be shocked at a few of her man's youthful escapades, but she wasn't, really. Barbie had been in the biz; she knew all about musicians.

And there had been the road, twelve long years of it. Denny's face and talent had gotten us signed, had made us famous, and the four of us had toured the world. We'd lived the dream of every kid with a good voice or a pair of sticks or an axe, like Katie – and there really wasn't a bad memory to be recalled, as long as we carefully avoided remembering our young, love-struck road dog. As long as we didn't talk about how the dream had ended.

So we didn't. Even though the memories were somewhat censored, it was great reliving them with my old Sony rep and God's bass player. I didn't feel like I was slighting Elise's memory by not mentioning her. She'd always live in my heart. There was no use in marring the walk down Memory Lane by talking about things that were beyond our control.

The three of us got mellowly drunk. Lenny directed me to the guestroom and I fell into the big, comfy bed. Once again, there were no dreams.

We all slept through the dawn's early light. Barbie made us a big, hearty, chuck-wagon brunch of bacon and eggs and biscuits and gravy and then Lenny took me out to the paddock to show me his horses.

Yep, they were horses. There was a black one and a white one, and a black and white one. Lenny cut up an apple and gave it to them. We patted them and then they wandered off. We stood with our elbows on the rough fence and looked at them for a few minutes; then my old friend's curiosity peeped out and positively blinked at me.

"So what're your plans now, Cal? You gonna go on tour with your band, conquer the world, make a million bucks? Again?"

"They're not my band, Lenny."

"Ernie's band, then." He smiled, but he was watchful.

"They're not even signed yet." Phenex's lack of talent hung in the air between us like a small swarm of gnats. "They're waiting on your woman to accomplish all that."

"She'll kick their demo upstairs. But nowadays . . . They don't need to be signed to tour. You and Ernie can buy 'em a bus, impress the local promoters –"

"Ernie can buy 'em a bus. They're not my band, Lenny," I repeated, a little bit more emphatically. "I don't think they're all that good. And either do you."

"Does Ernie?"

"Ernie's bored. He's tired of Azomite, but he's not tired of the road. He has enthusiasm for being behind the scenes for a change, but then, this is what he's got to work with. He tries to see them as better than they are, I think, and sometimes he succeeds."

"Ernie's not one to kid himself. Especially not as far as some nobody band's talent is concerned."

"It's not just some nobody band, Lenny. It's his kid. It's his . . ."

"His what? His woman?" Lenny snickered unkindly. "I'm not going to say Ernie's not ever gonna settle down, Cal. But if he does, he's gonna start out on the beginning of the end with someone a whole lot younger than old – and I do mean *old* – Marcie, there."

"Candy."

"Whatever."

I could've mentioned that Candy and Barbie were about the same age, but it wouldn't have made any difference to Lenny's scenario. Candy was old, especially for Ernie's tastes, because she was trying so hard not to be.

"It's his daughter's band," I stated simply. "He wants to help her out."

Again Lenny shook his head. "I don't care if she is his kid. It just doesn't seem like him. Like you say, they're all right, but Ernie's gotta know that they're not gonna go anywhere. The kid might've, but Mom shot all that down by not letting us back her in the studio."

"That was because of the demon Phenex," I told him, attempting a straight face. "It's gotta be them, his namesake minions. Not us unbelievers." Even if we were vastly superior musicians.

"Yeah. Ernie told me about all that. He told me how the kid came to be, reminded me of the red splotches on him in Frisco. I saw the goat on the wall."

"Yeah. They're into it." I shook my head. "It's ridiculous."

"Maybe Mom put a spell on him." Lenny snickered again. "Maybe that's why he's so down to waste his time and money on this?"

I shrugged. Ernie and I – that's all we had. Time and money. Not that much of the former and more than enough of the latter.

"Ernie's amusing himself, Lenny. He's hoping to play road dog. He wants to try his hand at being promoter. He wants to go back on the road."

"He was just on the road. What happened to Azomite?"

"On hiatus."

Time and money, I thought again. Ernie had filled up his days recently, and mine, with this mediocre band. The idea of taking them on road had fired Ernie up, enough to make him overlook their mediocrity. And Lisa . . . Lisa had fired me up, put thoughts in my head that perhaps the end of my own road might contain a little joy at last, and this idea had led me to overlook the impossibility of the whole thing.

Lenny's watchfulness remained. "What do you want out of it, Cal?"

I raised an eyebrow, shrugged, hoped I was the perfect picture of no-plans-at-all. "You know me, Lenny. I'm just along for the ride."

"You should get a place like mine," he suggested, no longer looking at me. "Out in the boonies, just the two of you, where no one will judge . . ."

I glanced at him, immediately erecting my I-have-no-idea-what-you're-talking-about face. It was my first time using it, except on Sonny, and he'd shot it down. Still, I figured it would get a lot of mileage. I even backed it up with the words: "I have no idea what you're talking about." But Lenny, my old friend, could read me better than I would've imagined.

"This is what I'm talking about, Cal. You and that girl."

I persisted, expressionless. "What girl?"

What did he think he knew? Was he just fishing? Was he just fucking with me? The last time he'd seen Lisa, it was before we'd even –

"How many girls do you know, Cal?"

"What are ya trying to say, Lenny?" I asked with mock offense, trying humor to deflect him.

"I'm trying to say that you've been a loner for damn near as long as I've known you. But now . . ."

That was all true. There had been a few, like I say, before the band hit the big time, but none of them had lasted. They'd all been just *meh* to me, and I'd been the same to them. There'd been Elise, my best friend; then she was gone.

And then one day you find, ten years have got behind you . . . No one had missed the starting gun more than me. Having a significant other – I'd always believed that ship had long ago sailed for me.

Until now.

But I would make Lenny say it. "What?"

"You and that girl. Ernie's daughter. Leesy."

I'm sure I flinched. *Leesy* had been what I'd called Elise. "Her name's Lisa."

"All right." Lenny smiled. Apparently my knowing her name equaled a confession to him. And he started in on the secluded cabin in the woods shtick again, secure from the prying eyes of a not understanding public. "There's actually some acreage for sale just up the road . . ."

I remained determined to not discuss this. I wasn't ashamed of Lisa. I was ashamed of myself, and the idea that I would indeed like to settle down somewhere with her and simply be in love with her until the day I died, the ridiculous maudlin impossibility of all that – how could I talk about such boyish stupidity with someone I'd known for more than twice as long as she'd been alive?

So I played dumb. "I have no idea what you're talking –"

"I saw how she looks at you. That could be one-sided – but it's not. It's written all over you, my friend. I can practically smell it on you. How long have the two of you been –"

"Not long." Why deny it anymore? He could *smell it* on me.

I looked over at him to gauge his opinion, and as was not unexpected, Lenny was not judgmental, any more than Ernie would be, if he found out. Yet I sincerely didn't want him to find out.

It wasn't the thirty-seven year age difference. Christ! Even forming the words for that was a study in insanity: the *thirty-seven* year age difference! Lisa's daddy and Lenny and I were well on our way to middle-age when she was born. If you don't think so, take those thirty-seven years and double them. How likely was it that any of the three of us would live to be seventy-four? We were middle-aged when she was born.

The fact that Lisa was not yet old enough to buy a drink and I was five years into my AARP years was not the problem, was not an issue to either Lenny or myself. Perhaps being musicians, our morality was lax; perhaps we'd known since we were young men ourselves that a lack of years on a young woman's part did not mean a lack of experience.

Regardless, I was sure that Ernie would see absolutely no problem whatsoever, but Lenny was like me. It was not the age difference that was the reason he looked at me with a slightly pained curiosity. He saw the problem as I did: he saw me making a fool of myself over a girl whose interest I could not possibility keep once the apparent novelty wore off. He was suggesting a way to prolong it, by whisking her away from the real world, from men her own age, from anything else that might show her the error of her choice.

"She's a musician. Lenny. She wants to go on the road, just like we did. She wants to be a rock star."

"So you're gonna go with her. You and Daddy Dearest."

I shrugged. "They're not going anywhere yet."

"Ernie'll see to it. If Sony passes, he'll just pay to get them to open on somebody's tour. Some other semi-unknown." Lenny grinned. "Phenex will have better accommodations than the headliner."

Again I shrugged.

"And you're gonna go with 'em."

It irked me that it was a statement, not a question. How did he know I'd go with them? I'd never been that much for the road – the only thing that had made it bearable, really, was Elise's company.

Oh, yeah, that's right. Lenny could *smell it* on me. Lisa's company would be so much better than my platonic friend's had ever been.

"Can't leave Ernie out there as road dog all alone." No sense in lying to Lenny or myself. If Phenex went on tour and Lisa wanted me with her, I'd go. Like a groupie. Like a camp-follower.

"I wish you luck, Cal. It could work."

"But it ain't likely, is it?"

Now he shrugged. "Enjoy it while it lasts. *All you touch and all you see –"*

"Right."

Again he looked inquisitively at me. "Why do you have such a pessimistic attitude about it?"

"Gee, Lenny, I dunno. There's the age difference –"

"So what? She obviously likes you –"

"For the moment." And when the moment ended – I couldn't talk to him about what the pain was gonna be like.

"You're liable to drop dead tomorrow, my friend."

After the last couple of days – you have no idea, I thought.

"So, why worry about it? This little chickie likes you –"

"She thinks it's destiny."

"Don't they all? So why put a cloud over it by worrying how long it's gonna last?"

And just like that, I saw that he was right. Lisa would change her mind someday, but it wasn't going to be today, nor tomorrow. I had to stop anticipating that, and do as Lenny said: enjoy it while it lasted. I smiled gratefully at him.

Lenny gave me a sidelong glance. It was curiosity of a different sort now, mixed with a little bit of old-fashioned envy. Surely, he loved Barbie and all, and he wouldn't ever dream of such a thing himself. Or maybe he had dreamt it, just for a split-second now and again, as the years accumulated. There had been the adventures of the good old days, overseas, but they were past.

"Ya gotta tell me, Cal. What *is* that like?"

"Just like it used to be."

I spent the remainder of the weekend with Lenny and Barbie. I rode a horse. It was fun. They invited me to stay the week, or for as long as I liked. I got the impression that it was an unusual pleasure for them to have company, and the three of us discovered that we'd missed each other.

But on Monday morning, I was summoned. Lisa's text said, *We're back. I've just washed the camping grime off. I hate 2 camp. I miss u so much! When can u b here?*

The message arrived while Lenny and I were in the barn, preparing for another ride. He said something to me, and when I didn't answer – I was looking at my phone – he grinned and said, *"His master's voice."*

There was no sense taking offense. Lenny understood, and was nothing if not a little bit envious. I grinned back at him. "His master's text." I showed it to him.

"I miss you so much." Lenny stopped saddling the horse. "Come on, I'll walk you out to the Caddy."

"I don't have to leave right this –"

"But you want to." He grinned again. "Bring her with you the next time. I'll tell Barbie goodbye for you."

TWENTY-ONE

I arrived in Riverside a changed man, transformed by my old friend's advice. I would live this dream to the fullest, pretend that it was absolutely *no thang* to be keeping intimate company with a woman so much younger than myself. It was a common rock star phenomenon, after all, going back at least as far as Jerry Lee Lewis and his fifteen-year-old cousin-wife. Ronnie Wood, Nikki Sixx, McCartney, Rod Stewart, Clapton. The list of hoary old rockers with nubile young brides went on and on.

Unlike myself, most of these musicians had produced children in their youth. Then, by virtue of their fame and wealth, they snagged young women in their dotage, and were able to pass on their genes again. It was the new evolution: not survival of the fittest, but survival of the richest. So why should I be so hung up about it? Was I not a rock star, too? On the drive back to Riverside, I almost began to think of it as my right. As destiny.

I had texted Ernie, asked him what he was doing, but had received no response. He wasn't at Phenex's abode: the grassless backyard of the clinker-brick house was devoid of vehicles when I arrived, except for the van.

Its hood was open, and it was up on jack stands. Roy and James peeked around from the front of it, to see who had driven up. They were filthy, hands and faces and clothes begrimed with dirt and grease, and it occurred to me that both of them looked like they were in their element. They'd always struck me as unlikely musicians; as mechanics, they looked much more at home.

They greeted me and explained that they were changing the starter on the van, and giving it a preventative maintenance once-over. *To be ready for the road* went unsaid, but the hope for such an unlikely thing, the anticipation of it, was almost palpable. Candy had probably scryed again, and Phenex had no doubt reassured her of his namesake band's imminent fame.

I looked into the van's engine compartment with no other curiosity besides a brief concern as to whether or not it was safe to have it running while it was up on the jack stands. Cars and their workings, especially old, common ones, interested me even less than Lenny's livestock. But these were supposed to be my fellow musicians – I'm sure they thought of themselves as such, even if I didn't – and it would've been impolite to just ignore them and go on into the house.

The Accord and the Triumph being gone, to make a little conversation, I asked, "Where is everybody?"

"Candy went to the mall," Roy supplied, sticking his greasy hand into the rattling chaos, making some adjustment, unconcerned with the whirring fan. I figured he knew what he was doing, that mechanics took such stupid risks. I thought that Candy would be supremely pissed if she returned home to find a nine or eight-fingered bass player, however, and grinned to myself.

"Sonny went to visit his mother in Barstow," James told me. "He left as soon as we got back from your house."

"That's a long trip on a motorcycle," I commented.

James exchanged a glance with Roy. "We worked on it for him before he left."

So Sonny was like me, no mechanic. I opened my mouth to make further small talk, perhaps to ask them if they'd seen Ernie, but the slam of the side door stopped me. I glanced in that direction; Lisa didn't approach, but simply inclined her head to indicate that I should come to her.

"Good luck with . . . this," I told Roy and James. They didn't look up from the engine, didn't watch my hasty trot across the yard.

Lisa smiled and opened the door. Once inside, she grabbed my hand and pulled me toward the staircase off the cavern in which the band rehearsed. "Come and see my room, Cal. Let me show you how much I've missed you."

I hesitated, looked over my shoulder toward the mechanics. Lisa shook her head. "They wouldn't dare disturb us."

Her voice was colored by a small portion of her mother's command, and I realized that Roy and James were Lisa's minions, too. Like the queen, the princess viewed them as little more than servants. God, what a weird scene it all was!

I'd never been upstairs before, but now I allowed her to lead me, my newfound decision to go with the flow permitting me to give in to my eagerness. I'd missed her, too.

Lisa locked the door behind us and immediately kissed me, wrapping her arms around my neck. Then she pushed me bodily across the room, until I fell backwards onto her soft bed. I was enveloped in her scent, from her sheets, from herself as she climbed astride me. It was something else I'd never forget, after her voice: the fresh, wholesome, alive smell of her.

Afterwards, I watched her get dressed, and had my first chance to look around the room. It was cluttered; clothes, whether clean or dirty, I couldn't tell, were piled up on a chair beside a dresser crowded with make-up and hairbrushes and girl-things. Posters from bands covered nearly every inch of wall space, some new, some old and curling around their thumbtacks. To my chagrin, I discovered that I had been watching myself, as had Lisa's daddy: an ancient Sonic Daydream poster hung directly beside the bed.

Ernie and I grinned at me arrogantly, but the brothers Whitly were obscured by a Jurassic-era Van Halen poster. Michael Anthony offered me a toke; Eddie held his axe in one hand and pointed at me with the other, but not accusingly. Diamond Dave presented me with my fellow drummer, Alex. It was from *Women and Children First,* and I'd had the same poster on my own bedroom wall. The album was released in 1980, when I was seventeen, and I had already believed then that I could out roll Alex Van Halen any day of the week.

What a long, strange trip it's been.

I slid my hand under the shot of Van-Halen-from-irretrievably-younger-days and lifted it, to get a look at the rest of my own band, from less than ten years later, when we'd been just as young and no less successful than Diamond Dave and his crew. Lenny held his black Warwick, and glared solemnly, smokily at me. I just had time to muse that I'd bet he wished he still had half that much hair, before I noticed that Denny's face had been obliterated from the picture, X'd out repeatedly with big black slashes.

I glanced at Lisa; she was looking back at me. She shrugged. "It was Mom's poster. She doesn't care for Dennis Whitly. But I liked how you looked in it, so I covered him up with Van Halen."

It was a little distressing, Candy's hatred of my former frontman. I didn't care for the guy either, that was true – but I had reasons not to like him, let me count the ways: his heartless disregard for Elise's obvious love; the way he'd kept her on the road with us regardless, because she was a peerless road manager, when he should've sent her home so she could forget her obsession with him and get on with her life; whatever he'd allowed to happen between them on that last night – I was pretty sure what it was – that had driven her to suicide and attempted murder.

I had plenty of reasons to hate Dennis Whitly, and I'd spelled them all out in *Sonic Nightmare.* But I'd never really hated him, surely not like this, enough to black out his face on an old poster.

Hatred was not an emotion that I wasted any time on, just as I'd never wasted any time on love, until now.

It was true that I never wanted to see Dennis Whitly again, never wanted to speak to him – what did I possibly have to say that hadn't already been said? But I didn't hate him – hating him wouldn't bring Elise back. She'd made her decision, and even though I knew that it was Denny who'd driven her to it, it had, in the final analysis, been *her* decision. I felt a profound pity and sadness for Elise and her self-chosen doom, and I'd always feel an utter disgust and disrespect for Denny's weakness about the whole situation. But I didn't hate him.

On the other hand, Candy hadn't known Denny. Her overwhelming dislike stemmed from one reason, inconsequential, selfish, irrational: he had killed her favorite band.

I forgot all about Denny, and Candy's hatred of him, when Lisa leapt upon me and kissed me again. "Come on, Cal! Let's play!"

"But you just got dressed." I knew that I couldn't stay in bed with her all day, here, like I had at home, but a few more minutes might be okay . . .

"Not that," she said and kissed my nose. "Mom'll be home soon, and I don't think you're quite ready for the big reveal. You wouldn't want her to catch us."

"Lisa, I'm ready. Whatever you want to say –"

"Later." She extricated herself from my embrace, from arms that would've kept her there, if only for a few more moments. "Let's play music."

"James and Roy are –"

"We don't need them. Come on."

With the beat kept, her guitar and her voice were indeed all that was necessary for our little jam. Now I smiled in return when she wiggled her eyebrows invitingly as she sang to me. It was just the two of us in the big room, after all.

We ran through Phenex's own brief catalog, then, like The Piglets in their garage, we covered a cross-section of genres, of eras. It was a joy to play with her, even without a bass or second-guitar, because she was a fair-enough guitarist in her own right, and her voice was stunning.

At last she grew tired of singing and texted her mother, asking her where the hell she was. Candy returned that she had corralled the world's greatest guitar player for lunch – I imagined that she hadn't mentioned that she'd be showing up solo – and since they were just sitting down, it would still be a hot minute before she and Daddy returned to the demesne.

Lisa looked up from her phone and said, "Well, if that's the case, then I think we should go back upstairs."

I immediately laid James's chewed-up sticks down on the snare and stood, because Lisa's wish was indeed my command. But at that moment, Phenex's drummer and bassist entered the room.

Roy grinned and held up his blackened hands. "I'm too greasy to rehearse now."

Lisa regarded him expressionlessly. "That's okay. We've just finished anyway." Then she turned and smiled brightly at me. "You wanna go to the beach?"

Like I've said, I hate the beach, but since Lisa and I wouldn't be going upstairs again now, and since I wasn't looking forward to hanging out with James and Roy, I nodded. I hadn't been to the beach since before she was born, since the last time the band met at the oceanfront manse that Denny used to own in Malibu. Maybe it had gotten better since then.

Roy told her thanks for the invite, but he and James had to finish working on the van. Lisa cast a sidelong glance at me – she hadn't invited them, and her devious expression told me that if they'd tagged along anyway, she would've thought up some way to ditch them.

Roy and James each offered me a pair of board shorts for the occasion, but it was like Goldilocks's choice: one pair was too big and one too small, neither anywhere near the neighborhood of just right. I told them that I'd just pick up a pair at a surf shop once we got to Newport.

It was really too late for the beach; the day was more than half over by the time we found a place to park. Lisa and I walked barefoot in the sand until the sun began to set, then drove up the coast a tad and got a room at the Hyatt Regency at Huntington Beach, because I hadn't stayed in a hotel in years and Lisa had never stayed in one, and that way she'd be able to go back to the beach first thing in the morning. We got in the car and shopped briefly at Fashion Island so we'd have something nice to wear to dinner, and proper swimwear for frolicking in the surf on the morrow.

Lisa left one of the many bags in the car and I went back out to get it for her. I passed two longhairs carrying guitar cases, accompanied by a guy a few years younger than me. They smiled, and then the older guy said, "Excuse me. Aren't you Cal Bascomb?"

When I got back to our room, Lisa's expression wondered what had taken so long.

"I ran into a band in the parking lot, on their way out. Their manager recognized me . . ."

"That's all right, we know where you've been." She blinked languid blue eyes at me, pretended that she couldn't be less impressed.

I shrugged, knowing that despite her insouciance, it was the kind of thing that wanna-be-famous musicians such as herself longed for: recognition from strangers. *"Give me the beat boys and free my soul . . ."*

Her eyebrow lifted at this ancient, fairly obscure oldie, but still I could tell that she knew it. She riposted with, *"Turn me on, turn me on, Mr. Deadman."*

Sensing my unfamiliarity with the tune, Lisa smiled and sang raucously, *"Yeah, I want it, I need it, to make a million; yeah, I love it, a fuckin' rock star."*

She arose and embraced me. I wasn't a rock star to Lisa; I was just her new, old boyfriend. I hadn't been a rock star for some time, so this novel role was good enough for me.

Lisa tried to tug me toward the bed, but I pretended not to know what she wanted. It had just been a couple hours; I wasn't eighteen after all. I nodded toward the dark beach outside the window. *"If you like piña coladas and getting caught in the rain; if you're not into yoga, if you have half a brain . . ."*

Again the raised eyebrow, the grin of recognition. *"If you like making love at midnight . . ."*

Once more I nodded at the window. *"In the dunes of the cape . . .* You're the one that wanted to go to the beach, baby."

"I'm the love that you've looked for, come with me and escape." That wasn't quite how it went, but Lisa had succeeded in pulling me back onto the bed, so I didn't correct her.

TWENTY-TWO

The next morning, we sat on the beach beneath a garish yellow and white umbrella. There was the broiling sun, the pounding surf, the annoyance of the sand. Yep. I still didn't like the beach, but it was almost okey-dokey because of the company. I grinned to myself.

Lisa frowned at her phone. "The bassist from The Perfect Americans just died. Heroin overdose."

I'd begun to kid myself that thirty-seven years wasn't that much of an age difference in the great scheme of the universe. You're as young as you feel – and Lisa certainly made me feel young – and all that utter nonsense. But here it was in my face again. I considered myself still hep as far as music went, but she'd sung one I'd never heard of yesterday, and today, I had no idea who The Perfect Americans were.

To cover my ignorance, I said, *"If there's a rock n' roll heaven, you know they've got a hell of a band."*

"They've all found another place, another place to play."

She amazed me. There might be some holes in my repertoire, especially as far as new bands went – The Perfect Americans? Really? But Lisa was like my old friend Elise. She knew 'em all.

She smiled in delight at me. "Have you ever thought about that, Cal? The perfect band? If you could put anybody together, from any era, alive or dead, who would make up the perfect band?"

She'd already filed The Perfect Americans' not quite so perfect junkie bassist under *The Sad, High Price of Fame,* and I was glad at the change of topic. I grinned back at her. "There's already been plenty of perfect bands. Pink Floyd."

She considered. "Gilmour is the greatest guitarist, I've said that before. And Waters, the greatest lyricist. *Pink isn't well, he stayed back at the hotel.* If I was gonna start a Pink Floyd tribute band, you know what I'd call it? *A Surrogate Band."*

She giggled prettily, and my heart rejoiced. She was just so perfect, a dazzling young woman who knew as much about music as I did. *Maybe more,* I thought, recalling The Perfect Americans.

"Floyd was one of the greats," she continued. "One of my favorites. But they weren't perfect. Waters wasn't much of a singer; he was a little . . . shrill."

Rogers Waters shrill? I didn't think so. *"The lunatic is on the grass . . ."*

"Why are you running away?"

"That was the emotion of the song. I wouldn't call it shrill . . ."

Lisa shrugged. "They were great, but not perfect. There are much better singers."

I grinned. "Like Dennis Whitly."

Lisa made a face. She and her mother weren't fans, but, "He was never shrill."

"I thought you said Sonic Daydream was the greatest band in the world." *Repeatedly.*

"But that didn't make you *perfect.* There are definitely better guitarists . . ."

I had to agree with that, regardless of where *Rolling Stone* had put both Denny and Ernie on their hallowed list.

"And as far as drummers go . . ." Lisa eyed me innocently, to see if I would defend myself.

"Definitely better drummers." My dad had once told me, *Whatever you're good at, there's somebody that's gonna be better.* He thought Buddy Rich was better than him, and I always thought that Dad was better than me, though I also considered myself better than Buddy. My bank account told me how good I was, and new-band managers asking for my autograph. These truths lent me a little bit of a rock star's ego, but not much.

Lisa threw a towel at me. "You're all right."

For an old guy, my resident demon said.

"I've never studied drummers too much. Until now." Lisa squeezed my thigh. "So I suppose some are better than others . . ."

"You're saying that like your basic, A-side buying fan, you just bob your head, and don't pay too much attention to the drum solo –"

"Is that how you see me? As a basic, A-side buying fan?" She arched an eyebrow in feigned offense.

"Not at all. But you still have to have a drummer in your perfect band."

Lisa waved her hand, dismissing me and my fellows. "It's the singer, the songs, the guitarist that makes the band." Out with baby, bathwater, Bonham, Barker, and me, went God's bass player and all his four-string brethren.

"What I'm saying is that there've been great singers with so-so lyrics; great guitarists with so-so singers *and* so-so songs. Chris Cornell had a . . ." Lisa paused, consulted her phone. *"A near four-octave vocal range.* His voice was absolutely phenomenal. But some of his lyrics? What does that mean, *I'm looking California, and feeling Minnesota?"*

Lisa shook her head, and was I surprised when she didn't comment further on the great frontman's tragic, bitter end. She just continued with her analogy. "But imagine if Waters had written the songs and Cornell had sung them?"

I was rather nonplussed at all this. Floyd was awesome, Waters was not shrill, and Chris Cornell's lyrics spoke directly to me right at the moment: *Show me the power, child, I'd like to say that I'm down on my knees today . . .*

Lisa was remarkable, wonderful. How did one teenage guitar player become so opinionated on the greats of rock and roll? It was the kind of conversation I'd never been able to get out of my multi-platinum bandmates. Only Elise had ever talked about the what-ifs of mixing different musicians from different eras. Dennis Whitly was of course always ultimate singer, supreme guitarist . . .

"So who would be the singer for your perfect band?"

She grinned. "Paul Rodgers. No one sings like him. *Ye-e-e-a-a-ah, yeah!"* she wailed, and two young guys walking down the beach turned and looked at her. *"It's all part of my fantasy.* Singer, songwriter. I've got that position covered."

"I dunno, Lisa." There were certainly no flies on Bad Company's excellent frontman, but . . . "What about Robert Plant?" To show her that I was technically savvy for an old guy, I took out my own phone and called up Wikipedia. *"In 2011, Rolling Stone readers ranked Plant the greatest of all lead singers.* Led Zeppelin – there was your perfect band, right there. They were the epitome of rock and roll."

Lisa shook her head with the contempt of a conversant purist. I recognized the expression: it was like looking in a mirror. "Rock and roll? Now who's being a basic, A-side buying fan? Led Zeppelin was all about the blues, Cal."

I couldn't argue with that; again I thought it was strange and superb that an eighteen-year-old girl would know it.

She smiled guilelessly. "Did you know that Limp Bizkit covered Zeppelin?"

I knew they'd covered The Who's *Behind Blue Eyes,* but Zeppelin? I guess I could've missed that one, but the twinkle in Lisa's eye led me to believe that she was having me on.

"No. I can't say as I do."

She giggled. "Well, it's not really a cover, per se, more of an update. Are you familiar with *Nookie?"*

My grin curled like the Grinch. I was indeed familiar with it, though I had to admit that the refresher course she'd recently been giving me had put glorious new spins on old concepts.

She pinched me on the lovely sunburn I was already developing. "I mean the song."

"Oh. Yeah. Of course. The song. Yes. I'm familiar with the song."

"Well, *Nookie* is the same song as *Hey, Hey, What Can I Do?* They're practically identical."

At first I thought that Lisa must be referring to some kind of sampling/plagiarism issue. Zeppelin themselves had been caught up in one of those a few years before. The article on the internet had asked, *Does this sound like Stairway to Heaven?* The song, by some long ago disbanded late-sixties act, was awful, but after an interminable, high-pitched intro of violins and cellos and flutes, when the guitar at last came in, it was unmistakable. To my musician's ear, it was *Stairway.* But the jury didn't hear it that way, and the suit was later dismissed.

I must've missed Page and crew being on the other side of the courtroom from Fred Durst for . . . Maybe I was confusing *Nookie* with another one of Fred's tunes, because it in no way sounded like Zeppelin's *Hey, Hey, What Can I Do?* Or any other Zeppelin tune I could think of. It just wasn't the same kind of music.

But Lisa was grinning, so I finally said, "What are you talking about?"

"Okay, basically they're both about a guy with a cheating woman, right?"

"I got a woman that won't be true."

"It takes them both a minute to realize . . . Plant says, *Sunday morning when we go down to church, see the menfolk standin' in line; they say they come to pray to the Lord, but when my little girl looks so fine.* Ol' Redcap is a little more direct." Lisa again consulted her phone. *"I'm the only one underneath the sun who didn't get it.*

"They both consider forgiving her: *I walk the town, keep a-searchin' all around, lookin' for my street corner girl.* And: *Maybe she just made a mistake, I should give her a break.* Then they both wise up: *Ain't nothin' gonna change,* and *Gonna pack my bags and move on my way."*

Lisa concentrated, warming up to her analysis. She smiled at me. "But in the end, they're bragging about the whole thing, Cal. Plant says, *I thrill to her every touch.* Fred's a little whinier: *She put my tender heart all in a blender, and still I surrendered.* This girl was worth it, even if she was a cheater.

"Plant's inflection, the last time he says, *I gotta woman wanna ball all day* – he's saying, *Don't you wish you had that?* The sentiment is exactly the same as, *I did it all for the nookie.* They're both saying, *Yeah, she cheated on me, but I got mine.* So it's all okay. They're bragging. It's the same song."

It was hands down the most bizarre comparison I'd ever heard, but I had to admit that it had some merit. Neither Fred nor Zeppelin's legendary frontman had come off as too broken up about their similar situations.

"Here's another one," Lisa said with another girlish giggle. "Sonny said to me once, 'Quick, who sings *Paradise City?*'"

I opened my mouth to tell her that, of course, Guns N' Roses sang *Paradise City,* everybody knew that, but she held up her hand.

"I drew a blank for a second, then of course, I knew. I could see the video: the tour bus, the giant stage being set up, in quick motion. The crowds coming in, the comedy and tragedy masks, the band walking down the hall. The roadies dragging the girls away from *exquisite,* blonde, Vince Neil . . ."

Vince wasn't so exquisite anymore. He was older than me. Wait a minute. "Vince Neil? What?"

"Oh, yeah. I was hearing Axl Rose, but I was seeing the video to *Home, Sweet Home.* So I said, 'Mötley Crüe did *Paradise City.*'" Lisa smiled faintly at me. "Sonny looked at me just like you are, like I was dumb or something. He said, 'No . . .' And I said, 'Yeah. Mötley Crüe sings *Paradise City.*' I was so sure, because I could see the video in my mind.

"Sonny said, 'No. You're so wrong. How can you be so wrong?' He looked at Roy and James. Roy agreed with me. It was Mötley Crüe. James agreed with Sonny.

"I was so convinced – the whole mood of the song – *Oh, won't you please take me home?* It was all in that video. So I said, 'Ya wanna bet?'

"Sonny said, 'Yeah. If Mötley Crüe sings *Paradise City,* I'll tune your Strat. If it's Guns N' Roses, you tune my guitar.' I agreed, and Sonny said to his phone, 'Ok Google, who sings *Paradise City?*'"

She mimicked the monotone reply. "*'Paradise City* was recorded by Guns . . . And . . . Roses.' I still didn't believe it. I called up the video, still expecting to see the comedy and tragedy masks . . . I realized I'd forgotten the video to *Paradise City.* Of course it's Guns N' Roses. But it's the same goddamned song, Cal. It's the same video. The stadium, the band walking around, then onstage, the crowd. Axl performing."

Why I'm even here, I can't quite remember.

"So I tuned Sonny's guitar. But it's the same damn song."

I didn't agree with her on this one so much; the Crüe's tune was about touring – *Just one more night, and I'm coming off this long and winding road* – and Guns N' Roses was just bitching in general. But the videos were the same. I could see how she could've mixed up *Oh, won't you please take me home?* with *home, sweet home.* Especially since all of it, Vince, Axl, both songs, both videos, were from a good twelve or fifteen years before she was born.

She regarded me intently, curiously. "It's really like that on tour, huh? The stadiums. The girls . . ."

I shrugged. "The girls came to see Denny, but . . ." *He was a coward.* "He was married. So they settled for Ernie." I grinned. *Like your mom did.*

"You didn't . . . partake?"

"I kept Elise company."

Lisa leaned over and kissed me. "Now you're keeping company with me." Still the curious stare. "What would you do with a girl like Fred and Robert's, Cal? *A little woman that won't be true?* Are you the madly jealous type?" She squeezed me to indicate that I didn't have to worry about her fidelity, what with destiny and all.

I shrugged. *Easy come, easy go,* I thought. I was falling for her already – how could I not fall for an eager young woman, who was also a musician that liked to talk in-depth, what-ifs about bands? But still, I knew it could never last. It would hurt when she eventually found someone else . . . But, no I wasn't the madly jealous type.

I said, "I'd just do what ol' Bobby Plant did, I guess. I'd *leave her where the guitars play."*

****

I found that I liked the beach better than I had in the past, entirely because I was with Lisa. I liked it so much, in fact, that we stayed at the Hyatt until Thursday afternoon. We would've stayed through the weekend, maybe, or for as long as she liked, had it not been for the texts we received.

Candy's to Lisa was brief, mysterious. *U need 2 come home right away.*

What's going on?

I can't tell u over the phone. But u need to get back asap.

Lisa read her mother's words aloud, and I said we could go if she wanted to. We were packing up our new clothes when Ernie's texts began.

Dude.

?

I got a copy of the demo this morning.

And?

☺ It's great. And even better than that, I got em a gig.

Where?

Where r u right now?

I'm at the beach.

There was a pause, then, *Really? What r u doin at the beach?*

I looked at Lisa, stuffing our new clothing into multi-colored shopping bags. What was I doing at the beach, and with Ernie's daughter? Having the time of my life, that's what I was doing.

Where r u? I texted back. The reason why I was at the beach (and with whom) would have to wait for a face-to-face meeting.

I'm in Big Bear. Meet me at the house. I'll explain everything when I see u. Don't tell em anything about the demo or the gig. I want it to be a surprise.

I told Ernie *OK,* and put my phone back into my pocket. Lisa had just completed a final scan of the room, and satisfied that we weren't leaving anything behind, she was ready to go. We dropped the keycards at the desk, retrieved the Caddy, and headed back to Riverside.

It was dusk when we arrived at the closed gate, but it seemed that full darkness had already settled on the old house. Not a single light shone from the top of the short hill. I pushed the intercom button and the gate began to clank open. There had been no comment from inside.

The light between the crossed-neck Gibsons was shining dully, but it came on when the sun set. Lisa opened the door to a wall of blackness. She switched the hall light on and tentatively called for her mother. There was a soft reply of, "We're in here," from the kitchen.

The kitchen table was situated in a large nook, with a bench on either side of it, attached to each wall. Candy and Roy and James were all grouped on one side, their faces illuminated only by a selection of colored candles on the table.

"Why are you sitting in the dark?" I reached for the light switch.

Lisa said, "No. Leave it off," and quickly crossed the room.

Candy rose and embraced her, sobbing. I looked at Roy and James for explanation; their faces were big-eyed and somber. I turned to flip the light switch on again, and this time Candy croaked, "No. The candles are to help guide his soul."

"Whose –?"

"Sonny's dead, man," Roy whispered.

Candy's knees buckled; a sob escaped from Lisa as she helped her mother back to the bench, then collapsed beside her on it. They held each other and cried.

In open-mouthed shock, I stared at them, then at James and Roy. At last Roy arose and bid me follow him out to the band room. He flipped on the lights and threw himself into one of the folding chairs, never returned back upstairs after Phenex's audition for Barbie.

Roy ran his hand from the back of his head and then down over his face. He sighed, then looked up at me. "He was coming back from his mom's, last night. Late, like two am. His mom told Candy . . . I guess there was a witness. This guy was behind him on the freeway, and he told the cops that Sonny suddenly swerved, like there was something in the road in front of him. But the guy said he couldn't see anything. Sonny lost control, dumped the bike . . . At that speed, he died instantly."

TWENTY-THREE

Ernie imitated Ricky Ricardo. "L-u-u-u-cy! I'm home!" He barged down the darkened hallway and flipped on the kitchen light before Candy or Lisa could object.

Roy's head was down on his folded arms on the table. Beside him, James leaned back against the wall and stared sightlessly at the ceiling. Candy was on the end of the bench, facing the door, her elbows on her knees, her head in her hands. I sat on the opposite bench, cradling Lisa in my lap. Her arms were around my neck, her head on my shoulder.

Ernie's eyebrows went up in surprise at this last part, and he opened his mouth to speak, then closed it again. "What's going on here? Why are you sitting in the dark? Where's Sonny?"

At the mention of his name, Candy burst into tears again. She leapt up from the bench and threw herself into Ernie's arms. He looked at her in alarm, but she had buried her face in his shoulder, put her arms around his neck. She sobbed uncontrollably, and he tentatively, clumsily put his arm around her for comfort. He looked at me.

"There's been an accident, Ernie. Sonny's . . ."

"Sonny's dead!" Candy wailed.

Ernie's mouth worked in silent disbelief. Then he carefully sat Candy back down on the edge of the bench, gently removed her arms from around his neck. He squatted in front of her and took her hands in his. "Tell me what happened, Candy."

But she could not. She just shook her head and cried harder.

Ernie released her hands and stood. He again took in the tender picture of his bereft daughter perched in my lap, clinging to me, but he couldn't be concerned with the surprise of that at the moment. I was about to repeat what Roy had told me, when the bassist himself spoke, without raising his head from his arms. "He dumped the Triumph on the 15."

"What was he doing on the –"

"He's been in Barstow all week." Roy sat up. "He was up there visiting his mom. He was on his way back."

Ernie asked all the incredulous questions, and Roy supplied the answers, as he had heard them from Candy, as Candy had heard them from Sonny's mom, as she had heard them from the CHP cop who had rung her doorbell and discharged his sad duty; as the cop had heard them from the witness who had seen Sonny go down.

Then we sat in silence again. Candy put her head on her arms on the table now; Ernie sat beside her and put his arm around her shoulders. Lisa got up and turned off the kitchen light, then resumed her place in my lap.

We remained like this until after midnight, until the candles finally guttered out. I wondered if that was supposed to mean that the soul of the departed had completed its journey, if God was exercising mercy in his judgment, as Sonny had often wished. It was all bullshit to me. I had no hope for Sonny's soul, any more than I had hope for my own, seeing as how I was unsure either existed. Just like my parents, who had lived long and fulfilling lives, and just like Elise, who had not – Sonny was dead. That was the only truth I knew.

James had not said a word the entire night. Now he gently nudged Candy and softly asked to be let out. Ernie arose, as did Candy, and James and Roy left the booth. Roy said, "I guess we'll see you in the morning," then the two of them shuffled quietly away.

Candy again put her arms around Ernie's neck, although she had at last stopped crying. He was uncomfortable that she clung to him in her grief; he didn't know what to say, or how to comfort her. He looked at me helplessly. "I guess we should go, too, Cal."

Candy raised her puffy, tear-ravaged face from his shoulder. "I was hoping you'd stay, Ernie. I don't wanna be alone . . ."

Before he could give full thought to the implications of this request, Lisa stirred. She hadn't said anything all night either. "There's a spare bedroom upstairs, Dad. I'll go make it up for you."

"Ah, honey, you don't have to –"

But she had already stood up and wrapped her arm around her mother's shoulders. Like Roy and James, they silently left the room.

Ernie looked at me helplessly again, then after a moment, a question began to form in his eyes. Unlike Lenny, I wasn't going to make him say it.

"Look, Ernie. About me and Lisa . . ."

"I'm glad you were here to comfort her."

Now I was the one who felt helpless. But he had to know. "You don't understand, man. She and I . . . we've . . . we're . . ."

Comprehension flared in his eyes, and his mouth fell open. "You and . . . Christ, Cal! She's my daughter! When did you . . . Was it tonight? Because she was sad about . . ."

What kind of a monster did he take me for?

"No, Ernie. It was last week, after you guys went back to Riverside." It had actually been before that, when Mommy and Daddy and the rest of the band had been sleeping under the same roof. Ernie didn't need to know that. "It was when she stayed at my house –"

"She stayed at your house? When was this?"

"Where've you been all week, Ernie?" *While my life has finally taken on some meaning?*

"Answer my question. When did Lisa stay with you? When did you . . . *seduce her?"*

I couldn't've quite put into words how I thought my old friend would take the revelation of my *relationship* with his daughter, but it surely wouldn't have been like this. His paternity seemed to have made him forget who he was, who he'd always been: Ernie LaBelle, groupie-slayer par excellence. Mr. Anything for a Good Time. Had he forgotten how his offspring had come into existence?

An ugly word formed in my mind: *hypocrite.* But I wouldn't say that to him. We'd been friends for too long, and I was sure that this had to be just a momentary lapse of reason on his part, an unfamiliar spike of paternal pique. Now that he was a daddy – this was the way he thought he was *supposed* to feel, the manner in which he thought he *should* act. But it wasn't really him.

It was all ridiculous: Ernie didn't even know this headstrong young woman whom his own insouciant, rock star's arrogance had led him to unknowingly sire, lo, these many years ago. If he did, then he would've seen the way that she'd looked at me, he would've known that she was not a baby that had fallen into my evil web of seduction, the moment his eagle-eyed daddy's attention was diverted. My friend was absurd. He was suddenly become a poseur.

Your darling baby girl came on to me, old man, pressed her naked body against my clothed one, kissed me in my very own bathroom, and didn't object in the least when I – How many girls have you accommodated in the very same way, in how many anonymous backstage bathrooms, in hotels and the occasional tour bus, across this wide, wide world? Some perhaps as young as your daughter, perhaps as recently as Azomite's last tour? Where ya been all week, Ernie?

I would sound as preposterous as he did, if I said any of that to him.

So I said, "It was last week. Remember? She came back to the house with me after breakfast? And then she . . . stayed. We've been at the beach all week."

"So Candy knows?"

"I don't know what Candy knows," I told him truthfully.

Ernie opened his mouth, but like a toddler about to wail, no sound came out. I didn't think that I was gonna like what he was gonna say, thought it might end our long friendship, so I cut him off.

"I love her, Ernie. And she . . . Bless her heart, she thinks she loves me."

He searched my face to see if I was kidding, to see if I was making some kind of dirty joke. Love was not unknown to Ernie – he'd loved them all. But he knew that I was not like he was, and that such a statement coming from me wasn't a joke. If I said I was in love with his daughter . . . Well, hell. There was a first time for everything.

Ernie's paternal umbrage deflated as quickly as it had puffed up. He put his hand on my shoulder. "I guess I couldn't wish for a better man for her than you, Cal. If you think you love her – I know you'll never hurt her."

He smiled for a second, then he remembered the night's tragic news and shook his head. "Poor Sonny."

I nodded. "He had a lot of talent. It's a shame."

"I liked Sonny a lot, Cal, and I don't want to sound callous, but his troubles are over. We've got our own problems now. I got Phenex a gig, and not a bad one."

I didn't think Ernie was callous. He was a musician, and the story was the same for us as it was for actors: *the show must go on.* He knew that I knew it, that Sonny would've wanted it that way. He wouldn't have wanted Phenex to miss their first break because of mourning for him.

"Phenex needs another guitarist," I said.

Again Ernie opened his mouth to speak; this time he was cut off by Candy's wraithlike reappearance. She paused in the doorway to the kitchen and piteously said his name. He glanced over his shoulder at her, then quickly back at me, and I could read his thoughts as if I were clairvoyant.

He rolled his eyes – *I think I know what form Candy wants my comfort to take, dude. I don't want to leave her all alone in her grief, but Christ! I don't really wanna do that either. The poor kid's not even in his grave yet . . .*

Hail, hail, rock and roll, I thought. But I couldn't say that either.

You'll be back tomorrow?" he asked, putting off the inevitable. There would be tears, and it would be sad, but it would be what it would be in the end.

Lisa glided across the kitchen then. She made only brief eye contact with Ernie, then leaned against me. I put my arm around her.

"I'll see you in the morning then." Ernie sighed, then turned to meet his un-looked-for fate.

TWENTY-FOUR

I was up before the rest of the household. I put on a pot of coffee, sat down at the kitchen table and wondered what the day bring.

Ernie soon joined me. He silently poured himself a cup and sat down across from me. I waited for him to speak, but for several long seconds, he wouldn't even look at me. Then he stood up abruptly. "I'll be right back. I've got something to show you."

Christ only knows what this is gonna be, I said to myself as he left the kitchen. I didn't think I could take too many more surprises at the moment.

Ernie returned with a manila folder. He resumed his seat and finally looked at me, though his expression remained unreadable.

"Phenex's demo." He extracted a CD case from the folder. The tracks and times were listed in Oscar's instantly recognizable, backward-slanting, lefty's handwriting. Ernie had apparently rushed him; he hadn't even had time to print a proper label. Or maybe it was as Lenny believed: the engineer had simply wished to rid himself of Phenex at the earliest opportunity.

"And now the good news." Ernie grinned humorlessly. "The cosmopolitan city of Riverside is about to have its very first outdoor rock and roll music festival."

My eyebrows went up in surprise and a little glee sparked in Ernie's eyes. He was a Riverside native, just like I was, as the Whitly brothers were, so he knew that I knew that there was no place in our hometown to have an outdoor festival, or an indoor one for that matter. The biggest venue was the Municipal Auditorium, and true, it had hosted a few washed-up old rockers on their geriatric, we-need-to-pay-the-IRS, come-back tours. But sold out, it couldn't seat more than twelve or fourteen hundred people, and there was absolutely no place to park.

Now Ernie read my mind. "Where, you ask, is such a momentous event to take place?" He extracted a flyer from the folder. *ROCK INVADES RIVERSIDE!!* it screamed, in garish, drop-shadowed font. In smaller font: *Saturday, September 15th, Ryan Bonamino Park. Featuring* – again the font grew – *THE RACECATS!!*

"Who?"

"You haven't heard of The RaceCats?" Ernie asked in utterly put-on amazement.

He produced a concert flyer: The RaceCats had appeared the previous weekend, two shows only, at – surprise, surprise – The House of Ale. I assumed that the grainy black and white photo of four young guys with their eyes covered by black strips, like old-timey porn, was the band, but nowadays, one couldn't be sure.

I shook my head. "Nope. Never heard of them."

My old friend's grin returned, genuine now. "Yeah, me either. But they're on their way, I understand. They're signed with EMI."

That was fairly impressive. "So why play here?"

"You really aren't hep, are ya, Cal? Haven't heard of The RaceCats, don't know that they're Riverside's newest favorite sons." He winked at me. "And being such, and being but *newly* signed with EMI, they have agreed to headline this extravaganza, to kick off their first tour."

"Who else is playing?"

"Who cares? An all-day list of local nobodies. But Phenex is gonna open for them. It's not the Hollywood Bowl, but it's a start."

It certainly was. "How did you arrange –"

"Here's the best part." Ernie produced a third flyer, which informed me that the day after Riverside, The RaceCats were headlining another all-day outdoor festival at nearby Glen Helen Regional Park. It was the same location where Candy and Lisa's Lammas celebration had been held. The place was huge, with campgrounds and a lake and a giant amphitheater. Both of the US Festivals had taken place there in the 1980s.

This event that The RaceCats were headlining was significantly smaller, of course, but the clever promoter was still playing off the name. They were calling it the Just Us Festival.

Maybe I really wasn't hep, but I was surprised that the Inland Empire had enough fans in residence to support two outdoor events on the same weekend, especially featuring the same semi-unknown headliner. I said as much to Ernie.

"It's a different line up of bands at the second show."

"But the same headliner."

Ernie grinned again. "And the same band opening for them." He produced a fairly thick sheaf of papers from the folder now. "Here's the contract. I took the liberty of signing it for them."

This was certainly great news, but Ernie hadn't answered my question, had in fact cut me off in the middle of it. How had he gotten Phenex on to open for a signed band at two festivals in a row? The ink was barely dry on their demo – Ernie said that he'd just received it. How had he pulled this off?

"Bianca says she might be able to get them to open at a few other shows up the coast –"

"Bianca?" The plot thickened.

"Ah, Cara Mia, Bianca." Ernie glanced over his shoulder to make sure no one was about to come strolling into the kitchen, and lowered his voice. "File this one under *It's A Small World After All,* dude. Do you remember the little girl from The House of Ale?"

I blinked. Ernie and Lenny were going to have to be a little bit more specific with their use of the term *little girl.* Lenny had originally referred to Lisa as such; and now Ernie was referring to some chick from –

"You mean the bartender?"

Ernie nodded. Yes, there was definitely a need for some semantic clarification here. Katie was a little girl. Lisa and the young woman that tended bar at The House of Ale were not. At least not to me. Not anymore.

"So I had lunch with Candy there last week, then after she left, I get to talking to the bartender. Her name's Amber. Anyway, come to find out – remember we signed an autograph for her mom? Come to find out, not only is her mom a big fan, she works for some assorted branch of EMI. Not for them directly, I don't think – but she works for the promoter in charge of The RaceCats' tour. Or at least the Southern California part. I don't fucking know. All that Byzantine who's who bullshit used to be Lenny's job."

"And Elise's. And now it's yours."

"I signed on the dotted line, didn't I?" He grinned. "Anyway, all this interests me, and Amber gets on the phone and relays my interest to her mom, who just happens to be in town at that very moment. Twenty minutes later, Bianca is sitting in the booth with me at The House of Ale, reminiscing about the days of our misspent youth, telling me how she'd always wished she'd misspent some of them with me. An hour or so after that, I'm following her up the twisty-ass 330 to her secluded mountain retreat in Big Bear."

"The Porsche could handle it."

"The Porsche *loved it.*" Ernie's grin was infectious now; I was pretty sure how the rest of the story was going to unfold. "So, yeah, Bianca and I got to talking and I told her about Phenex, and she said she could definitely squeeze them in to open for a couple of shows."

So that's where Ernie had been all week.

"Wait – you said you didn't get the demo 'til yesterday. Bianca *squeezed them in* without even hearing them?"

"She's not A&R, dude. She's some kind of scheduling wheel. She doesn't care what they sound like. She mostly did it as a favor to me." He looked at the kitchen door again, then again grinned. Bianca had done it *entirely* as a favor to him.

"She did get to hear them, though. Oscar called me on Wednesday afternoon and said that the demo was ready. I had him send it up to Big Bear via courier. Bianca heard it the same time I did. Christ, was it only yesterday?"

"What did she think?"

Ernie shrugged. "I think it's all the same to her. She said, 'They're no Sonic Daydream,' and then we went out to the hot tub."

I realized that the powers of persuasion between an old rock star and an old, big fan were not to be underestimated. The memories of adolescent yearnings were strong and sweet. The kinds of favors I could no doubt elicit from Katie's mom, even at this late date, popped into my head for a second. No wonder her husband frowned at me.

"Did you tell Candy? I mean . . . about the gig?"

Embarrassment clouded Ernie's features, and he looked away. "Not yet. We didn't talk a lot last night. I wanted to tell them all together, anyway."

There were footsteps in the hall then. Candy and the remaining members of Phenex shuffled into the kitchen. Ernie and I arose to let them sit down. Lisa squeezed my hand and smiled sadly at me; love for her and pity for her grief welled up and practically choked me.

She and her mother and Roy and James assumed the same positions from the night before, morose, red-eyed, silent, looking at anything but each other or me, or Ernie.

Ernie and I made breakfast, as we were the only ones capable of doing so. They started to eat, still not speaking. The oppressive weight of their wordless grief finally became too much for me, so I said, "Did Sonny's mom say anything about services?"

"No services," Candy said around a mouthful of scrambled eggs. She might be grieving, but it hadn't affected her appetite. "At least not for us."

I waited for an explanation, but Candy remained interested in her plate. I glanced at Lisa.

"Sonny's mom doesn't care for our beliefs. I don't understand why he even went up there to see her. They haven't ever spoken for as long as I can remember." She looked questioningly at her mother, but Candy was entranced with her eggs and still refused to look up.

I thought that maybe Sonny had mended fences with his mom because he'd believed that Candy was done with him. *I get the feeling that I'm not long for this band.* Maybe he'd asked if he could come back and stay with her until he got a regular life again, because if Candy dumped him, Sonny would've been like that guitar player in the old joke: homeless.

I wondered: had some kind of break actually occurred, like he was sure it would? James had told me that he'd left as soon as they got back to Riverside.

But none of that seemed likely. Even if Candy didn't want him as a boyfriend anymore, I thought that her ambition for the band would've prevented her from firing its most talented member, when they had just cut a demo, when she believed that they were *on the cusp of fame,* as the demon had promised.

And then there was Ernie. Sure, it had been obvious at times that Candy yearned in his direction, but Ernie couldn't be less interested. Even now, after he had *comforted* her, I could tell: an entirely uncharacteristic awkwardness wreathed his features. Now that Candy was sitting right there beside him, he tried his best not to look at me, and if I did manage to catch his eye, I found a type of shame there. Ernie LaBelle had never been ashamed of anything in his long and chequered life. He had been in this for the new thrill of helping a band from behind the scenes. He had never wanted Candy; he still didn't want her.

Candy was strong-willed, that was true, and she considered herself to be worlds more attractive than she actually was. But it would've been clear to even the most casual observer that her baby-daddy wasn't having any. So I found it hard to believe that she would cut Sonny from her life, from her band, just on the off-chance that Ernie would change his mind once her former boyfriend was out of the picture. If he hadn't died, if she wasn't grieving, if Ernie wasn't big-hearted and feeling sorry for her – it wouldn't have happened like that. I knew it, and Candy had to know it, too.

Maybe Sonny had gone to Barstow because his mom had contacted him first. Perhaps she was sick or something, or perhaps she'd just wanted to see her boy again after years of banishment.

Maybe she'd had a change of heart about his *beliefs;* maybe she'd simply missed him.

I hoped that their reunion had been joyous, full of forgiveness and love. I hoped that it had been even better than my partial rekindling of friendship with Lenny and Barbie. There were still issues to be addressed there, but there'd be time yet for Lenny and me to clear the air. Time had run out for Sonny and his mom.

"She'll have him cremated," Candy said softly.

"We could sprinkle his ashes at Randy Rhoads' tomb," Lisa said.

Appalled, I looked to see if she was kidding, attempting some kind of macabre joke. She looked back at me as if to say, *What?* To her, it was a perfectly apt way to honor Sonny.

I looked at Ernie, and he seemed to agree with her. They wouldn't have far to go: the famous guitarist was buried just up the road in San Bernardino, in a giant, white marble mausoleum, complete with musical notes etched beneath its Doric columns.

I knew because I had accompanied Ernie and Lenny on a pilgrimage to it, not too long after Rhoads' interment. As in all things, I just went along for the ride. Guitarists were all the same to me, and dead ones even more so.

There but for the grace of God go I, was my own guitarists' solemn attitude. Unspoken and perhaps even unrealized (but present nonetheless) was another sentiment: There, if God were graceful to a little three man combo from Riverside – there might we all go, and what a way to go.

My bandmates were shocked and amazed at Rhoads' utterly bizarre rock and roll ending. Sabbath's tour bus driver was a former pilot. Coked up, he stole an airplane, and with Rhoads aboard, he attempted to buzz the bus wherein the rest of the band slept. One of the plane's wings clipped the bus, and it crashed in a nearby field, killing pilot, Rhoads, and another passenger.

It was a tragedy, true, a great talent ended too soon – but something in my guitar-playing fellow musicians couldn't help but point out to them that it sure beat dying in your sleep of old age. Tour buses, stolen airplanes, what must all that be like? *Rock and roll will never die,* even if its gods occasionally crashed and burned. In this case, literally.

The three of us couldn't have been much older than Lisa at the time. Denny hadn't been with us. He was about Katie's age then, but unlike her, he hadn't yet discovered Rhoads' hallowed instrument, the six-string that would change his life. Dennis Whitly's picking up a guitar would change all our lives.

"We won't be getting anywhere near Sonny's ashes." Candy reiterated, "His mother doesn't like us."

Maybe Ernie was picturing his own musically-adorned marble tomb; maybe he imagined crossed Gibsons and cryptic runes, like over the back door. Maybe he was tired of talking about dead guitar players. Whatever the reason, he changed the subject. "I got Phenex a gig."

Eyes brightened around the table and attention zeroed in on him.

Ernie opened his mouth, but Candy held up her hand. "We must perform the ritual first."

Ernie looked at me, and I looked at Lisa. "The Lesser Banishing Ritual of the Pentagram. It's to clear our environs of chaos and impurity." She gestured for us to follow her mother out to the band room.

Lisa said, "Stand within the circle." There was no circle and Ernie squinted and looked askance at her. "Just stand in the middle of the room with Roy and James."

We did as we were told, and when Candy produced a dagger from I knew not where, I was reminded of Ernie's long-ago groupie's large pair of scissors.

Lisa indicated the small circles, painted near the ceiling on each wall. Sonny had pointed them out to me – Ernie had not noticed them before. "These represent the four cardinal directions, the four elements, and the four archangels. Mom will now perform the ritual. As she gestures in each direction, imagine a ball of cleansing white light, descending. Or . . . just stand still and be quiet."

Candy intoned, "In the Name of God, the God of Yisrale, may Michael be at my right hand, Gabriel at my left, Uriel before me, Raphael behind me, and above my head, the presence of God."

I recognized the names of the archangels, as Lisa had said, but that was the extent of my familiarity. There were no daggers in the church of my childhood. Candy began humming unintelligibly; she made gestures and pointed at the yellow painted circle, then turned in the direction of the next one, painted blue, and performed the same things. Roy and James and Lisa joined hands and closed their eyes. They also hummed.

Then Candy said, "Before me, Raphael!"

Roy said, "Behind me, Gabriel!"

James rumbled, “At my right hand, Michael!” He pronounced it *Mik-ay-el.*

Lisa said, “At my left hand, Uriel!”

Then, in unison, “About me flames the pentagrams, and in the column shines the six-rayed star!”

Candy performed more gestures in the air with the dagger, then stamped her right foot. Lisa smiled at me. Apparently, the ritual was concluded.

Ernie raised his eyebrows and would’ve said something derisive, but I gave him a disapproving look. He didn’t care what these people believed, but they obviously did believe it, so it would be rude to mock them. Even if they were ridiculous to both of us, deserving of mockery.

“Now, Dad,” Lisa said, taking his arm and leading him back to the kitchen. “What do you have to tell us?”

TWENTY-FIVE

The following week we auditioned guitarists.

They came in all shapes, sizes, races, genders, and ages. Again I thought of Goldilocks' dilemma, this time from a musical perspective: some were too hot, some were too cold. All of them were awful; none just right.

We had a lesbian punker with a Mohawk and a Ferdinand the bull ring though her nose, who looked at Lisa as if she might eat her, like with a knife and fork. Not surprisingly, she chose Iggy and the Stooges' *Penetration* for her audition.

James shook his head; he didn't know that one, so I took over. I didn't know it that well either, but a punk beat is a punk beat. Unfortunately, the punker girl seemed to know the tune the least, and on top of that, she made the mistake of trying to sing it. She glared hungrily, droolingly at Lisa, but only got through one or two *So fines* before Ernie made a throat cutting gesture and said, "Thank you, we'll be in touch."

There was a graying longhair that gave us a fair rendition of *Bad Moon Rising.*

Ernie said, "Not bad, dude. What else can you play?"

The guy smiled; he was missing a few teeth on one side. "I can play anything you want, man. But I was wondering – do you think we could smoke a joint first?"

"Next!" Lisa said immediately. She had no use whatsoever for drugs.

The gentle-looking kid with the big cow eyes talked to his guitar, and only played a few scales as an audition. "We need you to play a song, dude," Ernie prompted.

"Well, we're kinda just learning. Isn't that right, Mary?" The guitar's name was Mary, and she answered with a short riff. "If you've got the sheet music, I'm sure that we could learn –"

Now it was my turn to say, "Next!"

"It's okay, Mary," the kid said. "We've got two more auditions today."

Two guys and a girl that showed up might've been good, or maybe not. Each of them recognized Ernie and subsequently me, and dissolved into giggling, autograph-seeking fans. They became too nervous to play and eventually, after Ernie signed their axes, they just left.

By Thursday evening – the show was Saturday – in an attempt to lighten the black, panicked mood, I told Ernie, "You know, I know a guitar player. What she lacks in experience, she makes up for in attitude. As a matter of fact, she's your biggest fan. Wants you to school her on the breakdown to *Cerulean.*"

Their tired eyes all lit up with hope, and I realized that my joke was going to fall flat. "Unfortunately, she's only fourteen."

"Shit, man, if she's any good –"

"I think the load-out would keep her up past her bedtime, Roy. I was just –"

"Fuck this," Ernie said, not even slightly amused. "I know a guy. And I think he might just be available. In the meantime, you need to rehearse. We've wasted enough time on this bullshit already."

"But we can't rehearse without a second-guitar, Dad."

They could; they just didn't want to. I thought that Sonny's empty place, and the wondering about who was going to fill it, haunted them.

"I'll stand in for right now. Until I talk to my guy."

Thus spoke Ernie LaBelle, and they all believed him implicitly. He had bankrolled a professionally produced demo for them; he had pulled two opening-for-the-headliner gigs out of thin air. If he said that he'd get 'em a guitar player, then, by God and the archangel Mik-ay-el, they knew he would.

I needed to make a quick trip home, to check on the hacienda, and grab some clothes, so Ernie walked me out to the car. I asked, "You got this?"

He nodded.

"Who's your guy?"

Ernie was frustrated about the horrible auditions, and he still frowned. "Allow me to surprise you."

I missed Lisa, but it was nice to spend one night alone in my own bed. The status quo had shifted without comment at the clinker-brick house: I was now with Lisa, and Ernie, though I could tell that it was not to his liking, was with Candy. She had apparently taken Roy and James in hand at some point: nary a snicker nor a surprised expression had come from either of them.

The door to the room that had been Sonny's stood closed during the week of auditions. When I returned from Temecula, it was open, and the room was empty, clean – almost sterile. In my absence, they had gotten rid of everything that he'd owned. I looked at Ernie, and he shook his head; this had all occurred while he had visited his own house for the afternoon, while he'd no doubt been getting in touch with his guitarist.

Like something out of *1984,* history had been rewritten. Sonny had never existed; it had always been me and Lisa, and it had always been Candy and Ernie.

TWENTY-SIX

I arrived back at the band house early Friday morning. As I said, I found that Sonny's memory had been expurgated, and also that stage-fright, almost visible, had descended like a cloud upon Phenex.

Candy was in the kitchen. She was of course clad in her normal groupie uniform concert tee – it was AC/DC this time, and I wondered if she owned a single one featuring a band from this century – but I was jarred into a double take to see that she was also wearing a frilly pink apron. And she was cooking.

Two cakes awaited frosting, and several racks of cookies cooled on the counter. Lisa was sitting at the table, playing with her phone, and she seemed relieved to see me.

"I gotta get out of here," she whispered. "Mom's freaking me out with the desserts."

It was Candy's way of banishing the butterflies. In the band room, Roy was lying on the floor, pushing a Hot Wheels Corvette back and forth, like he was six. James sat on one of the folding chairs, now a permanent fixture in the room, and bounced a tennis ball, and I thought unkindly that it was the most rhythm he'd ever demonstrated. Lisa took her mike off its stand, but didn't turn it on, and began to pace.

Ernie sat next to James, frowning into a large, white, softcover book. I was amazed that he could concentrate on reading beside the bouncing tennis ball, but then I recalled his ceaselessly playing *Tetris* on the tour bus. He would just shut out the rest of the universe and concentrate on making the blocks line up.

"What are you reading?"

"Christ, I thought you'd never get here." He closed the book and stood up. Ernie wasn't nervous; Ernie had never been nervous, and it wasn't like he was gonna be the one onstage tomorrow, trying to impress a big crowd, who were really just waiting for the headliners. Ernie wasn't nervous. He was bored.

"Where's Lenny? I thought he was gonna come down for this. And Barbie, too."

"Lenny's not feeling well. Barbie called me this morning – said he was feeling dizzy yesterday. She said he suddenly felt weak, almost fell off his horse. She made him some tea and put him to bed. She said she thought he'd probably gotten a little too much sun on the trail. He's not as young as he used to be."

"None of us are." Ernie studied me for a moment, trying to ascertain if I thought Barbie was lying for our old bandmate, giving him an excuse to not do something he didn't want to do.

I shook my head. "She tried to play it off with the too-much-sun thing, but I could tell she's concerned. You know – Lenny's never been sick a day in his life."

"I'll give him a call later. See how he's doing."

I asked him again what he'd been reading and he showed me the cover. There was a line drawing of some Egyptian-looking sun-thing with wings at the top. *777 And Other Qabalistic Writings of Aleister Crowley* was flanked by two strange columns.

I cocked an eyebrow questioningly, and he explained. "I found it in the bathroom. It makes absolutely no sense whatsoever."

"It's very dense," Lisa agreed. "Maybe you should try something a little lighter, Dad, like –"

"Like the *Malleus Maleficarum,"* Candy recommended, entering the room with an overflowing plate of chocolate-chip cookies. Her suggestion of reading material brought a grin to the faces of the demon's band; its humor or significance passed Ernie and me right on by.

"We'll make a warlock of you yet," Candy added. This remark produced a titter from the little-boy bassist playing with his toy on the floor.

"Right," Ernie said. He looked at me in exasperation, then a thought occurred to him. "Let's go to Guitar Center."

"You guys go," Candy said. "I've got a pie in the oven."

We went outside, and Ernie frowned at the van. Since the news of Sonny's death, it seemed that all he ever did was frown, unless he was talking about the gig. This road dog shit was about to get real, and I thought he was beginning to realize that some pressure might exist. He wasn't feeling it yet – Ernie was the most unconcerned, ain't-life-a-bowl-of-cherries? individual that I'd ever known. But maybe he was sensing that all of this wasn't going to play out exactly like a Sonic Daydream or Azomite show.

"You guys follow us," he instructed. "We've got another stop to make first."

I got in the Porsche with him, and as we pulled out onto Arlington Avenue, I asked, "Where's your guy?"

Ernie didn't look at me, concentrating on maneuvering the fast car through traffic. Heads turned as they always did, as he passed everyone by. "Other obligations today, dude," Ernie said, still frowning. "But the guy's got chops. He'll be there tomorrow. Don't sweat it."

I didn't worry about the guy's chops: if Ernie had a fellow guitarist up his sleeve, I had no doubt that he had talent. Maybe it was Scott Toombs, his bandmate from Azomite, although that seemed unlikely, as Scott had a wife and kid in Sacramento, and was no doubt up there with them. But even Steve Vai would've needed a moment to rehearse, to pick up the tunes. I shrugged to myself. Ernie wasn't in a mood to discuss it, and this was his band, his responsibility. He told me not to sweat it, so I didn't.

The other stop we made was at Hertz, where Ernie rented a roomy, shiny white van. He had apparently decided that he couldn't allow Phenex to show up for their first real gig in their own primered wreck, that he did, after all, have a reputation to uphold. Bianca might regret her helpfulness if the band looked as ratty and inexperienced as they really were.

I said as much to him when we were back in the 911. "Oh, Christ, I forgot about that."

Good ol' love-'em-and-leave-'em Ernie. Next!

"If we're gonna get 'em some better equipment, I thought the doors on the van should lock," he explained. Maybe he didn't care about appearances after all. "Bianca won't be there. I hope. She hasn't even texted me."

"She knows you're busy with the band," I opined.

"She's busy, too, with the line-ups and all. But I don't think she's actually gonna be here. She's up in Big Bear. On the computer. On the phone." He grinned. "Some younger chick'll be the one standing out in the heat checking off who shows up."

Ernie got on the freeway, the band following in the rental. Their van had been left behind in the Hertz parking lot. The nearest Guitar Center was in San Bernardino, probably not fifteen miles away from Randy Rhoads' final resting place. I hoped that Ernie's mind had left remembrances of dead guitarists, and apparently it had, for he made no mention of another pilgrimage as he headed up Hospitality Lane.

Once upon a time, Ernie LaBelle would've been mobbed at Guitar Center, and it occurred to me now, that he would *still* be mobbed at Guitar Center, had it been announced that he would be putting in an appearance there. He and Lenny and I had our fans, surely, but it had been Dennis Whitly that had been the face of Sonic Daydream. When the band was mentioned, people immediately thought of him, and the rest of the band, well, this many years down the line, our faces weren't as readily remembered. But had there been an announcement, the old fans would've crawled out of the woodwork to see Ernie, even if they couldn't quite picture what he'd looked like on the drive over.

Ernie was in incognito mode today, anyway. It was really his S.O.P. He wasn't a braggart by any means; he didn't seek recognition, wasn't like the baseball player in the old Springsteen song. Ernie was seldom the first one to bring up the glory days, unless it was to reveal the startling truth to some pretty young thing that had caught his eye. At Guitar Center, when one of the older salesmen looked curiously at him and nudged his buddy, Ernie just nodded guilelessly at them and went about his business.

And he was all business today. This was not the time to idly peruse the big amps and sparkly drum kits. It was not a day to impress the salesmen with the pretty young girl's ability to play the breakdown from *Cerulean.* This was not a day to shop. It was a day to buy. Ernie's band was playing a gig tomorrow, and he had just realized that their equipment was as shabby and worn as was their transport.

Ernie instructed me to pick out a suitable kit for James, and with the silent redhead in tow, I found the drum salesman. There was no fear of recognition here: the kid couldn't've been more than twenty-two, and his knowledge of once-famous drummers' faces didn't extend to back before he was born.

"We'll take that set over there."

"You'll . . . take 'em?" Dollar signs flashed in his eyes. "The whole set? You don't even want to try 'em out?"

"We're playing a show tomorrow. I'll try 'em out then," James said with a rare smile and an even rarer flash of humor.

The kid ignored him. The big redhead with the scruffy biker's vest and the stained jeans and the goat's head tattoo on his muscled shoulder might indeed be a drummer – maybe some kind of deathdoom shit, by the looks of him. And maybe he really was gonna play a show tomorrow. But Big 'Un wasn't going to be the one paying for a full set of brand new drums. That would be the old guy, the one now idly twirling an outrageously expensive stick, the one that hadn't even glanced at the price tag on it or on anything else.

"You have this in stock, right?" The kid nodded, gulped. "The distinguished looking older gentleman that came in with us," it was tough to keep a straight face, "is also picking up a couple of guitars and a few amps, so just send the boxes on up to the front." I handed him the stick and turned to go join Ernie.

"Do you want these, too?" the kid called after us.

"No," I replied, not bothering to turn around. The sticks I'd been twirling were a little delicate for James. "Pick me out four or five sets of Vaters. 5bs."

As James and I approached the guitar section, we had to pause while two smiling employees trundled a cart up the aisle. Upon it were two huge cardboard boxes with *Marshall* emblazoned on the sides. I smiled. Ernie wasn't fucking around.

We found him and his guitarists still in conversation with a white-faced salesman, not much older than the drum guy, and just as disbelieving of his luck. Roy had a slick red Warwick, the great grandson of the one that Lenny played. He held it carelessly, and I again thought that Roy was not much of a musician. He didn't recognize quality, even when it was being handed to him.

Lisa didn't have an instrument, just a bunch of packages of strings.

"Nothing for Daddy's little angel?" I whispered to her, sotto voce.

"I like my Strat," she said. "It's a good guitar."

It was indeed, the only instrument in Phenex's arsenal that rose them above the level of The Piglets.

"Besides, Sonny gave it to me, for my sixteenth birthday." She paused. "I know Mom paid for it and all."

Because Sonny had been just another minion with no income of his own, subject to Candy's patronage. I wondered again if he had ridden his old Triumph all the way to Barstow because she had ended it.

"But he picked it out, just for me," Lisa was saying. "I love that guitar." Tears welled up in her eyes and she quickly, savagely wiped them away. The pain remained, however, when she whispered, "I miss him so much, Cal! Everything I know, Sonny taught me."

She leaned her head against my arm for a moment. Lisa wasn't enjoying this Christmas-come-in-September shopping spree the way James and Roy were, the way I was. All the twinkling instruments, all the potential they contained; the idea that tomorrow she'd be onstage, where she'd always wanted to be, and Sonny wasn't going to be there with her – she couldn't shake the tragedy of that.

I realized that Ernie would never really be a father to her. He was kind and he was funny and he was helping her band, and she might grow to feel some kind of blood kinship to him someday, but there wasn't a whole lot more that he could teach her about the music that she loved. Sonny hadn't been blood to her, and he hadn't been old enough to actually be her father, but I knew that he'd held that role for her, nonetheless. It had been Sonny that had shown her how to tap into the potential of the genes so carelessly passed on after a Sonic Daydream show in a tiny apartment in San Francisco. Lisa held more love and respect and sorrow in her heart for Sonny than she would ever encompass for Ernie LaBelle.

Lisa composed herself. She glanced up to find the guitar salesman looking at her worriedly, wondering if her sadness might perhaps cause this old guy to change his mind about his purchases. She narrowed her eyes as if to say that she just might make it so if he didn't stop staring at her, and he abruptly turned back to Ernie. "Will there be anything else?"

Ernie grinned. "What do you recommend?" The kid opened his mouth, but no words came out. "If we need anything else, we'll order it online," Ernie told him.

"I'll just check you out then."

We followed the guitar salesman to the cash register, and he rang up the bass and the packages of strings. The amps and the boxes of drums and the sticks were on carts at the front of the store, with the drum salesman waiting patiently beside them. He no doubt had to enter his name into the cash register somehow – his commission was going to be hefty indeed, and he wanted to make sure it was credited to him. But just as the guitar guy finished hitting the amp boxes with the scanning gun and handed it to his colleague, the manager appeared.

"I'll finish ringing this up, Tom," he said, and the drum salesman's mouth dropped open. "Don't worry, I'll make sure you get the sale," he added tersely, then made a shooing gesture. "Go on, you have other customers." He also glared at the guitar salesman. "You, too, Tony. I'll take it from here."

Ernie turned to the banished underlings and told them thanks for all their help. They eagerly shook his hand. When the manager glared at them again, they quickly slunk away.

"Now then. Will you be putting all this on your Guitar Center Gear Card, sir?" The manager smiled expansively.

Ernie looked at me, then at the band, then back at the manager. "My what?"

"Your Guitar Center Gear Card. Since you're making such a large purchase, I figured that you must be a musician."

"Something like that," Ernie said.

"It's Guitar Center's line of credit." When Ernie just looked blankly at him, the manager asked, "Would you like to apply for a Guitar Center Gear Card? You'll get zero percent APR on major purchases for –"

"That's okay. Just put it on this." Ernie handed his American Express card to the manager. "I don't think we'll be making any more major purchases for a while."

The manager looked at the name on the card, and I must say that his next words were cooler than any I'd ever heard, once the person realized to whom he was speaking. "No, I don't suppose you will, Mr. LaBelle. I imagine you have all your guitars custom-made."

Ernie grinned, shook his head. "Actually they were all off the rack. I did have 'em delivered, though."

****

The rest of the day was spent assembling James's new kit, stringing and tuning Roy's new Warwick, restringing and tuning Lisa's Stratocaster and warming up the tubes in the new Marshalls. Candy paced back and forth ceaselessly, stuffing her face with the cookies she'd made and encouraging us to do the same. In an attempt to get rid of her, Ernie asked her to run over to Staples and pick up a set of stencils and a can of white spray paint so he could put the band's name on the new amps. She said she couldn't, because there was another pie in the oven, so Roy went instead.

Candy seemed to be waiting for something, and it wasn't just the pie. About the time we started loading the instruments into the van, it arrived.

A FedEx truck rumbled to a stop in front of the gate and honked. Candy told James, "Hold out the big drum," and practically ran down the hill. She returned moments later, out of breath, with a cardboard box, thin, flat. It measured about two feet on each side, and I knew immediately what it was. I rolled my eyes and looked at road dog Ernie, but he hadn't a clue.

Candy gingerly tore the box open, and sure enough, she proudly presented him with a big, round, bass drum-sized sticker. In a black-outlined box, it said *Phenex* in, Christ save us, I kid you not, italic Comic Sans font. They were a not a metal band, after all; Phenex's catalog consisted of playful, catchy, marketable, Sonic Daydream knockoff tunes. And thereby, even though they were sponsored by a demon, Candy hadn't wished them to come off as too demonic. There was no money in that kind of music after all. Phenex's sigil, no doubt stolen directly from the internet, climbed around the band's name, however.

"Ah, Jesus, Cand, that's so small time," Ernie said.

It was true. After our first tour, when I bought my first kit of exceptionally good drums, I had ditched the band-name-on-the-bass-drum habit. It said *Sonic Daydream* on the tickets, right under *One Night Only!* It soon said it on the marquees, on the cover of the *Rolling Stone,* on the platinum records. The only sticker we'd ever needed after that was the one that said *Sold Out* on the posters at the entrances to the arenas.

"They're small time, right now," Candy replied, reading the instructions for application on the back of the sticker. She gestured for James to lay the bass on its rim. "I want people to remember their name."

"And remember how it's spelled." She spared me a glare and proceeded to affix the demon's sigil. Annoyed, Ernie shook his head and walked away.

TWENTY-SEVEN

Phenex was scheduled to go on at 3 o'clock in the afternoon. The band, chomping at the oft-mentioned bit, were ready to go by ten, but Ernie played rock star and didn't get up until eleven-thirty. I thought they might lynch him as he sat at the kitchen table leisurely enjoying a cup of coffee, but when he reminded them, "This ain't my first rodeo, dudes," they stopped pacing fitfully.

Candy nixed his half-kidding idea of summoning a limo. "I'm sure The RaceCats don't have a limo. They don't even have a Wikipedia page yet."

No one seemed in the least bit upset that the second-guitar had not yet put in an appearance.

"Relax, my brutha," Ernie told me with his irrepressible, trademark grin. "This ain't his first rodeo, either. He'll meet us there."

Ernie drove the van, with Candy, drummer, bassist, and instruments, and I followed with Lisa in his Porsche.

There was a hand-lettered sign that said *BANDS,* and a wilted looking young man in a reflective vest. There were no other bands in line ahead of us waiting to check in; this was the reason for Ernie's making Phenex wait. It was indeed not my old friend's first rodeo.

Ernie showed the kid some paperwork, and nodded behind him. He handed us each a lanyard with a back stage pass in it and waved us on through.

Ernie parked the van across a field from the stage, amid a motley array of fifth-wheels with trailers, other vans, campers, and pick-ups. The RaceCats didn't need a limo; they had a modest black bus with their name skillfully airbrushed up the side.

"EMI money," I yelled above the band currently onstage.

Ernie leaned close to my ear so he wouldn't have to yell. "I bet that paint's still wet."

Candy stood beside him, shifting from one foot to the other in a welter of anticipation. The band onstage paused; there was a small cheer and then relative quiet while the singer spoke to the crowd.

Ernie seized the moment for instruction. He handed the paperwork to Candy and told her, "I want you to go over and find the guy wearing a big pair of headphones, not plugged into anything." He winked at me. "It might be a woman. If you can't find him, ask somebody for the stage manager." Candy nodded, looked at the stage, looked back at Ernie, eager to be released. "Tell them Phenex has arrived." He grinned at his band. "Find out what time we're supposed to load-in. We'll be over there." He pointed to several piles of equipment, the instruments of the bands next in line to take the stage.

"Okay, Ernie." Candy started to fly to her task, but Ernie grabbed her arm. "See if you can find us some roadies. It's hot and Cal and I are entirely too old for this shit."

"Right. Roadies." Ernie released her arm and Candy skipped joyfully toward the stage.

Ernie opened the doors to the van. "All right, boys. Fame awaits."

By the time we had the instruments on the ground, Candy returned, accompanied by two tatted-up roadies. "They want us to start *loading-in* no later than 2:45." She rolled the common term around on her tongue like ice cream, and Ernie's eyebrows went up in amusement. "This is Mike and Hotdog."

"My bruthas!" Ernie clapped them heartily on the back. He'd always been fond of roadies, since they'd always served him so well as groupie-procurers. But those days were long gone. He was stuck with his Number One Fan now, for the duration.

Ernie was still talking animatedly to the older roadie, so Hotdog addressed the rest of us. "Right this way, gentlemen. And lady." He simultaneously bowed and leered at Lisa.

I knew she'd be getting a lot of that, but just like Elise before her, a raised eyebrow and an expression of supremely bored disinterest told the roadie all he needed to know, even if it wasn't precisely the truth. She was with someone in the band.

Hotdog and Roy began pushing the amps on their dollies across the uneven grass surface. I carried his bass and its stand and James's shiny new high-hat. James grabbed his freshly decorated bass drum.

I glanced at Ernie and the other roadie, thinking that we could've managed the whole set-up in one trip if they decided to help. But Ernie and the guy were in conversation – I noticed that he was about our age – so I figured that Ernie knew him from the old days. Someone needed to stay with the van to make sure that the rest of James's kit didn't sprout legs and walk off by itself, anyway.

The camaraderie in the line-up backstage was infectious. Nobody here was even remotely famous; no rock star egos were on display. We were all just a bunch of musicians out to do what we loved. A mustachioed longhair put out his cigarette and helped

Hotdog and Roy with the amps. A shorn young guy with enormous eyelashes like a camel took my equipment from me. He shook my hand, told me his name was Boston and that he fronted for a band called Manhattan. He noted the name on the drum as James set it down, and told me that they were scheduled to go on immediately ahead of us. Two punk-looking girls approached Lisa and introduced themselves. They began to chatter excitedly together and I left the band to the festival ambience and went back to the van.

Ernie was gone – off to locate his mysterious second-guitar, I hoped – and the grizzled old roadie was sitting on the bumper of the van. He studied my approach and when I got up close, he continued to stare at me. Finally he said, "You don't remember me, do ya, Cal? My name's Mike."

I ran through the gallery of Mikes and Joes, Bills and Freds that had served as roadies for Sonic Daydream over the years. There had also been guys named after cities like Boston, guys named Killer and Bearclaw and Spike. Perry had traveled with us, and he had supervised the local crews that worked for the venues. Ernie made sure to learn all of their names, and Lenny had been pretty chummy with them, too.

But Denny tuned his own guitars, and always fled back to the bus or the hotel right after the show, sometimes taking his Les Paul or his Strat with him. *Run to the bedroom, in the suitcase on the left, you'll find my favorite axe.* But not one single groupie had ever accompanied him. Nor had any accompanied me, as I had kept company with Elise. So I hadn't had a lot of interactions with the roadies.

For several seconds, Mike allowed me to be discomfited with my inability to remember him. Then he smiled and flashed the devil horns at me. On his palm was a tattoo of a pentagram, and I placed him immediately.

"Mike! From Black Winter!"

Ernie had mentioned him at our initial reunion, when he was making the point that there were a lot of witchy-types in the diverse world of rock and roll, and who cared what these people believed?

"Your drummer's name was . . ." My memory again failed me. It had been long ago and far away, in Portland, on our very first tour.

"Louie. He OD'd about ten years ago."

"Ah, I'm sorry to hear that, man." He was the one that had clued me that Lars Ulrich had sold his soul for metal immortality.

Mike shrugged. "I didn't put the needle in his arm."

I didn't know what to say to that, so I said, "So you're a roadie now?"

I hadn't intended it as an insult, but it might've come out that way. "As are you, or so it would seem."

I smiled and shook his hand. He wasn't insulted. "It's great seeing you again, Mike."

He nodded over his shoulder. "Here come the young guys. Let's let 'em earn their money. Come back to the camper with me, Cal. I've got a scrapbook." When I hesitated, he added, "And beer. And air conditioning."

It was at least a good, solid forty-five minutes before Phenex was scheduled to perform, and a beer and AC sounded awesome after my brief but unaccustomed stint carrying instruments. Hotdog and James arrived to fetch the rest of his kit. It was a good thing that Mike had stood by the open van and waited for someone's return, because Ernie had the keys to it.

I told James this and he shrugged, as was his wont. I told him that I'd join them backstage in a minute and walked along the line of parked band transports with Mike.

TWENTY-EIGHT

His camper was ancient, tiny, something called a Scamp. It was attached to a truck older than we were. A house-room air conditioner, attached to a running generator, was duct-taped into the side window.

There was a dining table and seats at one end, a small bed at the other. A stove and tiny bathroom were on one side, and a sink and hotel-room sized fridge on the other. The interior was astonishingly well preserved, immaculately clean and neat as a pin, which seemed a little bit at odds with the dusty, tatted-up longhair beside me.

"It was my dad's," Mike explained. "I promised I'd always keep it nice."

He fetched me a beer and indicated for me to have a seat, then opened the opposite seat. He rummaged around under there for a minute, then produced a battered, faded photo album.

"The good old days." He replaced the seat and handed the album to me, then got himself a beer and sat down. "My girl Trish kept it up for us." He sighed. "She's gone, too."

I didn't want to explore whether he meant *gone* as in *dead,* like Louie the drummer, or simply *gone,* as in having taken a different path in life, so I gave my full attention to the pictures. The first couple of pages showed the guys from Black Winter, jamming on stage, or arm in arm, flashing the rock and roll devil horns and grinning in front of various bars and small-time venues. I recognized the marquee to the Roseland Theater, there in Portland, where Black Winter had opened for us, and the big stage at the Edgefield, where we'd played our first outdoor event, on our second tour.

I turned the page and was astounded to see a shot of Sonic Daydream, standing on the redbrick sidewalk outside the Roseland's floor to ceiling windows. I remembered that Sophia had caught a heel on one of those bricks, and I had prevented her from crashing to the ground by catching her. It had to have been just before, or just after this picture was taken.

The memory came back clearly. Black Winter's bass player – Sandy? Andy? – had volunteered to run us all by the venue for a quick look see, and we'd all piled into their van. We already had a bus then, a modest one, like the RaceCats', but Lenny hadn't been able to scare up the driver. He'd run into Sandy/Andy in the bar, and away we went.

Christ! How young we all were! When this snap was taken, Elise was not even seventeen, and we hadn't yet embarked on our unlikely friendship. Denny had one arm around Sophia – then his brand new girlfriend – and the other around her gleefully smiling little sister.

All that bullshit would cease soon enough. Like I say, for twelve long years, Denny managed to spend not one second more in Elise's company than was absolutely, unavoidably necessary. Yet still she worshipped him, worshipped the very ground upon which he walked, the sidewalks and hotel hallways and backstage passages that he always used as a quick escape route away from her.

It tugged at my heart to see this picture of her, a completely new shot, one I'd never seen before. I had my own pictures of Elise, in an old shoe box in my closet. In my drinking days, I used to take them out and pore over them, asking myself over and over again why I hadn't tried harder to dissuade her in her fruitless obsession with Denny, why I hadn't really lifted a finger to try to save her from herself.

My sense of self-preservation had been silent then, had let me feel guilty, had let me wallow in drunken self-pity. It had let the dreams practically consume me, re-enacting over and over again that night in Kansas City (years after we'd left bands like Black Winter behind), the one and only time I'd tried to talk her out of her madness.

The tour was almost over. Elise's time alone with Denny – except that Denny made sure never to be alone with her – was running out. I'd decided to try to sneak up on the whole hopeless situation, tried to tell her that maybe she'd be better off in Riverside, leading a normal life.

Now I relived the scene as it had occurred, sitting here at Mike's tiny Scamp table. I relived the repeated dreams I'd had of it. But I also realized with a little shock that Lisa had said the very same words.

When I'd suggested that she might be better off at home, Elise had called Sonic Daydream the greatest band in the world, just like Lisa would, almost two decades later.

How could I suggest to Elise that she quit touring with us? What was there for her back in Riverside after the thrill of the road?

"How ya gonna keep 'em down on the farm, after they've seen Paree?"

Elise always told herself that it wasn't just her yen for Denny that kept her with the band. It was the road. It was the biz. It was rock and roll.

But I had persisted. "Maybe this isn't the life for you. Maybe, when we get back home, you should . . . I dunno. Stay there. Go to school. Find somebody . . . Find somebody that's gonna love you back."

Elise was silent for a minute. "Life is long, Cal. Denny . . . All you guys. You need me right now. The tour –"

"The tour's almost over, Leesy. We're taking a year off, remember? To record? So Denny can get a chance to be a daddy, to dandle his daughter on his knee?"

"That won't last."

There it was, the insanity that she spoke aloud to no one but me. "Why won't it last, Elise? Surely, you have to see that Sophia and the baby aren't gonna just disappear –"

"Denny's stuck now, Cal. He's saddled with these . . . *responsibilities.* But what use are they to him? She can't even come with him anymore. Life is long. Someday, he's gonna see –"

"He loves her, Elise! When are you going to realize that?"

Elise smiled slyly. "Maybe. Maybe not. He's stuck with her now, true, but . . . Love can be a tricky thing, Cal."

I'd felt so unutterably sorry for her then. I asked, "What do you know about love, Leesy?"

"You love me, don't you, Cal? You're just trying to look out for me."

"I would love you, Elise, if I thought it would make you forget about Denny."

I had said those words to her, and they would come back to haunt me in a thousand drunken dreams. Because I hadn't meant it. Not then. I didn't love her. I pitied her.

She'd smiled at me, that scrappy, determined, Elise grin. Lisa had the same qualities in her smile.

"I love you, too, Cal," she'd told me. "You're the only friend I've got. Like I say, life is long, and I've got this hope inside me . . . You can't honestly expect me to go back to the old boring life, now that I've toured with –"

"The greatest band in the world. I know."

I had seen the futility of it then. Elise would never stop, never give up her delusion.

I didn't bring the matter up again, and for eight long years after she died, I tortured myself about it. Drink and guilt and bad dreams, her last voice message, reciting Justin Hayward's timeless lyrics: *Just what you want to be, you'll be in the end.* Goodbye, Cal.

And I love you, yes, I love you, oh, how, I love you. Oh, how I love you.

And once I realized that I had indeed loved her, my self-preservation reasserted itself, spoke long-winded, stentorian speeches about how none of it was my fault, how Elise was strong-willed, weak-minded in her obsession with Denny, how there was nothing I could've done to prevent what happened.

If there's blame to be laid, you know where to lay it.

And so I did. I wrote *Sonic Nightmare,* published it, making myself a pariah in the eyes of my bandmates. But that didn't matter; we had pretty much drifted into separate lives by then, anyway. Denny had Sophia, Lenny had Barbie, Ernie had Azomite. What I had was no more bad dreams. Elise's ghost was appeased.

My life was so much better now, I thought, as I turned to the next page of photos. Ernie and Lenny and I were friends again; I had Lisa. I was sitting in a postage-stamp-sized camper with an old roadie, talking about the good old days. *Yeah,* I told myself, *life's great.*

But the progression of the pictures depressed me. Black Winter continued to pose in front of the same little venues – it was apparently a tradition with them. The band had obviously never played anything bigger, never even came anywhere near the neighborhood of the kind of success Sonic Daydream had enjoyed. The venues remained small in the photos, got even smaller, seedier; and the guys from Black Winter got older and more tired. The bassist grew corpulent from drink – I recognized the bleary-eyed, hung-over expression in the pictures from the one that had looked back at me from the mirror for a lot of years. Conversely, Mike and Louie became wizened, skeletal druggies.

The last picture was dated from fifteen years before. When I came to it, like a good storyteller, Mike supplied the ending, and the denouement.

"Yeah, that was the last show, at some little firetrap in Seattle. Louie and I got in a fist fight over whose turn it was to score the dope. That was the end. I never talked to either of them again. Andy left a message with my sister when Louie OD'd."

At my pained expression, he smiled grimly. "It sounds like a country tune, doesn't it? Death and disillusionment." His smile became more cheerful. "But it all has a silver lining, Cal. Without a band, I didn't need a guitar, so I hocked it. Gave up the dope – I'd probably be dead now, too, if Black Winter had gone on. I got a job shoving amps for a local promoter, and the rest, as they say, is history. I'm still in the life, still digging the road. My sister's boy – his name's Horus, if you can believe that –"

"What is that, Greek? Roman? Wasn't he some kind of poet or something?"

Mike shook his head. "I dunno about all that. He's named after the Egyptian god."

I remembered the Egyptian-looking sun-thing with wings at the top on the occult book Ernie had been trying to decipher at the band house, remembered the pentagram tattooed on Mike's palm. His nephew was named after an ancient, pre-Christian deity. Apparently the witchiness was all in the family.

"The laddie reckons himself a poet." Mike grinned. "That much is true. He's a songwriter, and plays guitar, just like his Uncle Mike. He's only nineteen, and he's in between bands right now, so I got him on as a roadie for The RaceCats. But he's good, Cal. Reminds me of a young Ernie LaBelle." The old roadie winked.

There was a knock on the door. Mike opened it – it wasn't like he had far to go – and Hotdog peeped his head in. "Phenex is on in five. They're almost done loading-in. They asked me to find the drummer."

Mike looked at me in surprise. "Are you drumming for Phenex, Cal? I thought you were the roadie." He grinned.

"I am. The big redhead's the drummer." I arose and stepped out of the little space. "But it's me they're looking for."

As the three of us walked toward the stage, I asked Hotdog, "Did you see another guitar player with them?"

He shrugged, shook his head. "I've been looking for you, man."

I mounted the staircase on one side of the stage and beheld Candy and the members of Phenex standing in the wings on the other side, hands clasped together, eyes closed. Hotdog and Mike strode out and began the sound check. Ernie came up the steps behind me and slapped me on the back. I glanced behind him, but there was no one behind him.

"Where's your guy?"

The smile Ernie gave me was like looking back in time. It was the same grin he'd evinced in the picture in Mike's album: confident, gleeful, devious.

"Hep is not exactly your middle name, is it, dude?"

I frowned. "Hep me, Ernie. What the hell's going on?"

Ernie held up a red Charvel. It was familiar; I'd seen Perry tune it, watched Ernie play it, in a thousand towns around the world for a lot of years.

Then Ernie sang, reminding me that, alternating with Leonard Whitly – at the time, not yet proclaimed God's bass player, because neither *Rolling Stone* nor anybody else had heard of us yet – he'd once been the front for a little garage band called Sonic Daydream. Back when baby brother Denny was still in high school, still locked up all by himself in his bedroom, practicing *Baba O'Riley* in front of his mirror and trying to get the chords straight to *Smoke on the Water.*

"Here I am, on a road again
There I am, up on the stage
Here I go, playing star again
There I go, turn the page."

Ah, another rock star lament of yesteryear, Bob Seger whining about the cold, unfriendly road, neglecting to mention the money it had made for him. I grinned at my old friend, and he continued in his smooth, deep voice,

"But your thoughts will soon be wandering, the way they always do

When you're riding sixteen hours and there's nothing there to do

And you don't feel much like riding, you just wish the trip was thro-oo-ugh."

But that was all bullshit. Ernie had never wished the trip was through. He paused, then began another tune. *"Now the seats are all empty. Let the roadies take the stage –"*

"Ah, shut up." Once upon a time there had been a bunch of songs about the hard life and travails of a traveling musician. *I am just a new boy, a stranger in this town.* Ernie had given me *Turn the Page* and *The Load-Out.* I thought that if he started *Johnny was a schoolboy when he heard his first Beatles song,* I just might punch him.

There was nothing about being in a successful touring band that didn't beat the hell out of a day job. Any musician that told you otherwise had never held down a day job, so he didn't know how good he had it. I thought again for a second about Black Winter, and what could happen to bands that never made it. But I pushed the thought away, because even I was feeling a little bit of the old excitement.

"And now, ladies and gentlemen." Mike the roadie looked over and smiled at me. "Put your hands together and welcome to the Rock Invades Riverside stage . . . *Phenex!"*

There was a smattering of applause as Lisa and Roy and James walked out from their side. Nobody had heard of Phenex, after all. Ernie ran out from his side. There were no still no cheers. There would've been, had he been introduced, but none of the young RaceCats fans in the crowd recognized him.

But it didn't matter. Ernie was in his element. He had always loved the road in the Sonic Daydream days, and with Azomite, too. I should've known he'd never stay behind the scenes with Phenex, if he had a chance to be out there in front of the crowd.

Good ol' Ernie, I thought with a grin, *you're a simple creature. Rock and roll will never die.*

But then I thought of the mournful sax solo that was the intro to *Turn the Page,* and I thought of Sonny, and how Ernie had come by this opportunity to be onstage again, with a new band. My smile evaporated and took my elated mood with it.

But as Phenex's set progressed, by mood lightened again. Sonny would've wanted it that way.

After the first three of their six tunes, the singer said, "I'm Lisa Corson and we're Phenex." There was a whoop from the crowd that could only have come from Candy, and then a nice, appreciative spate of cheers.

Phenex finished their set, and while the applause was not by any means deafening, it had grown since Lisa had introduced the band. Phenex had performed quite well, and the audience had liked them. All around, an excellent first showing.

Hotdog, assisted by Roy and James, began moving Phenex's equipment off the stage; The RaceCats' roadies began moving the headliner's in to replace it. *Workin' for that minimum wage,* I thought. Other personnel attached to The RaceCats began filling the wings. I strolled down the steps to look for Phenex's road dog/interim guitar player. To congratulate him.

Once backstage, I saw Mike introducing another roadie to Ernie – this must be his ambitious, oddly-named nephew, Horus. Mike slapped the kid on the back, then yelled a few orders to the rest of his crew. I started to walk over there, but then Lisa materialized out of nowhere.

She grabbed me by the hand and pulled me around to the side of the stage. She pushed me up against it and started to kiss me. Her face was hot, almost feverish. She tangled one hand in my hair and pulled herself roughly against me with the other. She bit my neck, murmured breathlessly, "Oh, my God, Cal! That was so awesome!"

It was the thrill of the live performance, a feeling unequaled, craved by musicians and actors, preachers and politicians, public speakers. The incredible, electrifying energy of the crowd – and this was not even an exceptionally large crowd, nor were they overly receptive to Lisa and her band. But still the power pumped with her blood, sang in her nerve-endings. She felt extraordinarily alive, high like from no other drug, ecstatic.

Like a million performers before her, now she wanted to continue the amazing sensation on a more personal level, and lucky me, I was to play the groupie role. We were around the corner from the immediate backstage area – our own people couldn't see us, thank Christ – but we were still out in the open, exposed.

"Honey," I murmured against her insistent lips. "We can't do this here –"

"You gotta find some place, Cal." Her whisper was like a moan. "Right now."

But where? Home was too far away, and how would we get there? Ernie's Porsche . . . Still too exposed, too cramped. The van? It would be like a pizza oven in the van, and the band would be returning with their instruments.

Lisa continued to grind herself against me, and it wasn't helping me think at all. Then someone cleared his throat. I glanced up from the hot, panting young woman in my arms; Lisa stopped kissing me and looked over her shoulder.

Mike was standing a few feet away, smoking a cigarette. How long he'd been there, I couldn't say. He dropped the cigarette in the grass, snuffed it out. He offered the devil horn salute to Lisa, pentagram on display, and said, "Hail." She blinked, took her arm from around my neck and returned the international gesture of rock and roll.

With just the slightest of smirks, Mike reached into his pocket and arced his keys through the air to me.

"If you can't find me, give 'em to Chrissy. She's The RaceCats' road dog. And stage manager today. I'll see you guys in Berdoo tomorrow." His smirk widened as he started to walk away, then as an afterthought, he added over his shoulder, "Don't make a mess."

I grabbed Lisa's hand and ran with her across the field to the roadie's air-conditioned Scamp.

Put another dime in the jukebox, baby.

TWENTY-NINE

The RaceCats' set was over; they had already left in their cute little black bus. I had entirely missed the first show of Riverside's newest favorite sons' first tour, and didn't feel bad about it in the least. Maybe I would catch their act tomorrow, but probably not. I might have to play groupie again.

The crowd was dispersing, some on foot, the rest amid honks and taillights. The roadies and a few carpenter types were already beginning to dismantle the stage. I knew it would be a long night for them. *Now roll them cases out and lift them amps, haul them trusses down and get 'em up them ramps.* They'd have it all *set up in another town,* in Glen Helen, while I was still curled up in bed with Lisa tomorrow. I didn't see Mike, so I gave his keys to harried, worn-looking Chrissy, and Lisa and I started back across the field.

Halfway there, I noticed young Horus, leaning against the van, reverently strumming Ernie's Charvel. Then the old guitarist reached for it, and handed it up to Roy. Ernie clapped him on the back, shook his hand; then the kid ran off across the field and went back to work.

Lisa's phone beeped. She was looking at it when I commented, "Maybe Daddy found you a new guitar player."

Lisa was returning a text. She answered absently, "It's just for tomorrow's show. It's not like he's gonna join Phenex and go back on the . . ." She stopped and glanced quickly up at me, with an almost guilty look on her face.

But I didn't have time to wonder about that, because Candy came bounding across the field, as joyous as a black Lab puppy. She embraced her daughter, squealing, "You were so good!"

Lisa said thanks, and we continued toward the van. "And you're gonna be even better tomorrow!" Candy gushed. "Ernie said something about another guitar . . ."

"Horus," I supplied.

Candy's smile faltered. "The roadie's kid?"

"His nephew, actually. I hear he's pretty good."

Candy was unsure for a second, then her smile and her devotion returned. "Well, I'm sure Ernie knows." She hugged her daughter again. "You were great, baby! What was it like, being up there, in front of all those people?"

Lisa shared a sly glance with me, then told her mother, "It was awesome, Mom. Absolutely awesome."

THIRTY

Everything was bigger at the Just Us Festival.

It wasn't Wembley, but the stage was wider and higher than the one at Rock Invades Riverside. The park was exponentially bigger, as was the crowd. There were a couple of other modest tour buses this time, though I recognized none of the band names. The members of Phenex had resumed the same rock star insouciance they had exhibited at the recording studio. *Who cares about these other guys? We're opening for the headliner.*

Mike and Hotdog came over to the van to help us load-in. I just had the chance to tell him thanks for his perfectly timed loan the day before, then Ernie put his arm around his shoulders and, Charvel in hand, took off with him across the larger, dustier field toward the bigger stage. I figured that they were going to scare up Horus; Ernie was probably going to quickly teach him the tunes. It seemed a little rushed to me, but there was still quite a while before Phenex was scheduled to go on, and if the kid was any good, he should pick 'em up. *I'm sure Ernie knows,* I thought, and ceased to sweat it.

Neither Ernie nor Mike returned, but the time passed quickly. The band ahead of Phenex finished their set. The cheer was louder than at Riverside the day before, even though it wasn't really any more enthusiastic. It was just because the crowd was bigger.

Lisa had gone off with Roy and James and Candy about forty-five minutes before. As Mike and Hotdog and Horus began bringing their equipment onto the stage, I saw the band on the other side, hands clasped in their prayerful circle, invoking their demon. Ernie was with me on this side of the stage again, as far from the solemnities as possible. Deadpan, he remarked, "Did I ever tell you that Lars Ulrich sold his soul to the devil for metal immortality?"

"I have heard that, yeah," I replied, and we had a good laugh.

I wondered if such a thought had ever occurred to Candy, selling her soul to ensure Phenex's success, seeing as how she actually believed in souls and the arch-fiend and all that witchy mumbo-jumbo. "Some prophecies have been fulfilled," she'd said once, after she'd *scryed.* "Others await fruition. Rituals must be performed, and sacrifices must of course be made."

Whatever's clever, I thought, and watched the roadies.

To my surprise, they set up three guitars. Ernie's and Lisa's, and another one, on the far side of the stage. Apparently, Horus hadn't learned all the songs well enough: Ernie was gonna back him up a little bit.

I smiled to myself. The kid was obviously a Sonic Daydream fan. His guitar was a nice black Les Paul. It was a common enough axe, surely, but one just like it had appeared on the cover of our third album.

Mike the roadie didn't introduce Phenex this time. This was a bigger festival; there was a master of ceremonies. The band ran out on stage, again to mildly interested applause. To my continued surprise, they started in on their first song without Horus. He was nowhere to be seen; the black axe remained untouched on its stand.

This continued through the next two songs. I figured maybe the kid had been seized by stage-fright. I'd never had a problem with it myself, nor had any of my bandmates, but I'd seen more than a few famous and not so famous musicians, consumed by nerves, puking in garbage cans backstage right before they went on. But they always went on.

Phenex finished their fourth song; still no Horus. Then Ernie played the familiar intro to *Tomcats;* he looked over and gave me an apologetic grin.

Then I heard a miked voice, also familiar: "I heard this band likes oldies."

And then the owner of the voice swaggered out onstage.

Someone on the rail recognized him immediately, said something to her buddy like, *Oh, my God, Becky! That's Dennis Whitly!* and the roar of admiration swelled, raced backwards through the crowd in a wave and then moved toward the front again, breaking over the stage in a staggering cheer.

Sonic Daydream hadn't toured since 1999, hadn't released an album since the *Greatest Hits* in 2005. These people might be young and Denny was old, but all it took was one fan to recognize him, one fan to whisper his name, and the spell was cast. Dennis Whitly, guitar god, had descended to earth, had ascended the stage with a bunch of opening-for-the-nobody-headliner, also-nobodies called Phenex. The crowd, as the saying goes, went wild.

Denny picked up the black Les Paul. Yeah, it had been on the front of our third album; on the back had been a picture of him holding it. Never in a million years would I have expected Ernie to pull something like this – but I should've recognized Denny's guitar.

He and Lisa sang *Tomcats* together. The delighted crowd sang along. I remembered what Lisa had told me, that Candy had a video of her at five years old, playing a plastic, toy guitar and singing just this song, because she had been born into Sonic Daydream fandom, had she not?

I saw the truth of that uncomfortable phenomenon, undeniable now: Lisa's eyes were shining, and her grin was a mile wide. It was as much of a thrill for her to be onstage beside the famous frontman as it was for the stunned crowd to be watching him. Who'da thunk it? For the measly $25 gate to a local music festival, they were getting the once in a lifetime chance to see rock legend Dennis Whitly! Wait 'til Mom hears about this!

The song ended and the cheers were positively ecstatic. Denny acknowledged them with his trademark crooked smile; the crowd roared again. He waited for the noise to subside, then gestured across the stage. "Ernie LaBelle, ladies and gentlemen."

Another earthshaking cheer. While Ernie took a bow, I imagined that all the wanna-be four-stringers in the crowd were peering offstage, waiting for God's bass player to make an appearance. I saw a girl in the front point at me, standing in the wings. I stepped back where I couldn't be seen. This wasn't a Sonic Daydream reunion. I didn't want anyone cheering for me, because wild horses couldn't drag me out onto the same stage as Dennis Whitly; all the applause in the universe couldn't compel me to perform with him. Never, ever again.

He smiled at Lisa and said, "I was actually thinking of something a little older."

And then to my utter amazement, James – of all, people, humorless, plodding James! He wasn't miked, but I was close enough that I could hear him shout Bonham's count in. *"We've done four already but now we're steady and then they went, one, two, three, four!"*

And then mediocre Phenex, may Christ have mercy on my soul, with Lisa playing lead, swung into Led Zeppelin's *The Ocean.*

I dragged my hand across my face in pained disbelief. Elise had been the only person I'd ever met that *whistled* this song.

The crowd was stunned into silence for a heartbeat; they were young and Denny didn't sing anything like Robert Plant. But it was only for a split second, then the cheers drowned out the end of the first verse.

Denny was a professional, and Lisa had been singing all her life, so it seemed as though they had rehearsed, even though I knew that was impossible. There had been no time for a rehearsal. Despite

Lisa's slip the day before – "It's not like he's gonna join Phenex and go back on the . . . *road with us,"* and the guilty look that had accompanied it; despite James's gleeful shouting of Bonham's count in – I didn't even know he could play this song – no, there hadn't been any rehearsals. Candy wouldn't have permitted Dennis Whitly in her house. She had to've been in the dark about this as much as me. But Lisa and the rest of the band had known he was going to be here, had known what the set list was gonna be.

Lisa was a shade late on the lengthy bridge; the crowd was oblivious, but I saw Ernie glance at her. She was right on time with the *Oooh, yeah!* however. Then the band stopped and Denny was singing the *la-la's* to her in his flawless voice, undimmed by age. And Lisa harmonized with him, smiling into his eyes, singing back to him in the same manner that she always sang to me.

James was half a beat late, but Denny covered for him as he began the last verse. When he put his arm around Lisa as he came to the line, *Now I'm singing all my songs to the girl who won my heart,* the words of the reporter from *Rolling Stone* came back to me: *Dennis Whitly broadcasts an easy availability, an irresistible, Hey, baby, ya wanna? attitude.* He did so even now.

Lisa smiled eagerly back at him. They did a kind of kick-line together at the end of the song, and she sang, *Oh, it's so good!* to Denny, the way she'd often whispered it to me, but with far more enthusiasm.

A hot, oily bubble of something akin to jealousy burst in me then, bitter and acidic. But it wasn't precisely jealousy. Jealousy would've been a new feeling for me, just like love and hatred. What had I ever had to be jealous about? I'd never had anyone, had never therefore had cause to fear that someone would take her. It wasn't jealousy: Denny wasn't going to steal Lisa away from me. He was fifty-one, happily married; he didn't want Lisa any more than he'd wanted . . .

Elise.

It wasn't jealousy that roiled my stomach, made me feel sickly, light-headed – it was something else, a kind of naked fear. The way Lisa looked at him – she was so much more enrapt with Denny than she'd ever been, *would ever be,* with me. The way she sang to him, the way they sang together; I couldn't sing.

The tune ended and the crowd again went nuts; Lisa put her hand on Denny's shoulder and said something into his ear. They smiled at each other and shared a laugh, like old friends, old lovers, and the intimacy of it tore at me. It was all part of the act to Denny, what the crowd expected. Here was the old tomcat rock star, easy and confident with the young singer. From the way she gazed adoringly back at him, they knew what would be going on during The RaceCats' set this time.

The crowd fell silent when Lisa took her mike from its stand and set her guitar down. Was she going to make some public declaration of love for the guitar god, was she going to announce that world-renowned Dennis Whitly and Ernie LaBelle and the drummer hiding in the wings would be joining Phenex permanently? I knew that wasn't going to occur, but it was obvious to the crowd from the way she looked at him that *something* had to be going on with the pretty, dark-haired singer – what was her name again? – and old lover boy Dennis Whitly.

Then to my continued amazement – I wouldn't've believed that I could've encompassed any more amazement – Horus walked out onto the stage and set Denny up with a twelve-string acoustic guitar. The crowd remained silent, unsure of what was coming, but I knew. Like *my little lover,* Dennis Whitly was a David Gilmour fan from way back. I thought, *Christ, it can't be, Phenex can't pull it off, they don't have any synths –*

Lisa breathed into the mike, "How about another oldie? From about the same time?"

And sure enough, the intro to *Welcome To the Machine* blasted through the PA. It was recorded; the whole piece was recorded, like some kind of guitar-less, voiceless karaoke tape. The set-up was strictly to remind the crowd of Denny's legendary guitar chops, to spotlight Lisa's voice; to showcase the two maybe-lovers in an unusual, memorable duet.

And memorable it was; my stomach seethed. Denny strummed. When Lisa sang, *"Welcome, my son,"* he looked up and squinted at her, as if he was indeed a nascent performer, paying heed to the cautionary truths that were to follow. It was pure showmanship on both their parts; the crowd applauded wildly.

Lisa circled Denny, singing to him. Denny strummed, accompanied the recorded bridge – insanely, a line from an ancient disco tune played quickly, raucously through my brain: *Love said, 'Let the music play, he won't get away . . .'*

I blinked, shook my head, and onstage, Denny was assuring Lisa: he smiled calmly, seductively – he was ready for the machine, was indeed welcoming it.

It was just like Elise had said about watching him; the way Dennis Whitly played his guitar was like the act simulated. Only this time it was a duet. He had a partner, and she was digging it.

The aching longing in her voice, in her eyes, knifed through me when she sang, *"You dreamed of a big star . . . He played a mean guitar."* The crowd again went intercontinentally ballistic: Dennis Whitly was undoubtedly the biggest star most of them had ever seen; his mean guitar was multi-platinum. And the girl – her dream of him was utterly apparent.

The song ended. While the crowd cheered – I thought that they could no doubt hear them back in Riverside – while Horus whisked away the acoustic and quickly hooked up Denny's Les Paul again, he again put his arm around Lisa; she kissed him girlishly on the cheek.

My feelings of helpless fear intensified. Like Lenny almost falling off his horse in Anza, I felt dizzy, like I might pass out. I staggered down the steps and fell into a folding chair backstage.

World-famous guitarists Dennis Whitly and Ernie LaBelle accompanied never-gonna-be-famous Phenex on their last two songs, while I slowly recovered. By the time Denny and Lisa flounced offstage, happily arm in arm, her febrile face smiling up at him, my sick fear had hardened into rage.

I stood, my hands balling into fists at my sides. Dennis Whitly and his guitar god's charm had destroyed Elise, my only friend in the world, someone whom I'd realized that I loved, all too late. He wasn't going to carelessly destroy the girl I loved now with it. I would kill him first.

Denny saw me and he stopped abruptly. The smile froze on his face, then fled. "Well, I'll be a son of a bitch."

"You've always been a son of a bitch, Denny, for as long as I've known you."

"You've never known me, Cal."

Lisa ceased gazing lovingly at him and looked guiltily at me. She opened her mouth to say something, then closed it again. What could she say? She thought she'd found someone new, and way sooner than expected. What she didn't know was that he wasn't going to return her devotion, not like I had. Not by a long stretch. *For who so firm that cannot be seduced?* Not even by an eager, eighteen-year-old girl? Dennis Whitly, that was who.

Ernie appeared at my shoulder, his guilty expression identical to Lisa's. I frowned in questioning, betrayed disbelief; he quickly looked away.

"What the fuck, Ernie?" Denny said in harsh surprise. Lisa disengaged herself from his arm and took a step away. He was ignoring her anyway. *Get used to that, honey.*

Ernie became the picture of caught-with-his-hand-in-the-cookie-jar guilt. He'd kept Denny in the dark about my presence, too, or else he never would've agreed to this cameo appearance.

"It's been a long time, Denny. I thought maybe it was time that you guys buried the hatchet."

I thought that if there was a hatchet handy, I'd like to bury it in Denny's head, and then in Ernie's next. His self-absorbed arrogance had exposed his daughter to ruin and heartache. He claimed not to have paid any attention to Elise's obsession; now he was going to see it all played out again, and he wasn't gonna be able to ignore it this time. Like an experienced drug user, he had offered a hit to the wrong newbie, and through this careless gesture he had addicted her.

Denny laughed without humor. "Don't hold your breath."

I had to agree with him on that.

He eyed me appraisingly. "I gotta say, you look great, Cal."

He did, too. From his performance, I knew that his talent and voice had remained intact. His face was mostly unlined, save for the inevitable crow's feet around his famous green eyes, that tattoo that Father Time inflicts upon all of us. Unlike his brother, he hadn't gained a pound, had kept all his hair. It had of course gone gray, and he'd cut it to a respectable length, as befitting the dignity of his years.

Yeah, Denny still looked great. He was become a silver fox, and he had, without any effort whatsoever, successfully raided the hen house. His perennial charm had ensnared my prize chick.

Denny addressed his old second-guitar. "I don't know why you'd – maybe you just feel sorry for him, eh, Ernie? Just another washed-up drummer, all alone in the world. You never did get another gig, did you, Cal? And I'd imagine that the studio work's coming few and far between these days. Can't twirl 'dem sticks like you used to."

By this time, the rest of Phenex had gathered around us, silently watching the confrontation. Even Candy was there, open-mouthed, the very definition of astonishment. Someone was running through The RaceCats' sound check onstage, but it wasn't Mike, because he was standing there beside Candy, watching. Waiting.

"I'd be careful, though, Ernie," Denny continued. "There's a reason why he's all alone, why no woman'll have him. Once a traitor, always a traitor. As soon as your check clears the bank – if I were you, I'd be looking over my shoulder for that knife, the same one this lying, chickenshit, money-hungry bastard stuck in my –"

I lunged at Denny then, swung on him, anticipating how good it would feel when my fist connected with his famous face, thinking about how much Lisa would love him with a black eye, thinking how well he was gonna be able to sing with a broken jaw. I'd be able to twirl my sticks again after my knuckles healed up, but Dennis Whitly wasn't gonna be so pretty anymore after I beat his insufferably smug ass.

But Mike the roadie had been in the business for as long as I had, and he had seen (and no doubt participated in) more than his share of fights between musicians. He'd seen it coming from a mile away, and when I lunged at Denny, he stepped in and held me back. Ernie, a heartbeat slower, assisted him.

Denny stepped up – he was only an emotional coward, after all, a coward with women – and James and Roy quickly restrained him. The two of us struggled against these calmer heads and hands, eager to get at each other at last, after all these years. Denny wanted to defend his dubious honor, wanted to pay me back for my betrayal, to force me to say that it had all been a lie, that I'd dreamed it all up to make a buck. He thought I wanted to punch him for his fresh insults, calling me washed-up, friendless, money-hungry.

But none of that even stung. I wanted to thrash him for what he'd done to Elise a lifetime ago. I wanted to kill him for doing the same thing to my Lisa now, carelessly. Instantaneously.

James and Roy's grip on Denny slipped; before they got a hold on him again, he got right in my face. "Fuck you, Cal. I hope you die all alone, because you don't deserve anything better. Then I hope you rot in hell, unmourned."

Ah, yes, the legendary Dennis Whitly. Always the poet.

"Get him outta here," Mike commanded, and Roy and James hustled the famous rock star to the far side of the backstage area. Denny shook them off; I watched both of them put their hands up in the classic gesture: *No offense, dude. We we're just saving you from yourself.*

Onstage, the MC's voice, amplified, enthused: "Ladies and gentlemen . . . *The RaceCats!*" As the cheer went up, I watched Candy trail after Denny, her worshipful, groupie-supplicant's glazed look of adoration already bloomed.

She might hate him in theory, might've blacked out his face on old posters. But this was Dennis Whitly, front to her favorite band, singer to her baby-daddy's second-guitar, legendary rock god, in the flesh. Her animosity toward his murder of Sonic Daydream was forgotten as the eternal groupie's question formed in her mind: *What's Dennis Whitly really like?*

He was here, couldn't escape her before she could corner him – and that's exactly what she did, catching up, stepping in front of him, blocking his escape route around the side of the stage. I was sure that there was a limo waiting for him in the dusty field, mere steps away. So close, but still too far. Candy had him – he would have to say a few words to her, his band's Number One Fan.

Ernie also watched her, and I wondered if he was reliving the days when the groupies had come to see Denny, but had accepted him as second choice. There had never been anything but a Dennis Whitly-shaped cloud left behind after a performance – he didn't even linger to sign autographs.

Denny would be gone, but the excitement of the show had always remained for these girls. *The trilling wire in the blood sings below inveterate scars, appeasing long forgotten wars.* It had been like a war, like a battle to the groupies: standing in line for hours so they'd be in front, on the rail, where they could see their god up close; enduring roadies' leers beside the barrier. They had been picked – when they discovered that Denny hadn't picked them, most of them remained anyway, just to see what would happen next.

Ernie would smile, chose one from the small crowd, ask her name. She'd smile back. What the hell, he was an awesome guitar player, almost as cute as Dennis Whitly, and the itch was still there, and he *was* with the band . . .

Ernie watched Candy, and he didn't care now any more than he ever had. He didn't really want her – he'd just fallen into the convenience of the whole thing – and he knew that Denny assuredly didn't want her, not in this lifetime. Let her talk to the rock star, get his autograph. She'd be back, and if he was in the mood, Ernie would allow her to take her groupie-lust for Dennis Whitly out on him, just as he had in the old days.

"Let me go, Ernie." I shouted over the blare of The RaceCats' set, in full swing now.

He and Mike released me. The roadie squinted at me, leaned in so I could hear him. "Are you back, man?" I nodded. He again produced keys from his pocket and pointed across the field. "Go back to the Scamp. Have a beer. Cool off. I'll call you when your equipment's in the van."

I glanced around. A couple of roadies idled, still looking at me curiously. It would be a tale told when they were working tonight. "It was the drummer, dude! The whole band was there, except for the bassist. Right before the headliner went on – the old drummer was gonna scrap it with Denny Whitly!"

"I would've liked to've seen that."

"Ah, it didn't happen. Mike and the rest of *Phoenix* broke it up."

Candy was still smiling and gesturing animatedly to the rock star she had trapped, no doubt talking Phenex up as best she could above the noise of The RaceCats' set. Roy and James stood on guard nearby, in case Denny should suddenly decide to come back and choose me.

Lisa was gone. As headstrong and bold as Elise had ever been when it came to pursuing what she wanted, I imagined that she was waiting in the limo for Denny. The driver would've admitted her to its cool, quiet, private chamber. She wasn't a groupie, somehow snuck past security; she had a lanyard and a backstage pass, and he would no doubt envy Denny his soon-to-be-possession of her.

I loped across the field in the opposite direction, the direction Mike had pointed. I was grateful to the old roadie, relieved to get away. My rage had dissipated, replaced again by that sick, fearful feeling. Like I say, it wasn't jealousy. I knew that Denny would kick Lisa out of the limo, none too gently if she resisted – how had Eminem put it? *Won't get out, I'll push you out.*

His lady-wife was no doubt waiting for him somewhere nearby, and the presence or even the smell of a girl in his limo – Denny wouldn't want Sophia to remember the old days, when the groupies had clamored after him, when his Number One Fan, her own sister, had driven his black Mercedes over a dark California cliff because of her fixation with him. Denny wouldn't want Sophia to know that after just one set, he had managed to garner yet another relentless, obsessed fan.

I unlocked the Scamp, and the air conditioning washed over me like a benediction. I got a beer out of the tiny fridge and collapsed into the seat beside the table.

I exhaled heavily, put my head in my hands, thinking, *that's just what Lisa's gonna be. Relentless.* I could see her, wheedling Ernie, begging him to get Denny over to the house to perform with her again. And Candy would be right there with her, her former dislike of Sonic Daydream's killer disappeared by the thought of his in-person, killer smile.

Baby-daddy would attempt to accommodate them: "Come on over and jam with us, Denny. Cal's not here . . ."

Ernie would be oblivious to the danger. He didn't care what Candy wanted, and he wouldn't recognize the groupie-lust in his daughter's eyes, just as he had missed her come-hither looks at me. But Denny would know, and chickenshit as always, he'd decline the invitation.

But I knew that Lisa wouldn't give up – she hadn't given up on her single-minded determination to seduce me, had she? She reckoned all that as destiny, and getting at Denny – I had seen the same desire in her eyes, intensified. This would be her new destiny.

If Ernie couldn't summon him, Lisa would take matters into her own confident hands. I imagined her stalking him, calling him, sending him texts. I imagined her finding out where he lived, driving Candy's ratty Honda past his house, maybe even getting out and going up to the door.

It wasn't jealousy I felt. Denny wouldn't even let her into the house. She was far too young, and he'd learned his lesson after giving in to Elise. He'd tell Lisa in no uncertain terms to *get the hell off of my lawn.*

Lisa was like Elise in so many ways – beautiful, willful; and now, so obviously besotted with Denny. She lived in the same kind of fantasy world as my deluded old friend had, where destiny revealed itself, where wishing hard enough for impossible things couldn't help but make them so. I didn't imagine that Lisa would take His Guitar-Playing Majesty's summary rejection any better than Elise had.

The door opened abruptly and she stepped inside the Scamp. She slammed the door and the little trailer rocked. Hands on hips, she glared furiously at me.

"What the fuck's wrong with you?"

"Hey, I know you," I returned mildly. "You're Dennis Whitly's biggest fan."

She stared at me for another second, panting in anger. Then something dawned on her, and her face went slack with wonder as she grasped it. She said, "Ah, Jesus, Cal!" and took a step forward. She grabbed me, fiercely pressing my head against her damp abdomen.

She took my face in her hands, gazed searchingly at me. "When I was onstage with him . . . You saw . . . you saw *her!* You saw Elise!"

I pulled away from her hands. "I saw something."

She sat down across the table from me. She smiled, but when I didn't smile back, her seriousness returned. She attempted to grasp my hands across the table, but I again pulled away.

"Since I was a little girl, I've often thought of myself as Elise, Cal. I tried to put myself in her shoes. And all the things Mom has drilled into my head . . ." Lisa let that thought die. "I'm sure that if Elise hadn't made that fatal decision, if she'd somehow gotten a second chance . . . She would've been way over Dennis Whitly by now. She would've woke up one day and . . . and saw . . . *you.*"

I had no response to this.

"If Elise had been granted a second chance, I'm sure she wouldn't want anything to do with him these days. She would hate him, just like Mom does, just like I –"

"You people have an odd way of showing hatred, Lisa. You looked like you wanted to fuck him right there onstage, in front of his *ocean* of fans. *He played a mean guitar.* Your groupie mother is more comfortable backstage, of course, and I was sure she was just gonna push him against the wall, drop to her knees and start sucking his dick –"

Lisa slapped me then, hard. She was surprisingly strong, having held a guitar for most of her life. In the small space, the sound of it was like a gun shot.

"Ernie's right. Sometimes you're just dumb."

"Fuck Ernie." I wanted to rub my stinging cheek, but wouldn't give her the satisfaction of seeing that it hurt.

"It was all an act, Cal. Stage presence. Putting on a good show."

A small spark of hope flared in me, like a tiny paper match struck in a deep, black cavern.

"I read your book. Dozens of times. I've always identified with Elise. How could you think that I could suddenly fall for the bastard that betrayed her, that drove her to kill herself? Even if he does *play a mean guitar?* I told you. I've never been much for musicians.

"And Mom – Mom hates his guts. She was just kissing up to him, in case he can do something for the band someday. It was all just part of the act, Cal. Surely, you have to realize that."

She reached across the table for my hands again and this time I allowed it. I remembered breakfast at IHOP with Ernie and Candy and the band – poor Sonny! – after Lisa had kissed me, pressed her flawless body against mine; after our incredible, spontaneous coupling in the bathroom. I remembered how she had effortlessly and utterly ignored me, so much so that I'd convinced myself that she'd regretted what we'd done, that she was going to end it the very next second we were alone.

But she hadn't ended it. "When we were at breakfast, that's when I pretended," she'd told me.

I realized that Lisa had been trained to be a musician her whole life, and more than that, she had been trained to be a *performer.* She had cultivated more than just her singing voice; she had become an actress as well, and a quite capable one, able to mimic whatever emotion was required for the scene.

How disappointed would the crowd have been, had she displayed her dislike for Sonic Daydream's famous frontman, whilst she was onstage with him? How much more had they dug it, believing that there was some May-December hanky-panky going on between the rock god and his nubile young acolyte?

I felt like an ass. "I'm sorry, Lisa. You played it to the nines."

She grinned. "That's what I do, baby. Give the people what they want." She hopped up and plopped down in my lap, put her arms around my neck.

She picked up my beer and sipped it, then set it down firmly. "Jesus Christ and all the saints, Cal! How could you think that I could ever . . . I can't stand him." Her grin turned crafty, and a dangerous, diamond-hard glint flashed in her eyes. "As a matter of fact . . . Pretend I'm the genie in the bottle and can provide your revenge." She kissed my nose. "What would you have me do? What spell would you have me cast to destroy Dennis Whitly?"

Without thinking, I said the first thing that popped into my mind. "Make him impotent." Hardy har har.

Lisa threw back her head and laughed. "So mote it be!" she declared and kept on laughing, so much so that I began to feel uncomfortable at the joy she was taking at the thought of hurting someone I didn't like.

Like I say, I had never hated him, and now that I realized that he had not ensorcelled Lisa after all – that was as clear as glass by her laughter – I still didn't hate him. But her glee, unhinged – for a moment, that was almost as bad as when I was thinking that she wanted him. It showed a cruel streak in her.

But then she squeezed me, and my discomfort was forgotten when she said, “Now kiss me. I love you. You know who I really want.”

I’d never believed in magical spells or witchcraft. Less than three months ago, all the crystal balls and Tarot decks, all the scrying and other dubious forms of divination to which the true believer ascribes – none of that could’ve been able to lead me to believe that I would soon have a beautiful, perfectly delectable eighteen-year-old girl, sitting in my lap, telling me that she loved me, demanding that I love her, and *right now,* once again in this tiny space.

Yet here it all was. I still didn’t believe in witchcraft. But maybe it was possible to shape one’s own destiny, after all.

THIRTY-ONE

The field where the bands had parked their numerous buses and transports was larger at the Just Us Festival. The crowd had been vaster, and now that the show was over, it would take considerably longer for it to dissipate.

Phenex's equipment was already stowed in the van, but Ernie was in no hurry to leave. Being always friendly with the roadies, I saw that they'd helped him out. He and Candy and the band sat on lawn chairs behind the van; Horus was over there with them. There was an orange cooler nearby, together with a small hibachi. No sense fighting the mindless traffic. Let's have a tailgate party!

The inviting smell of hamburgers cooking reached me as we approached, and I realized that the temporary lows and awesome highs of this incredible, rollercoaster of a day had combined to make me ravenously hungry.

While Lisa and I were still some distance away, Ernie arose and walked toward us. I stopped. Lisa squeezed my hand. "Forgive him, for he knew not what he did." A giggle escaped her, and she scuttled away toward the van.

Ernie also stopped, and for several seconds, like gunslingers, we stood facing each other across a distance of perhaps ten feet. Lisa patted his arm as she passed, but said nothing. Candy and the band had fallen silent, again watching and waiting. Roy and James stood, perhaps anticipating that they might have to break up another fist fight between aging rock stars.

But that wasn't going to happen. Most of the umbrage I'd felt at Ernie's outrageous stunt had evaporated. He'd invited Denny to appear because it was better publicity than money could buy for Phenex. There would be an article in the local paper – *Rock Legend Takes the Stage at Just Us Festival, Unannounced* – for the band's sake, I hoped they spelled *Phenex* correctly. Hell, it might even make a few lines in *Rolling Stone.* Candy would be beside herself with glee to see her band's name appear in the sacred mag, even if it was way before their due, incidental to a mention of an infinitely more famous musician.

I hoped that there had been no photographers present, that no reporters had overheard the roadie gossip. Then the headline might be *Geriatric Rockers Brawl at Just Us Festival.* But my brief *disagreement* with Denny hadn't actually escalated to violence, and it had occurred during the headliner's set. I figured that any reporter types would've been out in the crowd then, and would've missed the silly backstage goings-on.

Now Ernie closed the distance between us. He looked down, scuffed the grass with his toe, like a kid. I was reminded of Katie. "I'm sorry about this, dude."

"It's all right, Ernie," I replied, the milk of human kindness, of magnanimity, of being the bigger person, flowing from me. "It was all for the band. I know."

He looked up at me in surprise, instantly grateful. "Did you hear the crowd? Denny playing with them . . . People will remember Phenex."

"Let's hope they remember them without an *o* and an *i.*"

Ernie shrugged. The band's name and its spelling couldn't be helped.

Another thought struck me. "Denny's not planning to . . ."

I couldn't even say it. But it wasn't entirely outside of the realm of possibility. He wouldn't be the first big name to be bitten by the road-bug in his dotage, especially if his old pal Ernie was along for the ride. A new band, new opportunities . . . Who knew what Denny might consider, as long as he could be assured that I wasn't going to be there?

Maybe he'd just call his brother: "Load 'em up and move 'em out, Lenny. Remember that fire-trap we played in Frisco on our first tour? How'd ya like to squeeze your fat ass up on that little stage again, old man?"

But to my immense relief, Ernie shook his head. "It was a one off, dude." He grinned. "History will not repeat itself. I think I just caught him in a bored moment, so it was easy to talk him into it. But now . . ."

"Since you didn't tell him that I was going to be there . . ."

Ernie shrugged again. "Fuck him. He was never a lot of fun anyway, and I don't imagine he's gotten any more so."

It wasn't that Denny had been stern or judgmental. Being married, he just hadn't enjoyed the same kind of fun on the road that Ernie had enjoyed.

The thought occurred to me that Ernie's fun had been curtailed now; there would be no more hot tub adventures in Big Bear for the old groupie-slayer in the foreseeable future, not if Candy had her way. She believed that she had her hooks in him now. She wasn't gonna let Ernie LaBelle out of her sight. I grinned to myself; he was as good as married, just like the brothers Whitly, but not as happily.

I slapped Ernie on the back and we turned toward the van. I realized that my old second-guitar had made as big a fool out of his former frontman as he had of me, by neglecting to tell us that we'd be running into each other. But while Denny would be going back to the same life he'd been living for quite a while now, that life into which boredom might be at last creeping, I, on the other hand . . . Lisa smiled and kissed me on the cheek, handed me a paper plate with a fat, juicy burger on it.

Denny was going back to same-place-same-thing, whereas my life had become a great big bowl of ripe and juicy cherries lately. The sky was the limit. I reflected that maybe I could consider myself kinda-married, too, like Denny and Lenny and completely-reluctant Ernie. But I would give you better odds than Vegas that I was digging it more than the three of them combined.

Ernie accepted a beer from his woman – I again grinned to myself – and regained his lawn chair. Roy formally introduced me to Horus, and told me that Ernie had indeed tapped him to be Phenex's new second-guitar.

Mike's nephew was a roadie no longer. Gratitude fairly oozed from him, seeping out around the Egyptian gods and goddesses, the pyramids and winged thing-a-ma-jigs that he had tattooed in sleeves on both arms. "I told Mr. LaBelle –"

"Christ, will you quit calling me that, Horus?" I couldn't quite tell if his irritation was a put-on or not, because he was looking at his phone and I was unable to make eye contact with him.

"I told Ernie thanks for giving me a chance. You guys have a great band."

Something in my mind again resisted the appellation. *Phenex isn't my band,* I wanted to tell him. But instead I just said thanks.

I sat beside Ernie and took a bite of my burger. He was still immersed in texting, and didn't look at me. The burger was excellent, and I exclaimed, "Who's the great cook?" I was still feeling magnanimous; I knew it was Candy, knew she would appreciate the compliment. She smiled at me, and in the festive afterglow of Phenex's successful performance, I was even able to forget for a moment that I didn't really care for her.

"Hot damn!" Ernie exclaimed, startling everybody. He grinned at me, and his next words gave me a feeling of déjà vu. Moments ago I'd been picturing what Denny might say if he was trying to entice his brother to go back on the road with Phenex: *Remember that fire-trap we played in Frisco on our first tour?*

Ernie said, "Remember that place we played in San Jose on our first tour? The girl in the box office – remember? She wore a gypsy headdress – a big jewel hung down from it, in the middle of her forehead."

Ernie didn't remember the size of the venues, but he remembered the women, at least the odder ones. I didn't recall even seeing this one, but I did remember the club. "I think Lenny told me it burned down. The second time we were in San Jose."

"Oh, yeah?" Ernie couldn't care less about the fate of some dive we'd played a million years ago on our first tour. He was concentrating on his memory of the girl. "This headdress thing . . ." He described it in the air with his hand. "It jingled when she talked. She asked me if I wanted her to read my palm, so I said . . ."

Ernie glanced over at Candy, who frowned back at him. His smile didn't dim; he certainly wasn't going to pretend to be ashamed of his past, not going to start apologizing to her for his adventures, seeing as how she was just another one of the uncounted legions of women who'd gone out of their way to nail him, precisely as had the gypsy fortuneteller. But he did stop relating the details.

He turned his phone around and held it up. "How'd you like to open for The RaceCats in San Jose, dudes?"

Candy made as if she would snatch it from him to read the text, but Ernie snatched it back with a *Just what* in the fuck *do you think you're doing?* look of appalled amazement.

How did that poem go? *What a tangled web we weave, when first we practice monogamy?* I grinned at my own wit.

Ernie's expression was a warning; he was letting baby-mama know that his phone and its contents were sacrosanct. Not only was she gonna get her feelings hurt if she got it into her head to scroll through it; Ernie wouldn't care about that in the least. Her hooks might have penetrated, but they were far from set.

"I'll read it to you. My contact with the promoter –"

Your big fan with the hot tub –

"– says, *Phillip really likes the band.*"

"Who?" Candy asked.

Ernie gave her a withering glance. "Aren't *any* of you people hep?" He winked at me and his grin returned. "Phillip is the front for The RaceCats. My contact says –"

Ernie was good. He didn't say *she says.*

"Phillip really likes the band."

Candy snorted. "What difference does it make if the singer likes us?" She didn't know much about the music business, not nearly as much as she liked to think she did, but she was fairly correct here. Newly signed bands didn't make too many line-up decisions. If that were the case, there would be a lot of cousins' and girlfriends' brothers' bands opening for your favorite act on tour.

Ernie squinted in a kind of pained annoyance. He shook his phone. "May I?"

Candy nodded. They were like a bickering old married couple already. I again smiled to myself at the misfortune of my old friend's predicament.

Ernie again referred to Bianca's text. *"Phillip really likes the band. Chrissy agrees."*

"She's The RaceCats' manager," Horus volunteered.

"The two of them would like to know if you want to open in San Jose. Tomorrow night. And . . ." Ernie paused for dramatic effect. *"The day after that in San Francisco."*

There was a moment of stunned silence, then Candy said, "Denny–"

Ernie shook his head. "I told her, no Denny." The cat was out of the bag now. Ernie's inside man was a woman. "And I told her that we've hired a new second-guitar." He grinned at Horus and the kid returned his grin proudly. Ernie read from his phone. *"Phillip says he's okay with that. Chrissy liked your sound."*

Ernie waited. Candy whooped and hugged Lisa. "Oh, my God! Two more shows!"

"That's what I thought." Ernie pushed a button on his phone and held it up again, displaying an entire screen of tiny type. "I took the liberty of okaying the contract for you. It's not really official, but we can sign it when we get there. It's not much money . . ." Candy whooped again, and Ernie grinned at me. "But we're not in this for the money, now are we?" His money had been made years ago. "We're artists, are we not?"

The departing fan traffic thinned as the sun set, but the party atmosphere intensified backstage. Glen Helen was a campground after all, and even if this particular area probably wasn't designated for camping, some of the bands and a lot of the crew had opted to stay the night and celebrate.

Mike wasn't one of them. He worked for the promoter that worked for EMI that was paying for The RaceCats' tour, just like

Bianca did. He was pretty much as muddy on the connections as Ernie was, but he knew he had to go. The RaceCats had left hours earlier, right after the show, as befitted an up and coming band. They were halfway to San Jose by now.

Mike trundled his ancient truck to a stop in front of our waning tailgate party. The generator and the room air conditioner were lashed down in the bed; there was a piece of cardboard duct-taped over the window of the Scamp. Horus kicked over the mostly cold hibachi and poured the water from the cooler over the coals. He dutifully strapped cooler and grill in beside the generator and the AC.

"Don't forget your suitcase, boy."

As Horus went around and opened the passenger side door, I realized that he was coming home with us. He was a part of Phenex now.

"Take good care of him, Ernie." Mike reached out the window and ruffled his nephew's hair. "Keep him away from the drugs and the loose women."

"We don't do drugs," Lisa said with a smile.

Ernie shook hands with the old roadie. "I'll tell him what he needs to know."

"I'll see you in San Jose."

THIRTY-TWO

We went back to the clinker-brick house. Horus was appropriately awed by the dilapidated grandeur of its sprawling size, suitably grateful when they showed him to his very own room, the one that had been Sonny's. Then he surprised everyone when he volunteered to whip up sandwiches if anyone was still hungry.

"The ritual first," Candy said. She eyed Ernie and me with a kind of disdain. "We must give praise and thanks to Phenex. It's not necessary for you to attend."

"All righty, then," Ernie said, and I followed him down the hall to the kitchen.

He plopped down on the bench and said, "I'll take a ham on rye, Horus, if there's any . . ." He looked around me. "Where's Horus?"

"He stayed out there. For the . . . ritual."

"No shit?" Ernie shook his head in disbelief. "So he's one of them, too?"

"His name's Horus, Ernie."

"So what? My grandfather's name was Horace. He didn't twirl around with a dagger. He didn't invoke the cherubim and praise demons."

"The archangels."

"The what?"

I sat down across from him and asked Ok Google to tell me about the Egyptian deity known as Horus. I showed Ernie the picture of the falcon god, indicated the spelling, and he again shook his head. I quoted Wikipedia: *"Horus is one of the most significant deities in ancient Egyptian religion, who was worshipped from at least the late Pre-dynastic period through to Greco-Roman times."*

Ernie was unimpressed. "Don't quote me on this or anything, Cal, because you know I'm not sure, but I think all that was a long time ago, and therefore interests me . . . why, not at all."

I opened another page, entitled The Goode Witch. It featured a black background and a purple font that seemed to pulsate, or maybe it was just my old eyes. I informed Ernie, *"Modern witchcraft encompasses reverence for many and varied pantheons; one of the oldest is that of ancient Egypt."*

I pressed the screen for another link. *"The Eye of Horus –"* I showed him the picture *"– is often used as a talisman to keep negative energies away and attract positive energies."*

Ernie rolled his eyes.

"Oh, here's one that mentions both Horus *and* Phenex!"

It was mysteriously called Illuminati – 1b, and turned out to be a Christian site. I read aloud to my old second-guitar: *"Little do young Rock and Rollers know they are deceived by an unseen host of agents of the Devil."*

This kind of religious bullshit amused me even more than did the earnest occult sites, but Ernie just rolled his eyes again. *"There is absolutely nothing romantic about Satan,"* I told him. *"He will give some power to work miracles, but this is his way of deceiving. So to help a Bible student avoid falling into any of Satan's traps, one can learn from the Scriptures and from those whom Satan has already used, how not to become another one of his victims."*

"Oh, yeah?" Ernie said with mock interest. "What does it say about Phenex?"

Like the band's contract for the next two gigs, the font was tiny and closely spaced, not to mention boring and repetitive. So I put *Phenex* in the search box.

"Now, it just so happens that one of the old spellings of Phoenix is Phenex or Fenex in Greek transliterations. Like the name Lucifer, Phoenix means 'Shining One.'"

"Didn't we already know that? Demons, devils, *the* devil. What difference does it make?"

"It goes on to say that the equivalents for F-E-N-E-X in Numerology add up to 666."

"That book – *777*. It was about Numerology. I think. It was absolute gibberish."

I skimmed the rest of the page, which bashed peacocks and the Pope, NBC and ABC (that's where Horus and his all-seeing eye were mentioned), astrology, secret societies, and the Age of Aquarius. It warned of the evils of Spiritualism and the coming New World Religion.

I glanced up from my phone. Ernie had his head on his hand, pretending to be asleep. Now he pretended to snore. I nudged him, and he said, "Oh, I'm sorry. I seem to have nodded right the hell off." He grinned. "Remember the bumper sticker Lenny had on his guitar case?"

I nodded, and as our own little coven, their prayers concluded, trouped back into the kitchen, he said, "I think it sums up our present situation, my brutha."

I glanced at my young lover, and she smiled at me. Lenny's bumper sticker had read, *Yes, I'm afraid it's true. I've fallen in with the wrong crowd.*

Everyone passed on Horus's offer to make sandwiches, opting instead for slices of Candy's three different kinds of pies. Then showers were taken and love was made (where appropriate). But everyone was too keyed up to sleep, and by midnight, everyone had reassembled in the kitchen, and were once again considering the pies.

"Let's see what this trip is gonna look like." Ernie's phone told him that it was five hours and forty-two minutes to San Jose from Riverside. Its optimism made him giggle. Phenex went on at eight o'clock tonight. "I want to be on the road no later than noon."

"It's only an hour or so to Frisco from there," Candy said.

"Right. We can drive on through after the show." His calloused, guitarist's forefinger flicked across the phone's screen. "I'll get us a hotel. Then we can sleep in in the morning, maybe sightsee." I was amazed to see him smile warmly at Candy, his perpetual state of mild annoyance with her seemingly fled in the interim since we'd returned from the show. I supposed that quality time had its merits.

"I haven't been home to Frisco in a long time." She returned his smile and squeezed his hand.

"We should try to get some sleep," Lisa said.

"I'm not sleepy," Horus said. He grinned at each of us in turn. "I'll sleep when I'm dead."

I doubted seriously if the kid was quoting the old Bon Jovi tune, but hey, you never know. "If *I'm gonna live while I'm alive,* I gotta sleep now," I said. No recognition. *I'll sleep when I'm dead* was just an expression to Horus.

Ernie grinned. "Go get my axe out of the van then, tough guy. You can listen to the demo and rehearse." Lisa rolled her eyes, but Ernie shook his head. "No amp. I wanna get some sleep, too."

THIRTY-THREE

Phenex's first road trip began right on time. The seven of us could've crammed into the van with the instruments; there was a third seat that could've been folded up. But it would've been a tight squeeze, and Ernie LaBelle hadn't clawed his way to the celestial heights of rock and roll to be stuffed into a van in his old age. Instead he and Candy followed in the 911.

Perhaps I was only projecting my past perceptions onto my old friend. Ernie had never done the all-inclusive, band-plus-instruments-in-one-transport, painfully small-time method of touring, like I had, once upon a time, with those forever-unknowns that called themselves Scranton. Maybe he would've been down to rough it, to slum it with his new band. It was only two shows, then back home, after all.

But as we were preparing to leave Riverside, it seemed that the old groupie-slayer was in a mood for some alone-time with his groupie: Ernie seemed positively friendly toward Candy. *Maybe all this clean living's gone to his head,* I thought.

Ernie had discovered a ready-made family just a few short months ago; he'd never sought such a lifestyle. But like other things found serendipitously, maybe it was better than whatever it was he had been seeking out of life. Ernie's philosophy had always been *It's not having what you want, it's wanting what you've got;* he'd just been far more fortunate than most. Ernie LaBelle had always already had what a lot of dudes wanted, all their lives. So maybe he was ready to settle down with what the average Joe had. I couldn't say as I was overly thrilled with his choice, but who was I to judge?

I didn't mind riding in the van, because I was with Lisa. We didn't put up the third seat; James drove, Roy sat beside him on the bench seat, and Horus put a pillow against the passenger side window and went to sleep. Amp-less, he had practiced for the remainder of the night to Phenex's demo, and being a roadie, he knew how to get his beauty sleep in a moving vehicle.

I sat behind him and looked out at the road, as I had done on countless tour buses, foreign and domestic, for twelve years. Lisa reclined with her head in my lap, playing games on her phone, *while the miles rolled away.*

Remembering the old days, I asked her, "Do you happen to have *Tetris* on there?"

She held it up to show me that she was playing precisely that game. Like father, like daughter. I remembered Lenny always yelling at Ernie to turn that *mindless, electronic, Russian shit off.* At least Lisa didn't subject us to the sound effects.

Once we passed Gorman, we stopped to stretch and get something to eat. On the way out of the restaurant, my phone rang.

The tinny electronic signal was a surprise. Who could be calling me? Damn near all the people I knew, at least the ones most likely to call, were right there. Sure enough, it was another unfamiliar number. I said hello and a woman's voice asked if I was Cal Bascomb. I said that I was.

"My name's Diane, Mr. Bascomb. I'm a nurse at the Desert Regional Medical Center in Palm Springs. I'm calling on behalf of Mrs. Whitly."

Mrs. Whitly? Why would Sophia be in Palm Springs? And why would she be having a nurse call me? There was no possible way that Sophia could have my number, nor would she call it if she did. Sophia was more likely to dial up the demon Phenex than she was to summon me. But there was no other Mrs. Whitly; Denny and Lenny's parents, like my own, had passed years ago. Unless –

"You mean Barbie?"

"Yes, Mr. Bascomb. Barbie Whitly."

So they *had* gotten married, sometime in the intervening years. I'd missed that, too.

"I'm afraid there's been an accident."

The six most dreaded words in the English language. An anonymous nurse on the phone, a sad cop at the door in the middle of the night. *I'm afraid there's been an accident.*

"Is she all right? Is Lenny –"

"Mrs. Whitly has a broken arm and some cuts. Mr. Whitly . . . Mr. Whitly's in a coma, Mr. Bascomb. The doctor thinks he suffered a stroke. He was driving . . . Mrs. Whitly would like you to come right away."

"We're out of town, Diane. Tell her we'll be there as soon as we can."

"I'd advise you to hurry, Mr. Bascomb."

I told the nurse again that we'd be there as soon as we could, and thanked her for the call.

The band and Candy and Ernie were chatting cheerfully. Lisa was the first to notice my shocked expression, and she touched my arm and asked me with concern what was wrong.

"Lenny had a stroke." I glanced past her to Ernie. "He's in a coma. We have to go back."

To my utter amazement, Ernie looked at Candy, as if for guidance, as if he was become one of her minions, like James and Roy, like the late Sonny, like the newcomer Horus. My mouth fell open in disbelief.

"Go back?" Candy said with an offended giggle. "We can't go back. We're opening for The RaceCats tonight."

I thought for a moment that she had somehow missed what I'd said. But no – she just didn't care. I spared her a glance as if she was an insect, just that insignificant. If she thought I was gonna go on to San Jose with her no-talent band while my friend was lying in a hospital bed in the desert – I couldn't believe that the words had actually come out of her ridiculous, scarlet slash of a mouth. At her preposterous statement, she had ceased to exist to me.

Ernie hesitated for another heartbeat, still looking at her.

"Of course you have to go, Cal," Lisa said at last. "Give him the keys, Dad."

Ernie blinked in confusion, as if he had suddenly awakened and didn't know where he was. "Of course. We . . . we have to go see Lenny." A dark guilt stained his eyes. "Let me get the paperwork out of the car for them, Cal. Then we'll . . . go."

Candy huffed, and stomped off toward the Porsche. I wished mightily that her favorite demon would open up a chasm in the parking lot and suck her down to hell with him.

"Hold on just a second, Cal," Ernie begged, and chased after her. Roy and James and Horus, wordless, expressionless, followed, and climbed obediently back into the van. *To await direction,* I thought with disgust.

Lisa hugged me and asked for details. I told her what the nurse had said, all the while watching Ernie and Candy. She alternately leaned against the Porsche with her arms crossed resentfully across her chest, or gesticulated angrily at him. Ernie only shrugged, shook his head. He reached into the car and held the paperwork out to her, the directions to the venue, the hotel reservations, all the dead-tree necessities that he had carefully printed out at home. Elise used to handle all these kinds of tiresome nuts and bolts, and it was all on Ernie's phone, now. But he liked to see it in black and white.

"You understand, don't you?" I asked Lisa, prepared, resigned to dismiss her as summarily as I had her mother, if she didn't understand. If she made one syllable of protest, she wasn't the person

I thought I knew. She wasn't the one I thought I loved. If she didn't understand that I had to go see my old friend in the hospital, that there would be other shows – then she was just a heartless, unfeeling, ambitious bitch like her mother.

But Lisa understood. She nodded, hugged me again. "Mom's just . . ." She glanced at her mother, shook her head in embarrassment. "We'll be okay." Her big blue eyes were solemn and sympathetic. "I love you, Cal. I hope everything'll be all right. Call me when you get there, let me know what's going on."

"I love you, too."

Ernie squealed the Porsche in a tight circle and slid to a stop beside me. Heads turned in the restaurant. "Let's go," he said tightly, not looking at me. Lisa would've given him a kiss on the cheek, but he wouldn't look at her either. I hugged her quickly, and got into the car.

Ernie didn't speak for some time, weaving the 911 in and out of traffic, pushing it effortlessly into the eighties and nineties. When traffic accumulated, he downshifted savagely. When we slowed to a crawl, he glanced over at me with that odd mixture of confusion and dark guilt.

"I'm sorry, Cal." There was a touch of anguish in his voice, so foreign there that I blinked in surprise. "I don't know what I was thinking, why I . . . hesitated like that. Lenny's like blood to us, and she's just . . ." He shook his head. "I'm sorry."

I wanted to tell him that it was okay, that here we were on our way now, but the words were a long time in coming. His hesitation had indeed shocked me, the idea that any thought of Phenex and Candy and their penny-ante gig would cross his mind before Leonard Whitly, our lifelong friend. But it had passed quickly enough, and Ernie was sorry about it. He was ashamed. Finally, I said, "Just don't get us killed on the way."

A slim space between cars opened up, and he upshifted and shot the Porsche into it. "At one with the road, baby." He hurtled through another tiny hole, then upshifted again. The car leapt forward and we were free of the bottleneck. *"If you were a car,"* he said, paraphrasing the old commercial. I'd heard it before, and I smiled at him. *"You'd be a Por-sha."*

Ernie grinned back at me, then the fear and the worry about what we were speeding toward clouded his face. "Tell me again what they said."

I repeated the scanty details, and he suggested that I try calling Barbie to get an update.

"Oh, Cal!" she breathed shakily.

"We're on our way, Barbie," I assured her. I put her on speaker. "Are you all right? Tell me what happened."

"I've got a broken arm, some scratches on my head. But Lenny . . ." She sobbed, then took a shuddery breath and fought back the tears. "We were on our way to the feed store –"

"In the Jag?" Ernie asked.

"No, we were in the pickup. We'd probably be dead if we were in the Jag. No airbags . . ." She paused, sighed. "Lenny had been feeling dizzy, on and off, but he said he was okay then. We were heading down the road, talking, laughing. Then suddenly, he grabbed at his chest; he stomped on the brakes, and I was flung forward, against the dash. I hit my head. My seatbelt must not've been latched all the way. It seemed like he was having some kind of convulsion, Cal, like he'd lost all control. He hit the gas again, then the truck veered off the road. We crashed into the ditch, and the truck rolled over on its side.

"The next thing I knew, they were pulling me out . . . They'd already cut Lenny loose, the ambulance was gone. I was hysterical. They told me he wasn't dead, but I didn't believe them. They put me in another ambulance. I passed out again, or they gave me something. I woke up in the hospital and they'd already set my arm. I don't remember any of that.

"Diane, the nurse . . . She put me in a wheelchair and took me up to ICU. I told the doctor what happened, how he'd grabbed at his chest, but he said it wasn't a heart attack. It was a stroke, Cal. The doctor says he'll probably come out of it, that he might be okay, but he's . . . he's so still, Cal! And he won't wake up!" She started to sob again.

Ernie thundered past a semi. "Where's Denny?"

"Denny's in with him now."

Great, I thought. *Just what the doctor ordered.* I hoped Denny would be able to put aside our differences for his brother's sake; I hoped there wouldn't be another showdown at the hospital.

"We'll be there in a little while, Barbie. You just hold on. But we gotta go now." Ernie gestured for me to hang up. He pointed behind us and slowed the Porsche, moved into the slow lane, then off onto the shoulder. I looked behind us and saw the lights. We were getting pulled over.

"Okay, Ernie," Barbie sniffled. "I'll see you soon."

I clicked *End* and steeled myself for this next ordeal. Ernie asked me to get the registration out of the glovebox as the CHP cop approached.

But the bad luck that had so suddenly descended on the members of an old band called Sonic Daydream lifted somewhat. The cop turned out to be a big fan, and for the price of a few selfies with the rock stars and their Porsche, a few autographs, he didn't write Ernie a ticket. He was as concerned for Lenny's well-being as if he knew him, and I again marveled at that fan phenomenon. Their favorite actors and musicians – they were like old friends in the minds of fans. The cop even went so far as to tell us that he would radio ahead, and tell his fellows in law enforcement to let us pass unhindered.

"Just try to keep it in the low eighties," he advised.

Ernie said thanks and asked for his card, promising him a boxed set of our CDs, autographed.

THIRTY-FOUR

They had moved Lenny out of ICU.

I knew we had found his room because I saw Barbie and Sophia sitting in the hall outside. I stopped when Sophia glanced coldly at me. She used her cane to stand, and Ernie stepped up to embrace her.

Barbie arose and hugged me tightly with her left arm. "I'm so glad you're here, Cal."

There was a butterfly bandage on a mean-looking cut over her right eye, and her right arm was casted up from just below the shoulder; her thumb and fingertips, bruised and discolored, peeped out at the bottom. Someone had gotten her some clothes. I didn't think they were her own, because they seemed too big for her. Her face was pinched and colorless. She seemed grayer, like she had aged a decade overnight.

"He's awake now," she said, and relief washed over me. "Denny's in there with him."

I watched Sophia sit back down and fold her hands over the handle of her cane. She would carry it with her forever – the reminder of the injuries she'd suffered when Elise had driven her husband's car over that cliff.

Sophia didn't look at me. Ernie went into Lenny's room.

"I want to prepare you, Cal," Barbie said softly. "Lenny's awake. They've got him sitting up, but he's got all kinds of tubes and wires . . . The doctor explained . . . His face is slack on the right side. He has no control on that side yet. He can't walk or talk . . . Oh, Cal!" She hugged me.

Why I had become Barbie's rock in this tragedy, instead of her brother-in-law, I had not a clue. But she clung to me. She was piteously grateful that I was there.

"What did the doctor say about . . . Is he going to recover?"

As if on cue, the doctor emerged from Lenny's room and caught Mrs. Whitly's eye. I was left standing alone in the hall, mere steps from the other Mrs. Whitly.

To my surprise, she said my name, gestured for me to sit beside her. Then she got directly to the point. "I realize that now is really not the time to bring up the past, Cal. But there are things I've been wanting to say to you all these years. You were Elise's friend. Her only friend."

You were certainly no friend to her, I thought. Sophia could've sent her sister home from the road, in the beginning, before the obsession became so entrenched, before Elise became indispensable to the band. But she hadn't. Secure in Denny's love and loyalty, she'd allowed the love-sick kid to tag along.

"I want to thank you for being her friend."

I nodded, accepting her gratitude, sensing there was going to be a catch to it. Regardless, it was too little and way, entirely too late. "Like you say, Sophia, now's not the time –"

She shook her head, just once, resolutely. She held up her hand to silence me. "There are some things that you don't know about Elise, Cal. About our family history."

A tear traced its way down Sophia's pale cheek. Like Denny, she had aged well. She had kept her trim figure, and had laugh lines around her mouth and the inevitable crow's feet, but her forehead was as smooth as a girl's. She dyed her hair the same blonde of her youth, a subtle, honey-tinged shade. Despite the worry and sadness of the situation, Sophia looked great.

It had been a kind of asceticism that had kept me fit; my solitary, hermit-like existence. But it had been all that clean living that had kept Denny and Sophia looking youthful, all that true love. I thought fleetingly that maybe it was my turn now.

"And once I tell you, I think maybe you'll understand. The way Elise felt about Denny . . . There wasn't anything he could do –"

"Sophia."

We looked up. Denny was frowning sternly, the same expression he'd worn when he saw me standing backstage at the Just Us Festival. But there was no surprise now. My presence had been expected this time, and to his credit, Denny's eyes showed no resentment that I was there. I'd once been his brother's best friend, and I had a right to see him. Denny didn't begrudge me that.

It didn't dim any of his own dislike for me, however. His brother in a hospital bed wasn't going to point up to Denny how short life really was, wasn't going to move him to forgive and forget. I figured that was *his* right. I wasn't inclined to forgive or forget, either, not even with his lady-wife trying to explain to me how *there wasn't anything he could do* about Elise's obsession with him. That was all bullshit. He hadn't even tried to do anything about it.

I finally got to touch him again, after all these years, Elise had said in her final voicemail. *We were finally alone . . .* And then he'd told her that it would never be just the two of them, and then she had driven his big, black, luxury sedan over the side of Mullholland Highway.

And now her sister was trying to tell me that none of that had been her husband's fault. *The way Elise felt about Denny . . . There wasn't anything he could do . . .*

Right. And I'm a Chinese jet pilot.

Sophia obediently joined her husband. Denny turned his back on me and they stepped over to say a few words to the doctor and Barbie. I went in to see Lenny.

He was sitting up, as Barbie had said, and he was hooked up to various machines. But he was breathing on his own; if there had been any kind of a respirator, it was gone now. The left side of his face quirked up in a signal of welcome. He gave me a kind of wink. The right side of his face remained immobile, almost corpse-like.

I took his right hand. Ernie shook his head and gestured for me to go around to the other side of the bed. I'd forgotten already that Lenny hadn't regained feeling in his right side yet.

I glanced at Ernie as I went around: his face was white, almost as slack as our stricken friend's. Happy-go-lucky, ain't-life-grand? big-hearted Ernie LaBelle was having a hard time disguising the shock and horror and grief that he was feeling at seeing Leonard Whitly laid so low.

I said, "Hey, Denny wants to talk to you." Ernie nodded, not able to hide his gratitude at this opportunity to escape. He patted Lenny clumsily on the knee and fled.

I was a better actor than my old second-guitar. I was also appalled at Lenny's pitiful condition, but I was tougher than Ernie. His parents had both died peacefully, mercifully, slipping away to God's judgment in their sleep. My mom had suffered a stroke, similar to Lenny's, though more severe. She had lingered for several days before another one finally claimed her, and I had sat by her bedside and held her hand, looked into her still-alive eyes in her already-dead face.

So I smiled, put on the cheer for Lenny, as I had for Mom. Showing my own pain and fear was a kind of selfishness, and it surely wasn't going to help him.

"Damn, dude. I know Phenex sucks, but you didn't have to go to all this trouble just to avoid their gig."

He gave me that wonky little smile and wink again and squeezed my hand. His grip was strong on the left side, and it gave me a little hope that he might recover, that he might just walk out of here under his own steam.

I talked inanities about the band, told him in a low conspiratorial whisper that it had been Ernie's legendary way with the fans that had secured the two gigs in town. I told him that I suspected that it was the same that had also gotten them the two shows on the road, and Lenny laughed silently.

A nurse brought in a tray of food, all soft: mashed potatoes and a clear soup, some kind of juice and something that might have been applesauce. She set it up in front of Lenny, then took his hand from me and put the spoon into it.

He looked at her, then looked at me.

"He's not left –"

"He is for right now." The nurse smiled and patted him on the shoulder. "I know you can do it, Mr. Whitly."

She turned and with a look, said, *Or you can feed him,* and left the room. She hadn't checked any of the machines, so I thought that was a good sign. Maybe Lenny was gonna be all right.

He tossed the spoon onto the tray and pushed it out of the way. I thought about chiding him, telling him that he needed to eat, to build up his strength, all the platitudes that leap to mind when someone's in the hospital. But I had to admit that none of it looked very appetizing, not to someone used to Barbie's farm cooking, and I wasn't his mother. I was his friend. I made a joke about the food and asked what I could get for him.

Lenny formed his left hand around a non-existent guitar pick and made a strumming motion across his chest. The gesture was unmistakable: God's bass player wanted his instrument. I grinned. Lenny made a writing gesture, and I opened the little drawer in the stand beside the bed.

There was Lenny's wallet and his cellphone, but no pen or pad. I felt around in the drawer a little more – it didn't open all the way due to some kind of machine in front of it. My fingers scraped across something. Curious, I pulled on it, and was amazed, and utterly, to come out with a medallion, just like the one Roy and James wore, and poor, dead Sonny, and Sonic Daydream's famous second-guitar.

I held it up. Inexplicably, it was blackened on both sides, as if it had been passed through an open flame. I blinked at him, astonished. "Where did you get this?"

With only one working eyebrow, Lenny communicated, *Where do you think?*

"What happened to it?"

Lenny shrugged, pantomimed. He grabbed his chest, closed his eyes, fell back on the pillow. He was telling me that he didn't know what had happened to the medal, that all he knew was that he'd been wearing it when he'd had his stroke.

"It's supposed to be a good luck charm," I said with a grin, and held it out to him. "You want me to put it back on you?"

A flash of fear crossed the animated side of his face, then disappeared into the slack side. He shook his head.

"Christ, Cal," Barbie said as she re-entered the room. "Throw that ugly thing away."

"Where did you –"

"Marcie gave them to Lenny, when we came to hear the band." She rolled her eyes.

"Candy."

"Whatever. You keep it." She snatched the medallion from my hand, and snuffed it and its chain into my pocket. I felt my own flash of unreasonable fear, remembered Sonny's words: *Just don't take it. Don't carry it, don't put it around your neck –*

Barbie shook her head. "I can't stand all that new age, hippie Wiccan crap, Cal. My roommate in college, *Ahhhn-drea.* She was all about the Earth Mother. She shared all that out-of-date, free-love shit with all comers." I expected Barbie to grin, then, but she didn't. "Until one of them beat her almost to death. Strictly *Looking for Mr. Goodbar* stuff. Her crystal ball didn't warn her about that, and her goddess didn't save her."

She dismissed all of witchcraft, all of Lisa's and Candy's and Andrea's and the band Phenex's beliefs with a wave of her hand. She smiled at her love, *her husband.* "They're gonna let you go home soon, baby."

Barbie kissed him gently on the mouth, then pulled the tray back. She picked up the spoon and made as if she would feed him, but Lenny shook his head. He didn't want me to see that.

Ernie peeked his head into the room and called me. He smiled painfully at his old friend and his wife, and nodded for me to join him in the hall.

"There's nothing more we can do here, Cal," he whispered. The doctor was gone, and I noticed that Denny and Sophia had also disappeared. "I have to get back to the –"

"Jesus, Ernie!" I whispered back. "Barbie's gonna need some help. They're gonna cut him loose but he's gonna be in a wheelchair for a while –"

"It's just one more show, Cal. I'm already missing tonight's." When my expression of amazement didn't change, he showed a shade of resentment. "Lenny would understand."

"You go then. Take me back to Riverside to get my car."

Ernie's eyes were pleading with me; he was at war with himself. "I'll be back as soon as I can."

He was right and he was wrong. There wasn't anything he could do for Lenny; Phenex needed him. His old friend would appreciate his smiling face; Phenex would be all right on their own. But I didn't want him to feel any guiltier about the difficulty of his decisions.

"Go tell 'em good-bye, Ernie." *I'm not going in there while you explain it to Barbie, however.*

While Ernie made his excuses, I stood alone in the hall and thought about what Sophia had said to me earlier, how none of her sister's obsession with her husband had been his fault. I thought that whatever happened for the rest of our lives, this point would always stand between us. It would never go away, never be forgotten; bygones would never, ever be bygones between Denny and Sophia and myself.

I put my cheerful face on again and went back in to say goodbye to Barbie and Lenny. His goodbyes said, Ernie took my place in the hall.

"Ernie has a meeting with destiny in Frisco tomorrow night, but I say, ya seen one mediocre act, ya seen 'em all." The left side of Lenny's mouth quirked up; Barbie looked at the floor, chagrined that I would be so straightforward about Phenex's lack of talent, embarrassed that she agreed with me.

"I'm gonna go back to Riverside, then home and get some sleep. I'll leave you here with Barbie and all the pretty nurses, Lenny, because if I stayed, why . . . they might just ignore you." We all smiled at the ridiculousness of that. "Call me when you're ready to go home. I understand you need a ride, seeing as how you totaled the pick-up."

Barbie squeezed Lenny's hand, then went out into the hall with me. Ernie had begun to pace. "Call me when they're ready to release him," I told her again.

"I appreciate it so much, Cal." She hugged me. "The doctor says he's gonna have to have speech therapy, rehabilitation."

"But he's gonna be all right, isn't he?" The naked pleading in Ernie's voice cut me. "He's not gonna stay . . . like . . . like he is now? He's gonna get better?" He looked hopefully at me. "Denny said that the doctor told him that it had to've been a stroke, even though they couldn't find anything on the scan now –"

"Yeah," Barbie agreed. "That's what he said. They want to run more tests, but he said it wasn't a heart attack, that everything's functioning normally now. There's no discernable brain damage, even though he's . . . he's still . . ."

"So he's gonna be all right." Ernie was trying to convince himself, as well as Barbie.

I could tell – if Lenny wasn't gonna be all right, if he was going to spend the rest of his days in a wheelchair, unable to talk or walk – Ernie wouldn't be able to face that. He was a good guy, big-hearted, and Lenny was his friend, but on this front, Ernie lacked strength. He was a coward. He couldn't bear to see his friend as a speechless cripple. He wouldn't be able to bring himself to visit, to watch the inevitable deterioration. Ernie would slowly or probably quickly withdraw, and he would hate himself for it.

"We'll be back the day after tomorrow. I'll come and see how he's doing," he promised. But I knew that something would come up. When and if Lenny was up and around again . . . But until then, Ernie would be too busy for a visit. He just couldn't bear it.

For the first twenty minutes of the ride back to Riverside, Ernie begged me to reassure him that Lenny was going to recover. "He'll be able to walk and talk again soon, right? And ride his horses and play his bass?"

I knew that the fine motor skills were the last things to return after a stroke. Sometimes they never returned.

Ernie caught my frown. "He'll die if he can't play guitar, Cal."

I opened my mouth to object, to say that Lenny still had Barbie and those black and white horses, that there was a very good chance that he'd bounce back and resume life as he'd always known it. But I closed my mouth again, didn't say anything. Because while all that was true – Lenny might even play his guitar again – the chances were just as good that he wouldn't, and regardless, he'd probably not ever be God's bass player again.

All these maybe-facts were depressing, so Ernie changed the subject. He told me his immediate plans: would I take him to the airport? He was going to catch the next red-eye to Frisco and meet

Phenex there, then drive back with them after the show. And he had other news.

"I got another text from Bianca. She said that if things go well tonight and tomorrow, she might be able to get them in to open for The RaceCats in Vegas."

"When?"

"End of the week sometime. In fact, she said she might be able to get them on for the rest of the tour. Eight or nine dates."

I was amazed, because like I've said, in my humble opinion, Phenex just wasn't that good. I had not as yet had a chance to hear The RaceCats, either; maybe nobody was any good anymore. But EMI hadn't become a recording industry giant by signing poor bands. Maybe my tastes were outdated.

But on the other hand, Ernie had said that Bianca wasn't A&R; maybe she was listening to the more experienced opinions of Chrissy, The RaceCats' manager. Or maybe Bianca's affection for Ernie LaBelle was clouding her judgment. Either way, Phenex needed to take whatever they could get. Sometimes luck was as important as talent in this business, especially when a band was just starting out.

"Any talk of signing them?"

Ernie shook his head. "Not yet."

Ex-groupie favors aside, that would be the real test.

"The rental fees on that van are gonna bankrupt you," I commented.

Ernie shrugged. "We'll see how it goes. Maybe we'll pick 'em up something when they get back."

You got a mouse in your pocket, Kemosabe? I still resisted that *we.* Phenex was his band, not mine.

THIRTY-FIVE

It was past midnight when I got back to the McMansion. I was exhausted after covering what seemed like a zillion miles of California freeway: halfway to San Jose, then all the way to Palm Springs; back to Riverside, then to Ontario to drop Ernie at the airport, then back home to Temecula.

The hot jets from the shower helped clear the stiffness considerably, but still I reflected that I was too old for this shit. If Phenex was gonna go on the road, Ernie was going to indeed have to rent them a nice little bus. Maybe I'd be able to sleep on it now, even though I'd never been able to sleep much on the buses in the old days.

Despite being bone tired, I dreamed.

The demon Phenex had been described on the internet as a big black bird, like the more commonly-known, rising-from-its-own-ashes entity, the one spelled with an *o* and an *i.* He was said to have the sweet voice of a singing child, all the better to entice the unwary close to his mouth so that he might devour them.

But my mind gave him the more common form of the red-skinned, horned, Hollywood-style devil, complete with furry goat's legs, cloven hooves, and the inevitable forked tail.

In my dream, he was sitting on a barstool, tuning Ernie's red Charvel, like Perry the roadie had done in the old days. He looked up at my appearance and smiled, displaying jagged, snaggle teeth. He took a guitar pick out of his mouth and said, "'S'up, Cal?" personably enough. His voice was indeed low and melodic.

"'S'up, Phenex?" my dream-self replied. I wasn't afraid, or even amazed. It all seemed the most natural thing in the world, this manifestation of the band's namesake demon, the fact that he was tuning Ernie's axe, the idea that I was conversing with him. It was all *no thang.* You know how it is in dreams.

"Fame awaits." Ernie's words, just before the band had taken the stage at Rock Invades Riverside. "It's just around the corner now."

"Ya think so, Demon?" my dream-self retorted saucily. "I dunno. I think your band sucks."

He laughed, and it was the expected, devilish bass rumble, not childlike at all. "They won't be the first to succeed because of assistance from the forces unseen. Know thee not that Lars Ulrich sold his soul for metal immortality?"

"But Metallica didn't suck," I insisted.

The demon shrugged. "All that is immaterial," he declared, then repeated, "Fame awaits my band."

"It's Ernie's band."

He laughed again. "Ernie's mine."

I remembered Ernie's confusion, his guilt, and Trent Reznor sung in my head: *I broke apart my insides; I've got no soul to sell . . .*

But all that was just ridiculous. My old second-guitar was no demon worshipper. My dream-self repeated Ernie's words: "Yeah, that only works if you believe in it in the first place, right? Like voodoo dolls? Ernie LaBelle makes his own luck, Phenex. He doesn't need help from the forces unseen."

Phenex smiled, and like the ghost he was, Sonny coalesced out of thin air at his side. My mind showed him as he must have been after the accident: his hair was matted with blood; one side of his face was crushed. I'm sure I groaned in my sleep from the horror of it, tried to wake up. But I remained entrenched in the dream, because another part of my mind wanted to hear him speak again.

But Sonny just repeated the words he'd already said to me: "Ernie's already in way over his head. He just doesn't know it yet." Then, mercifully, he disappeared.

The demon next repeated Candy's words. "Phenex will succeed. Some prophecies have been fulfilled. Others await fruition. Rituals must be performed, and sacrifices must of course be made."

Now Lisa and Candy herself appeared at Phenex's side. He set Ernie's axe down on a stand that hadn't been there a moment before, and he put one beefy red arm around both of them. The three of them smiled at me.

"This one is also mine." He extended a lengthy tongue, reminiscent of Gene Simmons', and licked Candy on the cheek. She giggled. "She has served me willingly, eagerly, since girlhood. It was I helped her get this one." He smiled at Lisa and she returned his smile.

"'Twas me that revealed to Lisa what she is; 'twas me showed them both their path to immortality. Lisa retains her loyalty to me – that is inviolate. But in this incarnation, the rest of her is yours. I give her to thee."

Lisa approached my dream-self and put her arms around my neck. It was very real: I could feel the press of her hot flesh; I could smell her.

Again Phenex spoke. "I invite you to join us, Calvin Bascomb. Fame awaits. You, too, are already halfway mine. All that remains is for you to give yourself over." A chain and another copy of that vaunted good-luck charm appeared in his taloned fist. It glinted dully as he held it out to me.

Again, Lisa repeated words she'd said before. "The forces unseen aren't generous. But they can be persuaded, their favors bought with the proper sacrifices." Then Sonny's words: "The cards begin to fall. The day of reckoning draws nigh, the season of cosmic revenge."

"Revenge?" I asked again. "Against who? For what?"

There was a chime then, echoing, hollow. Like all this collection of words, it repeated, and I snapped awake.

It was the doorbell.

THIRTY-SIX

The doorbell sounded again and again, maddeningly insistent, and I got out of bed and threw on some clothes to go and make it stop.

Stomping down the stairs, irritated, I reviewed the strange dream, then dismissed it. It had been nothing but a collection of statements I'd heard before, nothing but witchy bullshit, true-believer's mumbo-jumbo, collated. No revelations from the *unseen forces* had been revealed, because I didn't believe in the unseen forces.

And because I was an unbeliever, the dream was absurd, laughable to me. Phenex had borne an uncanny resemblance to the cartoonish representation of Satan in *The Pick of Destiny,* and my mind had just given me back annoying facts I already knew: Candy worshipped a demon, truly believed that he would bring her so-so band fame, if she made the proper sacrifices. Lisa also believed it, and that was all good for them.

Ernie was indeed in over his head, but not in any soul-owning, hellbound manner, as Phenex had suggested. The fame that Candy thought she saw on the horizon, the prophecies she believed fulfilled on that score (because of this string of unlikely gigs for the band) – none of that had happened because of any sacrifices or the demon's influence. All these seeming miracles had come to pass because of a chance meeting: an old rock star's enduring appeal to an old fan, now matured into a woman of some influence with EMI and The RaceCats' tour.

And I thought that Ernie was going to have to service that valuable relationship to assure its continuance, or maybe Phenex would find themselves *not* opening for The RaceCats in Vegas. Ernie would have to take a little side trip to Big Bear again, or Phenex would not be taking their rented van on the rest of that eight-city tour. Ernie may have sold his soul, or at least pawned it, but it wasn't to the cloven-hoofed devil of my silly dream. And it wouldn't be Phenex's eternal wrath he'd have to suffer if the reasons behind the band's sudden bankability were revealed. It would be Candy's.

I opened the door. Katie was about to push the bell again. I resisted the overwhelming urge to demand, *What the fuck?* of her. But I stopped myself, thinking that using profanity with children might damn me to join Phenex and his laughable minions after all.

"I've got a surprise for you, Cal!" she enthused, jumping from one foot to the other.

"I'm about worn out on surprises, Katie. It's gonna have to wait on coffee." I held the door open, and she ducked under my arm and into the house.

Katie knew the way to the kitchen; the layout of my house was not too much different from her own, and she had been here before. Like a dutiful fellow musician, she'd asked to see my kit – her own drummer was too shy to put in an appearance, so she had volunteered to describe it for him. And on several occasions, we'd shared a few sodas and discussed the subtle art of rock music.

Katie was knowledgeable, conversant for a fourteen-year-old kid. She was as devoted a follower of Euterpe, the musician's muse, as Candy was of her demon. It remained to be seen if Katie's dedication to her guitar and to The Piglets would endure after her inevitable discovery of boys, but for the moment, she considered herself a serious musician. I liked that about her, and it was obvious that she liked me, if for nothing else than my own knowledge and experience with our shared craft. Even if I was only a drummer.

I began to make a pot of coffee, and Katie perched on one of the barstools beside the counter and attempted to be patient with this adult ritual, still meaningless and unnecessary to her. If Katie was going to keep up with rock and roll and its late night excesses, I thought that she'd acquire a taste for coffee and its effects soon enough.

I found myself in a surprisingly good mood, after the travails of the day and night before. The absurd dream, this intrusion from the littlest guitar player – it all made me smile.

When the coffee started to drip into the pot, I said, "Okay. Tell me about this surprise."

Katie took a green guitar pick out of her mouth and gestured with it. "I have to show you."

Again I smiled. It was something they all did, every guitarist I'd ever met, even the demon Phenex. If they set them down, they lost them, so they invariably put their picks in their mouths.

"Tell me, Katie." I thought of Lenny's pantomime in the hospital, and I copied it, theatrically grabbing at the front of my shirt. "I'm old. The shock might kill me."

"I'll give you a hint, then you'll know. Your boxes came yesterday."

"Boxes?"

"Yeah. Big UPS truck pulled up in your driveway. We were rehearsing."

Aren't you always?

"The guy got out and rang your doorbell, but I knew you weren't home. I waited for him to just leave whatever it was, but he started to get back into the truck, so I went over there and asked him what was up. He said he had some boxes for you, but they were C.O.D., so he couldn't just leave them."

I had no idea what she was talking about.

"I told him that I'd sign for them. He said, 'No, honey. C.O.D. means *cash on delivery.* You have to pay for 'em, too.' I asked him how much, and he looked at his little tablet-thing and said, '$215.98.'

"So I said, 'Hold on a second, Homie. Let me just go across the street and get my funds.'"

Katie grinned at my amazed expression.

"I ran over to the house. I've been saving up for a new amp, so I knew I probably had it. I busted open my piggy bank with Mom's rock-candy hammer, and sure enough, there was enough. I paid the man and had him put the boxes in my garage for safe-keeping."

It was shaping up to be another bizarre day in my had-become-bizarre-lately life. I pictured Katie counting out handfuls of change and a few wrinkled bills to the stunned UPS driver, for some manner of freight that I had not ordered.

"You owe me $215.98, Drummer Boy."

I grinned. "I'm a little short right now, Guitar Girl. Will you take a check?"

She shook her head. "Cash on delivery."

"I'll have to go to the ATM." Then I asked the most obvious question. "What's in the boxes?"

"You ordered them."

"I haven't ordered anything." And certainly not C.O.D. I'd never ordered anything C.O.D. in my life.

Katie narrowed her eyes, perhaps suspecting that I was having her on in some way. "Your name's on them. It says *Fragile, Musical Instruments* on the sides."

I poured myself a cup of coffee, added an ice cube or two so I could drink it quickly, but I didn't move right away. I hadn't ordered any instruments. Was it some kind of mix-up from Ernie's trip to Guitar Center? No. That made no sense. The shipment would've gone to his house. They had his credit card.

Katie put the guitar pick back in her mouth. "Let's go, Cal. I wanna see what you got."

I realized that I'd left my phone upstairs at her insistent doorbell ringing. "What time is it?"

"It's nine-ish. I've been up since six, but Mom said, 'You can't be ringing people's doorbells before nine. Go to school. You can tell him when you get home.'"

I had a feeling of unreality for a moment. What day was it? Phenex had played Rock Invades Riverside – that had been on Saturday. Then the Just Us Festival on Sunday. We had started for San Jose yesterday – Monday – and then I had driven back and forth and around, Gorman, Palm Springs, Riverside, Ontario, then finally home. It was like the days of touring with Sonic Daydream, trying to figure out what town we were in, what day it was.

It was Tuesday. "You're not in school."

Katie put her hand theatrically to her head, like a raccoon-eyed Scarlett O'Hara. "I told Mom I felt a fever coming on. She understood. She said I could stay home if I promised to wait until after nine to tell you. She said it could be a *Mental Health Day.*"

"Your mom's cool."

"And she likes you." Katie wiggled her eyebrows to indicate that she was more than willing to use her mother's fondness for me as an excuse for a day off school, for a *Mental Health Day.* Even if she didn't quite understand what Mom saw in an old drummer.

"Come on, Cal. I wanna see what you got."

There were several large, battered cardboard boxes, taped together with some kind of multicolored, Christmas-themed packing tape: jolly white snowmen on a red background went in one direction on the biggest box, and the message, *Special Delivery, Don't Open 'Til Christmas* went the other way. Reindeer and Santas held the other ones together.

There was no sticker proclaiming *Fragile, Musical Instruments,* as Katie had told me. Instead, the instruction was hand-lettered, in thick Sharpie, and it said *Fragell, Musical Instrumnts.* This C.O.D. was definitely not from Guitar Center.

I looked at the return label. *S. Conamay, Lenwood, CA.* It was meaningless.

"Donnie says it's drums," Katie said.

"Who?"

"Donnie. My drummer." She hefted one of the big boxes effortlessly. "See how light they are? Donnie says it's drums."

A scene from my dream played through my mind, bringing another smile: I imagined Phenex, goat's feet, tail and all, leaping from one of the beat-up boxes. I decided that whatever the mystery shipment contained, I didn't want to open it in my young neighbor's garage. Her dad didn't like me.

"Let's take 'em across the street."

"Are they drums?"

I picked up one of the smaller boxes and shook it; there was a faint metallic zing. "Could be."

Katie frowned, then smiled again. "Not this one, though." She picked up a thinner, weightier box, more heavily taped. "This is a guitar. I'm sure of it."

"Well, I guess we'll find out in a second."

We each carried a box across the street. I went into the house and found a utility knife, then opened the garage door, and we brought the rest of the shipment over and set it next to the Caddy. Katie was excited; the thought of new instruments danced like sugar plums in her eyes. *Don't Open 'Til Christmas* be damned. She wanted to see them now.

I had not a clue who S. Conamay was, or why he would be sending me *Musical Instrumnts.* And from the condition of the containers, I was pretty sure that they weren't new. But why ruin Katie's fun? I handed the orange knife to her. "Head on, Homie."

"We'll save the guitar for last," she said and slit the tape on the first box.

All that was visible at first was pistachio-colored packing peanuts. Katie gave me the knife and plunged both hands into the box, spewing dunnage over the sides. A breeze picked up a few of the peanuts and rolled them down the driveway, and I was glad that I'd decided not to open the boxes across the street.

Katie pulled a white snare out of the box, sending more peanuts flying. As expected, it wasn't new. In fact, it was beat to shit: there was a hole in the head. Katie frowned and set it on the floor.

"Why would someone like you buy used –"

"I'm telling you, I didn't buy them." I sliced open another box. It contained the bass drum, some cheap brand called an Enforcer.

Katie laid her box on its side and pulled out a floor tom, also an Enforcer.

After a few minutes, all the boxes were emptied, except for the one that may or may not have contained a guitar. Green peanuts, and pink ones, too, rolled through the garage, blowing gently out into the driveway and accumulating in drifts under the Caddy.

I took stock. We had a full kit, albeit an old, cheap, none-too-gently used one. There was the Enforcer bass, floor tom, and two power toms; a throne of the same brand, heavily duct-taped. There was the snare of indeterminate brand. A fairly pricey Zildjian hi-hat and ride. Lugs, bass pedal, and other hardware, plus an uneven number of chewed-up sticks, were in the last box we emptied.

Katie surveyed the kit with a contemplative frown. "Who would send this to you, Cal?" She irreverently stuck her finger through the hole in the snare. "It's . . . junk. Maybe some fan?"

I shrugged, as mystified as she was. I handed her the knife. "Here. You open the axe."

Katie giggled. "It's a guitar, Drummer Boy. An axe is for chopping wood." She shook her head. "You're so old. Nobody says *axe* anymore."

"It has been said that I'm not hep."

She looked up from deciding where to cut on the box. "Not what?"

"Forget it. Try the seam there."

Katie sliced through the layers of holiday tape. On top of the dunnage was a manila envelope with my name on it: *Mr. Calvin Bascomb.*

"Now we'll find out who it's from," Katie opined unnecessarily, and handed the envelope to me. But she didn't wait for me to open it. She wanted to see the guitar.

It had been packed more carefully than the old drums, covered around and taped with several layers of bubble-wrap, so much so that its brand and configuration was hidden. Katie laid it carefully on the floor and began gingerly cutting the plastic away.

I opened the envelope. There were some guitar picks and some other unidentifiable flotsam in the bottom, obscured by a single sheet of paper. I removed it and read the round, somewhat childish hand.

Dear Mr. Bascomb,

You don't know me, but I've heard a lot about you. My name is Sandra Conamay. My son was a big fan of yours, and he asked that I send –

"Oh, my God, Cal! It's a '52 Telecaster!"

Katie quickly removed the rest of the packing material and held up the Butterscotch blonde and black Fender. It was old, true, worn, but that only meant –

"It's real, Cal! Not a reproduction! A real, '52 Telecaster! The drums are shit, but this! This is awesome!"

I blanched. I realized that I hadn't had time to wonder what had happened to it, figured maybe they'd just gotten rid of it with the rest of his stuff. But that would've been stupid. Sonny's Telecaster was too valuable an instrument. I reimagined his trip to Barstow, to *Lenwood* – now I pictured him aboard his old Triumph, with this Telecaster strapped across his back.

There was another envelope, tucked into the strings of the guitar. Katie pulled it out and handed it to me, still marveling at the old axe. She gave it a test strum, then looked up at me, smiling.

At my stunned expression, she said, "You know who it's from now?" She nodded at the letter in one hand, the unopened envelope in the other. I quickly scanned the letter again.

My son was a big fan of yours, and he asked that I send his guitar to you in the event that something happened to him. It was like he knew, Mr. Bascomb. He had it all wrapped up and ready to go. I've sent his drums, too. They were his first set. I couldn't bear to look at them any more now that he's gone. I've also sent –

"Cal?"

I looked up from the letter.

"You know who it's from?"

"Yes. It's from . . . an old friend of mine. He's . . ."

I couldn't tell Katie the details. She was just a kid, didn't need to hear sad tales about a fellow musician dying on a lonely stretch of highway, about a mother's grief. She might understand, but still, she didn't need to hear about it.

"He's asking me to . . . store them for him." I waved the letter at her, laughed shakily. "'Take good care of my Telecaster,' he says."

"I would take good care of it," she said reverently. "It's awesome."

I had to get rid of her. If she stayed too much longer, my own grief would become apparent, and she'd know that I was lying about *storing* Sonny's instruments.

The obvious solution hit me. "I'll tell you what, Katie. You take that Telecaster on across the street with you. Give it a tune, if it needs it. I'm sure he won't mind."

And I was sure he wouldn't, even if he was still alive. Sonny would've liked Katie, too. He would've recognized another musician, and would've been happy to let the kid try out his Fender.

"Are you sure, Cal? If this was my guitar, I wouldn't let anybody get anywhere near it."

"I'm sure, honey. You can . . . you can play it for a few days." That would keep her out of my hair. "He won't mind."

"Thanks, Cal!" Katie gave me a completely spontaneous hug, then caught herself. She was lead-guitar for The Piglets, a tough girl, and it wouldn't be good for her rep to be seen hugging old drummers. "I'll take good care of it. I'll guard it with my life."

This promise made me wince. "I know you will, Katie. I'll get that money to you later."

"Whenever." She walked down the driveway with her prize and I quickly shut the garage door.

THIRTY-SEVEN

I sat on one of the barstools beside the kitchen counter. The coffee pot clicked, still heating the now forgotten pot, and I reached over and shut it off. No need for caffeine any more this morning. I was more than wide awake now.

I set the manila envelope down in front of me, as well as the other, smaller one, still unopened, and read Sonny's Mom's letter.

Dear Mr. Bascomb,

You don't know me, but I've heard a lot about you. My name is Sandra Conamay. My son was a big fan of yours, and he asked that I send his guitar to you in the event that something happened to him. It was like he knew, Mr. Bascomb. He had it all wrapped up and ready to go. I've sent his drums, too. They were his first set. I couldn't bear to look at them any more now that he's gone. I've also sent some of the little things that were in his drawer from when he was a boy, as well as the devil symbol that he was wearing when he died. My pastor said that I shouldn't keep it in the house, and since you are his friend, I thought you could give it back to the evil people he had fallen in with.

He said you weren't one of them, and I hope it's true. He talked about you a lot, said you were a good person and his best friend. I begged him to accept Jesus into his heart, and I advise you to do so, too. We prayed when he was here. He told me he would believe whatever I wanted him to believe, and I pray that it was true, because God called him home right after he left me.

But God is a good God, and Sonny showed he was a good boy by visiting me before the end. He knew something was coming, Mr. Bascomb, that the eye of Jesus was on him for communing with those bad people all these years. But I think he repented before it was too late. I am confident that he is at the right hand of the Lord right now, waiting for me to join him.

So I'm sending you this badge of Satan. I want you to throw it in their faces and tell them that they didn't get my boy in the end, because I am sure he repented his sinfulness.

God bless you for being his friend.

I upended the manila envelope. There were several guitar picks, and a rusted, tangled chain with a girl's name attached to it: *April.*

There was a St. Christopher's medal, and I thought with my customary apostasy that ol' Chris, patron saint of travelers, hadn't protected Sonny worth a good goddamn on his last trip, now had he?

Sonny's medallion clunked onto the granite, and I didn't know if I was surprised or not that it was blackened, the same way Lenny's was. I recalled that Barbie had stuffed that one into my pocket at the hospital.

I went upstairs and retrieved it out of my shirt in the dirty clothes hamper. I went back downstairs, regained my seat, and compared the two pendants. Except for the fact that Sonny's was older – he had obviously worn it against his skin for a long time, as some of the relief had worn down – they were identical, blackened like a dime or quarter that had been tossed into a bonfire and then raked out of the ashes.

I wondered if Ernie's was also turning black by now. Sonny had said something about them being made out of silver, but I doubted it. Silver didn't turn black. More likely, they were made out of the same amalgam that caused cheap jewelry to turn your skin green.

I set the medallions down beside all the minutia from Sonny's bedside drawer; I wondered for a second who April might have been.

I knew the other letter had to be from Sonny himself; he'd wrapped the Telecaster for shipment to me. His mom had just copied the address and sent the drum set along with it.

Her rambling letter about God and redemption and those evil people had been as saddening as it had been annoying. She obviously grieved for her boy, as any mother would, but I imagined that a lifetime of admonitions to take Jesus into his heart had been what had driven Sonny away from her in the first place, and into the arms of Candy and Phenex and all that witchy bullshit.

Yes, I'm afraid it's true. I've fallen in with the wrong crowd.

Sonny had gone the opposite way of his mom, had embraced the forces unseen, the ones feared and despised by her church. He seemed to believe it all as much as Candy did, with his admonitions to me against accepting cheap costume jewelry, with his mumblings about the cards falling where they would, his hopes for a merciful judgment upon his immortal soul. His conviction to his mother that the end was near made him seem like a true believer to me.

That his prediction came to pass didn't make me think that he had indeed known it was coming, however. All I saw was a tragic coincidence, the product of a dark road and an old motorcycle.

Sonny's beliefs were just as ridiculous to me as were his mother's, and therein sprung my hesitance to read his letter. I'd liked the kid; he'd been a singer, a talented, multi-instrument musician, and what was I? Just an old drummer, who'd been fortunate enough to have some good breaks in life. Yet Sonny had liked me, looked up to me, even, enough to bequeath his most valued possession to me. I thought I might retrieve it from Katie and hang it on the wall above the fireplace in the dining area, as a tribute to our short friendship.

I hesitated to read his letter because I didn't want my memory of that friendship to be marred by more supernatural ramblings. But what else could I do? Sonny had left me his guitar, and a letter to go with it. I owed it to him to hear what he wanted to tell me, no matter how far-fetched it was gonna be.

Dear Cal,
If you're reading this, then I'm dead.

"Christ!" I said aloud to the empty room, and ran my hand across my face in exasperation.

Dear Cal,

If you're reading this, then I'm dead. Don't mourn for me, though. I'm sure it was merciful and quick, as had been foretold.

When Lisa was just a kid, Candy summoned the demon. He told her what was to come, and he also told her that on the cusp of fame, one of us would be sacrificed. When Ernie appeared, I knew the prophecy was nearing its fruition. When Candy started staring at him, I figured it was me that would be sacrificed.

But I had a good time for the last ten years, like I told you, playing music, not having to work. These are the trade-offs. But since I'm dead, and no doubt doomed for my sins, as Mom says, then revealing the rest of the prophecy to you can't doom me any more, no matter what Candy says. And none of them need to have my guitar. I know you'll take good care of it.

Here it comes, I thought, the warning, poor deluded Sonny's attempt to save me. Even if I thought I needed saving, which I did not, I reckoned it would take more than one dead guitarist's counsel from beyond the grave to accomplish it.

Lisa is the key to your salvation.

Or to my damnation, I thought with an irreverent, completely non-apropos giggle.

Lisa is the key to your salvation. She believes that meeting you is destiny, the fulfillment of prophecy, proof that she was born into this world, through the intercession of the demon, to be the instrument of cosmic revenge.

All her life, her mother has indoctrinated her into this belief, Cal. Lisa has been taught that the soul which inhabits her body is damned, and to free it of its curse, she must curse another, to commit his immortal soul to its just desserts. Through her mother, Phenex has guaranteed Lisa that when she has delivered this man's soul to damnation, then he will assure her fame and success with the band. Roy and James believe this, too, and will fight to accomplish it. Seek guidance from a good witch to help you combat them. They are dangerous to you.

Lisa believes that you will support her in her quest, that you'll help her destroy the one that is responsible for the damnation of her soul. But I don't think you will, Cal. I think you're a good man, an old soul yourself, and I think you know that the key to salvation is forgiveness, and not revenge.

And since Lisa loves you – she has always loved you – I think that you can turn her from this evil path. Trust in love, Cal. It's your only salvation.

Pray for me.

Your friend, Sonny.

I folded his letter carefully. I left the medallions on the counter, but swept April's pendant and the old picks back into the envelope, and stuck it and the two letters into the kitchen drawer. My earlier surmise had been correct. I would've remembered Sonny better without all this talk of demons and salvation and damned souls.

I tried to go back to sleep, but couldn't. I kicked around the house, played a set; but I was bored. The sound of Sonny's Telecaster coming from across the street saddened me, even though The Piglets' lead-guitar played it well enough.

I called Barbie. She said that they were running Lenny through more tests, that he'd been in and out of his room all day, so it wouldn't really do for me to come out and visit. She said the physical therapist had gotten him to stand up and take a few steps.

"That's great, Barbie!"

"But he still hasn't got much movement back on his right side, and he still can't talk." She sighed. "He wants me to go get his guitar, Cal. I made excuses. I told him, *It's a hospital . . ."*

I was surprised at her reluctance. "It might help, Barbie."

"Or it might not, Cal. What if he can't . . ."

"Well, not right away, but maybe you should let him –"

"He's not left-handed, Cal. The doctor said . . . I don't want him to get frustrated. I don't want him to get depressed."

She felt the same as Ernie: Leonard Whitly would die if he couldn't play guitar. She loved him, and she didn't want him to find out if that was going to be the case. But he was going to have to find out sooner or later.

"I'd let him try, Barbie."

"I guess so." She was still uncertain.

"Call me when they're going to release him, and I'll take you guys home."

Ernie didn't return my text. I imagined that he was still asleep in San Francisco. Lisa confirmed it: she and the band and Candy were out sightseeing without him. She said that the show the night before had been awesome; she wished that I'd been there, and regretted that I was going to miss the one tonight. She asked me how Lenny was doing and I typed, *Better.*

Ernie's working on Vegas 4 us. End of the week.

I heard.

He wasn't working on it too hard, I thought, if he was asleep. Maybe it was already in the bag.

I love u, Cal. I miss u.

I love u 2.

An inspiration struck me, a way to alleviate my boredom.

I'm gonna take a ride up to Riverside & check on the house.

Mom'll appreciate that.

THIRTY-EIGHT

I was surprised at my own restlessness. I had at one time barely left home, associated with no one, except for the occasional musical question-and-answer confab with Katie, and going to the Y to give drum lessons. School was in session now and the holidays were coming, so I had a break from lessons, until about the first of the year. I wondered if I'd be in town to resume them, or if I'd be on tour with Phenex. Hardy har har.

I'd been happy enough, in my solitary existence, but now that I'd spent some time with people, with Lisa, I found that being alone was tiresome. I found that I craved company, conversation. I seemed to have lost the ability to amuse myself. So I hopped into the car, just for something to do, and headed to my hometown.

I by-passed the Tyler Street exit that would've been the directest route to the band house, instead opting to go on to downtown, get off there, and just cruise out to Arlanza. I passed The House of Ale, then turned the corner and passed Mohini's House of Dreams.

A line from Sonny's rambling letter played through my mind: if I was to fight Roy and James in the coming battle for my salvation, I was to *seek guidance from a good witch to help combat them.* I didn't even know what a good witch looked like. But since the bad witch was out of town, I decided to start my search at Mohini's, apparently the witchiest place in town, what with being an occult bookstore and all. Home-base for the local coven. It was a joke I told myself. I was bored.

The bell over the door tinkled, and the woman behind the counter smiled and bid me welcome. She was the most unusually gorgeous woman I'd ever seen. She wasn't young – she was my age, at least. She was statuesque, with yellow hair streaked with white, worn in a thick braid down her back. She had large, violet-blue eyes; she was a Valkyrie.

I just stood there staring at her in silence for a moment. At last she asked me how she could help me.

I approached the counter and said, "Hi. I know one of your co-workers. Candy Corson."

Her smile stiffened, chilled a few degrees. I mused that Candy had had a similar effect on me.

"She doesn't work here anymore."

Of course not. Candy had never needed to work in the first place, according to Sonny, and now that she thought that Phenex was gonna hit the big time . . .

The woman was staring curiously at me. "You say you know Candy, but you're not her . . . type."

"Oh, no, not me." I shook my head, entirely too vigorously. "Not her type, no. My friend –"

The woman smiled at my discomfort. "I didn't mean in a romantic sense, Mr. –?"

I told her my name and waited to hear hers.

She repeated, "I didn't mean that you weren't Candy's type in the romantic sense, Mr. Bascomb."

"Please, call me Cal." I sounded like a schoolboy to myself. She was that alluring.

She smiled, showing small, very white teeth. "Though obviously, you're not that, either. I meant that you're not of the blood –"

"I've heard a lot about it, though."

Surprise brightened the purple eyes. "Really? From Candy?"

"No. Mostly from . . . one of her friends."

The beautiful woman offered her hands to me, palms up, indicating that I should show her mine. I complied, and she grasped my left hand firmly in both of hers, ran one thumb from the wrist to the tip of my forefinger. Inexplicably, I felt myself shiver and hoped she hadn't noticed.

"I see that you're a musician." She dropped my hand and made an adorable drumming motion. "Percussion, is it?"

Could she tell from the callouses on my hands, different than a guitarist's, but there nonetheless? Or did she know because Candy had mentioned me?

It didn't matter, because her eyes were hypnotic, so much so that they led me to say something that I never say.

"Yes, I used to be the drummer for a little band called Sonic Daydream." One heartbeat. Two. "Perhaps you've heard of us?"

She smiled in cute embarrassment, at a loss. "I'm sorry, Mr. – Cal. I don't know very much about modern music. Were you . . . popular?"

My Ernie LaBelle-style ploy, never before invoked, had fallen flat. I smiled back at her. "Not at all."

"Since you're not actually looking for Candy, for . . . any reason, how can I help you today?"

"Well, it's kind of a long story, –?"

"Oh, how rude of me. My name's Iris. This is my store." She clasped my hand in both of hers and quickly shook it. "If you'd like to step into my office, I'd love to hear your story. Just allow me to lock the door so we won't be disturbed."

"Oh, you don't have to go to all that trouble . . . Iris." Her name was as beautiful as she was. A little old-fashioned, maybe – she hadn't heard of my band – but I liked it, and her, very much.

"It's time for a break, anyway." I watched her cross the shop and turn the lock, switch the sign around from *OPEN to CLOSED.* She was wearing a pair of crisp white jeans and a snug amethyst-colored polo shirt that brought out the color of her stunning eyes, and she looked just as good from the back as she did from the front.

I was a little ashamed of my appreciation, but my own resident, excuse-making demon piped up. *You've only recently gone in for the younger crowd, Cal, 'ol son. It's all right to look at a handsome woman your own age. Lisa wouldn't mind. I'm sure she gives the young dudes a once-over if they catch her eye, don'tcha think? Despite love? Despite destiny? It's all right. It doesn't matter where you get your appetite, as long as you eat at home.*

Iris stepped behind the counter and drew aside a midnight blue curtain patterned with yellow moons and stars. "Right this way."

The office was small, cozy. Bookshelves crammed with books and what I assumed were various magical accoutrements stood behind a desk with a laptop and an *In* box containing a few unopened letters. Iris plucked a chair from where it stood against the wall and set it in front of the desk.

She sat behind the desk and opened its bottom drawer. "Would you care for a drink? I know it's a trifle early, but I have an excellent mead. Your *friend* Candy's coven makes it. I understand she hasn't been out to see them much either, lately." She brought out a crystal decanter and two small goblets. "Honey and spices and magic spells, drawn off by the light of the moon and all that. My predecessor here, a storied old witch from way back, was quite fond of it."

Right. "None for me, thanks. I'm driving."

Iris laughed, and it was like droplets of glass breaking on stones. "Are you, Cal? But surely not before you tell me your long story?" She poured herself a glass, then paused, waiting for my response.

Was this lovely woman flirting with me? It certainly seemed so. My appreciation for beautiful ladies and my luck with them had certainly changed in my old age. Watch out, Ernie LaBelle!

I nodded and she filled a glass for me.

"To absent friends," she toasted.

The honey mead was crisp and sweet, not quite wine, but not beer either.

"Now. Tell me what you think I need to know. How can I help you?"

"First of all, are you a good witch, Iris? I was instructed to find a good witch to help me with a spiritual battle. For my salvation."

I grinned, but Iris did not. "You're not a believer, Cal, yet you bandy around these serious words. *Salvation. A spiritual battle.* You speak as if in jest, but someone of the blood has taught you these terms. Do you sense some threat?"

Did I? *They are dangerous to you.*

"Maybe I should start at the beginning."

"Maybe you should."

I started with Ernie's phone call. I told Iris about his daughter, how she'd been conceived after Candy had daubed him with some sort of red paint. "Ernie said that she told him that it was the blood of the firstborn of Egypt or some such."

Iris smiled. "I sincerely doubt that's what she told him . . . Please, continue."

I told her about the band, named after the demon Phenex. I expected some exclamation at this, but it only produced a slight raise of one of her exquisite blonde eyebrows.

But when I mentioned Ernie's good-luck charm, I had Iris's full attention. "You say they made it for him specifically?"

"Yes. They have some kind of a press. I've never seen it, but he described it. Lisa wears a similar thing, and all the guys in the band wear the same one as Ernie. The drummer and the bassist . . . I don't talk to them much. But the guitarist was my friend. He had one, too, and he warned me . . ."

I sighed and stopped. Now we were getting to the walk through the valley of the shadow of death, fatal accidents on dark freeways, places where I knew that someone *of the blood* such as lovely Iris would start to see portents and premeditations and prophecies fulfilled – just as Sonny had.

My hesitation caused her to look intently at me. "Why did you come in here today, Cal?"

"May I?" I indicated the mead.

"By all means."

I refilled my glass. The mead was tasty, the company intriguing. It had been a long, strange trip lately, and I realized that it felt good to tell all the bizarre details to someone. If I got too drunk to drive, there was a hotel just down the street, within walking distance.

Iris was waiting for my answer. "I told you, I was instructed to look for a good witch."

"But you don't believe in witches."

I shrugged, feeling put on the spot. "No, I don't. But my friend . . ."

I discovered that I was working out my motivation for stopping at Mohini's as I spoke it to her. It wasn't so much that I felt threatened, but, "My friend is dead, and he believed in witches. He believed he was some kind of a sacrifice. And he seemed to be okay with it. Maybe I'm looking for a little insight into how a person could come to believe in something like that."

"I'm not going to give you a treatise on faith, Cal." I blinked in surprise at this response. Iris smiled at my wonder and continued. "It would take all day, and we don't have enough mead."

She arose and walked around the desk, around me, collecting her thoughts. She ran her fingers lightly across the titles on the bookshelves.

With her back to me, she said, "You're not a child, Cal, so I'm not going to say, *Once upon a time, there was no science, so man made up stories about how the world around him worked.* Nor am I going to exhaust myself in trying to make you believe in the things in which you do not, things I know to be true. A simple demonstration will suffice to make you see the most basic concept at work here."

"Are you going to turn me into a toad?" Her loveliness and the mead made me glib.

"No."

She stepped closer to me, and with a quickness I would not have thought possible, she slashed down at my head with a long dagger. I instinctively put up my arm to deflect the blow and she stopped the knife's descent, a hair's breadth from penetration.

Iris grinned and her purple eyes glittered with a kind of wickedness. "Thus, my demonstration. A being will defend itself from attack by whatever means necessary."

She withdrew the blade and I lowered my arm. She placed it on the desk. I saw that the handle was inlaid with jewels, too large and bright to be real, lest the thing be worth millions. A frowning skull served as pommel. Iris seated herself behind the desk once more.

"Similarly, to achieve what it desires, a being will attack in a manner it believes will work. If I sought to slay you, and I thought that this garish weapon would suffice, it wouldn't matter that you are probably strong enough to fight me off, or that its flimsy blade might've snapped off when it connected with the bone in your arm. If I believed it would've worked, I would've tried it." Her wicked grin remained. "At the very least, you would've been wounded, and perhaps that would've allowed me the time to apply a more potent weapon." She nodded behind me, and I noticed for the first time that a Japanese katana was affixed to the shadowy wall. "Had you been prepared for my attack, however . . . No wound could've been inflicted. You would've disarmed me.

"So it is with witchcraft, Cal, with magic. Good witches, bad witches. We all encompass the powers of both. Just because you wouldn't've believed in a million years that I would attack you, unprovoked – it wouldn't hardly have changed the outcome if I had. You'll accede to this fact?"

I nodded dumbly. I still didn't believe in the forces unseen, or that anyone's beliefs in them could be used to harm me. But I saw her point, nonetheless. Any physical attack, unexpected, could be deadly. James was big and Roy was sneaky. Why they might want to attack me remained a mystery, however, past Sonny's ridiculous mumbo-jumbo.

"Now." Iris steepled her hands, like a patient schoolmarm, but the impish darkness remained pooled in her eyes. "I ask for a suspension of disbelief on your part. Your friend is dead. What matter is it if I say that his demise was accomplished through magic? Dead, as the poets say, is dead.

"I want you to accept – if only for the moment – that there are forces at work here beyond your ability to quantify with science or the laws of physics as you understand them. I want you to give me that an attack is an attack, regardless, and forewarned is forearmed.

"It may be a spell, a charmed amulet – things whose powers you don't believe in – or it could be a dagger. Will you allow me to help you anticipate the threat? Will you accept that, although you don't believe, they do, these makers of *good-luck charms* – and thereby, they will use any means possible to achieve their ends?"

I nodded, still silent. What else did I have to do today?

"Good. First, let us examine this amulet, this *good-luck charm,* as you term it. Can you describe it for me?" She opened the top desk drawer and extracted a lined pad, then fished around another moment and found a pen. "Can you draw it?"

I said I would make the attempt, and while I applied my dubious artistic skills, she again arose and consulted the bookcase, finally selecting a volume and paging through it. She looked over my shoulder as I scribbled, but before I deemed my creation complete, she bid me stop.

"Is this it?"

The picture was similar, if not identical. I nodded.

"Remember now, Cal, you are suspending your scientific, modern-man's disbelief." The wicked grin flashed, then the schoolmarm was back. "When there is a master and an acolyte, there is a ceremony. They enter into a pact. The acolyte pledges his soul to the master."

Metallica's renowned drummer smiled, and played a short roll in my mind. I couldn't resist. "Like selling your soul to Satan? For metal immortality?"

Iris blinked. "For what?"

"It's not important. You were saying – the master and the acolyte . . ."

"You said, *selling your soul to Satan for* . . . something. That's a literary stereotype, an analogy, used to demonstrate that people will give up everything, even their own basic goodness, to get what they want. I'm glad you brought it up. Keep that kind of single-mindedness in your head. You don't believe in Satan, or your immortal soul, but you'll agree that people will make many sacrifices to achieve their goals. The businessman who neglects his family to rise in the corporate world, things like that?"

I had no further flippant comment, so again I nodded silently.

"So here we have the master and acolyte. Let's say that it's Candy and her –"

"Minions." I thought of James and Roy and Horus, and almost Ernie, doing what they were told.

Iris's smile flashed. "A delightful word. And apt! We'll make a warlock of you yet, my friend!"

"Don't say that, Iris." I remembered my dream, all the conversations, the words, rehashed. "Candy told Ernie once –"

"You say he wears this amulet? But he's a non-believer?"

"Yes and yes."

"We'll get to him in a minute. First – tell me about Candy's *minions.*"

I briefed her on James and Roy, quoting Sonny's words: "They're just her companions, she said, along on this path to help her look after her daughter. And now there's another one. Horus."

Iris grinned. "The son of Osiris. How quaint."

I told her that people had probably been misspelling it his whole life, just like *Phenex.*

"You said there was another? The one that is . . . deceased?"

"Sonny. He was more than a companion to Candy."

"A lover." Not a question.

"That, and a music teacher for her daughter." I frowned. "He was so talented."

"Yet Candy dispatched him."

I looked at her sharply. "It was an accident, Iris."

"A convenient one? That served Candy's further purposes? And you said that he believed he was to be sacrificed."

"My mother believed in the resurrection and the life. That don't make it so. It was an accident."

Iris shrugged. "Yet dead is dead, Cal. And Candy's purposes . . ." She waved her hand. "So these companions all wear this amulet. And her dead lover. And your friend."

"And God's bass player."

Again Iris showed confusion, so I explained. "Ernie had another guy from our band over to listen to Phenex." Her lip curled at the mention of the demon's name. "His name's Leonard Whitly. Once upon a time, long ago and far away, a magazine about music referred to him as *God's bass player.* Apparently, Candy gave him and his wife one of those medallions, as gifts, in gratitude, I imagine, for giving the band a listen. Barbie doesn't go in for all this witchy sh . . . stuff, so she didn't wear hers. But Lenny did. He had it on when he had his stroke."

An expression of pain. "Is he dead, too?"

"No. He's recovering. The doctors say that he might be okay –"

"Does he still wear the amulet?"

"No. It's at my house. Barbie said it was ugly. She stuffed it into my pocket at the hospital, told me to throw it away. It had turned all black, just like Sonny's."

Again, the lifted eyebrows, the deepening frown. More dire implications from the spirit realms.

"The master and the acolyte enter into a pact, Cal. The acolyte relinquishes control of his soul – he gives the use of its energy to the master, so that she may pool it with the energies of others, similarly given, to work powerful spells."

I couldn't hide my disbelief, and Iris reminded me once more to suspend it. "As I say, this pact is entered into knowingly, willingly. Even eagerly. The master promises the acolyte the moon and the stars, of course, in exchange for the use of his immortal soul. She promises him whatever he desires, because the master also now has the power to discharge the energy of the acolyte's soul, for her own uses." Iris paused to let the consequences of that sink in. "It gives her the power to end him, should she so choose."

I rolled my eyes, and she held up her hand. "These pooled energies . . . They allow the master to also extend her power to the souls of those who have not knowingly entered into the pact. Such as your friends."

I remembered my dream. "Phenex said about Ernie, 'He's mine.'" I giggled. Dead was irreversibly dead, that was true, but this was all just ridiculous.

Iris didn't smile. "What?"

I told her about my dream, all the repeated words and phrases, how Phenex had given me Lisa, how he'd invited me. *"Join us,"* I hissed, à la one of the demons from *Army of Darkness.*

"Who is this Lisa again?"

"Yes, well . . ."

I was uncomfortable for a moment, about to disclose my outrageous May-December relationship to this woman my own age. But then I discarded my embarrassment. I wasn't ashamed of Lisa, and I wasn't ashamed of myself anymore. Despite the age difference, we were simpatico.

"Lisa's Candy's daughter. The one who wrote to Ernie, told him he was her daddy."

"Oh yes, that's right. I think I may have met her once." Because I was expecting some kind of judgmental reaction, Iris refused to give me one; instead she only looked at me blankly for a heartbeat. "So the demon offered you this young woman, but said he retains her loyalty." Now she squinted at me curiously. "And all of this strikes you as merely coincidental? You see no guiding hand, no –"

"Lisa thinks its destiny. She and I. She's one of you people, and believes in things such as destiny. I, on the other hand . . ." I shrugged, smirked.

Iris cut through my smugness. "You're just enjoying her youthful adoration."

She was casting me in Ernie's role, as taking advantage of that groupie-lust, and my excuse-making demon objected, compelled me to leap to my own defense. "It's not like that. We're . . . we're in love."

Now I just sounded silly, and again Iris's eyebrow arched at my schoolboy's declaration.

"Why does this young woman believe that your relationship was predestined?"

"That's an even longer story."

"I have nothing but time. And mead." She filled my glass and her own. She waited.

I told the tale as briefly as possible. "I was in this band. There was a girl named Elise. She was my best friend. She was in love with our singer, but he was married to someone else. Her sister, actually. She killed herself over him."

The eyebrow rose again.

"I wrote a book about it. Candy was a big fan of the band – so much so that she got herself knocked up with our guitarist's kid. She read my book to the kid – Lisa – when she was little, making the whole thing sound like some kind of tragic fairytale. Denny was the bad man. Lenny's his brother. Ernie was her daddy. That left me, Elise's friend, the teller of this sad tale." I paused. "Lisa grew up with the story, grew to . . . love me. So when we actually met, she saw it as destiny."

Another heartbeat of silence. "And how do you see it?"

I liked Iris. I could tell that she was intelligent, despite her silly beliefs. She was quite beautiful, and in another world, I would've been moved to make a play for her. Even after this short conversation, I considered us to be friends. So I told her exactly how I saw it.

"I don't know if I believe in destiny, but this girl . . . I've been a loner all my life, Iris. Elise was my friend, and after she was gone, I came to realize that maybe I'd loved her. But there had never been anyone else, until this girl. I want to spend the rest of my life with her. She's brought me a kind of happiness that I didn't think I'd ever have."

The purple-eyed witch-woman considered these further boyishly maudlin affirmations of devotion for a moment, but then made no comment about them. "Who was it that told you that a spiritual battle was coming? Who told you to seek out a good witch?"

"It was Sonny. When Ernie came back around, he was sure that he was losing Candy, so he went to visit his mom. She said he believed that something was going to happen to him. He wrapped up his guitar and put my address on it. When he crashed his bike, she sent it to me. There was a letter."

Iris sensed my reluctance to go into Sonny's supernatural warnings, all this hocus-pocus that she knew was all bullshit to me. She waited.

"He told me . . . He talked about Lisa. He said that she believed that her soul was damned because of . . . Ah, Christ, Iris! It was all gibberish to me."

Her incredible eyes were solemn. "Try to remember, Cal."

I concentrated. "Sonny said that Lisa believed that meeting me was proof that she was born to be . . . *the instrument of cosmic revenge.* He said that Candy had told her all her life that she was damned, and that the only way she could free herself was to curse someone else."

"Who?"

"He didn't say."

"Was it to be just a random soul, or some specific individual?"

I shook my head, repeated, "He didn't say. He said that after Lisa had damned this person, in return, Phenex would make her band famous. Sonny said that Roy and James believed all this claptrap, too, and that they would fight to get it. *They are dangerous to you.* He said I should *seek guidance from a good witch* to help me combat them.

"Then he said that Lisa thought I would help her to destroy this person . . ."

Since Iris seemed to think it was important to identify the victim, I concentrated again, reaching for Sonny's exact words. I snapped my fingers. The Alzheimer's wasn't setting in quite yet. *"The one that is responsible for the damnation of her soul.*

"Then Sonny said that he didn't think I would help her, however. He said that I would show her that she should forgive, and not seek revenge. I could turn her from her evil path through . . . my love for her. Then he asked me to pray for him."

Now I waited. Iris mused for what seemed like a long time. "And you have no idea who this person could be? *The one that is responsible for the damnation of her soul?"*

"Not a clue. Maybe . . . maybe I should just ask her."

"Maybe you should." Iris studied me for another moment. "I'd like to do some research on this, Cal. See if I might be able to ascertain –"

"Are you going to scry?" I grinned.

She smiled indulgently. "Perhaps." She drew the pen and pad across the desk to her. "I was thinking more along the lines of examining the natal charts of some of these people." She then asked me my birthdate, and Lisa's.

"She was born on Valentine's Day. 2000. She has the symbol for Aquarius tattooed at the base of her neck."

Without looking up from the pad, Iris said, "How quaint."

She asked for Ernie's birthdate – I told her it was the same year as mine, but I was unsure of the month.

"Sometime in April, I think."

She asked me Elise's date of birth, and again, I knew the year, but not the exact month and day. "September. Or maybe it was October."

Iris met my eyes. "When did she die?"

Because that date was seared into my mind forever, I repeated it immediately. "May 7th, 1999."

Iris jotted the information onto the pad, then drew a few lines, made a few calculations. She chewed pensively on the end of the pen with her tiny, perfect teeth.

"Did you know that Lisa was born nine months after Elise died? Almost to the day?" She looked keenly at me, waiting for a surprised reaction, but I disappointed her.

"Yes, I knew that. Lisa was conceived the night of our last show, in San Francisco. Candy caught Ernie backstage, and . . . well, the rest is history. The next day, we went back to LA. Denny was alone with Elise that night . . . then she drove his car off a cliff."

"Denny?"

Hep is not exactly your middle name, is it, my lovely friend? I smiled inwardly. But if she'd never heard of my multi-platinum band, then she'd never heard of its world-famous frontman, either. "Dennis Whitly. He was our singer, our lead-guitar."

"When's his birthday?"

"He's four years younger than me. I don't know the month." I grinned at her. "But you can Google him. *He's kind of a big deal. People know him.*"

Iris smiled blankly at me; this pop-culture reference also passed her by. Then she studied me intently for another moment. "As a favor to me, would you also wear an amulet?"

I smiled in surprise. "Are you co-opting my soul, Iris?"

She returned my smile warmly, then cast her glance coquettishly downward. "Only with your freely-given permission, my friend."

"Then I so give it."

"Ah!" She sighed gloriously, and the light in her eyes danced. "Unfortunately for me, it's not that kind of charm." She fished around in another drawer, drew something out, enclosed in her fist. The chain hung down over her wrist. "It's not even custom-made, but it should suffice. I am not without powers of my own."

"So you *are* a good witch?"

She grinned mischievously. "I certainly can be." Iris closed her eyes for a moment, marshalling the forces unseen to my aid, then opened her hand and offered me the charm.

It was a small Eye of Horus. I grinned. *"To keep negative energies away and attract positive energies."*

Her wondrous eyes lit up further. "We'll make you into a –"

"Don't say that, Iris."

She walked out with me and unlocked the door. We had exchanged phone numbers; she'd promised to tell me what her research revealed.

"What do you use for magical research? A Ouija board?"

Again, that indulgent smile. Iris wasn't offended by my disbelief. "More comprehensive than the Library of Alexandria or the monkish tomes of a thousand plague-doomed monasteries. I use the internet. Which reminds me. Where can I get a copy of your book?"

"I'll send you one. Better yet, I'll bring you one." What else did I have to do today? The band wouldn't be back until sometime tomorrow, probably not before noon. I was, as my grandmother used to say, *at odds and ends* until then.

"In fact, I have an even better idea. Would you care to take a little ride with me, Iris?"

"Certainly."

"I've got a few copies at home. You can see my house . . ."

"Your . . ." She made that adorable drumming motion again.

I smiled, nodded. Enthusiasm flowed through me, like a child might experience. I'd made a new friend.

THIRTY-NINE

Upon arrival, Iris asked to see my drums, asked me to play something for her, something from my *group.* I ran through *Tomcats* and *Cerulean.* She smiled and tapped her toe, bobbed her head politely. But of course, she recognized neither of them. Iris had never heard of Sonic Daydream.

"Any requests?"

She pondered. "Do you know *The Battle Hymn of the Republic?"*

In utter surprise, I played the rolls, and was even more amazed when Iris sang it, in a clear contralto.

"Civil War buff are ya, Iris?" I asked, after the last *His truth is marching on* faded away.

She smiled. "I like a good gospel tune. Don't you?"

I put my sticks down and came around to her. I put my arm around her shoulder, in a friendly, host-like manner, and guided her back down the steps.

"I consider *The Battle Hymn of the Republic* more of a martial song."

She shook her head. *"The Star-Spangled Banner* is a martial song. It should have the same kind of drums, the same kind of . . .?"

"Rolls."

"That's it. *The Star-Spangled Banner* should have the same kind of rolls as *The Battle Hymn of the Republic.* It's a war song, but it's seldom performed that way nowadays. It's only modern arrangements that gospel-up *The Star-Spangled Banner,* whereas *The Battle Hymn of the Republic* is really a gospel, set to martial music."

This was a fair assessment, and I said, "So you do know about music."

"I know what I like." She added quickly, "Your group's music was . . . nice."

"You flatter me." Dennis Whitly's *Tomcats* and my drum solo from it were surely not *The Battle Hymn of the Republic.*

"Is my flattery working?" she asked brightly, with no hint of innuendo. Just friendliness.

"It warms my immortal soul," I returned theatrically.

"Jest not about thy immortal soul, Apostate," Iris said, only half kidding now. "Such is blasphemy. You risk damnation."

"Speaking of which . . ." I offered her a seat at the kitchen counter. I opened the drawer and handed Sonny's and his mother's letters to her. While she read them, I asked if I could get her anything. "I don't have any mead . . ."

Iris glanced at the wine rack below the counter, randomly selected a bottle. "This will do."

I found a corkscrew.

"You're not having any?" she said, when I poured only one glass. "Oh, that's right. You're driving." Her laughter, again like the tinkle of expensive glass, breaking.

"Are you trying to get me drunk, Iris?" I asked with a playful kind of exasperation.

"Of course I am, Cal, but not to any improper purpose." She winked. "It's such a long drive back to Riverside, and you have such a lovely house. We're having such a nice conversation. I was hoping that I might remain your guest tonight in order to continue it."

Once more, there was no innuendo, no veiled come-on. I got the impression that she wanted to watch over me, to protect me from the forces unseen.

"But of course." I found another goblet and poured myself a healthy portion. I looked at the bottle she had chosen. It was some Chardonnay, off-the-shelf, as were all my wines. As with cars and livestock, I was not a connoisseur of the vine. I'd just purchased a bunch of bottles at the supermarket once upon a time, to fill up the rack that came with the kitchen decor.

Iris finished the letters without comment, so I said, "Sonny's mom's something, huh? All that talk about Jesus." I rolled my eyes.

"One shouldn't mock others' beliefs, Cal. It's –"

"Blasphemy. I know." I smiled at her. "There was an old song, Iris." I cleared my throat and tried out my singing voice. Don MacLean wasn't going to lose any sleep over my skills. *"Do you believe in rock and roll? Can music save your mortal soul?"*

"And can you teach me how to dance real slow?" Iris grinned in delight. "That one I do know!"

"Music has always been the closest thing I've had to a religion, Iris. There's no deity to worship, just an eternal, changeless scale. A beat that runs through . . . through *my* soul, I guess. There's no blasphemy, unless you count . . ." I grinned. "Whatever style you don't like."

"Yet music celebrates God, Cal, even modern music." Iris sang the last verse to *American Pie:*

"And the three men I admire most
The Father, Son, and the Holy Ghost
They caught the last train for the coast
The day the music died."

"Music celebrates *life*, Iris," I insisted. "It's not confined to one narrow dogma. *The Father, Son, and the Holy Ghost."* A new thought occurred to me. "So you believe in God? I wouldn't've thought –"

"No, you wouldn't've. They say the two things one shouldn't discuss with strangers are politics and religion, Cal."

And music, for that matter. "I was kinda thinking we weren't strangers anymore."

Iris smiled. "And so we aren't. I believe in God, though not quite the one with the flowing white beard and the *narrow dogma.* I also believe in other forces. I believe that these can be touched, bargained with. I believe that I can compel them to do my bidding.

"This is also what Candy and her minions believe. You've been granted a glimpse of the unseen yourself. Phenex showed himself to you, tuning a guitar. Perhaps he, too, is a musician. He *is* said to have a glorious singing voice."

I grinned at her over my wine goblet. "The better with which to devour me."

"The wages of sin is death . . ."

"My point exactly." I searched for another one of my mother's Bible verses, another one to illustrate the wrath of her supposedly good and beneficent deity. *"God judgeth the righteous, and God is angry with the wicked every day."*

"But I will forewarn you whom ye shall fear: fear him, which after he hath killed, hath power to cast into hell. Yea, I say unto you, 'Fear him.'"

I hadn't heard that one, and told Iris so. "Regardless, it's all the same bullshit. Gods, demons; they all want me to obey, or else they're gonna punish me. And it's all to some standard that I might not necessarily think is –"

Iris held up her hand, cutting me off. "I'm not going to get into a discussion on the nature of sin with you, either, Cal." Now there was a hint of off-color slyness to her smile, but just a hint, and it vanished immediately. "I imagine our views would be similar.

"My beliefs are simple, simply summed up: *Be just and fear not.* Your *friends* talk of destiny. But destiny is non-judgmental. It can't be bought. It neither punishes nor rewards; reward and punishment are a result of the decisions we make.

"But Candy seeks to control destiny, to bend it to her will, with the help of a demon, and by any other means necessary. You don't believe that her means are viable, even though you dreamed of the demon. He spoke to you."

"I *dreamed up* the demon, Iris. I'd had a rough day. He could've been a product of whatever I ate in Gorman. What does Scrooge say? *There's more of gravy than of grave about you, whatever you are!"*

Iris smiled patiently. "I don't know too much about music, Cal, but I do like movies. I want you to think of Candy like the Terminator. The damnation of this man's soul, the appeasement of Phenex, the fame of her band. Her ambition – what does the guy from the future say? *It can't be bargained with. It can't be reasoned with. It doesn't feel pity, or remorse, or fear. And it absolutely will not stop, ever, until –"*

"You are dead. You think it's me that they want to damn?"

Iris shook her head. "Sonny said Lisa will want you to *support her in her quest.* She's going to expect your agreement. Your help."

"He thinks I can talk her out of it."

Iris regarded me solemnly. "From what you've told me, I doubt that."

I could not be solemn, what with the wine and the attractive company. "Love conquers all, does it not? I'll just ask Lisa." Like I was asking her, *What time is it? Who am I supposed to help you destroy?*

For the first time, Iris spied the medallions sitting a little distance away on the counter. She plucked a knife from a nearby block of them and somewhat clumsily slipped the blade through one of the chains. She held it up at eye level and examined it.

I asked her what I'd asked Ernie. "Is that a real language? What does it say?"

"It's Hebrew. On this side, the acolyte speaks: *My soul is thine.* On the other, the master: *Thy soul is mine."*

A bark of laughter escaped me. I covered my mouth in embarrassment. I didn't want to offend her, but, come on, really?

"I'm sorry, Iris. I pictured one of those necklaces that teenage girls wear. They say *Best Friends,* and are shaped like a heart. There's a break in the middle, though, and one wears one half and the other one –"

"This isn't child's play, Cal. Sonny pledged his soul to Candy and Phenex, and they took it. Through this device. That's why it's discolored. *The all-consuming flame . . .*" Iris nodded at the remaining medallion on the counter. "And she tried to take your other friend, too."

"Lenny's old, Iris, just like me. Things wear out, and people do, too. We all gotta go sometime." I felt ridiculous myself, suddenly, repeating trite clichés. "What I'm trying to say – Lenny's fifty-five. He's fat. He had a stroke. There wasn't anything magical about it."

Iris returned my gaze expressionlessly. I wasn't going to convince her, and she wasn't going to convince me, but I tried one more time. "Why would Candy want to steal Lenny's soul? Ernie, I can understand. She's apparently always been obsessed with Ernie. But what did Lenny ever do to her? What does she want with him?"

Iris shrugged. "Because he was handy, maybe? Because he accepted her gift? I don't know all her motivations, Cal. Maybe Phenex prefers the souls and energies of musicians? And you said he was an accomplished one. What did you call him?"

"God's bass player."

"A coup indeed to deliver God's anything to a demon."

I realized that lovely Iris was completely serious. Not in a fervent, missionary, I-must-convert-you-and-make-you-see-the-light kind of way, like Sonny's mom, advising me to accept Jesus into my heart. Iris didn't care if I believed or not, because her belief was second nature to her.

She wouldn't go out of her way to explain to me how gravity worked; I could see it in action for myself. So should I be able to accept the reality of current events: Candy had expired Sonny to use the energy of his soul for her own diabolical ends, and she had attempted to do the same to Lenny, but since his medallion had been removed, the evil was somehow stymied. All this was fact to Iris, completely plausible cause and effect. But I simply didn't want to discuss this ridiculous mumbo-jumbo anymore.

"I'm protected now, right? By the Eye of Horus?" I touched my own amulet through my shirt.

"Somewhat. I have to do more research –"

"Great. In the meantime, would you like to take a swim? The pool's heated." I reached for the blackened medallion, to put it back on the counter with its fellow, hoping to divert Iris from all this serious talk of souls and the taking of them, all stuff in which I still didn't believe, despite her solemn warnings.

Iris jerked her hand back; the chain slid forward off the end of the knife. She jumped out of the way as it fell to the floor. I bent to retrieve it and she grabbed at my arm. "Don't touch it, Cal."

"Don't be ridiculous, Iris." I picked up the medallion, and Ernie's words returned to me a third time. "I'm sure it only works if you believe in it in the first place, right? Like voodoo dolls?" I scooped up the other one, and put them and Sonny's and his mother's letters back into the drawer.

Iris's lip curled deviously. She regained her barstool, and reached across the counter for one of the canisters beside the coffee pot. She removed the lid, peeped inside. "In the world in which you live, in the belief system you inhabit . . . It would be safe to assume that this is sugar, right?"

I nodded.

"But if I replaced this sugar with, oh, say . . . cyanide, and you spooned it into your coffee, your belief that it was sugar wouldn't save you, now would it?

"I tell you those devices are now poisoned, and just because you can't see it, don't believe it . . . It changes nothing. *They are dangerous to you.* I recommend you rid yourself of them as soon as possible."

I want you to throw it in their faces and tell them that they didn't get my boy in the end . . .

But Iris was telling me that they had gotten him. I sobered at the vehemence of her belief, of her obvious desire to protect me. But only for a moment. It was all just insane.

"I'll get rid of them. But for right now . . . Do you want to take a swim?"

My maid Amanda sometimes took a dip in the pool. She kept her suit in the closet by the washer, and I didn't think she would mind if I lent it to Iris.

FORTY

We had an enjoyable afternoon and evening together. The subjects of magic, of ambitious, evil witches, deadly medallions, and the current and future threats to my immortal soul were dropped. We had pleasant, sparkling conversation about other things.

We swam, cooked dinner. We watched a movie. We got drunk.

Finally, I showed Iris to the room that Lisa had used, still the farthest from my own. It wasn't that I thought I would be tempted, and I was sure she wouldn't be. I could tell that Iris was very fond of me, despite my utter apostasy, but if there was any desire in her past a platonic friendship, she kept it hidden. She knew that I was in love with another, after all.

Or I might have been imagining Iris's affection for me, because I certainly felt an affection for her. It might've been the wine, gone to my head.

I even had a very nice dream about her; idyllic, tranquil. There was a tire swing suspended from the thick branch of a massive, flowery tree; Iris was wearing a demure white gown with a scarlet sash, and I pushed her to and fro. Then we were on a lake in a rowboat. Iris smiled at me and trailed her fingers languorously in the water, flicked me playfully with it. I rowed through dappled sunshine, then under a low, wide, tunnel-like bridge.

I mention these gentle, friendly images of myself and Iris to underscore their purity, because my dream soon changed to something else entirely.

All at once, Iris was gone, and I found myself in a darkened room of indeterminate size. I glanced to my left, and there was the demon Phenex, one cloven hoof braced against the wall behind us, his powerful arms crossed contemplatively across his chest.

He eyed me with a sort of embarrassed amazement for the span of maybe three heartbeats, then took a guitar pick out of his mouth. His black, curving talons reminded me of Candy's long, black-painted fingernails.

"Just what is it that you think you're doing, Cal?"

I considered the demon mildly. It seemed that we were buddies. "I have no idea to what you're referring, Phenex."

"Just how many women do you reckon you need all of a sudden, Lover Boy? Why are you making time with a shriveled-up, haughty old witch like Iris, when you have this?"

A spotlight split the darkness, revealing a stage and a stripper pole. Then Lisa, naked except for a pair of high heels, stepped out of the shadows and twirled around it for some moments. It was impressive; I'm sure I stirred in my sleep. Then she stopped and gazed invitingly at me, lips parted, flawless breasts heaving ever so slightly from the exertion of spinning on the pole.

"Didn't you give her to me?" I asked the demon, again with only mild interest. "Isn't she already mine? What are you trying to say?"

Phenex shrugged helplessly. *"Heaven has no rage like love to hatred turned, nor hell a fury like a woman scorned.* If she finds out that you've been having sanctimonious sorceresses stay overnight – who does Iris think she is, anyway? Telling you that your own people are out to get you?"

"They're your people, Red," I replied. "And it was Sonny that told me."

Phenex nodded at the stage again. "I wouldn't let her find out what you've been doing, my friend."

Lisa now had her hands on her hips. She pouted.

"I haven't been doing anything. I'm allowed to have guests, Phenex."

"You're allowed to do anything you want, Cal. The Lord, thy God, has given you a free will, has he not?

"It's all up for interpretation – the motivations for the actions that we take. You say it's all okey-dokey to have strange witches stay overnight when your girlfriend's out of town. But maybe Lisa wouldn't see it the same way. So I advise you to keep it all on the down low, just to be on the safe side. I advise you *to enter ye in at the strait gate: for wide is the gate, and broad is the way, that leadeth to destruction."* He grinned at me, showing all his snaggle teeth.

"I'm not sure Lisa would take too kindly to news of another bitch swimming with her man, drinking with him. Giving him advice. Staying overnight with him." The demon inclined his head toward Lisa again; her pout had morphed into an angry scowl.

"I'd keep it to myself, if I was you. If you tell her, she might just think, hell, what's sauce for the –"

"I don't even know what that means, Phenex." For *a Great Marquis of Hell,* he certainly could be annoying. "I don't have anything to hide. I haven't done anything –"

"Whatever you say, Homie." He held his hands up. I noticed that there was a pentagram tattooed on one red palm, like Mike the roadie's. "I'm just saying. You wouldn't want her to feel like she had to get even. That she had to *reciprocate.* You know how much she likes old guys."

"I haven't done anything –"

"Enjoy the show."

I looked at the stage again. From behind, a man's arm slid across Lisa's belly; his other arm crossed her chest. Lisa turned in his embrace, welcoming. The spotlight brightened to reveal the man, as naked as she was. Lisa wrapped her arms around his neck, leaned into him with a slow kiss.

I was not surprised in the least to see that it was Dennis Whitly, his old guy's head transplanted onto the lean, glistening body of a decades' younger man, a man Lisa's age.

I glanced over at Phenex to tell him that I wasn't worried about Denny and Lisa, because Lisa didn't care for him, and much more importantly, Denny wasn't having any. But Phenex was gone.

When I looked back at the stage, Denny's youth had been restored, crow's feet erased, hair once more long and brown and shaggy – he was again the god of a million groupie fantasies. A bed had replaced the stripper pole, and he and Lisa were going at it quite vociferously now, and even though I wasn't jealous of Denny, it really was no fun at all watching him, young or old, fuck my girlfriend; it was no fun watching her enjoy it quite so much.

I wasn't jealous. I was annoyed. But I couldn't seem to look away, couldn't seem to make myself wake up.

Phenex's voice said, "If I was you, I'd keep my choice of overnight guests to myself . . ."

"Oh, all right. I'll keep it to myself."

As if released, dismissed, I woke up.

FORTY-ONE

I pondered this dream as I got dressed and went downstairs. It was becoming a habit: weird dreams of red-skinned Phenex, contemplation of same as I padded down the steps. The first one had been amusing – my initial introduction to the band's namesake demon, my mind's imagining of him as cartoonish; my collation of previous conversations of witchcraft.

But what was my subconscious trying to tell me now?

Surely, I was fond of Iris. But fondness was no sin, and I hadn't dreamed of *her* naked and spinning on a stripper pole. I wouldn't trade what I had with Lisa for all the world, no matter how brief our time together might turn out to be. She was everything I'd ever wanted, without even realizing that I'd wanted it: youth, exuberance, musical knowledge and talent. And most importantly, it seemed that she loved me back.

The guilt that Phenex had attempted to engender in me about having overnight guests seemed to come from some external source, because I felt no guilt at my actions. Even though I flattered myself that I could've accomplished it, I hadn't entertained a single adulterous thought about Iris. Even my sweet dream of her had been innocent. I had not one thing to feel guilty about.

Enticing smells met me as my feet hit the hardwood on the first floor: bacon, coffee, something that smelled like fresh bread. Iris had been busy in the kitchen.

She met me with a smile and a steaming mug of coffee. She indicated for me to sit, and set a plate before me containing a fat Denver omelet, and a pile of hash browns, and yes, those were made-from-scratch biscuits. I realized that no woman had catered to me in this manner, made me breakfast, since my mother, when I was in grade school.

I thanked Iris profusely, told her she hadn't had to go to all this trouble.

"Your kitchen is wonderful, Cal. So large, so many gadgets. I love to cook, and you have so much food . . ."

"It's my maid. She does the shopping. Keeps everything stocked. She knows I don't get out much. I think she's afraid I'll starve."

"An admirable woman."

I nodded, and tucked into my breakfast, made appreciative *mmm* sounds at its deliciousness.

Iris eyed me inquisitively over her coffee cup. "Did you have pleasant dreams?"

Keep it to yourself, Phenex's rumbling voice said in my head. Iris continued to stare expectantly at me and inexplicably, I was struck with the impossible idea that she already knew exactly what I'd dreamed.

"Silliness," I replied, gesturing with my fork. "Meaninglessness. Trivialities."

"One of your rational man's gods, Sigmund Freud, said, *Dreams are never concerned with trivia.*"

I couldn't shake the impression that Iris was aware of what I'd dreamed, so I just went with it. "I don't have anything to hide, Iris."

"Freud also said, *How bold one gets when one is sure of being loved.*" She broke eye contact, busied herself with topping off my coffee. She asked if I wanted more sugar.

"As long as it's not cyanide."

"Nor aconite." She smiled mysteriously at my ignorance. "Wolf's bane. The queen of all poisons. More readily available than cyanide, and you'd be dead within the hour."

I didn't even pause, but spooned some into my cup. "I trust you, Iris."

"And I assure you that you can." Still she stared at me. "I also advise you to trust in your dreams, Cal. Sometimes the subconscious mind is aware of truths that the conscious mind ignores. My grandmother always said, *The biggest mistake you can make is believing that everyone thinks the same way as you do, and acting on that thought.*"

"Was she also *of the blood?*"

"From birth."

Jesus, I thought, *the entire universe, the demon Phenex, and my own unconscious mind are conspiring against me, trying to make me feel guilty over nothing. Iris is reading my mind.*

I had done nothing wrong, but maybe the unseen forces of my unconscious, and Iris, too, realized something that I consciously had not, and I paused to ruminate on it. Lisa was young, of a different generation. Perhaps her sense of propriety was indeed different than mine, perhaps she would not take into consideration my age, the fact that my curiosity about a beautiful woman in my house overnight would not extend to actually finding out about it. Another quote from the esteemed *Herr Doktor* occurred to me: *The virtuous man contents himself with dreaming that which the wicked man does in actual life.*

Besides loyalty to my relationship with Lisa, and respect for Iris, it hadn't been virtue that had stayed me from making a pass at my charming friend, however. Like most musicians, my virtue had always been dubious at best. It was age and experience that had made me immune to Iris. She was beautiful, true, and I was fond of her, but she didn't have anything that I hadn't seen before. *Making time* for its own sake had never been my thing.

I realized that such a truth might pass Lisa by, however. A younger man, young like she was, might've acted differently. I surely would not've been too happy to hear that Lisa had spent the night alone in a big ol' house with Horus or Hotdog.

It's all up for interpretation – the motivations for the actions that we take, Phenex had said. And even though I knew Phenex didn't exist, that his words were just my own words, filtered through the mysterious workings of sleep – maybe he was right. Maybe I should just keep the presence of the beautiful, *haughty old witch,* alone with me in the McMansion overnight, to myself.

My phone beeped.

We'll b home in an hour or so, Lisa's text said.

I looked at the time. It was barely ten.

Wow, I texted back. *U must've left Frisco early.*

It's a long story. Mom's pissed. I'll tell u when I see u.

Iris was loading the breakfast things into the dishwasher. She pushed the button, then said, "I understand there's a train nearby? If you would just take me to the –"

"That's not necessary, Iris. I'll drive you back home." Once again, our shared guiltlessness struck me. Why did she want to sneak out of here like a whore?

She nodded at my phone. "It doesn't take divine precognition to imagine that you've heard from your young lady." She smiled fondly. *"The minute I heard my first love story, I started looking for you, not knowing how blind that was. Lovers don't finally meet somewhere, they're in each other all along.* I wouldn't want to delay your reunion."

I shrugged. "Her mother's coming along." I realized that I sounded like a teenage boy, disappointed that there was going to be a chaperone for my *lover's reunion.* My own words embarrassed me.

Iris pretended not to notice. "All the more reason for me to go. Candy and I didn't part on the best of terms, Cal. She kind of left me short-handed at the store."

I sensed that this wasn't the only reason for Iris's distaste, and said as much. "And her . . . *methodologies* differ from yours. Candy's not a good witch."

Iris's tinkling laughter. "Indeed!" A smile, a pause. "I'll enjoy the train ride, Cal. Really. I insist."

I returned her smile. "So mote it be."

On the way out to the car, Iris stopped. "You've forgotten to give me a copy of your book."

The entire reason for her visit.

I went back inside and located the box of them, sent from the publisher a million years ago. It was half empty. I had given away a few copies here and there over the years. I wiped the dust off of one of the remaining ones and went back out to the driveway.

Iris was already in the car, a pen in her hand. "Of course you'll autograph it for me?"

I was at a loss for a moment. *To my good friend, Iris, thanks for all your support* – what I signed for strangers – seemed anonymous, as I felt that she really was my good friend. It seemed trite, almost insulting. *Long live rock and roll* would be lost on her. Finally, I wrote, *To Glinda the Goode Witch, from your faithful acolyte,* and signed my name.

She smiled brightly, as if it were poetry, and I felt like I should've put more thought into it.

"Now I have something to read on the train."

When I got back to the house, I texted Lisa, realizing that I had completely forgotten to do so earlier. *Can't wait to see u guys.*

Then I took a shower, and went back to bed for a little nap. I wasn't as young as I used to be, and I'd been up late, drinking and having pleasant conversation with my new friend. There were no dreams.

FORTY-TWO

My phone beeped. *We're here.*

I hadn't intended to sleep until they arrived. I pulled on clothes and stumbled down the steps, feeling fuzzy. I opened the door, and Lisa's expression of annoyance faded immediately. She smiled and hugged me.

Wordlessly, Candy stomped into the house, and I recalled Lisa's text: *Mom's pissed.* Lisa closed the door behind us, and Candy stopped in the entranceway, suddenly alert like some kind of animal.

She whirled on me. "Your maid's taste in perfume has gotten more expensive, Cal."

I looked at her, nonplussed, expressionless, still not all the way awake. Lisa sighed, rolled her eyes. Her annoyance returned.

Candy ignored her, actually sniffed the air. "Yes, an ethereal fragrance, faint, yet . . ." Her eyes widened, then narrowed accusingly. "A witch has been here!"

"Jesus Christ and all the saints, Mom! Just because you think that Ernie . . ." Lisa looked at me and explained. "So we were onstage in Frisco. There was a glassed-in booth, upstairs. From backstage, Mom saw Ernie up there, talking to the lady from EMI –"

"She doesn't work for EMI," Candy spat. "She's just a pencil-pusher, a scheduler –"

"Mom decided Ernie and this lady were a little too cozy, and now she's imagining whores and witches and groupies everywhere."

A line from Shakespeare played in my mind: *And thus thy fall hath left a kind of blot, to mark the full-fraught man and best indued with some suspicion.* Yet I marveled at Candy's intuition: Ernie had been cozy with Bianca recently, if not in the glassed-in booth in Frisco, and a witch had been here.

"I told her that she was imagining it," Lisa continued. "Ernie was just talking to her. There wasn't anything funny going on."

Now it was Phenex that spoke in my head, reminding me of the fury of a woman scorned.

"We left Frisco early because Mom was arguing with him. Christ! I'm so glad I was in the van instead of the car they rented, so I didn't have to listen to it. I told her –"

"Shut up, Lisa." I noticed that, at her side, Candy's left hand had formed the Evil Eye, the devil horns, and she unconsciously pointed them at her daughter.

"I told her that he was just talking up the band."

"Are you on for Vegas?"

Lisa glanced at her mother. "Not yet."

"Forget about Ernie," Candy said. "I know a witch's been here."

"Not just one, Candy. A whole coven. The Temecula Chapter of the Hot-to-Trot Sisterhood of Sonic Daydream Fans paid me an unexpected visit last night. They brought . . ." I grinned. "They brought stripper poles and did a quite rousing routine to *Me So Horny.*" I winked at Lisa. *"I won't tell your mama if you don't tell your dad."*

Lisa grinned in delight and hugged me. *"I love you long time."* Her knowledge of music was encyclopedic; she was even familiar with the filthy old rap song.

Candy was not amused. "Whatever. You and Ernie – you don't know who you're fucking with."

I was surprised by the profanity, as was Lisa. She told her mother to shut up.

"Whatever," Candy repeated, falling effortlessly into ignorant, slighted groupie mode, becoming in an eye-blink a slutty, been-around-the-block-on-her-back teenage girl, trapped in a middle-aged woman's body. She sneered at her daughter. "You're safe. You've had your shots. But just let me remind you, musicians are all the same."

You oughta know, I thought, and grinned brightly, innocently, at her.

She glared at me. "It'll all even out in the end. You just see if it doesn't."

She pushed past us and fled out the front door, giving it a good, solid slam. As the reverberation died out, I heard the squeal of tires and the unmistakable roar of Ernie's Porsche. Evidently, Candy wasn't so pissed at her baby-daddy that she was above borrowing his car.

Now Lisa herself quoted the Bard. *"O, beware, my lord, of jealousy. It is the green-eyed monster which doth mock the meat it feeds on."* She smiled at my surprise. "We of the blood always have the benefit of a classical education, Cal."

At her mention of her fellow witches, I looked to see if there was any suspicious searching in her eye, and was pleased and satisfied that there was not. Candy's intuition might be spot-on, but her daughter put no faith in it. And it wasn't like I had done anything wrong. The demon's advice and Iris's had also been spot-on: I surely wasn't going to mention it now.

"Come on, Cal, let's take a swim." I wondered – without any guilt, damn it – if Iris had returned Amanda's suit to the closet beside the washer. But I immediately forgot this possibly damning detail as Lisa started walking toward the patio, doffing her clothes as she went.

By the time she reached the sliding glass door, she was naked, and she turned and smiled at me smugly. She was proud, and rightfully so, of her youthfully perfect body, knew the effect it would produce in me.

I fought it for a minute. "Lisa, the neighbors . . ."

She opened the door and looked outside. "No one's peeping through the fence. Come on." She crossed the short patio and dove into the pool, not waiting for my response.

Life is good, I told myself. I took off my Eye of Horus pendant – another piece of evidence that a witch had been present – and put it in my pocket. I followed her outside.

We took a swim, and lightly, playfully did what comes naturally in the pool. Then we went back into the house and proceeded more seriously. Lisa had played two shows, and had not had an outlet for the inimitable thrill she felt from performing, so by the time the sun slanted in from the west, we had delightfully broken in damn near every room in the big house.

The day was as glorious as the week we'd spent at the beach, and more so, because we had the opportunity to again actually play music together, instead of just swapping lyrics. There were no guitars in my house, however, so we weren't much of an act. I kept the beat and Lisa sang.

I considered crossing the street and retrieving Sonny's Telecaster for her, but decided against it. I didn't want to put up with Katie – she might insist on a guitar duel with Phenex's pretty singer, just to check out her chops – and I didn't want to bring back Lisa's sadness when she saw poor Sonny's guitar. I also didn't want to answer her questions about how I'd come into possession of it.

As with Iris the night before, Lisa and I cooked dinner, watched a movie. I marveled at what a splendid host I'd become, entertaining comely and attractive witches, one right after the previous.

But I didn't sleep alone that night, as I had when lovely Iris had visited, and I didn't dream. Nor was Lisa the cook that Iris was, which I couldn't help noticing when she made me breakfast the next morning. But of course she had other charms, and they were quite enough to make up for her culinary deficiencies.

FORTY-THREE

When we got back to the clinker-brink house in Riverside, the baby-blue 911 was not present, and the mood inside was tense. Lisa hastily joined James and Roy and Horus in rehearsal, and Candy informed me tersely that my former second-guitar was *working on Vegas,* her expression daring me to make any comment whatsoever about all of that. I simply nodded, so Candy plopped down into one of the folding chairs and watched her band, and ignored me as if I'd ceased to exist.

I sat next to her and texted Ernie. I reveled in this aspect of the modern age that had turned us all into snarky teenage girls: the ability to talk shit on someone without them knowing it, when they were right there in the room.

Hell hath no fury, my brutha.

My last nerve, Cal. She's on it.

What did Bianca say?

She surprised me, being in Frisco. But she's not mad. I told her that our thing, that was before Candy had come along. I didn't go into how it had only come about because of Sonny dying, but I made it clear that our thing was first, & that this other thing wasn't anything that she needed 2 concern herself about. I told her that I hadn't been aware that she'd wanted our thing 2 continue. ☺ She understood. She's in the biz. She knows how groupies r.

The teenage girl in me said, *Oh, no, he didn't!* with a kind of mean-spirited glee. But he had. He'd called a spade a shovel, as my dad had always recommended, had called Candy what she was, to Bianca, and he was repeating it to me. *She knows how groupies r.*

I saw that Candy's angry, unwise possessiveness had killed Ernie's budding *minion-hood.* I smiled at my own cleverness. Ernie had regained his worldview. His baby-mama was just another one of legions of women that he had known. Bianca was another one, but she hadn't gotten all uppity about sharing, so he had a modicum of – for lack of a better word – *respect* for her.

What about Vegas?

I'm in Big Bear w/Bianca right now.

Maybe he hadn't been making time with Bianca in that glassed-in booth in Frisco, but once Candy had started bitching at him about it, Ernie had decided that it was once again time to play ball with a friendlier teammate. Forget God's commandments, or even Phenex's for that matter. Candy had unwisely accused Ernie of an infidelity that he hadn't committed, and now she was learning a more important commandment, and the hard way: *Give not Ernie LaBelle the name, lest you want to watch him play the game, and right in front of you.*

I just signed the contract 4 all 8 gigs. And more: a rep from EMI's gonna meet us in Vegas. They're gonna record Phenex, Cal. Sign em.

I glanced up from my phone as Candy yelled at her daughter, accusing her of being flat. Lisa wasn't off-key; Candy was just still in a pissy mood at Ernie's absence. It didn't matter that he was still working hard for the band. She undoubtedly suspected just how hard he was working, and in the face of that, her impotent anger remained.

U haven't told Candy?

U tell her. & tell her she's welcome. The show's Sat. Load em up 4 me, will ya, Cal? I'm gonna stay here til 2morrow.

I grinned. Ernie was most assuredly back. By staying away and with another woman, he was reminding Candy of her place in the universe. A worn-out old groupie wasn't going to dictate to Ernie LaBelle, even if she was his daughter's mother.

Ur gonna have 2 face the music sometime.

I'll b back 2morrow afternoon & then we can go on 2 Vegas. I'll get us a hotel. The meeting w/EMI's at 4 on Sat, show's at 9.

U want me 2 tell Candy about getting signed?

Do u want 2?

I thought that I'd enjoy seeing Lisa's eyes light up. Getting signed was the most fevered dream of every musician. I knew that it wasn't all it was cracked up to be, however. Once they put their names on that dotted line – Phenex the band wouldn't belong to Phenex the demon any more, at least not in this world. Phenex the band would belong to EMI, and they would step and fetch and dance to the corporate tune. They would get to make a record, but they'd also appear when and where the industry giant told them to, and they'd open for whomever EMI saw fit.

And if their first record – it would be eponymously titled, I was sure of it – if their first record failed to make the requisite profit, there wouldn't be a second one. EMI would drop them quicker than they had so surprisingly picked them up.

I saw a parallel between Iris's tale of masters and acolytes, of souls given over knowingly, willingly, eagerly. EMI would soon own this band, more completely than in some witchy compact with the forces unseen, solemnly made by the dark of the moon. EMI would own them legally, in iron-clad, airtight black and white. And if Phenex failed to perform financially as EMI's unimaginative accountants deemed fit – if they weren't *so happy they could hardly count* – it wouldn't take a spell or a blackened medallion or a dark highway for Phenex to be *sacrificed* back to Black Winter-style oblivion.

But the arch-fiend record company's puppeteering control of Phenex was still in the future. That they were gonna get signed would be nothing but the absolute best news in the world to them right now, and like I say, I knew I'd enjoy seeing Lisa's joy. But I figured I would see it, regardless of who broke the awesome news.

It's all u, Road Dog.

Ok. I'll text her. I'll see u 2morrow. We'll take my car. She can ride with the band.

I grinned. *U don't know who ur fucking with, Ernie.* Then I sent him a smiley face to let him know I was just kidding.

Right. This whiny shit's gonna stop, Cal. Any word about Lenny?

They're still running tests. But Barbie says he's walking.

That's great! I gotta go.

The hot tub beckons?

☺ Something like that. I'll text Candy real quick. I'll see u 2morrow.

Have fun, my friend.

☺Always.

Even though I was a ghost to Candy, she was sitting right beside me, so I heard her phone ring over the din of Phenex's rehearsal. The tone was the breakdown from *Cerulean.*

I watched her curiously, wondering what form her elation was going to take. Prophecy had been fulfilled: Phenex *had made the big time at last.* Whether they would endure – which I doubted – or become just another shooting star, remained to be seen.

I expected Candy to leap to her feet, to whoop ecstatically. To my surprise, she just grinned with an air of vindication. She caught Lisa's eye, and made a throat-cutting gesture.

Lisa ceased singing; the rest of Phenex jangled to a stop.

"We're on for Vegas. Saturday night."

Lisa encompassed the reaction that I'd expected from her mother: she cried *"Yesss!"* and whomped Horus on the back; he almost dropped Ernie's Charvel.

I thought vaguely that there would have to be another trip to Guitar Center soon to purchase an axe for Horus. But on the other hand, guitars had always been just guitars to the legendary Ernie LaBelle, and perhaps he'd already simply gifted this one to his worshipful apprentice.

"Denny's partial to his Les Paul, and he's got a great Strat," Ernie had said once in one of his many *Guitar Player* interviews. "He's got a few others, too, but not too many. I've got a closet full of guitars, dude. The manufacturers send 'em. They're all pretty much the same to me. It's a poor carpenter that blames his tools, and if you know how to play . . . Well, you get my point."

The interviewer had gone on to note, unnecessarily, that Ernie could no doubt elicit his trademark magic from a cigar box, a broom handle, and some rubber bands, and I remembered thinking that the gal from *Rolling Stone,* the one that had longed for Dennis Whitly's non-existent *availability,* couldn't have argued with that.

Lisa and the band were talking excitedly about Vegas, and I waited for Candy to drop the other, much more exciting bomb. After several seconds, unable to believe that she wasn't telling them that they were gonna get signed, I said, "Did Ernie tell you about . . ."

Oh, shit, was I letting the cat out of the bag? Maybe Ernie hadn't told her.

"Did he mention EMI?"

Candy eyed me icily. "Ernie's become a man of few words lately. He can't even take the time to call anymore." Then her expression became the very dictionary definition of smug. "He *texted* me the good news. I'll tell 'em on the way tomorrow. No need to disrupt rehearsal."

Whatever, you controlling bitch. I wasn't gonna tell them. Phenex wasn't my band.

They rehearsed for the rest of the afternoon, then Candy instructed Horus to lay out cold cuts and whip up some mac and cheese. Her need to busy herself in the kitchen had been a product of her nervousness before Phenex's hometown debut, and now that they were (to her) a successful, about-to-be-signed, touring band, she delegated the task of feeding them to her newest minion.

Lisa was again nervous, however – without even knowing about getting signed, she saw Vegas as the first big step on the road to fame. And she was also still on the outs with her mother. I noticed that they only exchanged frowns, and didn't do a lot of talking. So I was more than happy to take her home with me when she asked to go.

Lisa had brought a swim suit this time, and when we got back to the McMansion, she commenced to swimming laps in the dark. She said that the exercise helped her to think, helped to burn off the excess nervous energy. I sat in a deck chair by the pool and watched her.

FORTY-FOUR

Barbie called at 9 am the next morning, and told me that they were finally releasing Lenny from the hospital. She said that he was walking on his own, but still couldn't talk.

"He's very weak, Cal, but he refused a wheelchair. I made him take the walker they offered. He wants to go home."

He wants his bass. I told her I was on my way.

Lisa was arguing with her mother. "Oh, for Christ's sake, Mom! Just meet him at his house, then! Or better yet, just leave him alone until tonight. He's gonna go to Vegas with us, and then he won't be able to get away from you – hello? Hello?" Lisa rolled her eyes. "Mom just hung up on me. She said Ernie's coming home soon, but says he wants to go to his house to pack. She thinks he's avoiding her."

I blinked blankly, unwilling to comment. "I have to go pick Lenny and Barbie up in Palm Springs and take 'em home."

A shadow crossed her face. "Is it okay if I stay here, Cal? I don't really know them . . . They're your friends, and they probably wouldn't want a stranger just showing up with you."

"You're not a stranger."

"But still, I feel uncomfortable. He's just out of the hospital . . . I'll go visit them with you after they're settled back in."

You gonna go on tour with your band, conquer the world, make a million bucks? Again? Lenny had asked me. I doubted that there were gonna be any millions. I doubted that there would even be another record, or another tour. But Lenny had guessed right. I would be along for the ride for this one. I realized I wouldn't be seeing my old friend again until Phenex finished their eight-city tour.

"I'll take another swim," Lisa was saying. "I'll pack you a suitcase for Vegas. I'll be fine while you're gone. Go see your friends."

****

Lenny and Barbie were waiting outside when I arrived at the Desert Regional Medical Center. She set the walker in front of his wheelchair, and he grimly maneuvered it across the short sidewalk to the Caddy. Barbie opened the door for him, but he pushed her hands away when she tried to help him into the backseat. He slammed the door and she sighed, handed the walker to me.

As I stowed it in the trunk, she whispered, "The therapist said he might get frustrated. He has to take things slow. I'm so glad you're here to take us home, Cal. He kept asking if it would be you coming to get us."

I was touched by Barbie's gratitude, flattered that Lenny wanted me to pick them up instead of baby brother Denny. But on the other hand, Lenny and I had been friends for a long time. He knew that I was tough, tougher than his wife and Ernie and maybe Denny, too. He knew I wouldn't coddle him like Barbie was already trying to do, wouldn't let my own sadness and pity for him show.

I went through Bakers Drive-thru for him so he could get some real food. It was our favorite of old, so I knew exactly what to order. But then the bitching started immediately: Barbie said something about the unhealthiness of the food, how the doctors had said that he should start being more careful about his diet. Lenny leaned forward, tapped me on the shoulder, and when I looked at him in the rearview, he inclined his head toward his spouse, shook it.

I took a deep breath, decided to level with her for her marriage's sake. "Don't mommy him, Barbie," I told her, as if he wasn't sitting right there. "He's not going to change what he does, what he eats, just because –"

"I know, Cal." A tear ran down her cheek, and Lenny rolled his eyes.

Lenny made a writing gesture and Barbie took a pad and pen from her purse and gave it to him. He braced it clumsily on his knee with his useless right hand. At least he could move his arm now – that was an improvement. *I feel better,* he painstakingly scrawled. *Lets eat.*

Lenny slowly pushed his walker across the uneven ground of the dooryard to his house. I was glad that there were only two steps up to the front porch. It took him a minute, but he made it, then collapsed into a chair. Barbie unlocked the door. Lenny pushed the walker away until it was almost out of reach, then glared expectantly, defiantly at his wife. He struggled to take the pad and pen out of his pocket. Barbie flinched to help him, but then stopped herself.

Lenny was not left-handed, so he wrote very slowly. He held the pad up. *Bass.*

"I'm going to go check on the horses. Will you get it for him, Cal?"

Bitch! Lenny slowly wrote, and shook the pad at her. But she had already turned without looking at either of us and was halfway to the barn.

I picked up the pad from the little table there, where he'd dropped it in disgust. I tore the page off and stuck it in my pocket. I glared at him, then went into the house to get his axe.

I held it out to him; he was at a loss for a moment as to how it take it from me. He searched my face suspiciously for pity, so I remained expressionless. Finally he grasped it by the neck and folded it across his chest. By a force of will, he crooked his right arm and held his hand against the head. He strummed once with his left hand, tunelessly, then grinned his wonky, lopsided smile at me.

He'd just wanted to hear the tone. He knew he wasn't going to bust out the bassline to *Money* or even *Tomcats.* Not yet. He'd just wanted to hold his old friend for a second.

He went to set it down and I made to take it from him, but Lenny shook his head. He wanted the stand, so I went in and fetched it for him. He put the bass on it, then moved the whole thing closer, nearer to him than was the walker. He ran his fingers across the strings, and just looked at it for a second. Leonard Whitley's bass had been his friend longer than Barbie had been, longer than I had been. Like Ernie had speculated, its absence would leave a hole in his life; he needed to have it nearby, more than he needed Barbie or me. He winked at me. It would be a long road back, and Lenny might never be God's bass player again, but as long as he had his instrument, he was ready to start the journey.

He nodded for me to sit in the chair on the other side of the little table; Barbie's place. He reached for the pad, then looked at me and blinked in surprised astonishment. Some wonderful idea had struck him.

Lenny held his hand up to the side of his head: the universal gesture for a telephone.

"I dunno. Barbie probably has it."

He nodded at my pocket, so I handed him my phone.

He set it on the table and began pushing buttons, then abruptly held it up.

Now I can talk. Only need one finger to type.

I grinned, relief and love for him washing over me. "Yeah, but I'm gonna need my phone back."

Fuck u. That wonky smile.

I laughed, then Lenny tilted his head sideways and studied me; his half-a-face expression was now unreadable. At last he typed, *How's ur band?*

"They're not my . . ." I sighed. "They're great. They're gonna get signed."

Lenny's left eyebrow went up. His right one tried to join the party; another good sign. He nodded questioningly toward the barn.

"When did she have time to worry about Phenex?" I asked him, and it came out harsher than I had intended. He'd been at death's door and he thought his wife had been off getting some no-talent band signed. "It was all Ernie. That's why . . . That's why he's not here. He knows some woman from EMI."

Knos her well?

"Well enough, it would seem. It's not who you know, or how you –" Barbie came around the side of the house and I shut up.

I love you, Lenny typed, and held the phone up to her.

Barbie was speechless. She smiled, as if it was the first time he'd ever said it to her. The small triumph of the moment was beautiful. She kissed him, told him that she loved him too. "I'll leave you boys to talk, now that you can." She wiped away a tear of hope and went into the house.

Again Lenny stared at me for a moment, then he typed, *Right before the accident, I mustve been thinking about ur band. I saw a big bird.*

Like a cliché: "A bird?"

Lenny typed, scrolled. He held up the phone and showed me a picture of a brown bird with red wings and a red head, standing amid yellow and orange flames: Wikipedia's depiction of the legendary *Phoenix.*

Lenny typed again. *But it was all black. Feathers were falling out. It came outta nowhere, in the middle of the road. It seemed so real. I stepped on the brakes so I didnt hit it.*

Roy's voice in my head: *This guy was behind him on the freeway, and he told the cops that Sonny suddenly swerved, like there was something in the road in front of him. But the guy said he couldn't see anything.*

I blinked at my mind's silliness, at its trying to make some connection. That was just ridiculous. There was no connection. There were no spells, no magic, no cursed medallions, no harvesting of souls. Lenny lived in the boonies, and surely birds flew out in front of trucks here all the time, even big, black, Phenex-looking birds. But the words were out of my mouth before I could stop them: "Did Barbie see it?"

Lenny managed a shrug, with both shoulders. Another good sign. He shook his head. *I dunno. I saw the bird, tried 2 stop, then I felt like something was squeezing my chest. Don't remember anything after that.*

Lenny eyed me intently again, then typed, *Funny, huh? Guitarists anywhere around ur band, just droppin like flies. Ernie better watch his ps & qs.*

"They're not my band, Lenny," I whispered. I was stunned that he'd somehow made the same connection between himself and Sonny that Iris had made.

Maybe theyre bad luck. How could demon worshippers b anything but bad luck?

"How do you know about the demon?" I asked, shocked. Had Lenny been having dreams, too? Had Phenex asked him to *join us?* But that was just crazy.

Ernie told me, remember? Said Marcie told him the spirits helped her get pregnant, that she & the band worship Satan.

"Candy. And it's not Satan. It's Phenex."

He's a bird, right?

I laughed shakily, nodded. "But surely you don't believe in all that horseshit, Lenny! Are you getting stupid in your old age?"

Lenny shrugged again, unoffended at my insult. *Theres more things n heaven & earth, Cal. May b u should b careful.*

I was nonplussed. *"Really?"*

This frightening but not uncommon health event, this brush with death, had my old friend believing in devils, had made him suddenly, unaccountably fearful. *Repent, the end is near!*

"You want me to get you a priest, Lenny?"

Maybe u should think about getting urself one. What could it hurt?

Barbie came out on the porch, skillfully balancing two glasses of lemonade and a cellphone. It was quite a trick with her casted-up arm. She set the glasses on the table, and I watched Lenny carefully erase what he had typed before exchanging my phone for his.

I sipped my glass, marveling silently to myself about Lenny's warnings, so like Sonny's and Iris's. I again thought that the whole world was conspiring against me, that everyone had lost their collective mind, that everybody I knew suddenly believed in the forces unseen.

He's a bird, right?

Barbie smiled at me apologetically. "Denny's gonna be here in a little while, Cal."

I rose without even realizing I'd done so, unexpectedly glad for an excuse to get away. "That's my cue."

Denny didn't believe in the powers of the forces unseen, either, but we weren't likely to sit around and have a conversation about that, or anything else. I suddenly wanted to hear a voice of reason in this sea of hocus-pocus. I wanted to have a good laugh at the spirit world. I wanted to talk to my fellow apostate, Ernie LaBelle.

Fuck Denny, Lenny typed. *U dont have 2 leave.*

"He's your brother," Barbie scolded.

There was that motherliness again, surfacing in her tone. I remembered the notebook page in my pocket, Lenny's scrawled *Bitch!* Then, moments later, his typed declaration of love for her. I figured his mood was going to yo-yo like that for a while, depending on his level of frustration at the moment, on how much she was trying to mommy him at the time.

Yeah, the two of them didn't need the kind of friction that would spark if Denny and I crossed paths again so soon. Lenny's slow road to recovery was going to be difficult enough on both of them, enough of a strain on their marriage.

"I'm gonna be out of town," I told Barbie regretfully. "But if you need anything before then . . . I can always fly back."

"Denny's gonna stay with us a few days."

Her expression communicated that thereby, her husband would be in the best possible hands. I was no longer needed. I was dismissed.

I got the impression that Barbie thought that Denny would be on her side, would help her to coddle Lenny, help her to spoon feed him. Denny would help keep his brother away from his axe, show him that he wasn't ever going to be the same again, and that he'd better start accepting it. I didn't know if Denny would feel this way or not; but grasping that this was indeed Barbie's attitude shocked and saddened me.

"I'll text you," I told my old friend. "I know you can do that. And I'm gonna wanna hear at least *Another One Bites the Dust* by the time I get back."

Lenny gave me his wonky smile. *I'll b ready to audition for Bela Fleck. Victor who?*

FORTY-FIVE

On the way back home, I discovered that I was in a bad mood.

There was Barbie's motherliness – I felt a different kind of pity for her husband now. Lenny was gonna be all right, if he was allowed to have his bass and progress at his own pace. But I could see that Barbie was gonna hold him back, help him with the wrong things. She would want to dress him and feed him – I realized suddenly that her husband was going to be the stand-in for the child she'd never had. I found myself reluctantly, unwillingly putting my hope in Denny. He was a musician. Surely he wouldn't keep his brother from our craft?

And then there was that other craft, the one that Lenny had all of a sudden seemed to put so much store in. I thought of Iris's Eye of Horus charm, in my pocket in the dirty clothes hamper, and wondered if wearing it would put me in a better mood. I doubted it.

Now that Lenny had realized that he could effortlessly communicate through his cellphone, I saw him with it in hand always, and when he wasn't telling his wife *I love you* or *I hate you,* he'd be reading Wikipedia pages and Googling witchcraft practices. Maybe he'd done so already, before the accident. Maybe he'd been curious about the weird medallion *Marcie* had given him, had done a little magical research of his own, reading up on the symbolism of his old second-guitar's band's odd name. *He's a bird, right?*

Whatever. Here was one part of Barbie's stubbornness that would prove beneficial: if her husband suddenly started texting her hysterically about big black birds and dead guitar players, she would quickly put the kibosh on all that. Barbie didn't go in for all that new age, hippie, Wiccan bullshit.

And then I was confronted with it all further when I got home, and my mood worsened. The house was redolent with incense. Lisa was sitting at the kitchen counter, palms flat on it in front of her, eyes closed. Two fat candles burned. She had to have brought these accoutrements with her in her bag.

When I came in, she remained in prayer for some moments, not acknowledging me. Annoyed, I finally growled, "Amen," to end her ritual.

She remained motionless for yet another heartbeat, then at last opened her eyes and looked expressionlessly at me. "It's rude to interrupt the devotions of the initiated, Cal. It can be dangerous, in fact."

My temper broke. "You know what I find dangerous? Clogged arteries and old motorcycles. Father Time taking his toll. *Destiny is a rising sun,* Lisa. Time marches on. Things and people just wear out. Accidents happen. All this other stuff . . ." I waved my hand, and the thin cloud of incense roiled. "Thinking you can change what happens in the world, control it – you're just talking to yourself."

To my utter surprise, Lisa paraphrased Iris's words. "Everything that's happened in your life, lately – and really, for the last eighteen years, since . . . It's all been just a series of coincidences to you, hasn't it? You see no guiding hand."

I was harsh with her. "That's right. No guiding hand, no conspiracy, no witchcraft. You people are nuts. There's cause and effect to everything, true, but there's no such thing as destiny, Lisa, no predetermined rewards and punishments based on sacrifices and chants to the forces unseen."

Now I quoted Iris, but I turned her words around to suit my purposes. "Reward and punishment are a result of the decisions we make. Concrete, physical actions. Yes, I'm going to sleep with you, no I'm not gonna smoke that. But the decisions are mine. I'm influenced by nothing except my own past experiences and my own current desires. You can pray to God on high or Phenex below to intercede and control my actions, but none of it is going to make one bit of difference, because none of it's real. Thinned out blood vessels and worn out tires are real, and they'll blow when they blow. But there is nothing that you can chant about that will make them blow. Nor can you keep them from blowing when time – not any kind of guiding force, just plain old mindless entropy – decrees that they will."

She was unimpressed with my tirade. I got the distinct impression that I was talking to myself, now. "Ya got a minute, Cal? Have a seat."

Lisa gestured at the barstool beside her, and I was put in mind of all those *To Catch A Predator* episodes, Chris Hansen bidding the perverts to *Have a seat* in big, well-lit kitchens, just like this one. I'd always wondered how the would-be child molesters had failed to notice the hundreds of watts of stage lighting as they came up the hall.

I sat.

"Let me tell you a little story about coincidences. Once upon a time –"

"Once upon a time is how fairytales begin, Lisa. Fiction." I was still annoyed.

"You're not going to believe me, anyway, so why not begin it like a fairytale?" she retorted. "May I continue?"

I nodded.

"Once upon a time, there was a family. You know one of its members already. My mom."

I couldn't help but roll my eyes.

"You wanna know why I believe in the forces unseen, don't you?"

"Yeah, I guess I do." Just like I'd asked Iris how Sonny could come to believe that he was a sacrifice, how he'd been all right with it. Some cause and effect, some series of explainable events had caused Lisa to believe in the unexplained. And of course it would start with her mother, the biggest influence in her life.

"Okay, then. Shut up and listen." Lisa didn't smile. I had caused her mood to be as testy as my own.

"Mom lived in the house in Arlanza when she was a little kid. She lived there with my grandmother and my grandfather, and my great-grandmother. My great-grandmother was my grandmother's mother." She studied me as if I was a particularly dull child. "Are you getting this so far?"

Offended by her patronizing tone, I said, "Maybe some names might help, Teacher."

"Of course. The cast: my grandmother's name is Amelia. She lives in San Francisco, somewhere, or maybe she's passed. I don't know. I've never met her. Her mother's name was Cecelia; I met her a few times, but I don't remember her very well. She died when I was eight. My grandfather's name was Barrett. He died long ago."

Some snatch of conversation with Ernie tried to impress itself on my memory, something he'd said about Candy's father, but it failed to register.

"So once upon a time, they all lived together in Arlanza. Barrett was a musician – the grand piano there in the band room was his."

I had it then. Ernie had said, *Her daddy was some blues piano player who OD'd when she was a kid or something.*

"He was not a good man," Lisa was saying, "but his daughter loved him. He would play for her, try to teach her, but the notes on the sheet music never made any sense to her. 'They seemed to swim and jump and get all turned around,' Mom told me once. I think maybe she's a little dyslexic."

Or a little lazy.

"Barrett would get angry and yell at her when she couldn't play, but after a while, he gave up, and just played *for* her, and Mom liked that better. The happiest memories of her childhood were when she was sitting on the bench beside Daddy, listening to his music."

Lisa sighed. "But these memories were few. Amelia regretted marrying a musician. She went out to work every day, while he slept in after his late-night, ill-paying gigs. Amelia's own father had died when she was a child, too – he'd been a recovering alcoholic, and had preached the evils of drink to her throughout her childhood, so Amelia didn't go to the clubs where her husband played."

In the bars, with the men who play guitars, singin', drinkin' and rememberin' the times . . .

"Then why did she marry him?"

"He was charming. They met at a wedding." Lisa smiled, then sobered again. "Mom told me that they argued a lot. Barrett sometimes didn't come home after his gigs. Mom told me that she remembered an incident – Amelia wasn't home and Daddy was sitting at the piano with a young woman, laughing, playing for her. Then he left with the woman, leaving Mom in Cecelia's care. Then later that night, Mom heard Amelia sobbing in her room."

"Cecelia and Amelia didn't really get along, either. Cecelia was of the blood, and her daughter was an unbeliever, like you. She was just like you, in fact – exasperated and annoyed that her mother taught Candy all the old ways, that her little girl wore charms and read old books and made symbols in the air." Lisa smiled and forked the Evil Eye at me.

"Barrett Corson was a lot of things, but an alcoholic wasn't one of them." Lisa frowned grimly. "But he was frequently *sick.*" She made the quotation marks in the air. "When Candy asked her grandmother what was wrong with Daddy, Cecelia said, *We must pray for him, carry out rituals and sacrifices. He's in thrall to a powerful demon. We must seek aid for him from the universal forces."*

But it wasn't Phenex or even Satan himself that had him, now was it? And I bet that the universal forces were powerless against his habit.

It was as if Lisa read my mind. She shrugged in resignation. "Eventually, the demon claimed Barrett. Freed at last from this albatross around her neck – her talented, flawed husband – Amelia took her daughter and moved to San Francisco, away from the bad memories in Riverside, away from her crazy, witchy mother. Mom was about fourteen at the time.

"Mom didn't forget her grandmother, though. They wrote letters. Cecilia encouraged her to find a coven there in Frisco, to continue her studies. Mom did so, and it of course caused arguments with Amelia.

"'You're as worthless as your father, as crazy as your grandmother,' Amelia told her only child."

I realized again that I would never forget Lisa's voice. It was low and musical, and it accentuated her method of storytelling, the sing-song cadences, the pathos and bitterness.

"So the minute she turned eighteen, Mom moved out. She'd met a guitarist from some forgettable metal band, and she lived with him for a while. But he turned out to be a junkie, like her father had been, so she left him. She lived with two other witches for several years. She worked in a record store and also as a waitress, and finally saved up enough to get her own little place.

"All this time, she was of course a Sonic Daydream fan."

Of course, another record-store, waitress groupie. The saved-up nickels and dimes with which they'd bought tickets to see us had made me rich.

"Mom lived all alone for a long time. She'd never been able to find another musician who touched her soul the way Ernie LaBelle had."

I'm sure she auditioned quite a few before coming to that conclusion, however, I thought nastily.

"Mom told me that listening to your music . . . She was moved. She said that seeing Ernie up onstage . . . Her soul was transported."

Her and a million other girls. But mostly it was Dennis Whitly that had worked the transporter for them, his voice and his crooked smiles and his *mean guitar.*

Again, Lisa seemed to read my mind. "Mom said she never paid any attention to Denny or the bassist, or even you."

Especially not me, I hoped.

"It was always, always Ernie. Then Mom woke up one day with an odd feeling, that she was on the cusp of some great momentous event. She consulted with her friends, she dealt her Tarot –"

"She scryed."

Lisa frowned at my derisive interruption. "Sonic Daydream was coming to Frisco. Mom had tickets. What she had to do became clear. She would get a piece of Ernie LaBelle."

My eyebrows went up at this turn of phrase. *A piece* was certainly all it had been to Ernie, recalled years later only because of the bizarre ritual that had accompanied it, and the child it had produced.

"And so she did. She told me that the day she got the positive pregnancy test – she'd been sitting in the doctor's office . . ."

Lisa stopped and studied me closely for the span of several seconds. I was about to say *What?* but then she started talking again.

"Now we're coming to the part that you're going to try to lay off as coincidence, Cal. *Coincidences,* plural, because they happened one after another. But when I'm through with my story, I think that even you will be forced to see the hand of destiny at work. You won't be able to deny it.

"So six weeks or so after her interlude with my father, Mom is sitting in the waiting room of an obstetrician's office, trying to find out for sure whether he was indeed gonna be my father." Lisa grinned at the whimsy of this statement. "She sees a copy of *Rolling Stone* – have you ever seen a copy of *Rolling Stone* in a doctor's office, Cal?"

"I haven't been to too many obstetricians, honey."

Lisa ignored my flippancy. "Mom pages through it and finds the article: *Sonic Daydream Loses Road Manager in Horrific Crash.* There was a picture of the band, but they only interviewed Dennis Whitly."

The picture was something Sony had sent along. I didn't even know about the article until after it came out. Like Lisa said, they hadn't spoken to anyone but Denny.

"That was because Elise was his sister-in-law," I told her. "She was more than just our road manager. She was –"

"She was nothing to him," Lisa spat. "And you know it."

I shrugged. That much was true, and Lisa was aware of it because she'd read my book.

"Anyway, Mom reads the article. They described Denny's house in Malibu, said it was up the beach from the actor Sam Elliot's house. They mentioned how the accident happened not too far away, on Mullholland. In the article, Denny says that in the wake of the tragedy, Sonic Daydream would be taking some time off from touring." Lisa looked at me significantly.

"We put out three more albums," I reminded her.

"But you never toured again."

"Nope." It was not the earthshaking, history-altering event that Lisa – through her mother's opinion of it – was making it out to be. Just another example of entropy. Things wear out. Bands quit touring. It was not a tragedy; the tragedy had been Elise's suicide, Sophia's injuries.

"So, yes, indeedy, Mom's pregnant. Yay!" Lisa grinned. "She decides that she wants to pay her grandmother a visit, so that they can discuss the future of this great musician that has been created through –"

"Through the intercession of the demon."

Lisa tilted her head curiously at me, narrowed her eyes. "That's right. How do you know?"

"Ernie told me."

"Who told him?"

"You did. In your letter. You told him that Candy had decided, *with the help of the spirits,* that his son would be the greatest musician ever."

Through the intercession of the demon had been Sonny's expression, but I didn't want to bring up Sonny at the moment. Lisa was telling the story of why she believed in the unseen forces, and maybe the part about her quest would come up on its own. Maybe she'd just come right out and tell me about her supposed damnation, about the mystery person she had to give over to save herself.

I wondered if I could keep a straight face through it. Already, she'd given the sordid tale of another groupie nailing Ernie LaBelle a melodramatic flourish that it just didn't deserve. I enjoyed her voice, her theatrical phrasings, but there wasn't anything at all about the tale that pointed to a guiding hand.

Lisa still regarded me curiously. "Yes. I suppose I did tell him." She paused, remembering where she was in this epic saga. "Anyway, when Mom's about six months' pregnant, she decides to come down to visit Cecelia. And she decides to make a side trip, to see if she could find Denny's house in Malibu, to see if maybe she might be able to glimpse my dad."

Like we all hung out together. It was another groupie fantasy, the boys in the band just lounging around, making up tunes, enjoying each other's brotherhood-like company. More bullshit: each of us had our own homes, our own lives, when we weren't on tour. And in the six months after Elise's suicide and Sophia's devastating injuries

– none of us visited the house in Malibu too often. We'd see Denny again after he moved back to Riverside, to record, but that was about it. After Elise's suicide, the band was pretty much done.

"What do you think happened, Cal?" Lisa was saying.

Candy didn't find Ernie, I thought about saying. But I decided to just let her tell the story. The less I talked, the quicker it would be concluded.

"In your world of random coincidences, how likely do you think it would be that Mom would find the exact house she was looking for?"

I shrugged again, unconvinced. I thought about suggesting something about maps to the stars' homes – if you located Sam Elliot's house, Denny's was just one more up the beach – but again I kept my mouth shut. My bad mood had made this conversation entirely too adversarial, and I didn't want to make it any worse.

"There was a moving van out in front of one place, so Mom just told the moving guy, 'I'm looking for Dennis Whitly's house,' and the guy said, 'Well, you found it.'" Lisa grinned. "But yeah, I know, that's all just coincidence to you.

"'Look, dude,' Mom said to the moving guy. 'I just breezed in from Frisco, and to tell you the truth, I'm all out of money. I've just got enough gas to make it home to Riverside, but I'm a little hungry. I'll help you do this job if you could slip me a few bucks.'

"Mom had plenty of money. She wouldn't've come down the coast, unprepared, six months' pregnant. The baby inside her, Ernie LaBelle's baby, was the most important thing in her life. And so I have remained." Lisa smiled proudly, her love for her mother shining through.

"But Mom wanted to get into the house, you see. She wanted to see if maybe Ernie was hanging around.

"'I dunno, honey . . .' the moving guy began, but then one of his associates requested a word, and before you know it, Mom's hired to help. They didn't know she was pregnant. They just thought she was chubby."

"What did the moving guy say?"

"The boss guy didn't say anything else. The guy that had spoken up for Mom asked her if she was a Sonic Daydream fan. When she said yes, he took her into the truck and showed her some of Denny's guitars. Mom said that they were in there for a little while, and it was very hot . . ."

It suddenly dawned on me that Candy hadn't gotten hired on with a professional moving crew, at the drop of the hat, just because of her sad story and her chubby-at-the-time good looks and charm. Lisa knew it, too, even though it was obvious that she didn't want to draw me a picture. I wondered if Candy had actually described it to her, or if she'd just guessed.

Once a groupie always a groupie, and the moving guy had recognized it immediately. Girls that looked like Candy didn't just waltz in off the street looking for Dennis Whitly's house because they knew him. I felt a wave of disgust. It had been hot in the moving van, and they'd been in there for a while, because a moving guy was kind of like a roadie, and for a few favors, a roadie would let you see and maybe even touch the rock god's axe, might even let you backstage, or in this case, into the house.

Iris had said that Candy's ambition was like the Terminator: *it doesn't feel pity, or remorse, or fear.*

Or shame.

Candy was obsessed with Ernie, and Candy thought Ernie might be nearby, and it wasn't like she was gonna get any more pregnant. *These are the trade-offs . . .*

"So Mom helped the movers," Lisa continued. "Denny wasn't home, nor was his wife. No Ernie, either. The only one there was a nurse."

Sophia's nurse.

"The nurse eyed Mom suspiciously, took her aside. 'You shouldn't be lifting heavy stuff in your condition,' she told her.

"Mom hadn't really been helping all that much anyway –"

She'd done all the heavy lifting she was gonna do with the roadie-surrogate in the moving van, to gain entrance to where the band might be. Yikes.

"– but she begged the nurse not to tell them that she was pregnant. She trotted out the I-need-the-money story again, a poor, broke, unmarried, pregnant girl, just trying to get to Riverside. The nurse was sympathetic.

"'Come with me,' she said. 'I have some lighter things for you to take out. Clothes and odds and ends. The rest of the stuff is going to the house in Riverside. But these things – they're putting it all in storage.' Mom followed her to –"

"To Elise's room!"

"Yes. But of course it was all just a coincidence." Lisa grinned smugly.

"And of course, the nurse told her the whole story."

"What she knew of it. At the time, it was just sad to Mom. There'd been an accident, Mr. Whitly's sister-in-law had been killed, his wife injured. They were putting the poor dead girl's stuff in storage, because he'd decided to sell the house and move back to Riverside.

"Mom told the nurse that she was also from Riverside. The nurse asked if Mom knew that Mr. Whitly was a famous musician. She said no, she'd never heard of him.

"The movers packed the truck. Mom helped put Elise's stuff in there. Like I say, she wasn't even curious then. She didn't even peek into any of the boxes. The boss mover told her to follow the truck to Riverside, and once they unloaded what was going into storage, then he'd pay her.

"Mom helped unload the boxes at the storage place. When they were finished, the guy locked the door on the unit. He gave Mom a hundred bucks and told her to take the keys and the paperwork up to the office. I guess the office people were going to mail them from there to Mr. Whitly. The movers were in a hurry to get back on the road, and they didn't have time to stand around for this tedious detail. Mom said thanks for letting her help, and gave a fake phone number to the other mover, the one who had gotten her hired.

"She took the keys up to the office like she'd been told, but since there were two, she decided to keep one as a souvenir."

It's called a trophy, I thought, still with a kind of disgusted amazement. *Just like the kinds of things that the other kind of obsessive, the serial killer, keeps.*

"Mom went home to Great-grandma's house, and she stayed for a week, and they scryed and prayed. They discussed my future."

"All the time thinking that you were gonna be a boy."

Lisa shrugged, trying not to be defensive. "All mysteries aren't revealed." She squeezed my hand. "Aren't you glad I'm not a boy, Cal?"

I smiled.

"So Mom went back to San Francisco. I was born, not a boy, but that was okay, too. Mom sent me to music teachers. Then she met Sonny." A sigh escaped Lisa, for Sonny. "They formed the band, and they played a few gigs. Then Great-grandma died, and left everything to Mom. We moved back to Riverside. Your book came out, and Mom realized the significance of all the *coincidences* that had occurred in her life.

"She still had the key to the storage shed. All of Elise's things *are still there,* Cal. Dusty, forgotten. The remnants of his sister-in-law's life – it's just another bill Dennis Whitly pays at the end of the month. Mom and I have gone out there many times. Elise and I are the same size. I took some of her clothes. I looked at her high school yearbooks, the magazines and books that were in her room. She had some records –"

They'd probably belonged to her father, I thought.

"But no turntable."

"That would've gone back with Denny to Riverside. He likes records, too. He also built a recording studio in the –"

Lisa waved her hand. She didn't care about Dennis Whitly's studio.

"I took Elise's records from the storage place, so they wouldn't get ruined from the heat. There were also CDs, and I took them, too. Regular commercial issues, and ones she'd made herself. What did you old people used to call that?"

Lisa usually studiously avoided mentioning our age difference. But not this time. I was unsure whether she was kidding about not knowing the term, or if she was just being a little mean. I supplied the answer. "Mix tapes."

She nodded. "All the old music on them, Cal! They were all my favorites, stuff Mom played for me all my life. Like I say, I'd always identified with Elise, and seeing her records and her CDs . . . It was like she'd left them just for me. We liked all the same old bands. Do you understand why I believe now?" She hugged me unexpectedly. "Why I'm so happy? Why I know that you and I are meant to be together?"

You are young and life is long and there is time to kill today . . .

Life was indeed long, but I was no longer young. Ernie's daughter was killing time by trying to show me the hand guiding our destinies, but she was failing, and in the process, she was depressing me.

There had actually been few cosmic coincidences in Lisa's story, and even less evidence of a guiding hand. Candy had made the things happen that she'd wanted to happen, through simple, relentless, pathological obsession. She'd wanted Ernie's baby, so she'd wormed her way backstage to meet him, and later that night had accomplished a common biological process with him, something that happened every single day, all around the world, without the aid of one single supernatural entity.

Then Candy had read a sad story about a band she worshipped, in a magazine about musicians, one that had a global circulation. She'd driven down the coast, looking for the house that had been described, and had found it where it was supposed to be. These were not coincidences. These were studied actions.

Having located the rock star's manse, Candy had discovered that he was moving out of it – and again consciously schemed, this time to get inside, on the off-chance that she might run into Ernie. Since he was not present, she settled for stealing the key to Denny's storage unit, as a souvenir.

Candy was a big Sonic Daydream fan, so years later, she'd naturally read my book, as did a healthy share of other fans. No guiding hand there, just my publisher's shrewd promotion.

Candy's imagination had then transmogrified the bitter story I'd written into a fairytale for her daughter. And what better way to make it real for Lisa, than to allow her to touch and see and pilfer the belongings of the dead princess from that fairytale?

And then there was Candy's recent, angry admonition: *Just let me remind you, musicians are all the same.*

Lisa was the granddaughter of a musician, and even though *he wasn't a good man,* Candy had loved him, told his story to her daughter like it was another sad fairytale. Maybe Candy had also loved the junkie from the metal band that had been her ticket away from non-believing Amelia; she'd certainly loved Ernie, as only a groupie can. Maybe she'd loved Sonny.

Just like Elise, Candy had always had a thing for musicians, flawed though we may be. Despite our shortcomings, we'd been the only men for her, so she'd held us up as the standard for her daughter, and even though Lisa said she'd never been much for musicians, I was a special one.

I was the storyteller, and more: because she'd gotten inside Denny's house and his storage unit, Candy believed that she and her daughter had more of a connection to my band and me and my self-deluded, dead friend than she ever could've gotten from just reading my book.

And because I was the author of it – as I had at the beginning, once again I wondered about the quality of Lisa's love. I didn't doubt that she loved me – if anything, this reciting of Candy's life story had further cemented my belief in it. Lisa couldn't help but think she loved me.

I could see how, to her, it was indeed all so much more than mere coincidence – Candy finding Denny's house, getting the key to Elise's stuff – to Lisa, it was so much more than just her mother's devious, relentless obsession paying off. Candy had come up pregnant from a one night stand with her favorite guitar player; she had scoured the coast for his front's house and found it. She'd heard a sad story, stole a key; I wrote a book. It all fit together as the guiding hand of fate in Candy's deranged mind, and she'd passed this belief on to Lisa.

Ernie, and me, and Elise, too: Candy and Lisa felt as if they *knew us,* before we'd ever met. *We're like family to them.* Of course Lisa couldn't see a relationship between as anything other than destiny.

But to me, it was bullshit.

She looked hopefully at me, willing me to believe in that guiding hand. I thought of Sonny's Mom's letter: *He told me he would believe whatever I wanted him to believe.*

Lisa was my heart's desire. This incredible young woman loved me, and the demon in my mind put out the question: did it really matter that she loved me because of her delusion of fate? Wasn't love always love – precious, the thing that everybody longed for – even if its basis was misguided claptrap? Just like dead was always dead?

"Our lives were *brought* together, Cal," Lisa said, the avid light of the true-believer glowing like a fever in her eyes. "You've gotta see it now. You can't really believe that it's all just been random. Too many coincidences prove that nothing is a coincidence."

If I smiled at her, if I allowed her to think that she'd finally convinced me of our shared destiny, what could it hurt? Lisa believed like Iris did, and nothing I could say was gonna change her mind. Why continue to argue with her about it?

"Whatever's clever, baby," I said and hugged her. "Put those candles out so the unseen forces don't burn my house down, then let's go back to Riverside. Your destiny in Vegas awaits."

"It's *our* destiny, Cal. There are other aspects on the horizon –"

"Whatever you say."

Maybe she'd been about to tell me the rest of it then, and maybe things would've turned out differently if I would've just let her talk. But I couldn't take any more at the moment, not one more witchy word. I loved Lisa, and I'd felt a sharp pang of pity for her, pity for the craziness to which her mother had subjected her for her entire life.

Lisa said that she'd always identified with Elise. When I'd mistakenly thought her besotted with Denny, just like Elise, I remembered that I'd made my own comparison between them, had found them alike in so many ways. Both were beautiful, willful; both lived in the same kind of fantasy world, where destiny revealed itself, where wishing hard enough for impossible things couldn't help but make them so.

I had discovered a love for Elise, after she was gone. But I had pitied her while she was alive. I didn't want to feel pity for Lisa, too.

Our relationship was already lopsided enough as it was, her eighteen-year-old's wide-eyed belief in destiny, my old man's knowledge that there was no such thing. *Everything happens for a reason* was just the lyrics to a Limp Bizkit song to me.

She kissed me. "I love you, Cal!"

All that enthusiasm, all for a washed-up drummer.

My demon spoke up. *You know that one about looking a gift horse in*
the teeth, Cal, ol' son? Just like Lenny said, 'Enjoy it while it lasts. All you touch and –

"I love you, too, Lisa." I gritted my teeth. My ever-present, rationalizing demon quoting Pink Floyd was just a little too much at the moment. "Let's go back to Riverside."

FORTY-SIX

When Lisa and I walked into the band room, I had a spurt of déjà vu. James was once more sitting next to Ernie, mindlessly bouncing a tennis ball, and my old second-guitar was again frowning into a witchy tome, purple-covered this time, entitled, *The Cabalistic Encyclopedia.* Roy and Horus sat on the other side of James, completing the see-no-evil, hear-no-evil, speak-no-evil triumvirate of the band.

"Christ, I thought you'd never get here," Ernie said, as he'd said before.

He handed the book to James without looking at him, causing him to miss his bounce. The ball rolled over beside Horus's feet, and he picked it up and grinned. "Let's go outside. Play catch or something. I'm bored."

Deeming this a stellar idea, Roy and James followed Horus down the hall. Lisa went off to look for her mother.

When they were gone, Ernie said, "I get the feeling that my tenure here is about to be revoked."

I blanched, feeling a darker shade of déjà vu. Sonny had once said the same words to me, and Sonny was dead now. I shook my head, trying to banish all the talk of destiny that I'd been subjected to already today.

"But that's all okey-dokey with your friend Ernie LaBelle." He grinned without a trace of regret. "I got 'em what they wanted, right? But this me and Candy thing . . . That wasn't part of the deal. It's not, as the saying goes, working out."

"Have you told her?"

Ernie shook his head. "Why put a pall on the festivities?" He gestured around the room as if there were indeed festivities taking place. "I'm telling *you.* I'll go to Vegas, sit in on the meeting with EMI . . . I wish Barbie or Lenny could be there."

Or even Elise.

"How's he doing?" Ernie asked.

"Better," I said. I didn't want to go into it at the moment. It was depressing, and I wanted to hear more about his plans, now that he was through with the band's matriarch.

"I'll stay for the show, because Lisa's expecting me to," Ernie continued. "But after that, they're on their own. Candy wants to bitch at me, over nothing? Over women I was with before she came crying and begging me for *comfort?* She's gonna be here awhile." He grinned.

I grinned back. "There were a few."

He winked. "A couple. But she's just bitching about the last one." Ernie shook his head. "She also says she thinks she can manage Phenex better than me. I say let her. I've got other irons in the fire."

I was pretty sure those irons involved Bianca, *the last one.* But even if that wasn't the case, I liked what he was saying: getting away from Candy was all good. For him. But I didn't like it for me, because it didn't look like I was going to get away.

He read my mind. "I imagine you'll still wanna go on tour with them. To be with Lisa."

Did I? It was a short tour, and then she'd be home again. I was too old for the road, even if she was there, and maybe, somewhere in the back of my mind, I thought that it was something she should experience on her own, without her geriatric boyfriend along for the ride. Maybe it would give her another chance to reconsider *destiny.*

Besides, I couldn't shake the idea that there probably wouldn't be another tour. Despite this sudden, inexplicable attention from EMI, Phenex just wasn't that good. I knew it, Lenny knew it; Oscar Woodbine had recognized it immediately, and I think, deep down, Ernie knew it, too.

I took out a different thought and examined it, another one that had been rolling around in the back of my mind. Maybe, after this tour, I might suggest that Lisa come and live with me. She could still come to Riverside and rehearse with her band. They could play some local gigs, what with having a real record, and having once been signed with EMI and all . . .

But if I was honest with myself, I admitted that I wished that she'd come and live with me and give up her mother's demon-worshipper band. I was hoping that maybe this tour would be enough for her, that it would get that wanting-to-be-a-rock-star bug out of her system, seeing as how being a signed artist probably wasn't going to continue. If she wanted destiny, then maybe it could be just me and her.

Elise's voice in my head: *"How ya gonna keep 'em down on the farm, after they've seen Paree?"*

So I put that thought away.

I told Ernie, "I don't think I'll go if you're not going."

He seemed surprised, but not overly so. "Good."

So that's that, I thought. The prospect of being Phenex's road dog was not as exciting to my friend anymore, now that he'd discovered that his Number One Fan was a jealous harpy. I wondered about how Candy was going to take it. Was being Phenex's manager herself more important than being whatever she thought she was to Ernie? Would she choose her relentless ambition for the band over . . . what? Love? Affection? Obsession?

Regardless, I didn't think she'd take it well. Even if she was angry at him – she'd accused him of cheating on her when he hadn't done so, so he'd proceeded right on up to Big Bear and made her accusations a reality – unlike Ernie, I didn't believe Candy was ready to end it just yet. He'd been her obsession for a very, very long time; he was her daughter's father.

No, she wasn't going to take his abandoning the tour, and her, very well at all. When Ernie dropped the bomb, I believed he – and collaterally, me – were in for quite the blowback. *You and Ernie – you don't know who you're fucking with.*

My phone rang. It was Iris.

"The first crisis is coming, Cal." Her alliteration made me smile.

It had been a day full of supernatural rants, from God's bass player, from my sweet, misguided young girlfriend. I nodded at Ernie, letting him know I had to take this call. I went outside to listen to the newest rant. Mercifully, the boys from Phenex had gone elsewhere.

"What kind of crisis, Iris?"

"This whole thing – someone's damnation – it commences tonight. There will be several steps. Your friend – Eddie?"

"Ernie."

"Yes. The first one starts with an *E.* He's the initial key, the first lock. The next offering. Your friend Ernie is in danger, Cal. I have seen an . . . an end to him."

"Really?" I said, mostly just for something to say. I liked Iris a great deal, and didn't want to offend her, but I just didn't believe she could see anybody's end. I was just about fed up with seeing, and destiny, with guiding hands and big black demon birds –

"What's going on right now?" Iris asked suddenly, forcefully. "With Candy? With the . . . the group? The . . .?"

"The band? We're going to Las Vegas tonight. Then we're talking to the record company tomorrow. After that . . . Ernie says he's done, Iris. Maybe that's the end you've seen. He doesn't want to do this anymore. Ernie's got a friend at the record company, and Candy's jealous . . ."

I stopped talking. It sounded like high school hijinks, adolescent ridiculousness, jealousies and break-ups . . . and Iris was so serious.

"Does Candy need him to talk to the music people?" she demanded.

"After a fashion. He's expected." I giggled. "But I imagine if he drops dead, they could still sign the contract without him. The show must go on and all."

Then I felt a little guilty for my laughter. Iris was trying to look out for me and Ernie, and I was being rude to her. I'd been the one that had approached her, after all. I stopped laughing.

"They don't really need him for it, I guess. But he said he'd go, so he's going. Ernie's a man of his word." Again, I felt like I was mouthing clichés, but I didn't know what else to tell her.

"You watch over him, Cal. I won't go into detail – you won't believe me, anyway. But there he is one moment, then the next – he's gone. And then, your other friend . . . I see the Firebird . . ."

I suppressed another giggle, thinking, *Leonard Whitly wouldn't get caught dead in a Firebird, Iris. He prefers very fast, very expensive, English cars. And besides, he's not doing too much driving right at the moment.*

"Your other friend's fate – it's not as clear as this. This will occur first. I see that *E,* shining, alive . . . then blinked out in a heartbeat. You watch him, Cal. Whatever will occur . . . It will all be over by Sunday afternoon."

"I'll watch him, Iris," I promised.

"You'll survive what's to come, Cal. I've seen that far ahead. Although it's gonna go hard on you. Your faith . . ."

"I have no faith, Iris," I said softly.

She was silent for a long moment. "You must look out for you friends this weekend, Cal. Candy's ambition . . ."

I tried to break the heavy mood. "After all Ernie's done for her."

Iris ignored me. She was thinking her own thoughts, out loud. "There are still missing pieces to this. I just haven't got them all together yet. Who is the person that they want to give over to Phenex? Why does a young girl believe she's damned?"

"Is it Ernie they want to give over?" The words were silly in my mouth.

"No. Neither him nor you. Ernie's central. He's Lisa's father, after all. But still – I see him falling. Why would Candy want to sacrifice him? Why is he suddenly become expendable?"

"Erne's gonna expend himself, Iris. After the show tonight. He's done." I repeated, "Maybe that's what you see."

This seemed to have a certain logic to her, and her voice relaxed a little bit. "Perhaps. It's difficult for me to divine all of Candy's motivations, Cal. All her angles. I can't fathom why she would give Lisa's father over, but this whole situation is dangerous to your friends. That much is certain. The souls of musicians seemed to have a special significance here . . ."

I laughed again. "At least you believe that we have souls."

Iris sighed. "I'm sorry for all the histrionics, Cal, without having anything concrete to offer your see-smell-hear-taste-touch mind. It was a transitory thing, a black stain that spread acrost my mind's eye. I can't be any more specific than that. I saw your friend blotted out with that stain, ceasing to exist. It was frightening. Watch over him this weekend. By Sunday, all will have passed."

"Thanks for looking out for us, Iris."

"Text me, Cal. Let me know what's going on."

Ernie came outside and grinned at me. "All is in readiness, my brutha. Let's get this dog and pony show on the road, shall we?"

"By all means."

He texted Candy. She appeared promptly, followed by the rest of the band. I tried to watch their interaction, to glean if his Number One Fan realized that her rock star was now lost to her, but Lisa touched my arm.

"Are you stoked, Cal?" She squeezed me. "Mom told us about EMI. Just think – destiny!"

Christ, would I ever escape that ridiculous, meaningless word? I smiled blankly at her, then glanced over at Candy and Ernie again. She had one hand on his chest, the other on his arm. She whispered something into his ear, and Ernie's eyes narrowed, as if he was concentrating, maybe straining to catch whatever she was saying. Then she looked him in the eye for a heartbeat. Ernie nodded slowly and she kissed him quickly on the mouth.

I figured Ernie wouldn't tell her the bad news until it was time to come back home. *No sense in ruining the drive to Vegas. Or the show.*

Candy abruptly looked over her shoulder and skewered me with a *Now it's your turn* expression. I felt embarrassed that I'd been watching them, but she'd caught me, so I didn't look away.

She didn't have any whispered secrets for me, thank Jesus and all the saints. She just said, "Are we ready to go?"

"It's all on the Road Dog. He's calling the shots. I'm just –"

"Along for the ride. I know." Candy looked expectantly back to her baby-daddy.

"We'll do it like this." Ernie blinked, as if he was concentrating on some large problem. Then he shook his head. Whatever was on his mind, he squeezed his temples and came to a decision. "I'm getting a headache. I'm gonna ride in the van. You guys take the Porsche." He arced the keys through the air to me.

This was a change from *She can ride with the band,* but again I figured that Ernie didn't want to *throw a pall over the festivities.* Even though he laid himself out on the backseat of the van and put his head in Candy's lap, I knew he hadn't changed his mind. His thing with her had all been for convenience, but even convenience wasn't worth being bitched at. Ernie was, as the song said, *gone, gone, gone.* He just hadn't broken the news to baby-mama yet.

James and Roy and Horus dutifully climbed into the front seat.

"You got any aspirin?" Ernie asked Candy, before she pulled the door shut. "I don't feel so hot."

I thought of Iris's dire proclamations. I grinned to myself and reckoned that all those years of study, of scrying, of bargaining with the unseen forces had produced this. She had accurately predicted Ernie's headache.

FORTY-SEVEN

Lisa and I sang songs and chatted about the cities that Phenex might be going to play. I didn't think about asking her to come and live with me anymore; that was just a ridiculous schoolboy idea right now. I'd have to suggest all that unlikely happily-ever-after bullshit after the tour. I didn't let her know that I probably wouldn't be coming along when Ernie welshed, either. Why put a pall on the festivities?

Through Berdoo and Barstow and Baker, we caravanned to Sin City, across the alien moonscape of the Mojave. We arrived just as the sun vanished and the legendary lights came on. Ernie had booked rooms at The Golden Nugget, but it wasn't because he wanted to be near to old Vegas, because he wanted to soak up the Fremont Street Experience. It was because the hotel overlooked the venue, an outdoor, standing room only gem called the Downtown Las Vegas Event Center, the DLVEC for short.

Once upon a time, Ernie liked it best when the hotel was close to the venue. It allowed him to *slip on out the back door* with his chosen groupie after the show, with no running the gauntlet between the stage door and the bus, no screaming fans, no autographs. It allowed him to have his chosen back to his room before the load-out was half done, while all that after-the-show enthusiasm was still fresh and pumping. There were no groupies for Ernie at present; that would have to wait until he went back on tour with Azomite. But since he was booking the rooms now, he still liked to get as close as possible to the venue.

When we arrived at The Golden Nugget, Ernie, sound asleep, had to be roused from the back seat.

"What's wrong with me?" he asked groggily, as if I knew.

Would Iris know? a voice whispered in my head.

"I feel like I'm coming down with something."

"You're timing sucks, Dad," Lisa said expressionlessly.

"I'll be all right by the time you go on tomorrow."

Ernie had reserved three rooms: one for me and Lisa, one for himself and Candy, and like the nobody musicians that they were, one to share for James and Roy and Horus. We dropped off our suitcases, then regrouped in the lobby. It was time to check out the venue, which wouldn't take long, as it was just a big square of concrete next door, surrounded by high-rise hotels and office buildings.

I was surprised, but somehow not surprised, that Ernie didn't join us. Candy made excuses for him, telling us that he'd gone up to their room and passed right out again. "He says he doesn't feel too hot," she reiterated.

I thought that perhaps Ernie really was feeling sickly. Or, even though she'd no doubt caressed his fevered brow all the way across the desert, maybe he just didn't want to hang out with Candy any more than he had to.

I sent Iris a text. *Ernie's not feeling well. He's staying in 2night. He can't get in 2 much trouble sleeping in his room.* She didn't respond.

Candy skipped looking over the DLVEC; she and her minions immediately decamped to gamble.

Lisa and I walked down the sidewalk, past a tall, tasteful, wrought iron fence. If there was a show tonight, it wasn't for several hours yet, so the not-unimpressive stage was cold and dark across the empty expanse of concrete, but the monolithic, freestanding marquee on the corner was alive with light and moving pictures. We waited patiently through advertisements for the famous acts that were scheduled to appear in the coming weeks. At last, *Saturday, September 22nd* flashed by, and *The RaceCats,* followed by a larger than life picture of Phillip and the boys, with the little black porn strips over their eyes. In smaller font, and speeding by quickly, it said, *Featuring The Desperate Princes and Phenex.*

Lisa yelped and hugged me. It was quite the thrill to see her band's name in lights for the very first time, and I was glad to be there to experience it with her.

I wondered who the other act was, so I asked the lone security guard, "Is that a local band? The Desperate Princes?"

He eyed us for a long moment, then deciding that we were just harmless tourists, he smiled. "Beats me. I've never heard of any of them."

"You will," Lisa said.

"She's the front for Phenex," I told him with a grin.

The security guard looked her over again. "Is that a fact?" He winked at me. "Can I have your autograph?" He produced a pen, then patted his pockets until he found a folded piece of paper.

"What's your name?" I asked, because Lisa didn't. I thought perhaps a lesson in giving autographs might be in order.

"Ellis. With two l's."

Lisa wrote *To my good friend, Ellis,* then faltered.

"Long live rock and roll," I suggested.

Lisa frowned, shook her head, thought for another second. Finally she wrote, *Remember my name,* accompanied by a little smiley face. She wrote *Lisa Corson*, then as an afterthought, she added *Phenex* and drew the demon's sigil.

Ellis said thanks, and put the pen and scrap of paper back into his pocket without looking at it.

"It's been a while since I've been to Vegas," I told him. "It's cool that they built an outside venue right in the middle of everything. Has it been here long?"

"Since the last real estate bust." Ellis grinned, swept his arm to encompass the whole site. "The Downtown Las Vegas Event Center is the best failed hotel in town."

The lights and noise from Fremont Street, a block over, had captured Lisa's attention. "We'll see you tomorrow, Ellis!" she said, then pulled me across the street toward The Four Queens.

I thought it just as well that she was interested in the lights of old Vegas. She wasn't old enough to be on any casino floors; gawping at the weirdos on Fremont Street would have to be enough for an aspiring young rock star such as herself tonight.

We walked, we ate; we took the Deuce to The Excalibur and caught the last knights-on-horseback show of the evening, all the touristy things to do in Vegas if you weren't a gambler. We didn't see the rest of our party again that night, didn't see them at breakfast or lunch. We didn't see them again, in fact, until we assembled to meet with the record company reps the following afternoon at four.

Nor did we have far to go. Once and future rock star and neophyte road dog Ernie LaBelle had covered all the details. He'd booked a small meeting room right there at the hotel.

He collapsed into the first chair at the left-hand side of the large conference table and promptly put his head down on his arms. Lisa whispered to me that her mother had texted that he really was sick, that he'd been up most of the night throwing up, that he'd stayed in bed all day whilst she and the boys had been out gambling.

Lisa opined that her dad had a case of nerves, but I knew that wasn't it. Ernie had never been nervous about anything in his life, and besides, this meeting was all just a formality to him. He was through with this *dog and pony show* after the gig tonight.

But I was concerned about him. He was ashen, and dark circles underlined his vacant eyes. I knew it wasn't nerves, and I also knew Candy wasn't sticking pins in a voodoo doll somewhere as Iris believed. But Ernie was definitely sick. I figured that he'd perhaps come down with a moderate case of food poisoning.

Candy sat beside him. She had attempted to copy Barbie's businesslike attire for this meeting with the record company, with mixed results. The dark skirt and jacket combo were demure enough, but she'd left one too many buttons undone on her blouse, and had not let up on the raccoon-style eye make-up; the spiky heels were just a little too high for a business meeting. I thought the ensemble made her look like some kind a naughty teacher from a bad porn movie, but maybe that was just me.

James was beside her, then Roy, then Horus. They had all attempted to dress up, also. Horus was even wearing a short-sleeved, collared shirt and a tie. It clashed unmercifully with his Egyptian tattoos; long sleeves would've been a better choice, but it was hot in Vegas. Lisa was beside him, casual, in jeans and t-shirt, and I was beside her, dressed similarly.

Clothes might make the man, but it was dollar signs that made the band, at least as far as the record company went. I knew it matter not in the slightest how any of us were dressed.

The minute hand clicked over to the twelve. It was four o'clock on the dot, and like a suddenly animated marionette, Ernie straightened up. A little bit of color returned to his cheeks; he looked around at us as if he didn't know where he was, as if he'd just awakened from a dream and wasn't quite sure if he was in fact fully awake yet. Candy put her hand on his arm and was whispering something into his ear when the door opened.

Chrissy, the RaceCats' manager entered, and Phillip, their front. The kid enthusiastically shook Ernie's hand, and I recognized a fan, even from the other end of the table. He said a few animated words, praise, no doubt, and Ernie at last seemed to come out of his stupor, giving the kid an *Aw, shucks, we weren't that great* grin. To my surprise, Ernie looked pointedly at Candy, indicating for her to get up and move over. She did so without protest, and like a wave, we all got up and moved two seats down, so that Phillip and Chrissy could sit next to Ernie.

"Here's your lanyards for tonight," Chrissy said as she handed them out. She smiled at Candy and Candy smiled back. "No more stage managing for me. All we have to do is check in here."

Two slick A&R types came in and sat next to me, a guy in his late thirties and a striking young woman. Last but not least, an accountant and/or lawyer type, carrying a briefcase, took the head of the table. These people frowned; that was a bad sign. The young woman looked at Lisa and Candy with an annoyed, *You've got to be kidding* expression, and the guy almost sneered at Horus.

No. This was not a good sign at all. I hadn't really expected the reps to be offering around cigars to Phenex just yet, but I would've expected at least a little friendliness. It struck me that, starting with Ernie, the level of confidence in the band rose as you went around the table, then it fell off precipitously when you got to me, then plummeted to zero when you made it around to the other side. They faced each other almost like adversaries; the hopeful, smiling faces of Candy and Chrissy and the musicians, versus the frowning almost-resentment of the suits.

It was not what I'd expected. This wasn't multi-platinum Sonic Daydream demanding more money for the next sold-out tour, money that the record company would bitch about but in the end reluctantly pay; Barbie had frowned at us across the table at a few meetings like that, once upon a time. This was a meeting with a nobody band whom, I'd been led to believe, had been approached by the recording giant. Their confrontational attitude struck me as quite odd, therefore. I would've expected a little bit more of a welcome. I reflected that things had definitely changed in the biz over the years.

The lawyer/accountant type said his name was Stan, but failed to mention what his exact capacity actually was. Buddy and Sissy – I kid you not – were the names of the Artists and Repertoire crew to my right.

"There's been a change in the line-up for tonight's show and for the rest of the tour." Stan removed a thick sheaf of papers from the briefcase and pushed it across the table to Ernie. "Phenex will be opening for The Desperate Princes. The Desperate Princes will be opening for The RaceCats."

The question of the name on the marquee had been answered.

"Who?" Phillip asked.

"The Desperate Princes. They were supposed to open for you for the whole tour, but the . . ." He consulted his phone. "The drummer took ill. They're from the South."

"It's a good thing that we were available then," Candy said.

Stan made no comment. “Anyway, The Desperate Princes are ready to play now, so Phenex will be warm-up band for them for this tour.”

Ernie cringed at the term, but apparently neither Candy nor the members of Phenex cared that they had been knocked down a peg.

“The new contract reflects your change in pay, and so on. We’ll still provide accommodations of course, but whatever Bianca might’ve told you about a bus . . .”

“She didn’t say anything about a bus,” Ernie replied. He flipped through the contract, not reading it. He knew what it said: *Here’s a little money, we got ya’ll a room. But you’re now third string, easily replaced by any local band in any town, so don’t get uppity.*

Ernie wasn’t the uppity type; he was abandoning the tour anyway. “What about signing them for a record? Bianca said –”

“Ah, yes. Bianca said.” Stan sighed and removed a copy of Phenex’s demo from his briefcase. In its plain white sleeve, without any kind of graphics, it looked like nothing but a common mix-tape.

Buddy from A&R took the demo from Stan, turned it over thoughtfully in his hands. “Is it you playing second-guitar on this, Mr. LaBelle?”

Ernie’s eyebrows went up in surprise. “No. Our former guitarist met with an accident. That’s him playing on the demo.”

“I was just curious. I caught Phenex’s act in San Jose. I noticed a difference in . . . style.” Again Buddy frowned at Horus, the replacement guitar player.

“Horus had only rehearsed with us once when we played San Jose,” Ernie returned mildly. “He’s great.” The rock legend smiled at his protégé and at Phillip and Chrissy. They all smiled back. “So what about their record?”

“Who produced this demo?” Buddy asked.

“It’s awesome, isn’t it?” Candy enthused. She was not catching on to the antagonistic mood.

Buddy’s face remained grim. “Like I say, you sound quite a bit different live.”

“Oscar Woodbine produced it. He’s an old friend of ours.” Ernie glanced at me, as did all three of the unimpressed EMI people. They remained unimpressed.

“We’ll meet again after the tour to further discuss the record,” Stan said.

“But there will be one, right?” Candy piped up with a shade of concern. Now she was getting it.

"Yes," Sissy said with undisguised distaste. "Even though we had to revise your contract for the tour . . . We'll still produce and distribute one album for you. Bianca was adamant about that. Any other recording options . . ." She let that thought die, then laughed humorlessly. "Unfortunately, you'll have to settle with a lesser engineer than Oscar Woodbine. He's a little bit out of our price range for . . . new talent." She said *new talent* with open contempt.

I looked at Ernie in amazement and he winked at me.

"Of course," he said with an entirely smug grin. He wasn't at all put off by the tension in the room. "Phenex isn't Sonic Daydream, after all. Not yet."

Buddy sighed. "To tell you the truth, Mr. LaBelle, I find it unlikely that they . . . They're not really in the same –"

"Who the hell are you?" Phillip demanded, offended. "You don't know what you're talking about. Lisa's fantastic."

He stood and reached across the table and patted her hand. I was amazed to see the light of fan-love in his eyes. The RaceCats' front had a crush on my girlfriend! Wasn't that sweet?

Phillip regained his seat and turned back to Buddy. I grinned at Lisa. She shrugged; Phillip's affection was news to her, too.

"You didn't see the crowd react to her in Berdoo," Phillip accused.

"That was the crowd reacting to Dennis Whitly," Buddy said evenly. "We heard all about that." Now he considered Ernie, who grinned blankly at him. "More of your old friends."

"The crowd liked them besides Dennis Whitly," Chrissy countered. "In Frisco, especially. They've got a good sound."

Buddy waggled the white CD case. "I've heard it. And in my opinion –"

"Who are you, again?" Phillip said.

Buddy narrowed his eyes. "When I started in this business, you were still playing the xylophone in your second grade Christmas pageant, Phil."

Ernie winked at me again. *When we started in this business, this guy hadn't even been thought of yet.*

"The RaceCats are all right. That's why we signed you. This band . . ." Buddy took the time to look round the table at each of us, Phenex's members and entourage. He'd entered the meeting already on his A&R high horse, and now he was gonna tell young Phillip just how it was.

But then he sighed, shook his head. His tirade died unspoken. "You wanna know who I am, Phil? I'm somebody who does what he's told. It came from upstairs to sign your friends. So that's what we're doing. But I don't think they're ever gonna –"

Ernie clapped his hands together, making everybody jump. "We appreciate your vote of confidence, Barry."

"Buddy."

"Right." Ernie looked at Stan again, dismissing the A&R man and his opinions. "That's all you need from us, then? To sign this?"

"Yes. We'll have another meeting about the album when the tour's over." Stan watched as the contract was passed down the table. "Here's a copy of the itinerary."

Candy reached out and took it from Stan, because Ernie made no move to do so. I wondered if she knew already that he wouldn't be coming on the tour. I doubted it. Her mood was too light.

There was a moment of awkward silence, and again I thought it was the strangest meeting I'd ever attended. Apparently Bianca did work for EMI, over and above just The RaceCats' tour, and she had far more pull than I could've imagined, if her word had taken precedence over A&R. Things just usually didn't work that way, but on the other hand, what did I know? Like Barbie had said, the biz had changed.

Phenex was signed, was gonna do an eight city tour, opening for The Desperate Princes who were opening for The RaceCats. They were gonna cut a record that wouldn't sound as good as their demo, but it would have the EMI promotional machine behind it.

Maybe it would sell, but if it didn't, EMI wouldn't pick up any more recording options. Like Buddy, I didn't think Phenex would go any farther than what they'd signed up for today. After their first tour as a warm-up band, EMI would drop them, and they'd go back to Riverside, California obscurity.

Stan was a diplomat: he shook hands with everybody. The A&R couple were snobs: they managed to slip out without saying another word to anyone. Buddy wasn't quite finished yet, however. Through the open door, loud enough for us all to hear, he said, "I never thought I'd see the day that we'd sign someone based on some paper-pusher's blessing."

Sissy hissed, "That was Ernie LaBelle in there, Buddy. From Sonic Daydream. And the drummer, too. Upstairs is gonna listen about a pedigree like that –"

"Upstairs didn't listen to *them,* though. I did. You did." Buddy's voice was getting fainter as he and Sissy walked down the hall, but his final statement was audible enough: "I don't care if half of Sonic Daydream is backing them. They're no Sonic Daydream. They're not even in the same area code. And I can't understand why Bianca would be so insistent about producing a record for them when they're obviously –" Buddy and Sissy rounded the corner in the hall, and his words were cut off.

"Buddy's a bit of a hot-head," Stan said to no one in particular. "Whatever comes down from on high, if it differs from his opinion, well . . . He has yet to realize that it all pays the same."

We walked with him to the elevator, and when the doors opened, Stan smiled, sighed. "Welcome to EMI." Since it all paid the same, there was no sense in his being rude to Phenex, despite their mediocrity. "You all enjoy your tour. We'll talk about your record when you get back." He stepped inside, waved. The doors closed and he was gone.

We all looked at Ernie for some explanation. He shrugged. "Whatever's clever, kiddies. You're signed."

The elevator door soon opened again, and amid hugs and high-fives, we all got aboard.

Phillip asked Lisa brightly if she'd been backstage at the DLVEC yet. She put her arm around my waist and leaned against me, and told Phillip that she had not. He ignored her PDA and asked if she'd like to go with him to see it now.

I mused that the singer had to know that one of the old guys from the famous band was Lisa's daddy, but maybe he was unsure which one. Perhaps now he figured it must be me, and she was just showing a little daughterly affection. *Boy, are you gonna get your feelings hurt, Phil, ol' son.*

Ernie looked at me and inclined his head. We'd been friends for a long time, so I knew that meant, *I need to have a word with you.* Lisa opened her mouth, no doubt to turn Phillip down, and I said, "You guys go ahead. We'll be along in a minute."

The elevator doors opened and Lisa offered me a pouty glare. I grinned, squeezed her hand. If Phillip had it in his mind to confess his love already, she might as well get breaking his heart out of the way.

"Remember, you guys go on at eight o'clock now, instead of nine," Chrissy, ever the stage manager, told us. It was still three and a half hours away.

We walked the short distance to the venue; the Downtown Las Vegas Event Center was coming alive. Canopy tents now lined two sides inside the fence – merch booths and local radio stations and the bar. Just inside, past the glowing marquee, barricades and yellow-jacketed security guards awaited to wand the expected throngs. Someone was testing the stage lights: they blinked from red to purple to green. A DJ was onstage, playing videos from yesteryear. At the familiar intro to *Tomcats,* I looked over to see Dennis Whitly's smiling face, young again, twinned on the large screens on either side of the stage.

Our party stopped in front of the marquee, again looking at Ernie LaBelle for guidance. *You people better start getting over that,* I thought. *You're big kids now. Signed and all.*

He shooed them. "Go on in, check it out. We'll be back in time for the show. We've got a little errand to run."

There was a second's pause while Chrissy and Phillip looked at him in disbelief, but Phenex didn't seem surprised at all that he was sending them in alone. They knew he'd been sick. Maybe they thought that we old dudes needed to go back to the hotel and rest for a while before the show.

Finally Chrissy said, "All right, Ernie. We'll see you soon." She herded Phenex over to the barricades.

Now I waited for direction from my old second-guitar. He blinked at me, again with a look of mild confusion, as if he was just waking up, and again Iris's warning clanged in my head. *Watch over him, Cal.*

"Are you all right?"

"I don't fucking know, dude." He dragged his hand across his pale face. "I feel . . ." He gestured at the band, now through the barricades and halfway across the concrete. "I feel like this is all so . . . pointless." He looked back at me and demanded, "What's the point, Cal? Why did we do any of it?"

I blinked in utter surprise. Was Ernie having some existential crisis in his comfortable, wealthy, healthy old age? Was that what Iris had foreseen?

I clapped him on the back. *"It's only rock and roll, but I like it,* Ernie."

His face brightened suddenly, his smile bloomed. "Bianca . . . She's great, Cal. When I get back to town . . ." Then he winced, grabbed at his chest, his stomach, stumbled forward.

I put out my hand to steady him. Concerned now, I asked again, "Are you all right?"

His smile was wan. "Yeah. No strokes like Lenny. It must be something I ate. It comes in waves, this sick-to-my-stomach feeling. I think it's making me depressed." He stole another furtive glance toward the stage; the band was gone. "I gotta get away from here for a minute, Cal. So I can think. Where's my car? Let's take a ride."

We retrieved the 911 from the parking garage behind the Golden Nugget, and Ernie guided it silently, grimly through the always-killer Vegas traffic.

"Do we really have an errand?"

He shook his head. "I just have to get away. For some reason, I feel like I can't sit still."

Even though I knew it couldn't be so, I asked anyway. "Are you nervous about the show?"

He again shook his head. "Lisa's great. The rest of them . . . They're great for a warm-up band."

Was that resentment? I didn't think so, but . . . "Is it because EMI kicked them down –"

"No. They're signed. I got her what she wanted. Now . . . I just don't care anymore, Cal." He glanced over at me, and for a split-second, I thought I saw a flash of confused pleading in his eyes. Then it was gone. "For some reason . . . I just don't seem to care about any of it, anymore."

Ernie's dark mood was distressing to me. It was so unlike him, plus I had Iris's supernatural warnings, like a shroud, clouding my mind. But I just couldn't believe in her hocus-pocus.

"Maybe it's just because you're feeling sick, Ernie." He shot the Porsche onto the freeway, and I glanced over at the shining, coruscating lights of the gambling mecca. "Vegas is no fun when you're sick."

"Maybe that's it," he replied mechanically, unconvincingly. "Let's go lose some money."

Again I was surprised. Ernie was no gambler. Leonard Whitly was – *I got ta tell ya that poker's his thing.* And Denny, too. They'd *tucked their hair up under their hats,* and looking like *fine upstanding young men,* incognito, they'd hit the casinos after every show we'd ever played in Vegas. The Whitly brothers dug gambling.

But not me. I'd hung out with Elise, had walked the bright streets with her, just like I'd done with Lisa today. Elise had only taken one gamble in her life, her obsession with Sonic Daydream's front, and on that deal, in the end, she'd hit when she should've stayed.

And Ernie hadn't had time for games of chance, because he'd always had a sure thing waiting for him back at the hotel.

But he wanted to gamble now, so he exited the freeway onto the strip. *We ended up* not *at the Grand Hotel,* but at the Luxor. He handed the Porsche over to the valet, and I dutifully followed him into the hotel, as if I was his shadow. He obtained chips and I stood beside him while he joylessly played blackjack, losing prodigiously. Then as suddenly as the mood to gamble struck him, it decamped. We retrieved the baby-blue 911, he absent-mindedly tipped the valet with his last $50 chip, and we headed back to The Golden Nugget.

It was just another bizarre scene from a day that had only gotten stranger from the moment I'd hung up with Iris, back in Riverside, what seemed like a decade ago.

Ernie dropped me on the corner in front of the marquee to the DLVEC. We had successfully killed almost two hours; the band was scheduled to go on in an hour and a half. Ernie told me he was gonna stow the car, take a shower, then lay down for a little while to see if he felt any better.

"You've always been my best friend, Cal," he said seriously as I stepped out of the Porsche.

Nothing came to mind at first. It was just more oddness. At last I said, "Me and the ladies, Ernie."

He didn't smile. "Text me right before show time."

As he pulled away from the curb, his unaccustomed solemnity again brought Iris's warnings to mind. Well, I'd watched over him. He was gonna take a nap. Phenex would soon do their momentous first gig as a signed band. The next gig was in San Diego in three days, so we'd be heading back to Riverside in the morning. By the time we got home it would be Sunday afternoon and Ernie's crisis – whether supernatural, or existential, or just bad-food induced – would be passed.

FORTY-EIGHT

I called Lisa, but she told me that she was getting ready with her mom, that it was like dressing for the prom she'd never wasted time attending, that there were curling irons and hairbrushes, make-up and perfumes strewn all over our room. She giggled and said it was no place for the faint of heart, no scene for a man. She said she'd see me backstage.

I called Iris, but again got no answer. I walked around on Fremont Street, got a burger and fries I didn't really want. Soon the hour and a half I'd needed to kill before show time was expired.

The crowd was modest; I would've estimated that perhaps a quarter of the standing room was already occupied. I was pretty sure that no one had journeyed all the way from California to see unknown Phenex: these were probably locals, the kinds of fans that just liked to *go to the show,* regardless of who was playing. Or maybe they were fans of the mysterious Desperate Princes, or RaceCats fans, arrived early to take in all three bands and get their money's worth.

I held up my all-access pass to the proper authorities and was admitted backstage. Phenex had already loaded-in. The boys stood in a circle, holding hands with Candy. Their chant was inaudible above the din of the DJ, still blasting oldies-but-goodies onstage. Three unfamiliar longhairs walked past me, then out into the crowd – I figured this was perhaps the act on after Phenex.

Chrissy looked up from talking to a roadie, smiled, waved. Phillip frowned sullenly at me. I wondered where the rest of his band was. These kids were surely different than we'd been. After a show, we went our separate ways, true, but right before? Sonic Daydream, with Elise at our heels, had been inseparable.

Phillip followed The Desperate Princes out into the crowd. I figured that Lisa had told him the score, and he wasn't liking it, or me, too much at the moment.

At last I saw her, pacing by the back fence. She saw me at the same time, and ran over and hugged me. I held her at arm's length, drinking in her beauty. Her hair was a mass of wild black curls, the effortless look of youthful vitality that her mother tried so unsuccessfully to imitate. She was heavily made-up, something that she never did – red lipstick and lots of mascara and false eyelashes – but it looked great on her. She wore a black, spaghetti-strap shirt, and her signature khaki cargo pants. Not too sexy, but quite sexy enough. She was every inch the bad-girl rock singer, every single thing that young Katie back in Temecula aspired to be.

"I want to kiss you, Cal. But I'll muss my face."

I hugged her again, kissed the top of her head. "Break a leg, baby. It's all you." I nodded out toward the growing crowd. "I'm gonna play fan for this one."

Lisa's smile faltered for a second, then her confidence returned. "Okay, Lover." She pointed at the fence before which she had so recently paced. "Meet me right here after. I have no desire to see The Desperate Princes. I wanna go back to the room with you."

"Your wish is my command." I squeezed her again and went out into the crowd.

I was almost to the line of merch booths by the fence before it struck me that she hadn't asked where her daddy was. I texted him. *Wake up, Sleeping Beauty. Ur band's about 2 take the stage.*

I'll b right there.

I'm by the X107.5 radio station booth. In the back. I wanna see em from out front 4 a change.

I'll b right there, Ernie texted again.

FORTY-NINE

The DJ thanked the crowd for coming out. Then the stage went dark, and a heartbeat later, a disembodied voice said, "Welcome, Las Vegas – from Riverside, California, Phenex!"

The Party City crowd gave a hearty cheer, and Lisa began their set. The sound quality at the DLVEC was excellent, even in the back, and I had no trouble seeing my girl across the crowd. I realized that it had been decades since I'd heard any live band play from anywhere besides the wings or backstage. I'd forgotten what a joy it was to be in a receptive crowd, singing along, when you knew all the words. It was a one of a kind excitement, and I was transported back to high school, reminded of why Ernie and Lenny and I had sought to emulate those bands we'd seen onstage, to become one of them. I remembered something that I hadn't thought about in a long time: there were few things in the world as much fun as a rock concert.

The Vegas crowd cheered when Lisa said it was Phenex's first time in Sin City; they cheered when she asked them if they wanted to rock and roll.

And even though Phenex was still mediocre, I thought the boys were improving. Horus was not as good as everyone had said, not as good as Sonny, not by a long stretch. But unlike Sonny, he was a showman, pointing and smiling and winking at girls in the crowd. I thought that was Ernie's influence right there, although such antics had never been Ernie's shtick. He'd always distributed his charm after the show, on a more personal level. Denny had been the pointer, the smiler, the waver, and of course it had worked for him. Dennis Whitly's onstage persona had shot us to international fame. Denny had been better looking and a far superior guitarist to Horus, but the Vegas girls still responded, whooping and cheering for him during his solos.

Just like Ernie had always maintained, Lisa was great. She owned the stage, prancing and screaming, dueling with Horus. When their set ended, the crowd response was the best yet, save for the time when the legendary Dennis Whitly had appeared with them, and that time didn't hardly count. Phenex still wasn't very good for a signed act, but they were a spectacular warm-up band, and they were getting better.

I was pleased with their set, proud of them. The lights came up on the stage, so the roadies could load-out their equipment and bring on that which belonged to The Desperate Princes, so I started to skirt the crowd, angling my way slowly up the side to where there was an entrance backstage.

The big security guard waved me through, and the first person I looked for was Ernie. I figured that he'd decided to forgo the fan experience with me, the press of the crowd and all. It wasn't that he was a snob; it was that he'd been sick. I was sure I'd find him backstage, congratulating his daughter on a great performance, clapping the boys on the shoulders and telling them *Well done!* Ernie didn't have anything against the band, after all, and I was sure that he'd want them to see that he was proud of them. It would maybe ease the hurt when he told them he wouldn't be there in San Diego.

Lisa jumped into my arms, hugged me. I looked at her questioningly. "Where's Ernie?"

"I haven't seen him," she shouted over the ambient crowd noise. "I thought he was with you."

I shook my head and walked over closer to the back fence, out of the way of the hustling roadies. Lisa went to hug her mother and the rest of the band. I looked at my phone.

Right after Phenex's set had commenced, Ernie had texted. *I'm sorry, Cal. I just couldn't do it.*

Something about his use of the past tense struck me.

Where r u? I replied, but I was pretty sure I already knew.

In the desert.

Shit! I'd guessed correctly. Ernie hadn't gone back to his room at all. He'd dropped me at the corner and headed for home. He'd left me to ride back in the van, crammed in with Candy and Phenex, and he already had a good two hour head start.

Ernie was a lot of things, but a coward wasn't one of them, so I was having trouble comprehending this retreat. As I'd told Iris, he'd always been a man of his word, and he'd said he'd stick with Phenex through Vegas. But now he'd bailed, because he *just couldn't do it.*

What's wrong w/u, dude?

Nothing's wrong anymore. Once I realized what I had 2 do, the pain stopped.

What do u have 2 do?

End it.

The cursor blinked in the *Send Message* box below these two words, but I had not one single response. My first inclination was to think that Ernie was trying to make some kind of tasteless joke. But we'd all known a suicide, and it had never been a subject for jest for any of us.

I remembered his black mood, his bleak questions. *What's the point, Cal? Why did we do any of it?* I'd watched him wince in pain from this sudden sickness; he'd said it was making him depressed. But surely, happy-go-lucky Ernie LaBelle had to be kidding me. Out of a clear blue sky, surely he couldn't possibly be thinking about . . . I couldn't even form the words in my mind.

They were doing the sound check for The Desperate Princes onstage, so I stepped past another security guard, through the back gate to the DLVEC, out onto the relative quiet of Bridger Avenue. I started walking toward the hotel, to get away from the noise. I called Ernie.

He answered immediately. "You can't stop me, Cal. You're stuck in Vegas and I'll be home in a heartbeat."

I heard Elise's voice in my head, as it had come out of an old-fashioned cellphone speaker almost twenty years ago. She was already dead by the time I'd heard her message, lying cold and alone in some LA County morgue. *It's chickenshit to do it like this, but you would've just tried to talk me out of it, anyway.*

I hadn't heard the phone ring when she'd called – a cellphone was a new thing for me, a new thing for all of us, then. I'd left it on the coffee table or on the kitchen counter the night before, hadn't even seen her message until after Lenny had called me to tell me about the accident. My cell had not yet become a part of my person like it was now, never left behind, vital, necessary: wallet, keys, phone. I'd been unreachable when Elise had called me, unavailable to talk her out of it, to save her.

Now Ernie had put so many miles between us. He was just like Elise. He didn't want to be saved.

"Christ, Ernie! Why? Why do you want to –"

"I just got to thinking, Cal. My whole life's been a waste. I'm fifty-five years old, and what do I have? Nothing. I have nothing. Why draw it out any longer?"

"You've got me, Ernie. You've got Lisa. She loves you. Think of her, Ernie! You can't do this to –"

"She loves *you,* Cal. Nobody loves me."

"Oh, God, Ernie! Millions of people love you!"

He tried to laugh but it came out as a sob. "Millions of people love Denny, Cal. The music was all his."

Iris's words in my head: *Your friend Ernie is in danger, Cal. I have seen an end to him.*

Lenny's voiceless text: *Theres more things n heaven & earth, Cal.*

Somehow, Iris was right. Somehow she'd seen it.

You watch over him, Cal. There he is one moment, then the next – he's gone.

I had failed to watch over him, and he was indeed gone.

"Ernie, dude. Please don't do this. Wait for me."

Again, that sobbing laugh. "I'm an hour, an hour and a half from home, Cal. I gotta stop somewhere, get some pills . . ."

"Oh, God, Ernie! Please don't do this." I couldn't think of anything else to say, other than to plead with him not to do it. Reasoning with him wasn't going to work.

"You don't have to come, Cal. Stay with the band. By the time you get back, it'll all be over. I just can't go on anymore, not without . . . ah, I don't fucking know."

"Please, Ernie!"

"It's been great knowing you, Cal."

Elise's words: *I know you'll miss me – you'll be the only one.*

"Ernie –"

He'd hung up. I called again, but he didn't answer. So I texted. *I coming, Ernie. I'm gonna beat u there. I'm not gonna let u do this.*

Ur dreamin, Cal. There's no way.

Christ, I didn't want to make it into some kind of challenge, and if I kept telling him how I was going to somehow teleport myself to Riverside ahead of him, bend the laws of time and distance, that's just how he'd take it. He would put the pedal to the metal of his incredibly nimble German car, straighten out the curves through Cajon Pass and be home in no time to kill himself. Or maybe he'd just do it like Elise, and bust the Porsche right through the guardrail.

Lisa approached up the sidewalk, and the solution, in the back of my mind all along, clicked when I looked at her. "I gotta get to the airport."

"What?"

"Ernie's . . . I gotta go, Lisa." I started walking toward Las Vegas Boulevard. I knew I could find a cab there.

Like another cliché: "I'm coming with you."

I barked laughter at her. "You got ID on you?" She held up her lanyard and backstage pass. "No. Like a driver's license. You need ID to get on a plane."

She reached into one of the pockets of her cargo pants and produced a slim wallet.

"All right, then."

I stopped a cab on Las Vegas Boulevard and told him there was $200 in it for him if he could get me to McCarran in ten minutes. He said he could do it, told me to time him.

I tried to call Iris, got no answer, just a message that her voicemail box had not been set up. I texted her: *U were right. Ernie's on his way back home. He says he's gonna kill himself. I don't know the address, but if ur heading toward downtown, it's the first house on the right after Monroe. Long driveway. I'm gonna fly back. I hope u get this, Iris. I hope you can help him.*

I called Riverside PD, and they assured me that if I was worried that my friend might do harm to himself, they would drive by and do a wellness check on him. The fact that he lived on Victoria Avenue surely contributed to their helpfulness. They wouldn't've agreed to pop by the band house in seedy Arlanza to serve and protect quite so readily.

The dispatcher's public servant professionalism cracked a little, however, when I told her that they couldn't go now.

"He's not there yet," I told her. "He's coming back from Vegas. I am, too, but he's gonna get there before me."

"Sir, you'll have to call us back when you think he's here."

FIFTY

Forty-five minutes later, Lisa and I were on a Southwest flight to Ontario. I did some calculations: Ernie probably hadn't made it home quite yet. But he was close, no less than forty minutes by now. He'd said something about having to find pills. None of us had ever been druggies, but once a rock star, always a rock star: when you were in the biz, you knew who was, so I reckoned that obtaining the necessary narcotics shouldn't take him too long.

Lisa and I were an hour to Ontario, and another half an hour, forty-five minutes to home after that. As soon as we landed, if Iris hadn't got my texts, I was gonna have to call the cops again. I was gonna have to call somebody, get somebody over to Ernie's house to stop him. We weren't going to make it in time.

At last I had a moment to look at Lisa. She'd silently held my hand in the cab, wordlessly stood in line at the ticket counter, busied herself on her phone without comment while we'd waited for our flight. Now she gazed solemnly back at me from the window seat.

She smiled lovingly, squeezed my hand. I thought that somehow she must've missed the gist of the action, the reason why I'd had to flee Las Vegas as if I'd just robbed the Bellagio. Perhaps she hadn't been paying attention when I'd told the cops that they needed to do a wellness check on Ernie. So I spelled it out for her. "Your dad says he's gonna kill himself."

"It's all gonna be all right, Cal. All that has been foretold is coming to pass."

No alarm, no upset; only the devoted, fan-love brightness of her eyes, the true-believer's steadfastness lacing her words. The fact that she wasn't worried in the least about Ernie gave me pause, and the thought skipped through my mind that perhaps I should've taken pause some time ago. I'd been keeping company with a bunch of fanatics, blithely ignoring their strange rituals and beliefs, just as surely as I'd ignored the church bells on Sundays all my life.

Why didn't Lisa care that Ernie might be dead by the time we got back home?

My tired, exhausted, amazed mind suddenly decided to listen. I looked at Lisa's shining eyes, and her words echoed in my mind: *All that has been foretold is coming to pass.* Her smile was serene.

Iris had predicted that something was going to happen to Ernie. How? That didn't really matter, did it? I was flying across the dark desert right now, trying to prevent one of the happiest, most well-adjusted people I'd ever known from suddenly, inexplicably, without warning, killing himself. I was desperately trying to prevent dead is dead, and as Iris had said, what difference did it make how such a thing came to pass?

Ernie meant to *end it,* just as Iris had warned me. I couldn't worry about how she knew. I had to stop her prediction, *her prophecy,* from coming to fruition.

Now Lisa was talking about prophecy, too. Maybe, somehow, she knew that Ernie was gonna be all right. I still couldn't quite swallow all of the mumbo-jumbo I'd been force-fed about evil influences and the taking of souls, but I couldn't deny that Iris had called it, and Lisa was just as unconcerned as she could be. She hadn't said a word. She hadn't pestered me with any unanswerable *whys* or *hows.*

Now she was spouting the same old bullshit about foretellings coming to pass, but even though I was an old dog, one part of my mind could still learn new tricks. One part of my mind was no longer closed, smug, superior. It had adopted Hamlet's attitude, and Lenny's, that there were more things in heaven and earth than were dreamt of in an old drummer's philosophy, and this part of my mind meant to therefore, as a stranger, give these things welcome.

Iris had guessed that something was going to happen to Ernie. Maybe Lisa had guessed that it would turn out all right in the end. Why else would she be so fucking calm?

"What exactly has been foretold?"

She squeezed my hand again. "I wanted to tell you the moment I saw you, Cal. When I turned around and you were standing there in front of me at the house – I knew that it was all true, that everything Mom had ever told me was fact. You looked exactly as I'd always thought you would. You looked just like the picture from the author page of *Sonic Nightmare.*"

Right, a voice in my head said. Whether it was my old rationalizing demon or this new element of listening, open-mindedness, I wasn't sure. *You've never let yourself see just how crazy she really is, have you?*

And this was the very least of it. I looked nothing at all like I did in the thirty-year-old picture from *Sonic Nightmare.*

"I wanted to tell you everything right then, but Mom said no. She said that you were an unbeliever, that you'd laugh at me. And she was right." Lisa grinned fondly. "Mom's always right. You *have* laughed at me, all along.

"I wanted to tell you again, at your house . . . You were so adorable, so unsure, asking me if I'd wanted you to make love to me. As if I hadn't wanted that all my life." She caressed my cheek and the touch of her rough fingers, so much in contrast to her soft words, made me flinch. "But there wasn't any time to tell you then, and since then . . . I've see that of course Mom was right. You'd never see. Not until the truths were undeniable, even to an unbeliever."

Lisa sighed, stopped. I prompted her. "I still don't see. You're gonna have to explain what has been foretold and how it's been –"

"You were raised a Catholic, right?" she asked, changing the subject. I nodded. "Catholicism used to be a fine old dogma, black and white, with no shades of gray. Once upon a time it was, *Keep holy the Sabbath day,* and if we don't think you're keeping it holy enough, we're gonna burn your heretic ass at the stake." Lisa grinned, her eyes twinkling in merry amusement. *"Nobody expects the Spanish Inquisition!"*

She never failed to amaze me. "How do you know that ancient–

"The internet, Cal. All of history, music, anything that was ever funny. All you need is a guide, and Mom's always been great."

Lisa paused, then began again. "Sonny once pointed something out about modern Catholicism that really made me think, Cal. This latest Pope – Sonny said that he's trying to cater to everybody. Nothing's a sin anymore. Everybody's forgiven. Divorce, gay marriage . . . The new pontiff is just an old softie.

"'It's one more example of the general hubris of mankind,' Sonny said. 'God? What God? We'll do what *we* wanna do.'" Again, that gleeful grin. Lisa sang, *"There's no time for a conscience, and we recognize no crime."*

Yeah, we got dogs and Valvoline, it's a pretty damn good time. Christ, another obscure oldie from a decade before she was born, from a band called Toy Matinee. They'd been one of Elise's favorites. They'd only put out one record, and I wondered if Lisa knew the words to their one popular song because she'd found their CD among Elise's possessions.

"'But,' Sonny said, 'just because the Pope has decided to forgive his self-indulgent flock, doesn't mean the nature of sin has altered. Not in the least. To those of us of the blood, what was sin, remains sin.'

"'Such as infidelity,' Mom said." Lisa paused to let this proclamation sink in. "'And apostasy,' James added."

"Really?" I blurted out. Apostasy was a four-syllable word, a philosophical construct about turning one's back on one's faith, about *losing one's religion.* I wouldn't have believed James knew any four-syllable words, nor that he embraced any philosophies of any kind, seeing as how that was a four-syllable word, too.

"Oh, yeah," Lisa assured me. "James is rather unforgiving of heretics, of anyone who abandons our beliefs. It's like the mafia to him. Once you've been initiated into the mysteries, there's no such thing as renunciation. You might say that James has an old Catholic outlook about it. Heresy, apostasy – not only are these still sins to James, they're mortal sins. Unforgivable."

They are dangerous to you.

Now Lisa studied me carefully. "Did you know that suicide used to be considered a mortal sin, Cal? An eternal sin, really, as there was no hope of repentance?"

Lisa hadn't asked me why we had to get the hell outta Dodge. The new voice in my head ominously whispered, *Maybe it's* not *that she knows Ernie's gonna make it. Maybe it's that she knows he's gonna die.* But if that's what she believed, why was she so goddamned calm about it?

"It's not that way anymore, of course. The church coddles the grieving relatives, now. Let's all gather around and pray for forgiveness for the tormented soul, and because we're praying, he'll be forgiven. God does what he's told nowadays.

"No one makes anyone take responsibility for their actions anymore, Cal, not even the One Holy, Catholic and Apostolic church. I guess you can't really blame them, though. The suicide is gone, but the relatives, they're still around, tithing, coming to Mass.

"Having a suicide in the family used to be shameful, but not anymore. It used to be a sin. A suicide was once buried away from everyone else, in unconsecrated earth, because he had voluntarily chosen to go straight to Hell. He had chosen to damn himself."

Like James having a philosophy about anything, I wouldn't've suspected that young Lisa had such a firm belief in the final judgment rendered upon suicides. Was adherence to this stern, unforgiving, 14th century dogma the reason why she apparently didn't care about her father's insane choice? Had she already given up on him because she believed he'd chosen to damn himself? Had she already accepted that he was gonna succeed?

She's absolutely nuts, my new voice of open-mindedness said.

"So you think that Ernie's –"

"Ernie?" She frowned in irritation. "I wish you'd stop interrupting me, Cal. You're unaware of your importance in the great scheme of this, and I'm trying to explain it all to you." Now she smiled patiently at me. "I'm not talking about Ernie. What did you say to me once? *Reward and punishment are a result of the decisions we make?* There's a lot of truth to that. Ernie has reaped what he has sown." Lisa waved her hand sharply, dismissively. "I'm not talking about Ernie. I'm talking about Elise."

I blinked stupidly. Not one single word of response to this announcement came into my mind, because on the list of all the phrases in the vast universe that I would've expected Lisa to say, *I'm talking about Elise* wasn't even on the list. All my advisory voices, new and old, were silent.

But Lisa didn't proceed to talk about Elise further. Not yet.

"Mom had bargained with Phenex – if he'd grant her Ernie LaBelle's child, Mom had vowed that she'd devote that child's life to becoming a great musician in the demon's service. Phenex came through, and even though I wasn't a boy, Mom kept her promise, sending me to music teachers from the time I was in kindergarten.

"She told Sonny that the demon had led her to him, and that was good enough for Sonny, because he had faith in the universal forces once. When I was a kid, he was a true believer. It wasn't until later, when I was older, when Mom revealed the full prophecy to us, that Sonny began to fall off in his beliefs." She shook her head sadly.

I recalled James telling me how he and Roy had *worked on Sonny's bike for him* before he'd gone to see his mom, and I suddenly cast Phenex's drummer and bassist as avenging agents of witchy righteousness; my imagination even dressed them in pilgrim hats and buckle shoes, James's long red hair in a braid with a little bow. But they weren't witch burners. They were protectors of their own demonic faith, punishing heretics to it, sabotaging Sonny's Triumph and sending him to his lonely death because he'd fallen away from their beliefs.

It was my sudden open-mindedness that was suggesting such horrors to me. I shut down this new receptive attitude viciously. Better to be closed-minded than to be paranoid, to start suspecting . . . *They are dangerous to you.*

"So Sonny became my music teacher," Lisa was saying. "Mom couldn't be happier – a talented member of the initiated to instruct

Ernie LaBelle's child. Then came further proof that we were destined for greatness. Great-grandma Cecelia died and left everything to Mom. No longer would we have to struggle to make ends meet, James and Roy working odd jobs, Sonny bagging groceries, Mom waiting tables. That was no way for the favorites of a Great Marquis of Hell to be living.

"Now the five of us were set. The mundane physical needs of this plane would be provided. Our time could be spent playing music, preparing for the moment when Phenex the demon would thrust Phenex the band into our rightful place in the spotlight. As has now come to pass." Lisa grinned.

A little maniacally, my own resident demon observed. *She's nuts, Cal.*

"When your book came out, it was a revelation to Mom. It became clear that, not only had the demon helped her to get the baby she wanted, he'd led her to Denny's house to be closer to the lives of the members of the band she'd loved so much. She'd obviously been *destined* to have access to his dead sister-in-law's things, but why? The demon's full intentions were unclear to Mom. She'd have to seek to know his mind to figure it all out, to know what his plan actually was."

For my thoughts are not your thoughts, neither are your ways my ways, saith the Lord.

"It's dangerous to seek direct communication with a demon," Lisa informed me matter-of-factly, as if she was telling me that it was dangerous to go swimming after a heavy meal. "It's recommended never to commune with Phenex alone, as he's a trickster, and will try his best to entrance and then devour the supplicant. But Mom wasn't worried about any of that. On the one hand, she believed that Phenex was her patron, that he had plans for her. She'd pledged me to the greater glory of his name, but I was still just a little girl. Mom didn't think Phenex would be trying to eat her at the moment, even if she did have the audacity to request an audience.

"And on the other hand, Mom had faith in her ability to draw a faultless protective circle, because she'd already conjured lesser entities with Cecelia when only a child. If Phenex was annoyed at being roused, and decided to try to devour her instead of reveal his purpose – Mom was confident that her circle would protect her from such a whim."

The plane hit a spot of turbulence, bounced, jarring me back to reality from this crazy supernatural tale of the summoning of contrary, possibly traitorous demons. It was a reality that embraced laws of physics such as gravity, and loss of lift, and terminal velocity, and what a long way it was from here to the ground. I encompassed all the worries that stalk through your mind when the plane hits turbulence, but unlike my mother at similar times, no prayer formed in my mind. My own little devil cackled: *Cancel my subscription to the resurrection.*

"So Mom sent me to the mall with James and Roy and Sonny. She called Phenex – demons are bound to reply when properly called, Cal, did you know that? *They must appear.*"

Yeah, I'd heard something like that, yeah, I thought, but I couldn't speak, because Sonny's letter came back to me. *When Lisa was just a kid, Candy summoned the demon. He told her what was to come, and he also told her that on the cusp of fame, one of us would be sacrificed.*

I waited for Lisa to tell me what Phenex had pronounced, but she didn't mention sacrifice. Not yet.

"The demon's revelations were astounding, Cal. All was explained: Mom's access to Elise's things; your book. The very timing of my conception."

Iris's voice again: *Did you know that Lisa was born nine months after Elise died? Almost to the day?* Yup. I knew that. So what?

"I told you that I've always identified with Elise, have I not? Mom's fairytale version of your book brought her alive for me, and seeing and touching all her things . . . But Phenex revealed a deeper truth to Mom, Cal, and then she revealed it to me. You see . . . I am Elise."

A bray of laughter and one word – *"What?"* – escaped from me. My own voice seemed loud in the quiet cabin, and I looked around in embarrassment. A businessman across the aisle glanced up curiously over his half-specs, but when I met his eyes, he quickly went back to whatever he was reading. It was not a good idea to make eye contact with giggling fellow passengers on night-flights from Vegas.

I turned my attention back to Lisa.

"Time is like a picture window to beings such as Phenex, Cal," she told me solemnly. "Past, present, future – like a panorama. Mom believed that she'd just decided one day to have Ernie's baby, but Phenex already knew everything that was to come. Mom hadn't arrived at this particular decision at this particular moment all on her own. She had of course wanted Ernie since she was a teenager, but the knowledge that she could actually *get him* if she tried had never occurred to her before.

"It was because Phenex knew, Cal. He compelled Mom to act – I was conceived when I was, because Phenex knew that Elise's soul would be slipping its mortal bonds, not twenty-four hours later. He knew it would need a new vessel."

I looked for some twinkle in her eye to indicate that she was joking, but of course there was none. All this ridiculous insanity was gospel to Lisa, passed down from her equally deluded mother, based on a few coincidences of conception and death. They were calculations Candy had not made until eight years after the fact, conclusions she never could've drawn had she not read my book.

Therefore, *my importance in the great scheme of this.* If Phenex was the prophet, the seer of all that was to come, then I was his scribe. I'd told the story, mentioned the time of Elise's death, and the demon Phenex had then spoken, explained its significance to Candy.

She had then proceeded to feed her eight-year-old kid all kinds of ridiculous mythology. But this time, my amusement overcame my pity for Lisa's absurd upbringing. Even dark images of sabotage, of murderous punishments for imagined heresies, fled. I giggled; I guffawed. "Oh, my God, baby, you've got to be kidding! You can't possibly expect me to believe that you're Elise –"

"Silence!" Lisa whispered fiercely. He blue eyes blazed in exasperation. "We're going to land and you're gonna run off on some fruitless crusade. I'm trying to tell you that none of that matters anymore. The time has at last come. I am about to become the instrument of your revenge –"

"My revenge?"

"Will you shush? I'm trying to tell you. Phenex revealed to Mom that within me dwelt the soul of Elise Carlin. Mom told me about it gently at first. She sugarcoated your book – it was true that the sad girl had died, but everybody has to die eventually. And now the sad girl was getting another chance, a chance to live again, through me.

"And so it went, through grade school and high school. Mom played the old music – you'd said that Elise had known all the old tunes, so I knew that the reason I liked the stuff Mom played was because it was Elise's personality coming through. I wore her clothes. I felt honored to be the vessel of the soul of my favorite princess.

"You'd written her story so poetically, so I knew that someday, I'd get to meet you, and then the misstep of fate would be corrected. That's what I believed when I was a kid, Cal. The wheel of fortune had slipped – Elise had been destined *to be with you,* not Dennis Whitly. Didn't you say that she was your best friend?

"And someday, when I was old enough – Mom and I and Phenex were gonna set straight this glitch of fortune. Elise had been prevented from being with you in her first life – Mom once suggested that perhaps some other witch had put some kind of curse on her. But together, the three of us were stronger than that witch, and someday, soon . . . Elise had been reborn in me, and someday she – I – would get the chance to be reunited with you."

She is just as crazy as a March hare, my resident demon marveled. *Just as nutty as squirrel shit, dude. I know she's cute, and you've been lonely, but Christ-on-a-crutch, Cal, how have you failed to see how completely and irretrievably insane she is?*

"That's what I believed, Cal. Until . . ." Lisa sighed heavily, once more squeezed my hand. Her expression became almost apologetic.

"I have to admit that I forgot about our someday-to-be romance and happily-ever-after when I met Ryan. I didn't know you – all I had were some pictures, a couple of quick glimpses of you in Sonic Daydream videos." She studied me for a heartbeat, kissed me on the nose. "In my defense, now that I think about it, I gotta say that Ryan looked a little bit like you." She shrugged. "It was hormones. I was sixteen."

She said it like sixteen was a lifetime ago, like it was for me, instead of just a couple of years prior, like it was for her.

"I liked kissing him, touching him. I liked what he did to me. I closed my eyes and pretended he was you." She peeped innocently at me to see if I was buying it. "I thought maybe . . . I thought maybe I was supposed to experience love with someone else first, so I would be . . . prepared when I met you. Or so I rationalized it. It was all really just a spur of the moment thing." She sighed again.

Ships that pass in the night, my little devil said, and cackled again.

"But Mom set me straight on all that. She threw your book at me, told me it was a cautionary tale about love at first sight. So I actually read it myself, for the first time, and all the startling truths of what had really happened to Elise were revealed.

"After I read it, I remember walking into the kitchen. Mom was waiting for me. She said, 'Do you see now that you're meant for more than just whoring around with some worthless boy? Do you see the rare and wonderful opportunity you've been afforded?'

"I felt like I was in some kind of a dream. I asked, 'Why didn't you ever tell me that she'd killed herself?'

"'You were just a kid,' she said. 'It would've been a burden to you. You're old enough to handle it now.'

"'But my soul –' I began, and Mom finished for me.

"'Your soul is damned, yes. A suicide is always damned. But maybe not this time. Because of the intercession of Phenex, Elise hasn't been doomed quite yet. She doesn't yet suffer in eternal hellfire, but lives again within you. She's been given another chance, at least temporarily. Phenex has given you a mission, Lisa, an incredible opportunity to save Elise and yourself from damnation.'

"And then Mom told me what I had to do to save Elise's soul. Mom said that it was up to me to give over to damnation the soul of the man that had led Elise to make her fatal, irreversible decision. Then she and I would be redeemed. He had to be punished for what he'd done. That coward, that gutless, cheating bastard, just like you said, Cal. Mom told me, 'To save Elise's soul, your soul, Lisa, you must damn –'"

"Dennis Whitly." Of course. If she was Elise, it could be none other.

"Ah!" She gave me a noisy, sloppy kiss on the cheek. "He can be taught!" Her eyes glowed with gleeful enthusiasm. "I am the instrument of Elise's revenge, of your revenge *for her. Now we are become death,* Cal, you and me. *The destroyer of worlds.* How shall you like to see it done? What spell would you have me cast to destroy Dennis Whitly's immortal soul?"

There it was, everything that Sonny had told me in his letter. Of course Lisa thought I'd want to help her. She believed that she was Elise reincarnated, and who had loved Elise more than me, who had brought her sad story to the masses? Who had deposited the blame for her suicide, her self-damnation, none too delicately at Dennis Whitly's feet? No one could want to see Elise revenged more than me. And since Lisa was Elise reborn – of course I'd be down to help her.

But I didn't believe in damnation, and I most assuredly didn't believe that my misguided, beloved Lisa was the reincarnation of Elise Carlin. It was so funny, how Candy had come to all these incredibly tenuous conclusions – she never would've dreamed any of this stuff up about an other-worldly connection between Elise and Lisa, if she hadn't read *Sonic Nightmare.* The irony of that was uproariously funny to me. I couldn't control my giggles. I tried, but I just couldn't. At last I sniggered out, "How is that you plan to damn Denny, Lisa?"

She smiled indulgently at me. "Ah, my darling. And we'd been having such a nice talk. Yet still you doubt."

The *Fasten Seat Belts Sign* came on and the pilot announced our descent toward Ontario International Airport.

"My powers are marshalling, as we speak, Cal. Like thunderheads. Soon, when all sacrifices have been completed, I'll simply instruct him. Once I've come into my full strength, he'll do what he's told, without reflection."

Just like I do, I thought. *Your wish is my command.*

Moments later, the plane bumped along the runway.

Lisa had told me all along that she and her mother hated Dennis Whitly, and now she'd told me the entirely insane reason why. It wasn't just because Denny had killed their favorite band. Oh, no. That was actually a perfectly legitimate reason, comparatively, a common fan complaint. No, they hated Denny because Lisa was actually my poor, deluded friend reincarnated. She was Elise returned from the grave to enact cosmic revenge upon the man who had driven her to damn herself.

And I was a Chinese jet pilot.

Still, that word, *sacrifices*, chilled me a bit. *She's nuts!* my demon said again. I'd have to swallow my pride and drop by Denny's house and let him know that he had acquired a stalker. If nothing else, I saw it as my duty to a fellow musician. I wasn't afraid for his immortal soul, but I thought that he should know that the cute girl he'd sung with onstage at the Just Us Festival had it in for him. And her groupie mother, too. I didn't believe that it was spells or marshalled powers that he had to worry about, but I did remember Iris's simulated attack with the garish dagger. When they found their hocus-pocus ineffective, Christ only knew what other methods they might employ to *damn him.* One had to be dead before one was damned or saved, right?

As we taxied to the gate, I realized that I was exhausted, in mind, in body, in spirit. My young girlfriend, the hope of my old age, was living under a fantasy far more outlandish than the one Elise had entertained. Elise had harbored the unlikely hope that Denny would dump her sister and take up with her. A pathetic daydream, but not uncommon, I imagined, among girls with sisters. It was only the lengths to which Elise had taken it that had turned it tragic.

On the other hand, Lisa's delusion could get her locked up. She wasn't so clichéd and commonplace as to believe that she was Napoleon reborn; instead she believed that she was the dead sister-in-law of a rock singer more famous that Napoleon, at least in the English-speaking world. I imagined armies of shrinks, salivating to sink their teeth into a case-study of such textbook proportions.

I hadn't been able to save Elise, but I thought that maybe I could talk Lisa out of her aberration – in a way, like Sonny said, I could use my love to dissuade her from her quest to damn Denny. I thought that maybe with the help of those same shrinks, I could make her see that there was no way she could damn Denny, nor did she have to, because she wasn't Elise. It was all just a fantasy that her mother had inflicted upon her, and I thought that with some therapy, she could be made to see the silliness of all of it.

But I couldn't worry about Lisa's mental health right at the moment, nor could I worry about Denny. I had to get to Ernie. More accurately, I had to get *someone else* to Ernie, because I was still too far away. If Iris hadn't gotten my texts, I couldn't risk the time it would take to try to save him myself. I was gonna have to call the cops again, get them to go out to his house to check on him.

But the minute I switched my phone out of airplane mode, Iris called.

"Oh, thank Christ! Tell me he's okay!"

"We're at Kaiser Hospital. They're . . . I think they're pumping his stomach. The doctors wouldn't really tell me anything."

"So you –"

"Are you alone, Cal?"

I glanced at Lisa, walking through the terminal beside me. She was studying her phone, trying to figure out what shuttle to take to the nearest car rental place.

"No."

"Don't say my name."

"Okay," I said slowly. "Is Ernie gonna be –"

"Ernie's in the capable hands of modern medicine. There's nothing more that we can do for him right now." She sighed. "Why didn't you make him take off the amulet, Cal?"

Jesus and all the saints, from every single direction, still more mumbo-jumbo!

I had to give it to Iris that she'd accurately predicted a totally unpredictable crisis. Maybe she *was* some kind of sensitive; maybe that was possible. I didn't have to understand it to be grateful for it. She'd saved Ernie's life. But all the rest of it – just like Lisa wasn't Elise reborn, Ernie's sudden decision to off himself didn't have anything to do with a piece of cheap jewelry.

"I guess I just forgot."

Iris was silent for a heartbeat. "Text me when you get here. I'll let you know where his room is."

"Okay, it should be about –"

But Iris had already disconnected.

FIFTY-ONE

The urgent need to hurry had evaporated. Iris had saved Ernie's life. He was in the hospital, but it was no longer necessary to break any laws to get there to him. I was too exhausted to speed anyway. Beside me in the rented car, Lisa played *Tetris* on her phone. She had not asked a single question about her father. He was okay; maybe she'd known all along that he would be.

"Tell me again how you plan to damn Denny?" I figured that I might as well get the full scope of the delusion, the methodologies, since I already had the whys and the wherefores.

She didn't look up from her game. "I told you. Soon, I'll be powerful enough that he'll be unable to resist my commands."

"What do you plan to command him to do? Jump off a building?"

Lisa paused her game. She smiled, caressed my thigh. "I love you, Cal. But Ernie was right. Sometimes you're just dumb. I didn't say that I wanted to kill Denny, or even that I wanted him to kill himself. Although it's probably not outside the realm of possibility to persuade him to do that."

She winked, and it was like a cold hand squeezed my heart. What had she said earlier about Ernie, the only thing that she'd said at all? *Ernie has reaped what he has sown.* Even if he was all right, had she no pity at all for him?

Lisa tittered. "I would seduce Denny, Cal. As simple as that. Or make him believe that I was going to. I wouldn't go through with it, of course. My loyalty to you is steadfast."

Me and Phenex. Lucky us. Oh, yeah. There was gonna have to be therapy.

"But I *would* lead him down the garden path. I'd make him want me. Once my controls have been fully energized, he'll be powerless. My merest whim will become his life's work.

"I'll make him believe he loves me, Cal. He'll call, he'll text. I'll answer sometimes. Maybe he'll write songs about me."

All the things he never did for Elise. Though this be madness, yet there is method in't.

"And then, when I tire of toying with him, I'll arrange it so his wife catches us in a compromising position. No consummation will have to occur, but she'll believe that it has."

Cruelty simmered in her blue eyes. "These two facets will be enough to destroy him, Cal, to make his life a living hell. His desire for me, unquenched; and the fact that he destroyed his beloved wife's trust without ever achieving me. The knowledge that he'd do it to her again, if I'd only give him another chance. Maybe he will opt for the coward's way out, then. Regardless, he'll be damned by his own self-loathing."

I chewed on my bottom lip until I was sure that I wouldn't laugh at her. "Two things," I said at last. "Why do you think that Denny'll let you get anywhere near enough to seduce him? He's a coward from way back about such things, Lisa. He'd make sure the two of you were never alone –"

Lisa clapped her hands and squealed delighted laughter. "How you do flatter me, my darling! You think I'm saying that I'll just waltz in and conquer Dennis Whitly based on my own inestimable charm? That only worked on you." She batted her false eyelashes at me. "No. You haven't been listening. If I could do it on my own, I would've had him on stage at the Just Us Festival.

"I'll seduce Denny with the aid of the forces unseen, Cal. They gather even now, and will soon be poised to strike at my command. He wears the amulet. Mom gave it to him after the show, as thanks for helping the band. I'll call to it, and it'll call to him. Its power will bring him to his knees before me."

I couldn't comment about my lack of faith in the likelihood of a piece of costume jewelry wooing Denny away from his beloved lady-wife. Not with a straight face, anyway. Ernie's medallion hadn't driven him to the brink of suicide, and Denny's wasn't going to drive him to adultery with a girl ten years younger than his daughter. It was a fairytale.

As we exited on La Sierra Avenue, I told her, "The second flaw I see in your plan is this. If you really are Elise reborn, as you say you are, and if you had Dennis Whitly on his knees before you . . ." I leered at her. "You're not going to stop there. If you really are Elise, you're going to *consummate* it." I wiggled my eyebrows at her.

"It was the one thing she lived for, and as far as I can tell, she only got to experience it once. If she's really come back from the other side, and the opportunity presents itself again . . ." I winked. "If you really are Elise, you're gonna go for it." I pretended to pout. "What about me? What did you say before? That infidelity is another unforgivable sin?"

"That misplaced desire was all in a previous incarnation, Cal. Maybe the result of a curse. Elise . . . She – I – *we* – have nothing but contempt for Dennis Whitly now. You're the only one we love."

I shook my head. "It was all she ever wanted, Lisa, for as long as I knew her. The only thing." I parked the car. "So now, if you're really her, I don't think that she – you – would pass up the chance to nail Denny Whitly, if he was defenseless before your seductive magic." Again I pouted. "It's clear that you – neither of you – care about me at all."

"How dare you doubt our love?" She raised her hand to strike me again, but I caught it.

The anger faded from her eyes and I released her hand. "I do love you, Cal. I've always loved you." When my expression didn't change, her annoyance returned. "But why should you believe any of it? You haven't before, even when the evidence has been incontrovertible." She giggled suddenly. *"There's no need for the jury to retire.* I am Elise, Cal, and both of us love you. And we will damn Dennis Whitly. Soon. Just you wait."

You don't know who you're fucking with.

"Whatever's clever, baby. I've got other concerns right now besides Dennis Whitly's damnation. I have to find out what the hell's gotten into his second-guitar."

I took out my phone and texted Iris. *We're here.*

He's in Room 426. I can't see ur girl, Cal.

I sighed and got out of the car. Of course not. Rival witches and all. Again the mental and physical exhaustion weighed on me like a blanket soaked in wet concrete. It was only the spark of anger that kept me going at the moment, my resentment against all this continuous, unrelenting supernatural bullshit.

Poor, dead Sonny and his mother, ranting at me from opposite ends of a theological spectrum that didn't even enter into my worldview. I believed in neither gods nor demons nor my immortal soul, and I was just about fed up with hearing about them.

Then there was Candy and the band, chanting to their namesake demon before shows, gesturing with daggers to the forces unseen in the incorporeal air, mumbling mysteriously about fame and the sacrifices necessary to get it.

And Iris, so lovely, but also so incredibly irritating with her gibbered warnings that the very landscape around me was booby-trapped with daggers and cyanide, all placed in my path as a result of Candy's Terminator-style ambition.

And Lenny, made crippled and mute by nothing more magical than a flaw in a blood vessel, suddenly blabbering on in text form about big black birds and priests, dead guitar players and the unluckiness of devil-worshippers.

It was almost a good thing that I had to deal with Ernie at the moment, because I was just about at the end of my rope, ready to lash out, say things to any and all of them that I would regret, because in addition to Candy and the band, Iris and Lenny, of course there was Lisa, the light of my life. If anyone was a victim here, it was her, not Sonny or Ernie or Lenny or Denny, or any other unknowing possessors of those supposedly cursed medallions.

Her mother had twisted her mind with tall tales of reincarnation and redemption, with instructions for quests she must undertake to save the damned soul within her, a soul which Candy had convinced her was not even hers. Candy had poisoned her daughter's mind against a man neither of them even knew, entrenched the directive in her that she must destroy Dennis Whitly or be destroyed herself, eternally. It was so insane, so antithetical to how a parent should behave – worse than leaving her child to be raised by wolves, Candy had become the wolf herself.

I looked over at Lisa as she walked beside me, busily typing something into her phone. Candy had given her daughter such a disturbing philosophy, and so completely – but she could be deprogrammed. As we walked through the automatic doors and down the short hall, as we got on the elevator, I vowed it to myself. I hadn't been able to save Elise, and I hadn't been able to save Ernie – thank Christ for Iris! But I would save Lisa.

I'd hire doctors: MDs, shrinks, whoever was necessary. I'd sit in with them in their sessions – Lisa loved me – I'd tell her that she had to listen to them, that she had to face reality, that there was no such thing as reincarnation, that Phenex was just a figment of her mother's imagination, that whatever sins Denny had committed, they had nothing to do with her. It was neither her duty nor her right to punish him for them.

The elevator dinged and the doors opened; we walked down one corridor and then another until we found the Nurses' Station near Ernie's room. Out of nowhere, Lisa suddenly stepped up, took charge. She explained that she was Ernie's daughter; she'd heard there had been some kind of . . . *episode;* she asked to be directed to his room.

The nurse glanced expressionlessly, silently, from Lisa to me and back again. I had time to think about ambulance rides and stomach pumpings, visiting hours and whether or not Ernie was under some kind of suicide watch, if the law would be wanting to talk to him. I had time to remember the old joke: *Why is suicide a crime? Because it's against the law to kill a taxpayer.*

Finally, without saying a word, the nurse pointed at the room farthest from the station. Lisa thanked her and strode purposefully toward it, and I followed. But then the headstrong, take-control daughter stopped unexpectedly, pulled up short on the threshold. Her resolve wavered, vanished. "You go in and see him first, Cal. I . . . I need a minute."

Ernie's room was tiny, exceptionally so, even by hospital standards. It seemed as though the architect had deemed one room too large, and had added a wall as an afterthought, making two rooms, one of which was definitely too small. There was barely enough space to walk around the bed.

He was asleep, the sheet neatly pulled up across his chest, arms at his sides. I was glad to see that there were no machines, just an IV. Ernie was not like Lenny, whose old body had failed him, whose vital functions had needed to be monitored. There was nothing physically wrong with Ernie anymore, now that whatever drugs upon which he'd attempted to overdose had been removed from his system. He was just a healthy old guy, sleeping it off, now.

But he was still an attempted suicide, someone that the hospital staff had stuffed into a closet-sized room, away from real sick people, people who actually deserved their attention. It seemed to me that the very smallness of Ernie's room was a demonstration that the medical profession looked upon those that would do harm to themselves in the same way Lisa's old Catholics had, and Lisa herself did: without a lot of pity.

I wondered what kind of counseling Ernie was going to have to undergo before they'd cut him loose. I wondered if any of it would have any effect. Again I asked myself what could have possibly triggered his sudden death-wish, and again I came up empty.

I stood at the foot of the bed, and reflected that it was getting to be a regular thing, seeing my old friends laid out beneath crisp, folded sheets, incapacitated. There was no plainer reminder of how old I was and of how close my own end might be, than this. I took a deep breath, shakily let it out.

"What the fuck, Ernie?" I said softly.

I jumped when his eyes snapped open and met mine. He looked at me questioningly, and when he didn't find the answers he sought, he slowly looked around the room. Then he opened his mouth to speak, but no sound emerged. He swallowed, tried again. "Did we crash? Is everybody okay?"

Before I could respond, there was a low, pitiful moan from the doorway. "Daddy?"

Lisa swept into the room, her face tear-streaked. She passed me without acknowledgment, took Ernie's hand, squeezed it. Gently, she brushed the lank hairs from his forehead, kissed him tenderly.

"Are you okay?"

I turned and exited the room so that this touching scene between father and daughter could play out just between the two of them. *Daddy?* I remembered Lisa on the plane, waving her hand sharply, dismissing *her daddy* without pity. *Ernie has reaped what he has sown.*

I could've told myself that she'd had a change of heart, that she'd realized that she loved him and felt sorry for him, that her plaintive cry of *Daddy?* proved it. But I was too tired to start having delusions of my own.

I remembered Lisa's look of undisguised desire for Denny whilst they were onstage together; I'd seen what a profoundly believable actress she could be. This was just another scene. Her pitiless attitude toward her suicidal father had not changed. I figured that she was just showing this sad face of daughterly concern because she knew it was how I thought she should behave.

While I was standing out in the hall, I got a text from Iris. *Is he awake? Did u talk to him?*

He's awake. Lisa's in there w/him.

Alone?

A tremor of anger shook me, passed through my person like a palsy. Iris was suggesting that Lisa was somehow a danger to her father, because she was the enemy. Ernie's daughter was from the witchy camp that Iris was convinced wanted to *end him.* I knew that I'd lose it if Iris was standing here in front of me, that I'd scream and rail about the insanity of all this preposterous, superstitious nonsense. I'd take every ounce of my frustration with it out on her. All this bullshit had to stop.

But she wasn't there in front of me, and a deep breath was all that was necessary to make me realize that I was too tired to launch into a texted tirade.

Yes. Alone.

Let me kno when u leave. I'm gonna stay by him 2night. He's not safe yet.

Again, a tremor of anger, but lesser this time. Iris was kind; she believed Ernie still needed protection from the forces unseen, so she was volunteering to look after him. She had a good heart, even if it was entirely misguided. I couldn't fault her for that.

I typed, *Ok. Where r u?*

I'm one floor down.

Lisa came out of Ernie's room, the tears fresh and wet on her cheeks, and again I thought about what a fantastic actress she was.

"I have to go, Cal," she sobbed. "I have to get out of here."

"Lisa, I can't leave him –"

"No, you can't." She swiped at the crocodile tears. "You have to stay with him. He's still talking about ending it, how nobody loves him. I told him that I love him, that Mom loves him, but he just shook his head. The doctors . . . They're not gonna let him out of here talking like that, and I just can't deal with my dad being in a lunatic asylum right now . . . I'm gonna take a cab back to the house. Mom and the band'll be home soon. I'll come back and see him again then, but I just can't stay here right now."

She threw herself into my arms and hugged me tightly. I squeezed her back, but I wasn't buying any of it, not the confused pain that *Daddy* still wanted to off himself, not the desperate need to escape from it. The girl that had blithely played *Tetris* on the way home from the airport was the real Lisa.

Through her mother's conditioning, she believed that a suicide was damned. If he still wanted to kill himself, then her father was a stranger to her now. I thought about how guilty and repentant she was gonna feel once the doctors and I showed her how deserving Ernie had been of her pity, how wrong she'd been in her dismissal of him.

But that was all in the future. At the moment, if I was honest with myself, I was glad to get rid of her. She was crazy and I could only deal with one crazy at a time, and Ernie's was taking precedence. I walked down the hall and put her on the elevator, told her I'd talk to her soon.

When the doors closed, I called Iris. "You can come back up now. Lisa's gone home."

Ernie was again asleep when I returned. I lingered in the doorway while a nurse changed his IV, plumped his pillows. A small piece of paper fluttered to the floor, and she picked it up, looked at it briefly, shook her head, and set it on the bedside table. She smiled a little sadly at me as she left the room. We didn't speak – what was there to say, really? Blood family had a difficult time discussing attempted suicide – what did two strangers have to say to each other about it?

I again stood at the foot of the bed. When Iris came in, I thought she looked how Ernie had in Vegas: pale, with dark circles under her huge, round eyes. She touched me briefly on the arm, and wordlessly handed me a folded sheet of paper. Then she sat by the bed in the room's lone chair and took Ernie's hand.

I read my old friend's suicide note. To my surprise, it was entirely about Candy. In the short time since he'd *once again discovered his love for her,* Ernie said, he'd become addicted to her. The note went on and on about how much he needed and wanted Candy, what a mistake he'd made in ever believing that there could ever be anyone else but her. He sounded not so much like a junkie deprived of his drug, however; instead, he whined and puled as though he was a flower deprived of his sunshine, his only sunshine. It was just that histrionic. He said he couldn't live without her, and since he could never be worthy of her again because of the sins he'd committed with that filthy whore from the record company, he'd decided to end it all. The last line said he was leaving everything he owned to her. His only child was not mentioned.

I sighed and folded the paper, put it in my pocket, reflecting that legacies bequeathed in suicide notes, especially exceptionally whiny ones, didn't have the oft-mentioned leg to stand on in court. Whatever depression had come over Ernie, the last sane thing he'd said to me was that he was through with Candy, and had he been successful in killing himself, I would've made sure that she didn't get a dime. All of Grandma's money didn't stand a chance against mine when it came to paying for lawyers. Whatever lunacy had seized him, I knew that in the end, Ernie wouldn't have wanted his assets going to her.

But that was all water under the bridge, now. He was gonna be okay. Just like with Lisa's delusions – when Ernie woke up, if he was still talking about suicide, I'd make sure he got the best doctors. I'd stay by him until this madness passed.

"I wanna thank you, Iris. For saving him."

Iris kept her gaze riveted to Ernie's still face. She whispered, "I was trying to be vigilant, but somehow, I fell asleep. I didn't get your texts when you sent them. I didn't think to look at my phone when I woke up, so I didn't see them until some time had passed. When I finally got out there, I sensed I was too late. The house was dark, but he'd left the front door standing wide open. I looked for him. I went from room to room, calling, downstairs, upstairs – he wasn't in the front of the house, wasn't in any of the bedrooms. I finally found him, in the back most place, where there were instruments."

"The studio."

It wasn't a recording studio, not like Sonic Daydream's famous frontman had built behind his house. It was as Iris described it, a small room with a sofa and a coffee table and a couple of chairs, a room full of Ernie's many guitars and a few amps, a drum kit, where he and Azomite rehearsed sometimes, where he played by himself, where he jotted down words and music. It didn't have a glass booth or a recording board, but he'd always called it his studio, nonetheless.

"There were pills all over the table, on the floor. *So many pills.* He was laying on the sofa with a plastic bag over his head."

I winced.

"I pulled it off, and that's when I saw the chain." Now Iris looked solemnly at me. "I told you, Cal, but you didn't listen."

"Jesus, Iris, not this bullshit again . . ."

With an expression of utter disgust, she turned away. "I yanked the cursed amulet from around his neck. He breathed then, deeply, suddenly, like a newborn babe, but he didn't wake up. His pulse was weak, uneven. I called the paramedics, told them that I was unable to awaken my friend. I cleaned up the pills, flushed them. I put the note in my purse. When the ambulance arrived, I gave the bottle to the man, told him that perhaps my friend had accidently taken too many."

She looked at me again. "But I think they knew, Cal. The paramedics cross-examined me, asked me if he'd been depressed, if he'd talked about suicide. I told them no, I said I'd just stopped by for a visit, it was just a lucky coincidence. I said that there was no reason to think that it was anything other than an accidental overdose."

Iris gazed back at Ernie again, squeezed his hand. "It wasn't me that saved his physical body, Cal. It was the doctors, the machines that sucked the poison out. The doctors saved his body.

"What I did for him . . . I broke the spell on his spirit, the evil that they'd attached like a parasite to him. They've been siphoning off his life-force, suppressing his will to live. They'd silenced the jubilant music of his existence with that amulet, Cal, muted all the joy and happiness in his life. It would be the same for any of us, if we couldn't feel anything good anymore, if our insecurities and regrets were allowed to take us over. We'd want to end the emptiness, too."

"Lisa says that he's still talking about killing himself."

Iris didn't look at me. "She's lying."

"For Christ's sake!"

"It was a spell, Cal, and I broke it. It's gone now."

Iris noticed the scrap of paper on the table then, the one that the nurse had retrieved from the floor. She released Ernie's hand and reached for it. With a hoarse, croaking cry, he came awake, sat straight up in bed. He looked at me and burst into tears, covered his face with his hands. I was worried that he'd dislodge the IV.

"Why did you stop me, Cal?"

Iris held the piece of paper in her hand for another second, then dropped it back onto the table.

"No, Ernie," she whispered softly. "It was me that stopped you. Now . . ." She took his hands from his face so he'd look up at her. She smiled kindly, and gently pushed on his shoulder. "You just lie back now. Everything's gonna be fine."

Ernie complied and Iris plucked at the neckline to his hospital gown. Her blue-lacquered fingernail caught a chain. In a singsong voice, as if she might be talking to a child, she said, "Let's just take this off of you, shall we? Doctor's orders. No jewelry. It . . . it interferes with the medical equipment."

She deftly pulled the chain and medallion over his head before Ernie could object. Without looking behind her, she threw it at me, and I caught it. The charm wasn't the one he'd worn before – Iris said she'd rid him of that one. This was of a slightly different design, but I recognized it immediately.

"It's Lisa's." She didn't wear it all the time, but I'd seen it often enough. Dangling down, it would sometimes brush against my chin or my neck . . . I cleared my throat. Now was not the time to be thinking about that. It was definitely Lisa's charm, though.

Ernie had closed his eyes again, and Iris was tenderly brushing his hair off his forehead, just as his daughter had done earlier. "You sleep now, Sweetie," she murmured to him. "Everything's all right now."

When she was sure he'd drifted off again, Iris scowled at me. She snatched the paper from the side table and thrust it into my hand. "This is hers, too." She inclined her head toward the hallway, and we left Ernie's room.

Iris strode down the hall to a small, darkened waiting room. She flipped on the lights, then rounded on me the moment I stepped into the room behind her.

"The first spell was thwarted, so your lover has just attempted to dispatch her father again, Cal. Her own amulet, coupled with the inscription on that paper . . ." She grabbed them both from my hand and shoved them into a trash container. "She aimed to take the remaining power of his soul, and turn it toward –"

I grabbed Iris by the shoulders then. I gave her one good shake, then released her. She stumbled backwards and dropped into a chair. Into her astonished face, I growled, "You have to stop with this senseless witchcraft bullshit, Iris! No one can steal anyone else's soul, not with inscriptions or with cheap jewelry, because there's no such thing as a soul! There's no such thing as magic or witchcraft or any of this other crap!"

"Did you go to university, Cal?"

I blinked as if slapped at this totally non-sequitur question. *We of the blood always have the benefit of a classical education.*

"What?"

"Did you go to college? Do you consider yourself to be an educated man?" Iris shook her head, indicated for me to sit beside her. "I want to tell you a –"

"I can't take this anymore, Iris," I said, and as soon as the words were out of my mouth I realized that I sounded like both Ernie and Lisa. But it was true. I couldn't take it. "No more black tales of the supernatural."

Iris smiled grimly, humorlessly. "But of course. I asked if you had attended university because I wondered if you had any literary education." She flounced her hand dismissively, and again I was reminded of Lisa, of her similar gesture. "Have you ever heard of Shakespeare's play, *Titus Andronicus?"*

I nodded. "What does that have to do with –"

"Bear with me for one moment, could you, Cal? Not unlike yourself, I've had rather a busy evening." She nodded in the direction of Ernie's room, and her grim smile expanded, without taking on any levity. "I think you can allow me a few moments' digression."

I sat.

"You say you're familiar with *Titus?"*

"Vaguely."

"There's one character – Aaron, the Moor. He's the embodiment of evil – he sets the queen's sons to rape and mutilate Titus's daughter. He frames her brothers for murder. These are just some of the atrocities he commits. Not only is he evil, he's *unrepentantly evil.* At one point he says that his only regret is that he hasn't been able to do more wrong in his life."

I waited silently for her to get to the point, to perhaps compare Candy or maybe even Lisa to this Shakespearian villain. She took out her phone and consulted it for a moment. I continued to wait.

"There comes a point in the play where Aaron bargains with his enemy to save his son's life. He promises to tell heinous secrets, if Lucius will swear to save the child." Iris looked at her phone. "Lucius says, *'Who should I swear by? Thou believest no god: that granted, how canst thou believe an oath?'*

"To which Aaron replies, *'What if I do not? As, indeed, I do not; yet, for I know thou art religious . . . Therefore I urge thy oath; for that I know an idiot holds his bauble for a god and keeps the oath which by that god he swears.'"*

Iris looked at me expectantly over her phone. I shook my head, shrugged in annoyed incomprehension. "I didn't go to college, Iris. I'm a musician. It's true, I know a little Shakespeare, and while I have heard of this play, I have absolutely no idea what you're trying to tell me by mentioning it."

"It's as simple as this. Since the moment I met you, you've made it crystal clear that you believe in no power that you cannot quantify with your senses. Yet at the same time, you've demonstrated to me that Candy and her minions are devout. So this is the question that I put to you now. I'm not concerned with what you believe, but tell me, Cal, would you say that Candy's daughter puts her faith in the forces unseen?"

"Absolutely," I answered immediately.

"This is the last thing I'm going to say to you about witchcraft, Cal. The act of giving Ernie her own charm, the sigil on that paper – in Lisa's beliefs, these things were designed to leach away his life forces, to drive him the rest of the way over the brink. She wants that power for her own.

"Now, I'm not asking you to think about what it would mean if any of that was true, or possible, if one person could control the actions of another through supernatural means. I know that your mind is closed to these possibilities. Like Aaron, you believe in nothing." That humorless grin. "I ask that you ruminate only upon this: Lisa left behind these devices because *she* believes they'd work. Whether they would or not is immaterial, especially in your philosophy. Yet even you cannot ignore that by leaving behind these tokens, it proves that she has no good intentions towards her father."

I opened and closed my mouth like a landed fish; once, twice, three times. Iris knew nothing of Ernie and Lisa's relationship beyond a necklace and a scrawling on a piece of paper, but I remembered her unconcern, her proclamation that he had reaped what he had sown. I recalled her false tears.

If Iris had translated the things that Lisa had left behind to mean that she'd summoned the demon to aid Ernie in his recovery to vibrant physical and mental health – it would still be more claptrap to me. But Lisa would've believed in the effectiveness of her well-wishes. And if these tokens had been meant to harm Ernie, I knew she believed in that just as much.

"Why?" I asked Iris. But I already knew why. I remembered her fevered affirmations about her mother and Phenex and the powers unseen. Destiny, the need for revenge. Since Ernie had chosen to take the quickest exit, why not just push him the rest of the way? This energy they all believed in – Iris said Lisa believed she could use Ernie's, and it would no doubt assist in the marshalling of her powers; her big-hearted daddy's departed soul would help her to damn Dennis Whitly's.

Lisa was far crazier, much sicker than I'd thought.

The silent nurse I'd encountered in Ernie's room earlier popped her head in the door. "Are you Mr. Bascomb? Mr. LaBelle is asking for you."

FIFTY-TWO

Ernie was sitting up in bed, seemingly fully recovered, fully himself. He even offered his inimitable tomcat's smile to Iris. "Hello, Pretty Lady. Are you my doctor?"

She smiled fondly back at him, shook her head.

"What the fuck, Cal? What's going on? Did we crash? Where is everybody? What day is it? There's nothing wrong with me – nothing's broken, nothing's cut. Why am I in the hospital?"

I took his weepy, maudlin suicide note out of my pocket and silently handed it to him.

"Yeah, that's right. *She's too good for me and I can't go on without her.* What kind of joke is this, Cal? What day is it? Where's my phone?"

I called up our texted conversation from Vegas on my phone. He read it without comment, then flicked back to the home screen. "It's *Sunday?* I missed the show?"

I took my phone back from him. It informed me that it was indeed Sunday, 12:19 am, September 23, 2018. It had only been four hours ago that Phenex had played the DLVEC. It seemed like a lifetime.

"What's wrong with you, Cal? Why aren't you telling me what's going on? Is everybody dead?"

"Nobody's dead, Ernie. There wasn't any crash."

"What's the last thing you remember, Ernie?" Iris asked him softly, again like she might be speaking to a frightened child.

Ernie responded with another big smile. He wasn't frightened, wasn't depressed anymore. He stuck out his hand. "I'm sorry, I didn't get your name. I'm Ernie LaBelle."

Iris shook his hand, introduced herself, as if the two of them were standing around at a cocktail party. "I'm Cal's friend," she added. "Can you tell us the last thing that you remember?"

Ever one to accommodate a lady, Ernie narrowed his eyes and concentrated; after a moment, he smiled again. "I told Cal that I was gonna hit the oft-mentioned ramp, right after the band's gig in Vegas. I told him that I was through with all of my . . . my daughter's mother's jealous bullshit. I told him I had other fish to fry."

"You said, *other irons in the fire.*"

"Whatever." He waved the suicide note at me, at Iris. "That's what's so hilarious about this fake letter. *I can't live without her?* I can't *wait* to live without her."

"That's the last thing you remember? Telling Cal you were going to leave Candy?"

"Pretty much. He got a phone call and went outside . . . and then I woke up here."

"That was from you," I told Iris. "On Friday." I showed her the call log on my phone. "You called to warn me about –"

"I remember why I called you."

I looked at Ernie. "Then you came outside. Candy whispered something in your ear. Then we went to Vegas."

"I don't remember going to Vegas. Did I drive?"

"No."

"Because that would be scary." He grinned at Iris. "Driving to Vegas and not remembering it."

"You said you had a headache and gave me the keys to your car. You rode in the van with Candy. You laid on the backseat and put your head in her lap." I realized that I was annoyed. "What the fuck, Ernie? You're telling me you don't remember any of that?"

He shook his head. He crossed his ankles under the sheet, laced his fingers in his lap. "Tell me what I missed."

"You don't remember anything else?" Iris asked.

Again he concentrated. "A dream, maybe. Some record company assholes. Phil from The RaceCats screaming at them." He studied the disbelief on my face. "Are you telling me that really happened?" He looked from me to Iris and then back to me.

"You rode to Vegas with the band, then went up to your room. Candy said you were sick. You slept until four o'clock the next afternoon. You were your normal charming self at the meeting –"

"Did EMI sign them?"

I nodded. "Knocked 'em back to warm-up band for the tour, though. For someone called The Desperate Princes."

"Oh, yeah, they're great."

"You've heard of them?"

Ernie winked at Iris. "No, Cal. I'm kidding."

"Well, I didn't get to hear 'em either, because right before their set, you started texting me that you were gonna –"

"What about their record?"

"One record. Bianca saw to that."

Ernie smiled fondly. "She said she'd get that for them. For me."

"But if the attitude from the A&R fluffs is any indication, I wouldn't hold my breath waiting for them to pick up the option on a second one."

Almost as if she was at a tennis match, Iris looked from me back to Ernie, because it was now his turn to speak. She had not a clue as to what we were talking about, but she was enjoying the cadence of our conversation nonetheless.

Ernie caught her attentiveness and again smiled at her. "So what happened after the meeting?"

"You and I drove around Vegas for a while. You wondered rhetorically what life was all about. *What's the point, Cal? Why did we do any of it?* You dropped about twelve hundred dollars at the blackjack table."

Ernie's smile evaporated.

"Yup. At the Luxor. Then you took me back to the venue, said I've always been your best friend. You said you'd meet me to watch Phenex go on, but you never showed, because you'd already headed back home. You told me that you were gonna kill yourself. I went to the airport. I called Iris before I got on the plane. She went out to your house and saved you."

Ernie looked solemnly at Iris and she squeezed his hand. "It wasn't really me. I just called the paramedics. You'd taken some pills . . . They fixed you right up."

"Pills? And with that note . . . Am I in the Psych Ward?"

"Nobody else saw the note. Iris told them that it was an accidental overdose, so I don't think this is the Psych Ward." I glanced around at the proportions of the room. "The Psych Closet, maybe."

Ernie was not amused. "Christ Jesus, Cal! I don't remember any of it. Is it possible that I hit my head or something?"

"It was a spell, Ernie," Iris said slowly. I rolled my eyes, felt my anger return.

"A what?"

"Iris is a witch, Ernie," I told him, my voice full of mockery. "Just like Candy and Lisa and the boys in the band. She owns Mohini's House of Dreams."

"Candy use to work for you?"

Iris nodded. I said, "She believes Candy put a hex on you, on your good-luck charm."

Ernie felt the front of his hospital gown. "It's gone."

"Yes. Iris took it off of you to free your soul. The bad witches were drawing your life-energy away with it, making you want to kill yourself, so Lisa can go fuck Denny, damn him to eternal hellfire and all of that outlandish horseshit."

"It's Denny?" Iris's purple eyes flashed in amazement. "The singer from your book? The one that the girl killed herself over?"

"Oh, you haven't heard the half of it." Maybe it was from stress, or lack of sleep, or from just being fed up, but I felt a little hysterical. "Lisa isn't Lisa at all, you see. She's Elise Carlin reincarnated. She needs to marshal her forces to destroy Denny." Ernie blinked slowly at me, nonplussed. "So that's why, even though she's your own flesh and blood, when she came in here to see you, she cursed you with another evil charm. Of course, Glinda the Good Witch saved you from that one, too."

Ernie turned away from my tirade, incomprehensible to him. He asked Iris, "Where's that one?"

"I threw it away. In the waiting room. I was trying to explain to Cal –"

"Lisa actually put something on me?"

"You don't remember seeing her?" I asked.

"No. I don't remember anything after telling you I was done with Candy and the band, until I woke up, just now, and that dark-haired nurse was in here. I asked her what'd happened to me, and she said that a doctor would be in to see me soon. I asked her if Cal Bascomb was here – it was a shot in the dark – and she told me that she'd check and see if it was you in the waiting room."

"You don't remember talking to me earlier? You don't remember Lisa sobbing *Daddy?*"

Ernie shook his head. He said to Iris, "So Candy – she made me have amnesia?"

"It was her good-luck charm, Ernie. It sucked your will to live," I said sarcastically. "It made you want to end it all."

He considered me in silent amazement for a heartbeat. Ernie wasn't used to quite so much bitter derision from me. He again turned back to Iris. "Is that true?"

"In my belief system –"

Ernie shook his head, touched her arm. "Is it true?"

"Oh, for Christ's sake, Ernie!"

"What, Cal? I wake up in a hospital room with no memory of the last two days. You people say I tried to kill myself. Maybe it was some kind of hypnosis." He looked hopefully at Iris. "Maybe Candy waved that thing back and forth in front of my eyes . . . Maybe there was some kind of trigger . . ."

Iris nodded encouragement. "If it helps for you to think of it that way . . ."

"Go get it," Ernie said. "The charm, the one Lisa put on me. You said you threw it away in the waiting room? Go get it. I wanna see if you're right. If it'll have some kind of effect on me."

Iris's incredible eyes became fearful. "I broke the spell when I removed it." She laughed nervously. "Besides, I'm sure they've emptied the trash by now."

"I'll go get it. Just to prove that you're as nuts as everybody else, Ernie, taking this shit seriously. First Lenny, now you."

"That's not a good idea, Cal," Iris called after me, but I was already halfway down the hall.

I took the lid with its swinging plastic mechanism off the trash can; the charm and paper were right on top. Apparently, neither did the Psych Closet have too many visitors throwing things away, nor did they do too much housekeeping in the wee hours of a Sunday morning.

I gave the charm to Ernie. He clasped it in his hand, leaned back in the bed, closed his eyes. After about thirty seconds, he opened them again, shrugged. "I dunno. Maybe I feel a little sad." He grinned, not sad at all.

Ernie was no longer the lost, confused individual he'd been several hours ago, the one that had asked me plaintively, *What's the point, Cal? Why did we do any of it?* He was Ernie LaBelle again, happy-go-lucky. Mr. Anything For a Good Time.

I rolled my eyes.

"This is blasphemy," Iris said quietly. "It isn't wise to experiment with things you don't understand."

Ernie sat up. "I'm not gonna lie to you, Iris. I don't believe in hexes and curses any more than he does. However . . ." He dropped the charm and its chain into a small wastebasket beside his bed, and smiled at her once again.

"This is all I need to understand. I've lost two days. I'm in the hospital, for Christ's sake. That note, going on and on about how wonderful Candy is – that's my handwriting. Seriously, Cal? Tell Iris – would I ever leave all my assets to a groupie?"

I shook my head.

"Candy's pissed about Bianca, and something happened to me. Call it witchcraft, call it hypnosis. Maybe she drugged me. I don't fucking know. But I believe you when you say that they did something to me, Iris. I don't want to believe it, but . . ."

Ernie's face took on an uncharacteristic seriousness, almost the same sad and confused expression he's worn in Vegas when he was talking about the pointlessness of everything. Then it hardened grimly when he looked at me again. "Candy, and apparently Lisa, too – they've pointed a gun at me, my brutha. What difference does it make what it was loaded with?"

"How astute you are, Ernie," Iris said.

The hard expression evaporated and he smiled at Iris once more, reached out and patted her hand.

"What, because I'm smarter than him? That doesn't take much. He's always been a snob. But I know something that snobs don't consider: just because you think you're above somebody, that doesn't make you smarter than them." Ernie winked at me and I realized that he *had* always been my best friend. He'd always indulgently put up with me.

He continued, "I've told him all along – who cares what these people believe? I still don't care. But when I wake up in a hospital, I'm prepared to believe that I've made some enemies. Somehow – they put me here. The question is, what am I gonna do about it?"

FIFTY-THREE

The first thing Ernie opted to do about it was to sneak out of the hospital. He was feeling fine and he decided that he didn't need to talk to any doctors. His clothes were in the bottom drawer of the stand beside his bed – there was no closet in the tiny room – and he shooed us out while he pulled the IV from his arm and got dressed. Then he just sauntered out and joined us in the hall, and the three of us left the Psych Closet without a backward glance. No one noticed our departure.

Upon arriving at home, Ernie lost no time in scaring up his phone – it was dead, even if he wasn't – hardy har har. He plugged it in and stood there tethered to the wall while he called Bianca.

"I'm okay. It's an unbelievably long story. There are witches. I'll come see you in the morning." Ernie paused. "Okay. On Wednesday then." He mumbled something that might've been *I love you,* but my amazement that it could've been that made me unsure that I'd heard him correctly.

Ernie hung up and smiled with a happy kind of humbleness. "She was worried about me."

That's why she's still up at this time of the morning, I thought, *waiting for you to call.* I reflected that Candy's demanding brand of demonic witchcraft had failed to snare my old second-guitar, but perhaps some of that ol' black magic from a gentler source had found its mark. Who'da thunk it? Ernie LaBelle in love. The apocalypse was upon us.

In love or not, the devil-may-care Ernie of legend was definitely back. The near-miss of self-inflicted death and its subsequent stomach pumping – none of it remembered in the least – had served to energize him. Despite it being the wee hours, when all God-fearing good folk were snug in their beds – I told him as much – Ernie was making plans, concocting plots.

Since Iris had convinced him that Candy was indeed out to get him, it gave Ernie one more excuse to sever all ties with her. His daughter, well . . . he'd deal with her later. For now, she was in the same category as her mother: suspected.

As I'd maintained all along, a positive DNA test hadn't changed Ernie's personality very much. It was great that Lisa was his and all, she was an awesome singer, and he *had* felt pride and some kind of fatherly affection for her. He'd enjoyed helping with the band, and maybe he'd looked forward to enjoying family Thanksgivings and Christmases with her, if not with Candy. But seeing as how his own flesh and blood apparently had it in for him as much as her jealous mother, Ernie didn't mourn his daughter's betrayal. He was neither sad nor resentful, because he hadn't had enough time to get too attached to his role as Daddy. Things just hadn't worked out. It was time to move on, time to get on the bus and head on to the next town on the tour.

Now, planning his escape from the clutches of mère et fille and the whole demon-worshipping crew that had been his band became a kind of game to Ernie.

At the top of the list: he had to get the rental van back. He toyed with the idea of reporting it stolen, but decided that just wouldn't be fair, because they hadn't actually stolen it. He aimed to sneak back to the house as soon as they were back from Vegas and steal it himself. He'd drop it off at Hertz, and Phenex could figure out how to get their primered Chevy back on their own.

He plotted the immediate retrieval of my Caddy from the band house as if it was the raid on Entebbe, complete with silent utilization of the gate clicker and lightless creep of the rental car up the long driveway, with me riding shotgun and Glinda the Good Witch hiding in the backseat. I told Ernie that none of that cloak and dagger bullshit was necessary – Iris was visibly relieved when I simply had him click the gate open and drop me off at the bottom of the hill. She didn't want to get any closer to the evil lair than was necessary. They parked the rental car in a deserted grocery store parking lot around the corner and waited for me to get my car.

But I wasn't going to just slip off into the early morning like some kind of thief. The band wasn't back yet, but Lisa should be in the house sleeping, after her melodramatic flight from the hospital, so I thought I'd check on her. I didn't really know what I'd say – would she be happy or sad that Daddy was back to normal? I couldn't deny the idea that she hadn't cared what his fate was going to be, and Iris said she'd hoped to send him the rest of the way on to his reward.

I admitted that this was not a sane way to feel, and I laid the blame for it on her twisted mother. *The doctors'll help Lisa,* I told myself. *As soon as this tour's over, I'm going to get her in to talk to someone . . .*

Only the light between the crossed-neck Gibsons was on. I felt around behind the black one for the key, and despite the quiet and darkness, I encompassed not one spark of fear as I entered the house and flipped on the lights. There was absolutely nothing for me to be afraid of: I held a place of honor in Lisa's delusion. She might have in in for Daddy Dearest, but I was golden.

I called out. Silence.

It wasn't fear that preyed on my mind, but a growing sadness. The picture of the life that I'd envisioned with my young girlfriend was now clouded with the specter of mental illness. It was easy for Ernie to abandon his daughter to the craziness that she shared with Candy: he'd come into the game far too late to have developed a sense of responsibility for either of them.

But I loved Lisa. She was gonna be the light of my old age. And I knew that she loved me: it was part of her delusion to love me. Now I wondered if any of that love would remain after the doctors finished with her. After her mother's irrational doctrines had been expunged from Lisa's worldview, would she retain any of her affection for me, or would one necessarily have to go down the drain with the other?

Again the old resignation returned. Where once I'd thought that simple boredom – something beyond my control – would quickly lead Lisa to leave me, now a darker thought occurred. There was really no reason she would *ever* have to leave me. If I played along with her insanity, if I told her that I believed she was Elise reincarnated – then Lisa would continue to love me. She believed that she'd corrected a misstep of fate; she had achieved a metaphysical do-over. She and Elise were with the right man now. All I'd have to do was let her think I agreed with all of that.

I wasn't concerned that Lisa would be able to harm Denny in any way, and Ernie was mere steps away from excising himself completely from her life. So her delusion wasn't a danger to anyone, really, and if I let it continue, it would keep her with me . . .

I climbed the stairs to Lisa's room, but she wasn't there. I sat on the bed and hugged her pillow to me for a minute, taking in the faint scent of her hair, her perfume. All I'd have to do would be to let things ride, allow the absurd status quo to keep on keepin' on, and Lisa would continue to believe that we were destined to be together.

But I couldn't do that. If I did that, I'd be as sick as she was. I'd take her to see those doctors, and after they made her realize that the only evil there was in the world was the evil manner in which her mother had twisted her life – it wasn't gonna be boredom that took Lisa from me. It was gonna be a reinstatement of sanity. Once she saw that there were no unseen powers to be found in cheap costume jewelry, once the doctors convinced her that there was no such thing as destiny or reincarnation, it would only follow that she could also no longer have any use for an old, washed-up drummer. The entirety of her attraction to me had been part of her sickness, and it would pass, just like the fever did, once the sickness was cured.

I sighed. It hurt. But it wasn't like I hadn't known it was gonna hurt.

I texted Bonnie and Clyde that the coast was clear, that no one was home. I followed them to the rental car place and dropped the keys through the slot, then the three of us returned to Ernie's house to at last get some sleep.

FIFTY-FOUR

I was awakened by the sound of Iris screaming. It was three o'clock in the afternoon.

Ernie reached her first. When I got to her room, he was sitting beside her on the bed cradling her paternally, whilst she sobbed into his shoulder. He said gently, "Here's Cal, Iris."

She took a halting deep breath, turned her wet, frightened eyes toward me. "I've seen the Firebird again."

I fought to keep my expression neutral, noticed that Ernie was much better at it than I was. Iris, who'd been so kind, who'd saved his life, was obviously upset by something she'd dreamed. A Firebird was nothing more than an old Pontiac to Ernie, just like it was to me, but he held Iris close and comforted her, as if she'd been frightened by a flesh and blood intruder. It was real enough to Iris, and Ernie wouldn't let it show on his face that he thought she was screaming about shadows.

I had more trouble disguising my disgust. It seemed like this shit was just never going to end. I frowned. "I don't know what that means, Iris."

She sniffled, read my disdain, and her expression toughened. She instantly regained her composure. She thanked Ernie for running in to her, and it annoyed me that he lingered beside her on the bed, that he continued to hold her. She was obviously all right now. If I had any doubt, the austere, condescending tone of her next words confirmed it for me. As if I was the crazy person and not she.

"It's simple word association, Cal. The Firebird is another name for the Phoenix, the one that rises from its own ashes. The one with the *o* and the *i.* There is, of course, a symbolic connection in my mind between that one and the black bird for which your girlfriend's musical group is named. The demon Phenex doesn't appear whole and uncomplicated to me as he does to you. My dreams require some unraveling, some interpretation."

Ernie looked curiously from Iris to me, then back to Iris again. I watched him debate whether or not he really wanted to hear some new insanity about the demon Phenex appearing to me. He decided that he did not, because he said, "Why did you scream, Iris? This bird – whichever bird – why did it scare you?"

She turned away from my irritated disbelief, and my annoyance increased: Iris thought she might've discovered a supporter in Ernie.

He'd discarded his daughter's charm upon her advice. He'd accepted that his one-time womenfolk were out to get him, based solely on her interpretations, so maybe she could convince him of the validity of this new bullshit, too.

But I knew Ernie was no believer in the forces unseen. The only thing in which he believed was giving women want they wanted, and through years of practice, he could invariably guess what it was. Iris wanted comfort, so he'd hug her and nod and smile and listen, because these actions would calm her down, make her feel better. That didn't mean he was buying any of it, didn't mean he wouldn't snicker to me about the absurdity of it, later, when Iris wasn't around.

"On Friday, I saw . . ." She glanced at me again, and when I obstinately rolled my eyes, she again set her hopes on Ernie. "I saw something happening to you. These . . ."

"Visions?" Ernie prompted, and I wanted to punch him.

"These *glimpses* aren't ever concrete." Iris spared me a sneer. "But through a lifetime of study and meditation, I know that when I see an end, it means that an end is bound to occur."

"But it didn't occur," I pointed out.

"Because Iris saved me." Ernie hugged her in gratitude. Again I wanted to punch him.

"I saw something bad happening to you, and it was clear in its muddiness." She smiled fondly at him. "But there was something else, something separate . . . I dreamed of the Firebird.

"Now he's returned, and his symbolism is as simple and straightforward as hard, tumescent tree trunks and O-shaped swings and the guiding of rowboats through tunnels . . ." Iris paused again and stared at me, and I remembered my innocent dream of pushing her on a tire swing, of a pleasant day on the water, and I recalled that at the time, I'd gotten the impression that she'd somehow known what I'd dreamt. What kind of veiled Freudian symbolism was she trying to imply about that dream now?

She abruptly turned back to Ernie again. "I've just seen destruction visited upon Cal's other friend, and this time it's clearer than before. Some kind of disaster. Devastation. A blotting out."

"Who's his other –"

"She's talking about Lenny. She said you were gonna go first, then they were coming after Lenny."

"Why would they want –"

"Phenex finds the souls of musicians to be especially tasty."

"You're a poet, Cal." Iris smiled faintly. She couldn't find it in herself to hate me, even if I was a disbeliever. I again felt a little guilty about the vehemence of my cynicism. She was only trying to help, to protect my friends.

"Well." Ernie smiled blankly. It was all ridiculous to him. "It's easy enough to check on Lenny. We'll just call him. It's about time I called him, anyway, to see how he's doing."

Ernie paused for another heartbeat, then abruptly stood up, as if he was suddenly embarrassed that he was sitting so close to Iris. *Ain't no man more righteous than the fallen man reformed.* He was in love, after all, and maybe for the first time in his life, the idea of propriety meant something to him. He couldn't just be going around comforting every woman that desired comfort anymore.

Of course, there was no answer to his call: Lenny wasn't quite up to talking on the phone just yet. Ernie realized this before he left a voice message. He called Barbie next. Again, there was no answer. Ernie said, "Hi, Barbie, just wanted to see how you guys are doing. Please call me as soon as you get this." He winked at Iris. "It's important."

It was broad daylight in the middle of the modern century. Technological humanity had decades ago put a man on the moon, and nowadays, communication could span the globe in seconds. But despite all these commonplace miracles, the fact that neither Leonard Whitly nor his wife had answered Ernie's call was cause for superstitious dread for Iris. I could tell by the worried look on her face. The idea that maybe they were too busy living their lives to pick up their phones didn't seem to occur to her.

Ernie said that he couldn't remember the last time he'd eaten, and quickly made preparations to barbeque steaks. The opportunity to cook distracted Iris somewhat, but she still remained quiet and introspective. I could tell that Ernie longed to hear the whole story, to find out how I'd befriended Candy's former employer. He wanted to ask me all the details about how the beautiful, purple-eyed witch had come to predict his demise. But no opportunity for a private word presented itself.

I checked my phone. Lisa had texted at 12:30: *The band's back. I see u got ur car. How's Ernie?*

Several responses played through my mind, but I rejected them all. *Where were you in the middle of the night when I got my car? Do you really care how Ernie is? How are you gonna react when I tell you I'm not going on tour with you and your crazy, good-luck-charm-distributing mother?*

I replied, *Sorry I didn't answer sooner. Been sleeping. Ernie's fine.*

She replied immediately. *I'm glad 2 hear that. Mom wanted 2 take a ride, so we're not home. I'll text u when we get back. Miss u. Luv u.*

Luv u 2.

As I'd often done since cellphones had been invented, I marveled at the dynamics of texting. So much information could be exchanged, yet so much unpleasantness could be sidestepped, too. The pauses and inflections of a spoken conversation – those things that communicated far more than mere words – could be avoided. I didn't have to ask, *Why don't you wanna know more about your suicidal daddy? Why don't you wanna know where he is?*

These were questions that a normal, well-adjusted person might ask about a stranger, nonetheless a supposedly loving daughter about her father. But Lisa was anything but well-adjusted, and the glory of the text phenomenon was that I didn't have to deal with her disturbing brand of crazy right at the moment.

Iris and Ernie and I were just cleaning up the dishes after Ernie's excellent feast when Bianca called him. He went inside the house to talk to her, leaving Iris and me alone for the first time since the hospital. She wouldn't look at me, and I felt bad about that. I was very fond of her, and I didn't want our friendship to suffer because of my sarcastic outbursts about her beliefs.

"I'm sorry I'm so skeptical."

Now she regarded me silently for the span of several heartbeats, her fondness for me glowing mellowly in her beautiful eyes. At last she said, *"O thou of little faith, wherefore didst thou doubt?"*

"I doubted because . . . I dunno, Iris. What did you say to me when we first met? *I'm not going to give you a treatise on faith?* Faith is not my long suit. I doubt because I can't *not* doubt. I don't know how you knew about Ernie, so maybe I can believe that there can be some kind of sensitivity, somehow." I shook my head. "But all the rest of it . . ."

"I'm concerned about your other friend, Cal. If you recognize that I'm *sensitive* enough to've been correct about Ernie . . . Now I'm sensing . . . destruction . . ."

To soothe her – I could be comforting, too – I tried Lenny and Barbie again, but the planetary forces were out of alignment, because Iris had seen imminent doom: neither responded to my calls either.

When Ernie came back outside, all smiles after his conversation with Bianca, another thought struck me.

"Do me a favor, will ya? Give Denny a call? The last thing Barbie said to me was that Denny was coming up to stay with them for a few days. Maybe he's there. Maybe he'll answer his phone."

Ernie complied without comment. Denny answered immediately; the hex wasn't on him, after all. It was on his brother. The forces unseen had thereby allowed Ernie's signal to hit the repeater and connect with Denny's phone, where they had prevented his call from going through to the cursed one.

"I heard you're at Lenny's. How's he doing?" Pause. "That's great." A longer pause. Ernie frowned. "Hold on a second." He put his phone on speaker. "Say that again."

"I said, I was just gonna call you. Your daughter's here. Her and the whole band. Marcie said that they just decided to take a trip up to see how Lenny was doing."

Mom wanted 2 take a ride, so we're not home.

I automatically opened my mouth to correct Denny – what was it about the brothers Whitly that they couldn't get one old groupie's name straight? – but Ernie shook his head quickly, sharply. He didn't want me opening my fat mouth and letting Denny know I was there. He didn't want me resurrecting the feud again right at the moment.

"It was quite the surprise," Denny was saying. "We were just sitting here on the front porch, when all of a sudden this white van comes roaring up. I didn't even know your band knew Lenny, nonetheless where he lives."

"He and Barbie came down to listen to them once. Lenny probably told 'em where he lived. You know how proud he is of the ranch." Ernie looked at me. "Or maybe Cal told them."

"Fuck Cal," Denny said sullenly.

I glanced at Iris. She'd put her hand over her mouth. The enemy being at Lenny's house, all unexpected, was of course the worst possible news, because . . . it was expected. She'd seen destruction and they were its harbingers.

To take her mind off of her fear, I texted her, nodded in Ernie's direction at Denny's comment. *U read my book. U didn't think we're buddies, did u?*

"You know, I really think you guys should –"

"I don't care what you think, Ernie. I'm still pissed that you didn't tell me that he was gonna be at the gig in San Bernardino."

"You wouldn't've come if I'd told you."

"No, I wouldn't've, unless it would've been to kick his ass."

I texted, *My book was all lies, u see.* Iris smiled faintly.

"I'm sorry about not telling you, Denny," Ernie said contritely. "It was chickenshit of me. I wanna thank you again for showing up. Did I tell you EMI signed them?'

Denny surprise was undisguisable. "Really?"

"Yeah. And I'm sure it wouldn't've happened if you hadn't played with them."

"Probably not," Denny said off-handedly. "But it was the least I could do for your kid, Ernie."

Ah, that eternal Dennis Whitly ego, I texted to Iris. *As big as all outdoors.*

Denny's not unwarranted ego notwithstanding, it was true. Combined with Bianca's insistence, his legendary presence for just half a set had lent mediocre Phenex just enough marketable cachet for EMI to pick 'em up. Maybe there'd be a collaboration with the multi-platinum singer/songwriter at some future date, since he was buddies with the band, and that could mean bank for the record company.

"I appreciate it, Denny," Ernie reiterated. "About you and Cal –"

"Cal's a lying traitor, Ernie, and like I say, I'm not too thrilled with you either, right this minute."

Ernie laughed. "But you'll get over that."

Denny softened. "Yeah, eventually." He paused. They would always be friends. Ernie wasn't a lying traitor.

"Was that what you called for? To talk about Cal?"

"And to check on Lenny."

"Like I say, he's doing a lot better. He's walking. His face's almost looking normal. But he still can't talk, and he can't use his right hand yet." A note of pride surfaced in Denny's voice. "He's teaching himself to play left-handed."

"That's great, Denny," Ernie repeated. He looked significantly at Iris and said, "I was thinking of coming up there to see him tonight."

"He'd love it, Ernie. Like I say, he's coming along, but he gets frustrated. Do you want me to tell your daughter, have 'em wait –"

"No, no, that's okay," Ernie said quickly. "I was . . . I was supposed to go to the next gig with 'em, but . . . I've been sick. A little touch of food poisoning, I think. I wouldn't want them to know . . . If I'm well enough to come up to see Lenny, then they'll think I'm well enough to go to San Diego. And to tell you the truth, Denny . . . I'm not well enough for that, if you get my drift. Ya seen Phenex once . . . ya seen 'em."

"Just remember that it's you saying that, Ernie, and not me."

"I . . . you . . . *we* got 'em signed. And now . . . I've got other fish to fry."

Another pause, then Denny said, "Yeah, I won't say anything. They're getting ready to go, anyway. Barbie took 'em out to the barn to see the horses. Lenny seems anxious for them to go – isn't that right?" His brother must be sitting right there beside him, because Denny next said, "Ernie's gonna come up to see you." Then he said to Ernie, "I think Barbie's touched that they visited, though."

Once she found out they weren't there 2 bug her about getting signed, I texted to Iris. She shook her head, not understanding. *It's a long story.*

I imagined poor, mute Lenny, suddenly fearful after his stroke, even more fearful now that the very crew he deemed so inauspicious had, without warning, without invitation, descended upon his homestead. I wondered if he was texting Wikipedia pages to his brother, cryptic ramblings about big black birds and dead guitar players and bad luck in general.

Probably not, not with the devil-worshippers right there. It would require too much explanation for texting. I doubted if Ernie had taken the time to tell Denny about the supernatural leanings of his band; it wouldn't have helped to convince him to appear with them. Denny probably thought they were named after the town.

"We'll be there in a couple hours, Denny."

"We? You're not bringing Cal, are you, Ernie, for Christ's sake? Because like I say, I'm not in the mood for a reconciliation right at the –"

"No, no, nothing like that. Although I got five to one, he'd whip your ass." Ernie winked at me.

"You don't say," Denny commented drily.

"Actually, there's a lady I'd like you to meet."

I typed quickly on my phone and held it up. Ernie read aloud: "She's never heard of Sonic Daydream." Ernie looked at Iris in utter surprise. She smiled, shrugged, shook her head.

"That's great," Denny replied, unimpressed. "First you find Marcie, our biggest fan. Jesus, Ernie, I think she must've gone to every show we ever did on the West Coast. She told me all about 'em, every set list, what the weather was like, what you wore onstage . . . Now you go the opposite direction and find one that must've grown up under a rock."

Dennis Whitly. Poet, I texted to Iris. She giggled prettily.

"Variety and all, Denny," Ernie said and winked at Iris.

"Whatever's clever, Ernie."

It was so odd to hear Denny's familiar voice speak that expression! Once upon a time, he and I had been friends. I was a groomsman at his wedding; I smoked one of his Cuban cigars when his daughter Valerie was born. We'd been bandmates, had toured the world together for twelve years. I'd talked to him daily for a good portion of y life, and *Whatever's clever* had been something that he and his brother and Ernie and I had said to each other all the time. But besides the dust-up at the Just Us Festival, it'd been years since I'd spoken to Denny, yet here he was in this eavesdropped conversation, using the same old words. It took me back. It was a bittersweet feeling.

"I'll see you when I see you," Ernie said and disconnected.

Iris looked at me with what could only be called expectation, but I shook my head. "You heard the guitar god, Iris. He's not in the mood for me. You kids have fun. I'm gonna go home, maybe take a nap. Be sure to ask Denny for an autograph. He loves that." I winked at Ernie.

FIFTY-FIVE

The doorbell was ringing. It stopped, then began again. I looked at the clock on the bedside table. It was three o'clock in the morning. I staggered down the steps as the bell began to ring again.

Ernie was standing on the porch, wild-eyed, his face begrimed with black streaks.

"Lenny's house burned down, Cal."

Speechless with shock, I watched him stalk into the house, go out to the kitchen, start opening cabinets.

"You got anything here to drink?"

I shook my head, opened my mouth to speak, to ask the awful questions, but Ernie cut me off.

"Everybody made it out. Nobody's dead."

Since no liquor was to be had, Ernie busied himself with the mundane task of making coffee and I waited, still speechless.

"They're all at the hospital. They're okay, but the firemen said we should all get checked out for smoke inhalation. I don't like hospitals, so I came over here to tell you."

When the coffee started to drip, Ernie looked at me carefully for a heartbeat. Then he sighed, looked away to find himself a cup.

"Iris and I got up there, and introductions were made, blah, blah, blah. She commented that she could see the family resemblance between Denny and Lenny. She told Barbie that she had a lovely home, nice little friendly stuff. She and Barbie seemed to really hit it off. She didn't say anything about Candy or witchcraft or the Firebird."

They wouldn't've hit it off so well if she had, I thought. *Barbie doesn't go in for that supernatural shit.*

"But when she and Barbie and Lenny went out to look at the horses, I told Denny, 'Some weird shit's been goin' on.' I told him that I'd lost two days, that maybe I'd been drugged or hypnotized or something. I don't fucking know. I told him that I'd taken a bunch of pills that I didn't remember taking, that I'd wound up in the hospital, that Iris thought . . . that Iris thought that Candy had put me there, had somehow got me to do it.

"'What the fuck, Ernie?' Denny said. 'They drugged you? Why?'

"I told him about Bianca, that we'd . . ."

I could tell that his first choice of phrase was going to be *hooked up.* But Bianca meant more to him than that, so Ernie paused, searching for a more respectful expression. "I told him that I'd met Bianca before Candy and I hooked up."

There it was, what old rock stars and old groupies did. Fleeting. Meaningless. Good for a minute, but that was it.

"I told him that I'd seen Bianca again in Frisco, that we'd talked, that we'd come to . . . an understanding." Ernie grinned. "She's great, Cal. I didn't realize it before, how much we had in common, how cool she is, but after I saw her again. . ."

He sounded like a high school kid with his first crush, and I smiled back at him.

"Anyway, I told Denny that Candy saw us talking in Frisco, and she got pissed, jealous. I didn't say anything to Candy about me and Bianca, Cal, didn't say I didn't want to help the band anymore, or anything like that. I didn't get the chance. She just started in on me, bitching, accusing me of cheating on her." Ernie made a confused face. "Like we were married or something, like I had some kind of attachment to her, like I owed her something." He shook his head. "So I told Denny that Iris thought that, because she was jealous of Bianca, Candy had . . . tried to kill me.

"Denny said, 'Christ, Ernie! What kind of person would do something like that?' You know how he is, Cal. He never understood how nuts groupies can be."

He never let himself understand, I thought. *Until it was too late, and even then, none of it was his fault. Elise's fatal crush on him – none of it had been his fault.*

"Did you tell Denny that Iris thought that Candy had cursed you? With a piece of jewelry?"

Ernie shook his head. "No. He wasn't gonna buy that any more that you and I do. Why make Iris look silly? It was enough to tell him that Candy did something to me. He agrees that she must've drugged me somehow. He said that Lenny doesn't care for Candy either, that he was nervous the whole time she and the band were there."

Ernie poured himself a cup of coffee, put two big spoonsful of sugar into it. He again studied me, again sighed. "So, we sat around, visited, watched a movie. Lenny gets tired easily still, so we all turned in about ten o'clock. All the bedrooms are upstairs, right? Lenny and Barbie's room, and two guest rooms. Iris took one, and Denny the other one, and I slept on the couch in there with him.

"All good, right? We're nestled all snug in our beds, visions of sugarplums, etcetera. Then Iris starts screaming again, and Denny and I run in to her, and we smell the smoke.

"The whole ground floor was on fire, Cal. It was already starting to come up the staircase. If Iris hadn't screamed, woke us up . . . Barbie and Lenny had slept through that, too. Denny went in and woke 'em up, helped Lenny down the steps and outside. Denny snatched his axe off the porch and we ran out into the yard, just as the back part of the house – the roof caved in.

"We got out with nothing, Cal. Only Lenny's old Warwick. No cellphones. No fucking shoes. My wallet was in my pants or I wouldn't have any money, either."

I looked down at Ernie's grimy, bare feet.

"I'd left the keys in the Porsche, thank Christ. Denny's gonna have to get a locksmith out there to open the Benz. Lenny and Barbie have another truck, an old Ford. Barbie had a spare set of keys to it out in the barn, so she and Iris drove over to the neighbors' to call. Denny and Lenny and I just stood there and watched it burn. By the time the firemen arrived, there was nothing left but the barn. I helped Iris and Barbie with the horses – we actually rode them down the road to the neighbors'. They said they'd look after them.

"I took Lenny with me and Denny drove the girls in the truck. They're waiting for us at the hospital."

"Us? I don't think Denny wants to see me right –"

"For Christ's sake, Cal! I don't think Denny cares about that old shit at the moment. Iris says –"

"Oh, Jesus, Ernie, don't tell me. Let me guess. The demon Phenex, *come hot from hell –"*

"She thinks they came back and set it, Cal. She said . . . *You* said, something about Lisa's being out to get Denny. We know Candy's out to get me. We were all sound asleep. If Iris hadn't had another nightmare –"

"I really don't think that they're down to commit arson, Ernie. To commit murder."

"Why not? I almost killed myself, Cal. They made me –"

"They made you?"

"Look. I'm not saying it was witchcraft, like Iris thinks. I told you – I'm leaning toward that they drugged me somehow."

"To get you to kill yourself. To steal your soul."

"I don't know about any of that, either. But Candy's pissed about Bianca. She's . . . You know what she is. My Number One fan. Who knows what she might be capable of?"

Heaven has no rage like love to hatred turned, nor hell a fury like a woman scorned, Phenex rumbled in my head.

"Lisa's not your Number One Fan." My resident demon spoke up: *She doesn't really care for musicians.*

"But you said . . . This whole crazy thing about she thinks she's Elise, she's got it in for Denny? Like I keep telling you, Cal, it doesn't matter what they believe. But the coincidences are starting to pile up, don't you think? They just dropped in out of the blue to see Lenny, for a visit? They barely know him."

Mom wanted 2 take a ride, so we're not home.

"Maybe Candy just wanted to gloat about EMI signing them instead of Sony."

"It's a long fucking drive all the way out to Anza just to gloat. Iris saw destruction, and then Lenny's house burns down. Jesus Christ, Cal! It's just too much! Why won't you admit it? They're dangerous. I think we should call the cops."

"And tell 'em what, Mr. Attempted Suicide? Mr. Took Off from the Psych Ward Without Checking Out?"

"You said it wasn't the –"

"The cops'll lock you up, Ernie. You and Glinda the Good Witch, if you start blabbing about how some nobody band named after a demon is suddenly out to get the members of Sonic Daydream, out to steal your souls. *They will fucking lock you up.* It'll make *Rolling Stone.*"

"Christ Jesus, Cal, why do you keep downplaying all this? I almost end up dead, Lenny's house catches fire, with all of us inside. We all would've died, except for . . . except for you, because they knew you weren't there. I told Denny that you said Lisa wants to kill him –"

"Oh, God, Ernie!"

"He wants you to meet us at his house. Explain it to him. Sophia's out of town visiting Valerie. He's just like everyone else – he doesn't know her number, or Valerie's or anyone else's, because they were all in his phone, and it's a cinder now. He's worried about them. He wants to get home, find their numbers. He wants you to tell him what Lisa said."

"Are you serious, Ernie? I mean, really? You've got Denny believing that his family's in danger because –"

"Lenny's house is gone, Cal. It's fucking *gone.* Who knows what would've happened if Iris hadn't screamed? She saw it all ahead of time. You said Lisa had it in for Denny –"

"Here's what I'm gonna do, Ernie. Does Denny still have a land line? Call me when *the dregs of Sonic Daydream* get to his house." I found a pen and a piece of paper in the drawer and wrote down my cell number for him.

"In the meantime, I'm gonna drive back to Riverside. I am fed up. I'm tired of treating these nutcases like they have a right to ramble on about all this ridiculous bullshit. I'm tired of all the cauldron-rattling threats about sacrifices and damnation from them, and I'm tired of all the warnings and drawing of impossible conclusions from you and Iris and Lenny. Now you've dragged Denny into it, and I know I don't want to listen to his bullshit, too.

"I'm gonna get this shit all out in the open, tell Lisa once and for all that she's not Elise, that there's no way she can *damn* Denny. I'm gonna tell her –"

"What? That you're done? That you're not going to listen to threats against your band – because you refuse to see that they're not just threats anymore, but actions – are you gonna tell Lisa that you're not going to listen to her plot our doom anymore, not even in exchange for a young piece of ass?"

Again, I was like that beached fish, mouth working soundlessly, unable to think of one single thing to say to this. Could he be right? Could I be ignoring the danger to my friends because I loved Lisa?

At last words came to me. "She needs someone to show her that all this witchcraft shit isn't real, Ernie. I have to help her get away from her mother's insanity."

"But what if that's not possible? What if you can't talk her out of it? Are you just gonna keep making excuses for her until she succeeds the next time?"

"I don't know what happened to you, Ernie, but I don't think Lisa torched Lenny's house."

Ernie sipped his coffee and stared at me. "You know, nowadays, those arson guys – they can find the match. What are you gonna do if they say the fire was set?"

"That wouldn't prove that Phenex did it."

"Yeah, there's a gang of arsonists, roaming through the brush around Anza, randomly setting fires. That's more ridiculous than this curse bullshit. They've got it in for us, Cal – you just don't want to see it. But Iris saw it."

"Do you really believe that? Really?"

Ernie shook his head. "I don't fucking know, Cal. Iris knows these people –"

"She's one of them."

"All the more reason that I believe –"

"Jesus Christ, Ernie. Are you gonna tell me to get a priest, too?"

"What I was gonna say is this. Iris knows these people, knows what they believe. She knows what they're capable of. It doesn't have to mean that they pulled any of it off by supernatural means. Why do you keep sticking up for them? I mean – seriously, Cal? Whose side are you on?"

"Fuck you, Ernie. This isn't about sides. It's about calling your own flesh and blood a murderer."

"Yeah, my own flesh and blood. But you're a little bit more attached to her than I am, so you don't want to see –"

"I'm done with this shit, Ernie. I'm gonna get it all out in the open. I'm gonna take her to a doctor. The hell with the tour."

"I wouldn't go over there, Cal. Not alone. Wait till we get back to Riverside, till Denny gets in touch with his wife. Then the three of us'll go over there together. I'm sure Denny's got a few choice words for –"

"Fuck Denny. I'm gonna handle this. Call me when you get home."

FIFTY-SIX

Ernie went back to the hospital to gather up the refugees. I took a shower, made myself some breakfast, tried to figure out what I was going to say – all to kill time. No sense flying up to Riverside at four o'clock in the morning like a hysterical idiot when Phenex would still be asleep.

Even with all these self-imposed delays, even with Monday morning traffic, I still arrived at the run-down, clinker-brink nest of dangerous demon-worshippers just before eight o'clock. The tedious drive had lent me the time to take stock, had forced me to answer Ernie's admonition – just whose side was I on? I had to be on his side and Lenny's and even Denny's, because on the other side was madness. If I added up all the threats, the talk of sacrifices, the bestowals of cursed amulets – I had to face that Candy and Lisa's intentions toward my old bandmates were indeed bad, even if their methods were laughable.

The best course would be to follow Ernie's lead, to distance myself from these wanna-be-dangerous lunatics, and I would've done so, if it weren't for the fact that I loved Lisa. I wanted to save her, return her to sanity. I wanted to make her see that none of it was remotely possible, not witchcraft or demons or reincarnation.

I still wasn't quite sure what I was going to say about everything, but I knew that Candy and Lisa and the rest of the demon Phenex's namesake band weren't going to like it, so perhaps the forces unseen informed my subconscious that I might need to make a hasty retreat. Or maybe I already knew it and just didn't want to face it. *They are dangerous to you.* Either way, I parked the Caddy on the street and left it there.

I pushed the button on the intercom and Candy opened the gate. She walked out to the top of the driveway and watched my approach. I returned her expectant expression emotionlessly. I thought I could see the wheels turning behind her eyes: should she ask me about Ernie? And if she did, what kind of emotion should accompany the question? Should she fake concern, or unleash jealousy?

She hadn't tried to contact him since Vegas, and she probably figured I knew it. Maybe she should just let it ride about Ernie. Maybe she should just wait for me to say something, and then just take her cue from my mood. But we couldn't just stand there in the driveway staring at each other, and it quickly became obvious that I wasn't going to speak first. So finally she said, "What's up, Cal?"

"We need to talk."

There was a barely perceptible, suspicious narrowing of her eyes, but Candy endeavored to keep her voice light. "About what?" But she didn't look at me; she turned and led the way into the house.

I waited until we entered the kitchen. I waited until after Lisa, still wearing pajamas, jumped up from the booth and gave me a surprised hug. "What are you doing here so early in the morning?" she trilled.

"We need to talk," I repeated. "The three of us."

Lisa returned to the bench, and Candy sat down beside her. I sat across from them, and Candy immediately said, "So talk."

I was still unsure where to begin. Then inspiration struck me, and I started with the very least important detail. "Ernie wants the van back."

As an opening salvo, it was flawless, if I do say so myself. Candy could now lead the conversation in whatever direction she dared. She could put on hurt disbelief: why wasn't Ernie asking for it himself? Why wasn't he here? Whatever was wrong?

For a moment, Candy didn't respond at all – she typed something into her phone instead. Lisa simply stared steadily at me. The silence grew uncomfortable, but I didn't have anything else to say until this point was answered.

James stepped into the kitchen and looked expectantly at Candy, like a good butler waiting on his lady's instruction. He ignored me, and this gave me the impression immediately that my meeting with queen and princess was about to get frosty. James had never been one to slap me on the back and ask me how the hell I was, but he'd never ignored me, either.

"I need you to unload the van," Candy told him.

"But we're going to San Diego –"

"Ernie wants it back."

So that was how it was gonna be. Candy was gonna play it like the poor, wounded, abandoned innocent, used and abused by the callous old rock star. *What was your name, little girl?* She'd just muddle through somehow, just try to do the best that she could without the van, now that he'd left her out in the cold.

Now James considered me, and yep, his eyes were cold, resentful. "Fuck Ernie."

Lisa's suddenly laughter made me jump. "That's just the problem! Ernie doesn't want to –"

"You need to shut up," Candy hissed, and chastised, Lisa looked down at the table. But her grin remained. It amused her that Daddy had dumped Mommy.

She is just as crazy as she wants to be, quoth the little red devil in my head, not for the first time.

"Ernie wants the van back," Candy repeated to James. "So, unload it, and take it over to his house. Roy can follow you in my car."

"How are we going to get our equipment to –"

"Or you could take it back to Hertz," I suggested. "Pick up the Chevy. Take that to San Diego."

This was all just melodramatic bullshit. I knew they'd gotten an advance from EMI; they could buy a new van, or at least put down a sizable down payment on one. Candy just wanted to play the victim.

"There ya go, James," Candy said. "Please do that."

James hesitated for another second, as if he might be feeling uppity enough to say something else, but in the end he decided against it. He gave me another frown, then left to do as he'd been ordered.

Now Candy smiled tightly at me, still trying to maintain an air of pleasantness. "There. That's taken care of. What else?"

What else? It seemed that the time had arrived, and rather abruptly, for me to take the bull by the horns. To call a spade a shovel, as dear old Dad had been fond of advising.

"Lisa tells me that it's her destiny to destroy Dennis Whitly."

Candy looked at her daughter in furious disbelief, and again Lisa looked penitently down at the table. Apparently I wasn't supposed to know about Lisa's quest for cosmic revenge. Oops.

I used Ernie's expression now. "There's been some weird shit going on lately, Candy. Ernie's sudden depression –"

"What does that have to do with us?" she replied, way too quickly, and she couldn't stop the bitter vituperation there. "Maybe if Ernie would learn to keep his dick in his pants, he wouldn't have anything to get depressed about."

Lisa rolled her eyes, grinned at me.

I returned her grin, but if she'd looked closely, she would've seen that it didn't quite reach my eyes. "What happened to your necklace, Lisa? The one that hits me in the chin while we're –"

“I gave it to Dad,” she said quickly, cutting me off. Her grin faded, and her expression took on a kind of quizzical hurt. Why was I referring to our private business – why had I almost said the actual *term* for our private business – in front of her mother?

But Candy wasn’t concerned that her daughter’s boyfriend, who was a good solid ten or twelve years older than herself, had suddenly decided to describe sex acts at the breakfast table. The giving her amulet to Daddy thing – it was obvious that Lisa had done something else that I wasn’t supposed to know about, and Candy was again struck speechless that she’d let me find out.

“Why did you give it to him, Lisa?” I asked. “As another good-luck charm?”

“Why else?” Candy asked, again, far too quickly.

“I was told it wasn’t for good luck at all.”

Shocked amazement sparked in Lisa’s eyes. “Who told you?”

Candy laid a hand on her daughter’s arm. She studied me narrowly again. “I knew it. When we got back from Frisco – there’d been a witch at your house. I could smell her.” Now Candy grinned triumphantly at Lisa’s look of betrayed disbelief. “I told you, but you said I was seeing witches and whores everywhere. I believe the shoe is now on the other foot. How does it fit? I told you! Musicians are all the same!”

Tears welled up in Lisa’s eyes. “Cal? Is it true? Were you carrying on with some other woman when I was out of town?”

I reached across the table and squeezed her hands. “Not on your life.”

“Or on yours,” Candy sneered, all imitation of pleasantness vanished. “Like I told you then, Cal. You don’t know who you’re fucking with.”

There it was, just like Ernie had said: the threat. It didn’t amuse me this time, nor did it worry me. It just plucked at my native snobbery: just who in the hell did Candy think she was to be threatening *me?* She was nothing but an old groupie – and not even mine, at that.

“Don’t talk to him like that, Mom.”

Lisa’s sticking up for me was a completely endearing gesture and I couldn’t help but smile at her. I said, “Someone once told me that forewarned is forearmed.” I let my smile fade as I looked back at Candy. “Maybe you should tell me who I’m fucking with.”

“All right. I will.” Candy nodded dismissively at Lisa, like she was a misbehaving child. “First of all, I want you to know that all this her wanting to be with you garbage? That's all something that she's just made up in her head. When your book came out, when the miracle was revealed – I told her who she was, what she had to do. But all this happily-ever-after-with-you crap? This fantasy that Elise was meant to be with you all along? Lisa made all that up on her own.

"I never been supportive of it. I mean, you were her best friend in a previous life, true – but that was a long time ago. Sure, you wrote about Elise, the person that Lisa once was – but still, I could never understand how she translated all of that into a physical attraction to you."

"Stop talking about me like I'm not sitting right here, Mom. I hate it when you do that."

Candy glared at her daughter. "And now look what's happened! I've sensed a resistance ever since Ernie brought him over here. The prophecies were falling into place – Ernie returned to me, just like the demon promised that he would. But then you insisted on going through with this ridiculous . . . *thing,* chasing after this *old man,* like some kind of cat in heat –"

"He's my destiny, Mom," Lisa said quietly. She reached across the table and squeezed my hand. It was not expected; I flinched.

"Your destiny? You've almost derailed your destiny because of him. Did the demon's prophecy once mention him?"

"He wrote the book, Mom," Lisa said patiently. It appeared to me that they'd had this discussion before. "Cal was Elise's best friend, so now he's my –"

"So what? That doesn't mean you had to fuck him."

I was shocked but somehow not shocked at all by Candy's crudity. My resident demon asked, *What exactly did you expect from one of Ernie's groupies? Subtlety? Tact? Grace?*

"The demon never mentioned him, Lisa," Candy said again. "Everything else that he prophesied – it started to come to pass. Ernie returned to me just as Phenex had promised. I'd waited *so long* for him . . ."

Candy's eyes misted over for a split-second, then abruptly hardened again when she looked back at me. "Then you came along, and suddenly the balance was disrupted. Sonny would've gone, like he was supposed to, he would've stayed out in the desert with his holy-roller mother.

"But he thought that you were his new buddy," she spat hatefully. "He knew better than to come back here, but he thought he might come back to town anyway. Maybe you'd put him up. But I couldn't have him anywhere around, because if he was around, then Ernie would never . . . So it's your fault that we had to –"

"Sonny understood sacrifice, Mom," Lisa stated simply, and patted her hand. "What must be, must be."

The quiet horror of her words had barely scratched the surface of my brain when Candy hissed at me, "It should've been you."

In a long life spent in the business of rock and roll, I'd heard a few threats, especially in the early days. There was the big frat boy who hadn't appreciated how I'd smiled back at his drunken girlfriend. He'd felt duty-bound to jump bad with me about it after our set, just to prove to her how much he cared. There was the time that the band scheduled to come on after Sonic Daydream at The House of Ale thought we were a little slow clearing our instruments off the stage, thought we were cutting into their set time. My reply that he was more than welcome to carry my high-hat out to the truck if I wasn't moving quickly enough for him had actually incited the big bass player from this nobody trio to swing on me. It had been Denny who'd stepped in and broke that one up, before my smart mouth got my ass beaten for me.

And there had been guys in bars in the towns we played over the years that just hadn't liked my looks, had been down for a fight at the slightest imaginary provocation. *But you always seem outnumbered, so you don't dare make a stand.* That had never been a problem for me. I'd make a stand, because my bandmates would back me up. So at one time or another, all four of us had wound up in a couple of fist fights.

But this threat of Candy's whispered over my sense of self-preservation like a heavy, toxic smoke, riveting my attention, the way a drunken hillbilly with a busted beer-bottle might. *It should've been you.*

"If you wouldn't have been hanging around here," she continued, "Sonny would've just gone on his way. I should've . . . It should've been you. But she wanted you, so we had to –"

"It's destiny, Mom. Sonny understood."

They killed Sonny, a startled voice said in my head. It was that one voice that doesn't let you lie to yourself. *They are absolutely insane. They killed Sonny,* sacrificed him, *so that some hallucination Candy had once experienced, this prophecy of wish-fulfilment, would come to pass. Sonny had to die so that Candy would get Ernie and Lisa would get to keep . . .*

Me.

Sonny's letter – *And since Lisa loves you – she has always loved you – I think that you can turn her from this evil path. Trust in love, Cal. It's your only salvation.*

The love I felt for Lisa shriveled, curdled. They'd killed Sonny.

"The demon didn't say anything about him, Lisa. I think I've made a big mistake by letting you go on with this. Ever since he's been here, things have been falling apart." Now Candy was talking about me like I wasn't sitting right there.

"We're signed, Mom. We're gonna be famous."

"But Ernie's gone!" Candy wailed. Again Lisa rolled her eyes.

"You people tried to kill Ernie," I whispered. The threats, the evil purposes, the insanity: all of it was clear to me now. *They are dangerous to you.*

Lisa and Candy blinked identical, calm blue eyes at me. Lisa said, "What did I tell you, Cal? Ernie got what was coming to him. Some sins are unforgiveable."

"But Ernie escaped his just punishment," Candy said to Lisa. "And it's because you've chosen to have him here. I'm telling you, his being here is messing everything up. The rest of them . . ."

Lisa's reaction earlier had been right on the mark; it was extremely annoying to be discussed like you weren't even there. But having Candy turn her burning eyes my way was no thrill either. "How's Lenny, Cal?"

"I don't know. I haven't seen him. But I heard you did."

"Who told you that?"

"Denny."

"Since when do you talk to Denny?" Lisa asked.

"I didn't talk to him. Ernie did. Denny told him that you guys had stopped in for a visit."

Candy exchanged a glance with Lisa, and its meaning was as clear as if she'd spoke aloud. *Maybe he doesn't know yet. . .*

It was all true. They were insane. For the first time, fear laid a cold finger on my heart. I wasn't afraid of Candy, and Lisa loved me – but I wondered suddenly when James and Roy and Horus would be back. They'd do whatever Candy told them to do, whether it was to sabotage a motorcycle or drug a guitar player or set a houseful of people on fire. If they were lurking around somewhere – I was definitely outnumbered now. My sense of self-preservation told me precisely what to do, while I still had the chance, before this conversation got any uglier.

"Excuse me one second," I told Candy and Lisa. I texted Ernie: *I need u 2 get over here. The shit's just hit the fan. If I was smart enuff 2 b scared, I would b.*

I put my phone back on the table next to me, trusting in this indispensable modern technology. But just like the old telephone game with cans and a string, there had to be someone on the other end for the message to go through. Ernie had lost his phone in the fire, but he had to have a spare one at his house. Or he had to have stopped somewhere already this morning and gotten himself a new one. Ernie's phone was indispensable to him. He needed it to talk to his new love. He had to've taken care of replacing it before he did another thing today. I was counting on it.

Now that I'd secured a safe exit for myself – maybe – I decided that I had to find out the depth and breadth of their murderous insanity.

"Ernie told me that after your visit, there was a fire at Lenny's house."

The eagerness in their eyes, the anticipation, was wholly inappropriate and it was further proof that it was all true. But I couldn't back down now. "Everybody got out okay. The five of them –"

"Five?" Candy asked.

I nodded. "There was Lenny and his wife, and Denny, and Ernie and his friend –"

"From the record company?"

I smiled condescendingly, shook my head. "Really, Candy? Do you think that Ernie only has one friend?" I winked. "Anyway, they all got out safely."

"See?" Candy shrieked at Lisa. "I told you, I sensed a resistance to the flow of the prophecy – it's him! His presence – it's like a domino effect. He prevented Ernie from realizing the error of his ways, which allowed Ernie and his latest whore to be on hand to –"

"It was all Ernie's . . . *friend,* actually. She had a nightmare. Something about a black bird."

Why are you baiting her? some fearful, prudent part of my mind asked.

Why the fuck not? I answered. *She tried to roast my friends.*

"She woke up, screamed . . . Ernie smelled the smoke, and got 'em all out. Thank God for Ernie's friend." I smiled at their twinned disappointment.

How calm you are, my resident demon said. *Do you still think you're gonna be able to save Lisa? Her mother's just practically confessed to arson. Forget about Lisa – do you think you're gonna be able to save yourself? Do you think Candy's just gonna let you walk out of here?*

"This . . . *thing* with him." Candy gestured from me to her daughter. "It's a mistake."

Lisa sighed. "I can't be helped, Mom. I love him."

Candy laughed harshly. "For those of the blood, anything can be helped. You love him? Sure you do. You talked yourself into all that. And you think he loves you."

"Cal was Elise's best friend, Mom. He can't help but love me." She squeezed my hand again. I was ready for it this time, so I didn't flinch.

Candy grinned craftily. She might be nuts, but still she knew how things worked in the real world. She knew the logic of an unbeliever. *Just because you think you're above somebody, that doesn't make you smarter than them.*

Like a black net, Candy cast out the shadow of doubt before Lisa. "If he loves you so much, then surely he'll choose you over your common enemy?"

"Surely." Lisa's confidence in my loyalty was unshakable. For the moment.

"Tell him about the new plan to destroy Dennis Whitly. Tell him about his wife's car. See how much he loves you then."

Lisa smiled happily at me and again my resident devil pointed out that she was insane. "I thought about what you said, Cal, that Denny wouldn't let me near him. So when I left the hospital, I went over to his house. Rich people should really lock their cars up at night.

"I put an amulet under the seat of his wife's car, placed a welcoming spell on it. Phenex will claim her, and when she's gone, I'll go to Denny. I'll be his lifesaver in a sea of grief. Then when he loves me utterly, I'll abandon him, just like he abandoned Elise."

Candy grinned at me. "I know you wanna call Denny and warn him, now, don't you, Cal? Make no mistake: Lisa's amulet will call the demon; its spell has given him carte blanche to tear apart the puny metal contraption – she feels so safe in it – but Phenex wants the tender soul within, and through Lisa's magic, he'll get it.

"It's too late, of course. There's no way to stop it now. But you want to try, don't you? You want to call that cheating son of a bitch and warn him. You want to again try to turn aside the demon's plans. But you've interfered for the last time.

"My daughter loves you and she'd never forgive me if I got rid of something she loved just because you were an annoyance to me, but if you show her the truth, Cal, I don't think she'll miss you so much. I'm not saying that you just used her all along." Candy grinned smugly. That was exactly what she was saying.

"She's young and . . . accessible, so I'm sure you're at least fond of her. But love, loyalty, that's something else entirely. Dennis Whitly called you a traitor, and that's exactly what I think you are. But not to him. You goddamned musicians stick together.

"Go ahead, Cal. Call him. Maybe there's still time to prevent Phenex from flambéing Denny's wife, if only you call and warn him. Show Lisa how much you love her. Show her where your loyalty lies."

I heard the back door slam; a moment later, James paused in the kitchen doorway. Roy and Horus, shorter than the big drummer, peeped in under his armpits for a second, like Ignorance and Want clinging to the robes of the Ghost of Christmas Present. James looked to the queen for guidance; her return glance told him that a decision would be at hand momentarily. She waved them away and they moved off down the hall toward the band room.

Lisa looked steadily at me, waiting for my next move, and I realized that it was only her continued affection that was keeping Candy from throwing me to her minions. I thought of Iris's dagger again and wondered: *How the hell did I wind up here, trapped with a band full of lunatics that have it in for no less a person than my once-but-never-again friend, multi-platinum recording artist and notorious coward Dennis Whitly? What a long, strange trip it's been.*

"I don't know Denny's number." Which was the God's honest truth. I wasn't really concerned that Lisa's spell was going to in anyway affect Sophia's car, either, so I wouldn't've called him if I had it. Lisa and her love stood between me and the boys in the band and I wanted to keep it that way.

"Ernie, then." Candy reached across the table and took my phone, started scrolling through the contacts.

"No, Mom." Lisa continued to stare at me expressionlessly. "Let him do it himself."

Before she could give it back to me, my phone rang in Candy's hand.

She smiled at the caller ID and pushed the button. "Well, hello, Ernie, my sweet. We were just talking about you. I hear you're a little singed."

Candy grinned at her daughter, but Lisa was not amused. The question remained unanswered: would I betray her quest for revenge and warn Denny?

"He's right here." Candy handed the phone to me, and the two of them stared unwaveringly at me while I said hello.

"We're standing outside by the back door," Ernie said. "Me and a couple of bouncers from The House of Ale. My new best friends. Bianca's daughter called 'em for us."

"How nice of her to come through for you again," I said and winked at Candy. "I'll be right there. And if I'm not, well . . . the three of you just come on in and get me." I pushed the button and ended the call.

"I have to go now, ladies. Ernie's waiting outside for me." Candy reached for her own phone, and I said, "He brought some friends with him, and I'm not talking about other groupies. A couple of big boys. Your band's not gonna be able to tour if they get busted up, Candy. There's no one you need to call."

I slid out of the booth and asked Lisa if she'd come outside and have a word with me. She nodded, and went out of the kitchen first.

"I'll be seeing ya," I told Candy.

"You'd better hope not, Cal. Don't think this is over. Dennis Whitly is doomed. Him – all of you. The prophecy will be fulfilled."

"Whatever's clever, baby."

Lisa was looking at the ground, not at her father, when I stepped out of the door under the Gibsons. Ernie didn't care. It had all became a bizarre and unusual game to him – Ernie LaBelle versus the demon-worshippers – and he figured he'd won this round, rescuing me with the aid of the two tall, beefy young fellows that flanked him like members of the Praetorian Guard.

I nodded for him and his entourage to head on down the hill ahead of us, so I could talk to my young girlfriend for a moment. I put my arm around her. "I want you to come home with me. I want you – go back in and pack a suitcase. I want you to come and stay with me."

"We've got a show in San Diego tomorrow night, Cal."

Christ, how could I have forgotten about that? Could it be because her mother had just been threatening my life?

"Okay." I took her by the elbows, searched her face. "When the tour's over . . . Say you'll come and live with me. I'll get you some help. You've gotta forget about all this crazy –"

"No." Lisa pulled her arms down swiftly, like a bratty little kid, and stepped back away from me. "Mom's right. You're a traitor."

The tears fell, and seeing them tore at me. I still loved her, despite her murderous, desperate insanity. If I could only get her away from her mother . . .

"Lisa, please! You've gotta see that this is just nuts. All this hatred against Denny –"

"Denny killed Elise, Cal!"

"No, honey. Elise killed herself. You have to let this go. When the tour's over –"

"I love you so much, Cal!" She cried it so loudly that Ernie and one of the bouncers, waiting at the bottom of the hill, turned and looked at us. Lisa wrapped her arms around my neck, sobbed hysterically into my chest.

"I love you, too, baby. Come on. Come home with me now. I'll take you to San Diego to meet the band tomorrow . . ."

"No. Soon Denny's gonna be at the morgue. Then he's gonna go home, broken, and I'm gonna go to him then. Comfort him. He's just lost his wife, and I'm gonna be his replacement for her. He'll be so sad, but whenever he's with me, the sadness will be gone. I'll tell him that we'll be together forever, as soon as the tour's over . . ."

A chill ran through me, causing a violent shiver. Lisa's words were so similar to Elise's, the embodiment of her delusion: *Someday, Denny and I are gonna be together forever . . .*

"Of course you can't go on tour with us, Cal," Lisa said suddenly, as if I'd asked to go. "Mom's pissed that I told you about the prophecy. James tries to anticipate her whims, so I don't think you'd be safe . . ." Lisa's voice trailed off, her eyes became distant.

Had there been any nearby, the men in the white coats would've netted her up without a second thought. I'd never seen her more completely unhinged than at that moment. The threads of her mind were trying to knit together the dissonant ideas that she loved me, but I couldn't go on tour with her because her mother wanted to kill me. Lisa loved me because I'd loved Elise; her mother wanted to kill me because I was going to tip off Elise's betrayer. I was a traitor, to her and Elise, so Candy wanted me dead, so I couldn't go on tour with Phenex; but I couldn't be a traitor because Lisa loved me . . .

She shook her head, as if the physical motion would set straight these conflicting thoughts and emotions.

"And when I get back, you'll understand, right? I'll have to spend some time with Denny to . . . to set the hook, so to speak. And then I'll abandon him, and he'll be crushed, all alone, despondent. He'll want to end it all, just like Elise did."

Her demented smile blazed. "And after he does – then I'll come and live with you, Cal. We'll be happy together forever! You can come back on tour with us –"

Ernie honked the horn on Lenny's dusty old Ford truck, and Lisa's smile faltered, because here was reality intervening again: I was leaving with her adulterous father, switching sides, betraying her and Elise.

But she wouldn't allow herself to see any of that. She hugged me, kissed me quickly. "I'll text you every day while we're gone. I love you!" Then she turned and ran up the hill before one more shred of reality could intrude upon her twisted fairytale.

I reached the open gate. The bouncers were already in the truck. Ernie looked up from his phone, his face ashen with shock. "For Christ's sake, let's go, Cal! Sophia wrecked the car. Valerie's in a coma."

FIFTY-SEVEN

I followed Ernie downtown. It seemed like it took an interminable amount of time to make it to The House of Ale; it seemed like I waited forever while he said a few grateful words to the bouncers, slipped them a couple hundred bucks for their not-much-trouble, told them goodbye. It seemed to take years. I leaned against the fender of my car and waited. The pain and worry were like an acid in my mind, eating away at the years, bringing back all the cheerful memories, coloring them with agony and fear.

Valerie. Denny and Sophia's little girl. Not so little anymore: she was pushing thirty now, a famous computer prodigy, the visionary behind the hottest infotainment service in the world. Bigger than Facebook, more of a money-maker than Netflix, Valerie's Talk To a Movie Star (TTAMS for short) had a worldwide following. Subscribers paid $9.95 a month, and through the miracle of motion-capture technology, the operators to whom they talked appeared to be Hollywood's most famous, the living and the dead. Denny's baby girl was a genius and the service she'd invented had made her a millionaire.

Like her daddy, I hadn't seen or talked to Valerie in years, not since she *was* a little girl. Elise had committed suicide on Valerie's eighth birthday, and six months after that, Denny and his family had moved back to Riverside. Sonic Daydream had put out a few more albums, recorded in the studio he'd built behind the house. We never went on the road together again, and eventually we went our separate ways. Denny lived happily-ever-after with his wife and daughter. Ernie joined Azomite, Lenny retired to the ranch. I did a little studio work, and began my solitary existence.

So all my memories of Valerie Whitly were happy ones, of a sunny, joyous, blue-eyed, blonde child. *Uncle Cal,* she'd called me. She was the light of Elise's dark existence, and whenever we played a local gig, Elise would send a limo to the big house in Malibu, to make sure Valerie got to see us perform. I remembered those days, Valerie standing backstage wearing big headphones against the noise, holding Aunt Elise's hand. Their eyes shone with love, watching Denny sing.

Now she was in a coma.

I waited for Ernie to tell me the details. At last done with the bouncers, he sighed heavily, his face reflecting my own pain and fear. Valerie had called him uncle, too.

"They've got Valley and Sophia at Community Hospital."

"Sophia, too?"

The idea of my mother and Sonny's mother's God flitted through my mind, His supposed goodness and beneficence. I couldn't believe in Him now, any more than I ever could. Sophia had already suffered through one car accident. It had crippled her for life, had given her a cane as a constant reminder of how her own sister had tried to kill her. What kind of loving deity would bust up an innocent woman twice in one lifetime? It was all bullshit.

"I guess she's just cut up a little," Ernie said. "They were almost home. Sophia must've lost control on the off-ramp. She flipped the Volvo over the side. This was about the time the fire was going on. When Denny got home this morning – it was on the fucking news, Cal. *TTAMS's creator hospitalized after near-fatal crash."*

"I'll follow you over there."

During the short drive to Riverside Community Hospital, I remembered Lisa's deranged words: *I put an amulet under the seat of his wife's car, placed a welcoming spell on it. Phenex will claim her . . .*

I couldn't put it down to mere coincidence this time. Candy had told me that Lisa's medal would call the demon – *its spell has given him carte blanche to tear apart the puny metal contraption – she feels so safe in it – but Phenex wants the tender soul within, and through Lisa's magic, he'll get it.*

In Candy's silly, theatrical language, that was definitely the description of a car wreck, but I didn't believe for one second that the demon Phenex, called by Lisa's vaunted magic, had caused Sophia to lose control of her ultra-safe Volvo. Not for a minute did I believe it, not on your life. It wasn't spells or amulets that started fires or caused old Triumphs to suddenly crash on lonely freeways, and it wasn't magic that had caused Sophia's accident, either.

I remembered Candy's expression of worldly-wise cunning when she'd egged me on to warn Denny; the accident had already occurred by then. Maybe she'd seen it on the news, too. Lisa would believe that her spell had caused it, because that's what her mother had taught her to believe, but logically, it was much more likely that it was sabotage and not any kind of demonic sabbat that was responsible. Lisa had hidden her cursed amulet, made her invitation to the demon, and then after she'd departed, I imagined James sneaking up the darkened Whitly driveway and *working on* Sophia's car, just like he and Roy had *worked on* Sonny's bike. I couldn't begin to say what he could've done to it to make it fail – what did I know about cars? But I was immediately certain that's what had occurred. Lisa believed in the powers of the forces unseen, but Candy put her faith in James and a wrench to make goddamn sure the prophecies came true.

A plan began to form in my head. They had to be stopped. Fire, as the old saying went, could only be fought with fire. *And thine eye shall not pity; but life shall go for life, eye for eye, tooth for tooth, hand for hand, foot for foot.*

Ernie and I found a place to park in the hospital's big structure and walked through the echoing concrete levels and byzantine staircases to the front of the hospital. A Channel 7 News van inched its way past the front doors as we entered.

"Hometown boy's tragedy still makes the news, even after all these years," Ernie commented.

I shook my head. "You said it yourself. *TTAMS's creator hospitalized after near-fatal crash.* They're not here because of Denny. Valerie's famous."

"I guess you're right."

"Have you ever looked at her service? You can talk to Marilyn Monroe."

Ernie shrugged. "I've never been much for movie stars."

"Maybe she should get some guitar players on there, huh?"

He smiled faintly. "That would be cool. I'd surely talk to Randy Rhoads."

I imagined that Valerie would have to hire a whole 'nother arm of Research and Development to have operators masquerade as dead rock stars. "When she gets better, you'll have to suggest that to her."

The lobby of the hospital was crowded with people. We weaved through them, and Ernie said to the harried volunteer behind the counter, "I'd like to see Valerie Whitly. Could you tell me her room number, please?"

The young woman frowned. "Your name?"

Ernie paused, and I thought that it must be the very first time in his life, or at least since I'd known him, that he hesitated to tell somebody who he was. It was the crowd: some of them were surely reporters or whatever passed for reporters in the internet age, and he wasn't in the mood to talk to anybody. They were here for news about the condition of TTAMS's famous creator, but a little background interview, a little worried reaction shot from the guitarist from TTAMS's famous creator's famous father's once famous band would be a coup. It was a twenty-four hour news day, after all.

"Why do you need to know my name?" Ernie asked quietly.

"Ms Whitly's in ICU, sir. All these people . . . We have a list. We can't have the whole world peeping in at her."

"I'm family," Ernie assured her.

"I'm sorry, sir. I have to have your name." And since he was being so difficult, she added officiously, "And some ID."

This request actually pleased Ernie, because that way he didn't have to say his name. He showed her his driver's license and she checked the list, and told him the way to ICU.

Ernie thanked her, then turned and looked at me helplessly. We both knew that my name wasn't on the list.

"Just text me," I told him. I indicated a large waiting room off the lobby. "I'll be in there."

"I'll have Denny call down and put you on the list."

"Denny's got other things to worry about besides me, Ernie. I'll just wait. Text me."

FIFTY-EIGHT

The crowd in the lobby thinned. Valerie was stable, and if some of these people were reporters, there were other news stories for them to pursue.

I had time to feel guilt, to feel blame – all the emotions in which I'd wallowed after Elise's death: I hadn't stepped up, hadn't tried to show my best friend the impossibility of her dream. That was all true, but how effective I might've been in dissuading her was up for debate.

But my culpability in this new insanity was undeniable. *Sonic Nightmare* had been the key. The timing of Lisa's conception and Elise's death, the idea that it was Denny's betrayal that had caused Elise to kill herself – Candy would've known about none of these things if it wasn't for my book.

Grieving parents had once sued Ozzy, claiming that their troubled boy had been driven the rest of the way around the bend by the lyrics to *Suicide Solution.* The parents had lost, and my own case would fall out similarly: not a jury in the world would convict me as an accessory to Phenex's attempts to roast my band at Lenny's house or the attempted murder of Denny's wife through the sabotage of her car. But the fact remained that the queen witch would never have dreamt that these actions were prophetically ordained if it hadn't been for the words that I'd published.

I'd ignored Elise's obsession with Denny because there'd seemed to be no danger in it. I'd ignored Lisa's rambling supernatural threats for the same reason, basically – there had seemed to be no danger in the idea that one's hatred could manifest itself into action by the intercession of imaginary forces. But now I knew that, just as the Inquisition hadn't waited around for God to punish witches and heretics, my local witches hadn't waited around for Phenex to punish the members of Sonic Daydream.

They'd slipped some kind of drug to adulterous Ernie. They'd set fire to Lenny's house, because Lenny was complicit in Denny's crime. Not unlike myself, he'd stood by and done nothing while his brother drove Elise to suicide. Plus there was the added bonus that Denny the arch-fiend was there at the time, so Phenex had intended to literally kill two birds with one flaming stone.

James and his wrench had claimed Sonny, so the demon's prophecy of Ernie's return to his Number One Fan would come to pass. And since Denny had escaped the fire, James had done something to Sophia's car in order to facilitate Lisa's plan of soothing him in his grief and then abandoning him, damning him to a life of hopeless loneliness.

They are dangerous to you. Sonny had been mistaken on that. Phenex was dangerous to everyone but me, and I'd been too caught up in my love for the chief nutcase to allow myself to see it.

The old saying goes, *Speak of the devil and he shall appear,* and it played through my mind with disbelieving astonishment. I just happened to glance in the direction of the elevator and saw Lisa step off and cross the lobby toward the door. I arose and intercepted her.

The utter amazement on my face made it unnecessary to say, *What are you doing here?* It twisted my heart to realize that even though she was a murderous psychopath, we were so simpatico that she could simply answer my expression without words being necessary.

"What do you think I'm doing here?" She smiled brightly, kissed me quickly. "I'm completing Phenex's shoddy job. Mom says it's your presence that's dampening his power, but I think he's just testing my resolve, making me work a little bit harder to fulfill what's been foretold."

She giggled like a little girl. "Luckily, the security in this place is non-existent. It wasn't easy to slip into her room, ICU or no, but it wasn't impossible. I just put the amulet around her neck, slid it under her gown. Here, Cal. Take my hands. We'll call its power together."

But I already had my phone in my hand, was mentally begging Ernie to answer. I didn't believe in the power of Lisa's medal, but if she'd been in Valerie's room, she could've unplugged one of the machines . . .

"The mother was even easier," Lisa was saying. "She's not in ICU. She's on a different floor. Not so many nurses hovering around, and all the family's in the hallway near the daughter. I just walked right into her room, like I was a regular visitor. She was sleeping, but they'd set a food tray in front of her." Lisa grinned slyly, her blue eyes all a twinkle. I just had time to think how much I loved her beautiful eyes before she said, "I just poured the potion into her water carafe."

"Potion?"

Again my young lover giggled. "Not too mysterious. The main ingredient is wolf's bane. Fast acting. These doctors will never guess what hit her."

Iris's words came back to me: *Wolf's bane. The queen of all poisons. More readily available than cyanide, and you'd be dead within the hour.*

Ernie finally answered the phone. "Denny called down and put you on the list, Cal. Just tell the lady your name and come on up."

"Listen to me carefully, Ernie." A sudden calm had enveloped me. Screaming hysterically wouldn't do, because I had to get my point across immediately. "You have to get to Sophia's room. Take the food tray away, get rid of it and the water pitcher. Lisa's poisoned it."

"How did Lisa get into –"

"Do what I'm telling you. Do it right now. I'm coming up there, but you're closer. Remember Vegas."

"All right. I'm going right –"

Lisa slapped the phone out of my hands. Offense, outrage turned her eyes a darker shade of blue. "What are you doing, Cal? The prophecy –"

"You're insane." I couldn't look at her for one more second.

I picked up my phone, turned away to go to the front desk, to find out where Sophia's room was. I almost collided with Iris.

"I saw it on the news, Cal. I recognized your singer's last name, so I looked it up –"

"You!" Lisa hissed. Heads turned in the waiting room. She grabbed my arm, digging her fingernails painfully into my flesh. "Mom was right! She smelled the witch!"

I shook loose of her grasp, still not looking at her. I couldn't bear to. "We have to get upstairs, Iris. She's poisoned Sophia."

Lisa grabbed me again. "You *are* a traitor!" She sobbed. "How could you do this to me? How could you do this to Elise?"

Again I shook free. I took Iris by the elbow and hurried her out of the room.

"I hate you, Cal!" Lisa screamed after me, like a child having a tantrum. "Mom was right! You fucking musicians are all the same!"

FIFTY-NINE

Ernie met us in the hallway outside of Sophia's room. "It's all good, dude. If there was a food tray in there, they've already cleared it away. She's fine."

"It was in the water, Ernie!"

"There was no tray, Cal. Sophia's awake. I asked her if she ate anything, and she said she didn't see any food. There was a plastic water pitcher, like you said, so just to be safe, I dumped it out and threw it in the trash. Everything's fine." He smiled and said hello to Iris.

I had to see for myself, so I ducked into Sophia's room. She was indeed awake, and eyed me sullenly from beneath a bandaged forehead. She didn't care for me any more than her husband did.

"You didn't drink anything just now?"

"What the hell's going on, Cal? Ernie asked me the same thing, dumped my water out." She felt around beside her on the bed and pushed the button to raise it. "You people are crazy. I have to get out of here. I have to see Valerie."

Suddenly, out of nowhere, a sob shook me. The tears dropped down my cheeks. "Oh, my God, Sophia! I'm so sorry!" I collapsed into the chair beside her bed, took her hand.

Sophia recoiled at my touch. "What's happened, Cal? Is . . . Valerie – ?"

"Valerie's okay," I sobbed. It was a lie. I didn't know how Valerie was.

"Then why are you saying you're sorry? That goddamned car! The last thing I remember, the brakes locked up . . ."

I wept, buried my face in the sheet beside her hip. Surprised and touched by my grief, Sophia tentatively patted my head. "Are you telling me the truth, Cal? Is Valerie really all right? Where's Denny?"

I lifted my head, and even though she had every reason not to like me, she felt pity and tenderly touched my agonized face. I sniffled. "Denny's with Valley right now." The tears began afresh.

"You're scaring me, Cal. You say Val's all right, but –"

"This is all my fault, Soph. All of it."

And through sobs of guilt and tears of remorse I poured out the whole insane story to her. I told her about Ernie's biggest fan's pregnancy, about how Lisa's conception had coincided with Elise's death. I told her that they worshipped the demon Phenex, about how the demon had spoken to Candy after she read my book, how she'd convinced her daughter thereafter that she was Elise reborn.

I told Sophia that because I'd blamed Denny for Elise's damnation-by-suicide, Candy believed that he had to be damned himself in order to free Elise's soul, which now resided in her daughter. I told her that they'd killed their guitar player to make room for Ernie, that they'd tried to kill Ernie when he didn't toe the line. I told her that they'd set fire to Lenny's house, that they'd sabotaged her Volvo, that Lisa had just tried to poison her. I told Sophia that it was all because of *Sonic Nightmare,* that it was all my fault.

The tale of all the weird shit that had happened over the last couple of months poured out of me. Sophia, who I'd never seen as anything more than a wraithlike Yoko Ono to my band, Denny's milquetoast, saintly wife, became my confessor. I told her that I'd ignored all the warnings, all the hints, because I was in love with a young woman that was in love with me, whom I'd seen as the hope of my old age. I told her that I couldn't ignore it any longer, that the young woman was deranged. I said I was sorry again, and again buried my head by her side and sobbed.

In silence, Sophia stroked my hair for a moment. Then she said, "You certainly know how to pick 'em, Cal. I gotta say that for you."

I sat up again at this completely unexpected response. I swiped at the tears.

"I tried to tell you when Lenny was in the hospital. There are a lot of things that you don't know about Elise, about our family history. About our mother, the way she felt about our dad. When Dad died, Mom just stopped living. She just wasted away, until she was gone, too. There was nothing either of us could do to comfort her. It wasn't congestive heart failure or any kind of physical, medical thing. Mom died of a broken heart.

"You were friends with Elise. You think you knew her. You knew all about her obsession with Denny."

"So did you." The words just popped out of my mouth. Even in the throes of my guilt about the sabotage to her car, this eternal bone of contention came through. We were all complicit in allowing Elise's delusion to continue; none of us didn't anything to end it.

Unexpectedly, Sophia echoed my thought. "That's what I'm telling you, Cal. We all knew. And there was nothing any of us could've done to stop her. She never would've stopped."

"Until she did. Because Denny –"

"No, Cal. All those things you said about Denny in your book? About what you think went on between them that night? It was all bullshit."

My guilt at present events faded. Here were the old lies, the old excuses, again rehashed. "I know what happened."

Sophia lowered her voice to a fierce, hateful whisper. "You don't know shit, Cal. Elise didn't kill herself, she didn't try to kill me, *because Denny fucked her,* like you said in your stupid book."

The profanity from Denny's good girl shocked me.

"She killed herself because he turned her down. He'd managed to avoid it for all those years, and the minute I was gone, *the second . . .* " She shook her head in disgust.

"She put on her frilly teddy and trotted down to the kitchen in her bare feet, and she made a pass at her sister's husband. And he told her no, Cal. After all those years of hoping and waiting, of pouring her heart out to you, she got her final answer."

Sophia was wrong. I'd always believe that something *had* happened between Denny and Elise that night, something that had busted her insanity wide open, and I couldn't believe that it was just the man that was her obsession turning her down. He had in essence turned her down for twelve years, by ignoring her, by making sure that he was never alone with her. Once they were finally alone, why would one more turn-down send her over the edge?

But if he had given in, and *then* rejected her; if she'd achieved her dream and then he'd shattered it by saying it could never continue . . . That seemed a more likely reason for her final, irrevocable decision, and I'd said so in *Sonic Nightmare.*

I would always believe these things, and the Whitlys and I would never be friends again because they would both always deny them. Que sera, sera.

Sophia inhaled a long breath and let it out. "And then she was just like Mom. She just gave up. But she didn't waste away like Mom did. She just ended it, like ripping off a Band-Aid."

Sophia eyed me darkly. "Elise was considerably more than a bit little crazy, Cal. Her actions proved it. Denny didn't do what you think he did. It was a fitting tribute to Elise that you wrote something about her, about her relentless, groupie's love for a famous musician. *Sonic Nightmare* served well enough as a cautionary tale about that kind of delusional obsession. That she should've been pitied – you got that part right.

"But blaming Denny for it – your whole take on that was backwards. I've told you once, and I'll tell you again – there was nothing that Denny could've done about how Elise felt about him. Short of locking her up – she was just like Mom. She was crazy. This one-sided thing she had for Denny – it was her whole life. No talking cures, no anti-depressants, not your friendship, not a new man – nothing would've ended it for her. Until she ended it herself."

It was true what Sophia had said, that I'd never taken the full depth of Elise's craziness into account, but if she expected some kind of dawning awareness from me, if she thought I'd suddenly fall down on my knees and beg her and Denny's forgiveness, she was mistaken. No matter how deluded Elise had been, it had no bearing on the fact that Denny was still a coward.

I opened my mouth to reply, but Sophia shook her head. "This girl – the one that thinks she's Elise reborn?"

"Lisa."

"You say that you love her. Believe it or not, I loved my sister, and Denny loved her, too, in his own way, *like a sister.* Don't you think we would've talked her out of her obsession if we could've?"

"But neither of you ever tried."

"Didn't you try?"

I didn't try hard enough, I thought.

"It didn't matter," Sophia insisted. "This Lisa – I'm sure you've tried to talk her out of this irrational thing about wanting to hurt Denny. But it hasn't worked, has it?

"You were Elise's friend. You said in your book that you loved her, but all your love and my love couldn't save her from the demons in her head. You love this young woman – she believes in real demons. She believes she's Elise."

Sophia suddenly smiled. "That's why I say you definitely can pick 'em. You just can't seem to get away from the crazies, can you?"

Sophia squeezed my hand maternally. I realized that she was on some kind of pain medication, some kind of sedation. Some pharmacological means had to be making her so calm about all this. Some kind of soothing drug that was smoothing out the spikes of dislike and resentment that she'd felt for me all these years, lending her, if not exactly forgiveness, then at least unconcern. The past was past. It had all been so long ago. Elise was gone.

Then another thought crept into my head: Elise was nuts – Sophia had just proclaimed it, as if it was something that I hadn't known all along. Sophia was delusional Elise's sister; she was her mother-who-had-died-for-love's daughter. Maybe there was a streak of insanity in the whole tribe. I wondered fleetingly if Valerie had inherited any of it. They say that geniuses are always a little mad.

"Regardless, this whole senseless, homicidal – it's my fault, Soph. Because of my book . . . I'm sorry. I have to handle it."

"How are you gonna do that, Cal? You think the cops'll believe your story about demons and reincarnation?" These were the same words I'd said to Ernie.

"You know, not everybody loved Denny and your band. Interspersed with all the adoring fan mail over the years was the occasional death threat. Jealous boyfriends, misguided Christians. One woman wrote to say that she knew that *Cerulean* was an ode to Lucifer. Somehow, she'd convinced herself that Satan had blue eyes, and that Denny was going to burn in eternal hellfire for singing about them. Rock and roll is the devil's music, after all."

Sophia grinned brightly at my surprise, and I again thought that she was definitely medicated.

"These people that you know – they've just proven themselves to be a little more determined in their – what did you call it – their desire to damn him? We'll just have to watch out for them."

I shook my head. "I have another idea."

"Revenge is a dish best served cold, Cal." She giggled at that worn out old cliché. "I think your best bet is just to stay away from them. We'll be all right." She touched the bandage on her head. "I've been through worse than this."

But your brilliant daughter's in a coma because of them, I thought. *Because of me.* If Valley died – I saw the rest of my life filled with drinking and guilty recriminations again.

If there was any such a thing as destiny, as prophecy, here it was. I had to take action now. I hadn't acted to save Elise, and I'd only cleared my conscience by blaming her death on Denny. A band of crazies had taken my indictment of Denny's cowardice and turned it into a quest for revenge against him on a Biblical scale, something I never would've intended, not even in my most drunken, self-pitying binges. *Each man's soul's his own.* But I didn't hate him, and I certainly didn't want to see his family suffer. Sophia was Elise's sister. She had certainly suffered enough.

Denny didn't deserve to have to watch his back because of Candy's take on *Sonic Nightmare,* nor should his wife and daughter have to pay because of it. I would handle it.

SIXTY

Ernie and I went up to ICU, sneaking Iris along with us, but found the hallway deserted. I asked at the nurses' station and they told us that Ms Whitly had been moved. She was on the same floor as her mom now. She was awake.

Denny was standing in the hall outside Valerie's room. Her Uncle Lenny and Aunt Barbie were in there visiting with her. Denny scowled at me, just as his wife had done, but he thanked me for coming, nonetheless. I asked him how Valerie was, and he described her injuries: broken ribs that had collapsed her lung; a fractured skull. But the good news was that her lung was healing already, and the doctors had relieved the pressure on her brain; that had brought her out of the coma. The prognosis was good.

"We need to talk, Denny."

"Ernie told me, Cal. Your girlfriend thinks she's Elise reincarnated. She wants to kill me. He thinks she and the band set the fire at Lenny's house."

"I think they did something to Sophia's car."

Denny was expressionless. "But there's no evidence that they did any of it. Nothing that you could prove."

"I fucking told you, Cal." We all turned to look at Lenny, who had just come out of Valerie's room. The voice was garbled, rough, slurred like a drunk, but his words were clear enough.

Denny hugged his brother. "Welcome back, Leonard."

"I'm not back yet, Dennis." He held up his right hand, the fingers curled, still useless. But he could talk again.

"One day at a time," Ernie said, and also hugged him. He smiled, winked at Iris. "Look at us, all here together. I'm seeing a comeback tour."

Denny snorted laughter at the unlikelihood of that.

Lenny didn't smile. "I saw the black bird, Cal, and then when they showed up at my house –"

"You did?" Iris said in surprise.

He nodded. "Right before my stroke. When I got out of the hospital, I read up on it. There wasn't a lot else that I could do but read . . ." He frowned, told his brother what he'd learned. "Phenex is a Great Marquis of Hell. He's supposed to devour those who get too close. When the band showed up at the house, I knew that something else bad was gonna happen, but I couldn't *say* anything, and if I started texting it –"

"They really shouldn't let the impressionable read Wikipedia," I quipped with a smile.

Lenny stared at me, his expression sullen and angry, just as Denny's had been. "Is this funny to you, Cal?" he said in his gravelly, still slurry voice. "Valerie's in the hospital. My house burned down. Just because you're fucking that girl, does that make this all funny to you?"

My smile evaporated. "The Great Marquis of Hell didn't make you have a stroke, Lenny. The idea that you would even say that out loud *is* funny."

None of it – not the plots, the *actions* against my band – none of it was going to make me believe that there were supernatural forces at work. I believed in wrenches, drugs and poisons, but this witchcraft bullshit was just that. The odds were overwhelming that Phenex had torched Lenny's house, but there was no way on God's green earth that they had caused his stroke, no matter what he thought he'd hallucinated in the moments right before. Such things didn't happen outside of fairytales.

"They tried to kill me, too," Ernie said.

"With a cursed medallion, just like yours, Lenny." I waved my hands beside my head to indicate spookiness.

"What?" The disbelief in Lenny's strange voice was almost comical. "Why didn't you say something about this to me?"

Ernie shrugged. "You've been . . . sick. I didn't want to upset you."

I rolled my eyes. "You people can't really believe all this mumbo-jumbo –"

"None of this can be proven, am I right?" Denny repeated. "That they set the fire? That they fixed Sophia's car?"

"No. But they did it." Now all their eyes riveted to mine. "I don't think it's funny, Lenny. I think it's all my fault. This shit has all happened because the devil-worshippers have decided on a particularly insane interpretation of my book."

"What? Why didn't anybody tell me about this?"

"It's not important right now. This is all that matters. These nutcases have taken a potshot at all of you, but the fucking supernatural didn't have anything to do with it, and I'm just about goddamned tired of listening to you talk about big black birds.

"However . . ." I put my arm around Iris's shoulders and she jumped in surprise. "We have at our disposal, Glinda the Good Witch. She's a believer in the forces unseen, just like this band of lunatics that's out to get us."

"Us," Ernie stressed. "Not you. They're not out to get you. You wrote the book."

"Denny's always said that I'm a traitor, Ernie. And you and I, Denny, we're going to have to talk about that, someday, probably soon." I smiled with a fake sadness, for their benefit, although real sadness roiled in me. *Lisa . . .*

I shook my head. I couldn't bear to think about her.

"We'll talk about it someday, Denny. But not now. Now we have, as Ernie says, other fish to fry. I'm in this as much as you are," I told Ernie. "Lisa was standing right there when I told you about the poison in Sophia's water."

"What?" Denny gasped.

"Lisa told me that she'd tried to poison Sophia, so I called –"

"She might've made that part up, Cal," Ernie said. "There was no tray in Sophia's room. Just the water pitcher –"

"Now who's refusing to see, Ernie? They are absolutely schizo and absolutely dangerous, just like you've been telling me. And they're out to get me, now, just as much as the rest of you. I betrayed Lisa by telling you to help Sophia. She screamed that she hates me. I'm on the hit list now, too."

"And I am also," Iris said softly.

"Fear not!" I said and squeezed her shoulders. "You have the Knights of Sonic Daydream to protect you." I kissed her on the top of the head. "Just like you're gonna protect us."

Again they all stared at me, and I felt a kind of elation, borne of purpose. *I love it when a plan comes together.*

"It's like this, my bruthas. None of this supernatural mumbo-jumbo is real, but –"

"What the hell is this, Cal?" Barbie stomped out of Valerie's room. "Why would you give this stupid, ugly, witch-medal to Valerie?" She stuffed it into my pocket, just like she had Lenny's.

"I didn't –"

"Where did she get it then? When did you get superstitious, believing in good-luck charms? You're starting to sound like him." She nodded at her husband. *"Ernie's band's bad luck, Barbie,* he texted me, after they left. Turned out that the wiring in the kitchen was bad luck."

"I love you, Barbie," Lenny said in his drunken voice. She stared at him in astonishment, then hugged him, covered his face in kisses.

Despite the joy of Lenny's continuing recovery, I recalled Lisa's words: *Luckily, the security in this place is non-existent.*

"Lisa got into ICU, Denny. She put this charm around Valerie's neck." Denny was still speechless at the announcement that Lisa had tried to poison his wife. Now his mouth fell open in disbelief at this new action against his family.

"It's just like Iris told me one time." I squeezed her shoulders again. "These people can't be bargained with. They can't be reasoned with. They don't feel pity, or remorse, or fear. And they absolutely will not stop, ever, until we're all dead."

They stared silently, solemnly at me. I grinned. "But they ain't succeeded yet, have they?"

Candy had told her daughter that my presence was *dampening* Phenex's power. *Jesus Christ on a crutch, Cal,* my resident demon marveled. *Who'da thunk such absolute bat-shit craziness could exist in the modern world? Sophia hit it right on the head. You sure do know how to pick 'em.*

But I would dampen Phenex's power, all right. I'd thrown a cauldron-sized splash of cold water on the whole ridiculous pathology.

I told my old bandmates, "They believe in all this magical bullshit, and since Iris believes in it too, she knows what to do. We'll just start dropping a few magical talismans of our own, summon a few of our own demons. That'll keep 'em away from us. It's like voodoo dolls – it'll work because *they believe in it.* Isn't that right, Iris?"

SIXTY-ONE

I never did go in to visit Valerie. She undoubtedly saw me as a traitor to her family, too, and there was no need to upset her with my demon-dampening presence while she was injured, fresh out of a coma. Someday, I'd tell her the whole story, maybe, but for now, there was no need for her to see me.

I sat around in the hall and discussed witchy strategies with Iris – she was a stranger to Valley, and didn't go in to visit either. She was at first reluctant to contribute her invaluable knowledge to my plan. She of course saw an element of blasphemy, of heresy, in it: unbelievers engaging in sacred rituals to unnerve true believers.

But after a little coaxing, Iris grasped the method to my madness, agreed that it was the only way to keep Phenex's deadly minions at bay. They were single-minded: they believed that Denny's damnation was necessary to save Lisa's soul, and they believed that the demon would grant them fame once Sonic Daydream's frontman was burning in eternal hellfire. So the amulets and spells and covert sabotage attacks against all of us would never cease.

Iris also agreed that bringing in the law wouldn't help. If we accused Candy and crew of trying to kill us, it would only be good and free publicity for Phenex. The press would get ahold of it and it would play out like some kind of supernatural battle of the bands: secular and sane, world-famous Sonic Daydream versus righteously crazy, Satanic, but unknown Phenex. Their ticket sales would go through the roof.

Iris was fond of me, had always endeavored to protect me from her fellow witches, and this fondness led her to warm up to my plan after a few minutes. She had confidence in her own powers, and now that I was suggesting that she use them, a kind of smug righteousness surfaced in her.

Who, after all, was Candy? To me, she was nothing but a trampy old groupie, but to Iris – once the purple-eyed sorceress stopped and thought about it – Candy was nothing but a blight upon her faith, an uppity, too-big-for-her-britches, not-as-powerful-as-she-thought-she-was, neophyte of a witch. Candy was foolishly attempting to direct destiny with the assistance of some third-rate demon; Iris hinted to me that she possessed powers that Candy could not yet dream of accessing.

"Whatever's clever, baby," I told her. "You just tell me which direction to bow, which archangel to invoke."

Iris's vision of a Grand Guignol witch-fight faded. She frowned. "This isn't a joke, Cal. If we call on the unseen forces –"

"Seek guidance from a good witch to help you combat them." Sonny's words. I smiled at Iris. "You're the best witch I know."

Iris didn't smile in return at my compliment. "If we call on the universal energies to aid us in this – it's not a trivial thing, Cal. We'll have to sacrifice a little part of ourselves, all of us. I don't know if you're really prepared to do that. I told you before – you're destined to lose your faith."

"And I told you before. I have no faith to lose. What sacrifices do I have to make, Iris? What potions do I have to create? *Eye of newt and toe of frog, wool of bat and tongue of dog?* This shit has to cease. They have to leave us alone."

Still she frowned. *"O, full of scorpions is my mind,* Cal. You don't understand, because you refuse to understand. If we undertake to rid ourselves of them, it won't come without price."

"I don't believe that there's some risk to my immortal soul, Iris, because I don't believe in my immortal soul. What I do believe is that this is all my fault, and that I have to make it stop. If it takes throwing curses on Candy –"

"On Lisa." She watched me keenly.

I suppressed a flare of misery, made myself shrug like I didn't care. "It has to stop."

Iris stared steadily at me for a heartbeat. "I can make it stop, Cal. For good. Through certain rituals . . ." She searched my face, her amazing amethyst-colored eyes round and still with a kind of resigned sadness. "But once these actions are begun . . . *What's done cannot be undone."*

I patted her hand. I hadn't gone to college, hadn't had *the benefit of a classical education,* like those of the blood, but I had read my Shakespeare. *"The sin upon my head, dread sovereign."*

Iris smiled, but the sadness remained. "So mote it be."

A good-looking, black-haired kid in his early thirties stepped off the elevator and stalked down the hall toward Valerie's knot of well-wishers. He was followed by an attractive woman in a business suit, about the same age. Beside her was another black-haired guy, a little bit older, his features obscured by dark sunglasses and a hoodie. The young man spoke worriedly to Denny for a moment, then dashed into Valerie's hospital room.

Denny made introductions of the newcomers: the young man that had fled to Valley's side was her boyfriend, Brett; the woman was Joyce Vinson, her best friend and business partner. Joyce's companion took off his shades, and I was more than a little surprised to then be shaking hands with Mitch Barlo, star of stage and screen, her husband. They were newlyweds, or close to it: I remembered some headline about their nuptials flashing by on my internet newsfeed not long ago.

Valerie's revolutionary service had its home base in Hollywood, and concerned itself with actors, so I guess I shouldn't have been surprised that one of them would know her personally, would be married to her business partner. Plus there was the fact that her father was a rock star; celebrities knew each other.

There was now quite a crowd of the rich and famous in the hall outside of TTAMS's creator's hospital room, actors and executives and recording artists. All this famousness, uncorralled, with the hospital's non-existent security; there might be a riot. Authority was overdue to raise its ugly head, and as if on cue, a man in a suit materialized. I would've expected him sooner, actually, about the time that Channel 7 had been broadcasting from the parking lot.

"I'm Andrew Deane, Mr. Whitly. Director of Admissions." He shook Denny's hand, apologetically glanced at each of us. "I know that you're all worried. But could I possibly ask if some of you could perhaps go downstairs to our cafeteria while you're waiting to visit the patient? This many people in the hall all at once . . . Unfortunately, there are rules, fire codes . . ."

"We'll go, Denny," I volunteered. Iris nodded silently. She had a blank, stunned expression on her face, and I smiled to myself. She'd never heard of the world-renowned rock band Sonic Daydream, but she liked movies, and she was more than a little star-struck, standing so close to Mitch Barlo.

"Yeah, we'll come back later," Ernie agreed.

"I want to apologize . . ." the suit began.

"It's okay," Denny said. He turned toward Iris and Ernie and me, effectively dismissing the Director of Admissions. Deane did his own amazed double-take at Mitch, then scuttled away.

Denny offered me his hand, for the first time in decades. "We'll talk, Cal. Ernie's got my number. Thanks for coming. Thanks for letting me know about . . .

"All the craziness." I shook his hand firmly. "We're gonna handle it."

"Let me know." He shook hands with Ernie, told Iris thanks, gave her a friendly hug.

SIXTY-TWO

Iris had taken a cab to the hospital, so Ernie and I each volunteered to give her a ride back to Mohini's. She politely turned down my offer; with a little grin, she admitted that she liked riding in Ernie's sleek blue car. Then her smile faded when she said that she had to do some research if we were to combat Phenex's evil band.

"They'll be in San Diego on Wednesday," Ernie told her as we walked out to the parking garage.

I felt a flash of confusion again, like I used to when Sonic Daydream toured. What day was it now? It was . . . Monday. Only Monday.

Ernie said, "In fact, they're gonna be out of town for a couple of weeks." He winked at me. "I think we're safe for a while."

"Until they get back," Iris replied.

She abruptly stopped walking. Ernie and I proceeded a few more steps, then turned back to her. She gestured at his Porsche.

Incomprehensible scribblings adorned the driver's side window, applied with a Sharpie. I walked closer, looked at my own car, parked beside Ernie's. More of the same on the passenger side window of the Caddy, plus someone had keyed the entire length of it on that side.

I imagined Lisa in a jealous fury, stalking from floor to floor, combing the parking garage until she found Daddy's not-quite-one-of-a-kind-but-close-enough, rock star's German sports car, side-by-each with her traitorous lover's more sedate Detroit iron. I imagined her gesticulating to the unseen forces, raining down poisoned invectives and demon-backed curses upon our betraying heads.

But unlike other *rich people,* their cars parked in imagined safety in their driveways, ripe for sabotage, Ernie and I had locked up our transportation out in public. A little vandalism was all Lisa had been able to accomplish. She couldn't get into the passenger compartment to hide amulets, and she couldn't get into the engine compartment to pull out wires or hoses.

Ernie wasn't so sure about this last part. "You don't suppose she could've . . ."

I shook my head. "I'm pretty sure Lisa believes in her own powers. I think it's James that does the actual dirty work."

"Still –"

"Christ, Ernie." I pulled on the handle to the Caddy, above the vicious scratch on the door. "They're locked. She couldn't get in."

I watched him debate the possibilities, saw him reject the picture of Lisa rolling around doing mechanical mischief beneath our cars. He asked Iris, "What does it say?"

She smiled tightly, and willed herself to step closer to Ernie's car. "More of the same. Invocations for the death of your souls."

"Can you . . . say a few words? Nullify it some way?"

I realized that Ernie had decided to go with it. Since I'd suggested that the only way we could rid ourselves of Phenex was to fight witchy fire with more witchy fire, to trade them spell for spell, he'd decided to look to Iris as our leader in the supernatural fight. Our coven master. He'd pretend to believe it all, because they believed it. *Just like voodoo dolls.*

I rolled my eyes. "It's not anything that a car wash won't *nullify.*"

Ernie grinned ruefully, touched the angry gouge on the Caddy. "And maybe a little Bondo. A paint job."

"Maybe it's time for a trade-in," I suggested, even though the damned car was practically brand new.

We waited – Ernie more patiently than me – while Iris, like a faith-healer, closed her eyes and touched both cars for a second. *What a long, strange trip it's been.*

Ernie reiterated that he'd take Iris on downtown to her shop; I said goodbye to her and told him I'd meet him back at his house.

I watched them drive away. As soon as I was enveloped in the hot soundlessness of my disfigured car, the pain hit me. It felt like a hungry grizzly bear vised my chest in his furry paws; the tears again spilled harsh and hot from my eyes. I put my head on my arms on the steering wheel and bawled. It wasn't Phenex come to claim me, however; that thought didn't even cross my mind.

It was Lisa's irretrievable loss that wrung the agonized gasps from me, that made me cry with the same bleak hopelessness that I'd felt when Elise died, that I'd felt for so many years afterward. I hadn't saved Elise, and I couldn't save Lisa, either. Any hope that I could talk her out of her deadly insanity – that had all disappeared when I'd made the move to prevent her from murdering Sophia. I'd gone from cherished, predestined lover, to detested turncoat in the blink of an eye.

I'd taken a risk in loving Lisa; in the back of my mind I'd always known that it couldn't last. The years were wrong, a gulf that would've eventually filled in with boredom, with a resentment sprung from the undeniable fact that I'd already lived my life and she had yet to experience her own. But I'd risked it anyway, because she'd been so lovely, so perfect, and she'd loved me back. And because, also in the back of my mind, even though I knew it could never last between us, I'd entertained the hope that we'd always remain friends.

I'd rationalized that, like Bogie and Elsa, Lisa and I would always have that week at the beach, and I'd always get to hear her sing, even after she came to her senses and realized the impossibility of our May-December relationship. That it hadn't worked out would always hurt, true, but I'd clung to the belief that even after she found someone else, she'd still always be in my life, if only peripherally, as a friend. And that idea had contributed to taking the risk.

But all that was impossible now. Lisa was insane, unreachable; as unreachable as Elise, nearly twenty years in her grave. Lisa viewed me as her enemy, and more devastating – I sobbed, pounded the steering wheel in anguish – I had to accept the fact that she was also my enemy, indistinguishable from my host of other enemies: bitchy, controlling Candy and silent, vengeful James. Sneaky Roy and *of the blood* Horus. *They are dangerous to you.*

There would be no sad, inevitable drifting apart between us. It had been instantaneous, like a guillotine, like the loss of a limb, as if she'd died suddenly. My sense of self-preservation spoke, that voice that brooked no prevarication, no rationalization: *She hates you now.* Beautiful, utterly deranged Lisa believed I'd not only betrayed her, but the soul of my dead friend, too.

Perhaps more than she wished to damn Dennis Whitly, Lisa now wanted to see me just as damned. Just as dead. The idea that I now had to look over my shoulder for a knife in the hand of the person I cared about the most in the world – I cried for a good ten minutes.

Then, reminding myself that I'd always known it was going to hurt, I got ahold of myself and drove home.

SIXTY-THREE

For the first week after Lisa was gone, I had the dream.

I guess it was a nightmare, really, even though it always started out great. Lisa and I would be in bed, and it would all seem so incredibly real: I could smell her familiar scent, feel the velvety whisper of her lips, hear the low, intoxicating timbre of her throaty moans. I hadn't had such vivid sex dreams since high school, before I even knew what sex was about. But every time, right before the dream could erupt just like those embarrassing kinds that adolescent boys sometimes have, I would open my eyes (in the dream) to look at my perfect lover, to see that triumphant smile that she always gave me at that particular moment – and I'd invariably discover that she'd turned into some kind of monster.

My mother had been a staunch Catholic, but had never had too many worries about the presence of demons in real life. In her worldview, evil was what men did – she'd never been concerned that Satan was a concrete, cloven-hoofed being, alive and running around cozening souls, like those Christians that had written to Denny believed. She didn't think Hollywood's monsters-under-the-bed were in any way indicative of Satan-worship at Paramount or Columbia; my mom loved horror movies.

So as a kid, I'd seen them all, and now they all appeared in my dreams. Alternately, I opened my eyes to find that Lisa had turned into a rotting skeleton, a pus-dripping zombie, a werewolf, a putrid swamp-beast. A vampire, fresh from the grave. A fishy succubus. The first couple of times, the visions made me gasp and wake up, but after about the fourth time, I came to expect it. I just blinked at the monster, and he/she/it blinked at me.

Once I knew the scare was coming, the dreams became annoying. I thought of Lisa and the band holding hands and sending them to me – of course that was impossible, but it was just the kind of adolescent stunt that a jilted, vengeful teenage witch would think up, if it were possible. After a while, the dreams ceased. I missed the good parts that came before the monstrous reveals.

I got postcards in the mail with demonic sigils on them. I got anonymous texts with the same. When I forwarded them to Iris, she would call me back, concerned with what she called their *vituperative intensity*. She'd ask if she could come to Temecula to see me, or if I might care to make the drive to Riverside and spend the day with her. When I made up excuses about being busy – I lied and said that lessons at the Y had started up again – she told me that she'd channel healing thoughts in my direction. It reminded me of Sonny's mother's admonitions to take Jesus into my heart.

I didn't need healing thoughts and I didn't need Jesus. I needed Lisa.

Iris urged me to wear my Eye of Horus charm, assured me that its power was soothing. I had neither the heart nor the energy to tell her that I'd misplaced it somewhere.

I talked to Ernie and discovered that he wasn't being harassed by coded messages of execution by electronics, of attempted damnation via post. Phenex didn't have the brothers Whitly's cellphone numbers, but our enemies knew where they and Ernie lived. Yet none of the other former members of Sonic Daydream received any more supernatural threats. I was the sole target now, at least while the band was on tour.

Listless, out of sorts, bored but interested in nothing, I slept a lot after the dreams stopped.

Ernie had almost died, Lenny had lost his house, Denny had seen his family injured; I hadn't lost anything material, but I'd lost a part of my soul. I'd never believed I'd possessed one before, but the ache was above the physical, so with what little poesy I possessed, I assigned the agony to a vivisection of my soul.

From his newfound occupation of one-woman man, Ernie understood. He pitied me. He didn't have to lie about being busy, like I did. These days, he was spending all of his indolent rock star's time in Big Bear with Bianca, when she wasn't traveling for her job. But he still found a minute or two to call every day to check up on me. I acknowledged his concern and went back to sleep.

I recognized the symptoms of depression, even as they settled softly upon me, as choking and poisonous as volcanic ash. There was the practically round-the-clock sleeping. There were the wistful thoughts that perhaps things would be better if I just visited the liquor store and renewed my old acquaintance with *my pal Johnnie Walker and his brothers Blackie and Red.*

But even that's too much trouble. I think I'll take a nap.

It all signaled that commonplace situational malady, *clinical depression*.

I'd hooked up with a girl entirely too young for me and it had ended. Common, not at all unexpected. Waaah. You pays your money and you takes your chances. As the empty days progressed, the fact that it had ended not because of inevitable boredom but because she was a stark, raving, homicidal lunatic didn't really change the quality of the pain.

So, yeah, I was depressed. So what? *It ain't the first time, baby; baby it won't be the last . . .*

But I wasn't going to let the self-pity gallop through me, the way I had after Elise killed herself. I wasn't going to spiral into welcoming and comfortable alcoholism. And, of course, there were no thoughts of anything as maudlin and melodramatic as suicide.

Iris had accused me of believing in nothing, but she was wrong. I actually had one quite firm belief: that *the undiscover'd country from whose bourn no traveler returns* is simply oblivion. I had no *dread of something after death.* Dead was irrevocably dead, simple nothingness, no reward, no punishment, and certainly no rebirth. There would be no dreams.

This one life is all we get and reward and punishment are a result of the decisions we make. I had chosen poorly, but I wouldn't give up this vale of tears voluntarily. The pain was bad, don't get me wrong, and I knew that it would never go away entirely. But it was not unexpected; I'd suspected that I'd have to endure it eventually, but I'd gone on ahead and let her love me.

I knew the sadness would eventually let up enough to let me function again. Lisa wasn't dead, after all, not like Elise.

SIXTY-FOUR

The video was a surprise. Like the wishes and promises of my damnation, pictured in meaningless squiggly lines, it came via text from an unfamiliar number. But the players were all familiar enough.

It began with a small, partially darkened stage; I didn't recognize the last few chords of The RaceCats' tune, but of course I recognized Phillip. The crowd whooped appreciatively as the song ended, and he smiled at his audience.

"How ya doin' Tucson? We're The RaceCats."

Phil's second-guitar played a little breakdown, also unfamiliar to me, and again the crowd cheered. I thought, *Christ. Tucson.* I imagined what kind of a firetrap EMI had booked them at in *Tucson.*

"Before we finish our set, I'd like to bring on a guest singer. You saw her earlier. Please give another one of your great Arizona welcomes to the best songstress in the Southwest, and my close, personal friend, Lisa Corson."

You're a poet, Phil.

The crowd cheered dutifully. Lisa hopped on up onto the tiny stage, dressed as she had been in Vegas, all curly black hair and big black eyelashes. She took the mike from The RaceCats' singer, and Phillip casually embraced her, nuzzled her neck, to demonstrate to the fans just how personal a friend she was. There were scattered, coarse whoops, which translated from Arizona-ese to English as *Atta boy, Phil!*

"This song is about an old lover of mine," Lisa said, and again the crowd cheered lecherously. Of course the bad-girl singer from Phenex had had more lovers than just Phil, no doubt many more. Just look at her: young, beautiful, sexy. I imagined the dudes in the crowd, elbowing each other, talking about how they'd like to be next.

The stage went dark, then twin spotlights illumed Lisa, and Phillip with his axe.

I saw it all then, how the three weeks they'd been on tour had played out, just as Lisa – and maybe even smug Phil himself – wanted me to see it. It had started out innocently enough, but I'd lay odds that it had started after the very first gig in San Diego. Lisa had an idea for a song, had the lyrics in her head; maybe she'd even written them down. But since poor Sonny and that cheating son of a bitch Ernie LaBelle were gone, Lisa needed a little help with the music. Could Phil spare a few moments to help her come up with the tune?

Fucking A, Skippy, he could.

And it had progressed along well-worn lines from there. Like Johnny Cash and June, like Springsteen and Patti, Lisa and Phil had found solace from the loneliness of the road in songwriting and each other's arms. I saw the other members of Phenex crammed into the crummy Chevy again, or maybe they'd taken some of that EMI money and acquired a roomy new van, but Lisa had ridden from town to town curled up next to Phil in The RaceCats' slick little black bus. And I sincerely doubted if she'd shared any more hotel rooms with her mother.

Phil looked down at his pedals, and the spotlight glinted off the medallion around his neck; I was in no way surprised. Of course he'd wear it for her. I'd seen how he'd looked at her in Vegas. Phil would do anything for her. Lisa had captured his soul, too, I was sure, and she hadn't needed the cheap charm to do so.

Phil strummed, and Lisa began to sing.

"We were brought together
Twice but just one lifetime
I have always loved you
Forever we'd entwine

"Destiny pluperfect
Our words and laughing rhymes
I have always loved you
At last, the best of times

"Standing still beside me
I have to see it done
I have always loved you
You were the only one

"Shattered by my lover
A blonde to take my place
I have always loved you
Destiny disgraced.'

Phil's not-bad guitar solo played here, but I couldn't escape the fact that it bore an unmistakable resemblance to Denny's solo in

Sonic Daydream's one and only slow, sad ballad, a song called *Worlds Have Passed.* A spurt of amusement busted through my depression: I wondered if I should get Sony on the phone and have a little conversation about copyright infringement.

Lisa's song continued:

'Ours a love eternal
And played out once again
I have always loved you
Betrayal twice the sin

'Now I wail this sad song
The choice you made was wrong
I will always love you
Although I'll see you gone."

A few more chords from Phil and The RaceCats. The cheers from the crowd and another loving squeeze between singer and guitarist. Then the video went black.

I giggled. If Lisa had sought to incite jealousy or anger or further sadness by sending this clip, her stunt had utterly missed its mark. It was so juvenile, so adolescent: *I've got a new boyfriend, a younger piece of ass, how 'bout dem apples?*

I wondered where her former disdain for musicians had gone, and that thought made me giggle some more. *Here's a song to show you that I'm over it, with a little death threat thrown in just to make you believe it: Although I'll see you gone.*

The clouds in my head parted somewhat as a line from a far superior songwriter – he was the bassist for the singer that Lisa had chosen to front her perfect band, actually – played in my mind: *She's gone, gone, gone; I don't know if I'll cry, I don't know if I'll die laughin'.*

I remembered something that Lenny had said to me once upon a time, after Ernie's recounting of a particularly wild night with one of his fans. *Never sleep with anyone crazier than you, Cal, my brutha.* The loss of all that Lisa and I had had before the murderous insanity had begun, not to mention the loss of what might've been – it would always hurt. But Lenny's words were Truth with a capital *T.* Lisa was just as crazy as she wanted to be, and another truth made me smile: all her witchy beliefs, her chants and malefic dreams of damnation, her silly rituals and cursed medallions: they were all Phil's problem now.

Wait till Ernie gets a load of this. Feeling a whole lot lighter, I dialed his number.

"Phenex should be back in town in a few days, Cal," Ernie intoned seriously, as if four mediocre musicians and their overage groupie of a road dog were one of the ten plagues of Egypt. "But I've got an idea for their last show. It's at The Roxy."

The Roxy Theatre in LA was The Whiskey A Go Go's less famous, poorer cousin, just down the street from it on the Sunset Strip. Like The Whiskey, The Roxy had hosted its share of the greats back in the dim reaches of time, spanning many musical genres: Zappa and Etta James and The Sex Pistols. But despite its being on par with The Whisky as far as hosting big names once upon a time, nobody remembered that. The Roxy's primary claim to fame was an infamous one. The drug binge that had claimed John Belushi in 1982 had begun in the upstairs lounge of The Roxy, a members-only corner called On The Rox.

Sonic Daydream had never played The Roxy, because after our first or second tour, the place was too small to have hosted the kind of crowds we'd started to draw. *I guess they'll let anybody in there these days,* I thought nastily.

"Are you busy today?" Ernie asked brightly, and it sounded as if he really believed there was even the remotest possibility that I might be. He was almost as good at acting as Lisa. "The band's meeting at Mohini's. It's the other part of my idea. Your idea, actually."

"The band?"

Ernie paused and when he spoke again, there was a strange, tiny brand of what could only be called hope in his voice. "Yeah. Me and Lenny and Denny. And you, of course."

In character as Jake Blues, Belushi, dead for thirty-six years, spoke in my head: *We're putting the band back together.*

We're on a mission from God, Elwood added.

I guffawed out loud. "All right, Ernie. Is Iris gonna be our road dog?" He couldn't possibly be serious.

"It was your idea, Cal. You were the one that said we should start dropping a few curses of our own. Like those things they keep texting you."

"I think that's stopped, but I did just get a video. That's what I called you about. Wait till you see it. Lisa and Phil are the new power couple of rock and roll."

"What kind of video?" Embarrassed alarm tinged Ernie's voice, and I realized that he was imagining pornography, like the dream I'd had of a feeling-betrayed Lisa and a young-again Dennis Whitly.

"She wrote a song about our doomed love affair. Complete with a neat little death threat at the end. She sent a clip of her performing it, with Phil slobbering all over her onstage."

"How do you feel about that?"

"Dude. Really?"

"Don't give me *Dude, really,* Cal. I know what she meant to you."

Anything For a Good Time Ernie LaBelle was now an expert on love, on *feelings,* since he was experiencing some himself for the first time. But he was right. Lisa had meant the world to me. But I was trying to let it go, and her childish death-threat video, meant to inspire jealousy, had unintentionally helped toward that end.

I told Ernie, "Here's how I feel about it. I'm happy for them. I wish them many glorious years of writing bad songs, playing Arizona firetraps, and having acrobatically callisthenic sex together." I paused to let Ernie wince at that one. "Lisa's copying her mother – she's found the guitar player of her dreams. Now maybe she'll forget all this supernatural reincarnation-revenge bullshit and leave us alone."

"Do you really believe that?"

"I can hope, right?"

"God helps those who help themselves, my brutha," Ernie said with a giggle of his own.

"Are you hiring a priest for this Sonic Daydream reunion at the occult bookstore? Thirty pieces of silver and all to assure our betrayal to Satan of the demon-worshippers?"

"It was your idea, Cal."

"What was my idea?"

"Iris says she knows of a ritual we could do. She says we could tape it and send it to them. It could be just like this thing that Lisa sent to you."

Again I laughed. "And then they'll post it on the internet, Ernie, for Christ sake. We'll make the cover of *Rolling Stone* again. *Sonic Daydream Embraces Satanism, Plans Comeback. Ozzy Applauds.* Are you out of your fucking mind? What did Denny say?"

"They put Valerie in a coma, Cal. Iris says that none of our faces have to appear on camera. Nobody but Phenex will know it's us, and once they see it . . . She says it's really powerful. Denny's down."

"I'll see you in an hour or so." It had been my idea, after all, to dose Phenex with a little of their own ridiculous, witchy medicine.

And with my lightened mood, I discovered that I was looking forward to seeing Iris again.

SIXTY-FIVE

When the purple-eyed witch wasn't within earshot, Ernie referred to it as *The Great Inspired Ritual of We're Done Fucking Around.*

If one believed in Santa Claus and the Easter Bunny, the demon Phenex and the universal forces unseen, then, according to a quiet and solemn Iris, the invocation she had in mind to use against Candy and her minions was fierce in its awesome power. It would free us forever from their harassment.

The Knights of Sonic Daydream – which I insisted upon calling us while we engaged in this ridiculous claptrap – through Iris's help, would summon no lesser an entity than the demon Ashmedai. He was mostly thought of as a lust demon, *responsible for twisting people's sexual desires,* according to Wikipedia. Overseer of incubi, dealer at Hell's baccarat table – Wikipedia didn't just make this shit up – Iris assured us that he was also a prince of revenge, a heavy hitter, higher in rank than puny Phenex. Ashmedai was a King of Hell instead of a mere Marquis. When Candy was made aware that we'd called upon him to be our protector, she'd have no choice but to pack up her crystal ball and give up. Lisa would just have to save Elise's soul and her own by some other means.

"Get thee to a nunnery," Lenny said in his still odd voice.

It was so strange; I'd never expected to ever find myself in a room with my bandmates again. Ernie's latest call to me – which now seemed like it had occurred sometime about the time Rome fell – hadn't been totally unexpected, of course. He'd dropped a text or a call, paid me the one brief visit in the years since Sonic Daydream had called it quits.

Ernie had kept in touch, and my effortless reconciliation with Lenny had been a pleasant surprise. He'd refused to take on the role of his brother's offended keeper, and he and I had fallen back once again into the easy friendship that we'd shared as young men.

But here I was, sitting in a folding chair in Iris's office, and here was Denny Whitly sitting beside me. If someone had told me that I was destined to run afoul of demon-worshippers, that I was to find the young love of my life and then lose her again over a bunch of ridiculous supernatural hogwash; if they'd then told me that I'd be sitting next to my old singer, and we wouldn't have our hands at each other's throats – I would've taken the former as par for the course compared to the utter impossibility of the latter.

Denny wasn't going to be inviting me to Thanksgiving dinner with his still wounded family anytime soon, and he didn't take me by the hand and lead me down Memory Lane with nostalgic reminiscences of our band's heyday. But neither did he frown or sneer resentfully at me anymore.

Making me recant the suppositions that I'd put forth in *Sonic Nightmare* no longer seemed to be important to him. In the final analysis of past, present, and future, it was only Sophia's opinion that really mattered to Denny, and since she'd told me unequivocally that she didn't believe a word I'd written – Denny was content to cease calling me a lying traitor.

While his wife believed the truth he'd told her, I still believed the truth I'd told the world, however, so Denny and I were never going to be pals again, if we'd ever been pals. But we had this new absurdity to deal with, so we treated each other politely, as if we were merely acquaintances with neither shared past nor contentious disagreement.

And added to that, I caught a glance from him every now and then, as we sat listening to Iris's lesson on the ritual summoning of Ashmedai. My old friend Ernie had never been one for keeping things to himself, so it was inescapable that he'd told Denny about the extent of my love for Lisa, especially since he understood it, now that he had Bianca. So the expression that I saw cross Denny's face was a mirror of Ernie's pity.

I remembered his words backstage at the Just Us Festival, and it was clear that he remembered them, too. *I hope you die all alone, because you don't deserve anything better. Then I hope you rot in hell, unmourned.* The look on Denny's face said that he regretted these cruel words because it was now obvious that they would come to pass.

I wanted to tell him to save his pity, because I'd done it all to myself. *For long you live and high you fly, but only if you ride the tide.* I'd gambled, I'd lost, and I'd live with it. At least I hadn't been a coward like he'd been. There was no forgiveness on either of our parts, and there never would be. That kind of uplifting redemption only happens in the movies. But I was glad that we weren't going to fight anymore over something that could never be settled.

Iris said, "As part of the ritual, I'll need something from each of you. Some possession that's precious to you, something that's difficult for you to part with."

"Like what?" Lenny asked. "I don't have much left."

Iris smiled kindly at him. "Once upon a time, it would've been a valued fruit of your labor. You remember your Old Testament? Cain and Abel?"

I rolled my eyes. "Me, maybe. Not them. Godless heathens. All three of them."

Denny favored me with a mild smile, but still I saw that pity in his eyes.

Iris ignored me. "Briefly, and for my purposes, Cain and Abel brought offerings to God, and Abel's were accepted, while his brother's were not. Abel brought his best to the Lord, but Cain didn't." She smiled at our blank looks.

"I'm telling you to not be like Cain, gentlemen. When I tell you that Ashmedai requires something that is dear to you, I'm asking you to choose something that is actually dear to you. That's why they call it a sacrifice."

Lisa's words: *The forces unseen aren't generous. But they can be persuaded, their favors bought with the proper sacrifices.* It seemed that every discussion I had with these people about their absurd beliefs repeated some previous conversation about the same stupid bullshit. All their arguments were circular. Based on the same idiot premises, they revolved mindlessly, like medieval wrongness, the sun orbiting the Earth instead of the other way around, the transmogrification of lead into gold.

Iris told us to go home, choose our sacrifices. She encouraged us to meditate on the actions we were about to take, again cautioned us that once begun, the ritual could not be stopped. Once Ashmedai had been invoked as our protector, his influence could not be rescinded. He would block all threats to our well-being, whether astral or material.

"He'll *loose the fateful lightening of his terrible swift sword?"* I grinned at my own cleverness.

Iris didn't return my smile. "This is just what I'm talking about, Cal. Even though you don't believe, you're embarking on a course . . . Candy and Lisa will believe in the power, the *finality* of our sending. It's not a joke – it shouldn't be to you, and it certainly won't be to them."

"In other words, don't stick those pins in that voodoo doll unless you're sure you want to inflict pain," Ernie said and winked at Iris.

Still she didn't smile. "Maybe this isn't such a good idea."

Legendary singer/songwriter Dennis Whitly spoke up. "It's not a joke to me. My daughter still has staples in her head. I'm not saying that I believe it'll really work, but I'm willing to try. I'm willing to curse them as thoroughly as this guy is able. What's his name again?"

"Ashmedai."

"I'm willing to invoke Ashmedai or Satan himself if it'll get them to leave us alone. I'm willing to stick pins in voodoo dolls. If they believe that what we're gonna do has the power to hurt them, then I say head on."

Ernie and Lenny nodded. Dennis Whitly had spoken, and his word was still law, just as it'd been in the old days. I'd always chafed a little bit under this autocracy, but I didn't argue this time. The whole thing had been my idea, after all.

"Can we do this at your house, Cal?" Ernie asked suddenly. "Like, in the garage, Iris? Would that work?"

She nodded.

Denny didn't have a garage: he'd converted it into a recording studio. Lenny didn't even have a house anymore. Ernie's fine old place was built at a time before a three car garage was necessary. He had a little barn in front and a little left of the house. It was scenic and lovely, but Ernie didn't even use it as a garage. He always parked the Porsche in the driveway directly in front of the house.

And once again, this idea to fight Phenex on their own terms had been mine, so I said okay. Sonic Daydream and Glinda the Good Witch would invoke Ashmedai, Prince of Revenge, at my McMansion in Temecula.

SIXTY-SIX

The Knights of Sonic Daydream arrived promptly at ten o'clock the following morning. I was tidying up the garage, had the door open, and watched their caravan-like approach down my quiet street: Denny in his black Benz and Ernie (with Iris) in his recently detailed, de-spelled Porsche, followed by Lenny in his old truck. I was pleased to see that Lenny was able to drive again.

The famous guitarists parked their German cars side by side in the driveway; Lenny left his Ford behind my Caddy out on the street. There was a tarp covering something in the bed, and seeing it took me back to the old, old days, the days even before Denny had joined the band, when we used to strap down all our equipment in the back of my old Dodge truck, and cover it similarly with a tarp.

Ah, the good old days, my resident demon began, but then a bitter reflection snapped like a firecracker in my mind, quick but still acrid, and shut him up. At least I'd had Elise for company in the good old days. Now I was alone again and would that way remain, whilst my three former bandmates were only alone for the day. Each had a good and loving woman waiting for him back at home.

Lenny and Barbie were staying with his brother and lady-wife for the duration, until their house was rebuilt. Bianca was either staying at Ernie's or he was staying in Big Bear. I wondered if maybe the six of them had all had a pleasant little couples' dinner party the night before, after Iris had dismissed us. Another thought: of course Ernie and the brothers Whitly would want to engage in this demon-invoking lunacy at my house. I had no one; no curious girlfriend to wonder what four old musicians and a purple-eyed witch were up to in the garage.

Iris carried a large, oblong satchel. It clanked when she set it down on the concrete floor of the garage, and I suddenly pictured the mythical accoutrements of the vampire-hunter: metal chisels for prying open the doors to mausoleums, for lifting off the marble slabs of tombs; wooden stakes and the hammers with which to pound them in.

Iris told us to go on into the house, to make ourselves a cup of coffee. She said it would take her a little while to purify the space, to chalk out the sacred circle on the floor. I pushed the button and the garage door clanked shut.

"Give me about forty-five minutes. Please knock before you come back in," Iris requested, then shooed us out through the other door, into the house.

"We don't have to wait until nightfall?" I said to Ernie. "The dark of the moon and all that?"

He returned my non-believer's smile, but before he could answer, the doorbell began to ring, insistently. Short, staccato bursts. *Nobody expects the Spanish Inquisition!* I thought, and felt a tiny pang that the last person who'd said that to me had been Lisa.

I opened the door and Katie gazed up at my face for only a fraction of a second before peeping around me at the unbelievable assemblage standing in the entranceway.

"Shit!" she whispered in undisguisable awe. She'd seen Ernie's Porsche, had seen the other members of Sonic Daydream stroll nonchalantly into the garage.

"Won't you come in, Katie?" I said to the top of her head. She stepped inside, took a few hesitant steps forward, then stopped again. Never would she be a groupie, but Katie still couldn't speak. She was in the presence of rock and roll deities, and stared at them in wordless idolatry.

"Gentlemen, I'd like you to meet my good friend, Katie. She's lead-guitar for a local band called The Piglets."

"I've heard of them," Ernie said immediately. "They're great."

Now the littlest guitar player looked at me in disbelief, and her voice was an acolyte's whisper at witnessing a miracle. "You played him our demo, Cal? You played our demo for . . . *Ernie LaBelle?"*

I tried to place what I'd done with The Piglet's CD after I'd tossed it onto the passenger seat of my car, but I came up empty. In my mind's eye, the pink pig on the sleeve flipped me off sullenly. The demo had probably fallen down under the seat; it had definitely been forgotten sometime during the billion years of geological time that had passed in my life since she'd given it to me.

"Not yet, Katie," Ernie said. "We've all been a little busy lately. But he's told us all about you."

"As a matter of fact, kid, today's your lucky day."

Katie's eyes bulged; her mouth fell open. The man himself, the one and only Dennis Whitly, had just addressed her. Then he went it one better: he stuck out his hand and said, "Hi, I'm Denny."

Lenny rolled his eyes at me as Katie reverently shook the legendary guitar god's hand. We were only the bassist and the drummer, so we were relegated to nobody status before a little girl's worship of her favorite guitarists, and both of us could hear her telling the story to the rest of her band later: "And then he says – get this, Casey! He says, 'Hi, I'm Denny.' Like I didn't know who he was!"

Ernie said, "What kind of axe you got, Katie?"

She glanced at me, and I smiled smugly. I imagined a new term entering her lingo, a very old term. An axe was no longer a tool for chopping wood if Ernie LaBelle still referred to their shared instrument as one.

"She's been using Sonny's Telecaster," I told him, and his face went as blank with amazement as hers.

"Where did she get –"

"It's a long story."

I'd donated Sonny's sad, cheap first drum kit to Goodwill, because, not unlike his mother, I couldn't bear to look at it, and in the eon of time that had passed since Katie and I had opened the boxes of *Fragell Musical Instrumnts,* I'd forgotten all about his Telecaster. In all this excitement, as Dirty Harry said, I'd also forgotten to tell Ernie how Sonny had foreseen his own death and mailed his axe to me ahead of time. All Ernie knew was that Sonny was dead – it'd been Lenny who'd connected the guitarist's demise with Phenex the big back bird and his own string of bad luck.

"Go get it," Denny suggested. "I'd like to hear you play." He smiled at Katie and I thought she might faint. It was a moment she'd remember for her entire life. "Don't worry about an amp."

"Cal doesn't have any –"

"Step outside to my office, Katie," Ernie said, and she accompanied him and Denny back out the front door.

I looked at my fellow nobody again, and Lenny closed his good eye, the one on the side unaffected by the stroke, and squinted at me. "Ernie didn't tell you, did he?"

It struck me that my old second-guitar had always been closed-mouthed about his plans until they started to happen – *What's up Ernie? I don't fucking know, dude.* When he'd known all along. He'd gone on tour with Azomite before any of us had even heard that he'd joined the band. There was the stunt he'd pulled asking Denny to appear with Phenex in San Bernardino. He'd run off back to Riverside to kill himself. I shook my head, unable to imagine what Ernie had up his sleeve this time.

Lenny stepped to the front door, made a sweeping gesture so I'd look outside. Denny had pulled the tarp off the back of the truck, and he and Ernie had already put one of the three moderately sized amps in the street. I whirled on Lenny. What I'd remembered being under the tarp in the old days was exactly what was under the tarp now.

"The little girl started to say it. *Cal doesn't have any amps.* The guitars are in the trunk of the Benz."

I did that fish out of water thing again, mouth opening and closing, no sound. Try as I might, not a word came to my mind. What Lenny was trying to tell me just couldn't be. Too many years had passed.

"You know how Phenex is playing The Roxy tomorrow night?" There was still just the tiniest slur to his voice, but he was almost back to normal. Nobody would even notice it except for people who knew him.

I nodded.

"Except they're not. We are."

He might as well have been speaking in a foreign language, in the Hebrew stamped on Candy's cursed medallions. I just wasn't getting it.

"Ernie thinks the whole video-the-ritual idea is good and all. But he wanted to add a little real-life kick to it, on the off chance that, despite what Iris says, the crazy bastards won't be any more impressed with it than we are.

"So Sonic Daydream's gonna do a little super-secret set for the lucky crowd at The Roxy, and because of time constraints, blah, blah, blah, Ernie's girlfriend bumped Phenex. They're not going on because . . . we are."

Lenny winked at me and walked outside to join Katie, who was standing in the street next to a PA, destined to amplify Dennis Whitly's famous voice. Ernie and Denny were carrying an amp up the walk. When they got to the door, I finally found my own voice. "Are you out of your fucking minds?"

"Scared, Cal?" Denny asked. "Afraid they'll hex you good if you see 'em in person?"

"This is to demonstrate who's boss," Ernie said. They set the amp down. "The spell deally is all good, but the one thing Candy's the most concerned about is being famous, right? They've got a contract for a record; there was really no way to screw 'em out of that. But this last show? Bumping the warm-up band, and for *us?* That's all covered under contingences or whatever they're called.

"It's just a gesture, Cal, but really, so is this ritual thing. To show 'em that we're in no way afraid of their hocus-pocus, even if they have hit us pretty hard by surprise. To show 'em we've got magic of our own? Wasn't that your plan? That's what the invocation is for.

"But this other thing – we're reminding Phenex just who they're fucking with, in the great scheme of rock and roll. When Sonic Daydream breezes into town and decides to play a set, all unannounced, EMI and the management at The Roxy trip over themselves to do whatever we tell 'em to do, the least of which is bumping the warm-up band."

"That's music biz magic," Lenny said.

"It's just a gesture," Denny repeated. He featured me with his world-renowned sly smile. "Are you in?"

"Is that why you brought . . ." I gestured at the equipment. "To *rehearse?"*

The idea of a Sonic Daydream rehearsal made the very word alien in my mouth.

"What are we gonna do for real equipment? How are we gonna . . ." These were just practice amps, not big enough for an actual show. The logistics of Sonic Daydream playing a set in Los Angeles, and *tomorrow night,* again rendered me speechless. It was impossible. It was insane.

"Poor, deluded Phillip has of course gone over to the dark side," Ernie said. "He just doesn't know how far over."

"Sonny said the same thing about you, once upon a time," I told him.

"Poor Sonny." Ernie frowned. "I wish I would've know him better."

"He had a lot of talent."

"How did the little girl wind up with his guitar?"

We watched the little girl and God's bass player carry another amp up the walk.

"He sent it to me," I told Ernie, then said again, "It's a long story. She doesn't know about . . . what happened."

Ernie nodded. His smile returned. He looked in the direction of the drum room, at the top of the house. "I don't suppose you have a dumbwaiter or anything to get these up there?"

I shook my head. "I think it's time for a roadie union break." Ernie sat on the little amp, and Lenny and his brother went out to get the last one, with Katie following like their shadow.

Ernie said, "So Phil is in the dark about this gig, just like Phenex is. It's all going to be a great, big, last minute surprise."

"How are we gonna –"

"We're gonna use The Desperate Princes' equipment. Their amps, their drum kit. You're not too much of a snob for that, are ya?"

"I guess not."

"Bianca told me that the news from the road is that no one is more happy to see this tour end than the southern boys. Something about Candy making eyes at their bassist in Albuquerque, and the all-around creepy vibe that they got from the big dumb drummer and rest of the band. The Desperate Princes desperately want to go back to New Orleans where they came from, where the voodoo's in the bayou and not appearing onstage ahead of them. So they're more than glad to let us use their equipment. They're honored, in fact."

Ernie LaBelle, who had been a road dog for the very briefest of times, had it all figured out, had all the angles covered. Just like he always did.

And of course he was right. Invoking Ashmedai was all well and good for the astral plane. But bumping Phenex from their last show – from what might be their last show ever as a signed band, for no other reason than because it was entirely effortless for us to do so – that was just the kind of recording industry *fuck you* gesture that ambitious Candy would not soon forget. I again thought of the smirking pink porcine on The Piglets' demo.

"So we have to rehearse." It was a statement for me now; it was sinking in as a concrete concept. *My band has to rehearse.* I looked at them, Lenny and Ernie and Denny, and Katie smiling so widely that I thought that her face would hurt later. It was Katie's smile that made it real for me. A legendary band, defunct since years before she was born, resurrected right here before her eyes! Oh, my God, she was going to get to watch Sonic Daydream *rehearse!*

"Go get your guitar, Katie," Ernie told her. "I understand that you can play *Cerulean.*"

The look on Katie's face communicated that she couldn't be more thrilled, yet the thrills kept coming.

"OMG, Cal! Mom's gonna kill herself!"

"What?" I started at this declaration, all the amusement I'd been feeling at her joy draining away. Even the merest mention of suicide would forever have that effect on me.

"She went to visit my aunt in Poway. She's missing this! She's missing her favorite band!"

SIXTY-SEVEN

Iris emerged from the garage just as Denny and Ernie started up the second flight of stairs to the drum room with the last amp. She closed the door carefully behind her, and looked with trepidation at the little girl clutching the guitar.

"This is no place for a child, Cal," Iris whispered to me, sotto voce. "The power of the ritual . . ."

"Go on upstairs with the band, Katie. Show 'em what you can do."

The Piglets' lead-guitar gave me an impromptu hug and gleefully skipped up the stairs.

I grinned at Iris. "Not to mention the fact that her daddy would have me arrested for exposing her to Satanism."

"It's not Satanism, it's –"

"Witchcraft. Bargaining with the forces unseen. I've heard." I was in such a good mood, I gave her shoulders a little squeeze. "I'm sorry. She just showed up. She saw the band . . ."

Iris smiled tightly. "It's okay, Cal. All has been prepared. Just let me go and put out the candles, then we can begin whenever you guys are ready."

"I'm sorry," I repeated. "They want to rehearse . . ." That alien word again. *Sonic Daydream wants to rehearse.* It reminded me of the cleverest title in rock and roll history – after a hiatus of fourteen some odd years, the Eagles' reunited for the *Hell Freezes Over Tour.* I wondered vaguely if I would go along if Denny suggested that we take to the road again. *Sonic Daydream Buries The Hatchet, Live!*

What else did I have to do?

Nah, that'll never happen. This Roxy gig was just one set; the secular half of Ernie's *Great Inspired Ritual of We're Done Fucking Around.*

"It's the thrill of a lifetime for Katie," I explained to Iris, as someone plugged into an amp upstairs and strummed a few reverberating chords. It was good to hear a live guitar in the McMansion, for the first time ever.

Perhaps I looked wistfully in that direction – there were four guitar plunkers up there, but not a single drummer – because Iris laid her hand on my shoulder and said, "Go ahead, Cal. I'll just put out the candles and join you. I guess it should be a thrill for me, too, hearing . . .?"

"Sonic Daydream."

"Hearing Sonic Daydream play." She smiled blankly. Iris didn't care about hearing us play; she wanted to invoke Ashmedai and deliver us from evil. But she was going to try to make the best of it, since it was unavoidable.

It wasn't a real rehearsal. Ernie picked up on Iris's need to achieve our protection, and Katie would've just been in the way. So he catered to her for a few minutes, adjudging her rendition of *Cerulean* to be sufficient for her to take his place.

I had to hand it to Katie: she didn't hesitate to play with a world famous band. She had confidence in her chops, and I was proud of her. She even told Ernie, "I know *Tomcats,* too."

"You heard the lady, my bruthas." Ernie sat on Denny's amp, and I counted off.

We were of course incredibly rusty, and God's bass player was still learning to play left-handed; we weren't really up to much more than a fourteen-year-old guitar player, at least for *Cerulean.* But we improved immeasurably for *Tomcats,* perhaps because it had been our biggest hit. Denny's voice was all that it had ever been, and my girl didn't even miss a chord when he smiled his famous smile at her. And when Ernie took over for *Down the Center* – he played Sonny's Telecaster – we sounded just fine. We were a bunch of creaky old guys, but we'd been great for a lot of years, and the greatness was still there. We just needed to blow the dust off of it.

The brief rehearsal concluded. Selfies were taken with Katie and the band. I thought that Denny had enjoyed the audience, worshipful, like in the old days, but without the groupie-lust aspect to it, so I told Katie that we had a little business to conduct, but she come could back when she heard us playing again.

"Are you getting the band back together?" she asked, and again I was reminded of Jake Blues. A pair of Ray-Bans, a fedora and big black sideburns sprouted on her head in my imagination.

"Maybe," Ernie said, and I watched him glance hopefully at Denny for a split second. "How do you think we sound?"

Katie pointedly avoided looking at God's bass player, who had been the weak link in Sonic Daydream's performance. "Maybe a little more practice," the honest young musician opined.

Ernie smiled and patted her fondly on the shoulder. "My thoughts exactly. Come on back later and see what you think then."

SIXTY-EIGHT

Denny had brought a curious modern device, an odd little tripod to hold a cellphone for the filming of the ritual.

Iris agreed to appear on camera, because despite the damage that Phenex's namesake band had already inflicted on four old rockers from Riverside, California, Iris believed that she was the more powerful sorceress. Not to mention her confidence in the righteous purpose of the ritual, and Ashmedai's precedence over the black bird Phenex in the rollcall of Hell's royalty.

There was an old wooden table in the garage, an antique of dubious provenance that I'd been meaning to refinish. Iris had dragged it into the center of the chalked protective circle and covered it with a black cloth. A small black brazier stood on spindly legs in the center. I couldn't help but grin at the silver faces of the demons that stared out contemplatively from the four cardinal points around it. An entirely mundane can of Sterno awaited flame at the bottom.

Iris removed the two candles that she had lit previously and replaced them with unburnt ones, explaining that now that we were all present and ready to begin, new candles were necessary to dispel any spiritual vibrations that may have been present when she had worked alone in the garage earlier. She explained that the candles were blue, denoting inspiration, occult wisdom, protection and devotion. I could only hold Ernie's gaze for a second, lest I bust up. It was all so ridiculous. The pointless gesture of an unannounced Sonic Daydream set at The Roxy seemed like sound business strategy by comparison.

Iris had already cautioned us to give the ceremony the respect it was due. "I want you to behave as you would if you found yourselves in a church or synagogue or mosque. No silly faces or smiling. *Assume a virtue, if you have it not.* As you would in the house of any faith, let your faces show polite interest, contemplation of the truths to be revealed."

She had schooled us in the four basic pillars of the ritual, the cornerstones of her belief in the unseen forces in general. Each of these would be covered in microcosm in the ceremony, and I was put in mind of the familiar practices of the Mass that I'd attended as a child. Everything was always the same: *May God be with you. And also with you.* Kneel, stand, sit, kneel. Only the sermon differed from week to week.

The first part of the ritual reinforced the principle of knowledge, and The Knights of Sonic Daydream fell irretrievably already, despite our polite, interested expressions. As if we were black-cowled believers standing before her in some dark forest, Iris extolled us: the core of magic was to know that it existed. Of course we believed none of it, but politely and with feigned interest, we responded at the appropriate time that we were confident in the universal energy that surrounded us.

The next part of the sermon – uh, the ritual – built upon the first. Since we had pledged that we knew that magic existed, now we would expound upon our will to wield it to our own ends. Since we acknowledged that the forces were there, as real as gravity and the revolution of the planet, now we aimed to petition them to do our bidding.

Iris grinned assertively, admitted to the incorporeal air that the five of us knew the risk we were taking. She bade the invisible forces to behold the daring of true believers, to grant our audience. This was the third pillar.

Again I heard Lisa's words: *It's dangerous to seek direct communication with a demon,* but they were bound to reply when properly called. Now came the actual invocation of Ashmedai, the display of the fearless moxie of the practitioner. At Mohini's, Iris had warned us not to step outside the protective circle on the floor, lest we be consumed – Ernie had threatened to push me out, just to see if it would work.

Next came the call for our sacrifices, the recompense for the demon's services. He was present, if Iris was to be believed, waiting. Yet I didn't feel so much as a lifting of the hairs at the back of my neck. It was all so much bullshit.

We had already given to Iris those possessions that were precious to us, those things with which it was difficult to part. She had them in a black velvet bag, and with a flourish, she opened it and set it on the table. Then she lit the prosaic can of Sterno with an equally prosaic Bic lighter, to heat the brazier to receive our offerings for burning. I watched as she lit a few strips of paper and threw them into the brazier, to make a live flame inside. The papers were thin, with small, closely printed words, and my not-polite and not-at-all-interested resident demon asked me if I thought that Iris had desecrated a copy of the Bible to aid in our protection. *What would your mother think?*

What a long, strange trip it's been, I replied.

Iris placed her hand over the mouth of the bag and asked Ashmedai to welcome our gifts. I noticed that her long nails were no longer sky-blue: she had painted them black for this serious ritual, like Candy's. Like the demon Phenex's in my dreams.

Ours were old men's, rich men's sacrifices: not valuable in and of themselves, because things of intrinsic value could always be replaced. No jewels or gold, no coveted electronics or thirty pieces of silver: each was simply a memento – fragile, paper remembrances – cherished, irreplaceable, yet worthless to anyone save ourselves.

Denny had contributed a childish rendering of a bunny rabbit, complete with glued-on, cotton ball tail. The spindly, blue-crayon scrawl said, *Happy, Eastre, Daddy, I love yuo,* and I wondered if computer-genius Valerie may have been afflicted with a touch of dyslexia, at least in pre-school, like loathsome Candy and her tragic inability to read music. Iris applied the lighter to this icon of Denny's baby's childhood and dropped it into the brazier.

Lenny had lost all of his possessions, treasured and otherwise, in the fire that he was convinced had been set by our enemies. His contribution had been hanging on the wall at his brother's house, and now it was to be tossed to the flame also. It was a photograph, showing a grinning, impossibly young, gloriously happy Lenny – had he really ever had so much hair? Standing beside him was Flea.

I remembered the night the picture had been taken; again, it was from Portland, from our first tour. Like a scene from *Hedwig and the Angry Inch,* the Chili Peppers had appeared that night at the Rose Garden Arena, one of the town's largest venues. Sonic Daydream had done a little better than Bilgewater's, but the Roseland Theater was not the Rose Garden Arena, not by a long stretch. Venues of that size were still in our band's future.

Our set was late; we went on at the Roseland long after the Chilis had finished their show, and Flea, apparently looking for something to do, had just wandered into the club. Nobody recognized him while he was out in the crowd, certainly not me, and not even Lenny. It was not until after our set that we realized that we had been observed by rock and roll royalty: Flea took the time to come backstage and tell the not-yet-proclaimed God's bass player that he liked his licks.

Lenny had of course been flattered beyond the pale; the look on his face in the picture was identical to the slightly dazed look of wonder that had been Katie's stock expression whilst she rehearsed with us. Since he had nothing else left, the picture of Lenny and the famous bassist was indeed one of his prized possessions.

Ernie gave up the CD of our first demo, pre-Denny. This item had a little bit of real-world value – the copies of it that we had once handed out for free at The House of Ale now fetched exorbitant sums on eBay. But this was the original, recorded in my parents' garage in Riverside, a lifetime ago.

My own contribution to the ritual was like my bandmates, just a memento of a snatch of time, a relic of happier days, a memory of a person that no longer existed.

Once upon a time, on the tour bus ride from Frisco to LA, neither Elise nor I could sleep, mostly because it was broad daylight. But neither could we talk, because it would've awakened the rest of the band, each deep in the dreamland of siesta. So to pass the time, we'd played a little game, the result of which I now condemned as sacrifice to forces in which I refused to believe.

On the back of a flyer for some forgotten band, Elise had written a line from *Tomcats: Kitties and cats wanna do their thang, been thinkin' 'bout lovin' since the school bell rang.* She underlined *bell* and whispered to me that it was now my turn, that I had to come up with a line from another song that used that word.

Amused, I wrote, *But he could play a guitar, just like a'ringing a bell.*

Elise had given me her delightful, devious grin. She wrote: While my guitar *gently weeps.*

Break it to me gently, I'd written next. It was the song that Lisa would sing to me a lifetime later, the song that would capture my attention, make me notice her, make me want her.

Elise had giggled, looked over her shoulder in mock alarm, to see if her laughter had disturbed anyone. Ernie and Lenny and her beloved Denny snoozed on. She wrote: *And if my day keeps going this way, I just might, break your fuckin' face tonight.*

I didn't recognize the lyric. I would of course hear the song a million times afterwards, but *Break Stuff* was newly released at the time.

In her round, school girl's hand, in explanation, Elise had written *Limp Bizkit.*

Next I'd put: *Oh, what can it mean, to a daydream believer and a homecoming queen?*

Elise had frowned playfully, whispered that I was cheating, that *day* and *daydream* were not the same word. Then she wrote: *She's a killer queen.*

We'd filled up the whole back of the flyer in this manner.

When we got to LA, I roused my sleeping bandmates, and all of us went into a tall building for some perfunctory meeting with Sony. Denny and Elise cut out early and took a limo home. She'd given me a cheerful smile and a wink, as Barbie droned on meaningless details about the next tour, a tour that would never be. It was the last time I'd ever see Elise. She'd kill herself later that night.

As Iris chanted and the smoke from our dubious sacrifices roiled upwards, I reflected that none of them were truly lost. Ernie had copied his priceless demo onto his computer; not only it, but all the other homemade, pre-Oscar-Woodbine-mixed cuts we'd ever recorded could fit on a modern DVD nowadays. Lenny had scanned his precious photo with Flea, as I had my last happy memento of Elise. Denny had photographed his baby's cute bunny rabbit. Ashmedai and the flames got the originals, but our little tokens would be forever electronically preserved.

Iris finished the ritual: she banished the demon as she had invoked him. After the interval of a few silent heartbeats, she adjudged that he was indeed gone back to Hell, and it was therefore safe for us to leave the protected circle. She again shooed us from the garage in order to erase the evidence of our ritual. Sonic Daydream went back upstairs to rehearse.

Far away, across the fields, like *the tolling of the iron bell,* the noise of old hits, played live by their originators for the first time in decades, *called the faithful to their knees, to hear the softly spoken magic spell.* Katie brought her mom with her, breathless and flushed with the unbelievable anticipation of seeing her favorite band reconstituted, and right across the street. Apparently, Katie had informed Allison of the once-in-a-lifetime opportunity she was missing, and the visit to Poway had been immediately curtailed. She'd made excuses to her sister and returned immediately.

Even Katie's dad came over. We were at last formerly introduced – his name was Steven – and after he perceived that I had no interest in his wife (despite the way she stared at me – she was my fan, after all), he relaxed. He was about as impressed with our act as Iris was: Katie whispered to me with a little moue of disgust that Dad had always liked country music.

A party atmosphere reigned. Ernie actually asked my permission to invite Barbie and Sophia and Bianca down from Riverside to join us, instead a springing another surprise on me. It was still early afternoon, and as always, my pantry was stocked. Why not have a barbeque, a little impromptu, Sonic-Daydream-reunion celebration?

Whilst we waited for the ladies' arrival, Lenny told me that Bianca had become fast friends with Barbie and Sophia during the weeks of my self-imposed, depressed seclusion. Barbie and Bianca had the music biz in common, and all three of them, being the women of famous musicians, had immediately bonded. They took the train down from Riverside, so they could each ride back home with their man. *Isn't that cute?* my resident demon commented sourly. Denny went and picked them up at the station in the Benz.

It was fun. Like her husband, Sophia had buried her dislike of me; she featured me with a smile, a friendly hug and a kiss on the cheek. Barbie also hugged me, then held me at arm's length and solemnly asked me how I was doing. I told her blithely that all was well, and for the sake of the guests present, she pretended to believe me.

I was at last permitted the supreme pleasure of meeting Bianca. I had expected nothing less than an exotic and stunning woman to have at last ensnared perennial playboy Ernie LaBelle, and his lady-love did not disappoint. She was striking: a tall Negress of about forty-five, with flawless skin the color of milk chocolate, and positively mesmerizing tan eyes. I was immediately smitten, dumbfounded by her beauty.

She smiled and hugged me like we were old friends. Even though I knew that Ernie had no doubt told her the sad tale of my recent, doomed love affair, there was no pity for me in Bianca's conspiratorial expression. *Fuck all that,* her laughing eyes said.

She gave Ernie an affectionate kiss and told me, "Ernie says you know the oldies. So I know you'll feel me when I say, *The future's so bright, I gotta wear shades.*"

I smiled at her, although I was uncertain about the brightness of my future. Once they all went home, I would be *alone again, naturally.* My ever-surly demon said, *How's that for an oldie for ya, Bianca?* But I silenced him, and watched Denny smile at her also. Bianca had quoted one of the few songs in the entire catalogue of rock and roll that he'd once graced with his highest praise: *I wish I'd written that.*

Steven proved himself to be an excellent hand at the art of outdoor cooking, and of course all the sides that Iris and the other ladies whipped up were scrumptious. There was some perfunctory discussion of designated drivers, until I invited them all to stay the night. Then the drinking commenced.

The McMansion was full, overfull really, every room occupied. Denny and Sophia shared one of the small bedrooms; Ernie and Bianca took the one that poor sacrificed Sonny had shared with Candy on the long-ago night after Phenex had recorded their demo. Lenny and his bride occupied the room on the ground floor, off the hallway where once I'd gone back three times to peep through the open door at a naked, sleeping teenaged girl.

I lent my own bed to Iris, and went up the last flight of steps and passed out on the couch in the drum room. It was large and comfy and I dreamed.

A woman walked toward me down a brick-lined corridor. The ceiling was arched and the space was very narrow: the woman bent her arms and trailed her fingers along the bricks on either side of her as she approached. She was backlit; a silvery glow shone palely through the gauzy whiteness of a modest dress, immodestly revealing the curve of her hips and the length of her long legs, but her face remained in shadow. She paused before stepping out into the light, but my dream-self knew already that it was Iris, clad once again in the demure white gown with the scarlet sash.

As if it was the most natural act in the world, I embraced her. She smiled fondly at me, put her arms around my neck. I got the uncanny impression that it was not so much a fantasy of sleep as *a sending:* one floor below me, Iris was dreaming the same thing, and it was an invitation. If I woke myself up and quietly padded down the stairs, she would not be surprised to see me. She would welcome me into my own bed . . .

But even asleep, I didn't really believe in sendings and shared dreams, so I didn't wake myself up. I decided to just go with it as it was, as a product of my own subconscious; I was fond of Iris, and I was free now, after all. It was more rational than the risk of just be-bopping on down the stairs uninvited and waking a confused and perhaps outraged woman in real life. That would just be silly.

But as I went to kiss Iris in my dream, there was a bright flash of light, a clap of thunder, and Lisa appeared beside us, emerged from a theatrical puff of smoke. She was dressed as she'd been the day we'd met: white tank and tan cargo pants, without make-up, her black tresses caught up in a high pony-tail. She glanced at Iris with a smug, young woman's disdain, and wiggled her nose like Samantha of *Bewitched* fame. I even heard the tinkling bell.

Then Iris in her chaste white dress was gone from my arms, replaced by Lisa, now wearing a short, sexy, curve-hugging, red satin number. My brain's simple, laid-on-with-a-trowel symbolism was clear: the white and the red, the pure and the carnal, the good witch and the very bad one.

Lisa smiled curiously at me, as if playfully asking me what all that hugging the old broad had been about. This was what I wanted, and she knew it. She whispered, "I've been reassessing destiny, Cal."

And like all the dreams I'd had of her, it was so realistic that I shivered at the feel of her soft breath in my ear, at the pleasure of the sorely-missed music of her low, lyrical voice.

"I've come to the conclusion that the only part that matters is that we were meant to be together. To hell with Denny's damnation." She giggled prettily at her own devilish pun. "I love you. All is forgiven. Now kiss me."

The taste of her exquisite mouth was as intoxicating as it had ever been. But because it was only a dream, I snapped awake. For a moment, I didn't know where I was – was Lisa here beside me? I inhaled and thought I could still smell her familiar perfume. But then my drums resolved themselves in the dimness of the room, and realty returned. I was all alone, sleeping on the couch like an orphan in my own house. The band and their ladies (and Iris, too) were downstairs. Sonic Daydream was playing The Roxy tonight. We'd invoked the demon Ashmedai as our protector.

Lisa's voice, repeated from the outskirts of sleep: *I love you. All is forgiven.*

But a dream was just the random firing of synapses during sleep, interpreted by a wishful-thinking mind. It had no more bearing on real life than did invocations or curses or anti-good-luck charms. I sighed, wishing that it could be true – *Now kiss me* – but knowing that it wasn't, I turned over and went back to sleep. Lisa still hated me. I had betrayed her. Mercifully, there were no more dreams.

The morning dawned as it inexorably will, but both host and guests missed it. As befitting old guitarists and their women, a washed up drummer and a purple-eyed witch, after an unaccustomed night of drinking and socializing, we all slept in until noon.

After a tasty brunch, the ladies prepared to decamp, and I discovered that they had not taken the train down so that they could return to Riverside with their men, after all. I was sure that it had been at Ernie's direction: Sophia and Iris left in the Benz, Bianca took the Porsche, and Barbie the truck, leaving the equipment.

Sonic Daydream needed to rehearse yet, and the four of us could take the Caddy to The Roxy. What with all the supernatural machinations in the works, the ladies had declined to attend the unannounced reunion on the Sunset Strip. They would meet us back at Ernie's hacienda after the show.

SIXTY-NINE

The infamous On The Rox Club was on the second floor of The Roxy, in the front part of the building. I looked curiously down the darkened hall that led to it. A bouncer from the club shook his head and pointed in the opposite direction, told us to enter the first door on the right.

There were a couple of green rooms here in the back part of the old building, and of course, one of the world's most successful bands merited the best one: it had the unique feature of a little window in the wall that overlooked the stage below.

The brothers Whitly plopped down on a couch; Lenny propped his feet up on an ancient, scarred coffee table in front of it. He said, *"Johnny looked around him and said, 'Well, I've made the big time at last.'"*

Ernie giggled. He closed the door and hovered beside it. I sat in a very old, very worn recliner and looked through the hole in the wall – there was no glass – and pondered that some of the greats of yesteryear might've sat in this very chair and done the same thing. *Johnny's life passed him by like a warm summer day; if you listen to the wind, you can still hear him play.*

To my utter surprise, I saw Lisa standing on the stage, looking right at me. She inclined her head, a curious, questioning glance, and my dream came back to me in all of its crystal clarity.

A knock on the door made me jump, diverted my attention from her. Ernie opened it to reveal Chrissy standing in the hall, speaking in a loud voice not to a bouncer, but to an officious-looking management lackey: "It says *all access,* son, and that includes – oh, thank Christ, Ernie!"

She stepped into the room and gave him a big hug; still in the hallway, the lackey gesticulated apologetically. "It does say *all access,* Mr. LaBelle."

"She's all right, Ricky. Just keep the rest of them out. Mr. Whitly doesn't feel like signing autographs right now." Ernie shut the door in the lackey's face.

As was his due as a rock legend, Chrissy spared Mr. Whitly a gawp of awe. But she was a professional road manager – and already good friends with Denny's equally famous second-guitar – so her amazement was brief.

"What *the fuck,* Ernie?" she exclaimed and hugged him again. "What's been going on since Vegas? Candy said you abandoned the tour because you guys broke up, and I shouldn't text or call you –"

"It was quite a bitter break up," I said and smiled at her.

Chrissy didn't return my smile. I saw that familiar flash of pity in her eyes: just like everyone else, The RaceCats' road dog knew that the end of my thing with Lisa had to have been hard on an old guy. Then a type of embarrassment veiled her expression and she quickly looked back at Ernie. It was bad enough that it was over, but perhaps I was unaware of the insult that had been added to my injury. Maybe I didn't know about the on-the-road hijinks taking place between my former lover and her band's frontman.

"Candy and I – it was never like that, Chrissy."

"She surely thought it was."

"I broke a thousand hearts before I met you," Lenny crooned in his still-odd voice. He had a million of 'em this evening.

Ernie shook his head with mock sadness. "I was just trying to help out my daughter's band, Chrissy."

"Then you fell off the world."

"Almost literally," I said, but Chrissy still wouldn't look at me. She didn't trust herself to do so. She didn't want to be the one to let the cat out of the bag that my former girlfriend had already moved on.

"And then you show up here with . . ." Chrissy again blinked in disbelief at Dennis Whitly, rock star, and his brother, God's bass player. "And it's all on the down low? No one's supposed to know that you're gonna do a set?"

"Who told you?" Ernie asked.

I raised an eyebrow at this. Who did Ernie think told her? Chrissy was the headliner's road manager, and she was also no doubt more or less responsible for all three of the record company's interests on this tour. Candy surely didn't know anything about looking after a band on the road, and like Sonic Daydream of old, I'd heard that the bass player for The Desperate Princes handled their business.

"I got an email from Sissy at EMI. It was like a fucking telegram. She's too busy to be clear in what she had to say. All that was missing were the *stops* between the little sentences. *Line-up change at The Roxy. Big act playing after The RaceCats –"*

"Bump Phenex." Ernie grinned.

"Right." Chrissy studied him suspiciously. "I don't like being in the dark about shit like this, so I wheedled it out of Kevin, the boss here. Out of a clear blue sky, Sonic Daydream decides they want to reunite and play The Roxy, and it just happens to be on the night that Ernie LaBelle's kid's band is gonna be there."

"So now everybody knows?"

"Nobody knows, Ernie," Chrissy returned irritably. "Kevin said it was all on the down low, so I didn't say anything yet. Phenex's hanging around downstairs with my band. They were all told that the green rooms weren't ready yet. The Desperate Princes went down the street for a drink. Phenex is gonna get the bad news when they go to load-in. So, I'm asking you again. What the fuck, Ernie?"

"Just call it an old man's whim, and leave it at that, Chrissy."

"Where's your equipment?"

"We're gonna use the southern boys'."

"You let a bunch of backwater hillbillies in on all this weirdness, but not us?"

"It's just a whim." Ernie glanced at us and grinned. "I'd say we're entitled to it, wouldn't you?"

Chrissy shrugged. "Whatever. It all pays the same."

Lisa knows we're here. I peered out the square hole in the wall again; she was still gazing up at me with that adorable curious smile. I watched Phillip cross the stage, speak to her, attempt to embrace her. She sidestepped his hug and held the flat of her palm up to his face; the archetypical demonstration of the old 90s expression *talk to the hand.* I grinned. Could there be trouble in rock and roll paradise already?

Phillip said something else, but Lisa was steadfast. Whatever he wanted her to do, she wasn't in the mood. After a second, he shrugged and hopped off the stage. Lisa's mysterious smile lingered. I realized that I wasn't sure if she could actually see me or not: I thought the glare from the overhead stage lights was wrong, and she wasn't precisely making eye-contact with me.

She tilted her head a little to one side and her smile became more welcoming, again, just like I'd dreamt. Whether she could see me or not, I was sure she knew I was there. *Come on down and see me, Cal,* she seemed to say. *I miss you. All is forgiven.*

I actually started to stand up from the old recliner, to go to her. Then I sat back down, then stood all the way up. Hell, yeah. Why not? What was she gonna do, stab me in the middle of The Roxy?

"Who wants a drink?"

"They're gonna see you –"

"Nobody's seen the rest of you," I told Ernie. "If they see me, they'll think I'm just here because I want to see . . ." I shook my head. "It's a free country. I'm of age, I can be in a bar. They'll get the bad news when they go to load-in, just like Chrissy says. Who wants a drink?"

"I sure do." The RaceCats' road dog plopped down in the recliner I'd just vacated. She glanced out the square hole in the wall and opined that maybe she'd just watch the whole weird-ass gig from up here.

The brothers Whitly raised their hands for a drink, and Ernie followed. We'd traveled together for a long time, had once been best friends. I remembered what they all drank.

Lisa was waiting for me at the foot of the stairs. As if he was a stone statue, she ignored the bouncer who was guarding access to the inner sanctum from whence I descended. Lisa was above arguing with bouncers about where she was and wasn't allowed to be.

If there truly was anything like witchcraft, then this was it, my dream re-enacted. She knew that I'd come to her if she smiled at me, or if she just smiled in my direction. I glanced up and found that the little window to the green room was visible from this angle, but I still didn't think it could've been seen from where she'd stood onstage. Yet somehow, she'd known I was here. I didn't believe in dream wishes or any kind of precognition; I figured that perhaps Chrissy wasn't as closed-mouthed with her buddy Candy as she wanted Ernie to believe.

Lisa wordlessly took my hand and led me down a corridor behind the stage. She was apparently known to the bouncer guarding this passageway, as he let us go by unchallenged. She pushed open the back door, and I just had time to think that it was gonna lock behind us, that I was gonna have to go around to the front of the club to get back in, but no one was gonna recognize an old drummer, anyway, garish Roxy All Access Pass around my neck or no . . .

Then Lisa roughly pushed me up against the building and started to kiss me: hard, urgently, like she had after her first performance before a big crowd.

I let her kiss me for a moment, reveling in the sorely missed glory of it; her scent, the thrill of her perfect young body grinding against mine. But when she bit me on the neck and whispered that she wanted me, I couldn't resist.

"What about Phillip?"

"Who?" She grinned, and the reflection from the streetlight made the white of her teeth glisten. "This is destiny, Cal." She tugged me across the narrow concrete to a van, new. It still had paper license plates. It amused me that it was baby-blue, the same color as Ernie's Porsche. The windows were tinted as black as the pitch of legend, as black as Candy's jealous, unforgiving heart. The demon's sigil graced a magnetic sign pasted on the side.

Lisa embraced me again, put one hand into the back pocket of my jeans, gave me a little squeeze on the ass to let me know she was glad to see me. She paused long enough to slide the door of the van open. Then she shoved me playfully, but with definite, delightful intent. I climbed into the van, and before the door had clunked all the way closed, Lisa pushed me down on the long bench seat and climbed astride me. Before the overhead light winked out, I just had time to note Phenex's equipment, still stowed in the back.

There's not gonna be any load-in tonight, I recalled, and wondered for a split-second how quickly Lisa's newfound forgiveness and familiar friendliness were gonna evaporate once she found out that age and treachery had once again outfoxed youth and not-too-much skill; that Phenex wasn't going to perform tonight because a much better band had exercised their well-earned prerogative to take the stage in their stead. But I didn't think about it too long, however, because she started kissing me again.

I had an inkling then of how my good friend Ernie LaBelle had lived his life. Not that he was ever suspicious of his groupies – Ernie was the least suspicious person I'd ever known – but *the so many women, so little time* reality of his touring years had to have lent him the kind of detachment I was experiencing at that moment. I was suspicious of Lisa, and inescapably: there was no reason for her delusion to have abated, no reason for her to have forgiven me. She had to have some ulterior motive for this unexpected show of affection, so I held on to a separate alertness. I was sure that the same kind of thing had to have also accompanied Ernie's adventures in groupie-land.

Don't get me wrong, I was digging it, but there was a distinct lack of *Can You Feel The Love Tonight*-style hope and joy at the sudden and unanticipated return of Lisa's desire for me, dream or no goddamned dream. There was the very real possibility that she might at any second attempt to slit my throat, let me bleed out all over the slick backseat of Phenex's brand new tour van – nobody would be able to see my body through the blacked-out windows, and they'd just toss me in an anonymous LA dumpster on the way back to Riverside.

And there was also the idea of Lisa's recent *collaboration horizontale* with young Phil. She hadn't been thinking about our destiny then.

Hey, hey what can I do? I got a woman who won't be true, but there was no reason not to take advantage of my turn, just like Fred and ol' Bobby Plant had done. Once Lisa found out that Sonic Daydream would be preventing them from performing their last show, just because we could; once she viddied our recorded invocation of Ashmedai – yeah. Despite whatever it was she wanted to call what was taking place right now, Lisa was gonna hate me again in the very near future. So I might as well enjoy it – it was *so* enjoyable – because it was undoubtedly gonna be the last time.

Lisa had always been not-shy, but to hear her tale, there had only been Ryan and me. And now, of course, there had been her close, personal friend Phil. But Lisa tore at my clothes with a gusto that I would've expected from a girl with much more experience in these things. It was so strange – if I was inclined to believe any of this reincarnation bullshit, this would've been the moment. Lisa was suddenly like Elise had described herself, before she'd begun her forever celibate, bride-of-Christ worship of Dennis Whitly. Elise had always been the initiator with her boyfriends, or so she'd told me.

And now, Lisa seemed the same way, almost brutally aggressive, and that was why I was put in mind of her insane claims of reincarnation: it was as if all the desire, overwhelming, relentless, that long-dead Elise had harbored for Denny had coalesced in the very air. Lisa was now, inexplicably, feeling it all for me.

I understood Ernie's perennial confidence, his wonderful, insufferable ego. Since my romantic ideals of love for Lisa were held in suspicious suspension at the moment, I was able to look at her the way Ernie had looked at his groupies: there was all this mad desire to *get at* lil' ol' me, when, right then, I could take her or leave her.

But her desire was an incredible balm to my sore ego, powerful, almost better than the sex itself. Amid the techno beat of a drum machine, the theatrical piano slides, Bonnie Tyler rasped urgently in my head: *He's gotta be sure, and it's gotta be soon, and he's gotta be larger than life.*

Lisa needed a hero? I was certainly down, even though there was no reason whatsoever to believe that she'd given up her insane quest; no reason to believe that *all had been forgiven.* I'd betrayed her, gone over to the enemy camp, so the part of me that had become aloof, emotionally detached from this young woman I'd loved so completely – that part kept its figurative eye peeled for a weapon. Other than that, *I dribbled off my Bobby Brooks and let her do what she pleased.*

I won't lie and say that my emotional indifference made the act last any longer than was befitting a man of my years, surprised by the young lover that he'd believed he'd never touch again. Chris Cornell wailed in my head: *Is this a cure or is this a disease?* But unlike my recent dreams of her, it did come to fruition – I saw that triumphant glint in her blue eyes, even in the darkness of the van – and she didn't morph into one of the Universal monsters.

But neither did she have time to speak, to explain her change of heart. She collapsed on my chest, panting; and before I could sigh, *What's it all about, Alfie?* her thrice-damned mother was hammering on the side of the van.

"Open the fucking door, Lisa!"

"Jesus, Mom!" she yelled back, and the noise was deafening so close to my ear. "What are you, my shadow?"

"Christ, you are so stupid!" Candy pulled on the door handle. In a life devoid of miracles, I thought that now I was surely witnessing one. Despite her urgency, Lisa had been insightful enough to lock the door.

"Hold on a minute, Mom!" Lisa stood up as best she could in the van; she threw my pants at me, then motioned for me to sit up. I complied, and like teenagers busted by the law, we quickly wriggled into our clothes. *Outta the car, Long Hair!* I almost giggled aloud.

Lisa unlocked the door and yanked it open. The overhead light revealed us in all our disheveled glory. I grinned at Candy.

She didn't grin back, nor did the rest of the band, standing behind her. The cool night air hit me, and coupled with the menacing stares of James and Horus and Roy, all the warm feeling engendered by the previous few minutes drained slowly away. *They are dangerous to you.*

There would be no Ernie and two bouncers to save me this time. My old friend was upstairs, oblivious, probably wondering where the hell I was with his drink. But he wouldn't come looking for me. His appearance too early outside the green room would kill the surprise.

"You are so stupid!" Candy screamed. "He's just used you again! You're just a dumb –"

"Hey," I objected, not wanting to hear the profanity.

"Shut up!" Candy shrieked. The boys in the band moved restlessly behind her, and I knew all it would take would be a nod from this insane harpy, and they'd be on me like ugly on a bulldog.

"Christ, Mom!"

Lisa jumped from the van. I thought it best to stay put. It would buy me an extra second of maybe-someone'll-happen-along if they had to drag me out to commence punishing me.

"What's wrong with you?" Lisa asked. "You're acting like I'm fifteen. I'm a big girl. I'm allowed to –"

Candy slapped Lisa so hard across the mouth that it knocked her to the ground. I flinched in her direction, but at a warning glare from James, I sat back down.

A thin line of blood ran from the corner of Lisa's mouth, and insanely, I remembered the dreams in which she'd turned into a vampire. She wiped her hand across the blood, then looked at it. "What the fuck is wrong with you?" she growled at her mother. There were no tears. Vampires don't cry.

"Get up," Candy ordered. James offered Lisa his hand; she took it and he hauled her to her feet.

"This son of a bitch," Candy seethed.

She narrowed her eyes, and I thought that if looks could kill, I would indeed be dead already. I believed that it was coming, regardless. If Lisa had forgotten my treachery in the throes of missing me, her mother harbored no such warm feelings.

But like a villain in a bad movie, Candy would explain why first, otherwise Lisa might object. Maybe. *My daughter loves you and she'd never forgive me if I got rid of something she loved just because you were an annoyance to me,* Candy had told me once. *But if you show her the truth, Cal, I don't think she'll miss you so much.*

I wasn't copping to anything. *Come on, Ernie, come find me. Aren't you wondering what happened to your Scotch on the rocks?*

Candy took a deep breath, but her fury remained. "This *bastard.* And you just go right ahead and –"

"Will you get to the point?" Lisa demanded.

"We're not going on tonight. He and Ernie and that insufferable bitch from the record company! 'Just leave your stuff in the van,' Chrissy said. 'The line-up's been changed. Not enough time for your set. You can go on home if you want. Sonic Daydream's going on tonight.'"

Lisa's face went blank in disbelief. The pink flush of recent passion drained away; the smear of blood below her mouth looked like a crumbled rose upon new-fallen snow.

Yup, yup, yup, my resident demon cackled. *Ernie was definitely right. This stunt done pissed off the demon-worshippers, and mightily. I think you're about to die, Cal, ol' son, or they're gonna make you wish you were dead.*

Phenex stood motionless for a heartbeat, all eyes on me. They were waiting for me to try to explain, to try to snivel my way out of it. Candy wanted to see the disgust in her daughter's eyes when I begged.

A cartoon I'd seen once flashed through my head, and I marveled at the things that come to mind when you're about to die. In the background, it showed an eagle swooping in for the kill, mouth agape in imminent triumph, cruel talons extended. In the foreground stood a mouse with his back to the viewer, facing his certain demise, all Mickey ears and human hands. Like The Piglets portly pink mascot, the mouse was flipping off his impending doom. The caption read: *The last great act of defiance.*

I shrugged, grinned at Lisa. "I don't know what to tell ya, baby. *It's hard out here for a pimp.*"

Her eyes narrowed, just like her mother's, and that was the signal. James grinned hungrily at me, and again I had time to think of vampires. His hand actually fastened onto the front of my shirt, but then the cavalry arrived from a completely unexpected source.

"What the fuck, Lisa?"

I'd never been so glad to hear that expression in my life.

As a unit, Phenex looked over their shoulders. James let go of my shirt and I leaned over to peer past them at my savior.

Phillip was standing under the naked bulb above the back door of The Roxy, his hands on his hips. To my utter surprise, the *dregs of Sonic Daydream* were lounging against the wall behind him, like something out a Sony publicity still. Phil didn't know they were there, because he jumped when Lenny said, "Come on, Cal, you dumb son of a bitch. The Princes want us to hear their sound check."

As goes without saying, nobody had to ask me twice. I leapt spryly from the van and sprinted the short distance across the parking lot without a backward glance.

Denny grinned at me in unabashed glee. *"In a town without a name, in a heavy downpour, thought he passed his own shadow . . ."*

My band looked at me, and it didn't appear that they were gonna move until I said, *"By the backstage door."*

Ernie knocked on it, and I felt like I was in the Twilight Zone when I saw a small slot slide open, like something out of a Prohibition-era speakeasy. The bouncer opened the door. Ernie clapped me on the back; the brothers Whitly spared Phenex a smug smile.

As we entered the welcoming darkness of the corridor, I asked Lenny, "How long were you guys standing there?"

"Ernie snuck downstairs, looking for his drink. He saw Candy yelling at Chrissy, with the rest of the band. No you, no Lisa. So he came back up and got us. We followed them outside, just to see what was up."

"So how long were you gonna let it go on?"

"Not too long," he replied.

"Maybe just a few minutes," Denny said with his inimitable grin.

"Oh, hey, hold on." Ernie paused behind the stage, took his phone out of his pocket. "I damn near forgot, what with Cal's almost getting his ass handed to him. They're pissed now, and here's the coup de grâce." He pushed the requisite buttons and sent out the video of Iris's ritual.

SEVENTY

From my crow's nest vantage point, The RaceCats' set sounded all right. Despite an enthusiastic, more or less hometown crowd, I thought there was a distinct lack of triumphant-return-to-Southern-California hilarity in Phil's desultory between-song banter, however. I almost expected him to whine to his fans, to explain that a record-company betrayal was to blame for their opening for some *backwater hillbillies* that no one in the cosmopolitan City of Angels had yet heard of, instead of the other way around. But he didn't go that far.

The Desperate Princes shared the green room with us while The RaceCats were onstage. Whilst I watched Phil's bitter performance through the hole in the wall, they talked and laughed with the rest of my band, as if we were all old friends. Lenny gamely autographed the bass player's axe with his left hand. I watched the young, good-looking longhair murmur something aside to Ernie, and when Ernie rolled his eyes and slapped him on the back, I knew that they were talking about Candy.

The RaceCats' set ended, and the *wild-eyed southern boys* went downstairs to load-in. At one point, I looked down at the stage to see Phil offer the stock obscene gesture to his betters waiting upstairs in The Roxy's green room. I realized with a smug grin that he hadn't even been permitted the opportunity to come up and see it.

The Desperate Princes were good. Their sound was tinged with a little bit of Molly Hatchet, just a trace of the Allman Brothers, as all rock music from below the Mason-Dixon Line inevitably is, even all these decades later. Reminiscent of an old-timey Son of the Confederacy, their front's name was Beau Champlaine, and when their set ended, he told the crowd not to leave just yet.

"The Roxy's got a big surprise for ya'll," he told them. "They've got a new act for ya."

The crowd had paid to see three bands, so there was an uncertain smattering of applause. I doubted that any of them had missed Phenex. That thought, though perhaps unfair, made me grin again.

The Princes and the staff roadie from The Roxy set up my friends' guitars onstage. The lights dimmed mysteriously and we snuck down the stairs, with me carrying a pair of sticks that the southern boys' drummer had reverently handed to me earlier. We took our places and the lights came up.

Denny smiled at the crowd and said humbly into the mike, "Hi, Los Angeles. We're Sonic Daydream."

It wasn't until halfway through *Down the Center* that the stunned crowd began to cheer.

Our exit down the dark backstage corridor and out into The Roxy's tiny parking lot was a swift one. There was no big, safe tour bus waiting for us, no beefy bouncers or barricades to keep back the fans. Before the screaming and the deafening applause had wholly ceased, three guitars were stowed in the trunk of the Caddy; Sonic Daydream was already blocks away down Sunset before the amazed crowd started to spill outside onto the sidewalk.

The drive home was a lot of fun, like old, forgotten nights, like the days before we'd hit the big time. Just another nobody band, leaving an ill-paying gig in the drummer's car. Lenny apprised our set as adequate. He was the first to admit that he still felt like a left-handed beginner.

"The crowd didn't notice," his brother assured him.

"It was good enough for a surprise," Ernie agreed. He peeped over at me. "Too bad Phenex and The RaceCats missed it."

"I'm sure they'll read about it tomorrow." I eyed our famous frontman in the rearview. "Two unannounced Dennis Whitly performances in one year. *Rolling Stone's* gonna smell a comeback."

"Some reporter did call me after Berdoo, said Barbie gave him my number." Denny glared good-naturedly at his brother. "I think he said he was from *Rolling Stone.* Or maybe it was *Guitar Player.* I told him not to hold his breath." But I noticed that he smiled.

"Ernie could do double duty," I suggested. "We could open for Azomite."

We all had a good laugh at that one.

SEVENTY-ONE

Ernie's house was ablaze with welcoming light.

His lot was wide and spacious, but mostly it was long: the house was set at least half a football field's length back from the street. At the turn of the previous century, the builder of the old manse had owned the acres and acres of orange groves that had once dominated the area. The house and barn and distance to Victoria Avenue remained, but the land had been subdivided and sold off, the orange trees making way for more big houses. The lots were still large and private: a massive wall surrounded Ernie's lot, and there were still a few orange trees in the back behind the pool and patio.

The barn had long ago been converted to a small garage. It stood a little in front of the house and to the left, blocked from view from the street by another small grove of orange trees. The space on the right side of the driveway was cleared, with a lawn as verdant as any golf course. I often chided Ernie that he had to keep touring with Azomite to pay for the water to keep it so almost-supernaturally green.

There was a small section of driveway in front of the barn/garage, and it also curved in front of the house. I passed this darkened building and turned to the right, then backed the Caddy into the little space between it and Denny's Benz, so it was facing toward the street.

Ernie had been texting with the ladies on the trip home; Iris and Bianca came out of the front door and walked out to meet us. Iris smiled at me through the car window and said, "Leave the lights on, Cal. We want to take a video of your group all together. Bianca wants to say a few words for posterity."

I did as she bid and she set Denny's little tripod thing with her cellphone in it on the hood of the car. Sonic Daydream emerged; we linked our arms in camaraderie with Iris and Bianca and smiled at the camera. We waited for Bianca.

We were standing directly in line with the darkened part of the driveway in front of the barn.

I digress with all these tiresome descriptions of the layout of Ernie's property, who was there and where we stood, in order than you may better comprehend what happened next, seeing how it almost defies comprehension.

Bianca spoke to the camera. "Hi, Buddy. Sissy. I made the acquaintance of an unsigned act in Los Angeles tonight."

It was true; our contract with Sony had long expired, although they still kept the rights to our old stuff. Any new stuff, however . . .

Bianca gave Ernie a little squeeze, a smile, then looked back at the camera. "Have Stan crunch me some numbers. I'm thinking twelve cities, at least one new record –"

I didn't have time to wonder if any of this was true, if the never-to-be-underestimated Ernie LaBelle had really talked Denny into a comeback tour, because at that instant, there was a blaze of light, the roar of an engine, and Phenex's baby-blue van shot out at us from in front of the garage.

We looked to our left and were pinned by the lights like oft-mentioned deer, unable to move, to react, to get out of the way. We would've been mowed down in a line: me, then Iris, then Ernie, then Bianca, Denny and Lenny, if it weren't for the fact that at the last possible second, the van jerked to the right. It passed so close to me that I felt a breeze.

It careened toward the first of the orange trees, then jerked drunkenly back onto the driveway. We turned to watch it. The engine screamed, the van accelerated and shot out onto the street. A second before impact, the passenger side door opened.

Then, like an old silent newsreel I'd once seen of a staged train wreck – it said *State Fair Special* on the side of one of the locomotives – the van crashed into a huge, ancient, sturdy eucalyptus tree in the median. The noise was incredible, a booming, thudding, *folding* sound, and the complaining twang of instruments sliding forward then falling back. The back wheels went airborne from the suddenness of two tons of metal hitting an immovable object, then bounced back down onto the ground.

Then all was silence. We were too far away to hear the sizzling of escaping water or the tick of burning oil.

"You guys stay here," Denny told us, and he and his brother loped down the driveway. Ernie and I were unable to move, anyway. We didn't want to see . . . Nobody could've survived . . .

Iris was also rooted to the spot. It was as if she was sister to the great tree, now with a *puny,* inconsequential piece of metal crumpled against it. The tree would stand, probably for another hundred years, and it seemed that Iris would be right there with it, just as immobile. I touched her on the shoulder, asked her if she was okay. Her purple eyes were round and huge, and she didn't speak, didn't look away from the carnage at the end of the driveway.

Bianca snatched Iris's phone from the tripod and called 911, told them there'd been an accident, then handed the phone to Ernie to give them the address. Sophia and Barbie had run out at the horrific sound. They saw the back of the van; they looked at us in questioning fright.

"It's Phenex," I said.

Ernie ended the call and tried to hand the phone to Iris, but she just stared straight ahead. There were no theatrical flames, just a thin miasma of hot and oily steam from the busted radiator and the dislodged engine block. I again thought of the smoke puffing out of the stacks in the staged train wreck.

When Iris wouldn't take her phone, he gave it to Bianca instead, and stepped resolutely toward the house. "The cops are coming."

"We have to help . . ." Bianca began.

"There's no way we can help," Sophia said softly. She'd been in two car wrecks, and the thought skittered across my mind that she knew a fatal one when she saw it.

"Denny and Lenny went down there," Ernie said. Tears rolled down his face. "They've all gotta be dead. I don't wanna see that . . ." Bianca embraced him and led him the rest of the way into the house.

Barbie gazed helplessly at me, and I thought I could see an agony of post-traumatic stress syndrome play across her face. She'd been in a car accident recently, too. Like Ernie, like Sophia: Barbie didn't want to see either.

I nodded at Iris, who still stared straight ahead in horror. Barbie and Sophia enfolded her in their arms and led her back inside.

I stood and gazed down the driveway for what seemed like a long time. There was no movement to be seen, not even the brothers Whitly. The scream of the sirens entered dully into my head; when the red lights splashed the back of the van, turning the baby-blue to a pale lavender, I took a few steps forward. Then I stopped. Ernie was right. They were all dead. I didn't want to see, either.

SEVENTY-TWO

The eight of us sat arranged on couches and chairs and watched two of RPD's finest study Ernie's platinum records. A third asked questions. Ernie did all the talking. He lied.

"Yeah, we did a show together tonight, in LA."

Denny and Lenny, in the arms of their women, stared straight ahead, as Iris had done in the driveway. They had seen, and remained lost in the horror of it.

"Then – I don't fucking know, dude." Ernie ran his hand through his hair, rubbed his eyes. "They took off to go home . . ."

"Way too fast," Bianca finished for him.

Except for the in-shock Whitly brothers, we all stared silently at the patrolman. There wasn't anything more to it than that. The band had missed the turn because they came out of the driveway way too fast; they had crashed into the tree in the median. That's what Ernie told the cop. That's what he wrote down.

What the patrolman told us: all five of them were dead. James and Lisa had been ejected through the windshield; Candy and Roy and Horus, without seatbelts, had been tossed around inside the van, mangled by the laws of inertia and further crushed by their amps and instruments.

And Denny and Lenny had seen it all; Lenny had identified the bodies for the cops.

"And the other kid? He's also in this band?" The patrolman consulted his notes. "Phenex?"

Ernie shook his head. "He's from a different band."

The bright spot in this unimaginable pall of death was Phil. I'd seen the passenger side door open; what I hadn't seen was Phil bail out, milliseconds before impact. Lenny found him in the street. He was busted up, but he was alive. The cop said they took him to Kaiser; everybody else went downtown to the morgue. No sirens. No lights.

The cops told Ernie that they were sorry for his loss, that someone would be in touch about releasing Candy and his daughter's bodies to him. Bianca gave them a list of numbers to try in order that they might locate Mike the roadie for Horus. None of us knew anything about next of kin for James or Roy.

Bianca was able to function better than the rest of us – she knew about the witchy machinations of Phenex, and they'd almost run her down, too, but she'd never met any of them. They had been just names on paper to her, made strange and vaguely threatening by Ernie's stories of chanting before shows and cursed medallions. But that was amusing to Bianca, too, as it had been to me, right up until my deranged lover had bragged about poisoning Sophia, because she thought I was down to help her.

It had gotten real for me then. I didn't think it was real for Bianca yet. She hadn't known these nutballs before, and now she would never know them. So she was acting as polite and efficient hostess. She thanked the cops and walked them out to their cars. We stared at the door until she came back in.

"They tried to kill us," Ernie told Barbie and Sophia. This met with more abject silence; the brothers Whitly had already told their women, in whispered asides before the cops got there. It was a little tidbit that Ernie had left out of his official statement to the law. His daughter's band had tried to run us down. But there was no reason to mention it. What possible difference could it make now?

"Why didn't they kill us?" Lenny asked. "Why did James turn away at the last second?"

"Ashmedai," Iris said in a breathless, frightened whisper.

Their women knew all about Sonic Daydream's foray into the astral realms; they agreed that it was a viable sally against an inexplicable enemy that believed in such things. But none of them believed in it themselves. The only one of us that leaned even remotely towards belief was Lenny – he believed that Phenex was definitely bad luck – but even he didn't put any faith, so to speak, in Ashmedai's patronage.

But Iris believed, so we each gave her a condescending smile and changed the subject. Speculation on the real reason Phenex's drummer had at the last possible second decided to spare all our lives would have to wait until the true believer was absent.

SEVENTY-THREE

By the time Ernie and I left to go visit Phil in the hospital the next morning, the efficient authorities of the City of Riverside had cleared away most of the evidence of the tragedy. The van was long gone, towed away to its own graveyard. All that was left to mark its demise, as well as the endings of five human beings, was an angry chunk taken out of the eucalyptus tree, a little broken glass, a few blackened splotches of blood in the dirt.

Ernie didn't even glance at the scene as we pulled out onto the street. An uncharacteristic solemnity had descended on him; it was readable as a thorough dose of *There but for the grace of God go I.* It was as simple as that: Phenex was dead, but it could've just as easily been us. That was a sobering thought for my ol' happy-go-lucky second-guitar. *It could've been us.*

Beyond that, he entertained the same old Ernie LaBelle indifference. He embodied Tyler Durden's philosophy, *the ability to let that which does not matter truly slide,* better than anyone I'd ever known. Bitterness was something utterly foreign to him. Sonic Daydream almost got run down like so much money-crop before a thresher – but the aggressors were gone, so Ernie didn't ponder the great metaphysical unknowables that had sicced them on us in the first place. I'm sure he felt sad about Lisa, but on the other hand, maybe not. He'd never had that much time to get to know her; the novelty of whatever fatherhood was supposed to mean to him had not yet worn off before he discovered that his baby girl was out to get him. Ernie had already written her off before Phenex attempted to murder us, so his sadness was minimal.

Still, Ernie couldn't look at the place where the wreck had happened. He wasn't bitter and he had little grief. But the valley of the shadow of death was right across the street from his house; they had died *right there.* Ernie couldn't look at it. Not out of superstitious dread – Ernie would never be superstitious – but out of just regular ol' dread. Phenex had crashed; they were dead. It could've just as easily been us.

I was the very opposite. I couldn't look away from the site. The love of my life was dead, and I wondered – philosophically and without really caring one way or the other – had she hated me in the end? When she saw that tree rushing up, did she damn me with her last breath?

Surely she hated me; her band had tried to run mine down. All that was left of Phenex now was a scarred tree, and I felt appallingly unaffected by the whole thing. I hadn't seen; maybe if I had, it would hurt more now. But there was no searing empathy in me for their abrupt, bloody end; my resident demon commented that it had probably been merciful and quick, no doubt painless, and the rest of me agreed with him and didn't reflect further upon it.

I didn't think of the funerals that were to come, although I knew that Ernie would no doubt spring for all of them. I didn't even dwell on the fact that I would never, ever see the hope of my future again. At the moment, consideration of my future brought only . . . *meh.* The premier idea in my mind was that the insanity was over. The demon-worshippers wouldn't be bothering us with homicidal sneak attacks anymore.

Life goes on. *Shorter of breath and one day closer to death.* I kept waiting for the hurt, the agony at the realization that Lisa was now dust. Not a ghost, nor a celestial being on the astral plane; not with God in heaven nor with Phenex in Hell. Just dust.

I waited for the arrival of some sense of respect for the dead, the thought to emerge that, even though she was a homicidal maniac, I had completely loved her. And now she was irrevocably gone. I waited for the pain, but it didn't come. *I don't know if I'm happy, I don't know if I'm sad.*

SEVENTY-FOUR

The RaceCats' fortunate frontman wasn't in ICU. Somehow, when he'd disembarked so astutely from the doomed van, he'd managed to tuck and roll to protect his fragile melon from the unforgiving asphalt. He hadn't sustained a skull fracture like Valerie; here were no staples in his scalp. Not a scratch on his incredibly lucky face.

Phillip was lucky, but not unbreakable. You don't just bail out of a moving vehicle and hit the ground running. He sat up gingerly in the hospital bed, shirtless. He was still wearing the medallion Lisa had gifted him. I wondered vaguely what promise she'd given to him with it, but discovered that I sincerely just didn't care.

The nurses had balled up a pillow and stuck it behind the small of Phil's back for a little lumbar support. It was the only part of his back and shoulders that didn't look like hamburger from the road rash. He'd broken his collarbone, shoulder blade, and both bones in his lower arm, all on the right side. It was gonna be awhile before right-handed Phil played guitar again.

But it was better than the alternative.

When we walked into his room, the first words out of his mouth were, "Are they all dead?"

Ernie nodded.

"Nobody here would tell me." Phil sobbed, and a single tear traced slowly down his cheek, for Lisa. I commiserated silently with him as much as I could. It wasn't much, seeing as how she'd been a member of the party that'd tried to run us down.

Ernie asked the obvious question. "What happened, Phil?"

The kid licked his lips, sneered. "I'm so glad you asked, Mr. LaBelle, sir. Because it's a helluva unbelievable story, right from the beginning. Sir." He considered me for a second, included me in his scorn.

He took a deep breath and began. "This fucked-up adventure of a lifetime began when Chrissy told us that Phenex was getting bumped by Christ-on-a-crutch Sonic Daydream, of all fucking people. I thought she was having us on, but she said that it was for real. I couldn't find Lisa or any of Phenex in the club, so I went outside.

"I saw them all standing by the van so I called to Lisa. Then your bassist spoke up and I saw you, and then Dennis Whitly, standing around looking like a fucking rock star. So I knew it was true. *What the fuck?* I thought. I was pissed. It was Lisa's last show and her own dad was bumping her band . . ." Phil sobbed, then shook his head to stop the tears.

I was surprised at my own lack of pity. Phil had probably thought he loved Lisa, but unlike myself, he was young; and unlike myself, there'd be other Lisas for Phil. This love he wept for – he hadn't known her long enough to love her the way I had. She hadn't tried to kill him.

"When you guys went back inside, I told Phenex that this was bullshit. I said I'd see if there was anything I could do about it. I went back into the club and ran into Craig –"

"Who?" Ernie asked.

"Craig Price," I supplied. "The drummer from The Desperate Princes."

Phil frowned at our interruption of his recital of *this fucked-up adventure of a lifetime.* When he saw that he had our attention again, he continued. "I said, 'What the fuck is going on, Craig?'

"He said, 'It's Sonic Daydream, man.' Then he grinned like an idiot and said, 'They're gonna use our equipment. How do ya wanna do this? You wanna go on first?'

"I asked him what the fuck he was talking about, and he said, 'There's no reason to load our shit in and then load it out for yours, then load it back in for them.'

"I said, 'We're the fucking headliner, Craig. We play last.'"

My, my, my, quoth my little red demon. *Where is all this bitter resentment coming from? Could it be that this is the first time The RaceCats got bumped outta the headlining spot? I think that just might be it! You'd think after all that's happened, the kid would just feel lucky to be alive.*

"Craig says, 'They're fucking Sonic Daydream, Phil. They're the headliner now, and nobody's gonna remember if you opened for them or we opened for you or any of that happy horseshit, now are they? So what d'ya wanna do?'

"So I thought, *what the fuck ever.* If Phenex was bumped, then they were probably going home. If we played first, I thought that maybe I could get Lisa to wait for me. We were going home after this fucked-up gig, too, so I thought that if I could get her to wait through our set, then maybe she'd come home with me . . ." Phil's sob had now resolved itself into just a heavy sigh. Yeah. There'd be other Lisas for him.

"I went back outside; they were standing around deciding what to do. I told Lisa we'd open for the fucking Desperate Princes, just to get it over with, if she'd wait for me. Before I even finished talking she said, 'Okay. And afterwards, you can come home with me if you'd like.' She kissed me."

Phil spared me a smug smirk; then his mind must've reminded him that Lisa wouldn't be kissing him or me or anyone else ever again. He exhaled another shuddery sigh; I couldn't tell if it indicated the return of his sadness or a continuation of his bitchy anger.

"So we all went back into the club, and James and Roy and Horus and the fat guy that works there helped us load in. We played our set on that shitty, fucked-up little stage. I don't care how famous that place is supposed to be. It's a dump. Then they helped us stow our shit in the side of the bus and I told the guys I was going home with Phenex.

"Andy said, 'Chrissy wants you to –' and I said, 'Fuck Chrissy. She let this shit happen.' I told him I'd talk to him in a few days and I left with Lisa."

Phil took another deep breath and sighed it out again. I wondered if all this rancor was helping with his pain.

When he started talking again, he addressed Ernie. "On the drive home, Candy starts bitching about how it was your fault that they got bumped, how you're screwing some whore from EMI, and she'll do anything you say." Now Phil grinned slyly. "There's more than a couple whores at EMI, let me tell ya, so I asked Candy which one. Why didn't ya tell me you were doing ol' Bianca, Ernie? She's like a boss. I woulda asked you to get us some better gigs. Fuck The Roxy."

Before Ernie could reply, a nurse came in. Phil grinned at her and told us that we had to wait out in the hall for a quick second. "It's time for my shot. They're giving me morphine. Every two hours. Can't miss that."

In the hallway, Ernie said, "Christ! Is he a whiner, or what?"

"The new generation of rock star," I replied.

"If he thinks this is the only shitty gig he's ever gonna do . . ."

We shook our heads at the feelings of entitlement of a just-barely-signed, still-a-nobody singer from Riverside, California. My phone rang. It was Lenny.

"You're not gonna fucking believe this, Cal. Why isn't Ernie answering his phone?"

"Where's your phone, Ernie?"

He patted his pockets, shrugged. "I don't fucking know, dude. At home probably."

"I'll just tell you and you can tell him," Lenny said. "After you guys left, Denny tried to go out the kitchen door, but there was a deckchair wedged against it. That was odd, so we went out the front door, walked around the house. You ever heard of The Smokey Valley Muzzle Loaders, Cal?"

I sighed. I had witnessed more than a lifetime's worth of death and destruction in a very short period of time, and Leonard Whitly wanted to play 20 Questions. "Are they a band?"

Lenny chuckled without merriment. "No. They're a black powder shooting club. Dad used to belong to it when we were kids. Denny and I used to go with him sometimes –"

"Is there a point to this story, Lenny?" I asked irritably.

"Yeah. Here's my point, Cal. Since you're in a hurry, I'll make it quick. Dad belonged to this club. They shot old-fashioned guns. No shells. You poured gunpowder directly into the barrel, tamped it, loaded a ball, and so on."

"And? So?" I thought I felt the beginnings of a headache.

"So, Denny and I, we know what gunpowder looks like. It was all around the foundation to Ernie's house. Fucking *inches* of it in a few spots. And shit was piled up against the side door, just like the chair outside the kitchen. There was gonna be another fire, Cal. But no one was gonna get out this time. Anybody they didn't run down was gonna burn."

I was too exhausted to repeat this newest horrific wrinkle. I handed my phone to Ernie.

After he hung up, he said, "I might just have to break Phil's other arm."

"You think he was in on it?"

"There's only one way to find out." Ernie smiled at the nurse as she exited Phil's room, then turned to me again. "Don't they say confession's good for the soul? Since he's lucky to be alive, maybe he'll just tell us."

"Now that he's properly medicated."

"Or maybe I'll just beat it out of him." Ernie was feeling a little resentment now.

We went back in to get the rest of the story. Phil looked at us blearily, but he smiled. The morphine was working. "Where was I?"

"You were coming back to Riverside with Phenex."

"Yeah. Candy and Horus and Roy were in the back, and Lisa and I were in the front. James was driving. We stopped at the McDonald's over there by the Home Depot to get something to eat. Before we went in, Candy showed them all something on her phone. They laughed. 'Like that's gonna work,' Lisa said. I asked her what, but she just shook her head, told me it was no big deal.

"All the time we're in McDonald's, Candy continues to bitch about how you ruined our gig."

Now Phil turned his drugged eyes to me. "Then she starts telling me about how you're an asshole. How you'd taken advantage of Lisa, how when she'd said that she liked your band, you'd used that as an excuse to get in her pants. Then you'd dumped her, right after Vegas. I knew you guys had broken up, but . . . Christ. You're old enough to be her father."

Ernie grinned, slapped me on the back. "He's actually a couple month's older than me." After Lenny's news, whatever grief he might've harbored at the loss of his homicidal only child was completely gone.

Phil didn't smile. "I asked Lisa if it was true, that you'd taken advantage of her."

I discovered that his use of this archaic term annoyed me. If anyone had *taken advantage of Lisa,* it had been him, when she was on the rebound from our breakup.

What is this, high school? the omnipresent voice in my head asked. *On the rebound from your break-up? Phil didn't take advantage of Lisa and neither did you. She was take-advantage-proof. She played both of you.*

"She wouldn't answer me," Phil was saying. "She just looked away, like she was ashamed."

I'd like to thank the Academy . . .

"Then I was really pissed, so when Candy said something about teaching the old rock stars a lesson, I was down. She said we'd just park next to your garage, and when you got home we'd jump you. She said it was even enough. There were four of you and four of us . . ." Phil seemed to realize he was rambling and paused to collect his thoughts.

"So when James doused the lights and creepy-crawled the van up this long-ass driveway, I figured we were at your house."

I started at Phil's phrasing this time. I'd only been six years old when the Spahn Ranch crew had struck, but I'd read Bugliosi's book in high school. *Creepy-crawling* was the term they'd used for the burglaries they'd committed around the LA area before the murders. A shiver passed through me: Candy's minions (and her daughter, too) had been just as devoted to her and her homicidal commandments as had been Manson's family.

"There were lights on inside, but we knew there was no way you guys coulda beat us home. James eased the van up and slowly turned it around and backed it in in front of the garage. Once we were hidden, they all got out, except for Lisa. I got a little worried – I don't have anything against you, Ernie, not really."

You didn't bump his *band,* I thought.

"My beef was with this asshole. Because of what he did to Lisa."

"I didn't do anything to Lisa, Phil. She was –"

"It doesn't really matter now, does it?" he said softly. Then he sighed again and continued. "James opened the back of the van. I couldn't see what he took out, but all of them outta the truck made me nervous, so I asked them what was going on. Candy said they were just gonna have a quick look around."

I exchanged a glance with Ernie. The *incendiary device,* the gunpowder, was already in the van; setting this new fire had been premeditated. Phenex had planned to murder Ernie and whoever was at home with him tonight, even before we played our little trick on them at The Roxy.

"Candy closed the back of the van and the lights went out. Then Lisa starting kissing me and I forgot about them. The band was gone for a long time, long enough for us to . . ."

I believe they call that sloppy seconds, Phil ol' son, I thought emotionlessly.

"I'd say at least twenty minutes. Maybe a half hour," Phil concluded.

Whatever's clever, my resident demon opined.

"Then they all got back in the van and we waited. Candy said that when you guys pulled up, when you got out of the car, we'd just jump out and start swinging."

Ernie and I shared another glance. He said, "But it didn't go like that."

Phil shook his head. "It was crazy."

His eyes widened. I noted that sweat suddenly beaded on his forehead.

"Bianca and the other lady came out of the house as you guys pulled up. You guys all stood in front of the car together." Again Phil shook his head. “Candy said, ‘There’s that bitch that took Ernie away from me. Run ‘em over, James. All of ‘em.’

“I looked over my shoulder at her because she sounded so fucking serious – then, Jesus, Christ! It all happened so fast! But somehow, it also seemed like slow motion.

“James fires up the van, turns the lights on. He guns it, slams it into drive. There was enough time for me to see everyone look to see where the light was coming from. Then the van was . . .”

Phil put his hand, the one with the IV in it, to his forehead. He took a deep breath. “Just before the van woulda hit you, James cranked the wheel hard to the right.”

Phil shifted his eyes from me to Ernie.

“So hard that his head slammed into the driver’s side window. I saw a splash of blood on the glass. It was crazy. Lisa slid into him and I slid into her.

“Candy screamed, ‘Why didn’t you hit them?’ We were in the grass heading toward the trees, so James jerked the wheel back, got us back on the driveway. He slid halfway across the seat into Lisa, who slid into me.”

Phil licked his lips again. “The van shoulda stopped then, because James couldn’t’ve had his foot on the gas anymore. But it didn’t stop. It didn’t even slow down. James dragged himself fully back in front of the wheel and starts stomping on the brakes. Candy is screaming for him to stop.”

“He must’ve hit the gas by mistake,” Ernie said.

Phil shook his head. “I saw him jerk his leg up and stand on the emergency brake. Nothing. We’re almost to the end of the fucking driveway. I can see that big tree straight ahead. James hauls on the wheel and . . .” Phil dragged his hand across his face.

“I swear, Ernie. I saw another spray of blood hit the windshield. James hauled on the wheel and the skin came off of his palms and his blood sprayed the windshield, *because the fucking wheel didn’t move.* When the tires hit the street, I opened the door and rolled out. I heard them hit the tree, but I didn’t see it. Then I woke up in an ambulance.”

Phil looked at us expectantly, clearing wanting comment. So I said, “Why do you think James didn’t run us down?”

Phil grinned harshly. “You’re a fucking genius for a drummer, you know that, Cal? That’s the million dollar question, isn’t it? Why didn’t James run you down, when he obviously planned on doing just that?" Phil's voice had risen to a shrill, almost-shriek. He gulped a mouthful of air and calmed himself.

"It's just like I said. It was the weirdest fucking thing I've ever seen." He studied us for a moment, then said softly, "I'd seen them chanting before their sets. Lisa gave me this necklace, told me it meant we would be in love forever."

Not even a hitch in his voice at that sad, now never-to-be occurrence. Maybe Phil *was* just glad to be alive.

"Lisa told me that they believed in unseen forces."

Ernie didn't even look at me now. This wasn't news. "So?"

"That's what it was like, Ernie," Phil said, again with a tinge of hysteria. "It was like some unseen force jerked the wheel. It was like it made the van keep going, even though James was stomping on the brakes. He tore all the skin off his hands trying to turn us away from that tree, but it was like something was keeping us going, right into it." Phil tried to lean back in the bed, but the pain from his own ruined skin made him sit up again.

"You know they were into all that witchy shit. I'm just saying, maybe it got away from 'em somehow." He looked nervously from Ernie to me, then back to Ernie again, willing us to say something. Anything.

Ernie let him wait; I watched the clock on the wall behind Phil's bed click off a good fifteen seconds. Then he grinned, shook his head. "You've been through a lot, Phil. You almost died. They've got you on the good drugs. You just think you remember it that way."

"No, dude. It was like something else was driving the van. Candy was screaming. James tried to stop, but it wouldn't let him."

"It?" Ernie shook his head at the singer's morphine-induced fantasy. "It was just an accident, Phil. Tragic, but not the result of witchcraft gone awry." He offered me an unreadable glance. "James lost control of the van. That's all."

"That's what I been trying to tell myself. But it wasn't like that, man, it was like something else was –"

"It was an accident, Phil," Ernie repeated emphatically. He glanced around the hospital room, a couple of floors away from the one he'd recently occupied, but bigger. "You start telling people it was anything else but that, they might not be so eager to let you outta here." He tapped his temple. "Survivor's guilt and all."

Phil tried to lean back again – the morphine was kicking in fully now – but again he sat up. He nestled over on his mostly undamaged left side. "I guess you're right. It couldn't have been how I remember it. Could it?" His eyes pleaded for agreement.

Ernie smiled paternally, which gave Phil the agreement he needed. I nodded over my shoulder; the rest of The RaceCats stood in the doorway, pale with concern. They seemed impossibly young to me, nothing more than boys.

"Call me when you're feeling better." Ernie paused, glanced quickly at me. Then he told Phil, "I'd take that medallion off, though. I hear they're bad luck."

SEVENTY-FIVE

Back in the Porsche, Ernie shook his head. "Wait 'till Lenny hears *this* story."

"He's really started to believe all this witchy bullshit, hasn't he?" I remembered my bass player's slack face, his text. *How could demon worshippers b anything but bad luck?*

"He's like our narcotics-influenced friend back there. He says he knows what he saw, right before his stroke. He saw the demon Phenex."

He's a bird, right?

Ernie shook his head. "It was probably just a big crow. And then, just like Phil, once he was in the hospital, once he was medicated . . ." Ernie shook his head again, tapped his temple. "Lenny's imagination just took over. I believe that the crazy bastards drugged me, set the fire at his house, and like you say, James fixed Sophia's car. There was nothing supernatural about any of that. And the rest of it – Lenny's stroke, their wreck . . ." Ernie suddenly laughed harshly. "Maybe that *was* supernatural, huh? Maybe that was karma. What goes around comes around? Maybe the unseen forces paid Phenex back for all the fucked-up shit they tried to do to us."

I grinned. "Maybe it was Ashmedai."

Ernie also grinned, at the ridiculousness of that. Lenny might be at least a partial convert, but like myself, it all remained absurd claptrap to Ernie.

"It was just an accident, and now – we don't have to worry about any of it any more, do we? Lenny's almost back to normal. Denny remains undamned."

"You've got Bianca."

Ernie's smile bloomed again, then he peeped over at me guiltily. "I'm sorry about Lisa, Cal. For your sake. I know how much she meant to you."

He appraised my expression, waited for a reaction, so to accommodate him, I tried to summon up an emotion about it. I tried to remember the beach, Lisa's smile, the velvet of her kiss. But all I could see was the cruel narrowing of her eyes, right before James reached for me in the van at The Roxy. The big drummer was gonna beat me to death, and Lisa was gonna stand by and watch it. She was gonna *like it.*

She was gone, and there was no sense in mourning over something between us that had died before she did. I had no doubt that she'd cursed me with her last breath. *Ain't talkin' 'bout love,* Diamond Dave wailed in my head. *My love is rotten to the core.*

But Ernie wanted a response. I thought of all the years since our band broke up, all the time when the brothers Whitly and probably Ernie himself had thought of me as a traitor, if they thought of me at all. Phenex had tried to murder my friends, and somehow, it seemed that if I still felt any love for Lisa . . . I just didn't feel it anymore. It was gone. I was no traitor.

"She tried to kill us, Ernie. I won't go so far as to say that I'm glad she's dead . . ." But was that exactly true? Was I glad? The whole black fairytale had been my fault, because of *Sonic Nightmare.* I felt nothing. "But as far as any love for her goes . . . it's gone."

Ernie looked at me doubtfully for a minute, then he shrugged, convinced. Ernie might be a little devious, but his motivations always came to light in the end, and he expected no less from others. If I said I was over it, Ernie saw no reason not to believe me. He was assuredly over it.

We drove in silence for a minute and I reflected, again tried to feel something, anything at all, about the joy I'd once had with Lisa, or even for her murderous insanity, for her tragic end. But I got absolutely nothing. It was all as transitory, as meaningless to me as any other fairytale. I sighed inwardly and felt one little feeling at last: gratitude. I was over it.

When we got back to Ernie's place, we found our party sitting around on his back patio, having brunch. The concrete and vegetation around the house was raked clean, hosed down, as if an army of landscapers had descended whilst we were away. Two fat green lawn and leaf bags stood grimly at the foot of an orange tree, on the other side of the pool, filled with gunpowder and any detritus that the regular landscapers had missed the last time that they'd cleaned around the foundation of Ernie's house. It was the only reminder of Phenex's plan to immolate us, the dregs of their foiled *last great act of defiance.*

Bianca greeted her lover affectionately, and asked about Phil.

"He'll live," Ernie said simply. "He's a little confused right now, but once they take him off the morphine . . ."

"They only give it to you for twelve hours." Sophia, veteran of two horrific car wrecks, knew wherein she spoke. "Then it's Tylenol and your own guts."

"And bad dreams," Lenny said darkly.

Ernie ignored him. "Phil's gonna be all right. What have you lovely ladies fixed? I'm starving."

SEVENTY-SIX

The conversation around the table was subdued at first: the disbelief at the idea that Phenex had tried to kill us, the very real possibility that they might've easily succeeded had it not been for James's inept driving skills, the inescapable fact that they were all dead . . . The mood was decidedly dark.

But Bianca was a sunbeam. She hadn't known these evil people, and since they were gone . . . *fuck all that.* She asked Ernie what he thought the chances were of Azomite leaving Sony – she winked at Barbie – and coming over to EMI.

"I don't fucking know, baby. Scott handles all that road dog shit." Ernie's road dog days were over.

Bianca teased Denny about the possibility of a Sonic Daydream reunion tour. He deflected the idea for the time being, but to my surprise he said that The Roxy gig had been a lot of fun.

I marveled at how effortlessly Dennis Whitly could ignore the bad parts of any situation. He'd always had the ability: he'd ignored Elise's fatal infatuation with him for twelve long years; he seemed to have forgotten all about his dislike of me. He'd enjoyed playing the infamous old club on the Sunset Strip, and had simply allowed himself to forget that the nobody band we'd bumped out of spite had tried to kill us, that they were all dead themselves now.

The mood lightened. I listened, contributed to old stories of Sonic Daydream's touring heyday. Iris also listened politely, added a comment or question where appropriate, but several times during brunch, I caught her staring at me. It was impossible to escape the feeling that she had something to say to me, and it had nothing whatsoever to do with the glory days of an old musical group that she knew absolutely nothing about.

Brunch concluded, and the ladies cleared off the table. The boys in the band stood around the pool, but we didn't say much. There was the shock of recent events, and the fact that we really weren't used to each other's company again quite yet. Ernie grinned at us: the playful but-maybe-not-impossible idea of a reunion tour flitted in the air like a butterfly.

Iris came out of the house and stood beside us for a moment. She made eye contact with Ernie; I saw him nod. His smile evaporated. "Show me where all this gunpowder was," he said to the brothers Whitly.

Denny blinked in surprise. He thought the discussion of all that unpleasantness was passed. He'd already put it out of his mind. Ernie looked at him significantly, and Denny walked away with him without further comment. Lenny followed.

Iris and I were now alone, and I realized that whatever she had to say to me – I had an inkling of what it was going to be – she was going to spill it without further ado. I sighed in anticipation, pre-empted her. "It was an accident, Iris."

Her incredible purple eyes blinked in surprise. "I always sensed a little shine to you, Cal, despite your stubborn disbelief. So you know what I'm going to tell you?"

"I don't have to be psychic, do I? You think Ashmedai protected us."

A shadow crossed her face. "I'm ashamed to admit that I entered into Ashmedai's summoning without faith. That was a grave error." She smiled ruefully. "Didn't you tell me that you were a churchgoer as a child?"

I heard Lisa's low, melodic voice in my head: *You were raised a Catholic, right? Catholicism used to be a fine old dogma, black and white, with no shades of gray.* I had no feelings for her anymore, but I would never forget her voice.

I nodded at Iris.

"Do you remember your Proverbs? *The king's heart is in the hand of the Lord, as the rivers of water: he turneth it whithersoever he will. Every way of a man is right in his own eyes: but the Lord pondereth the hearts."*

I shook my head. "It was a long time ago, Iris, when I went to church." *A million years ago,* I thought, *a million years of rivers of water, all passed under the bridge.*

"The verse is about the mind of the supplicant," Iris explained. *"The getting of treasures by a lying tongue is a vanity tossed to and fro of them that seek death."*

Again I shook my head. "What are you trying to tell me, Iris?"

She sighed. "I had little faith in our invocation to Ashmedai, Cal. I didn't think that my belief alone would be sufficient. The four of you are unbelievers. *The sacrifice of the wicked is abomination: how much more, when he bringeth it with a wicked mind?"*

Again I shook my head, again she sighed. "I wouldn't have summoned Ashmedai had you been believers, like Candy and her group. If the four of you had truly believed, I knew that his vengeance against them would've been absolute. His power is vast, implacable. I knew that they would heed it, because they were true believers, so I thought, what could it hurt? There was no danger. The ritual was empty, meaningless, because the four of you have no faith."

"But they didn't heed it. Phil said they laughed."

"They were prideful."

The phrase smacked of that old-time religion and I grinned, despite the severity of Iris's expression. She didn't smile back and my own smile fled after a moment. She was just *so serious.*

"They were stupid, and I was foolish. I never should've invoked such a massive power, but I had no faith in it. I just didn't believe that Ashmedai would aid unbelievers."

I sighed. It was all over, and her gravity annoyed me. "Ashmedai didn't aid us, Iris. Why do you refuse to see that? You say I'm stubborn – you're just ridiculous. It was an accident. The van was new, James was unfamiliar with it. It was going too fast, and he lost control. They crashed. It happens every day."

Iris narrowed her eyes shrewdly, and I saw a new angle forming in her mind. "You only believe what you can see, am I right, Cal? Yet you believe in some invisible forces, like gravity, the turning of the seasons . . ."

"I can see them, too, the evidence of their existence, the scientific basis –"

"Ah, there's a word! Evidence!" Iris shouted, and I jumped at her sudden vehemence. With a theatrical flourish, she pulled her cellphone from her pocket. "Watch, *see,* Darwin's scientific monkey! Behold, powers beyond your ken!"

Clumsily, Iris pushed buttons on her phone. She was excited now, and the mundane operations of the new-fangled electronic device flustered her for a moment. A cellphone was neither bell, book, nor candle, but after a few fits and starts, she invoked what she wanted me to see.

In the video, the glare from the Caddy's headlights illuminated the members of Sonic Daydream, smiling, arms linked. Bianca spoke to the camera. "Hi, Buddy. Sissy. I made the acquaintance of an unsigned act in Los Angeles tonight." She gave Ernie a little squeeze, a smile, then looked back at the camera. "Have Stan crunch me some numbers. I'm thinking twelve cities, at least one new record –"

There was a blaze of light, the roar of an engine, and Phenex's baby-blue van shot out at us from in front of the garage. The video showed only the corner of it, where it had almost clipped me.

We turned, parted. The driveway was dark and empty for a moment, then the van clunked drunkenly back onto it, back into the frame. Iris's cellphone had captured its rocketing, relentless, arrow-straight flight. The brake-lights flashed on, lit up the night. The flare of light confused the sensor on the camera and there was a kind of blur while it adjusted to the brighter illumination.

But the van didn't slow, didn't stop, didn't dive forward or skid as it should've from the sudden application of the brakes. It continued, it accelerated. The brake lights stayed on. Phil's words: *I saw him jerk his leg up and stand on the emergency brake. Nothing.*

I again heard the booming, thudding, *folding* sound as the van connected with the tree, the twang of cymbals and guitars, all faithfully captured by this modern miracle, this tiny, inexpensive electronic device. I again heard, saw Denny. *You guys stay here.*

I watched him and Lenny run toward the steaming wreck. The brake lights were still on. Then Bianca's stunned face, her hand reaching for the phone on the tripod. The video stopped.

"You believe in the mechanical operations of your mechanical world, Cal," Iris whispered fiercely. "Friction, hydraulics. It was a brand new van, you said so yourself. The brake lights . . . Why didn't it stop?"

As if on cue, a diversion broke Iris's ridiculous tirade. Ernie stuck his head out of the back door. "How does a barbeque sound?"

"Christ, Ernie. We just ate."

"I don't mean right this minute, my brutha. Later." He grinned from ear to ear. "Bianca's got Denny talking tour."

Here was real life, the suggestion of a busy future. I realized that I was down for it, that I'd been game all along, since our rusty rehearsal at my house. I forgot Iris's serious absurdity, and grinned myself. "Really?"

"Yeah." Ernie's smile faltered at Iris's inability to hide her annoyance. He gleaned that he had interrupted something. "Come on in when you're . . . done. We'll go get steaks."

Ernie didn't wait for a response. He hastily closed the door so Iris and I could conclude our tête-à-tête in private.

Iris waited a heartbeat. The fire of belief in her eyes was tempered with sadness. With guilt. "I'm sorry, Cal. I shouldn't have invoked Ashmedai. His power . . . I knew that he wields death easily. But my faith in his willingness to aid unbelievers . . . I'm sorry, Cal."

"The Lord works in mysterious ways." I patted her shoulder patronizingly, then I felt bad about it immediately and removed my hand. She had been kind, helpful, all along. She believed that the awesome power of her silly words had brought about the death of the love of my life, and she was apologizing for it. I shouldn't be condescending to her. I should be showing polite interest, contemplation of the truths she had revealed.

But it was all bullshit to me.

"In the mechanical world, mechanical things fail, Iris. Maybe they were just going too fast. Maybe the e-brake cable snapped. I dunno. But I see no guiding hand, no demon's revenge. Please don't feel guilty, don't feel that you caused it. It was an accident."

I hugged her, and after a moment's hesitation, she hugged me back. "It's all over now." I smiled and was delighted to see a small answering smile. "Come on. World-famous Dennis Whitly and band are talking tour. You can't miss that."

"The thrill of a lifetime," she murmured.

I gave her shoulders another friendly squeeze and stepped toward the door.

Iris gasped, a sharp, hissing intake of breath in the still air. "What's that in your pocket, Cal?"

I turned. Her eyes were big and round again, frightened.

"What?"

"I said, what's that in your pocket?" She gestured. "The scarlet . . . In your back pocket."

I patted the seat of my jeans. One pocket held my wallet. From the other I brought out a small, flat, round black stone, pierced through the middle. A short length of red ribbon was attached to it.

Iris recoiled a step. "More evidence," she whispered. "Ashmedai protected you, Cal. He protected all of us. Right now you should be weeping . . ."

It took a minute for me to figure out where this new charm had come from, how in the hell it had wound up on my person. *She put her hand in my pocket; I got a keepsake and a kiss.*

Lisa.

"What does this one mean?" I moved my hand and the dull black stone twirled one way on its red ribbon, paused, twirled the other way.

Iris's eyelids fluttered. "Please get rid of it."

For a moment I hesitated. It was my only memento of Lisa . . . "What does it mean?"

"It's similar to the one Candy gave to Ernie. Its spell is a variation on that which gave her ownership of his soul."

I rolled my eyes.

"Only this one is . . . Did *she* give it to you? The young –"

"Yes."

Iris lowered her lashes. "It doesn't matter now, does it? She's –"

"It mattered to her. What was it supposed to do to me?"

Iris looked out at the pool, at the orange trees behind it. "It's given by a . . . slighted party . . ." She trailed off, refused to look at me.

"What's it supposed to do?" I demanded.

"It is the doom of love, Cal," Iris said, and at last met my eyes. "The young woman wished to kill all the love you'll ever again possess. Love for others, love for self. Soon, your loneliness would've consumed you, a kind of cancerous self-hatred, like Ernie felt, but far worse. It's a death sentence."

"I don't believe in any of that –"

"But she did, Cal. I've only seen such a charm bestowed a few times . . . There is an unspeakable finality to it. Even the sender can't rescind it. She was wishing for your end, in the worse possible way . . ." I was surprised to see a tear run down Iris's cheek. "But Ashmedai protected you from this final evil, too."

Her expression changed to a kind of curiosity. "You feel nothing? No sadness at her loss?"

"She tried to kill us, Iris. How could I still love –"

"The heart rationalizes, Cal. She was everything to you. It shone from your eyes whenever you spoke of her. But she tried to turn that feeling into an acid, to corrode your heart, your mind. She was turning her back on everything you'd ever felt for her, pushing you into a black abyss of despair. And she would've succeeded if it wouldn't've been for the demon's vigilance. You should be weeping in hopelessness right now, in a depthless hole from which even his power, if called on after the fact, couldn't redeem you. You feel nothing because he's excised it all for you. The love, the hatred. The pain. Praise Ashmedai!" she whispered in awe.

Again I rolled my eyes, and Iris came back from her true-believer's fugue. "Please. Get rid of it, Cal. I would bury it for you, but I don't dare touch it."

I balled up rock and ribbon, and doing my best LeBron James imitation, I pirouetted on tiptoe, arms raised, and arced the cursed charm into the trash can behind us by the pool. It clinked companionably against the metal; the dark green lawn and leaf bag shivered. Nothing but net.

I recalled Iris warning me about a loss of faith. She undoubtedly thought that this would cause it. Lisa had tried to kill me via a broken heart, had wished me a lonesome, agonized death, and yeah, that was pretty hard to take. But when she planted the thing on me – by that time, I hadn't trusted her any more, not even whilst we made love in the back of the van. My emotional involvement was already gone. *It's hard out here for a pimp.* My love for her had packed its brand new suitcases – it hadn't been here for very long – and decamped when she'd tried to murder Denny's wife.

I'd already suffered through the depression of the loss of my future with Lisa, and I'd come through it. The desire to protect my friends from the craziness had sustained me; the need to act because it had all been my fault.

Maybe I had lost some faith that I hadn't known I'd possessed. Or maybe Lisa's charm had exacted some toll, because I felt nothing, just like Iris had pointed out. Lisa had cursed me and the love we'd shared, but so what? The only unspeakable finality was that she would neither curse nor love anybody ever again, and that really didn't have anything to do with me. Phenex wouldn't be bothering us anymore, and that was all that even remotely mattered to me.

"Praise Ashmedai, indeed, Iris, because I think I'm gonna be all right." But when I turned around, I discovered I was talking to myself. The purple-eyed witch had already slipped past me back into the house.

SEVENTY-SEVEN

In a tall glass temple in downtown Los Angeles, sacred to the gods and demons of the recording industry, the minions of Sony negotiated with the minions of EMI. Copyrights were invoked, contracts revised. That peerless sorcerer of sound, Oscar Woodbine, was consulted. A new album of hymns would be recorded. And to promote it, yea, verily, the souls of Sonic Daydream, those high priests of rock and roll, were again consigned to the road for a twelve city tour. With a big, ol' cushy bus and plenty of time to relax between gigs, we would once again *draw the faithful to their knees.* The coin of the realm would be their offering, and the forces of the universe would again smile and rain largesse upon our particular corner of the religion of the music business.

The night after we recorded the album, there was another party at the McMansion in Temecula. After the bestowal of all access backstage passes upon Katie and her parents for the first show at the Hollywood Bowl, after they toddled on home across the street, after my bandmates retired with their women to their assigned rooms, Iris and I finally got together.

It was slow and sweet, as benefitted our years. We'd always been fond of each other, and since all the other promises of the future had been swept away, at least for me, it was undertaken with a mutual feeling of youthful *why the hell not,* a giddy *yolo,* as the kids say. *You only live once.* There was passion, and an immediate sense of comfort between us, but from the very first moments, I felt Iris's caution.

Despite my claims of being all right, despite her belief that Ashmedai had saved me, despite my willingness to demonstrate my affection for her – proof that I could love again, and enthusiastically – I couldn't escape the idea that Iris also believed that I'd been touched irrevocably by Lisa's last act of hatred.

It was apparent in the veiled glances she gave me sometimes: she felt that the black rock on the red string and the wish for my doom that had accompanied it had rendered me incapable of loving her completely. So Iris held something back. She wouldn't allow herself to fully surrender to what we could have, because she was sure we couldn't have it. I was damaged, cursed. She had to protect herself from the possibility of her own heartbreak.

I couldn't deny that there was a kernel of truth to what Iris never spoke, but what was there in her eyes, nonetheless. I'd never love her in quite the same way as I'd loved Lisa; that was undeniable. I could love her as much, I thought, but differently. Isn't each love unalike from every other?

Lisa had possessed the inimitable drive and vitality of youth; she'd been a fellow musician. Iris was not young and knew nothing about music, and she allowed the ghost of what Lisa and I had shared – as musicians as much as lovers – to stand between us.

Iris's doubt manifested itself in little moments of quiet. At these times, I doubted that it would last, and it lent a bittersweetness to all the time I spent with her. Maybe I held back too, then, and Iris's unspoken prophecy was thus self-fulfilled. But most of the time we were great together, and I vowed that whatever happened, we'd always be friends.

SEVENTY-EIGHT

I'd never been able to sleep on the tour bus.

In the old days, Elise was there beside me, and we'd talk. I'd listen to her whispered aspirations about Denny – he would be just across the aisle, zonked out. Denny never had any trouble sleeping whilst we traveled. I imagined that Denny never had any trouble sleeping, period. His conscience was perennially clear.

Age had encroached, and Elise was long in her grave, so I got a little sleep on the reunion tour, albeit fitfully. Sometimes I'd wake with a start, and for a minute I'd think that I was dreaming: it was 1990 or 1995, and I was young again. I'd look next to me and sometimes I would actually *see* Elise sitting there. She'd smile and then she'd nod at something out the window. I'd look, catch my fifty-five-year-old reflection in the glass, and realize I hadn't been dreaming after all. Sonic Daydream was indeed on tour again, but a lifetime had passed since Elise had been sitting beside me. I'd look again at the place . . . of course it was empty.

It was a new tour, though the brothers Whitly once again snored in their seats; even Ernie slept these days, dreaming no doubt of Bianca. Good ol' Ernie, always lucky. The rest of us would have to wait till we returned home to see our ladies, but Bianca travelled for her job, so she was able to drop in on some of our dates to see him, as her schedule allowed. He would disappear back to his room after the show, like he had with that night's lucky groupie in the old days. We wouldn't see him again until the next morning when he'd trot out of the hotel, all smiles, pulling his battered rolly suitcase behind him like a kid with a red wagon.

In our heyday, Denny would also retire immediately, and Lenny would go back to his room and do paperwork or perhaps the rare groupie, if we were overseas. I would hang out with Elise. Nowadays, the four of us hung out together, or just me and the brothers Whitly, if Bianca was visiting our second-guitar. Sophia and Barbie and Iris waited for us at the end of the road; tour responsibilities were handled by EMI via the lightning-quickness of text and email. We travelled with neither road dog nor roadies. Ernie tuned his own guitars. The bus driver knew the itinerary; venue employees loaded us in and out. All we had to do was show up. It was the best tour ever.

We'd sit in a bar or a restaurant after the show, just four old guys that didn't even vaguely resemble the long-haired musicians we'd been in the old days, so we were seldom recognized. My conversations with Denny were tentative at first, anonymous, chit-chat about the venue or the crowd or the set list. I'd always been able to talk to our famous front about music, despite the fact that I'd always considered myself a purist and him a peasant. He insisted on calling *Baba O'Riley Teenage Wasteland,* for example, and all guitar players were pretty much the same to me.

But I spent a whole lot more time talking to Denny about music on this tour; there was no Elise for him to dodge anymore. It became clear that the whole misnaming of that famous Who tune had been Denny playfully fucking with me and my seriousness, and I was reminded of things about him that I'd forgotten through the years that I'd despised him. Chiefly: we hadn't become one of the world's premier rock bands because Dennis Whitly was just a pretty face. He was an accomplished, professional musician, a singer and a songwriter – two things that no amount of educated snobbishness about music had ever made me.

It dawned on me that I'd spent too many years scorning Denny to ever really get to know what he knew about music. He had ensorcelled the fans in our younger days, made us millionaires, but so what? There were dozens of rock stars that did the same thing, ones that didn't even know how to read music.

I'd never sneered at Denny's talent, but I hadn't really given him credit for it, either. *He could play a guitar just like a'ringin' a bell,* but I'd always figured that it was his looks that the fans appreciated most. Now that I finally talked to Denny, I found that he knew a lot more about the old sounds than I'd ever realized. He wasn't just an uneducated, pretty-boy guitar-plunker as I'd always pictured him; he was not indeed unaware of the great history of rock and roll that had come before us.

I'd never be buddies with Denny, would never kid with him the way I did with his brother; we'd never be close, not like I was with Ernie. When we looked at each other, Denny and I would forever sense Elise's ghost hovering just nearby. But I'd discovered a new respect for him as a musician, and maybe that Thanksgiving dinner wasn't the impossibility that it had once been.

I discovered that I'd missed being in a band. I'd once told Iris that music had been the closest thing that I'd ever had to a religion, and taking the stage again every other night gave me an inkling into what she must feel at the celebration of her faith, what my mother must've felt when the priest said, *Behold the Lamb of God, behold him who takes away the sins of the world.* If there was faith for me, this was it. *Music celebrates life,* I'd told Iris once, and I realized that I'd never felt more alive than when I was playing with these three guys. I'd never been happier.

Do you believe in rock and roll? Can music save your mortal soul?

It could, if there was such a thing. It did.

I thought about Elise a lot during the tour. In my more sentimental moments, I imagined her pride at Sonic Daydream reunited, the band she'd always considered *her* band, the greatest band in the world. Denny had fatally disappointed her, and she'd never cared for his brother or Ernie LaBelle. But she'd loved us as a unit when we were onstage together – we were her favorite band, and nothing's more fun than seeing and listening to your favorite band live. I liked to think that she would've been happy to see how much I enjoyed our reunion.

I thought about Lisa too, sometimes, on those nights when sleep was out of my reach. My young lover had not been my old friend reborn; that had been just a tragic delusion foisted upon her by her insane mother. But the one commonality between them had been the music; the thing that had initially attracted my attention to both.

Before there had been her obsessive love for Denny, Elise had already possessed a deep appreciation for the sounds and the tunes, just like I did. I'd had a pair of sticks in my hands almost before I could walk; Elise had once shown me a picture of a four-year-old girl wearing pink, footie-pajamas and a giant pair of old-fashioned, leather-cushioned headphones. She was smiling up at the camera, an expression of surprised delight on her face.

"That was the first time I heard *Riders on the Storm,"* she'd told me. Though she'd never picked up an instrument herself, music had been part of the very fabric of her being from that day to her last. It was really no wonder that she'd fallen for a guitar player.

But because Denny didn't return her love, she'd turned to me, and the two of us – all we'd ever really had was the music. If it wasn't for that, and each other, all would've been loneliness. It had been so for me, after she was gone, for so many years. Until I met Lisa.

I'd loved Elise, who'd only ever been a fan, and of course I'd loved poor, insane Lisa because she was actually a musician, and a pretty good one. She could've gone far on her voice alone, if she hadn't been dealt a hand full of deluded, demon-worshipping, homicidal maniacs for a band.

I'd ignored the craziness because Lisa had been just like Elise – she'd loved the old tunes; her knowledge of them was encyclopedic, and unlike Elise, she could also sing and play them. Also unlike Elise, she'd been attracted to me.

But if Lisa had just been some young thing that liked me – if Lisa had just been a groupie – I never would've gone for it. The week we'd spent at the beach . . . It was Lisa's own love of music and her fascinating, thought-provoking takes on it that had made me fall for her the way I did.

My tragic loves.

Take me to your heart, feel me in your bones, just one more night, and I'm comin' off this long and winding road . . .

Sleepless on the tour bus, I realized that the thing that I'd been missing all these years was the music. Playing by myself every day, giving lessons to uninterested teenagers at the Y, even the little bit of studio work I'd done – none of that had filled the trackless void that my life became after Denny ended Sonic Daydream.

But through the intervention of a no-talent band of witchy crazies, the tunes were back, the beat had been restored to me. That which did not destroy us had made us all stronger, or at least cognizant of what we'd been missing. Lenny could now play the bass ambidextrously: he had one strung each way. Ernie had always lived to tour, and this strange ordeal had given him the opportunity to play road dog, to get that tiresome bullshit out of his system. Legendary Dennis Whitly discovered that he was positively *digging* the road again, and even if that got stale, as it inevitably would – touring was a young man's game, after all – Sonic Daydream was a band again.

We were reunited, and even if we never did another tour, I knew we'd henceforth and forever sit around in Denny's backyard studio and make music, like we had since high school. And even if nobody ever heard it but us, I was looking forward to it. I'd recovered my band and my lost religion, and no longer would I die all alone, unmourned.

I think my old friend Elise would've been glad about that.

*****

Also by LM Foster

A Passing Resemblance
Contrariwise – A Tale of Twins
Corvino
Crypsis
Duck Feet
Peter's Sisters

Two Green Keys
Two Green Keys
Adapted for the Screen

One Wilde Ride Trilogy
Part One: It Might Have Been
Part Two: An Exceptional Boy
Part Three: What Should Never Be

Stars and Guitars
Talk To a Movie Star
Where The Guitars Play

Tom and Wiley
This Carnival of Strange
Wiley Royce
Generally Recognized as Safe
Wiley Royce Versus The Martians

Parker and Dunn Mysteries
Our Endless Needs

www.ingramcontent.com/pod-product-compliance
Lightning Source LLC
Chambersburg PA
CBHW051430260626
47162CB00001B/36